YOUNG MUNGO

YOUNG MUNGO

DOUGLAS STUART

THORNDIKE PRESS
A part of Gale, a Cengage Company

LIBRARY OF CONGRESS CIP DATA ON FILE.
CATALOGUING IN PUBLICATION FOR THIS BOOK
IS AVAILABLE FROM THE LIBRARY OF CONGRESS.

ISBN-13: 978-1-4328-9672-0 (hardcover alk. paper)

Published in 2022 by arrangement with Grove/Atlantic, Inc.

Printed in Mexico
Print Number: 01   Print Year: 2022

For Alexander,
and all the gentle sons of Glasgow

THE MAY AFTER

THE MAN AFTER

ONE

As they neared the corner, Mungo halted and shrugged the man's hand from his shoulder. It was such an assertive gesture that it took everyone by surprise. Turning back, Mungo squinted up at the tenement flat, and his eyes began to twitch with one of their nervous spasms. As his mother watched him through the ear-of-wheat pattern of the net curtains, she tried to convince herself that his twitch was a happy wink, a lovely Morse code that telegraphed everything would be okay. F. I. N. E. Her youngest son was like that. He smiled when he didn't want to. He would do anything just to make other people feel better.

Mo-Maw swept the curtain aside and leant on the window frame like a woman looking for company. She raised her tea mug in one hand and tapped the glass with her pearlescent pink nails. It was a colour she had chosen to make her fingers appear fresher, because if her hands looked younger, then so might her face, so might her entire self. As she looked down upon him, Mungo shifted again, his feet turning towards home. She fluttered her painted fingers and shooed him away. *Go!*

Her boy was stooped slightly, the rucksack a little hump on his back. Unsure of what he should take, he had packed it with half-hearted nonsense: an oversized Fair Isle jumper, teabags, his dog-eared sketchbook, a game of Ludo, and some half-used tubes of medicated ointment. Yet he wavered on the corner as though the bag might tip him backwards into the gutter. Mo-Maw knew the bag was not heavy. She knew it was the bones of him that had become a dead weight.

This was all for his own good and yet he dared stare up at her with a doleful look. It was too hot for his nonsense. He was fraying her nerves. *Go!* she mouthed again and took a swally of the cold tea.

The two men idled at the bend. They shared a sigh and a glance and a chuckle, before putting down their bags and lighting cigarettes. Mo-Maw could tell they were itchy to be gone — these narrow streets didn't like unknown faces — and she could see it took patience not to goad her boy on.

The men were canny enough not to pressure Mungo, not so close to home, not when he could still bolt. Their slitted eyes kept flicking towards him, watching, waiting to see what the boy would do next, while their hands ferreted inside their trouser pockets as they peeled their ball sacks from their thighs. The day would be muggy and close. The younger man fiddled with himself. Mo-Maw licked the back of her bottom teeth.

Mungo raised his hand to wave up at the window but Mo-Maw glowered down at him. He must have seen her face harden, or perhaps he thought waving was childish, because he aborted the gesture and grasped a fistful of air, which made him seem like a drowning man.

In his baggy shorts and his oversized cagoule, he looked like a waif dressed in hand-me-downs. But as he pushed the cloud of curls away from his face, Mo-Maw saw his jaw tighten, and she was reminded of the determined young man that he was becoming. She tapped the glass again. *Don't you scowl at me.*

The younger of the two men stepped forward and laid his arm across Mungo's shoulders. Mungo winced at the weight. Mo-Maw saw him rub at his sides, and she was reminded of the tender purple bruises that were blooming across his ribs. She tapped the glass, *Oh fur God's sake, jist go!* At this, her son lowered his gaze and let himself be led away. The men were laughing as they clapped her boy on the back. *Guid lad. Brave lad.*

Mo-Maw was not a religious woman but she stretched her pink fingernails to the heavens and wiggled them as she cried hallelujah. She tipped her tea into the parched spider plant, and filling her mug with fortified wine, she turned up the music and kicked off her shoes.

The three travellers caught a corporation bus into Sauchiehall Street. Glasgow was in a rare swelter and they had to push upstream through rowdy gangs of shirtless men already poached pink from the sun. City benches were lined with thick-armed grannies, proper in their hats and good wool coats, and sweating heavily across their top lips. As sticky-faced weans skipped across the street the women pulled their heads into their fleshy chests and dozed in the heat. They reminded Mungo of the tenement pigeons, big lazy doos with their eyes half-closed and their heads swallowed by neck feathers.

The city was alive with the sound of buskers competing with the battle rattle of a practising Orange band. Like chirruping songbirds, the Orangemen's piccolos made a sweet trilling sound against the heavy thump of a Lambeg drum. The tune was so affecting that an older, refined-looking gentleman was lost in reverie and weeping big dewdrop tears. Mungo tried not to stare at the sight of a man crying so openly. He couldn't be sure whether the man wept in anguish or with pride. There was the glint of an expensive watch band peeking from out of his suit sleeve, and Mungo decided, based on no other information, that it was too ostentatious, too indiscreet to belong to a Catholic.

The men lumbered in the sunshine. They were weighed down with armfuls of thin plastic bags, a satchel filled with fishing tackle, and a camping rucksack. Mungo could hear them complain of their thirst. He had known them only an hour, but they had mentioned it several times already. They seemed always to be thirsty. "Ah'm gasping for a guid drink," said the elder of the two. He was already beetroot-red and overheating in his thick tweed suit. The other man ignored him. He was walking bandy-legged, as though his tight denims were chafing his thighs.

They led the boy into the bus station and with a rattle of coins they boarded a coach that would take them out the north side of Glasgow and towards the green hills of Dumbarton.

By the time they fought their way to the plastic bench at the back of the bus the men were sweating and hard for breath. Mungo sat between them and made himself as small as possible. When one of them looked out the window he studied the side of their face. If they turned his way, he would feign interest out the opposite window and try to avoid their eyes.

Mungo braced his chin on to his chest and tried to stop the nervous itching that was spreading across his face as he watched the grey city go by. He knew he was doing that thing again, the crinkled nose, the blinking, the face that looked like he might sneeze, but never would. He could feel the older man's gaze upon him.

"Ah cannae 'member the last time ah came oot of the city." The man's voice had a raspy quality, like he had a throatful of dry toast. He would occasionally inhale in the middle of a sentence, wavering, like each word might be the last one he managed. Mungo tried to smile up at him, but there was something ferrety about the man that made it hard to look him in the eyes.

The suited stranger turned back to his window and Mungo took this opportunity to study the length of him. He was an angular man in his late fifties or early sixties, but the years had clearly been hard. Mungo had seen his kind before. The young Protestant hooligans off the scheme often hounded men like him for fun, rounding up the jangling drunks outside the working men's club, taunting them towards the chip shop and then swooping as the last of their coins fell from their burst pockets. Neglectful eating and hard drinking had withered and jaundiced him. There was too much skin over too little fat, his yellow face wrinkling like an overripe apple.

The man's tatty jacket was mismatched with a pair of dress trousers, the knees of which sagged like more stretched-out skin. Underneath his jacket he wore a T-shirt emblazoned with an advertisement for a plumber on the South Side, the neck was torn and separating from the body. Mungo wondered if perhaps these were the only clothes he owned; they smelled musty, as though he wore them through smirr and shine.

Mungo felt strangely sorry for him. The man was trembling slightly. Years spent hid-

15

ing from daylight in dark pubs had given him the nervous reactions of a whippet pushed out into the snow, and he had the small darting eyes and long twitching limbs of a mistreated dog. He seemed on the verge of bolting.

As the last of the high-rises faded from view, the suited man made some small sounds, filling the empty air, inviting the others to join him in conversation. Mungo braced his chin to his chest and said nothing. The younger man was scratching his crotch. Mungo watched him from the corner of his eye.

This man seemed to be in his early twenties. He wore indigo denims and his belt was laced under the logo so as not to obscure the proud Armani badge. He was handsome — or he must have been close to it once — but there was something already spoiled about him, like good butcher's meat that had been left out. Despite the heat he had been wearing a puffy bomber jacket. When he removed it, Mungo could see his arms were roped with lean muscle that spoke to a heavy trade, or years of fighting, or both.

His hair was clipped short. His fringe had been combed forward in a gelled line, the hairs formed little saw-toothed points, as though they had been cut by pinking shears. Mungo stared at the damaged skin of his knuckles. He was honey-coloured in the way Scottish people seldom were; perhaps his family were chip-shop Italian or Spanish by way of the Black Irish.

Any trace of that romance was lost as he said in flat, glottal Glaswegian, "Haw. Dinnae be botherin' wi' auld St Christopher." He spoke without looking directly at either of them. "He'd bore the arse aff a horse."

Mungo was left to ponder why he was on a bus with St Christopher, while the other man went back to picking his nose. As the man's pinkie searched the inside of his nostril Mungo noted how he wore sovvie rings on all of his fingers and that his forearms were snaked with interlocking tattoos. He was a man covered in words: from the logos on his chest, to his shoes, to his jeans, to his skin. He had written on his flesh with a sewing needle, women's names, gang names: Sandra, Jackie, RFC, The Mad Squad. Here and there, the blue biro ink had bled, it wept beneath his skin like a watercolour and tinted him a pretty violet hue. Mungo read his arms carefully. He committed as much as he could to memory.

St Christopher reached into one of the shopping bags, and with a sly wink he raised a half-dozen cans of Tennent's Super. Keeping his small eyes on the back of the bus driver's head, he broke two cans free of their noose and offered them to the boy and the tattooed man. Mungo shook his head but the young man took a can with a grateful groan. He burst it open and clamped his lips over the escaping foam. He drained it in three throatfuls.

St Christopher must have read the boy's mind because he said, "They calls us St Christopher on account ah go to the alcoholic meetings on Hope Street every Sunday and Thursday. Ah'm Sunday-Thursday Christopher, so as no to be confused wi' Castlemilk Chris or Wee Ginger-Heided Chrissy." The man took a slug, and Mungo watched his throat struggle to take enough in. "S-T Christopher, ye see?"

Mungo had heard something like that before. Mo-Maw herself was known as Monday-Thursday Maureen. That's who the other alcoholics asked for when the boy answered the hallway telephone. The callers wanted to be sure they hadn't found the house of "Maureen from Millerston" or "Wee-Mo frae the Milk" by mistake. These small distinctions mattered if they were to honour the code of anonymity.

"Sometimes ah have the shakes that bad,

ah should go tae a Wednesday night meeting as well. But well, ah just cannae." St Christopher made a sad frown. "Do you see what ah mean?"

Mungo had been working hard at seeing what people really meant. Mo-Maw and his sister, Jodie, were always nagging him about that. Apparently there could be some distance between what a person was saying and what you should be seeing. Jodie said he was gullible. Mo-Maw said she wished she had raised him to be cannier, less of anybody's fool. It was a funny thing to be a disappointment because you were honest and assumed others might be too. The games people played made his head hurt.

St Christopher was sucking down his can when Mungo said, "Maybe you should just go on Wednesdays too. Like, if you really need to?"

"Aye, but ah like ma handle." His hand reached inside his shirt and drew out a small tin medallion of the saint. He peered down his pockmarked nose at it. "*S-T Christopher.* It's the nicest thing anybody's ever said about us."

"Could you not just give them your family name?"

"Widnae be very anonymous wid it?" interrupted the tattooed man. "If ye start spilling yer guts and letting everybody know yer demons, then they'd be able to lift yer name out in the street."

Mungo knew fine well that people had demons. Mo-Maw's showed itself whenever she jangled for a drink. Her demon was a flat, eel-like snake with the jaw and beady eyes of a weasel and the matted coat of a mangy rat. It was a sleekit thing on a chain leash that shook her and dragged her towards things that she ought to be walking away from. It was greedy and it was cunning. It could lie dormant, wait for the children to leave for school, to kiss their mother goodbye, and then it would turn on Mo-Maw, throttle her as though she was some shivering mouse. At other times it coiled up inside her and sat heavy on her heart. The demon was always there just under the surface, even on good days.

On the days that she gave in to the drink, the demon could be quieted for a while. But sometimes Mo-Maw could get so far in the drink that she would become another woman entirely, another creature altogether. The first sign was how her skin grew slack, like her real face was sliding off to reveal this strange woman who lurked underneath. Mungo and his brother and sister called this slack version of her *Tattie-bogle,* like some heartless, shambling scarecrow. No matter how her children stuffed her with their love or tried to prop her up and gather her back together, she took in all their care and attention and felt as hollow as ever.

When Tattie-bogle spoke, her lower jaw would hang loose and her tongue would roll in her mouth in a dirty, lascivious way, like she wanted very badly to lick something. Tattie-bogle always suspected that she was missing some party, that something more exciting must be happening just around the corner or hidden up the next close. When she felt like this she would turn to her children and shoo them away as though they were drab little birds. Tattie-bogle believed that better things, brighter lights, bigger laughs were always happening to women who had no children.

Tattie-bogle would become best friends with women she had just met, and over a half-bottle of Black & White whisky she would betray her own intimate secrets, and then felt wounded when these new friends didn't share the same depth of feeling. Then when they fought, she dragged them, or she was dragged by them, across the carpet and down the stairs. In the morning Mungo would find tufts of perfumed hair, like the straw from a burst scarecrow, lying in the hallway, animated by the draught that whistled under the front door. Either he or Jodie would hoover it up with the Ewbank and say nothing more about it.

It was Jodie who had split their mother in two. In the cold morning light, this trick helped Mungo forgive Mo-Maw when the drink had made her vindictive and rotten. "It wasn't Mo-Maw," soothed Jodie, as she held him in the airing cupboard, "it was only horrible old Tattie-bogle, and she's sleeping now."

Mungo knew what demons looked like. As the bus trundled north, he sat quietly and thought about his own.

"Ah wish this driver would hurry the fuck up," the tattooed man said. He reached into the bag between his legs, the canvas strap was studded with brightly coloured lures. Rummaging amongst the spools of fishing gut he produced a pouch of tobacco. He rolled a fat cigarette, his tongue darting along the paper. The man took a deep drag and blew the smoke into his empty lager can. He cupped his hand over the mouth like he had caught a spider, but the stench of tobacco was already wafting around the bus. Several of the passengers turned and glared towards the back seats. Mungo leaned over him with a meek smile and unclipped the hasp on the thin window.

"Do you smoke?" the man asked between greedy puffs. His eyes were a rich green, glinting here and there with flecks of gold.

"No."

"Guid." He took another lungful. "It's bad for ye."

St Christopher reached out a trembling hand and the tattooed man reluctantly let go of the cigarette. St Christopher inhaled and filled himself up to the very brim. His dry lips were sticky on the damp paper. The tattooed man rammed his shoulder into Mungo's. "Ma pals call us Gallowgate on account of where I'm frae." He adjusted his sovvie rings and nodded towards the oblivious bus driver. "You're a nervous wee fella, int ye? Don't worry. If he gies us any lip, ah'll fuckin' stab him."

St Christopher sucked on the dout until it burned his fingers. "Do ye like tae fish?"

"I don't know." Mungo was glad to see the cigarette die. "I've never done it before."

"Where we're gaun ye should catch pike, eels, speckled trout," Gallowgate said. "You can fish the whole weekend and naebody will come by and ask for a permit. Ye'll be twenty, forty miles from the nearest soul."

St Christopher nodded in agreement. "Aye. It is as near tae heaven as ye can get on three buses."

"Four," corrected Gallowgate, "four buses."

The remoteness of it filled Mungo with a sinking feeling. "Do you eat the fish?"

"Depends on the size," said Gallowgate. "In breeding season you can catch that many that you'd need a deep freezer to keep them all. Does your mammy have a big freezer?"

Mungo shook his head. He thought of Mo-Maw's tiny box freezer, how it was thick with ice. He wondered if she would be happy with a fat speckled trout, but he doubted it. Nothing he did seemed to make her happy. He had been worrying her heart lately, which he knew because she had told him so. He had tried not to laugh when she had said it, but all he could picture was her heart walking around the living room in her chest and folding a white hanky in agitation. At the time Jodie had rolled her eyes and said, "Listen to yourself, Maureen. Do you even have a heart?"

Mungo picked his cheekbone as the bus passed Dumbarton and the ochre banks of Loch Lomond came into view. He remembered the heavy things Mo-Maw had said. He knew why he was here; it was his own fault.

"How auld are you anyhows?" asked Gallowgate.

"Fifteen." Mungo tried to draw himself up to his full height, but his ribs still hurt and the old bus had terrible suspension. He was average height for his age, one of the last in his class to take a growth spurt. His older brother Hamish liked to grip his chin and tilt his face to the light. He would inspect the fine line of dander growing on Mungo's top lip in the same way a gardener checks on a spindly seedling. He would blow on it just to irritate Mungo. Although Mungo wasn't especially tall, he was still taller than Hamish. Hamish hated that.

St Christopher reached out and circled the boy's wrist with his long fingers. "Ye're only a wee thing aren't ye? Ah would have put ye at twelve, thirteen, tops."

"Ach he's nearly a man." Gallowgate slung an inked arm over the boy's shoulders. He exchanged a sly look with his friend. "Have yer balls dropped yet, Mungo?"

Mungo didn't answer. They just sort of hung there all wrinkly and pointless. If they dropped, where would they drop to?

"Ye know, yer nut sack?" Gallowgate punched the boy lightly in the groin.

"I don't know." Mungo doubled over for protection.

The men were chuckling to themselves and Mungo tried to join in, but it was a self-conscious laugh, a half-beat too late. St Christopher broke into a hacking cough and Gallowgate turned back to the window in disdain. He said, "We'll look after ye, Mungo. Nae worries. We'll have some laughs, and you can bring yer mammy some fresh fish."

Mungo massaged his sore balls. He thought again about Mo-Maw's worried heart.

"Aye. Yer mammy is a good wummin. One of the few left." Gallowgate started biting the dry skin from around his index finger and spitting it on the floor. Suddenly he stopped what he was doing. "Can I see?" Before Mungo could protest, he hooked his hand at the bottom of Mungo's cagoule. He started to lift it and began undressing the boy. "Gie us a wee look then."

Mungo raised his arms and let the man draw his top up until the nylon cagoule covered his face and bathed everything in a calm blue light. Mungo couldn't see, but he could hear the men and the ragged patterns of their breathing. There was a sad intake of air, a pause, then a sigh. Gallowgate's fingertip was slimy where he had been chewing it. He pressed it against the blackening bruise on Mungo's chest, and Mungo felt it travel from his sternum, around the curve of his bottom rib, as though the man was tracing a map. Gallowgate prodded his ribs and then, as if testing their tenderness, he dug his finger into the bruise. Mungo winced and squirmed to get away. He pulled his clothes back down, certain his face was scalding. Gallowgate shook his head. "Terrible business that. Yer mammy telt us all about that mess ye got yourself into with those dirty Fenian bastards. Catholics, man. Butter widnae melt."

Mungo had been trying not to think about it.

"Dinnae worry," grinned Gallowgate. "We'll get you away frae that scheme. We'll have a proper boy's weekend. Make a man out of you yet, eh?"

They changed bus, and then they changed bus again, and then they waited nearly three hours for the next one. They were far beyond Loch Lomond now and Mungo began to think the men had no real idea where they were. It all looked the same to him.

The two soaks lay in the gorse behind the metal bus shelter and finished the last of the Tennent's cans. Every now and then

Gallowgate would throw an empty over the hedge on to the country road and ask the boy if a bus was coming. Mungo tidied up the rubbish and said no, "No bus."

Mungo shivered in the sunlight and let his face tic freely, free from the open-mouthed stares of strangers. When he was alone, he tried to tire out the urge like this, but it never worked.

It was colder out here in the countryside. The slow northern sun seemed stuck in the sky, but the heat it gave was stolen by the long wind that hurried through the glens. His nose began to drip. He might also be sunburnt in the morning.

He sank on to his haunches. There was a scab on his right kneecap, the skin was puckering and itchy. Mungo checked no one was watching. Then he put his lips to it, ran his tongue over it to soften it, and sucked it till his mouth filled with a metallic taste. Mungo knew he couldn't be trusted not to lick his scab again so he covered his bare legs with his anorak and, pulling his knees to his chest, he hid them from the warmth-less sun. It had been such a rare sort of heat on the scheme that he hadn't thought to bring more than his thin football shorts. Mo-Maw had given him no time to get his bag ready, and she hadn't stopped him as

28

he sloped, poorly dressed, out the door.

He pulled the thick Fair Isle jumper from his bag and slipped it on under his cagoule. The dry Shetland wool tickled as it came down over his face. Mungo checked the soaks were still lying in the gorse. Cupping the jumper up and over his nose, he ran his tongue along the inside of the knit. It still smelled of fresh air, sawdust, and the sour ammonia of the pissy doocot. It reminded him of home. Using his thumb, he stuffed the fabric into his open mouth and closed his eyes. He shoved it in until he gagged.

By the time the country bus arrived the men were deep in their drink. Mungo helped them aboard with their bags and fishing rods and then he waited patiently for St Christopher to pay the fare. The drunk man swayed and produced a handful of silver and copper shrapnel. Chapped-faced women huffed impatiently, their shopping defrosting at their feet, and Mungo felt his neck burn as he scraped the change from St Christopher's curled palm and dropped coin after coin into the tray. The boy could feel his eyes twitch, and he was relieved when the driver finally said, "Okay, okay, stop. That's plenty, son." He had been embarrassed that he couldn't add so fast. School had been scarce for him since Mo-

Maw had taken sick on drink again.

The driver released the handbrake. Mungo couldn't meet the eyes of the country women but he laughed as he heard St Christopher lollop after him and wish their sour faces a "glorious and happy afternoon." Gallowgate was already sound asleep on the pile of tackle and plastic bags. Mungo sat on the seat in front and picked at the black rubber sealant around the window.

The fat bus bumped along the serpentine road. It stopped every so often, and dropped little white women outside their little white houses. The diesel engine thrummed a lullaby and the boy could feel his eyes grow heavy from the day. A copse of pine and yew trees began to encroach on the road, their leaves mottled the sunlight on his face. Mungo laid his head against the glass. He fell into a fitful sleep.

Hamish was there. His brother was lying in the single bed opposite his own. By how the daylight reflected off his thick glasses, Mungo could tell it was early evening. Hamish was scooping spoonfuls of cereal into his mouth as trails of chocolatey milk streamed down his hairless chest. Mungo lay still, quietly watching his brother. He always enjoyed moments like this, when the person didn't know they were being observed. Hamish was smiling to himself. The left side of his face puckered in a dirty grin as he flicked through the pages of a magazine. Mungo could see the pained, painted faces of naked women, spread-eagled and grimacing back up at Hamish. Yet when Mungo brought his gaze back to his brother's face, it was Hamish who was watching him. He wasn't grinning anymore. "Tell me Mungo. Is it all my fault?"

Gallowgate shook the boy from his dream. His top lip was caught on the sticky film that had formed on his teeth and for a moment Mungo didn't know if the man was smiling or snarling at him.

As they tumbled from the bus St Christopher rolled his ankle and fell into the grass verge. They were on a section of road where a thick canopy of alders made the air green and damp and slow. St Christopher writhed in the dirt, pulling his suit blazer tight across his pigeon chest. "How come youse didnae fuckin' wake us!" There was angry spume in the corners of his mouth. "We're miles out of our bastardin' way."

"I don't know where we're going. It all looks the same to me."

Gallowgate stepped forward as if to strike the boy and Mungo instinctively flinched, his arms barricaded in front of him.

"Fuck's sake." His breath was sour with beer and sleep. "Calm down. It's no come to that awready." Gallowgate heaved some of the bags out of the dust and slung them over his shoulder. The man started walking in the direction the bus had come, sauntering down the middle of the road, daring any driver to hit him. "It's miles back, so let's get a fuckin' move on."

There were no cars travelling in either direction but Mungo and St Christopher struggled in the safety of the verge, their carrier bags snagging on bramble thorns. The boy fastened his blue anorak up to his throat and then continued up and over his mouth. He sank his head lower into the funnel and became a pair of downcast, twitching eyes.

They had been walking for forty minutes when St Christopher started to moan; the bags of supplies were cutting into his fingers, and his dress shoes were starting to rub at his papery heels. Gallowgate scowled at the pair of them like a father who could not get his children to behave. He yanked the boy's arm and forced Mungo's thumb out, and left him facing the non-existent traffic. Gallowgate slid down the embankment and the older man followed him, complaining all the way. They lay behind the drystane dyke as Mungo waited by the empty road and tried to hitch a lift. Nothing passed in either direction. Further along, the road was flooded with sheep.

Mungo didn't know what time it was, but it was cold under the canopy of alders. His bare legs were speckled blue, so he made a game of removing his cagoule and slipping his legs through the sleeves. When his ribs became colder than his legs, he unzipped the windbreaker again and put it back over his chest. An hour passed, then two. No cars came. He could hear more cans of beer hiss open behind the stone dyke. St Christopher stood up every now and then to offer words of encouragement. "Aye ye're doing a great job son. Really, truly, outstanding."

The mannish woman was visibly shaken to come across the boy in the middle of the road. Her surprise turned to fear and then disappointment, as the two alkies clambered out from the undergrowth. Mungo stood in front of her brown Lada, blocking her escape, smiling as warmly as he could. He made an unsettling sight, beaming with relief in the dim glow of her headlights.

The woman wouldn't let any of them sit up front. But in the back seat, crushed between the strange men, he was glad of the roaring warmth of their bodies. They burned blue with the alcohol and the tang of peat on their breath reminded him of winter fires. The cold had robbed Mungo of any notion of independence and he gladly let their bodies swallow his. Gallowgate uttered as many polite niceties as he could manage; Mungo listened to him struggle to sharpen his vowels. He asked the woman to drive them to the dip in the road where the fence was broken, and a mud track led down to the lochside. Mungo could tell that even in broad daylight this would be hard to find, never mind in the violet gloam.

The woman drove slowly, afraid of the men in the back seat, terrified to miss the break in the fence and be stuck with them longer than she needed to be. Mungo watched her eyes flit to the rear-view mirror and every time they made eye contact, he smiled his best school picture smile.

"I've never seen sheep before," he said.

The woman smiled, if only to be polite. Whatever Mungo was doing seemed to make her more uncomfortable. Her skin was leathered as though she worked in the wind and the rain. She wore horn-rimmed glasses over a hand-knitted Aran jumper, and over this humble garment she had carefully arranged a pearl necklace. Mungo watched her tuck the necklace inside her jumper.

"We're not related," Mungo said quietly. "These are pals of my mother's and they're taking me away on a fishing weekend."

"Wonderful," she said without any wonder at all.

"Aye." He felt compelled to tell her more, to let someone, even this snobbish woman, know who he was, who he was with, and where they were taking him. "They are members of Alcoholics Anonymous. S'pose my maw thought it would do us all some good to get some air about us."

The lady in the Aran gansey took her eyes off the road a moment too long, and the car swerved as she connected with the verge. A thumb, or maybe a Bic lighter, jabbed a warning into the side of his bare leg. It was clear Gallowgate wanted him to stop talking. Mungo could hear St Christopher huff; he was smacking his lips in agitation like a woman who couldn't believe the price of milk nowadays.

They crept along for several miles, searching desperately for the point Gallowgate remembered from distant memory. Yet when they finally got to the broken fence it was exactly as he had described it. The lady clamped her handbag between her knees before she let them out. She sped off in first gear as they gathered up their bags of lager and fish gut.

"Snooty cunt. I thought she was going to twist her pearly earlobe right aff," said Gallowgate with a chuckle.

St Christopher had been shaking over by the fence. His lips were still slapping together in agitation. "Mungo. You shouldnae break a person's anonymity lit that."

Mungo had to turn his eyes from the receding tail lights. "Sorry. I didn't know." Mungo had taken Mo-Maw to enough meetings on Hope Street to know fine well the Alcoholics' rule of anonymity.

"Whit dis it matter to ye?" said Gallowgate. "The wee man wis only bletherin'."

St Christopher was rattling like a fairground skeleton now. He took to muttering under his breath. "Ah'm jist saying you shouldnae ruin a person's reputation like that."

Gallowgate drew his eyes over the trembling man. There was mud on his good suit from where he had lain in the gorse and his "ten-for-a-fiver" white sport socks were ringed with dust from the road; there were scarlet blooms at the heels where his shoes cut his feet. Gallowgate shook his head. "Ah

36

widnae have taken you to have been marked by pride." From his jacket pocket he produced a Wagon Wheel and handed it to the boy. Gallowgate winked at him. It was an apology for the older drunk. It said that Gallowgate thought he was all right, that they'd suffer through St Christopher together.

It was getting late now. As they walked down to the loch, Mungo thought how the men made odd friends — but then he knew that drink was a great leveller, it always brought unlikely people together. He had seen that in his own home, how different folk could huddle in solidarity around a carry-out. He thought about all the aunties and uncles that crossed his door and had lain in waste with his mother. People she wouldn't have sniffed at in the street became like kin when they cashed their unemployment giros and turned them into a quarter-bottle of amber.

There was no path to the loch, the ground was obscured with a carpet of horsetail fern. In the last of the blue daylight, Gallowgate wove in and out of the birch trees, gliding downhill to a loch they could not yet see. St Christopher fell behind. Mungo could hear him muttering to himself, and he stopped now and then to smile back at the sulking man, but St Christopher only paused and picked at the downy bark like he was fascinated by it.

Mungo had hardly been out of the city before. He had never been any place where the greenery didn't eventually end. He had once roamed the untended fields around Garthamlock but they had been spoiled with burnt-out cars and burst settees, and you couldn't run through the long grass for fear of things that might cut into your ankles. Now, as they walked through the forest, he was dizzy with the thought that he was only one of a handful of people who might ever have been here. There were no sounds, no birds, no animals skittering across the forest floor. It was soothing to be part of something so unspoiled.

They came across the bleached skull and bones of an old sheep. Gallowgate ran his fingers over the curled horns and explained it was a ram, "a man sheep." Mungo fished around in his cagoule pocket until he found the disposable camera that Jodie had given him. The roll was half-spent already, wasted on silly snaps of Jodie experimenting with a home-cut fringe. The only sound in the understorey was the *scritch-scritch* of the film winding on. The flash stopped the leaves in their swaying. Even St Christopher stopped his lamenting.

They crossed a dim clearing in single file. Gallowgate squatted; he took the time to show Mungo what stinging nettles looked like, and when they came upon an ocean of the plants, he hoisted the bare-legged boy on to his back. Gallowgate charged through the undergrowth like a saddled mule. He whinnied as his jostling shook gurgling laughter from Mungo. The more Mungo laughed, the harder Gallowgate cantered, until Mungo's shrieks echoed off the thick canopy and Gallowgate was panting heavily.

It had felt strange at first, to wrap his bare legs around Gallowgate's waist, but he felt safe upon the man's back. As Gallowgate put him down again, he rubbed the chill from Mungo's shin bones, and Mungo wondered if he had read the man wrong. Mungo glanced up the path but he couldn't see or hear St Christopher behind them anymore. Gallowgate didn't seem concerned, he hauched into the ferns, and kept marching onwards.

The sun was dipping behind the hills by the time they reached the lochside. After the confines of the forest, the loch suddenly opened up and it was almost too expansive for Mungo to take in. He stumbled down to the shoreline.

The day was drawing in the last of her colours, and as the softest violets and apricots bled away into the horizon, he was sad to have not arrived sooner. Mungo tilted his head back and walked in a circle. The sky above him was a darkening blue smeared with faint streaks of lemon. He hadn't known that the sky could hold so many hues — or he hadn't paid it any mind before. Did anyone in Glasgow look up?

He let out a small awe-filled sigh. All this beauty in the sky was mirrored in the loch as though Mother Nature was bragging. Gallowgate grinned with pride. "Wait till you see the sky the night. Ye've never seen a black like it."

Gallowgate offered Mungo his shoulders to sit upon, so Mungo could glimpse the other side before it vanished entirely in the dusk. From this height Mungo thought the loch must be two miles wide and a hundred miles long.

On the far side it was hemmed in by stout hills whose slopes were split like the underlying rock had torn through the very fabric of them. All the colours were patchy and mottled. It seemed to Mungo as though the hillsides had been blanketed in some giant threadbare rug. The moss green and drab brown were rubbed away in patches to

40

reveal the grey granite as if it were the underlay of the land. There were scatterings of purple moor flower and golden gorse, and here and there were little pockets of white snow, clinging stubbornly to the deepest fissures.

The loch diminished out of view on the left. To the right it turned around a lazy corner and disappeared behind a wall of pine trees. Mungo thought how it was ten times bigger than his scheme, bigger, perhaps, than Glasgow herself.

He had seen the sea twice before. There the water was always shaking and churning. But here the tide was lazy and the surface was glassy as a puddle. Nothing moved except for the buzz of black midges that swarmed low and excited a ripple of hungry fish. The loch looked colder and deeper than he could say. It looked sad, like it had been forgotten. Quiet, like it kept its secrets.

Gallowgate lowered the boy. He rubbed his hands over Mungo's cold back and then hurried across the broken rocks that lined the shore. Tucked into a moss-covered slope was a pile of rough-hewn boulders that vaguely resembled a bothy. There were parallel walls and Mungo could still make out the crumbled doorway and a gabled far end. Outside the bothy was a firepit and a semicircle of larger boulders for sitting on. Thick biting midges thrummed in the shadows.

"Ye'll get used to them," said Gallowgate, handing the boy a large dock leaf. "Rub yer legs with this and ye'll be awright."

Mungo rubbed at his bare legs until they turned green and slick with chlorophyll. The biting flies seemed undeterred.

St Christopher hobbled out from the treeline. He plonked himself down by the lochside and dunked his feet in the icy water. With his angular bones and his grey tweeds, he was just another rock on the shoreline.

Gallowgate marshalled the setup of camp around the stone fire ring. He took off his trendy nylon bomber and the knees of his Italian denims were soon damp as he unpacked the pile of plastic bags. From the backpack he unfurled two thin-looking tents. The two-man tent he erected inside the abandoned bothy. The smaller tent he staked across the far side of the camp, on a bed of dry shingle, almost as far away from the other as possible. Mungo helped drive the curved metal pegs into the ground with a flinty rock. "Shouldn't the tents be closer together?"

Gallowgate looked at the boy and shook

his head. It seemed he meant it to be a friendly smile, but it was without warmth, and Mungo thought he saw a flash of menace cross his thin lips. Perhaps, like Hamish, he didn't like for his authority to be questioned.

"Naw. Better to be far frae the fire," Gallowgate said. He went back to pulling the guy line tight. He strummed it to check its tension. "Don't youse want to see the stars?"

his head. It seemed he meant it, to be a friendly smile. But it was without warmth, and Mungo thought he saw a flash of menace cross his thin lips. Perhaps, like Hamish, he didn't like for his authority to be questioned.

"Haw. Better to be far from the fire," Oatlovgate said. He went back to putting the guy line right. He strummed it to check its tension. "Don't you're want to see the stars."

THE JANUARY
BEFORE

Two

Their mother was surely dead. It had been over three weeks since her children had seen her, and Mungo could imagine nothing but the most gruesome of scenarios. Mo-Maw Hamilton had been raped and then she had been gutted with a steak knife that some long-haul lorry driver had bought using petrol station coupons. She had been trussed and the tips of her fingers hacked off before her naked body was slipped into the cold brackish water of the River Clyde. Mungo followed his sister from room to room, conjuring the worst.

"I just know she's dead."

"Maybe," soothed Jodie. "*Or* maybe she's just on another bender."

"But what if she is dead?"

Jodie sighed. "Look around. We're no that lucky."

The children had come home again from school to an empty house and an emptier fridge. Jodie was watching her brother pace back and forth in front of the bay window, imagining all the horrible things that might have befallen their mother, listing the reasons they should go to the polis. They were in their school uniforms, matching navy jumpers over a striped burgundy and gold tie, except Mungo's tie was wrapped around his head like a bandage to soothe the itchy feeling in his face.

"She's fucked off before," said Jodie. "Don't forget who you're dealing with."

Jodie crossed to where he had been ploughing furrows into the carpet. She wrapped her arms around him, tried to quiet the fluttering inside his chest. He was only a year younger than her, but he had taken a stretch; it had come late, but he was taller than her by almost a head now. Jodie laid her cheek against the nape of his neck, he was burning hot. "Any minute now she could walk through that door."

Mungo turned his brown eyes to the door, the tic under his left eye sparking out a telegraph. Jodie cupped his chin with her hand and manually turned his face away. He was like a dog, he could stare at something for hours unless you distracted him from it.

She pressed her fingers to his face. The

doctors had advised her not to draw any attention to his twitch, to simply ensure that he was getting enough magnesium and that he would grow out of it eventually — but he hadn't, and she doubted that he ever would. It was happening more frequently now. His nose would begin to crinkle, and then he would blink as though someone was flicking the power switch in his brain. If he was especially anxious, or tired, it manifested as a tug or a twitch in his left cheek. He had taught her where to press to try and calm the electricity. It was nothing but a placebo. Jodie came to understand that he just liked to be touched.

He had been clawing at his cheek again, the skin was chafed and angry. Jodie tutted. "You have to stop scratching at your coupon. You're going to leave a scar. *Haaah-ha.*"

"I can't help it."

There was a fresh sore on his top lip. He had taken to picking it when the sore on his cheekbone became too raw. "Oh, for goodness' sake. You're gonnae end up all pock-marked and snaggle-faced like that fella who works at the butcher's."

Her younger brother was a rare sort of handsome. His wasn't the usual blunt or rugged masculinity, and it wasn't the overpreened, over-musked, amateur-footballer style that the boys in her year aspired to. Mungo had high cheekbones and a refined brow that Jodie, with her plump cheeks and stub nose, would have killed for. There was a timidness to his gaze. His hazel eyes could bathe you in their glorious warmth, or he could dip them away from you and make you wish he would look at you again. If you could coax it from him, then there was a real reward in his cautious smile; to earn it made others feel instantly endeared towards him. His unruly mop of hair made women want to mother him.

Growing up he had always been the obedient groom that Jodie constructed play-weddings around. Jodie would nag, while Mungo, always agreeable, would do as he was told. He would stand stock-still as she and Angie Harms swanned around him, draped in mucky veils made from their mother's net curtains. He spent many afternoons kneeling, biting at the hair scrunchies they had wrapped around their puppy-fat thighs in imitation of a garter belt.

There was a gentleness to his being that put girls at ease; they wanted to make a pet of him. But that sweetness unsettled other boys.

Mungo had always been the bonniest of

the Hamiltons. His brother and sister shared his chestnut hair and light olive complexion, so different from their mousy, wan mother. Hamish, when he had wanted to get a rise out of Mo-Maw, had said at least their shared colouring proved they all came from the same father, that they'd gotten more from him than just his surname. Jodie had to admit that Mungo wore it the best. Where the freckles and the sallowness looked slightly grubby on her and Hamish, on Mungo it looked so creamy that you wanted to take a spoon to him.

Jodie had seen the inside of Glasgow Cathedral only once; she had been allowed to go on that particular school trip since she could walk there and it was all free. As the other girls took out their RE notebooks to rub at the stone carvings, Jodie found a stained-glass window of the patron saint, St Kentigern, or as he was colloquially known to Glaswegians, St Mungo. Here St Mungo was depicted as a melancholy boy, cradling a fat salmon, looking sorry that it was dead. Jodie had watched the afternoon light splinter through the saint and cross the dusty cathedral floor and thought of her brother. It was a peaceful window, somehow lonesome. Jodie had sighed before it. It was unlike Mo-Maw to get something so right.

When they were younger and Mo-Maw took them shopping on Duke Street, women would stop to suddenly admire Mungo. "Here now, what a good-looking wee boy ye've got there."

Hamish would step in front of Mungo and say, "Thank you missus, you're no bad looking yersel."

The clumsier of the women would tut and say, "Naw son, *no you.* Him! He's bonny."

Mungo always hated that. He didn't like anyone staring at him. He knew when they got home Hamish would batter him, stuff him between the bed frame and the skirting board, and then just stand on him till he was bored.

Jodie let go of her brother's face. "When you feel the need to pick at yourself you should just sit on your hands."

"C'mon. They make fun of me enough. Can you see me sitting on my hands when my face spazzes out? No fucking way." Mungo bent forward and lifted his sister off her feet. He wore her like a backpack and carried her, giggling, through to the narrow kitchenette. He dropped her in front of the electric cooker. "Feed me, woman."

Jodie extended two fingers and jabbed upwards into his ribs. "That shite doesn't suit you. So don't try it. *Haaah-ha.*"

Jodie Hamilton had a nervous tic of her own, although she would never admit to it. It could pass as an affectation, or perhaps girlish nerves, but after certain sentences she would pepper the air with a sputtering, snorting laughter. *Haaah-ha.* It was unexpected. It was odd. It burst forth with a wheeze and died with a chitter. She tried to chew the end off of it, as though her laughter had a tail she could catch in her teeth. When Mungo started his blinking, it elicited sympathy. When Jodie started her laughing, people told her to get a grip on herself.

Mungo knew she was powerless to it; it happened at the worst times, and he saw how it embarrassed his sister. But Mo-Maw said she did it for attention. *Haaah-ha-ha.* She could startle women in quiet post offices. She could make gangs of neds step away from her. Mungo thought it was brilliant, much better than his fidgeting, scratching face, which always made people come closer to get a better look. But Jodie's tic was pure magic. It pushed people away.

Mungo loved to watch her deliver bad news.

One morning she had found Shingles, Mrs Campbell's scabby tabby, dead inside the bin sheds, all stiff and covered in maggots. She had wrapped the dead cat in her school

53

jumper and chapped on Mrs Campbell's door. There were tears on both of their faces as they looked down at the poor, lifeless beast. Mrs Campbell was stroking the bald spot between his mushroom-coloured ears as Jodie was dripping great gobs of tearful snot on to her shirt. "I'm dead sorry, Missus Campbell," she choked. "I could tell he wisnae right even in the dark there. I think he must have gotten into the rat poison. There was a stinking pool of sick next to his wee face. *Haaah-ha-ha.*" Jodie couldn't help laughing, even at the worst moments.

Hamish never got himself a tic. When Mo-Maw would rub Mungo's back to try and calm his anxiety, Mungo watched his brother scowl, and he wondered if Hamish felt a bit left out. He rarely got any special attention from Mo-Maw. Maybe he should get a really unusual tic, like that one that made you fanny around with the electric cooker knob a million times. Mungo could imagine Hamish flicking at the big light switch while the rest of them were trying to eat their dinner. If he had one, his tic would certainly be the biggest nuisance. Or maybe it could be the one that Mungo had seen on the telly. The one where the boy from the Borders screamed the dirtiest things when people least expected it. *Fuckcuntfannybaws* when he was in the church, *Getitupyeya-hairypussy* in the doctor's office. That tic seemed gallus and violent, perfect for Hamish.

Jodie undid the school tie around Mungo's forehead. She studied the uncertain weather crossing his face. "What's going on in that hamster brain of yours?"

"Do you really think Mo-Maw might come home any minute?"

"I don't know, Mungo. I asked the vet, but he wouldn't let me put a collar on her."

"You could be nicer to h—"

"He wouldn't let me spay her either." Jodie took two thick slices of white bread from the bread bin, smeared them with margarine, and dusted them with white sugar. She folded a sandwich and handed it to Mungo. "Maybe you could go see Hamish and ask if he's heard from her. Anyhows, she needs to get her poxy arse back here soon. The council will pap us on the street if she doesn't."

"They will?"

"Well, technically you'll go into a home for waifs and strays and I'll be put out on the streets. But you get the gist." Jodie filled two mugs with tap water. "Still think she's the best mammy ever?"

They spent the afternoon finishing their

homework. Jodie did her own quickly and then she helped Mungo with his. He was drawing a diagram of a bee and had mislabelled the thorax and the abdomen. In frustration, she tore the jotter from him and did it herself while she watched the evening news. She had taken the same class only twelve months earlier. She drew it perfectly and barely glanced down at the page.

"Mungo Hamilton," his Modern Studies teacher often declared, "How come ye cannae be mair lit yer sister?" The little Napoleon had a mass of grey curls that he teased out on all sides in the hopes it might make him more imposing. He spoke in a gruff Glaswegian dialect. Mungo knew he faked it in order to appear authentic to the East End weans, and to subjugate them by sounding like their fathers. Many of the male teachers did this because their proper Queen's English stank of privilege and always elicited mockery when they raised their voices and tried to control their classrooms. The man drummed his fist on Mungo's forehead as if he was checking the hull of a leaky boat. "How can't ye be mair lit Jodie?" Mr Gillespie would pause — he liked an uncomfortably long silence — before he would dismiss Mungo back to his desk with a wave of his stubby hand. "Ah suppose at least yer fuck all like your Hamish, and that's better than nuthin'."

Mungo gladly let Jodie do his homework while he sat by the radio and recorded the top forty on to a cassette. When he grew bored of this, he found a balloon in the kitchen drawer and blew it up, then he and Jodie kicked it back and forth without letting it touch the carpet. Once or twice, Jodie swung her leg too hard and her tight pencil skirt caught her other leg and swept her to the floor. While she lay there laughing, he would sit on her chest and pretend to dribble spit on to her face. They didn't wrestle, and eventually their gaze would slide back to the television. Mungo would sit on her for a while, and Jodie would let him, until he became too heavy, or she needed to get up and go pee. She would be late for her shift at Garibaldi's Café; Mungo knew she would have to run all the way down Armadale Street just so Enzo wouldn't scream at her in Italian for twenty minutes straight. Still, here she was, kicking this stupid balloon and ripping the seam of her best skirt just so he wouldn't be lonely without her. She was good like that.

"What are you going to do tonight?" she asked.

"Mibbe walk about for a while."

"You need to try and make some frien . . ." When she saw his eyes were twitching, she trailed off.

He was standing on the balloon and trying to burst it.

"Listen, I'm not coming home after my shift tonight. Don't worry, I'll find you at lunchtime tomorrow and we can sit together. I promise."

"Where are you going after Garibaldi's?"

"Never you mind." He followed her as she started filling her schoolbag with strange things: hair tongs, corn plasters, a velvet dress she had ironed and hung on the back of the bathroom door. "I'm staying with one of the girls from my History class."

"But who?"

She tapped the end of her nose. There was panic rising inside him and she could see it clear as a bubbling pot. "But I'm not Mo-Maw. I will be back tomorrow. Promise."

"Okay." He tried to not pick at his face but he couldn't help himself.

After Jodie was gone Mungo stood at the window and worried for Mo-Maw some more. To kill the quiet, he took out his sketchbook. Letting his hand glide over the page made him forget himself. Jodie had been the first to notice it. One day she had grown irritated by his restlessness and had given him one of her old jotters and a half-chewed blue biro. When he couldn't concentrate or grew itchy, she opened it to a blank page, and he drew great sprawling patterns. He never drew figures, he just started in a corner with the indigo ink and let it wander where it would until he had filled the page with intricately swirling, interlocking jacquards: things that looked like peacock feathers, fish scales, or ivy vines, all looping around each other till no whiteness remained. There were wonderful patterns forming in his mind. They could look as ornate as the Bayeux Tapestry or as simple as Ayrshire lace.

But today the blank page could not hold his attention. His mind would not leave his mother alone.

It had been Mo-Maw's turn to mop out the close, which meant it became Jodie's responsibility. For the past two weeks Mungo had watched his sister skitter inside the close mouth and sneak up the stairs before any of the neighbours could open their door and shame her for the stour. It was unfair, Mungo thought: Jodie was run ragged, and all because she had a fanny.

With nothing better to do, he filled the tin bucket and poured globs of Jodie's conditioning shampoo into the water. He started on the top landing, outside Mr Donnelly's door, and washed each stone step on his way downstairs. The close soon smelled tropical with happy bursts of coconut and strawberry chewing gum, but the mop grew slick and several times he had to wash a landing again and again to calm all the bubbles.

The Hamilton family lived on the third floor of a four-storey sandstone tenement. The close wasn't fancy but it was well kept, and everybody went to the bother of leaving a clean doormat outside their door. There were two flats on every landing and each half-landing had a stained-glass window, a simple diamond pattern that let in light from the back green and cast a subdued olive and indigo down the stone stairway.

As he emptied the perfumed water into the gutter he watched gangs of young Proddy boys prowl along the road. They had their jackets zipped open despite the damp cold, and they hung off their thin shoulders in an air of gallus nonchalance. Without exception, they wore their hair parted in the middle and hanging over their eyes in heavy gelled curtains.

"Mungo!" they called at him. They balled up their faces, twisted them like wrung-out tea towels.

Annie Campbell was out on her landing by the time Mungo climbed back up the stairs. She was rubbing at the stone floor with her foot, her husband's moccasin slipper making a tacky, sucking sound. "Oh! Mungo son, what did ye wash this wi'?"

"Just shampoo, Missus Campbell." He had always liked Mrs Campbell. When they were younger, she had baked cakes. On dreich days, if she had heard them playing in the close, she would give them each a slice of Selkirk bannock and tell them how she missed her own boys, all grown and headed somewhere south to look for work. Mungo knew Mr Campbell used to work for Yarrow Shipbuilding, although he couldn't remember Mr Campbell ever leaving the house for work, not since Thatcher had stopped funding for the Clyde. Now Mr Campbell rotted away in an armchair that faced a hot television, and the Hamilton children slunk against the wall if they ever met him on the stairs.

Mrs Campbell swept Mungo's hair off his face. "Honestly son, ye are all kindness and no common sense." She dug around in her pinny and handed him a fistful of lemon drops. They were all congealed and stuck together as one.

"Ah havnae seen your mammy in a guid while. Is she keeping awright?"

Mungo picked the lint off the blob of sweeties. He wouldn't look at her.

Mrs Campbell sucked thoughtfully at her dentures. She took her cracked hands and put them on his narrow ribs. "Would ye do me a wee favour? Ah'm that used to making big dinners. Ah can never get it right since my boys are away. Would you come inside for a minute and have a plate of mince? It wid break ma heart to put it in the bin." She pulled a face that said it would indeed break her heart if the food was wasted.

Mungo thought about Mr Campbell. It wasn't that he disliked the man. It was just the size of him scared any wean that found themselves in his shadow. Years ago, any time he hung out of the window and scolded one of his own sons, the other children would stop their playing and hang their heads in a moment of silent mourning for the poor condemned Campbell. Something about Mr Campbell made Mungo nervous because he had never grown up with a man in the house.

Although he was hungry, he shook his head. "No thank you, Missus Campbell."

The woman tutted. She grabbed hold of his hand and pulled him through her front door. She looked as wispy as sea haar, but she was made of tough Aberdonian granite. "Ah'm done asking you nice. Ah'll be personally offended if ye refuse ma cooking again."

Mrs Campbell led the boy through to her front room. It was the exact same shape as his own, only one floor lower. Mrs Campbell liked to smoke and keep the windows closed. He had heard her say: Why would she waste something she had paid good money for?

Mr Campbell didn't take his eyes off the television as they entered. They were replaying the highlights from a greyhound race out at Ayr. Mungo watched the long dogs slice through the drizzle as they chased the mechanical rabbit.

Mrs Campbell pushed Mungo into her own armchair. She unfolded a small trestle table and pinned him in while she went to heat up a plate. The wall above the fireplace was covered in photos of the Campbell boys. They showed a time-lapse of sorts, every era of them clearly documented. Smiling, good-natured boys, grinning once a year against the marbled blue of the school photographer's backdrop. They were at least ten years older than Mungo and he didn't remember them too well, but he could tell from the boys' mouths that the photos didn't miss a moment: baby teeth, missing teeth, first big teeth, gappy teeth, and metal teeth. He saw the shy smile of silver braces and then the straight and confident grins of successful young men. Mungo touched his own mouth self-consciously. Mo-Maw wasn't a big believer in dentists.

"Has your mother gone missing again?" Mr Campbell didn't look up at the boy.

"Aye."

"Wummin don't know what nonsense to be up to these days. Too much choice. No doubt she'll show up when she dries out."

"Do you think so?"

"Aye." He scowled at the racing results. "Has your Hamish found work yet?"

"Naw."

Mr Campbell considered this for a moment. "Aye, well. Glasgow's done for. No coal, no steel, no railway works, and no fuckin' shipbuilding." The man's jaw set at a funny angle but he didn't stop watching the racing. "You tell him Mr Campbell said he should join the navy. He should ask to get stationed at Faslane and then drive one of thon nuclear submarines right up Thatcher's cunt."

Mungo tittered with nerves. "Don't you mean John Major's hole?"

Mr Campbell grimaced. "There's submarines enough for the lot of them."

Margaret Thatcher had not been Prime Minister for a couple of years now, even Mungo knew that. Yet every conversation about unemployment and the future still focused its ire on her. Mr Gillespie had told his Modern Studies class that Margaret Thatcher had been intent on closing all the heavy industry in the city. The English government had been frustrated with the growing power of the trade unions, tired of subsidizing Scotland to compete with cheaper foreign labour. He had said that it was catastrophic to put several generations of the same families out of work: men who had been bred to shape steel would be left to rust, whole communities that grew up around shipbuilding would have no paying jobs. He drew concentric circles like the ripples in a puddle and tried to have the class list the broader effects Thatcher's policies had on the city. How when the collieries closed, it had been the butchers and the greengrocer and the man who sold used cars who had suffered next. Mr Gillespie had said it was bad enough that the Conservatives had killed the city, but that it had been spearheaded by an English woman was an unspeakable insult. What had made her want to neuter the Glaswegian man? A thousand words due a week on Monday.

When Mungo asked Jodie what *neuter* meant, she had said Mr Gillespie drank too much. That if a man was in power, he would never have made the tough decisions that Thatcher had been faced with. Then she asked Mungo if he actually wanted to work down a coal mine?

"Naw."

"Then stop fucking blaming it on women." Jodie picked the chipped polish from her thumbnail. "Besides, ignore the old bastard. None of that Thatcher stuff is on the curriculum. Mr Gillespie is a flabby-arsed Marxist. Do you know how some men build model railways in their spare room? Well youse are his little green soldiers. He sees it as his wee project to stir up the proletariat in the East End, while he drives his Sierra estate to the Marks and Spencer out at Bishopbriggs and spunks his wages on baguettes and Merlot."

Mungo must have been squinting at her because Jodie sighed. "I saw him peeling a kiwi fruit in the staffroom the other week. So, up your arse with his voice-of-the-working-class nonsense."

Mungo bet Jodie would never say that to Mr Gillespie's face.

Mr Campbell was still talking. "Just like the fucking English, eh? First they let boatloads of the starving Irish bastards come over and take all the good work. Then they go and shut all the businesses and leave us jobless and drowning in dirty Fenians." He looked at Mungo now, his eyes were as clear and blue as a June sky. "Aye, very clever of the English that was. That's how ye keep the Scottish lion on its knees."

Mrs Campbell returned with a scalding plate heaped with boiled potatoes swimming in brown mince. The gravy was thick with onions, long and curved as a witch's fingernails. In the middle of the plate were two fluffy doughballs. She smiled as Mungo ate. Mungo chewed as quickly as he could, eager to be away from Mr Campbell. Only when he was finished did she take the trestle table away and free him. The woman dabbed at a gravy stain on his jumper. "That Maureen Hamilton, she was having a bloody laugh when she named you after a saint, eh? The cheek of it. Look at the state of ye." He kissed Mrs Campbell's cheek, his lips felt greasy against the parchment of her skin.

The man pointed at the ceiling but did not look at the boy. "When yer mammy shows her gallus face, ah'll nail her fuckin' feet to your carpet if ye want? That'll soon sort her."

"I'll let you know," said Mungo. He nodded quickly as he went out the door.

Afterwards, Mungo lay on his living room carpet running his hands across his happy belly. The day dimmed early and the orange street lights came to life all across the scheme. He lay there in the afternoon dark, humming to himself.

He heard Mrs Campbell climb up and down the close with her sloshing pail. Her knees cracked as she went. The mop head clipped the hard stone as she rinsed each stair clean of his shampoo. He felt bad to have given her extra work, but her voice echoed as she sang Tammy Wynette to herself and he decided that she sounded content enough.

When she reached the Hamilton landing the woman crouched at his door. The rusted spring whined in protest as she opened the letter box. Her voice was carried in on the draught. He could hear her clearly enough, as though she was in the room with him.

"Mungo Hamilton, ye're a useless wee scunner."

The letter box closed with a snap. Mungo sat up. There was a brief pause before it rasped open. "But I love ye." It snapped closed, and then sprung open again. "Ya wee arsehole."

Garibaldi's Café had been on the same corner for over twenty years. For sixty years before that, it had sat further along the road, at the base of a tenement the council had pulled down during the slum clearances, when they had sent the families to live in the new high-rise flats.

Jodie was out of breath by the time she raced through the front door. Enzo Garibaldi raised his head as the little bell tinkled. He scowled at the ornate clock that sat amongst his family photos; six generations of stern Italian men wrapped in jolly striped aprons. Jodie knew the clock ran fast but it was hardly worth arguing about. She tucked her schoolbag under the counter and pinned up her hair.

Jodie worked at Garibaldi's most nights after school; scooping hard ice cream into oyster shells and marshmallow-filled wafers, before pouring thick syrupy raspberry sauce over the top of it with a glurp. Garibaldi's ice cream came in only one flavour: sweet full-cream vanilla. Jodie had tasted real vanilla only once, and she knew that Garibaldi's was not vanilla. It was just white sugar and heavy cream, but it made housewives' eyes roll back in their heads and children behave at the mere promise of a pokey cone. There was a reason it had stayed in business for nearly a century; it made your teeth scream with delight.

It was a damp, uneventful evening and she passed the hours by breaking apart bulk crates of ginger so Enzo could sell them individually at a higher price. When Jodie finished her shift she locked herself in the bathroom. She stuffed herself into her velvet dress and then concealed the dress underneath her winter coat before she asked Enzo for an advance on next week's wages.

Enzo liked Jodie; she had the tint of an Italian and reminded him of his own adult daughters, grown and with families of their own. At least once a week he asked if Jodie was still planning on going to university, if her life remained *on track.* It was an odd euphemism, when what he really wanted to know was if she was letting any man get at her. But Jodie was glad that somebody cared to ask, even if she had to remind Enzo that she didn't come from university money.

As she folded her apron, Enzo beamed at her proudly and handed her an advance straight from the till. Then he let her heap two golden oysters for herself, dusted in flake crumbs and smothered in raspberry sauce.

As she crossed Duke Street, the faint rain shimmered like midges in the glow of the street lights. She walked up the hill towards the high school and stood on the corner taking care to hold the dripping ice cream away from her velvet dress.

The man had been parked with his headlights off, waiting patiently for her. When he saw her in the rain, he turned over the engine and pulled alongside the kerb. Jodie got into the car and kissed him. He didn't linger on her lips. He was annoyed that she would bring dribbly ice cream into his new motor. Rolling down his window, he took the oysters from her and dumped them out on to the street. Then he put each of her fingers into his mouth and sucked the cream from her knuckles.

Before him, Jodie had never been outside of Glasgow; she had rarely been out of the East End. She knew the West End was not for the likes of her, with its gothic spires and ancient university and outdoor cafés with vegetarian menus, and she never went to the South Side because Hamish had scared her with lies of what the Pakistani men would do to a wee white lassie like her.

As he drove her across the Kingston

Bridge the city was illuminated below her and she felt alive. They flew over the lights so quickly that in moments like this she believed she could belong anywhere, not just in a council tenement looking after her little brother. Jodie curled up into the leather seat and allowed herself the day-dream of a life at college, maybe not a university, but a good trade school, a technical college like the Building and Printing school or Cardonald with its plumbers and hairdressers.

The man took her hand in his and kissed the back of it. As the lights fell away she put her trust in him. She knew he wanted the same bright future for her. He had told her many times how clever she was, and that when she had her education, they could be together, even in the bright daytime, somewhere far away from Glasgow and the eyes of his wife.

Mungo pulled on his cagoule. It was a royal-blue ski jacket that he needed to wrangle over his head because the zipper only went halfway down and butted into a large kanga-roo pocket. He loved this jacket. He could carry all manner of things in the pocket, which opened with a Velcro flap at the top and you had to twist your body to reach inside. Often he found things, pocketed them, and then forgot about them for weeks until they brushed against his fingers again. When Hamish hung him by the ankles, his entire world would spill out like a confession.

For a while he wandered along familiar streets, winding back and forth, looking for a glimpse of Mo-Maw, lying to himself that he was not. The streets were narrow and the tenements were tall, making each road feel sunken, deep as a sandstone gorge. The sky was small here. It was hard to see what was coming over the horizon until it was directly above you. He had spent his whole life on these streets and some days it could make him feel like a mouse in a maze. He knew there was nowhere you could walk without people looking down at you, watching the sameness of the weather, passing the slow time. It was hard to feel alone.

The worst of the watchers was Mr Ogilvy. Ogling Ogilvy led the local Orange marching band and either he or his twin sons would stand at their window practising their fife and drums and letting the thin glazing shake in its putty. Today, the Ogilvy twins wore their regimental blues and their jaunty Tam-o'-Shanters. In their white gloves they looked as neat as porcelain ornaments, children dressed as romantic, hateful Union soldiers. The sharp song of their flutes carried out over the tenements, and behind them, echoing off the stone walls was the *thoom, thoom, thoom* of the Lambeg drum. Ogling Ogilvy hammered the heavy oak battle drum, and it thundered off the sandstone as the shrill piccolos played the melody to "The Sash My Father Wore." Two men had stopped and leaned on the rusted fence to listen, their eyes wet with whisky. Mungo hurried past the Ogilvys'. *Thoom, thoom, thoom* went his footsteps. He knew Ogling Ogilvy watched his every move. He knew he thought him a great disappointment to the Protestant cause.

Frowning, he reached the large patch of scabrous grass that separated the old tenements from the damp flats the council built in the sixties. The city planners had angled the new flats away from the greenery. They had faced them towards the motorway because they had thought that's what people would have wanted to see: progress, not skinny weans playing in the smirr. Mungo loitered a while and was happy for a moment to be unobserved. The grass was worn bald and muddy, and bands of older boys were playing football, running up and down after a half-deflated bladder. They had organized shivering girls into clusters of three or four and were using them as wide goalposts. Every now and then the ball would ricochet off the face of one of these girls, and she would fake tears until the required boy came and clamped his chapped mouth over hers.

On the other side of the waste ground, younger boys had collected discarded wood, old doors, and bits of broken furniture. They had dragged it all the way here and assembled the scraps into dens. Eight or nine of these makeshift homes clustered together like a shanty town and Mungo watched little boys go around making repairs and improvements to their castles. As he watched their industry, he was reminded of a video the substitute teacher had played in school to show the inner workings of a beehive. He knew some of the boys had hard men for fathers and they had brothers in the jail. He had heard that boys as young as eleven could make swords and charge at bands of Catholics who came on to their scheme: they split skulls, they slashed faces, they stabbed Fenians twice their height and all for the chuckles of it. As he watched them cooperate building their dens, it was easy to forget the cheerful violence they were capable of.

Mungo kept his head low and passed by the new flats. The pebbledash facing was so porous that even on dry days it looked like it was leaching rainwater back into the world. On the far side, behind fifteen-foot walls, was a builder's yard. The builders had ringed the top of the wall in barbed wire, but the local boys would not be deterred.

Mungo watched a cluster of young men mount their attack on the wall. They had roped together two of their mammy's wall-papering ladders and someone had stolen the duvet off their little sister's bed. They wanted to get in because inside were great beasts of heavy JCB machines that could be climbed and smashed and destroyed. Some-times, inside the cabin of one of the diggers, a workman would forget his tools and the boys would take the bag full of hammers and spanners and make great plans to weap-onize them back at the tenements.

Best of all was the time someone left the keys for the JCB digger in the ignition. The Protestant boys took the digger, and after ramming it into other machinery drove it clean through the padlocked gate and up and down the back streets. They were lifting a bucketful of young men up to a second-storey window to peep in at a chubby girl when her mother finally called the polis.

Mungo watched the young men prop their rigged ladders against the wall. Their leader selected the smallest of them to climb the length of it and test it for sturdiness. A ginger-headed youth wrapped a teddy bear blanket around himself and scaled the shaking ladders. When he was high enough to kill himself, the other young men took turns at kicking the bottom of it. It must have been a great entertainment, for they were whooping and betting money on him cracking his skull. They grouped together and pushed the ladder away from the wall. For a moment it stood on its own and the ginger youth teetered with the promise of a broken back. He let out a pathetic howl. The ringleader cut through the others and with one hand he pushed the ladder back against the wall.

"Fuckin' pack it in," threatened Hamish.

The ginger boy blanched and wilted like stewed cabbage. He flattened the barbed wire under the teddy bear blanket and stood a while checking for the security guard before he scaled the wall and dropped on to the corrugated roof beyond. Mungo crossed the waste ground and stood next to his brother as the others climbed their siege ladder.

Hamish half-nodded in greeting. He was

watching his troops very closely. Mungo knew he would give them harsh feedback later; he ran a neat, ambitious little army. It was important to expose the inadequacies of the men in front of the other men, for it kept them divided. It kept them trying their hardest.

To Mungo, his brother was simply Hamish — Hamey if he was feeling especially brave. But to his troops he was Ha-Ha, or the Big Man, despite his disappointing height. Ha-Ha watched the last of the troops scale the ladder before he addressed Mungo. "Whit's happenin' gobshite?"

"Nothing." Mungo shrugged. "Have you seen Mo-Maw?"

Ha-Ha shook his head. He looked up at Mungo through his thick government lenses, his eyes tiny behind the yellowing glass. As a boy he had been embarrassed by his free tortoiseshell frames, but Mungo knew his brother had mastered this shame, and now relished the chance of anyone calling him a speccy cunt so he could surprise them with the swiftness of his violence. Hamish loved traps: he particularly enjoyed the suspended moment when someone ran off a cliff and didn't know they were about to fall to their doom. He came to appreciate how his glasses disarmed strangers. Other men would foolishly let the wee wide-o in the pensioner's glasses get too close, and still thought they could get the better of him, right up until he was shattering their teeth on the kerb edge.

Hamish was not tall, but he was always ready and never, ever scared to hit first. He was wearing his denim jacket and a pair of jeans that were an identical shade of blue. He had buttoned the jacket up to the throat and turned the collar up. On his feet he wore a pair of triple stripe Sambas that looked brand new. Nothing on him was given to fat, every tissue was sinew and muscle. Everything was pulled in tight like he was ready to bolt. Ha-Ha never ran.

"On ye go." Ha-Ha pointed up at the rickety ladder.

Mungo stepped back.

"How?"

Mungo knew his face was electric. "I'm no in the mood."

Ha-Ha wrapped a hand around the back of Mungo's neck. He was going to say something further but instead he thrust his brother at the ladder and Mungo found himself scaling it.

The builder's yard was not large. The industrial vehicles were packed tight, like pieces of a board game in a box. It was all very neat and orderly: mixers, spreaders, heavy steam rollers, and sitting in the middle, like a band of brontosauruses, were the long-necked excavators.

The key to success at the builder's yard was not to raid it too often. If you thieved from it too frequently then the foreman would install a temporary night watchman to protect the equipment. He was always a temp, because the Protestant boys would not think twice about stabbing him, so it was hard for the foreman to retain someone full-time. However, if they raided it only once or twice a year, it became a strange sort of parasitic relationship. The boys smashed and stole what they liked, and the foreman claimed the damage on insurance and still came out in the black in his account books. Hamish knew there were times the canny foreman used the raids to replace outdated models, or tools that were half-broken and would cost more to mend than to replace. Hamish had seen him once, in the Louden Tavern, and the man had nodded a faint head bob of respect. Twice a year, no more. It was still cheaper than hiring a night watchman.

The young Protestants were standing on the corrugated roof of the main building; their breath misted the air as though they

were a string of Eriskay ponies. Mungo
watched their eyes scour the builder's yard.
None of the horses moved until Ha-Ha
scaled the wall. He stood amongst them like
a general, a stone-washed emperor.

"Hallo, Hallo, we are the Billy boys.
Hallo, Hallo, ye'll know us by our noise.
We're up to our knees in Fenian blood,
    surrender or ye'll die.
For we are the Brigton Billy boys."

Ha-ha knew what he was doing. The
Orange song filled them with pride. Any fear
the half-men harboured vanished on hearing it.

One by one they dropped off the guttering and hit the gravel like spears of rain.
Mungo turned to his brother but Hamish
had vanished, and Ha-Ha was in no mood
to talk to him. He was watching his soldiers
make the first sweep, seeing what could be
soundlessly liberated, before the fun of the
smashing started. Then Ha-Ha shoved his
brother and Mungo hooked his hands on to
the tin guttering and dropped the fourteen
feet to the ground.

The youths were ripping things out of the
cabins now, tearing up owner's manuals and
carelessly tossing screws like shrapnel. Of

all the things they did, this was the part that Mungo hated the most. He could understand the theft — stolen things were useful — but this was just mindless destruction. The ginger-headed boy had found a bright orange hard hat; it dwarfed him and made him look like a wean who was terminally sick. Mungo watched him hammer his head into the side window of a steamroller. He did it again and again until the glass cracked and he could push the rest of it in with his elbow.

Ha-Ha never came down to the ground. From time to time the squad would throw things up to him, forgotten wrenches or a rusting spirit-level. Behind his thick glasses he watched everything like a tawny osprey. He pointed from his perch and the boys scurried off, searching for the shadow of his talon.

One of the squad was being too considerate in rifling through a toolbox. He was sitting in the raised bucket of a digger, as comfortable as a new settee. He was a tall youth who wore his mousy hair long on the sides and softly feathered over his eyes. Mungo knew that he occasionally spoke in the Queen's English — not *hame* but *home,* not *didnae* but *did not* — and that it slipped out of him when he was tired. He had a proud mother and a working father who still lived at home. The others teased him for it. Ha-Ha's voice boomed over the gravel. "Haw Prince Charles! Can ah bring ye a cup o' tea? Ya fuckin' poofter."

The marauders stopped what they were doing, fearful that he should be naming one of them a deviant, an aberration amongst decent men. Ha-Ha pointed his finger directly at the youth and shook his head in shame. "Stop fuckin' wasting time like ye were choosin' carrots to shove up yer arse." The mousy boy scattered the toolbox as he tried to reclaim his manhood. The others tittered and went about ransacking the place with a sense of relief. There was nothing more shameful than being a poofter; powerless, soft as a woman.

Mungo hid in the darkened cabin of a backhoe, safe from Ha-Ha's glare. He watched the mousy-haired boy flush scarlet and then spray the box of brackets everywhere with a malicious kick. The others scavenged all the weapons and tools they could and when they were done, they started their smashing. A ruddy-faced youth swung a fence post off the window of the excavator. The safety glass made a satisfying crunch.

When they grew tired of this, they moved

on to the third stage, and, reverting to children again, they played. The young men climbed on to the roof of the smallest of the loaders and made a great circuit of jumping from one to the other, never touching the ground. They ran this obstacle course of follow-my-leader and climbed higher and higher. They found new ways to make it more dangerous. They took it in turns to climb the angled neck of the brontosaurus excavators, they crept upwards to the bucket and then they leapt, gliding through the air to the roof of a backhoe. If they missed, then it was a twenty-foot plummet to the ground. But they flew across the night sky like fearless angels, their tracksuits flapping behind them like flightless wings.

The machinery was wet with rain. Mungo watched as some of the boys slipped on the angled neck of the brontosaurus. One or two overshot the jump and slid across the wet backhoe only to catch themselves at the very last moment on the raised rubber seal of a window. It always made the others hold their breath and fall silent for a moment. As the lucky boy hauled himself to his feet they would whoop for their own immortality.

Ha-Ha stood on the roof smoking a short dout. He had transformed from an emperor to a bored dad who hated having to share custody. It was as though he was watching his weans work off a day of sugary treats before he could return them to their mothers. It was because Mungo was watching his brother that he saw the sky change. Ha-Ha saw it too, the rhythmic pulse of blue and white. The police cars had crept nearer without wailing their sirens. Now they were at the gates. Ha-Ha had let his weans play too long.

Mungo spilled from the tin-can cabin and started the quick climb from front wheel to back wheel to engine mount to roof. He was bounding across the yard as the polis burst through locked gates. Around him the squad leapt from the long excavator arm and raced to the guttering and on to the safety of the roof. They were squealing like six-year-olds at a fairground as they danced away from the bogeyman's grasp. Only when they reached the safety of the roof and the dauntless protection of Ha-Ha did they straighten up and become men again. They arched their backs and showered the polis with phlegm.

Six policemen arrived in two Rovers and one battered detention van. They caught one of the slower boys who jumped unwittingly into an officer's arms. He held him for a moment like they were startled lovers.

The ginger-headed youth twisted on the neck of the excavator, slunk to his nylon backside, and was about to slide down and away from the polis. Mungo was almost at the guttering when he saw the boy fall. The metal must have been wetter than he had thought, and he slipped off the high arm as gracelessly as a bag of flour falling off a shelf.

He didn't split open like a bag of flour and he didn't cry out, but by the way his arm crumpled beneath him and the odd angle of his hand, Mungo could tell he had broken his wrist, maybe even shattered his forearm.

Mungo could hear Hamish call his name as he rained rocks and shrapnel down on the polis. If Mungo stood up now, he could climb swiftly and be on the corrugated roof before they could catch him. "Jist leave him!" Hamish roared. It would be foolish not to run — the polis must have clocked all the boys — and even if they hadn't seen Mungo, they certainly had seen the bag of flour plummet to his doom. They would come looking for the burst boy soon enough.

Mungo heard the clatter of feet on the corrugated roof, the bravado and taunts retreating, and he knew the others were back over the wall and running for the safety of the scheme. They were leaving him.

The ginger youth was hard-hatless now, and there was a shallowness to his breathing. Mungo gripped him below his oxters and dragged him underneath the backhoe. It was dark away from the security lights, and they watched as police torches streaked the ground. The young man was whimpering. Mungo put his hand over his mouth. Any other time he would have leathered Mungo for touching him like this. Now he lay with his head cradled in Mungo's side and they watched the police lights strafe between the vehicles. Mungo recognized him then: he was Bobby Barr, the older brother of a boy in Mungo's class, the unlikely father of twins, and a famed destroyer of virginities. Now there was blood pooling out his jumper sleeve and from the smell Mungo could tell he had ruined himself with piss.

Other than the soft crunch of gravel it was quiet. The polis were stalking and had switched off the crackling static of their radios. Bobby was sobbing quietly to himself. Mungo's face short-circuited in the darkness. *"Don't leave us."* Mungo could feel the words reverberate through the palm of his hand; the boy's tears were pooling in the gullies of his fingers.

Torchlight streaked under the backhoe. There were hard hands on Bobby Barr's ankles. A policeman ripped him out in one smooth move, and the boy rolled away on the chuckie stones, like a mechanic on a wheel board. Bobby's good arm was ruined and his other was cradling it like a baby, so he could offer no resistance. Whoosh. He was gone, fast as any magic trick.

"There's another fuckin' basturt in there," screamed an officer.

Mungo pushed away from the light and scrambled across the stones towards the other end. He could hear them closing in on him, two on either side, running along the long sides of the machine. He found his footing, he wasn't as agile as the other boys who leapt like skinny cats from machine to machine, but Mungo was on the cab before the polis could round the corner. He knew he would never make the safety of the guttering; as his legs hung down, they would grab at him. So he made the half-turn to run for the open gate, but they cut him off. He was trapped.

"Ye little basturt. When ah catch ye, ah'm gonnae fuck ye!" A smug smile spread over the officer's face. He was climbing up towards Mungo while the others blocked his escape. "Ah'm gonnae fuck ye. Ah'm gonnae fuck ye." He was chanting it over and over.

Hamish would have told him the officer only wanted to break his nerve. That he wanted to belittle and intimidate him so that Mungo would come down from the roof and offer no resistance. But Hamish wasn't here.

"Ye'll like it," said the policeman. "If ye come down the now, ah'll spit on it first, so it hurts less." They were laughing amongst themselves now. He could hear the polis both protest and congratulate the officer on how rotten he was. "Ye goat any sisters?"

Mungo scurried higher.

There was a thud in the dark. He wasn't sure what had caused it. But whatever hit the officer stopped his taunting, sweeping his cap off his head and knocking him against the side of a mixer. There was dark blood on his face, as black as treacle in the gloaming. There were bits of him sprayed over the yellow steel of the machinery.

Ha-Ha was back at the top of his ladder and launching half-bricks down on the policemen. Mungo knew the Protestants had a stash for gang fights and were now passing them phalanx-style up the ladder to their emperor. Ha-Ha had a skilled arm for smiting.

"Well? Run, ya fuckin' bellend!"

Mungo saw his chance. He flew down from the roof and was out the open gate as a hail of bricks sent the policemen scurrying under machinery. At first he ran past it, then he skidded to a stop and dashed back to the meat wagon. He threw open the back doors. He didn't wait for the captured boys, but he heard the reassuring slap of trainer soles as they raced, lungs bursting, through the wet streets.

THREE

St Christopher was hunched by the edge of the loch, mumbling to himself and swatting at the biting midges. Mungo couldn't tell if he was sulking or just sobering up. The man had his back to them and was hunkered over like he might submerge his face or spit up the rising boak. The wind mussed his thin hair; it broke the lock of sweat and pomade and separated the tawny brown from an inch of pure-white roots. His vanity struck the boy. The old man had coloured it like Mo-Maw did, from a supermarket box. He must have sat on the toilet at home with a black bin bag over his shoulders to catch the drips.

Mungo could see he had already unpacked all the remaining alcohol and nestled it between two boulders in the frigid loch. A man with a single suit, and a bag full of drink. As easy as that he was settled.

Mungo gathered sticks and Gallowgate

showed him how to make a weak, coughing fire from damp wood and green limbs. They huddled upwind and let the billowing smoke drive the black flies away. Mungo added moss-covered branches until the fire danced brightly. Each time he added one, he looked at the man to see if it was okay. Gallowgate unwrapped three lasagnes that had long ago defrosted, and buried their aluminium basins in the glowing embers. Mungo pressed his hands to his empty stomach.

St Christopher held his distance. Away from the firelight it became a sleekit kind of dark. It was as though the sky wanted to be like the quiet loch: it crept in shades towards the water, until the sky and the loch became one, and St Christopher was swallowed by the inky night.

"That's a funny name. Mun-*go,*" said Gallowgate. He was sucking on a bent dout. He had crushed the hand-rolled cigarettes in the back pocket of his tight denims and amber tobacco escaped from the creases in the paper.

"I suppose." Mungo watched him cover the holes with his fingers, skilled as any flautist. "My father was a Nationalist. He wanted his boys to have traditional Scottish names."

"Aye, but Mun-go. Ah mean, for *fuck's sake,* that's pure child abuse."

"St Mungo. He was the patron saint of Glasgow. He started a fire from nothing, or . . . something, I don't really know." His understanding of the Glasgow myths was streaked with embarrassment. He couldn't count the times he had been dragged to the front of the classroom to read the history of the city aloud, blushing at the sound of his own voice, retaining not a single word of what he read.

The first time they had called him Mungoloid, he had come home in tears. Jodie had hidden with him in the hot airing cupboard. He was soothed by the happy click and whirr of the gas immersion as she dried his face on Mo-Maw's winter coat. She had told him about the myths of St Mungo: the bird that never flew, the tree that never grew, the bell that never rang, the fish that never swam. Of all the legends, he liked the one about the bird the best; how St Mungo had brought the little robin back to life after it had been killed by the cruel children. Jodie said that was his power, that after their father died, he gave life back to Mo-Maw when she had given up on it for herself. He loved Jodie. He forgave her when she lied to him.

Gallowgate raised his can in salute. His eyes were rheumy with drink. "It's a marvellous thing. Here, ah thought ah was only scum but turns out ah'm a blessed man indeed. Oh, to be protected by two saints on this fine bank holiday weekend. One to carry me safely across the water. The other to light ma fires as we go." He drummed his fist against his heart. "If only ah could find another to gies a loan of some money. Then ah'd be fuckin' whistlin'."

St Christopher came shivering out of the darkness. He waited on the very edge of the light, like a shy guest at a house party. Gallowgate belched, beckoned the man to find a rock to sit on. It was embarrassing to watch St Christopher pretend like he hadn't been sulking, to watch him try and catch the conversation, jump back on to it like it was a galloping horse. His feet were meatless and bloodless. The water was so cold they shone smooth as blue porcelain.

As St Christopher thawed by the fire, there was a smell of turned milk, and underneath that, something that smelled like dried goldfish flakes. Gallowgate wrinkled his nose, shifting upwind slightly to lie against the bothy wall. Mungo watched as he lifted his shirt and ran a hand across his taut, distended belly; even there, he was inked with words, signed like the inside flap of a school jotter. They sat drinking by the fire long enough for their eyes to begin streaming from the smoke. As each new lager splashed open, the conversation darkened and ratcheted downward. For Mungo it was like walking down a tenement close: every flight they descended, it got darker, the lights were less bright.

". . . So, ah took hold of her and she was pure gaggin' for it," Gallowgate was explaining in the firelight. "She telt me that her husband knew whit she was up to and didnae mind. So, ah thought to masel, if this cunt disnae mind then ah'm no going tae worry about leaving marks, eh?"

Mungo drew his knees up to his chest again. He didn't like the way the man was licking the back of his own teeth.

"So, whit did ye dae?" St Christopher spat, un-saintly, eager for the dirty details.

"Well, ah've got haud of her." Gallowgate leaned closer to the boy. "An' she's got oan this wee blue nightie, one of them cuddly kittens printed on the front. Ah didnae bother to undress her cos she was no Easter lamb ye understand, sometimes it's better no tae chance it. So, ah just got stuck in. Started going for it." His eyes were opals in the firelight. He held out a cupped hand.

95

"Ye know. Ah was rubbing away. Feeding the wee horse."

The question slipped out of Mungo. "Wait, the lady had a horse?"

The men blinked at him. They roared with laughter. "Naw, wee man. Her lady bits, her fanny. Next time ye put your hand over one, see if it disnae feel like a pair of horse lips."

St Christopher rattled his own lips and made a neighing sound.

Gallowgate laughed, the short dout hanging out the side of his mouth. Mungo had done it again, failed to see the difference between what someone said and what they truly meant. He could feel his eyes start their nervous blink. He tried to laugh through the tic, eager to stay on the inside and not the outside of it all.

St Christopher had no time for the boy. "Then whit?"

"So, ah put her on the couch and we start doing it, like *really* doing it, right? An ah'm up to ma nuts in her guts and she goes like, *'Ooooh let's go upstairs and do it in the bedroom.'* " He hauched into the fire, the spit sizzled a second and then disappeared. "So here's me, ah carry her up the stairs like she was an auld coat stuck on a peg."

Mungo thought about the coat hooks they had made in techy class at school. Twisted

G-shaped metal pegs, heated and dipped in powder coating and screwed to cheap wood. He bit down on his bottom lip.

St Christopher slapped his leg. "Ye're a dirty basturt."

"Ah get her up the stairs and ah must've gone into the wrong room, cos this is a teenager's bedroom. But she's clawing at me, and we're gaun for it."

"She's a filthy besom, right enough," said the saint. Mungo wondered if he knew this woman.

"Well ah've bent her over and ah'm doin' her on the single bed." Gallowgate stood up and began thrusting his hips in and out of the firelight. His pale face was bloated with alcohol, it floated like a moon in the sky. "And just then ah look at her carpet and ye're no gonnae believe it, right?"

"Whit? *Whit!*"

Gallowgate stepped closer to the firelight. He arched his back, and Mungo could see the swollen outline in his denims where his meat lay pressed against his hip bone. Mungo lowered his gaze. Gallowgate took a draw on his dout, holding the tension, savouring the impatience of his saints. "Well, as it turns out, ah've only bloody tacked out and laid that floral carpet in her daughter's room the year afore."

"Aye. *So?*"

"A guid carpet-fitter never forgets his work. It turns oot ah had shagged her wee lassie on it as well." Gallowgate tossed his head back in a smug way. He exhaled like a proud chimney.

It took a minute, then St Christopher let out a howl like a punctured dog. "Ah, ya dirty basturt." His broken teeth looked dangerously sharp. He slapped his knee. "Well. Ah've got nae memory for cunts. But ah never forget a well-laid carpet."

Mungo didn't understand the joke. He was glancing from one man to the other, but he knew now not to ask.

"Fifteen she wis. A wee ride just like her maw." Gallowgate took a bottle of whisky from the plastic carrier bag. He drank it down in gulps as though it were only ginger ale. "Ah learned early, it's the big fancy houses that ye've got tae watch out for. Wummin who nag their husbands for double glazin' probably aren't getting whit they really want." He grabbed at the front of his denims, stroked himself, then throttled it, like he was trying to strangle it.

St Christopher stopped his howling. "Ah didnae know ye fitted carpets."

"Carpets. Kitchens. Teenage daughters. You name it. Ah fit it." He chuckled to himself.

St Christopher nodded in quiet respect. "Must be grand, to be a young man with everything to play for."

"Aye, well. Ah've always been good with ma hands." Gallowgate wrapped his knuckles on the side of his head. "It's the rest of me that's been a fuckin' disappointment."

"Still, you've yer whole life ahead of ye." St Christopher reached for the whisky like a child demanding a bottle, his feeble fingers grasping the air. Gallowgate handed it to him and when he stopped his gulping and gasping he wiped his mouth and said, "Ye should never have been in Barlinnie in the first place. A young man like you, in jail?"

Mungo had seen Barlinnie Prison before. He had heard Mo-Maw threaten Hamish with it when he got too close to the law, with his stolen motors and bags of contaminated speed. He had seen it strike a muted fear into his brother.

Mungo's face must have framed a question because Gallowgate was watching him before swivelling his eyes back towards the saint. "What the fuck did ye have to go tell the boy that fur?" Gallowgate flicked his dout at the man. "Ye'll frighten the wee fella." But something in his grin told Mungo he wasn't angry with St Christopher. Nor would he mind frightening Mungo.

"Tell him whit?" The man hopped to his bare feet. He did a jangly dance as he searched for the lit cigarette in the folds of his dirty suit.

"That we were in the *jail.*" Gallowgate turned a sneering smile towards Mungo. "He'll think he's out here with a pair of right jakeys."

Mungo picked at the scab on his knee. He pretended to be engrossed in it. "What did you get the jail for?"

"Breaking and entering," said Gallowgate quickly. Something about him looked like he was lying, but Mungo could not tell for sure. "It was an accident. Ah fell through a skylight right into a warehouse. By the time ah found the exit ma arms were loaded with four dozen fitba tops."

The saint made a noise like he wanted to contradict him, but Gallowgate kicked at the pebbles and sent a shower of them flying in the man's direction. The swiftness of it made Mungo jump. "Aye. Breaking and entering, right enough," agreed the saint reluctantly. Something about how he said it made Gallowgate snicker.

"How about you?" asked Mungo. His scab peeled away from the skin. "Why were you in the jail?"

The saint looked at Gallowgate and then back to the boy. He did not answer. Gallowgate spoke for the man. "Vagrancy."

St Christopher looked offended but said nothing.

"They put you in jail for *that*?" said Mungo.

"Well, that and ugliness." Gallowgate laughed as he pulled the charred lasagne containers from the ashes. "Who's hungry?"

They were forced to wait a long time before the lasagne trays were cool enough to handle. The conversation ebbed as the men tried to eat around the burnt sections of meat and rubbery cheese. St Christopher put his dinner to the side like he was not interested. He took up the whisky again and filled his belly. Mungo thought the food tasted smoky and delicious. As the pasta expanded in his gut, he stared into the fire and thought about the jail and that poor woman and her horse. By the time he had swallowed the last of his dinner he was feeling heavy, tired from all the fresh air. His face must have been twitching freely because Gallowgate was staring straight at him.

"Ye must take some shite for that at school?"

"Sometimes," said Mungo. He put his

hand to his cheek and as the flesh twitched he began to pick at it with an index finger. He could feel the skin lifting away as he rubbed.

"Stop rubbing at yersel," said Gallowgate. "How does that help?" The man came closer. "Move your hand, ah want to look at it." Gallowgate cupped Mungo's chin in his rough palm. He tilted his face towards the firelight. "Ah think it's a wonder."

"Don't laugh at me." Mungo tried to pull away from the rough hand.

"No, seriously. It's like your face has a mind of its own. It's showing what you feel on the inside without ye even asking it." Gallowgate turned Mungo's cheek to the fire. The small patch where the boy rubbed at his skin was dry and chafed along the high bone of his cheek. He ran his finger gently across the bone. "Does this help?"

"No." Mungo sank into himself and slid out of Gallowgate's grip.

Gallowgate winced as though he had heartburn. "Imagine. God gives ye a beautiful face. Then he does that to fuckin' spoil it. What a spiteful bastard."

"Cruel!" sang St Christopher.

"Poor wee Mungo. Ye're wound so fuckin' tight." Gallowgate tilted his face towards the distant moon. Then he let out a sudden, terrible howl. It made Mungo want to run. Gallowgate lowered his smiling face to the boy, his sharp incisors snagged on his bottom lip. "Howl wi' me."

Mungo shook his head. Gallowgate stood up and held out a hand to the boy. He pulled him into the night. "Howl. Ye'll feel better."

Mungo tilted his head back. He hadn't noticed, but the sky wasn't absolutely black after all. There were stars in every corner you could see. Even when he thought he found an empty patch of nothingness his eyes adjusted and the sky filled with frosted stars and then what looked like the cream left by stars. He had never seen the night sky like this before. He had never seen it so cloudless, without the soft orange filter from the lights of the scheme.

He howled once. A timorous sound that hurried away at the end, his chin falling to his chest.

"No like that. Lit *this*." Gallowgate inhaled, he swallowed the night. Then he howled like a monster. It ruptured the stillness and made Mungo long for the return of silence. He peered into the dark loch, fearful that something might reply.

Gallowgate gave up. "Awright, if you won't howl, then jump the fire." He took a small run and leapt over the embers. "C'mon!"

St Christopher had been enjoying their foolishness but at this he sat up. "Take that nylon jacket off first, son, or ye'll be wearing it for life."

Mungo cast off his blue cagoule and could feel the chill coming off the loch. Stepping into the darkness he took a running leap and flew over the flames. He cleared the dying fire easily, relieved that he didn't embarrass himself. Something like happiness thawed out the cold inside of him. He followed Gallowgate in a looping jumping circle, the two whooping like a pair of maddies. The stars, the fire, the deep loch, it suddenly felt all right and for a moment he forgot all about Glasgow. He forgot why he had been sent away with these men.

They jumped the fire for a time, until Gallowgate started bumping into Mungo, and they were colliding in mid-air, moshing each other the way headbangers liked to do. Mungo stopped his jumping, pretending to have a stitch. Gallowgate sprawled out upon the shingle. He opened a can of Tennent's and nudged it towards the boy. "I'll boil ye some water in the mornin' but drink this for the now. It'll help ye sleep."

Mungo realized he hadn't drunk anything

all day, no loch water, no milky tea. He sniffed the can with its familiar yeasty smell. He could feel the men watching him nurse it, but he was wary of the drink. He had seen the awful sadness it contained, just beneath the happy foam. Slowly, he raised the can to his lips, the first sip soothed his parched throat, but the thick oaty taste made the boak in him rise. The men nodded in approval. Mungo found if he took a mouthful of the beer and held it in his mouth before letting it trickle down his throat, then it was less sickening, tasted less like mildew. If he sucked and sloshed it back and forth between the little gaps in his teeth, it lost its bloated heavy feeling and became like stale, sour dishwater.

The men passed the whisky back and forth, as Mungo stripped young branches for the flames. After a time, he turned his cold kidneys to the fire; there was nothing beyond this pool of dim firelight. His eyes were growing heavy when St Christopher spoke again. "So huv ye goat any pubes yet?"

The lager emboldened him. "Is that all you two talk about? Fannies and fitba and pubes?"

"It's just banter between the boys." Gallowgate snickered. "How auld are ye again?"

"I told you. Nearly sixteen."

"So ye've got plenty pubes?"

"Mibbe," Mungo sneered. "None of your business, is it?"

"No shame in becoming a man, ya big hairy beast. Happens to all of us." Gallowgate held out his hand in the American way for the boy to slap it. "Here, put it there big man."

Tired now, Mungo reached out for the high five. In a swift move Gallowgate grabbed the boy's wrist and with a wrench he spun the boy on to his lap and choked his forearm around Mungo's throat. The violence was sudden, his can of lager went rolling into the darkness. Mungo forgot about the stars and the firelight. Gallowgate took his thick fingers and stuck them in between Mungo's ribs. He found the old hurt. "If ah ask ye a question don't be so bloody cheeky."

"I didn't mean it."

The man released him as quickly as he had grabbed him. Mungo scrambled to his feet. He stood apart from the men for a long time, his eyes bloodshot from the smoke. He dared not rub them.

"Don't spaz out, wee man," Gallowgate gurned. He mocked Mungo's mutinous face. "Ah was only having a laugh."

St Christopher sat slurping his can and grinning like a halfwit.

Mungo didn't want to look like a baby, so he tried a casual laugh and pretended to be in on the joke. "Good one, Gallowgate." He felt the impression of Gallowgate's fingers still there, still on his skin, pressing into his tender side. Mungo slid into the darkness, pretended to go piss into the loch. As his eyes adjusted, the water gleamed the same colour as the sky, but it glistened slightly in the moonlight, the sky matte above it. The wind coming off the loch smelled like rain. Mungo waited at the water's edge a long time. He watched the illuminated men like they were part of a diorama: they drank, they smoked, they peered out at nothing. He was forming sentences in his mind, how to fold himself back into the group, when Gallowgate shouted at the dark, announced it was time for bed. St Christopher nodded in agreement.

Mungo emerged from the darkness and made for the red tent by the water with the single sleeping bag inside. Gallowgate tutted and said something about the wild deer and pointed him to the two-man tent inside the bothy. The boy was too tired to sulk. The sour lager gurgled in his belly and he lingered as Gallowgate stamped on their little fire with the heel of his trainer. Gallowgate pointed again towards the tent in the bothy. He watched with all the authority of a father as the boy crawled inside.

Mungo lay there in his football shorts and his blue anorak, scratching the midge bites on his legs. The ground beneath him was cold as kitchen tile and his heart sank as he thought again how he had no warmer clothes to change into, tonight or tomorrow. Rubbing his cold knees, he slithered into a sleeping bag, balling his fists and jamming his hands between his legs for warmth. It was no use. The earth below him was greedy; as fast as his body could burn, the stones leached the heat away from him.

At first, he mourned for the other, smaller tent with only one sleeping bag in it, but now in the pitch-black he was glad not to be alone. There was something terrifying about what might lurk in the loch beyond the fire, and the night was surprisingly cold. Mungo balled up for warmth. His eyes grew heavy as he waited for one of the men to come to bed. He listened to them walk to the loch edge and talk quietly while they pissed loudly into the water. The roar of the whisky didn't seem to give them any insulation. From the sharp way they were inhaling, he could tell they were as freezing as he was.

Gallowgate parted the tent flaps. It seemed a great effort to fold his drunken frame into the small space. He closed the zipper, and they were sealed inside together. Gallowgate collapsed on top of his dank sleeping bag, the wind pushed out of him with a wheeze. The tight space filled with the smell of him, whisky, cigarettes, dirty socks, and warm armpits. It grew damp as a closed mouth. "You awright, pal?" he asked quietly. His fingers searched the air for Mungo, pressing into the dark like a cautious typist. He searched for the boy, until his fingers found the side of Mungo's face, where the soft hair grew along his jawline. For some reason, the fingers kept moving. Gallowgate's ring finger brushed Mungo's bottom lip. His sovereign rings were cold against Mungo's cheek.

Mungo pulled away. "I'm fine. Tired."

"Ah, there you are."

Mungo could hear Gallowgate rub his palms together. He was blowing on his hands. "Fuckin' Baltic, int it?" In the dark he reached a thick arm out and pinned Mungo under it, pulling him against his chest for warmth. "It'll be warmer if we huddle the gether. I never was a Scout, but

109

I've seen enough films to know we better stick the gether or we'll be deid by the mornin'. Summer in Scotland, eh?"

The man pulled him tight and held him against his chest. Mungo turned away from him, but Gallowgate fitted himself against Mungo's back. Gallowgate was not a big man but every part of him was sinew and muscle. Even through the two layers of nylon, Mungo could feel his stomach expand to fill the small of his back, till there was nothing between them. "Won't St Christopher freeze?" said Mungo. "Don't you want to share it with your friend?"

"Naw. Dinnae grudge him his peace and quiet. This is a rare treat for that auld basturt."

"How?"

"Auld Chrissy has had a bad run of it of late. He spends most nights in the Great Eastern. Do you know that hostel? It's no for the faint of heart."

Mungo had seen the homeless shelter at the Wellpark end of Duke Street. It was an old cotton mill with an imposing Victorian facade that made it look like a prison, and now housed up to three hundred men a night in tiny sleeping cubicles. In the mornings they tried to discourage the men from loitering on the stone steps, but they lin-

110

gered like wraiths. It was one of the few buildings even Hamish crossed the street to avoid.

"Dinnae worry about auld Chrissy," said Gallowgate. "He's spent that many nights in the gutter he probably thinks he's in heaven now."

Gallowgate's arm grew heavy across Mungo's chest. The man's breath grew hotter and slower, Mungo could feel his eyelashes brush the back of his neck. "You and me, we'll just stick the gether. Just like the clans on the mountainside."

Suddenly, Mungo had a great desire to talk. He opened his mouth and the words tumbled out. He didn't even think about it, as though he had sprung a leak and out of him poured an endless story to fill the darkness. It came out in a whisper, without the burden of pause or punctuation.

"When I was six my brother taught me how to ride a bike my dad was already gone away so Hamish said he was going to teach me and he kept saying it but when I got a bike for Christmas he didn't teach me and finally by the time summer came he said I made him feel bad so he took me outside."

Mungo listened to the side zipper slide open on Gallowgate's sleeping bag. It was followed by the slow, tinny snickert of his own. Gallowgate's denims were unexpectedly cold against his bare legs. The man's arm moved down to the boy's waist. Gallowgate pulled himself tighter against Mungo's back. His fingers were splayed like a star on Mungo's stomach.

"Hamish didn't even let me try with the stabilizers he just took them off and said I was never to use them then he got on the bike and pedalled away from me he made me run after him all the way up to the top of the big hill and put me on the bike then he held the seat and right afore he let go he said he'd batter the fuck out of me if I fell off." Mungo kept on talking to the dark. "The bike was wobbly but I stayed on it for ages and ages then it got faster and faster and faster till I couldn't pedal and I had to lift my feet because the pedals were slapping my legs. I was happy for a moment." Mungo drew a breath there. He could feel the man's lips were slightly parted, they pressed lightly against the knuckle of his spine. "When I got to the bottom I didn't know what to do because Hamish hadn't shown me how to stop properly or how to turn so I just kept going and battered right into the red car it hurt my face and my arm and my knee and my bike took the hubcap off of one of the wheels I was lying on the ground crying with a nosebleed when Hamish came running and picked me up and we ran and hid behind the big green bushes."

Gallowgate let out a shuddering breath of foul air. Then he started snoring. Mungo felt the arm grow dead around him. He stopped talking. It was a lot warmer in the shared sleeping bag. He felt stupid to have worried.

There were rows of teeth marks on the windowsill, perfect little half-moons of anxiety. All afternoon Mungo knelt before the bay window and watched the street for her, his teeth sinking into the soft wood, the metallic taste of lead emulsion coating his tongue. The small flat was marked with his distracted grinding; the corners of towels were chewed and sodden, the hem of his school shirt was balled and stuffed into his mouth until he choked, the handle of the wooden spatula had a hammered pattern where he had clenched it between his molars.

After the trouble with the polis, Mungo spent a lot of time at the window. For days afterwards he avoided Hamish as best as he could, travelling in great wide arcs to stay far from his line of sight. It did no good.

Mungo came home from school one day and Hamish was sitting alone in the kitchenette. There were layers of clean clothes hanging from the laundry pulley above his head. Jodie had been busy keeping the house going, stripping beds, bleaching whites. Now Hamish sat beneath it smoking. He spoiled everything.

"Hallo." Mungo surprised himself with how casually it came out. There was a disappointment in seeing his brother, but also a sick sort of relief. His schoolbag slid from his shoulder.

"You've been avoiding us," said Hamish with a knowing laugh. There was fresh ink on his knuckles. Hamish liked to give himself tattoos using an old sewing needle and a burst biro. Curving across the knuckles of one fist was "Adri" and on the other "Anna," Adrianna, the indigoed name of his little pink daughter. "Funny that. I should be the one embarrassed to run into you."

Hamish's tattoos had a disjointed, improvised feeling. The shapes were primitive and the designs were never plotted out, or laid against some larger, cohesive plan. When Hamish got dressed in the mornings Mungo had tried to decipher them. The ox heads and daggers and coiled serpents appeared at random and were spread out across Hamish's pale skin from his nape to his kneecaps. He was punctured with a million

115

pinpricks, tiny bursts of blue ink, and the symbols seemed scattered across him like constellations in a night sky.

"Have you seen Mo-Maw?" Mungo opened the kitchen cupboards, one after the other, hoping they were not empty, but knowing that they were.

"No. She's probably done a runner. Does she owe somebody money?" He flicked his cigarette into the pile of dishes in the sink. "Leave a saucer of milk out for her, a packet of ten Regals. She'll be back when she needs something."

Mungo slunk out of the kitchenette. There would be nothing to eat until Jodie finished her shift. If she didn't come back tonight, there would be nothing to eat until the morning.

"You havnae thanked me for saving you the other night." Hamish was starting his menace. He followed his brother to the living room. Mungo threw himself on the settee and wished he would get on with it. "What the fuck were ye playing at? It wisnae *Apocalypse Now.* Why the fuck did ye no leave that ginger arsehole?"

"He was hurt."

"*So?* I put a brick into the side of that polis's face for you. I could get the jail and all because you were playing Florence

Nightingale."

"He nearly died. He was shittin' it. I couldn't leave him." Mungo kept his eyes on the blank television, it was better to watch Hamish in the reflection, not to meet the provocation of his gaze. "It just felt wrong."

Hamish pulled Mungo to his feet. He wrapped his tattooed hand around the back of Mungo's neck and put his forehead against his brother's. He must have seen it somewhere as a way for fathers to comfort sons, or to subjugate them. It should have felt tender, but something had twisted within him a while ago. Mungo tensed his stomach muscles and waited for the blow.

"The polis have been going door to door asking after us. They want to know who's been robbin' the builders. It's only a matter of time afore some spiteful auld cunt grasses, and all because you couldnae man up."

When the blow came it wasn't to the stomach as he had expected. Hamish reached out and wrenched his brother's nose. It was a dirty manoeuvre left over from their boyhood and Mungo, who was always prone to nosebleeds, began to gush. Bright tears filled his eyes but he wouldn't cry. He had learned not to give his brother the satisfaction. Hamish liked tears; if you showed any to him, he went out hunting for more. Mungo pulled the hem of his jumper up and balled it over his nose. The acrylic acted more like a leach than a plug.

"Stop greetin'. It's no broke." Hamish knuckled his glasses back up the bridge of his nose. He smiled, and in that instant, Mungo could tell he wanted to be friends again. Hamish was mercurial like that. It was what made him so dangerous. "Listen, I was watching you the other day. I wisnae impressed."

Mungo could picture him glowering on the roof, not missing a moment through his corrective lenses. "I shouldn't have even been there."

"That's the point. *You should've.* You're ma wee brother and it's an embarrassment to see ye carry on lit that."

"Like *what*?"

"Lit you were too good for it. Floating around like a wee fuckin' poofter." Hamish paused to see if the blow had landed.

Mungo was glad half his face was covered by the school jumper. He could feel the electricity start in his right eye. He pinched his bleeding nose.

"What do you think Da would've said? If the big Ha-Ha was still around he would

have leathered ye for yer nonsense. You didnae steal anything, you didnae fuck anything, you couldnae even run frae the polis
on yer own." Hamish picked a piece of
tobacco from his lips. "Too busy trying tae
cuddle wee Bobby Barr."

"That's no true."

"I feel like I'm failing you, Mungo. Like
I've no been showing ye how to be a man."
He looked genuinely disappointed at that.
There was a soft, round defeat in his sharp
shoulders that he would never have carried
out on to the street. "I feel like I've no been
raising ye right."

Mungo knew it weighed heavily on his
brother but it was foolish to think that
Hamish could have raised him. They were
too close in age. If you dropped a stone in a
puddle, it was as though the ripple in front
was expected to raise the one right behind
it. Mungo was not very bright, but even he
knew that would be impossible. A ripple
could do nothing more than let the next
ripple follow in its wake, no sense of where
it was headed itself.

Mo-Maw didn't like her children to call
her Mammy, nor Mother, and never just
Maw. She said she was too young for that
shite. She had just turned fifteen when she
came down with Hamish and was only

nineteen when Mungo was born. They all came out so close together, they might have been arm-in-arm. Mungo was the only one who hadn't burst forth singing. The other two came out raging, fists clenched and faces blue, but Mungo had just looked up at her in a sad way, she had said, like he was already expecting her to be a great disappointment.

Mo-Maw could pass for Jodie's elder sister — she reminded her children of that daily. Mungo could remember the time the four of them shared one single Irn-Bru while waiting in line for *The Jungle Book*. Mungo had set Mo-Maw's nerves on edge by asking for a hot dog from the corner cart.

"I *do* like mustard," he had protested. He was only five.

"Ye dinnae, Mungo," Mo-Maw had threatened him, but her youngest was not a big eater. She hadn't seen him eat anything of real substance in three whole days. He was a distracted little boy, more given to worrying and wandering and fidgeting than sitting at a kitchen table.

Mungo had turned away from the sweating hot dog cart. He floated over to the illuminated posters and she knew she was losing her chance to put something solid in his stomach. Mo-Maw had knotted her mouth, paid for the expensive hot dog, and smeared it with luminous yellow mustard. Mungo had taken one bite before his face flared a deep puce. Born stubborn, he held it in and tried to chew. Jodie said she would eat it for him, but Mo-Maw was a fizzy kind of angry and she'd thrown the whole thing in the bin.

Her hackles were up by the time the ticket girl asked what they wanted. "Four children's tickets," Mo-Maw had said, trying to pass for a child herself.

Hamish had been dazzled by the bright lights. Mungo could see his eyes were headed westward and skyward, but his mouth was tilted towards Mo-Maw. "Mammy." He knew better than to call her that, and now he said it clear as a bell. "Mammy, do you think we could have popcorn when we get inside?"

The ticket seller had sniffed and smiled a wry grin. She had a satisfied look on her face that said she was looking forward to passing this story around the usherettes during their tea break. Mo-Maw had taken a hold of Hamish's upper arm before he could even swivel his eyes away from the bright posters. As she spun him around there was both wonder and terror on his face. Mo-Maw was only a few inches taller than her eldest child even then, but she'd strung him up like a butcher's chicken. She held him on tiptoes, and then she leathered the back of his legs. *One, two, three,* Jodie counted. Mo-Maw's face was scarlet as she raised her hand again, full-swing, like a professional golfer. Mungo had stepped forward and stood in front of his brother. Mo-Maw's hand came down too fast and caught him in the soft of his belly. The sausage blew out of him. If he had bothered to swallow the hot dog it would have come up in the great pile of lurid sick.

"So, I've been thinking." Hamish's hand was already on the door handle. "I need to spend more time with you. I need to sort you out."

"I'm fine as I am." Mungo was still talking through the bloody school jumper. He sucked down a clot from his nose.

Hamish came uncomfortably close and stood on Mungo's toes. He readied his fist in a high arc and swung it towards Mungo's face. The boy flinched as Hamish stopped a half-centimetre from connecting with his tender nose. "Lesson one," he spat. "Don't fuckin' talk to me like that ever again."

Mungo had mixed feelings about the February half-term holidays. School provided a relief from worrying about Mo-Maw all day, and he looked forward to the free school dinners. With the school closed for a week, he was soggy with listlessness. Jodie had no time to distract him as she took on more shifts at the Italian café, her wages were barely able to cover feeding them both without Mo-Maw's benefit books.

Most days, Jodie let Mungo come and sit with her at lunchtime and together they shared a deep-fried pizza in one of the booths towards the back. Enzo took a frozen pizza and, cracking it over the bone of his knee, folded it in two. He dipped it in a batter, the same creamy gloop that smothered all the fish and sausages, and then fried it quickly. It ended up as a bubbling mass of glorious stodge and melted cheese. Mungo had to burst it open and let the magma cool before they could touch it. When they were finished eating they both felt greasy and tired, yet underneath this was the sensation of being completely full and there was a comfort in that.

Mungo swung his legs underneath the table and tested Jodie on her French verb conjugation. He was rotten at French; every sentence felt as though it was spoken by a manic stutterer and the idea that something as simple as a spoon had a sex left him feeling agitated and with the desire to break something. It was like a game no one would tell him the rules to. When he pressed Jodie on the rules, she just shrugged. When he quizzed Jodie, he got the French pronunciation wrong, so Jodie would correct the question and then provide a perfect answer. She was that good. He laid his head on the table and told her how she would go to college and live in a fancy house in the West End. She flicked her apron at him and went back to work.

After this, Mungo was left with the yawning gape of the day in front of him. Sometimes he chewed the windowsill, sometimes he bothered Mrs Campbell. He would chap her door and ask if she needed anything doing. She was a busy woman, happiest when she was being useful, so she mostly always said no. But sometimes, there on her doormat, she would run her fingers through his thick hair. He liked the way her short nails raked his scalp. It took him a few visits to realize that this was what he came for.

Once or twice Jodie came home with news of a Mo-Maw sighting. One of the ice-cream lickers had seen her in Haghill, or getting on the Barras bus with thick armfuls of shopping. These women had never spoken to her, they had just seen her, but they said she looked well, hale, freshly painted. Jodie would lie and smile and say, yes, *yes,* Mo-Maw was doing great. She was ecstatic to be a granny to Ha-Ha's little Adrianna.

When she was safe at home, these comments made Jodie apoplectic. As she sprayed her work shoes with deodorant she called their mother filthy names that made Mungo blanch. She was harshest on Mo-Maw in a way that only girls were allowed to be. She said it felt like having a lost dog you couldn't admit had run away, a wayward bitch that you hoped would come home when her heat broke. At first, these sightings were a small comfort to Mungo. For a brief flash they gave him hope that she hadn't been murdered, that she wasn't floating somewhere in the cloudy Clyde. But if she was alive, why didn't she come home? And after a while he also came to hate receiving news of her looking happy, stories of her whistling round the Trongate.

Over half-term he kept a wide berth around Hamish. He avoided the council flat where Hamish stayed with his girlfriend, his new baby, and his sort-of mother-in-law. He skirted the waste ground where the boys played football and set up turf wars with the Catholics from Royston.

Since the incident with the flying brick,

the polis drove up and down the tenement streets constantly. They would chap at the door of anyone who might tell them who the boys were that raided the builder's yard. Almost everyone knew it was Ha-Ha, but nobody would take the risk of grassing. The polis officer was still in the hospital. His jaw had been mangled and was hinged with four metal pins; he was left with a clamped mouth that wouldn't open wide enough for solid food.

There was a quiet, forgotten place behind the tenements, a scrabble of trees that sat between the edge of the motorway and the last row of sooty sandstone. The city council had fenced in as much land as they intended to care for, and opposite this the roads department had fenced in the rushing motorway. Between these two fences was a sliver of unclaimed grass, a purgatory only forty feet wide. Over the half-term Mungo sat on the grass, picking at the scraggly wildflowers, feeling guilty about the policeman. Sometimes old men with leash-less dogs would dauner by, but mostly, Mungo was alone. He took out his sketchbook and drew the grids and interlocking faces of the tenements. Without lifting his pen he filled a double page with a wall of bricks and windows with tightly packed venetian blinds. But the roaming pen could not calm his mind. He closed the sketchbook, and then his eyes, laid his chin on his clasped hands, and felt the breeze of the day trippers as the traffic sped past to Edinburgh.

There was a doocot at the far edge of the forgotten grass. A two-storey shelter, six feet by six feet, and fourteen feet tall. The rectangular turret looked hastily put up from old, corrugated iron, a set of heavy front doors and glossy melamine that came from dismantled cafeteria tables. The whole structure had a tottering angle but was sturdy enough; each seam was nailed or soldered firmly shut, and the roof was sealed from the rain with thick tarpaper. A sliding skylight was fixed on to this roof, and over this skylight was a wire basket that cantilevered and acted as a snap-trap of sorts. Although it was made of scraps, the tower had a house-proud feel. Whoever built it had taken great care; they had painted it in a drab olive colour, an unassuming tone that would camouflage it against the waste ground it sat upon. There was a working door mounted on to one face, and laid across this were three heavy iron bars each with a fist-sized padlock.

Mungo had been drawing in the grass for two days and now, on the third, the doocot door was finally flung open.

There was a young man, he was hauling his belongings out into the shy sunlight, as if to air them. He went through his routine with ease as Mungo watched him over the top of his sketchbook. The boy must have had a strong back to carry the large cages out of the doocot as easily as he did. Then he scuffed his toes, and stumbled with his long arms knocking at his side. From a distance, between his gangly arms and his skillful hands, there was conflict about him. He could be either a boy or a man, depending on how he turned, or how the light caught him.

He was wearing a heathered grey tracksuit of thick cotton fleece. On his head was a knitted fisherman's cap of deep navy-blue. His ears stuck out like two pale cabbage leaves and he wore the cap above them, hanging loose as if he couldn't force it down over them. He had a shock of dirty-blond hair and there was a look of the outdoors about him; a rosy colour flushed high on his cheeks from days spent in wind and rain. He reminded Mungo of a farmer: purposeful, solitary looking. He went about his routine with a semblance of deep contentment to be outside.

The boy had not seen Mungo, or had seen

him and didn't care. His face was turned to the sky, watching pigeons glide above the tenements. Something in the clouds caught his eye and he disappeared inside his tower. There were heavy footsteps on a ladder as the skylight slid open and he poked out of the roof like the captain of a wooden submarine. He was cradling something in his large hands. Mungo watched him caress it, whisper gently to it, and bring it to his lips for a kiss. He threw it into the sky and a pale pigeon fluttered away over the slate roofs of the housing scheme.

"Whroup, whroooup, whrooup." He was cooing after the bird.

His little bird whirled over the sandstone. It followed the other birds and they dipped for a moment out of sight. When Mungo looked back towards the doocot the boy was still hanging out of the skylight but now he was glowering down at him. The boy dropped back inside. He came out of the low door and started striding towards Mungo.

"How long are ye gonnae sit there?" he asked abruptly. Mungo could see the strength of his face now; he had muscles that ran from under his broad cheekbones down to his jaw, and while he waited for Mungo to reply, they moved and pulsed with life.

"What's it to you?" It was brave, and maybe a little stupid. His nose was still tender from Hamish and this boy was a good head taller than him.

What had looked northern and hale now puckered in uncertainty, and the boy looked his age again. His mouth was shaped like a wide bow, his teeth were large and white, but spread at intervals. "It's just if ma hen sees you sitting there," he motioned to the missing pigeon, "you might scare her off and she willnae come back."

"How can a bird be frightened of me?"

The boy worried the sky. He seemed conflicted. It would be mean-spirited to ask a stranger to leave and that didn't seem in his nature. "Listen, could you haud still? Put that book away, the flap of the pages might frighten it."

Mungo nodded and closed his book. The boy beamed down at him with relief. He was funny looking: gappy teeth, sticky-out ears, and a bent, Roman nose. But when he smiled he was disarming. There was something uncomplicated about him. As his eyes returned to the sky the smile never left his lips, and Mungo found himself staring. It seemed like this boy could not have spent a day on the same streets that Mungo knew,

130

never needed any of its callous posturing, the self-protective swagger, the dirty promise of hitting first. There was nothing guarded or fearful about him. Mungo couldn't help but smile back up at him. "I'm Mungo."

"I know fine well who you are," said the boy. "Your Ha-Ha used to kick the shite out of me for a laugh." The boy was still watching the sky, but he thrust a hand towards Mungo and hoisted him to his feet. He yanked so hard that for a moment Mungo was airborne. He could smell the fresh air on him as the boy clapped him on the back. "I'm James Jamieson. I live on the street ahind yours. I can see your Jodie dancing around her bedroom."

Mungo closed one eye and scratched at the back of his head. "Sorry. She had three weeks of highland dancing when she was eight. She cannae help herself."

"I don't mind," said James. "She's no very graceful. But she was always dead nice to us when I saw her in the street."

Everyone hated Hamish, but everyone loved Jodie. It spoke to her great-heartedness that people who could not stomach Hamish or Mo-Maw still held her in such high regard. Mungo didn't know where he fell in all of this. Sometimes he felt strangers looked at him like just another blemish on the life of this unstintingly good girl.

James led Mungo towards his doocot. About twenty feet away from the tower they lay down on their stomachs. James took a coil of white washing line into his hands. Mungo could see the rope snake through the grass back towards the tower. They were waiting for something to happen. James was purring lightly, mimicking the throaty, contented warble of a pigeon. *"Whroup, whroooup, whrooup."* With each coo he bobbed his head like he was catching a sneeze. His eyes were scanning the skyline for a glimpse of his blonde bird. A few times Mungo opened his mouth to speak but James put his finger over his own lips and Mungo sank back into the damp grass.

Eventually the blonde pigeon circled back over the tenement roofs. Relief flushed over James's whole body. *"Whroup, whroooup, whrooup."* He was kneeling now and bowing with each coo.

The pigeon landed on the doocot roof and still they waited. Another bird, slightly larger and more ordinary looking, circled the blonde doo. It landed on the tarpaper roof and began eyeing James's pigeon. They locked their hard beaks together in a wrestling type of kiss.

"Ahh, they're *nebbing*. Yes!" Mungo could feel James thrum next to him. James's bird flattened herself slightly and the interloper mounted her. The boy shifted and gave the rope a sharp tug. The wire basket snapped shut over the lovers. The pigeons fluttered wildly and then they settled. "Ya bloody beauty!"

James was racing towards the doocot. He had captured someone else's pigeon using the lure of his beautiful bird. Mungo followed behind him. Inside the doocot, a wooden ladder drew you up to a rickety platform that formed the upper storey, and then a second stepladder led upwards to the skylight. Set into the wall were dozens of cages framed out of scrap wood and covered with chicken mesh. Each cage was filled with a restless-looking pigeon. The stench was overpowering.

James Jamieson returned the blonde seductress to her cage. He was carefully backing down the ladder with the new pigeon in his hand. "I've been trying to catch this bugger for about two years. Look. He's a Horseman Thief." He was turning the grey bird, inspecting its beak and its arsehole. The bird was just blinking. "It's Wee-Man Flannigan's prize pouter. He's gonnae be pure

133

devastated. I wish I could see his face for maself."

"Are you not going to give it back?"

James stuck his tongue all the way out. "Am ah fuck! That's the whole point, that's what I've been trying to do all these years, have the best doocot in the East End."

He let Mungo stroke the soft downy feathers. The bird looked incredibly ordinary to Mungo, but it was chirruping happily and didn't look even slightly bothered to be in the stranger's grasp. "I've got to take my time and spoil him now. Ye know, bind him to me properly. Make sure that he disnae chase some other bit of fanny into somebody else's doocot."

"Don't you worry that you'll lose a bird?"

"Ach, I lose birds all the time. That's the game. When you let them go out on their own, they go as far as they want to go, you take a chance. If they want to come back, then they come back. If they don't, then you lose them."

"Sounds like a country and western song."

James shrugged. "I think it's honest in a way."

"What? To be led away for a mad shag?"

James looked at Mungo in a way that made Mungo feel childish. "If one of my birds leaves me, how can I be angry? It's

134

my fault for not making a good enough doocot for them. They must not have been happy enough to stay." Two pigeons were pecking at each other through the wire of their cages. James drew a hand between them and moved them apart. "You'd fuck off if you were unhappy, right?" he asked Mungo.

"Mungo! Mungo!" Outside the doocot, someone was calling his name. That was the thing with being called Mungo, when someone called that name, they were definitely looking for him. Jodie sounded like she was excited and annoyed at the same time. Mungo stuck his head out of the shelter. She was surprised to see him emerge from the doocot. "What are you doing in there?"

Mungo just shrugged and picked up his bag. "Why aren't you at the café?"

"Enzo let me away early."

James and Jodie barely acknowledged each other. James was still clutching his prize pigeon and looking like nothing could ruin his day.

"I've got news. Missus Campbell telt me something. You need to come with me."

Mungo slipped a strap over each shoulder. As he stepped away from the doocot James grabbed the spare fabric of his cagoule. "Haud on. Will you come back the morra?"

135

"Mibbe," bluffed Mungo.

James held the blinking bird out to him again. "*Ach, go on.* You must be guid luck or something."

They waited until the street lights came on, until good families had drawn their curtains and settled in front of their televisions. Then Jodie and Mungo left their tenement and headed along the main road. They walked westward against the brightly lit night buses that were bringing couples back from a night up at the dancing. Half-cut faces looked down on them as they walked alongside the busy road. It was late. Mungo took his sister's hand in his and walked against the kerb, keeping the worst of the bus grit and puddle spit for himself.

It was raining lightly, and the air was still sharp with the frosts of winter. By the time they reached the massive bulk of the Royal Infirmary, the night-shift nurses were already clustered outside, smoking cigarettes under the A & E awning. When Jodie was younger, the Royal Infirmary terrified her. To her it was a Victorian headmistress in the form of a building: strict and cruel and a warning to be on your best behaviour. It was built like a fortress and hung over the city in an imposing way. Thick turreted towers and balustrades running along the length of its roof gave the building a sense of confinement, like it was not a hospital but a prison. It was older than either of them could imagine and the western facade had collected decades of rain and car fumes until it bled pure blackness. It was not a place you ever wanted to end up. The pitted surface of the sandstone held shadows and gave a darkness to the city that filled Jodie's nightmares. It took her a long time to believe such a foreboding place could be somewhere people would come to get better.

Mungo put his arm around Jodie's shoulder. She hadn't been eating properly, neither of them had, but Jodie always let him eat most of their deep-fried pizza and Mungo couldn't remember the last time he had seen her eat a whole plate of her own food.

They waited to cross at the traffic lights that controlled the thick artery of the High Street. Directly across from the infirmary was a triangular island. The waste ground was bordered by a windowless pub and the indiscreet remains of a half-pulled-down tenement that made the island feel like a bombed-out warzone. In the midst of the rubble sat a white caravan. It spilled a sliver of light out into the wet night. Cars streamed by on all three sides.

The snack bar attracted a queue of lorry drivers waiting for their dinners and street cleaners waiting for their breakfasts. Men in short sleeves huddled under the plywood awning. They shivered as they smoked and danced from foot to foot, rain dripping down the necks of their shirts.

There she was, in the halo of yellow light, pushing hunks of meat around on a sizzling griddle. Jodie wanted to turn, to leave now, but Mungo held her fast and they waited patiently for the queue to move along. The woman looked content. She talked to the regulars with an easy familiarity that showed they already knew each other. Now and then she stopped her cooking and took one of their heads in her hands and asked how their sick wives were, or if their weans were behaving themselves. She listened intently as a bin man talked about his union dispute with the corporation. Mungo watched her ask insightful questions that showed how deeply she cared. Jodie turned to him and said quietly, "Please, whatever you do, don't let me laugh."

When they reached the front of the queue they stepped out of the darkness into the sickly fluorescent light. "Hiya," she said, as though they had met casually at a bus stop.

"What are youse two doing all the way out here?"

Mungo forgave her in that instant. He was flooded with profound relief. He turned to Jodie, but her jaw was locked tight and her eyes were nothing but knife slits. "Is that all you're going to say? Hiya? *Hi-fuckin'-ya?*"

Jodie tried to tug her arm free from Mungo's grasp, but he would not let go. He was staring up at Mo-Maw, gazing up at her in devotion. *Please,* he thought. *Just let me look at her a little while longer.*

"Listen, lady." Mo-Maw was pointing down at her daughter, the greasy scraper extended like the finger of God. "It's that exact attitude that has made me no want to visit."

"Visit? Visit!" Jodie rarely used to get angry. When they were younger, they often joked that Hamish had stolen both of their portions of anger. But now Jodie was angry all the time. Mungo was shaken from his reverence. He watched as Jodie's head snapped back and her wet hair flew wildly around her. "You don't fucking *visit* your own weans. Ya mad auld bitch. You come home every night and make sure they've been fed and cleaned and then ye tuck them into bed. You make sure they have done their homework and have had enough to eat for their lunch and then if you are fucking lucky ye get ten minutes peace to yersel afore ye start it all a-fuckin'-gain." She had been pointing a sharp finger back up at her mother; the griddle scraper and her finger almost connected. Her face started to twist into her nervous laugh. *"Haaah-ha."*

Mungo watched Mo-Maw wilt. Several of the taxi drivers were standing slack-mouthed, huge gobbets of half-chewed sausage sitting on their fat tongues. They were unsettled by this screaming ingrate. Then when she laughed, they could not see the joke. There were rivulets of tears on Jodie's face. "What you do not do — what you *absolutely* do not do — is leave your children alone while you disappear. You don't fuck off to get your hole and let them think you're dead."

"We just wanted you to know that we missed you." Mungo felt the sudden need to say it. He had been struck with a rising fear Mo-Maw would latch this trailer to a car and leave them again, standing on this traffic island surrounded by a dozen strange men. Jodie scowled at him like he was a traitor.

Mo-Maw leaned out the serving hatch. She placed a damp kiss on Mungo's lips. "Darlin'. Ah came by the flat twice to pick up clean clothes, hairspray and that. Ah'm sorry. Ah left a wee note."

Mungo's jaw hung open, he spun and glared at his sister.

"What? Would it hurt less to know that your mother couldn't even hang around for thirty minutes until you got home from school, eh?"

Mo-Maw closed the top two buttons on her blouse. She spoke over the heads of her children. "How about that, Johnny, eh? Ah gave up my figure for these ingrates. Now you see why ah drink." She looked down at Mungo. "Away and wait over there, and ah'll come see you when ah get a minute."

"But —"

"I'm workin'. Go and have a seat."

Mo-Maw couldn't come out of the snack bar and talk right away, but she handed them two floury rolls with bacon and black pudding and a cup of tea each. Mungo watched his sister hesitate before taking hers. The picnic table was slick with rain but the van deflected the worst of the wind. Mungo wiped a spot dry for Jodie to sit on. They cradled their hot teas and tried to pull warmth through the polystyrene. There was a sliver of pink jumper peeking out from Jodie's coat sleeve. When she wasn't looking, Mungo pulled at it, and hooked his fingers into the loose stitches. The late-night traffic flew by. Mungo tried not to make eye contact with the mothers who rubbernecked from warm Saabs.

"Jodie?" There was a tentativeness in his voice. "Try and remember the good bits, eh? She's not all bad." Jodie stared at him. Mungo went on and as he did, he counted off their mother's good qualities on his fingers. "She's funny, she doesn't always mean to be, but she is. She doesn't hold grudges or dwell on bad stuff. She hardly ever nags us. She is, she . . ." He paused. "What's that word that begins with *R*? You know when you get knocked down but you get back up again?"

Jodie didn't falter. "Rotted, rancid, rarelysober, reallyfuckingselfish?"

When the night-shift breakfast rush was cleared, Mo-Maw hopped down out of the small caravan. Mo-Maw looked nothing like her offspring. All the Hamilton children's swarthiness must have come from the Black Irish that ran through their father. Mungo had never seen any pictures of this man. At one time, there was the promise of an undeveloped roll of film lying in a kitchen drawer somewhere, but Mo-Maw could never seem to find it. His mother was shorter than Jodie — only five foot tall in her bare feet — but she heaped her mousy curls on top of her head to give her the illusion of height. She was small-boned and fine-featured with quick green eyes. She was paler than her children, fragile looking, but her brittleness was only skin-deep.

Their mother was wearing a greasy pinny and underneath that she wore a pair of cropped denims and a brand-new pair of white trainers, flashy Nike ones with the swoosh on the side. Mo-Maw noticed them eyeing this luxury. "Well, ma back hurts, standing at that hot griddle all day." She had a polystyrene cup that was bright with the molten orange colour of Irn-Bru. There was an astringent tang to it that smelled like alcohol, a strong medicinal scent that was noticeable despite the rain. Jodie was already picking at a splinter in the table.

"How long have you been working here then?" Mungo thought that seemed like a safe place to start.

"Two weeks, give or take." Mo-Maw sat close to Mungo and lit a damp cigarette that looked like it wouldn't take. "Jocky knows a fat Scouser called Ella. Big Ella owns a whole fleet of these vans and needed somebody to work the night shift here."

"Who's Jocky?" asked Mungo.

Mo-Maw pushed at the hair that hung

down the back of her neck; her old perm was looking tired and slack. Mungo thought that hair could grow a lot in a few weeks. "Jocky's ma new fella," she sniffed. "He runs the pawnshop down the Trongate. Oh! Wait till you meet him. He's a smasher, puts you in mind of a chubby wee Nicolas Cage. Fair loves his grub." She pushed Mungo's hair from his eyes. She liked to look on him, he was the bonny and, as of yet, unspoiled bit of her and Big Ha-Ha. He didn't have the sharpness of Hamish or the weariness of Jodie. "Do you want a Commodore 64? Jocky can get me one if ye want?"

Mungo shook his head. He didn't want a computer.

Mo-Maw rested her hands on the table. She noticed Jodie looking at her fingernails. Her nails appeared nude under the street lights, but as she waggled them Mungo saw their pearlescent shimmer. "Do youse like it?" she asked Jodie. "Ah felt yon *Raspberry Beret* was making me look a bit done-in. Aw the young lassies are wearing these nude shades the day. Took me a minute to get used to it, but I think it looks cleaner, younger. Din't it?"

Jodie stared at her mother with such intensity that Mo-Maw turned to Mungo and asked if she had something on her face.

"Are you living with him? This Jocky?" Jodie asked. "I mean, I suppose you are living with him, but why?"

"How no? Jesus Christ. Ah'm only thirty-four, Jo-Jo." Mungo knew his sister hated this pet name, she said it made her sound like a dancing monkey. "You'll be seventeen in a couple of months. Ah was potty-training Hamish when ah was your age. What's the harm in it, eh? Jocky treats me right, he takes me for a Chinese — starters and mains."

"Prawn crackers, too?" asked Mungo.

"Aye. And a banana fritter if I like." Mo-Maw turned her gaze back to Jodie. "Ah've got to try and squeeze a wee bit of happiness out of life while ah still can."

Jodie nodded across the table at Mungo. Her face was wet from the rain, it gave it a waxy pallor and her expression was alarmingly calm. "He's only fifteen. You're no done raising your weans yet, ya selfish besom." It was happening again. This pitched battle between Jodie and Mo-Maw over Mungo. He felt forever in the middle. At any moment they might both get on their knees and try to lure him towards one of them with a bit of salted ham hock, like a dog.

"Oh, gies peace. We both know ye love

145

playing at the wee housewife." Her cheeks were hollow sucking on the cigarette. Mungo searched for Jodie's feet under the table, he wrapped his legs around her ankles, ensnaring his sister.

Mo-Maw said, "Look, ah've goat some money now. No much, but some." They listened to the squeak of the new trainers. "Ah'll come round the house and pay all the bills. We can go down Duke Street and run the messages the gether. You can have all the chocolate biscuits ye want." She took Jodie's hand in her own. Mungo thought Jodie might stab her. "You need to stay on yer own a wee bit longer. Jist till I know where me and wee Jocky are headed."

It was becoming so late it was early. There was a fresh line of black hackneys pulling up on the kerb. They bumped up out of the flow of traffic and Mungo watched them heave with relief as pot-bellied taxi drivers stepped down into the rain. "Can we come visit? Can we see where you live now?" He could feel the side of his face start in a mutiny.

Mo-Maw put her chin on his shoulder. She strained to kiss his twitching cheekbone. "Naw son. No the now."

"How?" It was not a good enough answer for Jodie.

Mo-Maw leaned forward and clasped Jodie's hands in a way that startled his sister. "Wummin to wummin, ye might not know how men are yet, but ah need to make this easy on him. It's too early for me to be messy, to be a bother."

"A bother?"

"Ye'll understand one day. Ah need to keep it breezy a wee while longer, that's aw." As she rose to serve the men, she unbuttoned the top two buttons on her blouse again. "Ah need to find the right time to tell Jocky ah've got weans."

FIVE

Mungo had been summoned. He was hunchbacked in front of the television, drawing a tight spiral that he didn't know how to end. Jodie looked at him havering over whether to go. She turned off the television and reminded him of how much worse it would be if he didn't do exactly as Hamish asked.

Most of the time Hamish stayed in one of the damp council flats that were built in the 1960s. Mrs McConnachie lived on the top floor and since Hamish had impregnated her youngest lassie, Sammy-Jo, she felt obliged to let him hang around. Mungo could see his brother tried to be on his best behaviour when he was there. He acted in a constricted way, tight-faced, grudgingly patient. It served only to squeeze all the cruel bits of him into the part of his day when he was not trapped under the McConnachie roof. But Hamish knew better than to chance his luck further: Sammy-Jo was only fifteen, and Mrs McConnachie could have him jailed for molesting a minor. As it was, her doctor called the Social and the Social called the police. Sammy-Jo lied to them all; she said she didn't know who the father was, and on the birth certificate a civil servant had written *Unknown* in his finest calligraphy. Hamish had copied the script and tattooed the word behind his right ear.

Mungo stood on the threshold to Mrs McConnachie's living room. He hadn't been invited inside yet. The settee had six of the boys from the builder's yard crammed on to it. They were packed thigh to thigh and spilled over the arms of the small sofa. In their nylon tracksuits they looked like so many plastic bags all stuffed together; a flammable, noisy jumble of colour-blocking and sponsorship logos. There was the manic throb of techno coming from the stereo; someone had a bootlegged copy of a Carl Cox set from Rezerection. It sounded like the DJ was pressing an early warning siren over a stuttering breakbeat. It was so aggressive sounding — it moved so fast — that it made Mungo feel tense.

The ginger boy was the only one to look up at Mungo. He half-nodded and then

149

swivelled his clear blue eyes back to the daytime television. That was it, that was all the thanks Mungo would get for saving him. His arm looked mangled; navy-blue fingers blossomed from the end of a sickly pink stookie. The plaster was already covered in hand-drawn cocks, each throbbing vein painstakingly rendered in fat bingo marker, and signed with pride. The boy's eyes were a faraway blue, and there was a rash around his thin mouth from huffing a fresh bag of glue. His arm must have hurt awful bad.

One of the MacPherson brothers was sat on the settee. It was rumoured that there were four brothers in total, but at any given time there were only ever two MacPhersons on the streets of the scheme at once. They alternated in and out of Polmont Young Offenders so frequently it seemed like Mrs MacPherson was checking them in and out of a pawnshop based on how much she could handle at any given moment. Mal MacPherson sat on the broken arm of the settee, tapping his white drumsticks soundlessly on his legs: the left holding a rigid beat, the right adding the swirling thrill. He stopped and held the drumsticks aloft with a sense of ceremony. The sticks made a rigid line, the tips connected under his septum. He held it for a beat — Mungo could almost hear the pause in the marching tune — and then he proceeded to drum soundlessly again. The boy was dedicated. He was always practising for the Orange band competitions that took place in the Auld Resolute working men's club; a barricaded, windowless hall that sat defiantly in the Catholic end of the Calton.

On the soundless television, an English woman was dipping a vase into liquid and showing the audience how to crackle glaze the surface of it. Each one of the young men was staring slack-jawed at the screen. On the low table in front of them sat a bundle of folded nappies amongst a pile of stolen car radios, half-drunk bottles of MD 20/20, and one very large tomahawk.

The tomahawk was homemade. Someone had taken the handle from a ball-peen hammer and screwed it to a slice of sharpened metal. Mungo knew that one of the boy's uncles still worked in shipbuilding and would bring him offcuts of steel when he could. The axe looked like a medieval weapon that could cleave the arm off a man. The boy had polished it lovingly and then, using electrical tape, had wrapped the handle in blue, white, and red stripes. He had sharpened the blade to a shining point, it made a screeching noise just to look at it.

Mungo couldn't stop staring.

Sammy-Jo McConnachie was sitting on the armchair. She was drowned by one of Hamish's jumpers. She had their pink baby stuffed up underneath it, and was trying to get her to latch on. Mungo glimpsed the side of her breast. The swelling looked painful; there were angry veins bruising the underside of each tit, and it looked like two giant gooseberries had been stitched to a child's ribcage. The girl looked tired and seemed on the verge of tears. The baby was fussing and colicky sounding. Its five measly hairs were gathered together and bound with a jolly bow.

The woman stopped glazing her vase and held it out for the cameras to see the intricate swirls. The young men looked from one to another in amazement; white pearls of acne flushed across their foreheads. "That's pure beautiful," said the ginger-headed boy. They all nodded in agreement.

Sammy-Jo started buzzing around the room, trying to wipe the table before her mother came in from work. Mungo could remember her from school. She had been the year below him, boyish and slender in a way that hadn't hardened into a look of mannish starvation yet. She always smelled of fresh apple shampoo and was considered to be the prettiest girl in the whole scheme. Mungo had watched the boys from all the surrounding years try to get next to her, but of course it had been Hamish who had turned her head. Hamish was a challenge for girls; he could be so embittered, so antagonistic, that when they coaxed some small sweetness from him, they felt chuffed with their own allure. Hamish had told Sammy-Jo that he felt like a bigger man when she was around, that she, and she alone, made him want to get his life together. Mungo saw how she carried herself differently after that, she swanned around like a saviour in a B-cup. How could she resist him?

"Ha-Ha!" she shrieked. Hamish's handle always sounded strange to Mungo, like a bad actor forcing out a fake laugh. "Ha-Ha! Tell them to take their feet off ma mammy's good table."

Mungo could tell Hamish didn't want to leave the house. He didn't want to take the battalion of boys out to wander the smirred streets. It was too early for mayhem.

She was trying to tidy the pile of car radios, but the wires were roughly cut and they kept unspooling in a messy pile. The baby was huffing underneath her thick jumper. Sammy-Jo had been clever, Mungo remembered, she was one of those children who was so fluent in mathematical hieroglyphics that it seemed as if it were her native tongue. She began shaking the bottles of formula to see which still held the most. "Have ye goat any money?"

"I was gonnae ask you the same thing." His eyes were glued to the telly.

Sammy-Jo looked on the verge of hot tears. One of the boys had stopped watching the television and was openly staring at the underside of her swollen breast. "Ha-Ha!"

Hamish tore his eyes away from the television. He was angry about missing the crackle glazing. "Whit? Did yer granny no give ye something for the baby?"

"That's to get her ears pierced."

"Listen, I just need a couple of poun' for bus fare. I need to sign on up at Jamaica Street." He nodded towards the table. "I could even take they radios down Paddy's market and sell them afore teatime. Then we would have my dole money and whatever I got for these."

"Naw."

"Ye would have enough money to pierce her ears four times over."

It was unpleasant to watch Hamish have to barter and reason with someone. Mungo was used to him just taking what he wanted and he had seen him menace Mo-Maw and Jodie if they offered some resistance. Mungo wondered how long it would be until he hit Sammy-Jo.

A singer started screaming, *"You make me feel so real,"* over the techno beat. Mungo had been waiting in the doorway. It had been clear that he hadn't been given permission to talk yet. "I could give you money, Hamish," he said. "If you want?"

The boys all swivelled to look at him. No one ever called the big man "Hamish."

"Okay. I'll gie ye it back." Hamish scowled at Sammy-Jo. He never said please or thanks.

Mungo rooted around in his cagoule pocket. Jodie had given him money for school supplies and he hadn't spent all of it. Hamish jostled him out into the hallway, and they went through into the narrow kitchenette, where Hamish clouted him around the back of his head. "Don't ever call me that in front of them again. It's *Ha-Ha*. Four fuckin' letters, even you are no daft enough to get that wrong."

The kitchenette was narrow, smaller than even Mo-Maw's. Mungo knew Hamish had tried to put their names on a council list for a flat of their own. The female council officer had been horrified by him: fifteen-year-old girls should not be living with eighteen-year-old men.

Mungo poured the coins into his hand. "I have things you could sell, you know. If it would help the baby."

"Lit what?"

"Like a remote-controlled car and one of those Space Invaders games."

"Naw. I've selt them already." Hamish quickly changed the subject. "Listen, I have something for ye." He reached into the back pocket of his denims. He thrust something small at his brother, and with a snip, a three-inch blade shot out. Mungo fell backwards over the bin. He was holding on to the melamine counter and staring down at the short blade. Hamish was jabbing it towards his stomach and smiling with a demented pleasure. "After that fuckin' palaver in the builder's yard ye need a blade to protect yersel."

It wasn't much of a blade, small and silver with a fake onyx handle. It looked like it would keenly slice an apple or cut through a length of old washing rope. As if Hamish had read Mungo's thoughts, he stabbed the blade into a bag of white sugar. Once, twice, three times. The sugar poured out of the bag and glistened on the counter.

156

Mungo put his hands in his pockets. He locked his elbows to his side. "No way. I don't fuckin' want it."

"It's no a question." Hamish thrust the knife towards his brother.

"But what if the polis stop me? What if the polis find me with a blade on us?"

Hamish snorted. "Fuck sake, Mungo, look at ye. What would the polis stop *you* for? Ye're that soft I'm surprised you have enough bones to stand upright."

"I don't want a knife."

Hamish sheathed the blade back in its handle. He loosened the Velcro fastening on Mungo's cagoule pocket and dropped the knife into the kangaroo pouch. "Listen baw-jaws, the more involved I get with the Billies, the more the Fenians are gonnae want to hurt a Hamilton. Even if ye don't want it for yersel, haud on to it for our Jodie. You never know when ye might need to chib a cunt." He carefully sealed the Velcro. He was done discussing it. Hamish licked his finger and was dabbing the white sugar, it made a crunching sound between his front teeth. "One more thing, I'm gonnae need yer help on Friday."

"Me?" He motioned through to the living room, where he could hear the squeak and repetition of children's television. "Why can't one of the Billies help you?"

Hamish was going through the kitchen cupboards. He was looking for something sugary to eat, and for something electrical to pawn. "It's a guid opportunity for me and you to spend time the gether. I telt ye, I'm gonnae show ye how to be a proper man. I'll no have ye embarrassing me."

"But I was going to help Missus Campbell on Friday."

"Jesus Christ." Hamish was shaking his head. "Friday!" It had an underlined finality to it. His top lip curled back in distaste. "An if I have to come searchin' fur ye, ye'll be fuckin' sorry."

Jodie was having a difficult time concentrating over the cackling of the seagulls. She had spread her homework over the folding table, and knew she had only thirty minutes before her man would return with the fish supper, and she would have to hide all the childish reminders of herself. Only thirty minutes before the folding table would retract into a hard, uncomfortable bed and he would pull a fitted sheet over it.

Who cared about "the fatal mistakes made by the Italians while governing their colonies in Africa" anyway? Half the pupils in her class couldn't find Edinburgh on a map.

There was the crunch of tyres on gravel and she swept her schoolwork back into her bag. Like usual, they sat together, shoulder to shoulder on the top step of the caravan, and looked out over the Irish Sea. West Kilbride was the furthest Jodie had ever been from home. It was only forty-five minutes from Glasgow but it felt like a world away. The caravan park sat in a farmer's field and looked out over the slate-grey horizon. House-proud Glaswegians rented the caravans for the season. They covered the windows with net curtains and filled old car tyres with potting soil and forget-me-nots. They came with hopeful deckchairs and cars loaded with drink, happy to leave the drabness behind for a few hours of streaked sunshine.

It was cold here, much windier than the city, but Jodie loved how fresh and untouched everything smelled. Every breath felt crystalline, scrubbed clean with sea salt. They ate their fish suppers outside in silence, and while she watched the sea, he studied the side of her face, struck with a sense of luck that this bonny, tenacious girl could be his. When their lips were greasy with fat Jodie took the last of the charred batter and threw it high for the swooping birds. For a while, he held her cold hands in his, then he took her back inside, and folded the table into a bed.

When they were finished, he slept. He turned his pale back to her and she watched the curly black hairs on his shoulder blades dance in the breeze. It had already lost the excitement of the unexpected, was becoming too much of a routine. He would collect her in his car. They would come to this caravan. He would go alone to buy some food, and then he would sweat on top of her for four minutes and fall fast asleep. Jodie already knew that he would wake soon and get dressed quickly. He would tickle her bare feet and tell her he loved her. But already he would be looking at his watch, thinking about his own children and the roast chicken he needed to collect for their dinner.

At first he had promised he would leave his wife. But the more Jodie let him do his sweaty things to her, the less he seemed to promise that. She was surprised to feel so relieved.

Jodie lay there and carefully counted the blemishes on his back. Then she broke them into categories, separating the brown age spots from the blood-red skin tabs. She didn't want to come here anymore, but she felt compelled. He had bought her fourteen fish suppers, and being a bright girl, she knew the exact cost of it all. She lay behind him and spoke it quietly: "If a man buys a girl fourteen fish suppers at two pounds twenty-five a time, how long till the girl gives up? Show your working." It was a trick question, because she didn't know how much the girl also owed in petrol money.

She was smarter than that, after all. He had been the first to tell her of her potential. "Jodie Hamilton, if you apply yourself you could go all the way. How on earth have you been hiding in Hamish's shadow? It's like finding a diamond under a turd." He was smiling at her over the heads of the other fourth-years.

Boys her age didn't seem to notice her. Most of them knew the legend of her brother and would not dare. Others didn't like the way she would question the answers they gave in class. It was easier for these boys to latch on to one of the hubba-bubba girls and finger her around the back of the swimming baths than it would be to handle bossy wee Jodie of the famed Hamilton scum.

She rolled on to her back and looked at the panelled ceiling. She wondered if she was looking for a father. No, it was more than that: she wanted respite from pretending to be Mungo's mother. She felt tired all the time now. It was a transaction — she knew fine well — but for the three short hours that this man would take care of her, she could set aside all the burdens that were not hers. Three hours of peace in exchange for four sweaty, dirty minutes.

He didn't care anymore if she enjoyed it or not. At the beginning he would have asked if she was okay, worried that her tightness caused discomfort, but now he was delighted when it did. He would lie on top of her and look into her eyes with lust, and a kind of fear. He looked afraid that she would pull her knees together and ask him to get off. *Please let me finish,* his grey eyes seemed to say, and she could tell this was one of the best things that ever happened to him by the way he repeated "thank you, thank you, thank you" as he slipped in and out of her. She had liked that at first. Now he didn't ask her if he was hurting her, even as he thanked her over and over. He just did as he pleased and then kissed her, once, on the forehead. The greasy mark of it felt a bit like a red tick at the bottom of a test.

The man was awake again. He sat up. Mr Gillespie was tickling the bottom of her foot. He was missing all the teeth on the upper left side of his mouth and she wished he wouldn't smile at her over the crook of his shoulder like that.

When Mr Gillespie was first manoeuvring her into position, he took her to the Ayr fairground. With a crisp fifty-pound note he paid for her to go on all the rides: screaming, rickety rollercoasters, the heavy, pendulous pirate ship, and her favourite, the whizzing, spinning waltzers. The lights, the sugary candy floss and sweet peanuty smell of popcorn had made for a dizzying night far from home. Jodie could picture him now, paying for all the rides, and standing nervously in the shadows, like a divorced father, while she had her seventy-five seconds of fun.

There was another time he had brought her to West Kilbride. It was a damp evening in September and marked the first time she had kept her knees together from shame and from spite. Her bad mood had begun in his steamy Sierra. Mr Gillespie hadn't realized he had been talking too much about his own daughter, who went to Hutchesons' Grammar and was a shoo-in for Edinburgh University. She was jealous to see him boastful and proud of Gillian. It stung to think that no one felt that way about her.

"Do you think Gillian does something like this with her Modern Studies teacher?"

she'd asked as his hand worried the loose thread at the bottom of her school skirt.

The look of disgust on his face had pushed her deeper into the leather seat. Gillian Gillespie would never sink so low. Jodie had bitten her bottom lip, but she laughed anyway. *"Haaah-ha."*

"The sooner you grow out of that stupid laughter, the better," he'd muttered.

The firth had come into view. The low sun reflected on the sea and it shimmered like silver fish scales. Jodie had decided then that she would let him do whatever he wanted and just stop caring. She'd rolled down the window and laid her head on the door frame. The sea air cooled the burning in her cheeks.

Mungo pressed the grey pigeon flat against the board. He held it firmly like James had shown him, and the pouter bobbed but it did not struggle. James mixed the packet of hair dye that he'd bought from the chemist and smoothed it over the bird. There was a toothy American pin-up on the side of the box, and now the boys were matching her hair colour to the wings of a pigeon.

"Don't get it in her eye, I cannae fly a blind bird," said James.

In long, gentle strokes, he brushed the

sludge all over the bird. He plastered it over the wings until Mungo could remove his hands because the bird was pasted to the piece of salvaged plywood. It had the look of an animal tarred and feathered. Then they waited for the pigment to leach from it. "It's science, int it?" James grinned, shaking his own tawny locks. "Everybody prefers a blonde."

The doocot was sour with the tang of bleach. The acrid stench made Mungo's eyes sting, but his face was not twitching. He liked it here. James reached out a few times and tried to lick the thin dye brush against Mungo's temple. He had to keep dancing away, always careful to never let go of the platinum bird.

He had come to the doocot every day for the past week. James had been generous with him, happy to have someone other than his doos to talk to. He let Mungo hold the birds and let him feed them their diet of pellets and water. On the second day they sat on the damp grass and James shared his ham sandwich with Mungo. By the third day, James had made him one of his own, thick with butter, chewy at the crusts. Next to Hamish, James was straightforward and uncomplicated. When he handed him something, Mungo didn't need to flinch. He was sitting in the cold grass eating a salty ham sandwich when he realized with surprise that he would be sad to go back to school on Monday.

The pigeon didn't become the sun-kissed Los Angeles blonde that the box promised. It turned a pale soupy colour, like an old lady's tights, but James seemed pleased anyway. He took care to wash the hen carefully and rinse the last of the strong chemicals from her wings. When he put her back amongst the others they bobbed and eyed her lasciviously.

"I think they fancy her already," said Mungo, "but I reckon she fancies herself more."

James was busy putting pairs of cocks and hens together, letting them start a stunted round of courtship before separating them at the weekend and sending them out over the city, a hard-done-to feather ball of lustful confusion. If they were beautiful and horny enough they might attract another man's bird back to James's doocot and have the quick fuck he was trying to deprive them of now.

A bluish bird was strutting up and down behind his chicken wire. It was puffed up and bloated looking. It was keen to attract any hen that met its beady gaze. "He looks

166

full of himself, din't he? The big gallus smasher."

"What's his name?" asked Mungo.

"I dunno, I thought I would call him Archie but it doesnae feel quite right."

Mungo peered through the hexagonal wire. "Go on, call him Mungo."

James laughed, then he let out a sore rattling cough. Mungo noticed he did that a lot. It was an old man's cough, wet and phlegmy and deep set in his lungs. James picked up a smaller greige-coloured doo. It was a nervous-looking bird that was small enough to be female. "Naw, if anybody is to be Mungo, this is the bugger."

"He disnae look like he could attract a stuffed chicken."

"That's what ah'm saying." James lifted the brown pigeon and stroked its ruffled collar. "But watch yer language, Little Mungo can hear ye and he's a sensitive little prick."

Mungo peered at the small pigeon, he stroked its collar with his pinkie, and it flinched. He would have to admit the name suited the bird. "I've never met another Mungo before. I'm gonnae look after it and make him tougher than Dolph Lundgren over there."

James had lined the doocot in smashed

glass shards to discourage rats from eating his defenceless birds. There was a crunch of broken bottles underfoot as he did an excited dance. "That's it! His name is Dolph, it's no Archie." He turned to his bluish bird. "I hereby christen you: Dolph the Mad Shagger."

"Dolph Pidgegren."

"Naw, I'll get hammered up the meeting with a name like that. It has to be mair poetic like. Something that strikes fear into the heart of other doomen, *Champion of the Sorrowful Skies,* some pish like that."

"How about Conan the Sectarian?"

"No way!" But Mungo could tell that James liked it.

They stepped outside and gave the new couples some privacy. They lay on their bellies in the raggedy grass and listened to the faint roar of evening traffic. The last of the daylight had sunk below the fleecy clouds, for a few brief moments everything was bathed in a soft peach glow. Mungo closed his eyes and tried to feel its warmth. "How did you start the pouting anyhows?"

He imagined James shrugging beside him. "It was just something my da introduced me to."

Mungo felt everyone knew everything there was to know about the Hamilton family, but James hadn't told him anything about his family. "Is he a dooman as well?"

"Not really." James coughed again. "He was looking for something for us to do the gether. I think he felt guilty."

Mungo wondered what it would be like to have a father. "Do you look like him?"

"Aye."

"Do you act like him?"

"Aye. That's what my maw used to say anyhows."

"Does she no think so anymore?"

James looked at him, it was a fleeting glance like he was trying to find something in Mungo's eyes, some cruelty perhaps, or the narrowing that mean-hearted women get when they sniff a good story. "Sorry, I thought ye knew." He was ripping grass out by the roots. "There were hunners of big black cars, I thought everybody on the scheme knew." He slipped a blade of grass between his lips. "That's why he feels guilty, see. After my maw died he needed to go back to work. He works away a lot. He's a pipe-fitter on an oil rig. It's good money."

"In Scotland?"

"Aye, but right at the very top, it's nearly in Norway. He works two weeks on and gets two weeks off. But it often feels shorter. He says the paraffin budgie can't take off in the fog."

"The paraffin whut?"

"The helicopter. He's hunners of miles offshore, and they can't fly in bad weather. The sun lifts a fog off of the sea. He says some days you cannae even see Aberdeen for the haar. You'd think it'd be the winter, but it's not. It's the summer that's the worst." He met Mungo's eyes now. "Did ye really not see all the black mourning cars?"

"No," said Mungo, and he meant it. He had not known Mrs Jamieson was dead. "I'm sorry about your mammy. It must be quiet in your house."

"Sometimes."

"It's quiet in my house too." Mungo slipped a blade of grass between his fingers and tried to blow on it and make it whistle. The blade of grass made a thrumming sound and then let out a shrill song. "You know, you can come round anytime you like."

"Cheers. But it doesn't matter, I'm no gonnae be here much longer. Soon as I'm sixteen then I'm gonnae leave school and get out of this shitehole."

"Aye, but where would you go?"

"I don't know. Mibbe somewhere up north. Somewhere I could get a job working outside. I like being outside and any-where is better than here. Here I just feel like I'm playing at happy housewives for an auld man that's never home."

Mungo could barely imagine life away from Hamish and the constant fear of something bad happening to Mo-Maw. He tried to laugh. "Tell you what, if you hold on, ah'll come with you when I turn sixteen. I mean, I've never even been out of the East End. You could take me to Shettleston and tell me I was in Spain."

James didn't say anything to this. It made Mungo feel odd. He felt the seconds stretch awkwardly. He should have kept his mouth shut, but the words inside him wanted to fill the void. "You know, I thought my maw was dead too. But she wasn't. She was cook-ing black pudding outside the hospital." It was a stupid thing to say to a boy who had lost his mother. He lowered his face into the grass.

As the lights came on in the scheme Mungo helped James sweep out the last of the cages and lock up for the night. As they walked back to the tenements James handed him a long brown feather, one of Little Mungo's moultings. "Ye should have this."

Mungo turned the feather in his hand, it was soft and fluffy along the outer edge.

Little Mungo was still a squab, he had yet to mature. He was going to mention this to James, but James spoke first. "I'm gonnae see some lassies up by the old fountain. Do ye want to come?"

"Nah. I'd better not." He didn't like Jodie to come home to an empty house. He wanted to have the lights on before she returned from the café.

James started hacking again. He took a blue inhaler from his tracksuit pocket and drank in two large lungfuls. His woollen hat was sitting above his ears as it always did and the cold had chapped the tips of his ears. "Maybe you should go home, and just warm up a bit? Watch telly?"

"Naw. I'm no ready to go back to an empty hoose. Are ye sure ye willnae come wi' me? I know a lassie that will let ye finger her if ye buy her a Walnut Whip."

Mungo felt along the soft ridge of Little Mungo's feather again. He wondered if he would ever reach an age where that sounded like a nice thing to do. "Naw. No thanks."

"C'mon, man up," said James with a half-smile. But he'd already turned and was lurching towards the park.

By the time Mungo reached home all the lights were already blazing and she was sitting at the drop-leaf table in the kitchenette. She had kept her thick anorak on and was drinking whisky from a long-stemmed wine glass and using another as a lazy-man's ashtray. The line of her violet mascara was ruined and it gave an odd blue tint to her face. He knew she had been crying. She must have seen him gawping at her.

"Don't just stand there catching flies," sniffed Mo-Maw, "come and gie us a hug."

Mungo went to his mother. She pulled him on to her lap and she cradled him like the *Pietà*. He was almost sixteen now, much too tall to be babied, but he let her mollycoddle him anyway. He wrapped himself around her and sank his face into her hair. It smelled like sausage grease and loamy peat, cigarettes and Juicy Fruit, all the familiar smells he had missed. Yet as he snuffled into her crown, underneath it all was the scent of another person's soap, and there at the base of it, the smell of Jocky's house, the musk of a stranger's bath towel. Mungo tried to ignore it. "I really thought you might be dead."

"Ah-HA!" She shrieked and threw her arms wide like an Egyptian mummy. "Nae luck pal. *It's alive!*"

Mungo couldn't laugh yet. "There's been stories on the evening news. Some teenage

173

lassies went missing and it turned out they were murdered. I was worried about you."

"Och. That's a lovely thing to say." She tilted her face towards him. There were creases on her face that were not there the last time he saw her. Old make-up was ground into her fine wrinkles, it made them seem like veins. "If ye were a mad murderer yerself, do ye still think I could pass for a teenager?"

Mungo scratched his face. "Oh aye." He knew she would like this lie.

Mo-Maw stamped her small feet in glee. "Och. Ah forgot how much better ah always feel when ah'm around you." She kissed his cheek. It was a strange open-mouthed kiss. He could feel the wet tip of her tongue. She was already drunk. "If only ah could find a man as good as you. Ah don't know how ah never managed to make a mess of ye. Not like ah did with those there two."

"Jodie's awright," said Mungo. "She's gonnae be a doctor, or an astronaut. I think you should be proudest of her."

Mo-Maw made a disgruntled sound, then she grinned conspiratorially. "Disnae matter. Who likes a wummin that's no fun?" She poured a galloping stream of whisky into the wine glass. Mungo wondered if Tattie-bogle would come tonight, the dull-eyed monstrous side of her. He watched her closely, she looked like she was enjoying herself. Maybe it would all be okay. "Don't ye hate being cooped up all day here with *her*? She's no fun at all. Ah swear that scunner came out of me with a to-do list."

"We always have a laugh when we're the gether."

"That's another thing ah've never liked about that one. As soon as she was big enough to hold ye, she was running all over this scheme like ye were her wee baby."

"Mungo, you can't be burning all the lights . . ." They hadn't heard the key in the lock. Jodie was standing before them with a soggy pizza box in her hand. "What in God's name are *you* doing here?"

"What a way to greet yer own mother."

Jodie put the pizza box on the table. She took Mungo roughly by his arm and pulled him off Mo-Maw's lap. She dropped him into a seat of his own and pointed at the cold box. "Here, eat that." Mungo did as he was told. Jodie used her index finger and dipped it into Mo-Maw's elegant glass. She winced when she sucked it.

Mo-Maw's eyes were glassy, the whites were steeped in redness as though she had been too long in the local pool. Her jaw was set at a funny angle and she was scowling at

Jodie as she hovered over Mungo. The boy ripped a hunk of battered pizza and handed it to his mother. She reached out to take it, but Jodie drew back Mungo's wrist. "When you are full and *if* there is some left over, then she can eat — not before."

Jodie started gathering the dirty dishes. "So, to what do we owe this great honour? *Haaah-ha.*"

"Ah just thought ah would come and see ma weans." Mo-Maw was sitting upright in the kitchen chair, trying to gather some dignity in her own house. "What's the harm in th—"

"Spare me your nonsense, Maureen." It was cold, but without meanness. Mungo looked up at her — Jodie looked worn through. "What's happened with Jocky?"

"Nothing. Nothing's happened with Jocky. It's aw candy floss and winching in the moonlight. Ah just wanted to come see ma boy. My only true love." She reached across the table and interlaced her fingers amongst Mungo's. They mooned at each other like they were sweethearts.

"Great. So, this is just a flying visit then? I'm glad you could fit us into your diary." Jodie's hair was scraped away from her face; her ponytail hung down her back, thick as a hawser rope. The tautness made her stony-faced. Rummaging through the kitchen drawers, she produced a stack of papers and dropped them in front of Mo-Maw. There was angry red ink everywhere like the letters were shouting at them. "They're threatening to cut off the electric, the gas, *and* the phone. The housing association has written to us three times about the fact there doesn't seem to be an adult in the house. If you don't show yourself, they will call the Social and your precious boy here will be put into care."

Mo-Maw roared. "Ah wonder what grassin' basturt telt them that." She cast the red letters to the floor. "These fuckin' tenements! Ye cannae walk the length of the street without every clipe knowing yer business."

"You need to go in first thing on Monday morning and talk to the council."

"Aye, I'll get to it."

"No, you will go in first thing on Monday morning."

Mo-Maw put her hand up to cover her lips, she leaned across the table to Mungo as though Jodie was not even there. *"See, ah telt ye she was no fuckin' fun."*

Jodie closed her eyes. Mungo watched her hands go limp at her side. Mo-Maw tipped the cigarette ash out of her spare wine glass.

She filled it with whisky and poured sloshes of Irn-Bru in after it. She pushed it towards Jodie. "Here hen, maybe this will help ye loosen up a wee bit."

Jodie's eyes flew open. Mungo had never noticed it before, but now he could see the violence of Hamish in her face. Her eyes could fade to the same black and grey of Ayrshire flint, and her jaw locked in the way Hamish's did when he was going to punch something, hard. She extended her hand and swept the glass off the table and sent it flying into the wall opposite. Molten orange sprayed the white countertop.

"Ya insolent streak of piss." Mo-Maw did not like to see good drink wasted. "Ye're not too old to go over my knee, lady."

"Why did you come back?"

"Why did you come back, why did you come back." Mo-Maw was parroting her, turning it into a sour whine. "Well if you must know, it was your fault. Everything was going grand between me and Jocky until youse two showed up at the snack bar."

"Our fault?"

"Aye." Mo-Maw tipped her nose upwards and turned her body away from them as though she had been dealt a mortal insult. "Ah felt bad after ah saw yeese. Guilty like. So ah telt Jocky ah had weans, and he papped us. He said it was too much trouble. He said he didn't want a family."

Jodie rested all her weight on one hip. She squinted like she could smell something rancid. There was a long awful silence before she said, "See, I asked around and it turns out Jocky Dunbar has four weans of his own. Three girls and a wee boy, all of them still in school. *Haaah-ha.*"

"Well, ah didnae say he *didnae.*"

"You've been living with a strange man and playing house with his weans. Have you been cooking for them?"

"It wisnae like that. Ah wisnae there for them."

"Were you ironing their school uniforms? Making them sandwiches for their packed lunch?"

"No all the time."

"Wait, what?" Mungo looked from one woman to the other. "Maw —" she hated when he called her that — "Did you iron clothes for another boy?"

"Naw, Mungo." Mo-Maw reached out to him across the table but he pulled his hand away. Jodie laid her hand across the back of his neck, it was burning hot.

"I know you are not here because of us," said Jodie. "I know you've been playing pretend with some widower and his shiny

179

weans. I would bet Mungo's life on the fact that you are here now because he's chucked you for drinking too much. I bet he got sick of the state of you bouncing around the Trongate and disgracing his name."

"Ye've never loved me."

"I did once." Jodie nodded sincerely. She took Mungo by the arm and led him out of the kitchenette. "You can stay until after you've spoken to the council and then you need to leave. Ah'll come to the snack bar every Friday and collect money for the bills. You only need to pay until Mungo has his sixteenth birthday. Then you're free to destroy yourself however you like. Try and take the fast road."

Jodie wished her brother would cry. It was a luxury she never had. It had been different for her, she had no one to cry to — neither Mo-Maw nor Hamish could have offered any comfort. But Mungo had her. As they crouched behind the communal bin shed she wished that he would cry. She only had to think of Hamish and she could see the rage that built when you never let the hurt out. She knew too many knotted-up men. "You know she's a liar, don't you?"

Any other time Mungo would have defended their mother. That was his role in the family tragedy, to find the last scraps of good in Mo-Maw and forever be reminding his siblings of it. He knew his line, but he didn't have the energy to recite it.

"You know she will leave the minute Jocky phones for her."

Mungo looked thunderstruck, his mouth was hanging open. He didn't have the energy to argue anymore. "Did she really look after Jocky's weans?"

"Yes," said Jodie. "I noticed you've been at your mad chewing again. I couldn't bring myself to tell you."

They idled in the shadow of the midden as long as they could bear. It stank something terrible, but the longer they waited the more likely that Mo-Maw would have collapsed into a fitful sleep. They huddled together out of the wind until they startled Mrs Campbell as she brought plates of fish down for the tenement strays. Mungo had been telling Jodie about the pigeon boy when Mrs Campbell chased them out of the darkness and upstairs to their beds. All the way up the close she berated them. But Mungo saw the pity that sat in the corner of her mouth. "Ye're a right pair of buggers to frighten an aul' wummin like that." She slipped a chunk of bright orange cheese into each of their hands. She had produced it

181

from her pinny pocket, as though it was a very ordinary place to keep your cheese. It was cracked dry at the edges but she made them eat it before she let them go. "Pair of ye look like ye might come down wi' the rickets any minute."

"Thank you, Missus Campbell," said Jodie.

Mrs Campbell took Jodie's hand. She smoothed the loose hairs away from Jodie's face. "Listen, hen, if for any reason at all ye cannae sleep up there the night, ye just come back doon the stairs to me, awright? Ah can make up a wee bed for the both of ye, nae questions asked." Mrs Campbell paused, but she wouldn't let go of her hand. "Ah cannae be seen to be interfering in another wummin's business, ye understand that, eh? But youse just say the word, awright?"

Mungo stepped forward and gave the woman a hug. She spun him into a waltz. "Da-dee-da-dah. Aw, yer a pure sook, Mungo Hamilton. Last o' the great romantics." She shooed the children away. "Awa' wi' ye. Awa' afore ye make auld Graham jealous."

The Hamilton flat was quiet. Mo-Maw was in her bedroom, breathing heavily. They closed the door silently behind them. Jodie put her fingers to her lips but Mungo knew what to do. They had been playing this game for a long time: don't make a sound, don't wake Tattie-bogle.

Mungo had only been seven and Jodie had been eight and a half when they first met Tattie-bogle. Jodie could see her brother struggle with this other person, the angry, destructive drunk that came when Mo-Maw was lowest. They had been watching *Willo the Wisp,* it was only dinner time, but Mo-Maw had been drinking for long before they had come home from school. Hamish had asked for something to eat and she had laughed and told him how the electric cooker worked. In a fit of rage, Hamish had taken the bottle of whisky from her and poured it down the sink like it was cold tea.

When she was finished leathering him, a panic rose inside her: where would she get more drink? She telephoned a man who lived in the close next door. He came over and they spent some time in her bedroom with a bottle of fortified. Hamish had to lie on his stomach, the back of his legs scarlet with handprints. They sat close to the television and ate bowls of salted porridge that Jodie had made. When the man finally left, Mo-Maw was fully drunk and only half-dressed. She had gone past the point where she had been having any fun and now she was angry and lousy with a deep sense of having been swindled.

"Do ye know what ah just had to do?" she accused Hamish. They knew, although they didn't have the words for it yet. They'd had to sit cross-eyed before the television in order to not hear the man and his grunting. The children had been so close they could smell the static from the screen. "Well, that was all *your* fault, so it was." She pointed an accusatory finger at her eldest boy. The children sat clumped together, alert as three startled ferrets. That was the day Jodie invented Tattie-bogle.

When Mo-Maw finally passed out, Jodie rubbed some calamine lotion into the back of Hamish's red legs, while Mungo flicked through the channels on the soundless television. They were playing a werewolf movie: some comedy about an American teenager trying to cope with his terrifying alter ego. The three children sat open-mouthed, their heads lolling on soft necks, when Jodie quietly said, "Ah. That's like Mo-Maw. She's not the same person all the time. See."

Mungo and Jodie choked down the last of Mrs Campbell's dry cheese. They stood in their dark hallway and tried to decipher the message in Mo-Maw's uneven breathing. She was falling asleep. *Good.* Jodie hugged her brother goodnight. They parted to go to their separate bedrooms. They did not make even the faintest noise, but still somehow Mo-Maw stirred. Her voice was damp and claggy sounding in the darkness. "Mungo? Mungo darlin', is that you?"

Mungo looked to his sister; she was beseeching him to be quiet, all the colour had drained from her face. Mo-Maw stirred from her bed. There was the thump of a meaty foot hitting the carpet, and Mungo knew what he had to do to keep her safe, to hold her still. "Yes, Mo-maw. It's me. What is it?"

It took her much longer to think when she was rolling this deep. The children stood in the dark, waiting for her reply. "C'mon," said the pitiful voice. "Come in here and sleep with Mo-Maw the night."

You're too old for that, mouthed Jodie.

"I know." But he couldn't admit to Jodie how much he wanted to do it, how he wanted to be with his mother, and to feel safe again.

"Mungo, you can't sleep in with her," Jodie whispered.

"Munn-go, Mungo. C'mon-go, Mungo sleep in here the night," Mo-Maw whined.

Mo-Maw was slurring heavily. He could wait, he could do nothing, and she would probably fall asleep. But how could he tell Jodie this was for him as much as it was for her? "I should go. I can keep an eye on her. Make sure she doesn't go wandering in the night."

Jodie didn't say anything else. She turned away from him in disgust and slammed her bedroom door. He listened to the tiny snib catch. Hamish had kicked her door in once — right around the time Jodie had started her bleedings — and in revenge, she had taken all his trousers and cut the pocket bags out of them. For a long time after that Hamish had needed to carry everything he owned in his two hands like a beggar of Bethlehem.

Mungo poured Mo-Maw a tall glass of metallic tap water. He slid into the warm bedroom. "Lift your bum," he commanded, and she did a crablike pose on the bed, shaking, like she might topple at any moment. Mungo dug the tight elastic of her leggings out from her belly flesh and drew them off. Sighing with relief, she lay back on the bed and patted the sheets next to her. Mungo took off his own clothes, naked but for his boxer shorts, and climbed in beside her. Drawing the duvet over them, she pushed herself close to him and he wrapped himself around her small back. She was like a child in his arms, a drunk, sour-breathed, nicotine-coated child. Mungo pressed the warm tops of his thighs against the underside of her cold legs. He held her tiny feet between his and rubbed them gently until they felt less like ice.

"Ah'm no sleepy," she slurred.

"Do you want a story? I can tell you the one about the woman who wins the football pools and never needs to work another day in her life. You like that one."

Mo-Maw shook her head like a child. "No. Sing me something good."

"Like what?"

"You know hunners of good songs. Sing me something you've taped off the charts. Something about love."

Mungo lay behind her. He needed to keep her here with him. In a quiet voice he started to sing his love songs, unsure of the words, but certain of how they made him feel.

SIX

The orange Capri was parked under a broken street light. Some industrious youth had climbed the lamp post and disconnected the light so that he could kiss his girlfriend in privacy. The car sat in the shadows, near the breeze-block wall that separated the drying area from some muddy grass. It was a magnificent machine. Even in the half-dark it was a shade of pumpkin orange so confident that it defied the usual embarrassment of gaudy motors. It was a powerful-looking beast, the kind that Mungo only ever saw in toy boxes imported from America.

Hamish put his hand on the door handle and with a quick slice of a flathead file he released the lock and let himself in. Mungo slunk backwards into the shadows. By the time Hamish had coaxed the roaring engine to life he had pressed his entire back against the breeze block. "Get in, ya shitebag" was all Hamish would say. Mungo didn't think he could outrun the growling engine.

With its mirrored baubles and furred headrests, the inside of the car felt more like a seedy gentleman's club than a car interior. Hamish drove slowly through the back streets as Mungo sank down into the plush velour seat and tried not to let anyone see him in the stolen motor. When they reached the traffic lights of the Parade, Hamish slid the car out of gear and pumped the accelerator. It made a ferocious roar that echoed off the tenements and made people jump at the bus shelter. He did it again.

"I don't like that." Mungo's face was ticcing.

Hamish gunned the engine again. Oncoming headlights glinted off his thick lenses. "I won't stop doing this until ye sit up and stop acting like a fud."

"But you've knocked it."

The engine squealed again and the car lurched into gear. "So? Anybody that wants tae stop us has to fuckin' catch us first."

The lights of the Parade were beautiful at high speed. Bright chip shops and cosy pubs all reflected on to the damp streets. Tenements streaked by, and Mungo watched the lights change in synchronization in every one of the front rooms; happy families, tucked in from the cold, all watching the same channel. Soon, the tenements fell away and the low houses of Royston rose on the hill to the right: the land of Catholics, no place for a Hamilton.

Beyond these sat the broken promises of Sighthill. The high-rise towers were only twenty years old and were already in a state of disrepair. They were the tallest buildings Mungo had ever seen. The tops of them disappeared into the dense clouds, like a stairway to somewhere above the endless rain, or like a strut trying to keep the ceiling of dark cumulus from collapsing and suffocating the entire city.

The Capri knew how to fly. Every time Hamish paused at a red light and took off again, Mungo was pressed back into the seat, as forcefully as the times when Hamish would sit on his chest. Only this pressure felt like freedom. Hamish gunned the engine and snapped the steering wheel, and the car slid around the traffic island. While they paused at the lights Mungo pointed towards the illuminated snack bar. It was quiet and Mo-Maw was hanging out the serving hatch with the fluorescent tube light glinting off her pallid chest. Her boys watched as their mother flirted with one of the bin men. Hamish cranked down his window and pumped the engine again. He screamed over the roar, *"Getitupyeyaauldrunk, giesagobble!"*

Mungo slid down in his seat. He turned to apologize to Mo-Maw but they were already screeching towards the Trongate. Hamish was roaring with laughter, and despite himself, Mungo realized he was having fun. "Don't wet yersel, she'll no know it was us," said Hamish. "She'd never wear her glasses in front of men."

The orange beast roared down High Street and, turning right, it passed the newspaper works and went into George Square. Hamish drove like he owned the whole city, one hand high on the wheel, the other waving at scornful lassies out the window. Mungo laid his forehead against the cool glass and watched a thousand stories go by: young, underdressed women going for drinks after work, lines of animated art students talking with their hands, and the lawyers with their arms full of Manila folders, walking with a sense of their own importance. So many lives were happening only two miles away from his and they all seemed brighter than his own.

Hamish pulled the car along the wide artery of Argyle Street. The people seemed a lower sort here, people like them. They were closer to the River Clyde now and the shops were cheaper; the buildings not yet sandblasted back to their glorious golden colour. Glaswegians cut through the smirr without even looking where they were going. They didn't look up at the grand buildings, heavy with Corinthian columns, that the Tobacco Lords had built for themselves. Mungo felt envious. If he could walk these streets every day, he would never take the beauty of the city for granted.

"You awright?" asked Hamish. "Ye're no gonnae be sick, are ye?"

"I never get to see this. Don't drive so fast."

They cruised on for a while, winding up and down West Nile and Renfrew Street and then back along Hope Street. The car stopped at the lights by Central Station and they watched young women huddle together and make their way to the pubs and clubs. The tops of their soft arms were pink with gooseflesh and mottled with stubborn baby fat. Hamish pulled alongside them and brought the engine to a seductive susurration. The girls laughed at them.

Hamish flicked the fuel gauge. "Seems a shame to waste this beauty. How do ye fancy an adventure afore we get tae work?" He drew out a can of Special Brew from his tracksuit pocket and handed it to Mungo.

He took out another and slammed it off his brother's in salute. Mungo was sad to see gobbets of white foamy lager spill on the upholstery but Hamish didn't seem to mind. "Here's to us brave Hamilton men."

There was a stack of someone else's cassettes in the cigarette drawer. Hamish played the Pretenders and he mugged at Mungo to "stop his sobbing," bopping in time to the jangling chorus. Hamish looked happy, driving fast, with one hand gliding through the spitting rain, and the can of lager clamped between his knees. Mungo wanted to watch him in his rare contentment, but the city was already flying by underneath them. They took a bridge over the Clyde. They flew over neighbourhoods Mungo couldn't name.

By the time they reached the sea it was hard to see where the land ended and the water began. Hamish parked on the tallest hill and they sat on the bonnet. Below them were constellations of evening lights, lonely farms, and tiny clusters of villages sitting snug against the frigid Irish Sea. Hamish put his arm around Mungo. He almost apologized. "Mibbe next time we'll do this in the daylight, eh?"

Mungo didn't mind. It was the quietest

place he had ever been. "Can we turn the headlights off? Just for a wee minute."

His brother did as he asked. Hamish finished his lager, and then he finished Mungo's for him, as they sat together in the gloaming. After a while, he said, "Ah dinnae mean to be so hard on ye all the time."

"I know."

"I just feel a mental amount of pressure sometimes. You know, wi' the Billies, wi' baby Adrianna, and looking after you on top of it."

"I don't ask you to do that."

"S'pose you're the least of ma problems." Hamish was pulling gently on Mungo's earlobe. Mungo rarely heard his brother talk like this. At home, you couldn't admit anything tender. It was foolish to say something sweet that the scheme could use against you later. "We're in this the gether, Mungo. I'm just hard on you because ah cannae have ye turning out soft or nothing." He tugged Mungo's ear, then twisted it.

Mungo was sad that his real brother had crept back so soon. "I think something is wrong with Jodie. She's no eating properly."

"Aye?" Hamish sounded bored. "I bet none of the boys at school want to shag her."

"Wait, I thought we were in this the

gether? Three Musketeers?"

"That's a laugh! It's mair like the God-father and his two useless wallopers." Hamish crumpled his lager can, it sailed through the air. "C'mon. Want to see some braw magic?"

Hamish drove along a series of twisting roads. He drove fast and Mungo was reminded that his brother had been here before without him and the thought made him blue. The car banked around high hedges and farmers' fences until it came to a stop facing up a small hill. In the last of the violet light Mungo could see about forty feet ahead of them.

"Right," said Hamish. "What do you think happens if ye take the handbrake off on a hill?"

"That's stupid," said Mungo. "You would roll backwards."

"Right enough."

Hamish released the handbrake and Mungo braced himself, waited for the car to roll downhill backwards, away from the glow of its own headlights. Nothing happened for a while, then, very slowly, very surely, the car rolled uphill. Mungo could feel the heat of Hamish's broad grin. "How crazy is that?"

It was strange indeed. The car was accelerating uphill of its own accord.

"It's cursed or something. Anything ye put on this hill rolls upwards instead of downwards. It's an electric current. Freaky right?" Hamish put the car into gear and continued up the hill, but Mungo wanted to do it again and again.

They stopped at a small harbour by the sullen sea. Hamish bought them a poke of chips to share. He didn't complain when Mungo drowned it all in malt vinegar, he just said, "Don't eat them now. I know where we should go."

The soggy chips were still warm by the time they came to a long drystane dyke. Hamish pulled the car off the road and they scrambled over the high wall. It was pitch-black. Every so often, long ferns licked at their legs, and it made them dance with fear and delight. In the distance, about a mile away, was the faint glow of man-made light.

When they finally reached the glowing castle, Mungo had to ask what they were looking at because he had never seen anything like it. There was the Central Station Hotel, and the sooty sandstone of Glasgow Cathedral, but those places were built for the public or for day trippers. This house was all for one person. It was built for majesty and looked somewhere between a fortified castle and a grand, stately home. The main structure sat with its back to the breaking sea and the landscaping and crenelated walls wrapped around him as far as he could make out. The faint light from inside rippled against the mottled glass. The windows were generous, the rooms overfurnished, and Mungo could tell there was a world of beauty to look in and out upon.

"Smashin' int it? Culzean Castle." Hamish stood under the canopy of an ancient tree, his hands on his hips, proud as any laird. "Sammy-Jo wants to get married there." He whistled. "Do ye know how many stolen motors it would take to pay for that?"

Hamish pointed towards a bridge that arched over a sunken garden. The bridge had guard turrets on either side, long since put out of use. "In there is a good place for pumping lassies," he said, matter-of-fact. "Bring them up here wi' a bottle of Buckie and show them this castle. They'll let ye get both hauns up them after that." He was smiling. His mouth was full of yellow chips.

Mungo was watching Hamish dangle from a thick bough and thinking how much he enjoyed this playful side of his brother. Hamish was far from Glasgow and the glare of the Protestant boys who expected so much from him, and the rest of the scheme who expected so little. Here, Mungo could remember the boy Hamish had once been, mischievous and brave, full of impetuous ideas and never afraid of falling, so long as he could fly first. In this moment it was as if he had not yet soured. To see him carry on like a wean again was almost too much for Mungo to bear.

"Hamey?" Mungo knew he was pushing his luck.

"Whut?"

"I love you."

Mungo was watching his brother swing back and forth when he felt the hands on his collar. Why did they always grab you by the collar? The night watchman had slunk across the wet lawn, the dull churn of the sea had muffled all his footsteps. He slipped a tight arm under Mungo's chin and tilted his head backwards.

"Got you, ya wee fucker!"

Hamish had barely let go of the bough before Mungo did it. The violence sprang out of a lifetime of compacted instinct, hard-learned lessons from a sadistic brother. In one quick move Mungo pulled his head forward and then snapped it backwards. He felt the hard bone of the man's nose give way to softness and he knew that he had shattered it. He curled his body into a ball and shoved with all of his might, pushing the man off balance. The night watchman fell to the sodden ground. Mungo broke free of his grip and sprang to his feet.

The man was rolling on the ground and clutching at his smashed face as Mungo darted past Hamish, heading for the safety of the darkness. As he passed, Mungo grabbed hold of Hamish's slippery tracksuit and dragged him away from the man and back through the ferns. It had been easy to overpower the night watchman; maybe he was unaccustomed to Glaswegian schemies ransacking his castle. Yet as they scaled the drystane boundary there was a look of admiration on Hamish's face. Mungo could see his teeth flash in the moonlight. Hamish lived for the thrill of mischief. As he manipulated the exposed wires and started the car humming, he said, "Sakes, Mungo. You act all shy, but I don't think you know what ye're capable of."

They sang all the way back to the city. Hamish had been talking down the boasts of the Catholic fighters and beaming with pride at the tiny spark of violence inside his brother. "That was mental how ye decked that auld cunt." He grinned. "Next month, ye need tae gie us hauners against the

Royston Bhoys. The bastards willnae know what hit them. I cannae wait to see you bury a tomahawk into one of those Fenian wallopers."

Behind Sighthill there was a sludge canal that ran from the North Side to the Clyde, and at night, all the low industrial buildings that framed it were dark and locked tight. Hamish abandoned the Capri in the middle of the empty road. There was just enough petrol left in the tank to set it alight. Mungo had tried to reason with him. They had had their fun, could they not just return the beautiful motor undamaged and just this once not spoil everything good that came to them.

"How stupit are you? I'm getting paid eighty poun' to steal this motor and torch it. Joe Morrison will get mair frae the insurance than he would get for a trade-in."

Hamish lit the rag that he had stuffed into the petrol cap. He danced away from the Capri. There was a terrific explosion and the car was a growling ball of flames. It knocked the wind out of Mungo, and it shook all thoughts from his head. It was dazzling, how something marvellous could be destroyed so quickly and so completely. The brothers jogged away from the flames, sat on the wall of Sighthill Cemetery, and watched the tall plume of rubber smoke merge into the uplit clouds. Mungo felt sad that their night was over. Soon they would be back on the scheme. He wished they could get Jodie and go eat vinegary chips by the sea together.

They were watching knots of Sighthill weans move closer to the bonfire, finding things to throw on the roaring flames before the fire brigade arrived and doused the fun. Down the hill, the industrial buildings were illuminated by the strobing blue of the fire engines. The boys watched the lights wind their way through the maze of streets towards the canal. Hamish spoke first. "I was proud of ye, up at the castle."

Mungo didn't feel proud. He was repulsed by the way his hair was hardening from the man's sticky blood. "That's a sad thing to be proud of me for."

Hamish was holding a short dout between his second and third knuckles. The city was half-rotted below them. It wasn't only that Mungo was too young to understand, it was also that in fifteen years he had seen nothing but the half-dozen tenemented streets they lived on. Hamish clenched his left fist and tried to dampen his temper. It wasn't Mungo's fault that he didn't know more. "There's nae jobs here. Ye'll need to fuckin' toughen up. Like, what's even the point of you stickin' in at school?"

"Yeah, but you didn't even try." It was too quick. Mungo braced himself.

Hamish flicked the dout and the cigarette cartwheeled into the night. He folded in on himself like a half-shut blade and set off on the long walk home.

Mungo trotted behind him, a kicked dog at his master's heels.

Hamish scoffed. "Learn a trade, that's what the school telt me. I telt them I wanted to go tae university, learn all about the engineerin', and they said, 'You know, that's not for boys like *you*.' " Hamish feigned his best West End accent and Mungo knew by the way he sung it upwards that he was mimicking Mrs Newman, the overworked headmistress at the high school. "The sad thing wis, I knew what that sour cunt meant, but I goes, *'How no?'* And she sucked in her massive wobbling chins and goes, 'You're not cut from university cloth.' "

Mungo had heard Hamish say the exact same thing to Jodie; now he knew where the hurt began. "And you believed her?"

"No at first. Newman telt us if I liked buildin' things that much, to go down Govan, and apply for a shipbuilding apprenticeship.

She sent me down the watter one afternoon, paid my bus fare and everything. I came swannin' down the dockside in my best school uniform while a tide of men were pushing the other way. They had just been telt they were getting the sack. Their lunch pails were still full." Hamish stopped his long strides and looked out over the low city. "Grown men wi' greetin' faces, and here's muggins, in a school tie, asking for an apprenticeship. Three hunner and fifty men on the broo and I'm asking for a bus-fare allowance. It was a pure embarrassment."

"I'm sorry."

Hamish turned on his heels and rammed his finger into his brother's chest. They had crossed some kind of Glasgow boundary and it was like the angry man he had left behind had been waiting there for him to return. "I don't need you feelin' sorry for us."

The side of Mungo's face started twitching again. It had been calm all night, even as he broke the nose of the night watchman.

Hamish studied its familiar twisting and sighed. "Do you hate us, Mungo?"

"No!" It came out in a rushing torrent and it was true. Mungo bit the inside of his lip and added, "But I don't want to be like you."

He expected Hamish to clout him. But Hamish only turned away from him and laughed. Mungo took a half-step backwards to avoid any surprise right hook. "It's funny. Ah thought the same thing about Mo-Maw and look at me. I was an old man at fifteen and a dad at eighteen."

"Is that why you hate her?"

"I don't hate her." Hamish laughed, but it was sour. "Aye, mibbe I do. But don't we all blame her for somethin'?"

"I don't blame her. I just try to love her."

"You're still young, baw-jaws. Gie it time."

At that, Hamish turned back around and started to run as fast as he could. Mungo knew to keep up with him. Royston was not a place for a Hamilton to walk leisurely, Hamish had ruined even that. On the side of the low council houses someone had spray-painted a large green shamrock. The brothers didn't stop to consider it. They flew along the glistening streets, interlopers in the land of the Catholics.

SEVEN

Mo-Maw spent the morning trying to get into Jodie's good books again. She alternated between ironing the same four tea towels and staring mournfully at the telephone, but whenever Jodie came near, she rearranged her smile and covered the shame she felt at having been spurned. As if to prove her reformation, she then spent the afternoon slipping cubed steak and sausage meat into a pot of stovies. The kitchenette was damp with steam. The air was salted with beef stock and sweating onions.

Mungo lay down on the hallway carpet and propped his legs on the wall. He relished the happy clip of their one good knife, and the splooking sound made by the stirring ladle. Every now and again Jodie would step over him on the way to the toilet. Her rolling eyes implored him to grow up. "Traitor!" she crowed. "Have some self-respect." Eventually she gave up on scowling at him and started cuffing his flank with her toes — "Sorry. So sorry." — pretending it was an accident every time she passed. But Mungo was a loyal dog. He would not be moved.

He got up eventually and followed her around the house. Jodie had been drying her long hair and he floated into her bedroom silently, inching ever closer, till he was sat near her, then beside her, and until finally his left hand was upturned and she was dropping her hair clips into it. He quietly implored her to come to dinner, and it was clear that he would give her no peace until she agreed.

His sister joined them at the drop-leaf table. She sat side-saddle to the chair, like she might up and leave at any moment. It made Mungo itchy. Mo-Maw ladled out bowls of potatoes that were as big and white as snowballs and floated in gristly sausage meat: both the long kind and the chewy square kind. Then she drowned everything within a lochan of fragrant gravy.

His mother had washed her face since her last shift but Mungo could still see pockets of the ultraviolet mascara when she smiled. As they dragged their bread through the gravy, she made small talk, telling them about the characters that frequented the snack bar; the nocturnal feeders who spent their lives roaming around in the dark. They fluttered to her like moths, she said, and with no shame they told her all kinds of personal things they should never utter in the daylight.

"So, that's when Big Ella telt me that the last lassie she employed was selling mair than sausages and fried egg. The dirty besom had written out a secret price list and everything, and if ye bought ten, you got the eleventh wank for free." Mo-Maw was cackling at the story and for a moment she seemed happy enough for a heartbroken woman. "For the first three weeks ah had all these long-distance lorry drivers asking us what the *special* was. Ah kept telling them it was curry sauce and chips, and they kept looking at me like ah was stupit. 'Naw,' they'd say, 'the *special*-special.' "

Jodie folded her arms across her chest. "Mibbe you should give it a go."

"What? Ah'm no touching any man's boaby for a couple of bob."

Jodie's eyes darted to Mungo. They both knew the truth of it, that Mo-Maw had done worse and for less. His feet were searching for hers under the table, trying to kick her before she soured the meal. The edges of her lips were already curled in snideness. "Mibbe if you sold yourself by the ounce, you'd get a better price."

Mo-Maw dropped her fork. She pressed self-consciously on her small rolls of fat.

The women were both glaring, but not at each other. Mungo fretted to fill the empty space. Jodie had only eaten a few mouthfuls of the stovies and then stopped. "Are you not hungry?" he asked, mopping his own plate.

She looked a little green. "I don't seem to have an appetite."

He turned her plate slightly, as though this might help. "Just eat a few bites."

Mo-Maw lifted her fork again and ate without savouring the food. "Don't fuss, Mungo, if she doesnae want it, then she doesnae want it." She turned to Jodie. "Anyhow, now that you're a wummin, it'll no do ye any harm to skip a meal or two. You cannae eat like ye were a twelve-year-old boy. You know what they say about genetics?"

"Spell it," said Jodie quickly.

"Spell whut?"

"Genetics."

Mo-Maw snatched Jodie's plate from the table. She took the wasted stovies and poured them back into the pot.

The telephone began to chirp. Mo-Maw

gathered up her limp curls and caught them into a long banana clip. She never stood when she talked on the telephone. She treated every phone call as an opportunity to sit down, smoke her cigarettes, and converse at length. Wrong numbers were her favourite.

Mungo waited for their mother to leave the room. He laid his open hands on the table. "Sake! Why do you always have to start something?"

Jodie didn't answer him. She laid her head on top of Mungo's hand. The caramel silk of her hair was shiny and sweet-smelling. He could feel the beat of her pulse murmuring at her temple. She was burning up. They listened to Mo-Maw answer the telephone. She always recited the number back to the caller, an affectation that irritated Jodie. "Hello-o, Hamilton residence. *Five-five-four, six-one* —" The posh accent slid off of her lips. "Ah, for fuck sake! Oh, it's *you,* is it? What do ye want?"

The children listened as Mo-Maw fought with Jocky. It didn't take long. Her resolve had shallow roots. What started out as a frosty, stubborn blockade soon melted, and she was purring down the phone at him like a teenager. Jodie sat up straight and sighed once. Mungo helped scrape the old nail polish from her fingernails, and one by one, she repainted them in Mo-Maw's good polish. It was a powdery pink, the colour of a baby's earlobes.

Mo-Maw's face was flushed as she came back into the kitchenette. "It's not even been a whole weekend." She squeezed Jodie's hand, which surprised everybody. "Do ye think he loves me?"

Mungo knew his sister was going to ruin it for her, long before she actually did. Jodie allowed her mother a brief moment of reverie before she pulled her hand from her grip. "Surely you are not going to leave again?"

"How no? Am ah no meant to be happy?"

Jodie inclined her head towards Mungo. She said nothing more.

There was a brief moment where it seemed Mo-Maw didn't know where she was. Then she collected herself and cradled Mungo's head against her bosom. Mungo inhaled deeply, unsure of when he would be so near to her again. He felt her sink her weight on to her right hip as though she was grounding herself, then something shifted in her tone. All the earlier excitement was gone, her voice was flat, like someone had let all the air from a balloon.

"No, no. You're right, Jodie. I should stay here."

Jodie's eyes grew wide as china saucers. Mungo knew he should say something to move Mo-Maw back towards Jocky but he did not. He put his arms around his mother and said nothing.

Mo-Maw was talking back to a game show. She was counting the last of her loose change as Mungo pulled his cagoule over his head. He hovered around her, sleekitly checked that what she was drinking was only tap water. Then he told her he would be back in a few hours.

With the sudden reappearance of his mother it had been several days since he had last seen James. Mungo still felt terrible that he had mentioned Mo-Maw's return from Hades, with James's own mammy dead — real, non-refundable death.

James wasn't at his doocot, but a fresh spray of pigeon shit and sawdust said he had been there a little earlier. Mungo plodded back through the scheme. It was a dreich Sunday night, a perfect night for weekly baths and ironing work uniforms, and a lethargic malaise had fallen over the tenements. He knew the back of James's flat faced his own, but he didn't know the exact number. He tried to look casual as he dawdled along the empty street and checked each buzzer panelling for Jamieson. Mungo was about to give up when at the last close he found the name written in green ink on the top buzzer.

"Who is eht?" It wasn't James's voice.

"Hallo, is James there? Can he come out to play?" Mungo cringed. He was bad at this.

But the buzzer razzed and he was grateful to step into the dry close mouth. The close was lined to shoulder height in gold and brown diamond patterned tiles. Each landing had a floral stained-glass window that filled the stone stairwell with fractals of beautiful light. It was the same housing scheme as Mungo's, but he could tell the council agent who managed this close took more pride in its upkeep. The families who lived here were — by the slightest fraction — better off.

The Jamieson door was a broad set of double doors on the very top landing. James was leaning over the banister, barefooted, in a thick Aran gansey over a pair of nylon football shorts. He looked flat, tired, and stood with his arms crossed like a bored bouncer. He softened when he saw Mungo climb the stairs. Without a word in greeting,

Mungo followed him inside and sat down at the opposite end of the settee.

Horse racing highlights were on the television. James's father was packing a ripstop holdall and arguing with the list of winners. He didn't acknowledge Mungo as he came in. His horse had lost, and he was packing his bag without thought, like he had packed it too many times before. Mr Jamieson was tall like James, and broad too, useful-looking. His hair was the same flaxen hue but the sides shone with silver. He looked like a man who might enjoy a long swim in January; his face had a high, florid flush. Without taking his gaze from the television he pulled on his navy toque, and Mungo realized then that the hat that James usually wore was a tatty version of his father's.

When the man finally cast his eyes over his son, they were as grey as the North Sea. Then Mr Jamieson looked over Mungo. It was such a look of disdain that Mungo hid the scuff of his left trainer behind his right, although each was as worn as the other. He wondered what Mr Jamieson had heard about the Hamilton family.

James's father went out into the hallway. He ripped a wire from the wall and as he came back into the living room he was binding their cream telephone with its own cord.

He shoved it into his sports bag without looking at his son. "You know the rules. If you need tae call me, use Mrs Daly's phone." James nodded slowly. Mr Jamieson ran his eyes the entire length of Mungo again, and the boy felt an odd compulsion to open his hands and turn out his palms.

"Right." He zipped the sports bag closed. Reaching into a tight bundle of notes he peeled a stack of them away. He slapped the money on the table. "Three weeks, then. See if ye can no burn through it aw this time, okay? Try . . ." He started to say something, and then he cast his eyes over Mungo again and thought better of it. "Jist try your best to behave. Stick in at the school. Awright?"

He didn't hug James goodbye. He just nodded, as though they had passed each other on the street.

Mungo didn't speak until he heard the man go whistling down the close. "Wow. He's a laugh." But James was struck with a type of rictus. Mungo could barely recognize him without his usual carefree look. "You didn't tell me your da was home."

"He wasn't. He only came for the week-end."

"But I thought he got two weeks off?"

"Aye, he does. But he telt me he's met a

woman from Peterhead. He wanted to head north early and spend some time with her before going back to the rigs."

Mungo didn't know where Peterhead was. He said nothing.

"Apparently Caroline is a stewardess on the Auk rig." James paused. "Her and her daughter breed Yorkshire terriers. They have eleven of them. Big fuckin' whoop."

It seemed like James didn't want to talk anymore. He hammered the remote control, flicking between the same four channels so rapidly that Mungo had to hold his cheekbone and look away. He settled on some English comedy rerun. They sat in a heavy silence and watched as pensioners let a piano roll down a Yorkshire hillside.

The front room was the same shape as Mungo's although everything in it was plusher and of a much finer quality. There was a fitted carpet and a large wool rug. Someone had taken care to match the settee to the carpet and the carpet to the curtains. It had the luxurious feeling of having been purchased all at once, not laid away and added to, stick by stick. There were framed photos on the mantel: one of a family of four posing in a studio, and another of two children, James and a handsome older girl.

"I didn't know you had a sister."

He followed the line of Mungo's gaze. "Geraldine. She married a whisky distributor."

"Cool."

James snorted. "He's called Gerald. His name is *Gerry Berry*. Can you believe it? Pair of them are pure jokes, man. She thinks she's the dug's baws because she lives in a fancy house wi' satellite telly. But I know she's all fur coat and nae knickers. Mrs Gerry Berry likes to come on Tuesdays and Thursdays after work and bring me frozen dinners."

"Mibbe she wants to make sure you are eating right?"

"Really? I expect she feels guilty."

Mungo was thinking about Jodie. His next question seemed only natural. "Why don't you just go live with her?"

James turned and looked at him square in the eye. "Why doesn't she ask me to?" Then he turned his face back to the television. This was a different person, not the industrious, hearty, fresh-air-filled boy he knew from the doocot.

"C'mon, don't be like that." Mungo rammed his shoulder into his.

When he did this to Jodie, she would shove him back, and soon they would be tormenting each other until whatever had first ailed them would have dissolved for a while. Mungo rammed him again. James didn't move. Mungo felt foolish, pressed against his side. He was going to straighten himself when James shifted slightly. James raised his arm out from under the weight and draped it across Mungo's shoulders. It made Mungo flinch in anticipation of a blow, a flick, a chokehold. But as he waited for retaliation, it slowly dawned on him that no hurt was coming. Instead of rejecting him James had made more space for him.

Mungo slid into him and filled the cavity in James's side. There was a tide in James's chest, and Mungo bobbed on the swell of it. He was carried along by the slow rise and fall of his ribcage and comforted by the sigh at the edge of his breath. James's arm was heavy but Mungo liked the weight of it, he felt safe underneath it. The lanolin from James's Aran jumper tickled the back of his neck and he could smell the musk of his armpit, the sticky remains of soapy deodorant, the salt of rain-scrubbed skin. James's fingers danced in the air, they kept time with his distracted mind. Mungo closed his eyes and the fingers drummed a gentle beat on his chest.

Occasionally James would laugh at the

clumsy pensioners on the telly and the whole bulk of him shuddered. Mungo was muted. He couldn't focus on the programme, so he followed the patterns of James's laughter, always a half-beat behind. They sat like that for a long time. It all felt somehow wrong. Mungo worried that it would end.

"It's a lot of money, int it?" Mungo hadn't heard him at first, so James said it again. "That money, it's a fair whack."

Mr Jamieson had left what looked like two hundred pounds on the table. Mungo had been trying not to stare.

"He gets paid a fortune, that's the only reason he leaves. They pay overtime and danger money. He's got nowhere to spend it out in the middle of the sea."

"Is it to feed yourself with?"

"He never asks what I spend it on."

James lifted his arm and stood up. It was as though a thick blanket had been pulled away on a February morning.

In the veneered cabinet there were some crystal ornaments and several shelves of leather-bound books. They had a refined air to them, posh as any scholar's office. James took one down and opened it in front of Mungo. It wasn't a book at all, but a burgundy case for a videocassette. None of them were actual books.

Inside this fake book was a pile of crisp notes. "Two thousand and forty-nine pounds, give or take. I don't spend everything he gives me. I try to save most of it so I'll have enough to leave when I'm ready." He folded the new notes inside and tossed the book across the table as carelessly as an empty cigarette packet. He sat on the other side of Mungo now, further away, and curled his flat feet up underneath himself. He went back to staring at the television.

"How's Conan the Sectarian?"

James laughed, Mungo felt buoyed to see the happy-gappy teeth again. "Turns out his name was Caledonian Sun. He was famous. He wouldn't settle so I took him to a guy in Garthamlock. He gave us forty poun' for him, said Wee-Man Flannigan was gonnae stab me if ever he caught me."

"But you didn't steal the bird. Isn't that the whole point?"

"Aye, but some eejits take it awfy hard. You were there, I caught him fair and square. Flannigan can go fuck himself. *Whrooup, whrooooup.*"

"I'm sad you sold him."

James extended his foot and shunted Mungo. "You need to sell them. If ye don't the bird might try to make its way home and take your prize doo wi' it." He pulled his foot away. "You need to move them on. Confuse 'em. It's all part of the game."

Mungo's side felt hollow where he had been pressed against James. He had thought perhaps James had needed the contact, that perhaps he was lonely here all by himself, but perhaps it had been Mungo who had wanted the comfort.

"Are ye hungry?" asked James.

He wasn't — the stovies coiled in his belly as heavy as lead — but he followed James through to the kitchenette anyway. The cupboards were filled with colourful boxes. It was an Aladdin's cave of sugar, with every manner of prepackaged starch you could buy. Mo-Maw never went into those aisles at the shop, she stayed with the meats and vegetables and made it as far as the tinned soups. James looked at the hoard with a sigh of boredom.

On the wall above the small dining table was a collection of crucifixes. A collage of different palm leaves twisted into small crosses. The children's names were written on them in the same writing but different coloured pens. His mother must have collected them every Palm Sunday throughout the years.

"Fuck!"

"Whut?" James was eating two chocolate biscuits that he had sandwiched together.

"Nothin'."

The reason he could not quite place James was because they attended different schools; his was not just another unknown face, lost in the scrum of an overrun state school. James was a Catholic, and the Catholic was grinning as he poured two heaped bowls of sugar puffs and crumbled a chocolatey flake over the top. Mungo took his treat and tried not to look at the crucifixes. As milk dribbled down his chin, he resolved not to tell Hamish about the Fenian.

They spent the evening in the glow of the electric fire watching a Royal Command Performance on television. They lay on the blue rug and crammed an endless procession of buttery shortbread into their mouths. English comedians were notoriously unfunny. English comedians performing in front of the Queen were unfunny and slick with a strange kind of slithery smarminess. On top of this, the man now performing had gone all limp in the wrist and something about him made the boys uncomfortable. It was a loathsome sight, people were roaring at him, and the louder they laughed the more he swished and lisped.

"When you leave," asked Mungo, "where would you go?"

James turned away from the comedian. He lowered his cheek to the floor. "I told ye already. Anywhere but here. I want to live somewhere where people aren't always leaving. I don't mind being alone. It's the fact they keep fucking off, again and again." James looked at him. "Would you be awright if I left?"

He shrugged. "Do what you like."

James lay between Mungo and the television. He was searching Mungo's face in the flickering glow. "You are a bad liar, Mungo Hamilton." He tried to lay a thick finger on Mungo's cheekbone, right where the twitch had started.

Mungo slapped him away. "Why does every fucker want to touch my face?"

James propped himself up on one elbow.

Mungo was squinting, peering like he had an eye test. He started to laugh.

James looked behind himself at the bright television. He turned and looked at Mungo. "Who are you laughin' at?"

"I can see different colours through your big ears. They're pure glowing."

James flattened them against his head.

Mungo toed his hands away and the large ears sprung back to life. "You're like

Dumbo."

James lunged and caught Mungo's ankle sharply, twisting it. It cracked his knee and Mungo contorted to release the painful pressure of it. "Call me that again," he growled. "I fuckin' dare you."

"Dumb —"

But before he could finish James was on top of him. His knee was in Mungo's side and his left hand held his face against the floor. The thick carpet skinned his raw cheekbone. James twisted his arm behind his back. "I cannae hear ye? Speak up."

Most days, Hamish easily bested Mungo. Mungo learned quickly to offer no resistance because that would only prolong the beating. Roll into a ball. Tuck your elbows to your knees and cradle your face between your forearms. It stole the heat from Hamish. It was no fun to whale on a sack of lifeless meat.

"Submit," James commanded.

"Ah-yah! No way."

James wrenched his arm again. "Sub-mit."

"Awright."

He released him and Mungo scuttled away. He sat with his back to him, cradling his sore wrist. James had gone too far, he was no better than Hamish. The victor's smile slid from his lips. He reached out a hand to apologize. But as Mungo turned, he glowered at James from under his fringe and a grin broke over his face. "Dumbo. Dumbo. Dumh-boh. Ya big-eared basturt. Can you fly with them flappers?"

He could endure more than James could ever dole out. James would learn.

They roughhoused until the street lights flickered on. Mungo had stayed away as long as he could. He lifted his T-shirt and rubbed at his swollen belly, feeling sick on sugary shortbread. "I need to get back. Mo-Maw will be worried." It was the kind of thing Americans said on television. He liked the sound of it, though he knew she wouldn't be.

A tightness spread across James's face. He opened his mouth to say something but Mungo watched the words catch on his teeth as though he thought better of it. *"Whroup, whrooup, whrooooup."* He bobbed and cooed in reply.

"I'll come to the doocot after school the morra." Mungo tried to sound as casual as he could. He pretended he was looking in his cagoule pocket. "You go to the Catholic school, don't you?"

"Aye," said James. "I told you your Ha-Ha used to try and murder me."

Mungo looked up. He had misunderstood.

"I thought you meant that in a general way. You know, like a touch of casual murdering."

James sat up and pulled his knees to his chest. "Naw. Every day at four o'clock I had to bolt from him and the other Billies. For a speccy wee dwarf, your Ha-Ha can really fuckin' run."

"Aye, he's a man of wasted talents."

James was picking at his big toe. It seemed like he wanted to say something more, but several times he lowered his head and his hair fell over his eyes. When eventually he spoke, it was directed towards a tasselled table lamp. "Can I ask you a favour, Mungo? I don't mean anything funny by it. But would you stay, just a wee while longer? Maybe, if you like, stay here the night?" Mungo could see he was struggling. "I have a Christmas selection box, ye can have first pick."

"I can't. My maw." Mungo thumbed over his shoulder.

"Go on. Please."

Mungo exhaled. He knew what it was to feel this heavy.

The boys went one flight down and asked to use Mrs Daly's telephone. The woman seemed to have been expecting them and left them alone in her tidy hallway. The phone rang twice before Jodie answered. She sounded the same deflated way she often did after a long shift at the café. Mungo told her where he was, told her where he would stay, and said he would collect his uniform in the morning.

"Wait, do you *actually* have a pal?" She sounded both surprised and relieved.

"Is that awright?"

"Fine."

"Can I stay here then?"

"Aye. If I need you, I'll wave across the back middens. Look out for the smoke signals."

"Will you tell Mo-Maw for me?"

"I will," she said, then she rattled her lips together in an exasperated breath. "When I see her."

"What do you mean?"

Jodie was running a flat brush through her hair. He could hear the static crackle down the telephone line. "Mungo, did you actually think she was going to stick around this time?"

"Oh." Mrs Daly had so many cats that Mungo couldn't keep count.

"Never mind. She wrote a lovely note."

James's bedroom was a mess. The walls were thick with posters pinned layer upon layer. Clothes, clean and dirty, lay in heaps on the floor. In the corner of the room was a pile of old canary cages, modified to transport pigeons. Above these was a twitcher's map of Scotland, lochs and hillsides in glorious detail, each glen filled in with the type of bird an enthusiast could expect to find there. James had circled some far-flung places to disappear to.

The boys lay together, with James facing upwards and Mungo with his head at James's feet, head to toe in the single bed. They took great pains to not touch. If one moved his leg too close, the other shifted and hung off the side of the narrow mattress.

"What's your maw like?" asked James in the darkness.

It was hard to describe such a thing. You only got one mother, it didn't bear a comparison and she didn't come with a list of features like a new oven. "I dunno. She's just my maw." Mungo had never considered it before.

He could hear James picking an old sticker from his headboard. "Does she like to dance?"

"Aye."

"Does she like to sing?"

"More so when she's drunk." Mungo's

eyes were open in the darkness. The room looked strange and somehow familiar. He would have thought a Catholic's bedroom would have been bare, or perhaps with crucifixes everywhere, but there were none. He kept expecting to roll over and see Hamish eating cereal in his bed. "My sister says she's not a mother at all. She says we were just a mistake that happened to a stupid young lassie and that she has regretted it ever since. After my dad died Mo-Maw decided she was going to put herself first."

"That's not what mammies are supposed to do."

"That's another thing Jodie says." He didn't want to talk about them anymore. "What was yours like?"

"Oh, she was the business," James said very quickly. "Even when she was really sick, she pretended like she wasn't. Every day I came home from school she wouldn't let me out of her hug until I told her everything that had happened. If Geraldine got home after me she had to wait in line for her hug. It could take pure ages. My mammy called it the *juicin'*. She said if she didn't hold us tight, we would ignore her. She squeezed us as hard as she could to get all of the good stuff out of us. She wouldnae let go until ye telt her absolutely everything."

"That sounds nice."

"Aye. It was." James coughed like there was a clog in his throat. Mungo could tell he was breathing deeply to keep himself from crying.

Mungo didn't know what to do. He reached out a hand and felt the sharpness of James's shin bone. He made a fist and tapped along the bone, up and down, up and down, the way a doctor would probe a fracture. He waited for James to pull away. But he didn't, and Mungo folded first. He drew back his hand, laid it in the centre of his chest. "What was the best dinner she made?"

"She was a shitey cook." He sniffed. "But I miss that — not the food — but the feeling that she was here in the flat, looking after us. The flat never felt empty when she was in the kitchen. Ma da was on the rig when she died. She had told him she was fine, but she wasn't. They chartered a special helicopter for him and everything, but it still took him eight hours to get home after she was dead."

Eight hours. Mungo couldn't imagine a distance that far.

"I was sat here with her body. Just waiting

on him." James was swallowing harder now.

Mungo couldn't cross the distance between them. The best he could do was to lay his hand next to James's so that their little fingers were almost touching. They were close enough that it was as if they *were* touching. The heat from James's hand jumped the distance between them and flooded Mungo's entire body. He lay there, upside down and a world away, and listened to James choke up. He wanted to offer more comfort. The courage wouldn't come.

It was James that changed it. The pinkie that had lain next to his own crossed over and locked over his. The electrical current that had burned at the border jumped on to his skin and he was scorched.

Without questioning it, Mungo sat up in the bed and oriented himself to lie beside James. He pulled the boy on to his chest and felt the crumpled wetness of his face. He held him, just like Jodie would hold him, and let him remember his mother. It was good to put your weight on someone else, even if it was just for a short while.

EIGHT

Mungo stepped out of his school uniform and left it in piles across the living room floor. It was warm in the airing cupboard, it was peaceful, and he felt calmest here. He pushed his hand between a stack of towels and enjoyed the sensation that the cotton nubs left on his skin. He sank in all the way up to his armpit and it felt something like a hug. He'd been anxious all day, thinking about how James had been too embarrassed to talk to him after he had started crying about his mother.

Mungo had only wanted to help, but in the morning light, James couldn't look him in the eye. As the sun came up, James had gone to the doocot and left Mungo to have his Weetabix alone, feeling like he had done something dirty, something wrong.

Mungo came out of the airing cupboard and stood at the bay window. He dug his thumbnails into the soft wood and deepened the gouges he had been making over the past few months. He watched as a familiar man came along the street. Although the man kept his eyes downcast his spine was rigid and his crown was pulled proudly upwards to God. The man walked with nipped footsteps; he tucked his arms neatly by his side, careful to take up no more room than was his to enjoy. He never swung his legs in the way of most men broadcasting how they needed to make room for their cocks. There was a stiffness in his arms but there, at the tips of his fingers, was a slight feathering. You could barely see it. Everybody could see it.

Rarely did you see the man without bags of messages. Every day he went to the Co-op and bought just enough to last him to the next day. He stocked a bachelor's pantry: two sausages from the butcher's, small packets of teabags, and bags of frozen vegetables that could be kept fresher for longer if he resealed them with old elastic bands.

Some idling Protestant boys clocked the man. Tucked safely under the awning of the Pakistani shop they nudged one another and aped him as he walked along the street. If Charles "Chick" Calhoun knew they were mimicking him, he didn't acknowledge it. A rash-faced grease slick of a boy held his hand out in a vulgar way as though it had snapped at the wrist. He minced up and down in front of the neon star stickers that were advertising a great deal on yesterday's bread. The other boys sucked on their fags and cackled to themselves. "Cooieee!" he called out with a flutter of his fingers.

There were several housewives idling at their windows, drinking tea and waiting for their children to come home from school. Anyone who was watching poor Mr Calhoun sucked on their teeth in pity.

"Cooo-*fuckin'*-eeee, ah said." The ned was getting louder. "Yer no gonnae be rude and ignore us, ur ye?"

Mr Calhoun, as he was known to his face, and Poor-Wee-Chickie, as he was known behind his back, didn't break his stride. He didn't lift his eyes to his tormentors.

"Are ye looking at ma arse?" The ned tried an old tactic in order to provoke him. He turned to his friends. "Haw, did youse see that aul' feller look at ma arse?" They all agreed that they had. Like shell-suited apes they started pacing and gesticulating wildly at the solitary man. It was all they wanted, to bait him into responding, to insult him so profoundly he would let his guard drop. Then they could feign injury, batter him, and remind him of his low place, sub-human, sub-them. This one old man made them feel better. When everyone looked at them like they were nothing, like they had nothing, he still had less.

The man maintained his neat stride, the narrowest of smiles on his lips. Mungo had no way of knowing that Poor-Wee-Chickie was not in there; he was not present in his own body, having learned, long ago, the art of floating away above the tenements. It was his trick. As his body fought along the Parade, his spirit was flying over Duke Street, swooping and spiralling to the La Scala picture house where it sat in the dark, watching Anne Baxter, incandescent, in *All About Eve.*

Poor-Wee-Chickie lived on the ground floor left. It was a door the children all rushed past. A plain brown door like Mungo's own, that had a sad, degraded look from all the times it had been scrubbed clean of foul graffiti. Someone — a Proddy pal of Ha-Ha's — had found a half-dead can of spray paint in one of the middens. The wit had spray-painted *Child Mahlestur* in tall letters on Poor-Wee-Chickie's door. Jodie had tried her best to wash it away before Mr Calhoun saw it. She must have been scrubbing the paintwork raw because it was the sanding noise that finally brought him to the door. He found her there, her school uniform lousy with bleach and paint flakes.

"Ah, the poor beasts. They cannae spell for toffee. Personally, I prefer *kiddie fiddler* myself. It sounds somehow more genteel, more musical. Don't ye think?"

Jodie liked Poor-Wee-Chickie. She had endless patience for the lonely. But Mungo was wary of him; even though he knew better, he still believed the untrue things they said about the bachelor.

Mungo got dressed. He pulled on his cagoule. Perhaps the best idea would be to see James, and simply pretend none of the nonsense, none of the crying, had ever happened. As he went down the stairs, Poor-Wee-Chickie opened his door at the sound of his footsteps. "Ah, Mungo son. Thank God it's you. Can ye help me?" He was clutching Natalie in his arms, the fawn-coloured whippet he spent most of his disability allowance on. "I've had a wee spot of bother." He nodded out to the daylight and said no more. "Do you think you could let Natalie out for me? She must be bursting."

Mungo took the dog outside and walked her beside a line of parked cars. He tried to avoid the attention of the Proddy boys, now looking for their next target, but he could hear them moan, quietly enough that they could disavow it if he challenged them — he would never challenge them. *"Mongo, Mungo."*

The small whippet did not care for the smirr. She grimaced, did her business quickly, and dragged him back inside.

"Did she diddle?" asked Poor-Wee-Chickie.

"Aye, she diddled."

"Diddled and *doddled*?"

"Aye. Diddled and doddled."

He swept the dog up in his arms. "Guid girl. It's hard for a lady to doddle in front of a strange man."

"Really? You should see our Jodie. Sometimes she doesnae bother to shut the toilet door."

"Och, ye're a terror!" Poor-Wee-Chickie fluttered his hand like it was a fine hanky. "Can I bother ye for five more minutes? I jist need somebody to hold her still while I clip her wee claws. Every time I get near her wi' yon clippers, she bolts for the other side of the flat. Ma sister usually helps me, but she's taken up wi' a Pakistani widower, and she's never oot the hoose noo." He looked wistful for a moment. "Mind you. She does have lovely curtains."

236

Mungo must have nodded, because Poor-Wee-Chickie stepped to the side and let the boy into his flat. As he crossed the threshold Mungo tried not to stare at the ghostly words that still tainted the door.

The flat was smaller than the ones up-stairs, much of it was carved away for the stairwell and entrance foyer, so it felt like an old-fashioned room and kitchen instead of a proper family flat. Poor-Wee-Chickie was wearing a camel-coloured Lyle & Scott jumper. He had a strange habit of wearing all his clothes tucked inside his trousers, regardless of how thick the fabric was. Over the volume of his pleated trousers it gave him the old-fashioned look of having a well-defined waist. He always wore freshly pol-ished shoes, inside or out, and a thin belt with a shiny metal buckle. Poor-Wee-Chickie handed the forlorn whippet to Mungo. She folded into his arms easily, nothing but bones and ligaments, and he held her like she was a pile of jumbled kindling. She was the least cuddly dog Mungo had ever touched.

Mungo had never seen the man walk the whippet in daylight. Just last week, Mo-Maw had mentioned that she saw the pair of them wandering the scheme, alone on empty streets, both before and after her night shift. Mo-Maw didn't trust that about him, and said that he was "sneaking around like a grave robber." But Poor-Wee-Chickie preferred to go unnoticed. It was safer somehow, dipping in and out of shadows.

"This is a great help, son. I cannae be chasing her all around the place, no at my age." He took one of Natalie's paws in his hand and with a pair of loppers he clipped each nail in turn. "She's a daft bitch. Once a month for eight years we've been at this, and ye think she'd be used to it by now. Just goes to show ye . . ." He chuckled. "Even beasts never lose hope for a different outcome. I'm gonnae get her one of these days, and instead of cutting her nails, I'm gonnae paint them hoor's red. That'll show her." He kissed between her ears. "What would ye say to that, eh? Ya silly besom."

Mungo surveyed the room over the top of Poor-Wee-Chickie's head. The house was immaculate, everything economical and painfully arranged, not a speck of dust. Mo-Maw had said Mr Calhoun was a housewife, but a housewife only to himself.

"He's a bachelor," she'd said, as her children lined up at the kitchenette window and watched him peg out his sheets and socks on the washing line.

Jodie sniffed. "What harm is he doing?"

"Bet he wanks that much he needs to wash they sheets every day," offered Hamish with a sneer. "Rotten auld bachelor."

The only thing they had all agreed on was that Mungo should not linger outside the bachelor's door. If he had to play inside the close, he should play upstairs, between the Campbell and the Hamilton landings.

The nail clipping was swift. Mungo lowered Natalie to the floor. She ducked her head under her carriage and sniffed her own vagina. Poor-Wee-Chickie laughed. "It's a funny habit. She's checking ye've no stole it." Satisfied it was still there, the dog moped off to the settee and curled up in the corner. "Tek a wee glass of ginger, son. Just to say thanks."

Mungo started to refuse, but Poor-Wee-Chickie was already in the narrow scullery. The boy followed him through. There was a VHS player and a large colour telly next to the bread bin. He couldn't help himself. "Wow! Do you have two televisions?"

"Aye. I like to watch old episodes of *Sportscene* when I cook." He poured a tall glass of fizzy ginger. "Do you like the football?"

Mungo shook his head and looked at his trainers. It was a source of shame for him not to be good with a ball. He wanted to change the subject then, to pick at a different scab, one that was not his own. "So does Missus Calhoun do all the cooking?"

The man barely drew breath; he had a quicksilver mind. "Now, son, do ye mean my sister or my mother? Because I know ye don't mean my wife."

There was something about the way the smile slipped from his lips that told Mungo he had taken a step too far. Maybe he had wanted to see more clearly what they all squinted at from behind the net curtains. "Sorry, Mister Calhoun." Then he added, "It's jist I've lived above ye my whole life and I suppose I don't know ye."

"Don't ye?" He handed him the glass with a chuckle. "Well. At least yer the first to admit that. Usually people think they know everything about me."

There was a pigeon on the windowsill, a plain, unremarkable doo. Poor-Wee-Chickie went to the window to drop torn pieces of white bread through the slit for it. Mungo noticed then the smoothness of his face and the thickness of his fair hair. He wasn't as old as he pretended, older maybe than Mo-Maw but much, much younger than Mrs Campbell. It was an affectation, this old, shut-in pensioner. The man could still be out at his work, could still be of use. Somebody could love him.

"You awright, son?" He caught Mungo mid-thought.

"Aye. I was just thinking about pigeons." Then he doubled down on the lie. "I have a pal who has a doocot. He's interested in doo fleein'. I've been learning all about them."

"Is that right?" He dropped the last of the bread through the crack. "Ma father used to trap them right off the window ledge. Ma mammy used to make a gorgeous pigeon pie."

"That's minging. Don't tell my pal about that."

Poor-Wee-Chickie was laughing. "He'll no want my recipe, then? What's his name?"

Mungo wondered if it mattered. If the boy in the doocot was even his friend anymore or if he had done something wrong while trying to do something right. "James, James Jamieson."

"James, James Jamieson." The man repeated it under his breath and rapped his knuckle on the windowsill. "James. Old-fashioned and not very imaginative, but it's a good solid name. Jameses are very constant people. He sounds like a person you can trust."

"Do you think?"

241

"Aye. I like him already." Poor-Wee-Chickie pointed up to the top-floor tenement across the back middens. "He lives there, doesn't he? I used to ride the mornin' bus to work wi' his father. He was a miserable big bastard. Didnae have the time of day for anybody. Wouldnae smile at ye if you bought him a new set of teeth."

"He looked at me like I trekked dirt across his carpet. Did you used to work wi' him?"

"No. I was a slater for the council. He carried a union bag. Must've been some sorta shipbuilder. Mibbe a stager, or a caulkerburner." Poor-Wee-Chickie tapped his neat fingernails against the glass. The doo blinked. "I've seen that boy staring out his windae. He's there late at night. Sometimes he's there in the morning."

"I think he's looking for pouters."

Poor-Wee-Chickie nodded, but the jutting of his bottom lip said he thought differently.

"He's all right. He just keeps himself to himself." Mungo shook his head like he wanted to change the subject. "I dunno. He can be a laugh to hang out with up at the doocot. He never makes me feel bad." Poor-Wee-Chickie made a face that looked like he didn't quite grasp what Mungo meant. "See. You know how when somebody has something they love and they won't let you near it? Like, Hamish has an old Pink Floyd album he won't let me hold. It opens out into a great big picture and I only want to look at the drawings but he won't let me touch it. Or — *or* how Mrs Campbell does-nae like it when I touch the ornaments on her hall table. Well, James isn't like that. He loves his doos and spends all his time with them but as soon as I met him, he let me hold one. I think that was guid of him."

Poor-Wee-Chickie rapped his hand on the wooden sill again. "James-Guid-and-True." He thought for a moment. "What kind of roof is on that doocot?"

Mungo shrugged. "I dunno. Tarpaper?"

He ran a finger over his moustache. "No, no, no. That won't do. He'll be replacing that mair often than he should. What angle is it at?"

Mungo wasn't great with angles. He held his hands up in a triangular apex and shrugged. Poor-Wee-Chickie took his hands in his own and spent a great deal of time checking the exact pitch of the roof against Mungo's memory. He manipulated the boy's hands wider and lower until Mungo agreed about the fifteen-degree mark.

"No, no, no. That's no guid in the long run. Much too flat. A few hard frosts and the tarpaper will soak up as much as it repels." He was thoughtful for a moment and still holding the boy's hands in his own. The side of Mungo's face started stuttering and Poor-Wee-Chickie remembered himself suddenly. He let the boy go. "Sorry son. Old habits die hard. Roofs! I cannae help myself sometimes."

"It's okay," said Mungo, lowering his hands. "Thanks for the ginger, Mister Calhoun."

Poor-Wee-Chickie reached out like he wanted the boy to stay but then he thought better of it. "Will ye stop in again? I'll show ye a trick that Natalie can do for a bit of streaky bacon."

Mungo knew he would not, but he lied to be polite. "Aye."

"And tell James-Guid-and-True to nail some slate over that tarpaper. Everything that's built wrong gets ruined around here." He led Mungo out to the short hallway. The front door had five security locks and took an age to open.

NINE

Mungo had fallen asleep. When he woke upon the cold earth, the tent was alive with dappled light. Gallowgate was breathing unevenly; his breath was hot and yeasty. His arm was a dead weight pressing into the softness below Mungo's ribs. Their shirts had ridden up and Mungo could feel the sweat of Gallowgate's belly pooling in the cup of his lower back. The drink had paralysed the young man, but there were signs of a resurrection. Mungo could feel the swollen lump pressing against his buttocks and every so often it twitched and pulsed as Gallowgate filled with blood and strained against his Italian denim.

Mungo had been clenching his fists. They were bloodless, white, and as he unfurled them they tingled with relief. He counted. One Saturday sleep. One Sunday sleep. Then home.

In the hush of the morning, while the

245

shingles were still slick with mist, Gallowgate led Mungo down to the loch. He taught the boy how to prepare his line, threading the fish gut with weights and a buffer bead. He showed Mungo how to secure the barbed hook with a blunt knot and how to cast out into the darkest pools of water. For bait he produced some fetid lamprey chunks which had been sealed in a freezer bag. Gallowgate kept gulping to swallow the threat of his own bile.

Mungo took off his trainers and waded thigh-deep into the frigid loch. The cold made a castrato out of him; it made him want to sing. Except for the gentle lapping and the occasional swarm of midges, the loch was tranquil. Under the clear sky, the surface was shiny as a looking glass. Mungo wriggled his toes and could see them clearly beneath the water. Before him lay more emptiness than he had ever known.

The far side of the loch was walled in by the carpeted hillsides. Beyond these were jagged Munros, the denuded mountains stretching as far as Mungo could see. The sun illuminated the eastern face of the crags and left the other faces in deep shadow. These shadows held pockets of speckled snow that looked like flaking paint, like old coats of white emulsion that were peeling away from the moss-covered hills, as if it were the handiwork of a careless God. Each mountain appeared as though it had been chipped away from a larger piece of flint. Some of the ridges were so sharp they reminded Mungo of Hamish's homemade tomahawk.

A sharp wind blew across the loch and snapped the fabric of his cagoule in its hurry. The air was clearer than he had ever tasted, and when Gallowgate wasn't watching, he tilted his head back and put his tongue out into the breeze. It tasted green like spring grass, but there was a prehistoric brownness to it, as though it had searched an entire age through damp peaty glens and ancient forests, looking for its way to wherever it was going.

If he had known the words to describe it, he would have said he could smell the tang of the pine forests, the bright snap of bog myrtle, vetch, and gorse, and then underneath it all, the damp musk of dark fertile soil, the cleansing rain that never ceased. But to Mungo, it was green and it was brown and it was damp and it was clean. He had no words for it. It just smelled like magic.

Gallowgate was not moved by this magical wind. He spoiled it by hauching great gobs of phlegm into the water. They floated by Mungo like swirling nebulae. All morning the man had said very little, like he could not speak over the din of his hangover. He held his rod between his knees and lit his fifth cigarette. Mungo slid further out into the freezing loch. He wanted to keep the unsullied wonders for himself.

St Christopher was not moved by the majesty either. He spent the bright morning lying in the one-man tent, nursing his shakes. As the morning wore on, more drink left Gallowgate's blood and put him in a worsening state. The two men hadn't spoken since the previous night and by the way Gallowgate kept glancing at St Christopher's tent the boy could tell that he was in a foul mood and looking for a place to pollute with it.

Gallowgate lurched off into the long grass to take his morning shite. He took a meandering route past St Christopher's tent and kicked the guy ropes. The tent sank on to the sleeping man like a shroud. Mungo watched the thin nylon heave up and down, keeping time with the man's snoring.

The slow sun had shifted from the eastern side of the crags by the time St Christopher finally rose from the dead. In his wool suiting, he bent over at the loch's edge and lapped at the icy water like a beast. Sitting back on his haunches he blinked to himself for a long while. Gallowgate ignored him and busied himself with the campfire. He dropped two tins of beans into the flames and the three of them sat together and ate a measly breakfast. They had been an age trying to open the stubborn, scalding tins without a can opener, and when Gallowgate finally burst them on the edge of a rock, some of the beans had sprayed across the shingles. St Christopher used his yellow fingers to save the beans and scoop them into his mouth. Every so often he would eat a small stone by accident, and the grinding of the broken teeth would stop, and he would cough and spit the tiny pebble across the campsite.

Mungo sat apart as some thick clouds rolled in. The clouds had been locked out by the tall Munros, but now that they found their opening, they rushed into the peaceful glen. They gathered and thickened and pressed downwards, like smoke filling a room.

It was a strange thing to see; the wonder of the changing light and how it gave colour to the land. The morning sunshine had burned the hills with brackens and lichens and coppers. Now, the fleecy clouds fell like

249

heavy curtains, and they dampened it all to a lifeless grey and brown. It was as if the earth had no hues of its own.

As all the greens faded to grey he thought of James, and the way the light left his eyes without warning. He wanted to see those greens and golds. Then he pushed the thought away — he would never see them again.

The men were scratching through empty bags and rattling the crushed beer cans looking for a mouthful to kill their shakes. For the first time Mungo could study Gallowgate in the crisp daylight. He wasn't much older than Hamish. His flashy denims hung off his frame; his only remaining fat sat in paunchy bags beneath his eye sockets. He was hunched over, inspecting the last of their supplies, and laying them out on the rocks. There was a fair share of drink left: a noose of cans, a bottle of whisky, and a quarter of something clear. For food there were two chocolate bars; the kind with the painted frog on the side, the too-milky ones you gave teething toddlers. Mungo wondered if that had been his share. If that is what they'd brought to make this boy they didn't know fond of them.

Soothed by the fresh beer in his gut, St Christopher came down to the water. His shakes were softer now. He had brought some sprats from the city, a handful of half-rotted fish that he had wrapped in toilet paper for transport and carried in his breast pocket. It helped explain the unpleasant smell that emanated from him. Mungo tried not to inhale as the man showed him how to sink the hook into the fish's gullet. St Christopher cast out into the peaceful loch and put the remaining fish back into his suit pocket.

"Absolutely nuthin' better, is there? Just us boys and some good fishing, eh?" At least he was in better fettle than the sullen Gallowgate. "Cannae believe ye've never been at the fishin' afore. Shame that. Nobody tells wee boys how to fend for themselves anymair. Ah met a fella the other week who didn't even know how to fix a puncture on his bike. He just took the thing, flung it in the canal."

"Why?"

St Christopher shook his waddle. "Ah dunno. But ah waited till he was gone, waded in, and got twenty-five poun' for it at the pawnshop."

"I can fix a bike. I'm not great at school, but I can fix things. And I know about pigeons."

"Don't worry about school. Any man that

251

can use his hands will never want for work. Glasgow is the home of the working man."

Mungo thought about what Hamish had told him about the shipbuilders; the hundreds of men being put out of work every month. St Christopher was lost in another time. Mungo skimmed a stone across the water's surface. "What is this loch called, anyway?" He tried to sound casual, but he still didn't know where he was.

"Ah'm no tellin' ye," said St Christopher. "If I tell ye, all the schemie wee bams wid be up here, ruining paradise with their souped-up Escorts and BMX bikes. Aye, yer maw telt us aboot yer brother." He chewed on a thought for a moment. "How come yer brother couldnae teach ye how tae fish?"

"It's too quiet for him."

"And ye've no got a faither who could teach ye?"

"He's dead."

"Ach, ah'm sorry. A young gent like you. Ye must miss him."

Mungo couldn't say just how much he missed him. It was too big a feeling to put into words. "I was only wee."

St Christopher gave a pitying sigh. "Funny. Yer mother had the look of a divorcée to me. Angry wee wummin. She looks like she's been cheated out of something."

Mungo didn't know what to say to that. He was glad when St Christopher kept talking to fill in the silence. "Ah think ma own mammy was overjoyed when ma faither died. He wisnae a bad soul, he jist liked the ponies too much. At first ah thought ma mammy wid marry again. She was young enough, never much of a looker though." He turned to the boy. "Is that an awfy bad thing to admit about yer mammy?"

Mungo shrugged.

"No? Well it's true. She wisnae anybody's idea of a thrill, but she was companionable enough. A very well-read wummin." St Christopher turned back to the loch, he reeled the slack from his line. "Did your mammy ever marry again?"

Mungo shook his head. "She's been trying. How about yours?"

"Och, naw. This was years ago now. Right after ma faither died aul' Jeanette sold the family hoose and bought a one-bedroom flat in Govan. She gave us all a wee bit of cash, said she wanted to see us enjoy it aw while she could. In other words, 'here take this and get the fuck away frae me.' " He laughed. "She never remarried, ah don't think she let a fella inside her ever again.

But in the end she got what she always wanted."

"And what was that?"

St Christopher chuckled like it was obvious. "Peace from men."

Mungo skimmed the last of his stones out over the loch.

St Christopher drew his fishing line from the water. The sprat was gone; all that was left was a milky sac of tiny organs, faint lines of the red liver and heart that marbled the cloudy mucus. The hook must have been painfully deep to rip the insides from the twice-destroyed fish. "Basturt! He's away wi' ma lure. You were meant to be watchin' that. Ah bet it was a fuckin' pike. How did I no feel it pullin' on the line?" He posed the question more to the loch gods than to Mungo.

Mungo wondered if there was much the man could feel anymore. The blunted and cauterized veins on his face, across his hands, and down his forearms all looked like they were pushing to the surface in hopes of feeling something, anything. Even his jaundiced eyeballs were encroached with tiny blood vessels that put Mungo in mind of Garibaldi's vanilla ice cream; creamy yellow boules shot through with raspberry-red sauce.

St Christopher scraped the fishy organs off the hook and flung them into the water. He spat over his shoulder to Mungo, "It's aw yer fault. Gettin' me gassin' on about ma mammy lit that. Away wi' ye. Ye're bad luck." Then he added, mostly to himself, "I'm better at it than this."

Mungo didn't reply. It was hard to know if St Christopher was a ruin of a man, or if there had never been much to ruin in the first place. Teaching the boy the ancient skill of fishing had been the only contribution he had made to the trip so far. This water was hoaching with fish, all of Scotland was. But now the ripped-out guts of a supermarket sprat confirmed him to be a failure even at this.

St Christopher was rolling the sleeves of his blazer up. His forearms were so thin that he could turn the woollen fabric several times over, till it almost reached his elbow. Skewering another sprat on the line he cast it into the water. Instantly the float bobbed once, and the sprat was gone. "Cunnin' fishy basturts!"

The man was soaked to the knees. He took off his suit trousers and waded waist-deep into the loch. His underpants hung loose, like a loincloth made from an old sheet. With arms outstretched he stood as

255

still as a dead tree and when a fish came near, he made a pantomime of trying to scoop it out with his bare hands. He fell in, sinking under the surface. He flailed up again, sputtering and cursing, clutching his loose drawers to stop them sliding down his legs. Mungo laid down his rod and excused himself to the bathroom. He had to keep his back to the saint to hide his laughter.

St Christopher paid no mind as the boy wandered along the shore of the long loch. There was a copse of stunted trees that came down to the water's edge. Mungo weaved in and out of them, feeling the bog suck at his shoes and the mud migrate upwards on to his bare legs. He went deeper into the forest. It was quiet at the loch, but it was even quieter here without the gentle lapping of the water. He idled over mossy boulders and climbed carefully along fallen tree trunks, enjoying how the sun dappled the ground through the thin canopy. He hid himself but nothing stirred. Mungo wondered about the last person to see all this forgotten dell. It struck him then that he was totally alone.

He came to a gurgling river, a freshwater tributary that fed into the vast loch. The water frothed at the edges for the richness of the minerals in it. It swirled around boulders, and here and there it was thick with schools of brown fish, darting and happy and unbothered. Mungo waded through the waist-deep current; it was colder than the loch, coming fresh off the thawing peaks. He lost his footing on the mossy riverbed and the icy water knocked the breath from him. He jumped and squealed, suddenly very alert, clambering on to the next boulder. He crossed the river and the fat brown fish watched him go.

The trees thinned and he was back at the exposed lochside, far from the men. Mungo walked the shoreline, only stopping to fill his pocket with flat stones for skimming. As he turned a bend the ruins of an old castle stood before him. It rose from the same grey and dun-coloured stones of the hills around it, pushing up from the granite like a great rift in the earth. It must have once been a proud place, sprawling over several small hills down to a peninsula on the lochside. There still stood the three tall walls of a great hall, and another surviving wall had the vague shape of a tower, four or five stories tall, with the narrow slits of arrow embrasures.

Mungo clambered over one of the collapsed walls and stood in the gutted hall.

Part of the tall tower lay in the heart of the castle, where it had come crashing through its own roof. What remained felt thick as a fortress. Besides trespassing at Culzean with Hamish, he had never seen a castle before, much less been inside one. Mo-Maw had always kept him from school on the days the class would go to Stirling or Edinburgh. "Ah don't work aw the hours God sends so ye can be fingerin' some tapestries." There was always something more urgent to spend the four pound fifty on.

Fifteen years he had lived and breathed in Scotland, and he had never seen a glen, a loch, a forest, or a ruined castle. Actually, he had seen them, but only ever on biscuit tins or the side of tourist buses. Mungo lay down on one of the large hearthstones and let his head spin. It was hard not to feel a little drunk. "Halloooo." His voice echoed off the roofless chamber. *"Whroup, whrooup, whrooooup,"* he called to the sky.

He wondered how it would feel to go home, now that he had seen more of the world in a single day than in fifteen years — how could he stay on the scheme and not try to go beyond it? James had been right. Mungo wished that James was here with him, or Jodie, but mostly James. It would be grand to have someone to share all this newness with, someone who knew that he wasn't making it all up. Mungo picked at the ochre lichen and felt frustrated that he wouldn't have the words to paint it all again for Jodie or Hamish or Mo-Maw. Even if he could describe it, he knew that they wouldn't care anyway; they would make him get up off the clothes that still needed ironing or ask him to hold the box of car radios they had stolen. They would look at him with a bored chew and wonder when his stories of this golden-green place would be over.

But maybe James wouldn't. James would have listened to him tell his stories, and when Mungo showed him the photo of the ram's skeleton, James would ask if there had been a rancid smell (there had not), he would ask if there'd been any wool sticking to the underside of the carcass (there had been, it was cream-coloured and curly). He wished James was here. James would have cared.

Mungo tapped the back of his head against the hearthstone.

He shot to his feet. It started as a nervous canter. He needed to move, needed to shake the guilty thoughts of the Fenian out of his head. Standing by the rotted mantel he clapped the heels of his shoes together. He bowed to the empty hall and with a heel-toe-heel-toe, he galloped the first round of Strip the Willow. The school had taught the dance during a particularly nasty winter. They had grudgingly cancelled any periods of outdoor sports and the council estate boys — who had natural finesse when they were cracking hockey sticks across one another's skulls — were made to dance around the cold gymnasium in reluctant pairs. Mungo twirled with the memory of it. He had always liked the ceilidh lessons; he was just never allowed to admit it. He cantered around the ruined hall, spinning an imaginary Jodie at the end of his outstretched arms.

"You are guid at that," said a disembodied voice.

Mungo stopped his spinning. Gallowgate scrambled over the fallen wall, a cigarette clenched between his teeth, too sure of himself to take his hands out of his pockets. "Ah forgot this shitehole was here." His jaw was looser than it had been that morning. He produced a fresh can of lager and drank it in four gulping mouthfuls. "If ye dinnae want to starve to death we need to go find a shop." He crumpled the can in his fist and tossed it into the shadows of the crumbled hall. "*Or,* we could roast that auld idiot afore he frightens aw' the fish away."

Mungo had been hoping that they would never catch any fish. He hoped that the men would go to bed early, hungry and bloated on whisky.

Gallowgate clambered out of the castle. Mungo stalled, pretending to tie his shoelace, then he darted into the shadows and found the discarded Tennent's can. He hid it inside his cagoule and climbed up and out. Gallowgate was already swaggering back in the direction they had come. Mungo stood a moment and considered his castle. He wound on his disposable camera and took the time to frame a photo that no one would care to see.

He didn't have a watch, but it felt as though they had been walking for hours. They had tramped along the lochside, past the camp, and then kept on going. They walked far apart from each other and neither of them spoke. Mungo was dawdling at the back. He was picking the heads off wildflowers and filling his chest pocket for Jodie. As he plucked the flowers he made up their names: cowsbreath, ladies' bumholes, blue-granda-willies.

The village was no longer a village. It was a spattering of fieldstone houses, leftovers from another time. The three or four other houses they passed seemed like they had stood empty for a long time. Mungo peered in all the windows.

The house closest to the road was a single-room shop that doubled as a part-time post office but was chiefly the private home of an unfriendly-looking woman. Everything in the shop was coated with a fine layer of dust. Under the glassy eye of the well-weathered shopkeeper, Gallowgate bought some tobacco, her entire stock of pot noodles, and as many cans of lager as he could afford. The woman never once smiled at them. She spoke with a sing-song lilt the likes of which Mungo had never heard before. It was a beautiful voice and Mungo would have liked to hear her talk more, but she had taken an immediate dislike to Gallowgate and was in a great hurry to get them out of her shop so she might return to doing absolutely nothing. There was something about the thinness of the fabrics they were wearing that she disliked. It pegged them as outsiders. She made a disapproving face when she saw Mungo's gym shorts, his blue legs in his scuffed trainers. She narrowed her eyes when she first heard the flat, dull thud of Gallowgate's accent. *Glaswegians.* All she said was "You better tek all yer rubbish awa' wi' ye when ye leave. We dinna need city fowks treatin' yon loch lit it was one big rubbish bin."

When the teuchter woman wasn't looking Gallowgate gave her the middle finger and shoved a bar of chocolate up his sleeve. On the way back to the campsite he slipped the warm chocolate to Mungo. "Will that put a smile on yer face?"

They were leaving the cluster of cottages when they came across a red phone box. It was tucked under a clutch of yew trees and heavily overgrown. Mungo stopped abruptly. "Can I phone my maw?"

"Ah've no got any coins, wee man." He knew that Gallowgate lied. Mungo had seen the teuchter woman hand him his change.

Mungo's eye fluttered like it might spasm. He tried to focus his disappointment on searching his own pockets. He felt around in his cagoule and produced two silver coins. "S'awright. I've got some."

It was strange to be in a telephone box that did not stink of rotting piss. For comfort, someone had lined the floor in patterned carpet and put an old kitchen chair under the receiver. On the shelf that held the phone book was an air freshener and a real living potted plant. Mungo pressed the soil and felt the dirt spring back from being freshly watered.

He pumped in his coins. His fingers hovered over the dial long enough that the line went dead and the coins were belched back at him. If only he could call James; he was the only person Mungo wanted to talk to. He was unsure of the number, and besides, Mr Jamieson was sure to have confiscated the cream telephone in his rig bag. It was stupid. What would make him think James would want to talk to him now?

Instead he dialled his home number, then without waiting he hung up. The coins rolled free, he pumped them in and dialled again. Mo-Maw answered on the very first ring. Mungo was surprised to find her there, and not with Jocky and her new family.

"Hallo?" She sounded on edge already. *"Five-five-four . . . eh . . . six-one, eh . . . two-two."*

"Mo-Maw. It's me."

"Mungo. Mungo ma darlin', is that really you? Are you awright? Where are ye?" The questions were tumbling out of her too quickly.

"Aye, it's me. I'm fine." Mungo started to answer the last question and then realized he didn't quite know the answer. "I don't know where I am exactly. It's green, there's a deep loch and an old castle. It was nighttime when we got here so I didn't see any signs."

"Are they looking after ye?"

"Sort of."

She exhaled for what sounded like the first time. "That's good."

Gallowgate rolled his hand like Mungo should hurry up.

"I learnt how to start a fire. I learnt how to put bait on a hook."

"See!" Mo-Maw sounded like she was relieved. "That's what ah telt our Jodie. That's what ah wanted you to do this for. Masculine pursuits. It'll make a man out of ye."

Mungo turned his back to the window. He picked at the spider plant and whispered into the handset. "I want to come home now."

"Okay. Then come home."

He hadn't expected her to be so easily convinced. It unnerved him. It had all been her idea but now she was willing to fold it, throw the whole experiment in the bin. "I can't. It took ages to get here. They won't want to leave till Monday."

"Then ye jist have to tell me where ye are."

The telephone let out three little pips. The money was running out. He felt his tic spasm. "I don't know where I am."

"*Oh son.* Ah'm sorry Mun—"

The line went dead. He cradled it against his chin for a while, pretending she was still there while trying to calm the mutiny in his face. He stood like that until Gallowgate rapped his ring on the glass. "Jesus Christ. It'll be pitch-black afore we get back. The midges will eat us alive."

His legs were covered in raised bites by the time they got back to the fireside. Relieved to have procured more drink, Gallowgate was in a chatty mood, and he talked all the way back to the campsite. He said he would show Mungo how to gut a fish, if St Christopher had caught any, and then he would show him how to set a trap for rabbits. On Sunday night they would cook a big rabbit stew. Rabbit meat and instant noodles. Gallowgate promised it would be the finest thing he had ever tasted.

Mungo watched the man closely; he tried to smile in all the right places. It was the fourth different face Gallowgate had shown him, and he wanted to keep all of them straight. There had been the sullen man on the bus, the letch with the dirty stories at the campfire, the wounded fisherman by the loch, and now this person, his excited best friend, his false big brother.

He was always slow to realize when Hamish was manipulating him. It often dawned when Jodie would yell at Hamish to stop it, to stop using Mungo as his slave, stop saying nice things just so Mungo would do as Hamish wanted. This usually came right after Hamish had been incredibly, inexplicably kind to him. Mungo had started to become suspicious of the kindness of others, but James had changed that. Now he watched Gallowgate walk in a swaggering backwards fashion through the thick ferns. He was talking excitedly about building snares and box traps. "Ah'm gonnae show you everything ah know," said the man. "How lucky are you?"

St Christopher was drying his suit by the smoky fire when they finally reached the campsite. His underwear hung off of him and the knuckles of his spine pushed against his thin skin like snow peas in a pod. Mungo looked at the sharpness in his bones and felt sorry for the man. He looked like one of the weans he saw on the African telethons, except they had bloated stomachs and St Christopher's hollowed inwards under his ribs and almost reached his backbone.

He was happy to see them return. Drying on a rock were seven small fish, lined up

267

neatly, their iridescence already dulled and flaky. St Christopher circled them like a proud house cat. "It's no much," he was saying while taking each fish into his paw and stroking it gently. "But the morra we'll put them on the hooks and catch a perch or brown trout."

"Aye." Gallowgate rattled the plastic bags. "That might jist work."

St Christopher cracked open the last bottle of whisky in celebration. He took two long slugs and passed it to Gallowgate, who did the same. They held it out to Mungo and the boy put the bottle to his lips but held his tongue over the hole as a stopper.

Gallowgate clouted him. "Don't be a fanny. Get it in ye." He cradled the back of Mungo's head and tipped the bottle up to his lips. An angry, scorching wave poured down his gullet. It burned the air from his lungs. Gallowgate waited for the boy to stop choking before he tipped the bottle again. "Mair! Mair! Mair!"

Mungo was soon drunk.

He spent the evening pulling long branches from the forest and dropping them on the fire. One of the branches split like it had arms and he held it close like it was a fine lady. He turned and danced with it in the firelight. He was stumbling across the pebble shore and the men were watching him and cheering him on. They filled the empty bean cans with loch water and placed them amongst the flames to boil. Over and over they refilled the cans and poured it over the sweet and sour Chinese noodles. When they were done, each man had eaten at least two pots of the salty worms. They lay around feeling fat and content, their bellies lined with starch and full of firewater.

Mungo stared at nothing. His eyelids were growing heavy and he could feel his heart beating behind his eyeballs. Big gobbets of rain started falling and hissing on the campfire. The gobbets turned to a downpour and soon the men were scampering, saving the pathetic fish, the tweed suit, and what was left of the carry-out. They ran for cover and Mungo lost them in the sheets of sudden rain. The men crammed into the two-man tent by the bothy and he, alone, crawled into the half-collapsed shell by the waterline.

Gallowgate had given the boy a warm lager, and he was glad for the smoothness of its taste, how it was flat and soothing where the whisky had burned. He lay down and felt a rare peace. The ground was moving underneath the red tent. Streams of water coursed around his body, flowing towards the loch. He could feel the cold of the running water, yet he was not wet. He drank his lager. He closed his eyes. Drunk for the very first time, and carried away by the rain.

TEN

They had their ears to the carpet, their buttocks to the sky, and it looked like they were praying. The children knelt in the middle of the living room and listened as he swung his fist into her softness. He was hurting her. Each time he hit her, the woman cried out in pain. It was a tremulous squeak that ended in a chewed full stop, like she wanted to swallow the shameful cry as soon as it escaped her. Even as he was battering her, she worried about his good name.

"He's gonnae kill her," said Jodie. "Do something, Mungo!"

"Lit what?" He wanted to put his fingers in his ears.

"I don't know." The pages of her geography homework were creased in her fist. She was pacing and there was a panic in her eyes. "If Hamish was here, he would know."

Rangers had lost the Old Firm game. It had started as a fine spring day. All along the road the tenement windows were open and televisions and wirelesses were blaring the game out into the street. Big Ogilvy and his twins stood at their bay window in their regimental blues, *thoom thoom thoom.* They filled the street with Orange pride. But Celtic scored early and the street fell into a tense hush, even Ogilvy's twins stopped their peeping. Collins's goal in the first half was followed by another from Payton, putting Celtic firmly in the lead. Rangers brought on their golden boy, McCoist, but they struggled to get back into the game. When Hateley eventually pulled a goal back at the eighty-four-minute mark, the street erupted in desperate cheering. In the end it was not the fact that Celtic won — for they had no chance of winning the league — it was the fact that they ended a historic run of forty-five games unbeaten for the champs. All the Catholics would be celebrating in Baird's Bar. Mr Campbell had taken it heavy bad.

"We have to do something," repeated Jodie.

"What?"

"I don't know. God's sake. Can you just be a bloody man, for once?"

But Jodie Hamilton was her own man. She was out the door and down the close stairs as Mr Campbell was dragging his wife across the hallway carpet. Jodie hammered on their door like a Provvie debt collector. Mungo appeared, not quite at her side, but slightly behind her. He rocked on his heels, and it took effort for him to step in front of his sister. As the door opened Jodie realized Mungo had their mop and pail in his hand.

It was rare to see Mr Campbell standing these days. But when he opened the door he filled the frame from to doorstep to lintel. "Whit in bloody hell do youse two want?"

Jodie had the peculiar courage of a girl who never expected to be hit by a man — which was strange, because all three siblings had seen their mother suffer at the hands of her boyfriends. There was no man that Jodie would not answer back, and although Mungo admired that about his sister, he thought she put too much faith in the decency of men. This belief, this bravery, gave her a gallus tongue. When they were little, Jodie opened her smart mouth amongst gangs of neds and wrote cheques that Hamish would have to cash later. More than once, Mungo had been chinned by some boy he had never met, and then told to pass it along to his mouthy sister.

Mungo spoke before Jodie could say

anything. "Hallo, Mister Campbell," he said, as cheerfully as he could manage. "It's my turn to wash the close and I havnae any soap flakes. Do you think I could ask Missus Campbell for a lend of some?"

There was a deep lilac flush to the man's face. He had been sweating and moving more than he had in years and his fat-clogged arteries were struggling to let the blood around his mass. The thin hair of his comb-over hung loose. "Annie is unable to come to the door the now. She's no well. She's in her bed."

Mungo tried to look crestfallen, but adrenaline coursed through his veins. "Is she awright?"

"Whit's it to you?"

"If she can't come to the door can I come in? I know guid and well where she keeps her soapflakes. I'll be quiet."

The man didn't know what to make of the boy with the mop. But the way his face curdled in disgust told Mungo he had heard enough. "Naw, ye cannae. Gie that pail to your sister and fuck off."

Something was moving lower in the close. On the half-landing below them, a small face was peeking around the banister and watching the children at the Campbells' door. Nobody paid it any mind. Mr Campbell put his arm against the door, making to close it on them.

"Excuse me, but is everything all right?" Jodie had seen the chance slipping away and she would be more direct than Mungo. "I heard a terrible banging earlier. All ma mammy's Jubilee plates shoogled in the cabinet."

"Annie's had a wee fall," said Mr Campbell. "Ah've telt her no to dust standing on a kitchen chair." Then he smiled. "But she'll learn." He pushed against the door before Jodie could say anything more. It was almost snibbed when a voice rang out from the stairwell.

"Graham!" The voice had a clarity to it that gave it an authority. "What's all this racket?"

Poor-Wee-Chickie was slowly climbing the stairs to the Campbells' landing. He was half the height and half the width of Graham Campbell. He ran his finger around the belt of his trousers, tucking his thick jumper into the waistband. "Ye've had yer bevvy. Ye've had yer fun. It's yer bed yer needing now."

"Who the fu—"

"Don't come the wide-o wi' me." The bachelor cut him short. "Ye don't frighten me, Graham. I was raised by a wife beater."

"S'at so?"

"Aye. I have pent-up aggression. Dr Doak telt me so. Ye want to help me feel better?"

Graham Campbell had spent his life bending steel; the bones of Charles Calhoun would shatter like cold slate. Mr Campbell was swelling with rage, the lilac burned violet now and his fists knotted into ham hocks. He took a step towards the small man. "Ya cheeky wee poofter." There would be hometown glory in destroying this deviant. There would be halves of whisky and pints of warm lager at every bar north of Duke Street.

"Oh, sticks and stones," said Poor-Wee-Chickie, but he didn't step back. "Is this a cry for help? Ah've heard about those. Mibbe what you need is for me to come in there and hold you for a while." Poor-Wee-Chickie placed a hand on his hip, his tongue darted across his bottom lip. "Eh? Is that what you need? Do you need wee Chickie to put you to bed?"

It was kind. It was brave. It was undeservedly generous. It would destroy whatever was left of Charles Calhoun's good name. The halves of whisky and the cheap warm lager would still be waiting for Mr Campbell. He could still be a hero. *Ah was gonnae batter the little shit-stabber, but ye should've heard what he said tae me next. Gen up. Ah had tae get away frae him afore he tried tae stick a haun up my arsehole. Ah'm no a Sooty puppet. Dirty fuckin' reprobate.*

The Proddy neds would hear all about it. They would feast on Chickie's bones. *Haw! Haw! Mister Calhoun. Dae ye want to put me to bed an aw?*

There was a sharp intake of breath, as if someone had forgotten to breathe for a long time. Mrs Campbell appeared in the shadows of her hallway, as though she had been behind the front door the whole time. "Stop your nonsense, Chick. Ah'm fine. Ah've had a wee fall."

There was a blue bruise on her pale face that spread from her chin to her eye socket. The skin below her orbit must have split, for her hanky was spotted with blood. Her left arm hung limp by her side, and by the way her hand was crooked in the pocket of her pinny, it seemed as though he had broken her wing.

They were all silent for a long while. Mungo could hear the whispers, the shuffling feet behind all the peepholes up and down the close.

Jodie was the first to break the silence. "Oh, Missus Campbell. I'm nothing but a daft wee lassie, I've burnt the dinner again.

277

Haaah-ha." It was a lie, but no one had the heart to unpick it. There were tears on Jodie's face for Mrs Campbell, but it was easy to pretend she was worried about a burnt steak and kidney pie. "I need your help to fix it afore I get the belt." Jodie reached into the dark hallway. There was something about her small hand crossing the threshold that was bold and foolish at the same time. Mungo watched it slide past Mr Campbell and towards the woman. He held his breath lest Mr Campbell should take affront and snap it easy as a sapling branch. It felt like an eternity before Mrs Campbell stepped towards the outstretched hand, and when she did, Jodie choked with relief. "Oh, you're a lifesaver. I don't know what I would do without you."

"Right, hen." Sounding a little dazed, Mrs Campbell stepped into Jodie's arms and allowed herself to be guided upstairs, moving hesitantly as though she had forgotten the way. Mr Campbell was blocking all the light in the doorway. Mrs Campbell turned to him, with the hanky still pressed to her cheek, and said quietly, "Ye've had enough to drink, Graham. Away to yer bed, darlin'. Ah'll put yer dinner on when ah come back down the stair."

Poor-Wee-Chickie looked like he wanted

to say something more but thought better of it. He rapped his knuckle on the banister, and the knocking let them know that this was over, that they would not speak about this hurt, not today, not ever. The man turned and shuffled quietly downstairs. With Poor-Wee-Chickie gone, Mr Campbell retreated into the flat like some belligerent cuckoo.

Mungo followed the women upstairs. Jodie had her arm around Mrs Campbell. The woman seemed so small that Mungo could imagine his sister lifting her and carrying her the rest of the way. But Jodie did not rush her and they took it step by step, solemn as a funeral procession. Mungo watched Mrs Campbell's heels rise and fall inside her fleece moccasins. Her ankles were chalky blue from poor circulation, and he resolved that he would find her some thick sports socks when they got safely upstairs.

When they reached the half-landing, the light from the stained-glass window illuminated the bruise on her face with a sickly vividness. Mrs Campbell said, "He was always a wonderful dancer. Ye widnae know it to look at the size of him." She said it so quietly that it seemed like she was talking to herself.

Jodie exhaled sharply through her nose.

"Well, I think it's a bloody disgrace the way men get worked up over the football. What a bunch of sore losers."

Mrs Campbell twisted free of Jodie's grip. She climbed a few steps and then she turned. She looked confused. "No. That's no it at all."

"It is. The football is just an excuse for the men to drink and fight and get all their anger out —"

"Ye're too wee to know anything about men and their anger." Mrs Campbell took her damaged arm from her pinny pocket, she stroked it, cradled it as though it were a poorly lamb. "Every day for twenty-seven year that man went to the shipyards. Girders as big as corporation buses flying around on chains, a ton weight of steel dangling above his heid, and at any minute it could've dropped and kil't him, and left me wi' nothin' but three weans and a divot in the mattress. And he *knew* it. Aw those men knew it."

Jodie set her jaw. "Then he should be relieved that it's all behind him."

The woman's gaze travelled out the colourful window and into the back middens. She was bathed in a patchwork of green and blue light, which made her appear sectioned off like the butcher's guide to the very best cuts of meat. "Some of the men used to drink six, seven pints of lager at lunchtime. They only had an hour and yet they'd neck one pint after the other. Ah heard the barman would spend all morning pouring them, and he would line hunners, *thousands* of pints up along the bar so the men could just grab it and drown themselves as soon as the lunch bell rang. Oh and they ran for it! Does that sound like happy men to you?"

"I'm sorry, Missus Campbell. But I know plenty of unhappy people. That's no excuse for your . . ." Jodie nodded at the woman's face. It was like she couldn't bring herself to say it out loud.

Mungo watched as Mrs Campbell stared at and then through Jodie. Nobody ever looked at Jodie as if she was stupid, as if she was a know-nothing, and it surprised Mungo to see it now.

"When our Graham would come home, when we would sit down at dinnertime, ah would ask him how his day was, and all he would say wis 'Aye, fine. Aye, no bad. Aye, it was awright.' So ah would just start wittering on about so-and-so and her new fancy man, or how Mary McClure didnae like the new minister." Mrs Campbell shuddered as she sighed. "Imagine all that fear and disappointment clogged up in there, and nobody stopped to ask him about it, to ask if he was happy in his life, if he was coping. None of the men could tell ye how they really felt, because if they did, they would weep, and this fuckin' city is damp enough."

Mrs Campbell pressed her hanky to her cut. She lifted it away and considered the blood clotting upon it. "And whut did they get for aw their troubles, eh? They got laid off by some suit-wearing snobs in Westminster who couldnae find Glasgow on a map, who didnae give a flyin' fuck if the men had families to feed. They get telt that they're the problem wi' this country, that they're haudin' back progress because they're no afraid of hard work. Then some uppity ginger bitch decides that's the end of them with a stroke of her fountain pen. Done, finito, kaput."

Mrs Campbell had entirely transformed before them. All the earlier frailty was gone, and now she peered down at them with a fizzing anger. "So naw, Jodie Hamilton, it's no about the fitba. It's no about if he likes a wee drink, or doesnae like ma cookin'. Ye're nothin' but a pair of daft weans. Youse have no idea what it's all about. No idea at all."

Jodie clasped her hands. "Please! You're kidding yourself on. You're letting him get away with it."

Mrs Campbell started back down the stairs. Jodie reached out to her but the woman shrugged her off. When she was back on her landing, she turned and looked up at the Hamilton siblings. "Ah've known you since ye were in nappies, and ah've known that selfish mother of yours even longer. If anybody should understand making excuses for the person they love, then it's you two. Can ye no forgive me that?"

ELEVEN

St Christopher came to Mungo's tent in a sulk. The men had argued in the other shelter; the torpid, slurred fight of two soaks. It was a whiny, piteous argument, full of the poor-me's. He could hear them cast up slights from the distant past, dents to their tarnished pride, tallying their ledger of loyalties. They both sounded hurt. Mungo could only catch snippets of it through the downpour, but it sounded like St Christopher was sobbing — maybe they both were — then they were laughing together or laughing at each other, he couldn't tell. The boy rolled in and out of a stupor.

Now it was the saint in the damp suit who lay next to Mungo. This tent was too small for the both of them, but still the man had slithered in anyway. He had gone to the formality of donning his soaked blazer, but he wore no trousers, no socks, and his bloodied feet were swimming in his pair of good church brogues. St Christopher was watching him, not saying a word. Mungo blinked, he was confused at the apparition. His gut roiled with whisky. He wanted to retch in the hopes it would draw out the poison.

Mungo pressed his back against the side of the tent and pulled his knees up to his chest. He could feel the tapping sensation of rain falling on his skin, but he was strangely dry. In several places the rain pooled, and he had to press the tarpaulin to release it, to stop it collapsing on him entirely. St Christopher was staring at him in the gloaming, his eyes stagnant as puddle water.

Mungo wanted to fill the dusk. He started to tell the long lullaby about Hamish teaching him how to ride a bike. But St Christopher didn't want to hear his stories.

"Stop your talkin'." He drummed Mungo on the kneecap. At first it was a tap and then he balled his knuckles and rapped them hard against the bone. The old scab gave a dull throb. "Ah cannae sleep if ye are gonnae lie there wi' your sharp bones sticking into me."

"Why aren't you in the big tent?"

"He's a fuckin' louse. Always cheatin' us. That's how."

Mungo straightened his legs and the saint

made himself comfortable. He thought at first to lie on his back again, but it was a hell to have the man's foul breath on his face, rushing up inside his nostrils. Besides, the tent was too narrow for them to lie shoulder to shoulder. St Christopher huffed and pestered the boy till he rolled over, his face against the cold wall of nylon. The rain kept falling. The ground was disintegrating below them as an arm crept across him, just like it had the night before, but this time Mungo could tell the man was far from sleep.

Something tapped the back of Mungo's leg. It felt not unlike two fingers, searching him, and trying to push between his bare thighs. It was warm, sticky with its own tackiness, and for a second they stuck together, like when two skins of different temperature connect, one slippery and damp, one powdery dry. It stuck to him for a second and then it slipped in between his thighs. The man gasped.

At first St Christopher seemed content with that. Then the man started to saw back and forth. His foul breath tousled the boy's hair.

"Stoppit!" Mungo clamped his thighs tight, locked his ankles one over the other. "What the fuck are you playin' at?" He

286

twisted away from the man and St Christopher mewled in pain. Mungo was pressed against the tent wall. There was nowhere to retreat to.

All weekend St Christopher had seemed as hollow as balsa wood, famished and empty of any nutrition, any goodness. Now he seemed even hungrier than he looked, like he would not be starved any longer. The man wrapped his hand around the boy's throat; every finger felt like a vise. He dug his ragged nails into the larynx and tugged like he would separate the windpipe from the spine. Then he threw a bare leg over the boy and Mungo felt the stitching of the Goodyear brogue scratch his calf. "Don't be stupid, son. The mair you struggle, the longer it'll take."

"Please. Don't," gurgled Mungo.

St Christopher didn't answer him. He shoved the warmth between his thighs again and started humming to himself. He was pushing and pushing and humming and humming.

The suit jacket was rolled up on the man's forearm. He had bound both of the boy's wrists tight in one of his long hands. With the other he squeezed the air from his throat. In the very last of the daylight Mungo could see the hairs on the man's arm. The black hair stood against the pale skin like a forest in the snow. Mungo's strained breath caught the hairs and they changed direction, flowing away and twisting like the long grass in the trout river. He tried to think of the beauty in the hills. It was raining hellishly hard.

He was cooried into the far corner of the tent when Gallowgate pulled back the flap. It was almost completely black inside the red tent, but the faint embers of the campfire lit the side of Gallowgate's face. Mungo could hear St Christopher pissing into the loch. His humped back must have been arched with satisfaction, maybe relief; the high arc of his piss splashed noisily on the surface of the water. The man loosened his guts and farted into the night.

"Are ye awright?" asked Gallowgate softly. "Whut happened? Why is he whistling?"

Mungo shook his head. Several feelings he couldn't process all fought to push to the front of his mouth. He didn't know the words to explain what St Christopher had just done to him. Even if he had known, the shame clamped his jaw shut, the pain in his throttled throat choked the sound.

Gallowgate was dabbing at the sleeping bag. He rubbed something between the tips of his fingers, sniffed it, and recoiled. He left Mungo in the darkness as he went back out into the night. Mungo couldn't tell if he struck the man, or shoved him, but there was a panicked splashing, and a gasping as St Christopher struggled to right himself and make it back to the shore. Gallowgate parted the tent flaps again, he sounded genuinely angry. "You are well out of order! Ya dirty basturt. Ah'm phoning the fuckin' polis."

The boy could hear St Christopher chuckle; the slap of his wet blazer as he cast it on to the rocks. Then came the sound of his labouring to bend down and crawl into the other tent. The satisfied sigh as his weary bones hit the sleeping bag.

Gallowgate reached into the darkness and searched for Mungo. *"Here, here."* He was trying to be soothing, beckoning Mungo from the corner. "Ah'm dead sorry. Look, ah'll talk to him in the morning. It'll be awright."

Mungo's voice sounded faraway. His throat was inflamed with the throttling. It hurt to swallow. "It's no right. He fuckin' touched us! He shouldn't have done that."

Gallowgate had to come closer to hear him. "Ah know."

"My big brother will fuckin' kill him. *Mur-*

289

der him."

"Ah know."

"Please. I just want to go home."

"Ah know, ah know. We will. In the mornin'." He pulled the boy towards him and put his arm around his shoulder.

Mungo was soothing himself by telling Gallowgate all the things Ha-Ha would do to St Christopher. He could picture him with the tomahawk tucked into the waistband of his denims, doggedly turning out all the darkened pubs of the Saltmarket, the Trongate, near the Briggait, scouring beneath the railway arches, searching the faces of all the inebriates until he found the cunt he was after — and he always found the cunt he was after — then the keen edge of his tomahawk would sing.

Gallowgate listened patiently, sighed in all the right places, waiting for the boy to calm his breathing. He was running his hand along Mungo's back, soothing him like a patient father, patting him as though he were a child with trapped wind. They sat together in silence and listened to the noisy anorak rustle under his caress. Mungo picked his twitching face.

"Gallowgate?"

"Aye?"

"If I just wanted to leave now, like *right*

290

now, which direction should I walk?"

"Shhh, it'll be light again soon. Everything feels better in the light." Gallowgate's arm must have grown tired. The fatherly hand started moving in a circular motion. It moved round and round and lower and lower until it slid under the toggled waist-band of his cagoule. As it gently brushed the warm divot above Mungo's backside — the little valley where fine dander was just starting to sprout — Mungo flinched. Gallowgate's sovvie rings were chilled as they travelled up the vertebrae of his spine.

Mungo hadn't realized he had been crying until Gallowgate told him to stop. He had never been a great one for crying as a child. For as long as he could remember Hamish had taken a pleasure in trying to break his temper; trying to find and pierce the water balloon filled with tears that sat inside everyone. Hamish would sit on his chest and thump away with piercing fingers like his breastbone was a typewriter. At the end of every sentence he would twist his ear like it was a crank and with an open palm, clatter the side of Mungo's face. New sentence.

How am I, Mungo Hamilton, such a wee gullible fanny? Type, twist, clatter. New sentence.

Why do I, Mungo Hamilton, always get myself into bother? Type, twist, clatter.

Even Jodie had used his stoicism when it suited her. She would get Mungo to go into Mo-Maw's secret stash and steal potato scones for the pair of them. They would sit in the quiet of the airing cupboard and gorge themselves on the stodgy triangles. When Mo-Maw would catch them, Jodie would say it was Mungo's idea, and he would get the leather sandal across his legs. Jodie would hide behind his bedroom door and wait for him to come into the room smarting in pain, but dry-eyed. She would give him a hug and tell him that's why he could bear the blame, because he never cried, he never gave anyone the satisfaction of his tears.

Gallowgate hissed at Mungo to stop crying. He had his hand on Mungo's football shorts and was trying to pull them down. Mungo used all the strength in his body to clamp one hand on his waistband and brace the other against Gallowgate's chest. All the years of defending himself against Ha-Ha had given him a defensive sort of strength: muscular legs that could support another man's weight, a taut body that could curl shut, and clench tight as a clam. For a second it seemed like he could lift the weight of Gallowgate off him.

The last of the firelight caught Gallowgate's eyes. By the set of his jaw, Mungo could sense his determination. The man hammered his fist into Mungo's face, in a way Ha-Ha never had. He dropped his elbow on to his already bruised windpipe and pushed upwards until Mungo's head tilted all the way back. Then he turned the boy over.

TWELVE

In the weeks following Mo-Maw's resurrection, she was neither here nor there. Jocky would call and Mo-Maw would sweep her life into her handbag and run back to him. Every five days or so he would return her like an overdue library book, and she would appear so dog-eared, so sodden with drink, that it looked like she had been dropped in the bath. Jodie said she thought Jocky was a bad drinker too because he would call at any hour of the day or night. They could hear him as he told Mo-Maw, over and over, that she was lovely. Mo-Maw wanted to believe it, even though she knew she was not lovely, she told him she was too tired to be lovely now.

The night shift had made her nocturnal. More than once Mungo woke up for school and found the front door wide open and Mo-Maw sitting at the kitchenette table in her heavy coat.

The guts of her brown handbag would be spilled across the floor, out the front door, and dribbled the length of the close as she had stumbled home and searched for her house keys.

Mrs Campbell chapped the door twice in the one week. With her purpled face and yellowed eye socket, she asked Mungo how school was going. Without a word, or a downward glance, she took his hand and folded Mo-Maw's white bra into it, and still talking about the foul weather, she curled his fingers silently around it, and left without casting an aspersion on Mo-Maw's name. The next time she brought him a Fray Bentos steak and kidney pie, roasting hot from her own oven. Then, in a plastic bag, she handed him the debris Mo-Maw had dropped the night before: half a dozen panty liners, a bottle of Avon perfume, and a stack of defrosted square sausages.

Mungo closed the front door and carefully returned all of Mo-Maw's belongings to her bag. His mother had taken her bra off again, but that morning it was on the kitchenette table and she was shelling monkey nuts and dropping the shells into the upturned cup. There was an empty bottle of fortified wine on the table. She looked like she had been sat there smoking and drinking since before the dawn.

"Ah shut early," she declared, although he did not ask. "Ah jist couldnae be bothered anymore."

Mungo kissed her warm crown. She had tightened her perm with money they didn't have. Her scalp smelled like it had been burned with chemicals. He put on the kettle and poured her two strong mugs of black tea, just the way she liked. Her head was drooping on to her chest, it bobbed in bunting waves, like a toddler past bedtime. Mungo watched her fight sleep, he tried to take the ashy cigarette from between her fingers but she pushed him away.

"Stop hoverin'. Sakes. Yer like a wee wummin." She ashed on to her own leggings, then brushed it on to the floor. He dared not sweep it up.

Across the back green, above the cluster of communal bin sheds, there were already bright lights in the flats opposite. Mungo watched the light come on in James's house, a single light that he switched off whenever he left the room. Mungo knew he woke early to go to the doocot. He would spend an hour feeding and exercising the birds before there was any danger of another dooman sending a lure into the sky. That was the thing with the East End doomen:

they were mostly unemployed, so they didn't keep standard business hours.

James was silhouetted against the bright light of his kitchenette. He looked out and saw Mungo watching him. They still had not spoken, not even once, but he gave Mungo the thumbs up sign, with a face like it was a question. Mungo returned the salute with a definite thumbs down. James laughed.

"Come away from that window," said Mo-Maw. "Stop watching wummin get dressed for their work. That's aw ah need. To have raised a peepin' Tom."

Mo-Maw had taken to stealing meat from the caravan, arse ends of black puddings and half-defrosted bricks of sliced bacon. Mungo turned on the electric ring and prepared her a hot breakfast to line her stomach. The eggs rolled across the frying pan in a white greasy liquid of their own, catching bits of bacon fat and scraps of yesterday's black pudding in their wake. He waited until the centre filmed over before he flipped them gently. The plate made a chalky sound as he slid it across the tabletop towards her. It was exactly as she liked it.

Mo-Maw made a retching sound. "Ah cannae be looking at that."

"I could make you some porridge."

"Stop fussin'." She sounded tired but far from sleep.

"Maybe you want to go and lie down?"

She stubbed her cigarette into the egg roll. Her eyes cleared. The routine of the night shift was in her. "Ah want to go out."

She could barely walk. With her arm around his shoulders Mungo carried her down the stairs. At one point she climbed up on the banister, and she was so wilful that he had to hold her as she slid down it. *Wheeee.* Mo-Maw began cackling and it was impossible not to be affected by her glee. Jodie would be furious that he hadn't buffeted her from the door, that he hadn't used all his wiles to deflect her to the settee and make her sink into the softness that she couldn't rise up out of.

The early morning light was a pale-blue wash, it muted the vividness from everything it touched, it stole the life from the faces of passing strangers. He needed to put his arm around his mother to stop her from stumbling along the Parade. At times she leaned on him so heavily he felt like he had her whole weight against him. Then she would take a few shuffling steps and pitch the other way and he would stagger after her. It took all his strength and concentration not to tip them both into the gutter.

The early shift gawped down upon them from warm corporation buses. From the pity in their faces, Mungo could tell they made a sorry sight. Mungo tried to hold his spine straight and keep his eyes on the horizon like there was a purpose to their journey, but there was not; she had taken the notion for a walk and he had been powerless to stop her.

"We used to do this all the time when ye were wee." She wasn't any soberer but the cold had pinched her nose and now she looked fully awake. He was holding her at the waist and she had both her arms around him like they were young lovers. "Ah couldnae cross the doorstep but ye would be clinging to my skirt. The other two couldn't have cared less if I got hit by a bus. But no you, you were always there for me."

She had oriented their walk towards the city centre; maybe the casino would still be open, or the penny puggies under Central Station. Tattie-bogle liked lights. He had hoped she would lose heart, but she didn't. The drink could flatten her or give her a peculiar stamina. The terror lay in the fact he never knew which it would be.

To get to the city centre they needed to pass in the direction of the Necropolis. The air would be freshest there, the steep hill would be best for clearing her head. It would be quiet that time of the morning, when no one could see the strain or embarrassment on his face. He bumped into her like a gentle tugboat, and steered her towards the cemetery. The view from the Necropolis spanned the low city. He could see the tall fingers of Sighthill and the dense cluster of Victorian buildings that made up the centre of the city. The Tennent's brewery was already belching its yeast into the sky.

"Ah don't think Jocky loves me." Her American trainers were caked with mud by the time he dropped her on the steps of the John Knox memorial. "He's taking me for a mug."

Mungo crouched near the statue of a scowling clergyman to pick crocuses that were already past their peak. It was hard to find ones that had not yet collapsed in on themselves. "Maybe he doesn't like you when you're drinking."

"Sakes. Ah'm only thirty-four. All ah should be doing is drinking. Drinking and dancing and laughing." Her face looked sunken in the morning light. She took a bottle of fortified wine out of her bag. Mungo could feel his eyelids start to fill with electricity. He had emptied the drink from her bag before they left, but she had been wily enough to put it back in when he wasn't looking. "Ah bet that sounds dead old to ye, din't it? Ah wisnae much older than you when ah came down wi' our Hamish. Your father was stunned. Ye should have heard the terrible things his mammy called me."

Mungo couldn't remember his grandmother. He had a lingering sense of a Presbyterian snob, a woman that spread jam on salted crackers and pretended they were fancy biscuits. "Tell me what my father was like?"

"Oh, no this again." She struggled to light the end of a bent cigarette. Mungo worried she would forget he had asked about his father, but the nicotine seemed to focus her mind, and she eventually said, "He wisnae anything special. There was plenty better looking. But he was a cheeky and charming big bastard. A brave soul like our Hamish and soft in the centre like you." Her eyes were fixed, somewhere out over the snaking Clyde.

"Why did you let him fight in the gangs if he had weans?" Mungo had asked her this a thousand times before. All three of them had.

"Ah couldnae have stopped him. Ah tried, but he never belonged to me, no really. We

301

had only been living the gether for half a year afore he got stabbed. Jodie was still sleeping in a pram because we couldnae afford a bed for Hamish. We were only playin' at houses." Her eyes were rheumy with the cold. "Ah mean, ah wisnae even the first person that the polis told. Ah had to phone his mammy when he didn't come round that night. She was the one who telt me he'd been stabbed. Ah was at home in an unfurnished flat nursing his two weans and she didnae even think enough of me to phone me herself."

Mungo had been planning on giving the half-wilted crocuses to his mother. He let them blow away down the hill. "I didn't mean to make you sad."

She held her hand out to him and he sat beside her. "Don't be daft, ye've never brought me a minute's sadness in my life." He could hear her sniffling. "It was a lovely surprise to know you would be born. Ah buried him on a Tuesday and on that next Monday Dr Doak telt me ah was pregnant wi' you."

"You must have gotten a fright."

"Ah did. Seeing as how ah only went to see him for some anti-depressants." She flicked her dout out over the headstones. "They came to see me, ye know."

"Who?"

"The wee boys that stabbed him, a handful of wee Fenians. They'd taken the notion to wear their good communion suits, maybe their mammies had forced them to do it, but it was like a foreign delegation when they chapped the door. Awful brave for four wee Catholic boys to walk those streets after they'd killed the bold Ha-Ha. They must have felt guilty. Ah remember they were soaking wet and shivering. They'd waited till it was a pure belter of a storm. Safer that way."

"Did you want to hurt them?"

"Ah did at first. Ah was screaming and roaring. Jodie wouldn't latch on, she was always a fussy wee thing, and with everything that happened, ah was up to high doh. But these boys were all about your age, they looked so young standing at my door. Ah think they thought they were hardmen when they'd first stabbed him. It was in all the papers and in time their own mammies got on to them after they heard Ha-Ha had two weans and well, that's a rotten thing to bear. It was the wimmen who felt bad. They were only wee boys running wi' scissors."

"Hamish will get his own back one day."

"So he says. But a funny thing, they used to buy Hamish nappies. For a while they even sent me money, mostly Provvie checks and maybe an occasional tenner at Christmas." She drew a deep breath. "Aye, well, it's aw fun and games till someone loses an eye, eh?"

Mo-Maw had an affectation when she was feeling sad, a soothing tell of sorts. She spread the fingers on one hand and caressed each finger, rubbing the length and pressing into the soft webbing between each, tamping down gently, as though she were wearing fine gloves. Mungo was thinking about how he should save up and buy her actual gloves. But she straightened up suddenly, the stone step leaching the heat from their bodies. "Did I ever tell you how ye got yer name?"

"Aye, like a hundred times."

"Oh am ah boring ye? Ah must've been mad to give ye such a name."

"It's a Fenian name."

She waved her hand dismissively. "Naw. The saints belong to aw of us. But ah can remember the registrar staring at me like ah was mental. Ah *was* mental. Ah wisnae even a widow — ah couldnae even call myself that. Your father was always *'poor Jocelyn Hamilton's boy,'* he was never my man, never *'poor Maureen Buchanan's fella.'* Ah just felt ye needed somethin' of Glasgow. It was probably the only thing your father really loved. Ah thought it could help bring some peace."

"Not to me."

"But you are. You are my dear one." She rubbed the back of his hand. "It's a hard name, ah suppose."

"Stephen would have been fine. David. John."

Sat at the top of the hill, they could smell the sweet diesel in the crisp morning air. The Parade was already choked with congested traffic all trying to make its way into the grey city. Mo-Maw kissed his cold cheek. "It'll absolutely kill me."

"What will?"

"When you meet a lassie and leave us."

"You left me first!" His voice pitched higher than he would have liked.

She waved her hand like he didn't understand. "Ah can barely handle sharing ye wi' Jo-Jo as it is." There was truth to this. It sat uncomfortably between them. "Ah know she thinks ah'm a terrible mother. She doesnae miss a trick to remind me she could raise ye better herself. The judgy prig-faced wee cow."

"Maw!"

She slapped his knee. "Whit have ah telt ye about calling me *that*?" At least she rubbed where she had slapped. "But ah will. Ah'll die when ye start the winching." Without regarding her, he knew what would come next — she was not a woman given to subtleties — he could practically hear her eyes swivel towards his face. "So, have ye met somebody yet?"

"No." He pulled her tight to his side. "You're my only girl."

She wasn't laughing as she pushed away from him. "Darlin', ah'm starting to worry about you. Ye'll be sixteen at Christmas, ye should be chasin' lassies. Ah had every father from Govan to the Garngad at my door by the time Hamish wis your age." She went quiet for a moment. "Is there anything the matter?"

"No." He felt himself flush.

Mo-Maw looked uncharacteristically concerned. Jodie had told her about their possible eviction and she hadn't bothered her shirt. Hamish had gotten a girl-child pregnant and she hadn't ruffled a feather. But now she stared into his eyes and she looked genuinely worried.

"I'm just not that interested." Then he added hopefully, "Yet."

She sniffed. "*Listen.* Just cos ah've been away don't think ah've no been watching. Missus Campbell tells me everything ye've been up to. She telt me ye've been in at Poor-Wee-Chickie's."

"Mister Calhoun needed a hand."

"Aye, ah bet he fucking did!" The back of her jaw was jutted out to the battle angle. "And your soft wee hands will do very nicely thank-you-very-much. Stay away frae him, Mungo. Dae ye hear? Ah'll be damned if ah raise a bachelor."

Mungo was glad to stand up. He arranged the hood on her thin anorak. The fake coyote fur matched the speckled tones of her dyed hair. "Let's go home, you look done in."

"Thanks very much." Mo-Maw wiped the streaking mascara from underneath her eyes. He pulled her to her feet, and they almost toppled into the crocuses.

"Listen, ah need yer help. Ah need to cut out the drink. Nae kiddin' this time." Then, without any irony, she downed the last of her fortified wine. Mo-Maw pummelled her small breasts, hoisted them a few centimetres higher, and sighed when they drooped back into place. "See, ah cannae let Jocky get away. If ah do there might never be another go-around for me."

Mungo agreed to nothing. He led his mother down the boggy hill. When she slipped, he picked her up.

He did not go to school that day. While other children were running for the first bell, Mungo ran his mother a lukewarm bath. He put a stack of towels in the oven to heat them, and when he put her to bed, he laid the towels over her so she was warmed through. Mo-Maw was roiling and restless. Mungo took off his school uniform, and climbing in beside her, he held her till the shakes subsided and she fell asleep.

The sky had dimmed again by the time Jodie came in from school. She cracked the bedroom door and their eyes locked in the silence. He thought she would be relieved, but Jodie just looked her usual disappointed self.

When the evening news came on Mungo made a heaped plate of dry toast and sat with Mo-Maw while she ate as much as she could. He never let her from his sight, lest she find a secret stash of fortified and calm her tremors with it. He laid out clothes for her to wear and together they caught a corporation bus into the city and went to the meeting hall.

He had been to AA before, but rarely without Jodie. Mo-Maw had tried the

Twelve Steps over the years, but her sobriety had always been fleeting and vague. Like a gallus child that thought it could ride a bike without stabilizers, she pronounced herself *cured* after a few weeks, but soon crashed and skinned her knees on the drink again. She wasted a lot of breath arguing that there was a difference between *taking a drink* and *being a drunk.* Jodie had babysat him at the back of enough meetings for him to know that if you were an alcoholic, one or one hundred drinks were the very same thing. Mo-Maw disagreed; sobriety bored her.

The meeting room was at the back of an old Masonic hall. It felt like a school assembly, with painted floorboards that ran the length of the room, and a raised wooden stage. There was a connecting hallway leading to a small windowless kitchen and before and after the meeting the members liked to gather around the scalding tea urn. Mungo felt most comfortable there. He held Mo-Maw's coat and when the meeting convened, he leaned against the urn and let the warmth radiate through his body as he listened to everyone's confessions.

When the meeting was finished the alcoholics gathered around the folding trestle table. This particular meeting housed a tight community; humble folk who, regardless of the varying sizes of their wage packets, rubbed along with genuine empathy. Mungo liked to be amongst them and even though his eyes started to sting from the smoke, he liked the hugging sensation their puffy winter jackets gave him as he squeezed through the tightly packed crowd.

Mo-Maw took his hand and dragged him towards a cluster of women who were chewing on gammon sandwiches as they gossiped.

"*Weh-ll,* would ye look how big yer gettin'? And to think it was only the other day ye were doing forward rolls on my guid carpet." Every-Other-Wednesday Nora cupped his face in her cold hands. Her cigarette gave off a tendril of smoke. His eyes were twitching, not bad, but enough. Mo-Maw sighed.

"*Weh-ll,* is yer face still giving ye bother?" Every time E-O-W Nora saw him she asked the same thing. She was a stocky woman; a home help from Roystonhill who had searching eyes and skin that had yellowed like old kitchen paint. Her salt-and-pepper hair was clipped short and her mouth was puckered with fine lines from smoking forty a day for forty years. When she spoke, she prefaced everything with a long, drawn-out *weh-ll.* It served as a "who am I to say?" It seemed she said this as if to undermine her own opinion, in case God disagreed with her, and would crack the heavens and contradict her.

"*Weh-ll*, never mind the twitchin', son. You breakin' hearts yet? I bet the lassies have to keep their hands over their ha'pennies wi' you." She winked at Mo-Maw. This was another thing she said every time she saw him.

"Ah wish he would, Nora. It's a late bloomer ah've got on ma hands."

"Well, lucky you. Enjoy him while ye can. I never see my sons anymore. Ye should see the miserable articles they've married."

Mo-Maw pointed a finger at his crotch. "Ah had our Hamish have a wee look. Apparently, it's aw there and working fine."

"*Mammy!*" His voice pitched and broke. Several heads turned, cigarettes clenched between teeth.

"Ya wee bugger. If ah've telt ye once . . ."

The circle of women were appraising Mungo as though he was a second-rate bullock. E-O-W Nora put a calming hand on Mo-Maw's arm. "*Weh-ll*, yer wee mammy is just worried about ye, Mungo. It's hard raising boys when ye are a wummin on yer lonesome." Then she turned back to Mo-Maw. "Ah mean, look at ma

311

eldest boy, a brand-new motor, a glass conservatory, two weeks all-inclusive in Torremolinos, and here ah am sitting in the Garngad with kitchen wallpaper that won't stay on the wall." She dropped her dout into the polystyrene teacup. "As Rod Stewart is ma witness, if ah had it to do all over again, ah'd only have daughters."

Mo-Maw scoffed. "God. Anything but that."

THIRTEEN

Jodie stared out over the fallow fields of North Ayrshire. There had been a late frost and now the ploughed rows looked like stitched panels on a quilt, each channel picked out by snow-white thread. The brown fields rolled all the way towards the horizon where the charcoal sea met the flat dull sky. The suspension had worn out on the bus long ago and as they rattled their way towards this line of nothingness Mungo wouldn't talk to her. He drew his hood up over his head and couldn't bring himself to face her.

Mr Gillespie had run away. He and Jodie had such a habit of discretion that it was Mungo who told her that Mr Gillespie had disappeared.

Usually Jodie and the teacher haunted different wings of the sprawling high school. She preferred the quietness of the arts and languages prefabs while Mr Gillespie hid in the teachers' study. Occasionally she would look up and find him peering down at her through the wired safety glass at the head of the main stairs. A smile would ripple across his face, a spark of lust in his eyes, and then it would be snuffed. Jodie had liked that. She thought she was slick.

Thursday was their day to meet and fuck — and the occasional Saturday when he told his wife he was at the golf — but mostly Thursday evenings when they would drive to the tin caravan. He had stood her up before, left her standing in the shadows of the tenements, and later he would give her some excuse: a wean with measles, a wife with a sprained back. Then he would haunt her more that following week, floating down corridors in the cloud of her Cachet. Sometimes he would shout at her in the hallway, contriving some small infraction, anything that would allow him to drown her in his shadow and make her cast her hazel eyes in his direction.

This past week when he missed their Thursday at the caravan, she was glad of the peace. After the weekend, he didn't haunt her in the hallways, and when she went to the Modern Studies block, he was not there as usual.

Her brother was getting dressed in front

of the electric fire when he sang, *"I know something you don't know."* He was alternating between buttoning his school shirt and bending over and spooning heaps of dripping Weetabix into his gullet. He never took his eyes from the cartoons. "Are ye not gonnae guess?"

Mungo was bare-arsed and innocent as a wean. There was no heating in the rest of the flat, but it wasn't right that he was naked in front of her, not now he was fifteen. He was physically a young man, if not yet inside his head. A rash of light brown hair dusted his groin and thighs, and the round chubbiness of his buttocks was becoming lean and square with muscle. He waggled his bare arse at her.

"Stop your nonsense and put your underpants on." She mourned the sweet little boy that he used to be. At night she could hear him through the wall, rubbing fast and finishing much too quick. She knew what he was doing when his bath took an eternity and the immersion ran out of hot water. There had been a time she'd had to chase him with a washcloth just to get him clean.

"I know something you don't know." He baited her with a grin but Jodie would not guess. *"Fine!* Fat Gillespie has run away. Mr Goodart says he'll be teaching us from now

on. I heard him say Gillespie didn't show up for work, didn't phone in sick or nothing. He just vanished." Mungo was pulling on his long black socks. "Goodart asked us if Gillespie had given us homework and we fuckin' lied." He sank to one knee, strummed a fantastic air guitar. He didn't expect Jodie to start sobbing.

Jodie felt the floor tilt underneath her. Like a gable end slated for demolition, the front facade of her fell away and the private contents of her life rolled out. She was being torn down, and every mismatched bed sheet in her mind was to be exposed for all to see. She knew why the teacher had gone away. She knew what she had done to make Mr Gillespie disappear.

Mungo wouldn't sit next to her on the bus. He sat on the bench opposite and flattened himself against the glass, his eyes fixed somewhere over the black fields. Jodie couldn't remember a time when he had been this disappointed in her.

It was a long while before she could stop crying. Then she had told Mungo all about Mr Gillespie, about his holiday caravan, the frontier of the vast sea and the excitement of the screaming waltzers. For every thing she told him, there was a thing she could never tell. She didn't tell him how Mr Gillespie had said he believed in her. How easily he had groomed a daft wee lassie into believing that she might get out of the city; that she might escape the dreich streets that held them all stuck and be free, at last, from the burden of her brothers. She had a good brain, sure, *but she was nothing special,* not compared to these Perth lassies with their tutors, and the Edinburgh debutantes from the Mary Erskine School. She had a good head on her shoulders but he was the one who would make sure she would go far. How could she tell Mungo that as he was fingering her that very first time, she had already started to trust him and doubt herself?

Mr Gillespie had promised to help her get into Glasgow University, and she had doubted she was bright enough to manage that on her own. To Jodie, the university was another city altogether, one whose postcode was a moat that kept East End middens like her out. It was the ancient seat of learning that respectable Englishmen came to when they wanted a sense of frontier plus a top-drawer education, not to mention four years of shenanigans with local girls who liked to get fucked off their faces on eccies and pints of snakebite and black.

Hamish said he knew all about it. When he had a supply in, Hamish sold dank hashish to the university freshers. He cut it with plain rolling tobacco and crumbled a beef Oxo cube over the top of the mixture. He could make the smallest amount stretch across a whole class.

His timing had to be perfect. He had to catch them during freshers' week while they still had envelopes of money from their grandmothers and before they learned the hard lessons the city had in store for them. He always struggled to straighten his grin as Toby and Dom sniffed at bags of tobacco and Mo-Maw's out-of-date Bisto and exclaimed it smelled just as good as the skunk they had "that one time in Goa."

Hamish called this last week in September "Plum Season." You had to con the bastards before they got too ripe and Glasgow rotted them on the vine. Soon enough the city would show them its true nature and then it would be too late. But three years running, he made enough money to pay off all of Mo-Maw's Provvie loans; he even bought a video player and with the remainder he rented a full-body sunbed for Sammy-Jo.

The last time Hamish had come in the door buzzing and flush with freshers' money, Jodie was already lying with Mr

Gillespie and dreaming of making it to the West End. She was slack-jawed as Hamish talked in awe about the grand tenements the students lived in, the fancy ones off Byres Road, with their wide wood floors, high ceilings, and big centre lights that cast a sparkle upwards, not downwards from a garish bulb. It filled her head with day-dreams.

Every Plum Season, the English arrived in their mothers' battered Volkswagens, all the better to not flaunt their wealth — the good Mercedes was simply too much for the north. They slouched down the Great Western Road in balding corduroys and waxed Barbour jackets. Their hair was artfully unbrushed, an old Proust was dog-eared and protruding conspicuously from the flap of a canvas bag. They were dressed for shooting grouse in Aberdeenshire.

"Ah think they've had the Walkman too loud when their mammies were telling them about Glesga being full of peasants. Daft cunts thought she said it was full of pheasants." Hamish told that joke to every single one of his Protestant boys, and twice to Jodie. "You can only dress like ye don't care if ye have money. I mean serious, never-have-to-count-it money."

Glasgow teenagers in the very best of gear

they could afford and caked with make-up and body spray watched the slouching corduroys from the top deck of the bus and felt a spur of shame. It would be a dream to afford beautiful clothes. It would be another dream entirely to be able to shun it and dress however you pleased.

Hamish took their money quickly. He sneered as they told him they planned to visit their big sisters — invariably called Tilly or Tanya or Tess — at St Andrews or Robert Gordon's. They asked him the best season to visit Skye. "How the fuck should ah know?" he would say. "Ah'm no yer fuckin' ghillie pal."

These students went home for every holiday. Whenever anyone asked them where they studied, they would answer *Glasgow,* and the friend would nod approval; how bright and brave young Dominic Buxton was, and just the acceptable level of debauched. They always went home after graduation. They would never actually settle down here.

Yet to Hamish, the worst of them were not the English. The worst were the chinless lambswool milksops from the West End or Perth or Edinburgh. These Scots spoke the Queen's English with a snooty clarity that would embarrass even Etonians. They knew more than one Rabbie Burns poem by heart, and actually enjoyed ceilidhs and bagpipes without taking the piss. They knew all the best walks around Loch Voil and thought the Drovers Inn did the best Sunday roast, though it was "ruined by day trippers." To Hamish, these Scots let themselves be minstrel dollies. Middle-class Glaswegians were the worst; they had no loyalty, when it suited them they draped the city about themselves like a trendy jacket, but they knew none of its chill, none of its need. These Glaswegians were acceptably foreign and endlessly entertaining to the English. Their das were not being put out of work on the Clyde or pulling slag from the coalfaces in Cardowan. Their daddies were catching the commuter flight down to London and eating smoked Scottish salmon at business lunches in Canary Wharf. They preferred to take their oatcakes with French pâté and drank uisge beatha by the glass, not by the bottle.

Hamish took one look at them and knew he hated them. He was jealous in every way. Then, howling at their gullibility, he took their money and gave them a lungful of powdered beef.

He told Jodie that university life was not available to her. It was not for Glaswegians like her.

Jodie listened to the scream of seagulls and knew she couldn't explain any of this to Mungo.

What she had told him was enough. In the tenement, with milk pouring down his chin, Jodie had told Mungo about the baby Mr Gillespie had put in her belly. This was why he had disappeared. She told Mungo how Mr Gillespie had said it wasn't his. How he had screamed at her in a lay-by and panicked like a midden rat trapped by Staffordshire terriers. It was funny, she had thought then, for him to act so trapped when he wasn't the one who would be stuck. His knuckles were white on the steering wheel as he'd listed a long list of Protestant surnames, her classmates. He'd recited them alphabetically, gruffly, like he was reading the morning attendance.

"Was it McConnachie?"

"No."

"Neely?"

"No."

"Nicholson?"

"No-ooo."

"Rattray?"

"Nein!"

"Ahhh, come on now. Don't lie to me, girl. I bet it was Rattray. I've seen you all giggling and scratching his name on the inside of your desks."

"God sakes. No way." It was not the bold Rattray.

"Buchanan?" he asked. "Was it wee Buchanan then?"

"Wait, what? Buchanan doesn't come after Rattray," she'd sneered at him. "You're slipping."

Mr Gillespie had rattled the steering wheel. "Murchison?"

"No!" Jodie had let out a long sigh. "I have slept with nobody but you." His face blanched like over-boiled cabbage. "*Sir,* it's your baby."

Usually he liked it when she called him *Sir.* He asked her to call him that when he was on top of her. But not now. He would not believe that the foetus was his. "That's what lassies like you do, ye roam the streets like dugs in heat. Ah knew it. Ah knew ye were just like every one of those slags from the scheme." He was muttering over and over to himself, reprimanding himself for his stupidity. "Ye'll never get to university now."

She couldn't tell him that she hated lying underneath him — she had enjoyed it so little that it would be an age before she ever let another boy put himself inside her.

He didn't bring her back to the East End that day. He left her near his home, in the Cowgate out by Kirkintilloch. When she asked where she was — she knew nothing about this part of the world — he said "*Cow*-Gate" and slammed the door. She would have expected more maturity from any of the boys on his register.

Now Mr Gillespie was gone and they were on the bus to Largs, looking to connect to the next one to West Kilbride and then the caravan park. It had been Mungo's idea — it was a stupid idea — but she had none better.

Jodie slid across the aisle and sat next to her brother. She pressed against him until he was squashed up against the window and forced to acknowledge her. She expected him to look disappointed or angry; but when he looked at her it was with profound sadness and she found she didn't like the mirror of his gaze and wanted him to turn away again. Mungo uncurled his fingers. He had a handful of Jelly Babies and he had separated the red ones just for her.

Mungo had never seen the sea in the daylight. When they changed buses in Largs, he pulled her towards it and Jodie felt lousy that she couldn't let him linger. The next bus dropped them at the mouth of the caravan park. They walked the tarmac cul-de-sacs until they found the row of caravans that she knew best. Although it was still cold, Glasgow retirees were preparing for the short summer: replanting beds of dwarf geraniums in old whisky barrels, reconnecting frozen water lines. The retirees watched the children suspiciously and Jodie regretted that they hadn't changed out of their school uniforms.

It was a stupid idea to look for him here, but a part of her had half-expected him to be at the caravan, because she could not picture him anywhere else. She had few images of Mr Gillespie, except him standing in front of a pull-down map of South Africa or lying on top of her on the pull-down table. She had never seen him walking along a street. Did he whistle "Billy Boy" like Mr Campbell, or weasel and strut like Hamish? She had no real idea of him outside what he taught her in school and then what he did to her afterwards; what he gave to her mind and what he took back from her body.

The caravan was a beige tin can that was cold to the touch. They peered through the proud net curtains into the empty interior. Mungo started tugging on the door.

"What are you doing?" She knew a dozen

eyes were watching their every move; this schemie scum didn't belong amongst their manicured flower beds.

"He might have left a note inside," said Mungo, "or *mibbe* there's something with his real address on it. Some way we can find him and make him help you."

Jodie hadn't thought this far ahead. She hadn't imagined what she wanted from him. It was foolish, but she just needed to make sure he had understood, that it hadn't been a misunderstanding after all. It was a burden to have a trusting soul. Sometimes she just couldn't believe the worst in people. All these years with Mo-Maw should have learned her better.

Mungo tried pulling on the galvanized handle again. The door was thin and Hamish could have kicked it in easily, he would have known just where to aim his Samba. Mungo searched in the kangaroo pocket of his cagoule. He drew out the small knife Hamish had given him. He had no idea how to force a lock, but this was barely a lock. He jammed the knife behind the bolt and the door burst open.

It was clean and cold inside. The Gillespies had left just enough furnishings to sell it on to the next Glaswegians. With none of Mrs Gillespie's fussy knick-knacks it looked foreign to Jodie. She had to check again to make sure she had not mistaken the sameness of all the caravans. No, this *was* the one. She ran her hand along the underside of the collapsible kitchen table and felt the sharp pitted mounds of dried mucus. Mr Gillespie had liked to pick his nose after they fucked and wipe it on the underside of the veneer. This was the place.

"It's like a magician's hat in here." Mungo marvelled at the empty space. The Gillespies had two spoiled children; they had splurged on the deluxe upgrade.

Mungo found the chemical toilet and was pissing noisily into it. It sounded like a cheap plastic bucket. "Aw man!" he cried, lifting his feet high. "I don't think this is plumbed in." Pools of sugary yellow piss were leaking out around the base of the commode. Instinctively, Jodie found herself looking for a tea towel to clean up the mess.

"What are you doing?" asked Mungo, tucking himself away. Before Jodie could answer he took his hand and swept the last remaining photo off the wall. A twee thing, a black-and-white photo of Inveraray that had been tinted with watercolours. It smashed on the floor. He smiled.

Jodie filled with blood. She ripped at the sheets of the double bed; the bed that belonged to his wife, the same bed he wouldn't let her lie down in. Giro-Jodie had to make do with the folding table or the tweed banquette and its uncomfortable bouclé fabric, or if he was in a real rush, she would brace herself against the tin sink and listen to the jangle of cutlery while he hiked her school skirt up above her haunches.

Jodie ran her hand over his pillow. It was freshly laundered but so deeply slept on that it held the traces of his sweat and his hair pomade. She could smell him on it. She ripped the covers from the pillows and tore the goose feathers from their guts. She had disembowelled two whole pillows and was screaming, red in the face, before she finally ran out of breath. Her brother stood in the narrow doorway and watched her shoulders heave with the exertion of it, every breath rounding them a little more as the anger bled out of her. "Wait. You can get pillows full of feathers?" Mungo's eyes were wide with wonder. "Fuck him!" He picked up a pillow and bloofed Jodie with it. She fell against the rosewood wall and her shoulder burst through the veneer. He hit her again and the air filled with fresh goose snow. Jodie found her own weapon and they made a great game of climbing around the caravan, bouncing from bed to banquette and walloping each other without mercy. It was a far-roaming, rolling war and they destroyed everything in their path. The caravan squeaked and tilted on its tyres.

They only stopped when the last pillow was flattened. Jodie's left ear was bloody where her gold hoop had torn free, but she couldn't care less, she didn't even shout at Mungo. Every surface was thick with fibre and feather. "That's what he deserves," said Mungo proudly. But it was all too childish. It was not enough payback.

When they went outside, the winter sun was setting below the clouds, and Mungo could at last see the break between sky and sea. There were feathers in their hair and stuck to their school uniforms. Mungo crouched beneath the caravan and removed the brake bricks from the rear wheels. Jodie watched him do it with a nervous giggle. "You're wasting your time. He's gonnae sell it on. He's never coming back."

Her brother pondered it for a second. It was unfair to harm whoever the next holiday makers were. Hamish would not have cared. But it was cruel to send total strangers rolling and screaming into the Irish Sea.

"You're no fun," pouted Mungo, but he did not replace the bricks. He cantilevered the stand at the front and put the guiding wheel back in contact with the earth. The caravan shifted as he pushed it. It started rolling downhill, started gathering speed. "Ah, ah. Fuck!" he cried. "Run. *Run!*"

Jodie was curled up in the armchair and had been ignoring him as he tried to read John Donne. His face flushed with the effort but she was not paying attention to him. She was thinking about something else. He hadn't even noticed that she was crying.

"How the fuck can auld McGregor do this to us?" he moaned. "It's no fair to bully a Scotsman into speaking proper English and then throw it for a loop and saddle him with this shite."

Mr McGregor was notorious for it. For those *special* weans — the boys who were going nowhere in life — he prescribed "the Big Donne." The English teacher knew they were beyond his help. He administered the poet like it was a massive dose of penicillin for someone who had already withered with TB. If any child could not manage the curriculum, he was not going to waste any more time dragging them through *The Mayor of Casterbridge.* They were put to the back of the class and got the Big Donne.

Most of them spent the hour drawing on the inside cover. Mr McGregor didn't care.

"It suck'd me first, and now sucks thee,
And in this flea, our two bloods mingled
    bee;"

Mungo clawed at himself. "That wummin has scabies and he's writing a love song about it. And auld McGregor has the cheek to give you the ruler if you say *hame* instead of *hoh-m*. But this auld soap dodger spells any fuckin' word any fuckin' way that he likes and gets called a 'master.' " Mungo pitched the thin volume across the room.

"I like that poem," said Jodie, mostly to herself. She wiped her face and tried to smile. "The poet is trying to con a woman into sleeping with him. They should teach every girl that poem the minute we get a chest."

Mungo shook his head. "I'd like to dig up John Donne's bones and punch them."

"Punch? *Would you?*"

"Aye." He eyed her suspiciously. "What's wrong with you now?"

Jodie tugged at her woollen tights. She stood up and met him in the middle of the floor. "I'll make you cheese on toast if you do something for me?"

There was that sudden kindness; Mungo knew he was about to be manipulated. "I'm no hungry."

"I need your help. I need to ask you to do something and you need to be a man about it."

There it was again, that phrase. They all wanted to see this man inside him. "I won't agree until you tell me what it is."

"Well." She paused again. "I want you to punch me as hard as you can."

He laughed great ugly guffaws. But Jodie was not laughing. She took his hand and laid it on her stomach, over the nubby fabric of her acrylic jumper. It was taut feeling and it was radiating an even type of heat. "If I have this baby, I'll never get to read any more poems."

He pulled his hand away. "Are you mental?"

She held on to him. "It's nothing. It's not even a baby yet, it's only a wee tadpole. If I wait much longer it will have nerves. It will have earlobes . . ." Jodie had always been good at Biology. She was using what she had learned to pressure him. "Don't worry. It's only a sac of mucus and cells. If I get it out I can just flush it."

"I can't. It's a baby."

"It is not. And when all's done, it never

was." She sighed and tried to talk softly to him. "Mungo, if I have this baby, I'll be just like Mo-Maw. You wouldn't want that, would you?"

"Of course not. But mibbe I could look after it. I'm not going anywhere, so what's the harm? You can just still go to school. You can go to college. The council will give us a wee flat. We'll get brilliant benefits."

The thought chilled her. She hadn't imagined a life with her brother *and* a baby. "No. I'm not living like that. If you won't help me then I'll need to find work. They're taking on trainees at Maguires, I can fold cardboard." She stroked his bonny face and smiled. "But you'll help me. I know you will."

"I willnae."

Jodie stepped away from him. In one smooth motion she stepped on to a chair and then on to the windowsill.

"What are you playing at?"

She turned. "Do you remember Tattie-bogle, when she wanted Mo-Maw to jump? If I don't get this baby out of me, I *will* jump." He remembered well. He would never forget his mother on the wet window ledge, how she clambered up there every so often, any time she felt the children did not love her enough. A shadow crossed Jodie's eyes, a flicker that she sometimes got when she solved a particularly hard equation. "Huh. I understand why she did that now. I won't live like this."

Mungo put his arms around her waist and dragged her down. Then he shoved her so hard she flew back into the easy chair. The soles of her feet went skyward. "Fuck you."

"Mun—"

"Fuck you."

Mungo sulked in the dark kitchenette. He ran his finger around the field-flower wallpaper and enjoyed the way the pattern was padded to give it a three-dimensional feeling. He stared at the back of James's tenement. They still hadn't spoken since James had cried. He wished for a friend now.

The middle cabinet was full of pint glasses that Mo-Maw had stolen from the old men's pubs on Duke Street. He took one and into it he emptied all the liquids and condiments in his mother's kitchen: brown sauce, red sauce, yellow sauce, and sour separated milk. He added a raw egg, Askit painkiller powder, and half a shaker of black pepper. To the top of the sundae he added a long squirt of dish soap and a dash of toilet bleach. He topped it with a wad of his phlegm.

"Here, drink this." He handed the potion

to Jodie.

She was sitting on the windowsill looking out at the narrow street. She had been crying again. Then she laughed. But then she got herself stuck somewhere between tears and laughter. He stepped away from her, offended. "You asked for my help. Drink it."

Jodie wrapped her arms around his shoulders, she tousled the hair at the back of his neck. It felt good. "You silly eejit. Mungo, they are not connected. The uterus and the stomach. I'll likely shite myself, aye, but the blob won't shift." She put the foul glass on the windowsill. They could still smell it from across the room. "Punch me, or you can kick me, if you prefer. Just the once. I promise."

Mungo was ashen. He shook his head.

His reluctance confused Jodie. There had been wet summers where they had amused themselves by slamming the door in each other's faces, waiting till the exact moment their sibling was crossing the threshold and then *wham*. You got double points if they were carrying a mug of tea.

"All the hours," she began quietly, "all the afternoons I've sat in that airing cupboard and nursed your hurts. And you won't even do this one thing for me?" Jodie wiped her tears. "I thought you loved me. *Haaah-ha.*"

"I do."

"No, you don't. You only love what I do for you. You're as bad as the rest of them."

He pressed his thumb knuckle to his twitching eyelid. "Just once?"

She nodded. "Aye. Just once."

"Now, you said. Just. Once." He needed to reiterate it, to have it notarized.

Jodie pushed his hair from his eyes. She let him know it was okay. "Just once."

He spent a long time working up to it, never quite touching her, hoping she would change her mind. Jodie yelled at him. Eventually her brother drew his fist back and with a pained scream he struck her in the stomach. He had pulled it short. The blow didn't even dislodge the air inside her. But now Jodie had the momentum she needed. "Good. Again Mungo. Harder."

"But you said just the once."

"Aye, but you need to hit properly."

He hit her again, harder this time, but he let his wrist roll over the fist.

"Harder."

He hit her again. The gasping was all his, not hers.

"Harder."

He hit her again. She barely moved.

She gritted her teeth. "Please, Mungo. For goodness' sake. For once. Be a man."

He drew his fist back. All was white and red. He swung it into her, and he followed the curve of his fist with all the power in his narrow shoulder. It connected and the wind blew out of her. He hadn't expected what he felt; his hard fist against the tender pillowy-ness of Jodie. Her flesh had easily absorbed it and not resisted. As she bent double, he found himself marvelling at her; a woman's superior design, able to take the blows and reward them with a feeling of warmth and protection. It wasn't like when you punched a man. On the rare occasion he dared to retaliate against Hamish, Hamish's very fibre reached back out with bone and gristle and muscle to return the pain up Mungo's arm. When you hurt a man, he hurt you back.

He had a picture of Mrs Campbell then and he hated himself.

When she regained her breathing Jodie composed herself. She took Mungo in her arms. All the colour had drained from his face; even the tic, starved of blood, lay motionless. It was her with the bruised gut, yet she was comforting him again. As in everything in life, he couldn't be there for her. They both thought it but neither said it. *Useless.*

"Thank you, Mungo." She coddled him.

"Shall I heat some of Mrs Campbell's broth and we can have a wee cuddle? *Scooby-Doo* will be on in a minute."

In the end it didn't work, but Jodie didn't tell Mungo that. It was better they didn't talk about it again. She had asked for violence out of a gentle soul and it made her feel like she had trampled a patch of fresh snow.

It didn't work, her belly continued to swell. Poor-Wee-Chickie — always watchful behind his net curtains — noticed the happy girl no longer smiled as she came along the street. He told Mrs Campbell and Mrs Campbell brought Jodie a steak and kidney pie. The following week she did what girls in her day had done, and she took Jodie to see a Romany woman down in the Calton. The never-was baby was gone, and Mungo thought it was all his fault.

FOURTEEN

Mungo lay flat upon the earth. After the men had used him, he neither slept nor moved. He thought if he played dead, he could invite death to take him away. Several times he tried denying his own breath, not with a puffed-out chest, hoarding oxygen, in the way Jodie had taught him for swimming, but on the edge of his exhale he simply stopped breathing and refused to take more air inside of him. It never worked. His body was a treacherous thing.

The sun rose early. The rain had ceased but it left the air thick and moist to the touch. As the sun came overhead it illuminated the red tent and everything was bathed in a furious cherry glow. Gallowgate had not bothered to close the zipper when he left, but he had wiped Mungo almost tenderly and raised the football shorts back around his waist. Although the tent flaps blew loose, the air was stifling and hard to breathe. It stunk like sweated whisky, like blood and watery shit. Fat horseflies were landing on the nylon siding and fucking each other, inches from his face.

Mungo could tell he had a black eye; the slightest touch from his fingers made him recoil in pain. He hesitated before he searched the length of himself. There was a gash on his chin where the zipper on the sleeping bag had caught him and then the waterproof matting had rubbed it open. His ribs were tender and the hair at the top of his head sang where Gallowgate had gripped it and pinned him down. His legs felt wet and sticky with his own blood, and his own shit, and other things that were not his own. But the worst of the pain was deep inside him. Somewhere above his stomach and below his heart. He tried to search it with his fingers, but he couldn't get at it, and it grew.

There were no voices outside the red tent. All he could hear was the gentle lapping of the water and the lazy buzz of clegg flies. He needed to go to the lochside, to lower himself into the numbing water and wash it all away. He wanted to sink beneath the surface and never come up again.

Mungo rolled over. There was another sensation, a new feeling; like he needed to sit on a toilet and evacuate himself entirely. Mungo removed his sock. He used it to wipe the worst of the mess from his bare legs. Then he crawled out of the tent.

The men were sitting at the dead campfire in silence. The bars of toddler's chocolate sat on a rock, like a rabbit trap.

"Oh. What time do you call this?" St Christopher was looking Mungo straight in the eye, a face free from remorse. Mungo didn't want to, but he dropped his gaze to the ground. He wanted to look at the man in the face, make him drop his eyes, but found he couldn't. "Ah thought mibbe ye were gonnae sleep the whole day away. What a waste. We've got trout to catch."

Gallowgate had his back to the boy. He didn't say a word. St Christopher came closer, he squinted at the boy and considered his bruises. "Dear God, that's a fuckin' shiner ye've got there. Did we get that loaded?" There was an odd tone of pride in his voice. He seemed to be innocently enjoying the thought that they had become rowdy, and Mungo wondered what, if anything, the auld lush remembered. "Fuck me. Ah must've tain a bad blackout. When ah've got a drink in me, ah could start a fight in an empty coffin."

Mungo backed away without turning his

back on them. He was inching towards the tree line, back to the cool quiet place where he had felt unfettered and free the day before.

"Where are ye going?" asked St Christopher. "Ye've no touched yer pot noodle."

"I just need to —" Mungo gulped painfully — "to use the toilet." The sound that escaped his lips was hoarse, it lacked power. He touched his swollen throat.

Gallowgate was gutting a small perch. He turned slightly and watched Mungo recede into the canopy of trees. He spoke to the boy over the blade of his shoulder. "Dinnae go far, Mungo. Bad things happen to wee boys in dark forests."

Mungo went deep into the forest. He ran and ran till he came to his rushing river. He crouched in some tall ferns and let his body empty itself. It stung as it poured out of him, and he knew he was split. When he was finished, he took off all of his clothes and stepped into the torrent. Fresh violet bruises were rushing to meet the old blue bruises he had brought from Glasgow. Yesterday the frigid water had made him recoil and shriek. Now he plunged his whole body underneath the surface, and he could barely feel the cold for the scalding inside him. He searched the riverbed and found a porous stone. He scrubbed himself with it, dragging it like a pumice all over his skin, till he was pink and chilled and stinging from the roughness. It was no good. He felt filthy. He vomited then, big arching torrents of yellow and puce. He watched it float downstream to the loch.

"It was only a wee game," said Gallowgate. "It just got a little bit out of hand, that's all."

The man was leaning against a beech tree, near to Mungo's discarded clothes. He was smoking and digging the dirt out from under his thumbnail with the gutting knife. The blade caught one of the few rays that snuck through the canopy and glinted menacingly.

Mungo's bottom lip started to tremble. He pinched it, pushed his nail into it until it was steadied. "It wasn't a game to me."

"Ah, c'mon. You know what boys are like. Everybody does something lit this. It's all part of growin' up. It's easier than getting a lassie in bother."

Mungo was angry at himself. He couldn't look the man in the face and found himself talking to the river's surface. The raspy voice didn't sound like his own. *Just you wait. Wait till I tell my big brother what you did. He will fuckin' kill you. He has a tomahawk* and he'll split your stinkin' skull with it."

Gallowgate knew nothing about the legend of Ha-Ha. He chuckled as he fussed with his neat fringe. "Be a shame to ruin a guid haircut."

Mungo launched his pumice stone, but Gallowgate was too quick for him and dodged it. It clattered off a tree trunk and skittered through the ferns. The understorey swallowed all sound. They were alone again. Gallowgate folded his blade and tucked it away. "Look, it's possible that I went too far. But are ye sure you didnae enjoy it?" He was grinning now, small sharp teeth. "Even jist a wee bit?"

Mungo shook his head slowly. "No."

The man sucked in through his teeth. "Fuck, then I'm *really* sorry, pal." Gallowgate considered it for a moment, he even seemed a little remorseful. "But ah'm surprised to hear that. Specially after what Mo-Maw telt us about ye."

There was no blood at all left inside him, yet every inch of him felt bloated with a blistering rage. He blanched and flushed at the same time. "Whatever they say I've done — it was never anything like that."

"Z'at so?" Gallowgate looked contrite for a second, but the sharp point of his incisors stuck on his bottom lip and he became an animal again. "But that's no what ah've heard. It's the whole reason ye were sent away wi' us. To sort you out. To make a man out of ye."

"This is how ye make a man out of me?"

"Naw. S'pose not," he said. "But we're doing this out of the kindness of our hearts, taking a wee waif to gawk at the heathery hillside. So don't be ungrateful. Don't be so fuckin' stingy wi' the favours next time." Gallowgate picked up the boy's under-clothes, his T-shirt and boxer shorts. "In Barlinnie ye weren't allowed to wear yer own clothes. Ye were never given the same pair of underwear twice and by God, they never, ever fit right. Even when they had been washed ye could still smell some other fella on them, still feel the hundred fellas that had worn them afore you." He ran the grey cotton between his fingers, then he pitched Mungo's underwear into the river. "Ye should wash them. We cannae be carryin' on like pure animals."

Mungo had to flounder downstream to catch the discarded clothes. He regarded them, familiar things he had worn a thousand times and wondered who they belonged to now.

Gallowgate had become bored watching the boy flail around. He was irritable in his sobriety. "Anyhows, hurry up with that. Auld Chrissy is still gonnae show ye how to catch trout. It'll be a laugh if nothin' else." Turning back towards the campsite he stopped short and flicked his cigarette dout towards Mungo. "And jist in case ye take a funny notion, ye cannae tell anybody about what happened. Not yer mammy, not yer brother. Ye'll never be a proper man if they knew whit ye did and how much ye liked it."

"I did not like it." He spoke as clearly as he could manage.

"Really?"

It was then that something changed for Mungo. This was not something your mammy could kiss away. It was not a bully that your brother could chib with a blade. Nobody could make a pot of soup for it. The shame and the guilt were his to bear. Mungo knew Gallowgate was right. He couldn't tell anyone.

"Besides," said Gallowgate as he disappeared into the ferns, "everybody knows ye're a dirty wee poofter. A filthy little bender. It'd be yer word against mine."

Then he realized the men would do it again.

By the time he arrived back at the campsite

Gallowgate was emptying Mungo's back-pack, making it ready for a run to the village shop. Mungo watched him dump his sketchbook and the board game out on the shingles. These were things that belonged to a wee boy. Things that no longer felt like his own. It could all sink into the loch for all he cared.

Gallowgate had taken a survey of the leftover alcohol. When he saw it was only the dregs of whisky and a few cans, a panic had arisen in the men. They were circling and roaring, turning out every pocket. Everyone at the campsite had an empty stomach, but it wasn't until Gallowgate realized they would also have dry throats that he decided on another run to the shop.

Mungo saw his chance. "I could help you carry the drink," he said, trying to sound as casual as he could manage. If only he could go to the post office, he could ask the teuchter woman where they were. He could telephone Mo-Maw again and she could telephone Hamish, and then Hamish would come with his shipbuilder's tomahawk and chop these men to pieces. Mungo needed to get back to the little post office.

Gallowgate saw Mungo's wounded smile and laughed to himself. "Mungo. Ye cannae kid a kidder. Ye are not going to any shop wi' a face like that."

"How?" Mungo raised a hand to his tender eye. The socket was swollen and the eye was closing over. He was having some difficulty with his peripheral vision but his tic had been beaten into submission, the flesh too tender and damaged to misbehave.

"Never you mind *how.*" Gallowgate swung the empty bag on to his back. "That auld teuchter cunt already thinks we're pure scum. If she sees the face on you, she'll phone the polis and we'll get the jail for fightin'. Naw. You stay here. Make sure that idiot doesnae drown himself." Gallowgate turned and walked away from them. He stopped on the edge of the ferns and said, "Don't wander off. Don't try anything daft. It's yer word against mine, and yer family already knows what you're like." Then he disappeared into the trees.

Mungo slumped on a lichen-covered rock. He could walk, he could run, but in which direction? He wondered what Mo-Maw had told Gallowgate, he wondered what would make his family take this stranger's word against his own. As his face burned and his guts throbbed with pain, he pulled his knees up to his chest and rested his good eye on his kneecap. He suddenly felt alone again, not in the magical way he had yesterday, but in a way that stripped all the heat from his body. He had a feeling then, a fear that he might never go home, never see Jodie or James again.

"Cheer up, son. It might never happen."

He found himself watching St Christopher gouge tiny minnows with the hook and drop them into the loch. His nervous nature meant that he barely left the rods alone long enough for any fish to come near them. The man was hunched and searching for prey, his face too close to the surface. "Fuck it! There's no one single fish in this whole scunner of a loch." He was complaining to no one in particular. "Ah used to fish the Cart River every Saturday wi' ma faither. We used to take home big buckets full of perch, stinking wriggling fat buggers they were. We'd catch that many ma da would send me door to door, practically givin' them away." The man took off his bunnet and scratched at his bald head. "This loch must be fuckin' broken."

It would be a long time till Gallowgate would return and Mungo couldn't listen to this moaning. He thought to send the man away from him; it would give him a chance to think about what he should do next. "There's a river over there. It's teeming with some kind of fat fish." He held his hands shoulder width apart.

St Christopher's eyes grew wide. "That's where the buggers are hiding." He reeled in his line. "Show us, eh?"

It took longer to lead St Christopher through the forest than it had to explore alone. The man couldn't climb over fallen tree limbs, he had to stop, sit down on the tree, and then swing his legs over one by one. It was odd to see this man in his old working suit stumble through the thick carpet of ferns. Every now and then his fish hook would get caught on a branch or a leaf and Mungo would have to pick it out for him. The third or fourth time it happened Mungo studied the man's face for a long while as his dextrous fingers worked the knotted fish gut. Under the dappled canopy, the sunlight refracted off the man's eyes and they had a filminess to them Mungo had not noticed before.

Mungo knew now why the man lowered his face so close to the water, why he slipped on every single rock. His eyes were dying. St Christopher could hardly see.

As he followed Mungo to the river he talked non-stop. Mungo wasn't listening and didn't stop to consider the quiet magic of the dell. It had been ruined for him. Now he kicked the heads off fat bluebells and ran his hand spitefully up the fern stems, stripping them of all their fronds and leaving them to die.

They came to the river and found a spot where it was deepest. There was a widening where Mungo could see lazy fish eat skimming bugs. He pointed at the fish and watched St Christopher follow the arc of his arm. But the boy knew he couldn't see the fish for himself, not anymore. The man cast his rod downstream and secured it between two boulders. He took out a cigarette and lit it, then he thrust his hands in his pockets and waited like he was at a bus stop.

Mungo waded across the river. He wanted to be far from the stink of the man. He had been damp since that first rainfall, but this water did something for him; it distracted from the stinging in his face, and from the low throb that was now spreading across his ribcage. If you forged slowly, the footing was good, there was only one boulder that was unbalanced. Mungo felt it teeter under his weight and he quickly adjusted himself, careful not to topple over into the current. It was childish, but he made up his mind not to tell St Christopher about it.

On the far side there was a fallen log sitting in the wet mud. When Mungo stood on

it the ground let out a wet fart. He rocked
on it for a while, pressing and releasing the
sinking wood while he dreamt of bolting
into the understorey, wondering how fast he
could run through the ferns.

"It's no fuckin' use," said St Christopher
eventually. "None o' these fuckers are biting."

Mungo could see where the fishing line
bounced in the current. The man had
missed the place he had pointed to and the
coloured weight was bobbing too violently
in the eddy. "Why did you do it?" Mungo
asked.

"Ah thought that's where ye pointed."

"No. That's not what I meant. I meant
why did you do that to me last night."

St Christopher was only a short distance
away, the river being only twenty feet wide
at this point. Still, Mungo could tell the
man was not looking directly at him; he
thought he was, but he was not. "Have ye
never been a Boy Scout?"

Mo-Maw had never been able to afford
the uniform; what use were knot-tying and
astronomy badges on the streets of the East
End?

"Well, they're aw at it. It's what us boys
do when we're alone. A bit of fun. 'Asides,
it's like a tradition to some folk. You're jist

no supposed to mention it when you're poor, but when ye're rich, haw, haw, *haw*. It's what all they posh boys do the gether. Oxford is full of it. Aw they boarding schools. They all love a bit o' casual buggering down there." St Christopher took out the toddler's chocolate and held it out to Mungo.

Mungo wondered how many times St Christopher had told that story to boys. It slithered off his tongue so easily. How many times had he held out a chocolate bar to a greetin' wean? It made his head throb.

"You weren't in the jail for vaykri . . ." Mungo stumbled over the word.

"Vagrancy?" offered St Christopher quickly. "Naw. Ah wisnae inside for that."

Nobody said anything after that. The river rushed between them.

Mungo was afraid of Gallowgate. There was a swing to his head that reminded him of a fighting pit bull; there was a ragged muscularity to his body that made him look like he had been whittled with a dull knife without being sanded smooth afterwards. But St Christopher did not frighten him, not anymore. Now he was angry at what he had let the old man get away with. He swallowed once, shouted as loud as he could with his battered throat. "Why don't you take that chocolate and shove it up your arse."

The man laid the chocolate on the river-bank, as though Mungo was a dog he could tempt to inch closer. "Suit yersel. Besides, you should come to enjoy it. It's safer than getting a lassie in bother."

That lie again. Mungo thought of Jodie and her *bother*. He thought of her small, distended belly and he wondered if the man in the caravan had forced that into her.

St Christopher sighed. He scratched at his stubbled cheek and changed the subject as though they'd been discussing the weather. "Mungo son, where are these fishes ye promised me?"

Mungo was on the far side of the river. He could have turned then and slid into the tall ferns and been gone, St Christopher would never be able to follow him. But where would he go? For all he knew he was a thousand miles from home. Or the tene-ments could be just on the other side of the Munros.

Above them the leaves sounded the first tap-tap-tap of a heavy rain. Gallowgate would get soaked. Mungo pointed at the school of fish near his feet. They were not brown after all, but an iridescent shimmer of multicoloured scales. "You'll not get

354

them from over there. Your lure will be carried downstream. If you use those big stones you can cross and catch them from here." He turned away, not certain he wouldn't cry again.

He was stripping the heads of some bluebells when he heard St Christopher enter the river. The man let out a prayer as the frigid water knocked the breath out of him. Mungo allowed himself a smile for the man's discomfort. He was intent on macerating the blue petals into a thick paste as he listened to St Christopher push against the current, moaning "Jesus Joanie, Jesus Joanie," over and over. The man was almost at the far shore when the incantation stopped.

St Christopher had found the loose boulder. His leather brogues slipped on the mossy riverbed. The water was only waist-high, but he landed face first into the river and let go of the rod and the bag of fishing supplies. Mungo watched his wool bunnet float away as the man shrieked in fear and pain.

Mungo feared he might drown, and without thinking, he leapt into the water and waded out to him. The man flailed and swallowed a bellyful of water as he struggled to find his damaged footing. "Ma ankle!"

Mungo reached out and hooked him by his lapel. There was no weight to him, he was a sack of marrowless bone. Mungo steadied him in the eddy and using all his strength he hoisted the saint upright.

St Christopher was hacking water, his lungs were weak from years of smoking and sitting and smoking some more. Mungo hauled the man towards him and with his one good foot, St Christopher found his footing, and wrapped his fingers around Mungo's forearms.

There were so many details to consider: the graceless man, how the spears of cold rain made the river feel almost warm, the ruined fishing supplies, so many things to capture Mungo's attention that it was a funny, insignificant detail to fixate on. But Mungo stared. He found himself glowering at the man's hands and the way the long fingers wrapped around his forearms. These fingers that ended in nicotine-yellow pads, with grooved, bark-coloured fingernails; with black hair that sprouted above the knuckles and each knuckle that was as gnarled as a grafted sapling. These were the same fingers that had bound him the night before. The same dirt-caked nails that had pierced the skin at his wrists as the man had stuck his stinking, fetid cock into the warm space between his thighs.

There was a trick Ha-Ha had taught him once. It was a very clever trick. He called it the "Cheerful Friend"; a trick meant to disarm any wide-o or bully who sallied up to him looking to start a fight. Ha-Ha had shown him how he must look at the person square in the eye, with no twitching or signs of aggression in the centre of his brows. Ha-Ha had taught him to look at the person and smile with his mouth *and* his eyes, his widest, brightest smile. It had to be full and generous, the way you would look at a basket of puppies or a sky full of fireworks on Guy Fawkes Night. Then, when the wide-o was wondering why you were smiling like an imbecile, you hooked your right leg behind both their ankles and you pushed as hard as you could into their chest. Then — if you were carrying (and you should always be carrying) — you knifed them.

Water was dripping from the tip of the man's pitted nose. Mungo smiled. It brightened the dimming day.

Mungo hooked St Christopher's good leg, and with his hands on his lapel, he shoved the man backwards under the water. St Christopher let go of his wrists, his arms flayed out, searching for solid ground where there was only water. Mungo held him there and counted to five.

Despite Ha-Ha's lessons, Mungo was a deep well of goodness. He counted to ten and then he hauled the Saint by his lapels again and tugged him from the water. He had only wanted to scare him. He had only wanted him to take his hands off of his body.

St Christopher erupted like a geyser. His lungs burst with river water and he coughed and spat it in Mungo's face. His dull eyes were roving wildly in his head. He was desperate and panicked. *Good,* Mungo thought, *let him be feart.*

The boy opened his mouth to warn him, but St Christopher swung a loose fist at his face and connected with the tender skin under Mungo's bruised eye. The boy let go. He felt the riverbank under his torn backside, and as he spun under the water, the world dropped from view.

When he found his footing, he had a rock in his fist. It was a small rock, only about the size of a Christmas satsuma, but when he swung it, it cracked off St Christopher's temple and the man fell backwards into the water.

Mungo gripped his collar again. He put his knee on the man's chest and pushed with all his might. He shoved until he felt the man come to rest on the riverbed. Then he stood on him. The saint's fingers grabbed for the heavens, but Mungo denied them to him. After that, it didn't take long to drown St Christopher.

FIFTEEN

Gallowgate was quicker without the boy trailing behind him. On the far side of the loch, the clouds hung around the hills as though they were trapped and couldn't find a way out. The loch appeared restless, angry, as the wind hurried down the hillside and raised its hackles. The rain began to fall in sheets and by the time he reached the little shop he was soaked to the bone.

The teuchter woman watched him closely as he dripped up and down the only aisle, filling his arms with tinned ravioli and fruit cocktail. Her limited selection of alcohol made for a poor man's pantry. He was forced to choose a fine whisky that was too expensive for necking and a nooseful of lagers that had a thick coat of stour on the top.

"How much for a smile?" he asked, stalling for time. But the shopkeeper was immune to his charm. She sent him out into the pouring rain and locked the door behind him.

Gallowgate sheltered in the red phone box and squelched down upon the wooden chair. The rain rattled against the glass, but it was mostly dry inside. Taking the phone book, he laid his cigarettes out on the cover like little wounded soldiers. He tried to save them, and he burst the tobacco from the ones that were beyond repair and piled the loose baccy in his pocket. Blowing the stour from the top of a can of lager he took a long, grateful pull.

The sky had come low. The clouds closed completely and the last shafts of sunlight were gone. It would take a long time to stop raining. Gallowgate read the phone book. There were very few names here and what surnames there were repeated over and over. People tended not to move far in this part of the world. He chose a name at random and turned a coin in his hand. There wasn't much money left; they had gotten through more alcohol than he had budgeted for and when he counted his change, he realized he didn't have enough to get them all safely back to Glasgow on the bus. He thought about Mungo and wondered if that was a good idea anyway, to take the boy back to the city where he could tell his side of the story.

It happened all the time. Young boys from the city drowning in lochs, the water deeper and murkier than any chlorinated swimming pool. The evening paper was full of stories of inexperienced young men freezing to death on hillsides or caving their heads in on a steep Munro. It would be believable. It happened all the time.

Gallowgate pushed the coin into the slot. He dialled the number and waited. He was about to ring off when a faint voice answered at the far end.

"Hallo, is that Mrs E. Beaton?"

The woman sounded winded, like she had travelled a long way to reach the telephone. Perhaps it was another phone box that sat in the middle of a cluster of cottages, perhaps she had been in a hot bath. "It's Dokter Procter from the hospital. Ye know, the *big* hospital."

"What hospital, Doctor? I've never even been to any hospital."

"The biiiig hospital. The wan through in Edinburgh. Well, we got your test results back, *aye,* your GP sent us yer case notes. *Dr Deacon,* that's right. Well he sent us yer notes to take a look at and ah'm afraid we'll need to take both of them."

"Both of what?" said the woman. "I only

went to see auld Deacon about my cough."

Gallowgate was drawing flowers in the condensation. "That's the thing now, Mrs Beaton. We need to amputate both of yer legs in order to make your cough better. It's all connected see. Don't cry now. We could try and save them from the knee down but the surgeon couldnae say for sure till he had a look at ye himself." The phone rang its three pips and the call disconnected. Gallowgate sniggered to himself.

The rain was driving sideways now. The loch disappeared, then the white houses, then the yew tree. Gallowgate flipped through the phone book again. He found a name he liked the sound of and decided to tell its owner that he was their long-lost son. He hoped the woman was old enough, but then everyone up here seemed old; anyone with a spark of life had already left for the city or further south.

When he was in Barlinnie he had passed many an empty hour doing much the same thing. He had nobody of his own to call, so he dialled Glasgow numbers at random and talked to whoever should answer. The people were generally kind, a little confused maybe, but kind. They would go to their window and describe the weather to him in considerable detail. *Rain,* it was mostly always raining, but to hear the different strangers describe the thousand different types of rain gave him a calming pleasure. Some folks would open their *Evening Times* and read him the day's headlines. Occasionally they would forget who they were talking to and would stop halfway through a story about rape or murder and would try instead to find something about local politics. Lonely old men were the best company. These men would tell him about the Old Firm game, running through the match in such meticulous detail that he felt he had been pitch-side at Parkhead for Celtic's victory.

Other times Gallowgate had gotten a wean, a child who was home alone while her mammy ran some messages. Sometimes he got a wee boy and then, nearly always, he hung up immediately.

He was dialling the number and thinking about what this woman's son might be like, when he stopped. He waited for his coins to be returned to him, then he dialled a different number. Something from deep in his memory.

A young girl answered the phone. He could hear the tinny sound of a pop record blaring behind her, and from the tangle of different voices he could tell the house was full of people, and thick with happiness. *"Hallloo-oo,"* she sang.

"Jacqueline, is that you? It's me. It's Angus."

He could practically hear the girl's face harden, the song wiped off of her lips. "What do you want? I thought we telt ye not to phone here again."

"Ah know. Ah'm out though, ah'm on the outside and ah'm getting help. Ah'm getting better."

"Outside. Outside where? Where are you, Gus?" There was a tinge of panic in her voice. He could imagine her looking around herself like he might step out of the hallway cupboard or from behind the settee.

"Ah'm up north, ah've gone away for a fishin' weekend with a couple of the lads. Ah just remembered what day it was and ah thought ah should phone." He took a slug of the dusty lager. "Ah'm no drinkin' anymore, Jax. Ah'm past all that. So, can ah speak to Mammy?"

Jacqueline didn't answer. He heard her put the receiver gently on the table and talk to a person in the other room. There was a succession of doors closing and the pop record grew faint. There was a familiar voice on the other end. "Angus? What do you want?"

"Hallo, Mammy." He pumped more coins into the phone. "Ah just wanted to phone ye."

"Okay. Is that it?"

Gallowgate wondered what she looked like now.

He could picture his mother in happier times; a time when she had rented a cream and claret caravan down on the Saltcoats coast for the Fair Fortnight. She had taken the three of them away on the train, Angus, Jacqueline, and young Evan. The rain had fallen in solid curtains all that week. She had spent the first afternoon crying and staring out of the caravan window as the rain hammered a maddening drumbeat on the tin roof. He knew how hard she had worked to afford the week away. She had put money aside the whole year, saving what she could from her job cleaning the local school.

While the weans had jumped on the banquette she had left the caravan and gone down to the beach. She came back with buckets full of gritty, wet sand and upended them until there was a sandpit on the linoleum floor. All afternoon she went back and forth in the pouring rain bringing sand back to the caravan for her children. Gallowgate could not remember a happier time than the four of them sheltered from the rain and playing on their private beach. The steam rising from his damp mother as she knelt before the gas fire.

There was not a sliver of that warmth in her voice now. "I asked you to stop phoning here."

"Ah know. Ah wanted to tell ye ah was out of prison, Mammy. That ah was working at it."

"So I had heard."

He was rubbing his thumb against the mouthpiece. "Ah've got myself a wee job. Nothing fancy. Just laying underlay for a carpet fitters out on the Royston Road." He waited for her to say something, but she didn't say anything. "Ah've been going to AA meetings in the evenings. Ah'm trying my best to stay away from the drink."

"Where are you phoning me from?" He heard the same worry in her voice that had clouded his sister's.

"It's awright," he said. "Ah'm nowhere near the house. Ah'm away fishin'."

He had expected her to find a calming ordinariness in this. He was far away from the Gallowgate housing scheme. He could not be a bother to her. But instead of being calmed, her voice pitched and went up in tone. "Who are you fishing with?"

"Naebody special. Just an auld guy ah know from some of the AA meetings."

She must have moved her mouth close to the receiver because her next words had a muffled quality to them. *"Angus. Are there children there with you?"*

"No. I know the rules."

Gallowgate was a born liar. He had learned the skill when he was young, and he had found no better way to make the things he wanted come to him: sympathy, chocolate eggs, an afternoon off school, new Diadora football boots, or a look at the private place on the wee boy next door. For a time there was almost nothing he couldn't lie his way into. It had started insidiously enough but by the time he was sent down to Barlinnie it had become more than a grease to ease his way in life and was now a facet of his nature. Gallowgate was a born liar; his mother had learned that the hard way.

"Dear God," she whispered. "Angus, please don't hurt the boy."

He didn't know when she had stopped loving him, but he wanted to find out and go back to a time before it. She had accepted the real truth about his nature now. She had taken Evan's side, believed his brother's stories, and then she had called the police. Now, as Gallowgate let the last of the pennies die, he knew the four of them would never sit in a sandpit in a cream and claret caravan on the Saltcoats coast again.

The telephone let out three quick pips. Gallowgate savoured the last of his mother's sighs. There was a rasp at the bottom of her breath now, a sandpapery sound that said it was too late to stop smoking.

SIXTEEN

Mungo sauntered through the doocot grass. He stopped now and again, and pretended to be interested in something at his feet. He went unnoticed and for every minute that passed, he inched closer to the structure, until he was so near he could no longer pretend he was just casually strolling by. James was inside, hunched over a cage of brown doos. He was pouring medicine down a bird's throat, whispering to it as he squirted a syringe into its gullet. Everything around him was dim, drab, except for him and the fledgling, illuminated from the skylight above. He looked like an oil painting, as though the heavens were smiling down upon him. His hair shone like a crown spun from pulled sugar.

Mungo slouched against the door frame, he laid his cheek against the painted wood. "A woman I know was almost murdered by her husband."

James didn't flinch, he didn't jump at the voice. Mungo knew then that he had seen him orbiting the doocot and had not bothered to reach out.

Mungo searched around for something, anything, to talk about. In the corner, under the lowest bench, lay two piles of roofing slate. Mungo used them to pry open a conversation. "Did you buy roof tiles?"

James glanced at the slate. "Naw," he said, and that seemed the death of it. Mungo felt his fibre push away from the door frame. It seemed clear that their friendship was over, and it was time for him to go. Then James spoke again. "There was a couple leaning against the door one night. The next night there was a couple mair. They're dead heavy. It's the strangest thing."

"Just like that?" Mungo knew it was not just like that. He knew Poor-Wee-Chickie would have worked hard to bring the slate to the boy. It would have taken several nighttime trips to deliver the tiles, his shopping trolley squeaking in the dark, a nervous Natalie pulling on her leash and the pair of them staying to the shadows.

James handed Mungo a Manila envelope. Inside were countless slate nails, a tile punch, and a precise technical drawing of where to put the nails through the tiles.

Mungo unfolded the foolscap, it was drawn in a neat hand but it was unsigned. "Jeez-o. A slate roof. You'll have the nicest gaff on the scheme."

"Aye." But he didn't look happy about it. He could still not look Mungo in the eye.

Mungo understood that feeling of shyness and shame, and he felt a tenderness for James. "Look, if we plumb this doocot you could get forty-five pound a week for it. It's practically two floors. You could get a single mother, six weans, and four pit bulls in here, easy."

James didn't seem to be in a mood for jokes. He turned his back to him again, hunched over the doo, picking sawdust and shite out from between its claws. It seemed like he wanted to be alone.

Mungo turned to leave before his face started to sputter. "Listen, I don't know what I did, James. But I'm sorry. I really am." He scuffed his shoe, there was a crunch of rat glass underfoot. All Mungo had done was comfort his friend when he had been grieving his mother. There had been nothing dirty about it, but everything felt wrong.

"Don't be stupit." The light from the doo trap cast hard shadows across James's face. It made his ears stick out more.

"I'm not funny, if that's what you are thinking. It was only a hug. I didn't mean anything by it."

"I know." James sealed the envelope of nails and tossed it to the side. "You've been picking your lip again." He paused, then he added, "Do you want some cake?"

"Cake?"

James nodded into the corner. There was a white box on the bench. Mungo lifted the lid and inside was a Victoria sponge with whipped cream oozing from between its golden layers. There was a decorative teddy bear, and edible letters where someone had misspelt *Birtday Boy*. Mungo stared at it for a long time. He felt rotten. "Do you have a bike?"

"How? Did ye get me one?"

"James, I didn't know it was your birthd—"

"I'm only joking. Aye, I have a bike."

"Then let's just go somewhere."

"Where?"

"I don't know. Somewhere nice. Somewhere we've never been."

"But where?"

Mungo shrugged. He extended his arm and held out his index finger, he spun slowly. "Say when."

It was the first smile James had given him

that day. It was small and it was crooked but it gave off more brightness than the doocot skylight above them. "Ye're a fuckin' eejit." He watched Mungo spin for several revolutions. "Awright, awright. Stop."

Mungo stopped. His arm was pointing eastward. It was as good a direction as any.

They filled James's schoolbag with cans of sugary ginger and the white cake. Using a wheezy football pump, they reinflated the wheels of Mr Jamieson's Rattray. The bike was rusted from disuse and the rubber handles had worn away with sweat, leaving Mungo's hands black and sticky from just wheeling it out of the close. The white frame had been patterned with alternating stripes of gold and green plumber's tape. *Proud to be a Fenian.* James sensed Mungo's reticence to climb on to the narrow seat. "But it's been blessed by the Pope himself."

"It's a bit much. I'll get fuckin' stabbed."

James pedalled the old Rattray racer and Mungo sat pillion behind him. He held his body rigid and touched James's waist only slightly. James hunched forward and bobbed up and down, working hard to propel them both forward, pumping the pedals like a shire horse. At first, they glided up and down the familiar streets. They passed the same faces they saw every day, and Mungo alternated between fearing that James would stop pedalling and want to go home or that they would corner into Ha-Ha's crew and he would be beaten to death for riding behind a boy on a bike bright with Celtic colours.

"You're not doing it right. You *have* to go in the direction you chose. That's the only rule."

James huffed but he turned the bike eastward and when a street tilted the wrong angle, they took the next left, and kept cycling away from the afternoon sun. Several times James looked like he wanted to give up. At first the streets seemed to be getting worse. They passed tight-packed tenements that were heavy with a sense of lack and need. They rode between rows of bombed-out flats where all the windows were boarded up with protective covering. When James faltered Mungo dug his hands into his side. "Keep going, keep going, keep going." There had to be more.

Eventually the city started to expand as if it was breathing, the houses started to spread apart, and there was more sky than sandstone. The council houses changed to a four-in-a-block formation, but the small gardens were mostly untended and riddled with weeds. When they dead-ended into Barlinnie Prison, Mungo almost admitted defeat. James was panting from the hill, and they stood and stared at the barbed-wired monolith, massive and forbidding as a Victorian workhouse.

"My uncle, Paddy Grant, is inside for aggravated assault," said James.

"Mo McConnachie's there," said Mungo, "and Joe McConnachie as well." Everyone knew someone on the inside of Barlinnie.

Was this all there was? Was this what was at the end of the road, as far as their legs could carry them? Mungo could feel all enthusiasm ebb from his friend. He switched places with James, forcing the larger boy to slide back on the narrow seat. "Let me pedal for ten minutes more. If we don't see anywhere nice then I'll pedal all the way home. Okay?"

"Aye, okay."

They rode on, but slower now, heavier of heart. They debated whether to cross a bridge over the roaring motorway. Mungo had a distrust of bridges; it was only an overpass that separated the Protestant Billies from the Catholic Bhoyston. On the far side he could see another housing scheme, but beyond that was a low line of trees, and there were no tower blocks, nor gasworks, to spoil the horizon.

They rode to the line of trees and were delighted when they opened on to some grassy slopes. There was a golf course to one side, where plump middle-aged men looked as cheerful as bonbons in their pastel jumpers. Beyond this lay a large pond almost like a small lochan. The pond itself was choked with algae and filmy as a cataract, but pretty swans glided over the green surface. It was peaceful. It was theirs alone.

"See. Telt ye. Happy birthday."

James cuffed him in the side, "Jammy bugger," but he was smiling.

Mungo wove the bike along a path, cycling in great lazy circles, and tried to dip low enough that James would fall off. They spent time laughing and dragging each other to the water's edge and trying to pitch the other man into the swan scum. When the swans grew tired of them and floated away, the boys climbed a low berm and Mungo pushed the old racer through the long grass till dew glistened on all the spokes. From the top of the hill they could see the dense, grey city to the left of them; to the other side were new houses, half-built and generously spaced, made of bright orange brick, for families with cars and good-paying jobs.

James opened the box. The cake was flattened and the letters had bled into the sponge. It didn't matter. They shovelled sticky handfuls of it into their mouths, lay back on the grass, and let the warm cream choke them. James had a hidden quarter-bottle of Famous Grouse in his anorak pocket. He took a long slug and passed it to Mungo. "Put some hairs on yer baws. Go on. They cannae arrest us for drunk-pedalling an auld racer."

He only swallowed a dribble. Drink scared him but he didn't let James see that. The whisky tickled on the way down, but under the low clouds and on the fresh grass he liked how it tasted like woodsmoke and peat. It was like bonfire night, before they put old bike tyres on the flames, before Ha-Ha buried cans of hairspray and watched them whine and explode.

James took out a packet of crumpled cigarettes. "Watch this." He turned his head from Mungo, and when he turned back, he had four cigarettes in his mouth, each stuck between a different gap in his teeth. He grinned and rolled his eyes.

"Ye're a bam," laughed Mungo. "Honestly. I can't believe what a moody basturt you are. Laughing like an eejit. Two hours ago I thought you'd jump off the roof of that doo-cot."

"Well, ye've cheered us up."

James lit a cigarette and offered it to Mungo, but he shook his head. Anyone who had seen Mo-Maw hacking in the morning, ash-fingered and raking through the douts, would never smoke. He could hear Jodie's voice in his head. Jodie, the hypocrite, who had already done something much, much worse than smoking.

James frowned at him. "What's wrong with you now?"

Mungo hadn't realized his face was knotted. "See at your school, do the Catholic teachers try and shag the students?"

"Naw. Don't be daft. There was a Father Peter that taught fitba that we called Father Paedo but that was it. He stood in the corner and *monitored* us when we were in the changing rooms. But I just took it as him being a cunt." James blew smoke rings into the air. The boys watched them float down to the pond. "How? Are the Proddy teachers trying to touch yer ring?"

"No, not mine," said Mungo. "But I'd let them if it meant I never had to study Maths again."

"*Oh. Shove it in, sir. Just a wee fraction more!*" James laughed. They watched pensioners take slow laps around the pond. "I don't mind Maths. It's the languages that I can't stick. Priests fuckin' love their Latin."

"Do you have to go to chapel all the time?"

"No, but we pray most mornings at school."

Mungo thought about it for a while. They had weekly assembly in the Protestant school, and they were expected to recite the Lord's Prayer at lunchtime. So, what was it about Catholics that made them so different? What was it he was supposed to hate in them? "How do ye remember all the dance moves?"

"The rituals? Och, they teach ye all the moves when yer a wean. Ye just know after that. Catholics aren't all that big on freestyle, ye know." James made the sign of the cross. "At least it's just school. At home we don't go to chapel on a Sunday anymore. Not since my mammy died. Ma da doesnae like to get all dressed up to sit in the pew. He says it's like good china without a working teapot."

"What a poet. He's the next Rabbie Burns." James's eyes were bright under his flaxen hair. He seemed less like the sullen boy from the doocot. Mungo was sure James was happy again, and that he could take a teasing. Mungo put his hand on his hip, he did a fey half-dip and said, "Besides, you're the teapot. You big bender."

Something flickered between them. He had misjudged. He had gone too far. For a second he thought the shutters would come down over James's eyes again, that the bright eyes would fall back to the ground. He regretted having said it. Then James took a last draw of his cigarette. "Teapot? Aye. Well. Takes one to know one, eh."

It was what they didn't say next that made Mungo nervous. James didn't break his stare and he didn't say anything. His grin widened slightly and with each millimetre it grew, Mungo's smile widened to meet it. They sat like that, just grinning until their faces hurt.

"You look like your da," said Mungo eventually.

"Fuck ye, I don't."

"You do. You're friendlier looking. When you want to be." He picked at the grass. "You should try not to be so heavy sad all the time."

James reached up and pushed Mungo's hair out of his eyes. It was so quick it almost didn't happen. His hand was furtive and fleeting, like a darting doo.

A fissure Mungo hadn't known about cracked open in his chest; beneath it was a hollow feeling that had never bothered him before. It was an agony not to raise his own hand and touch the hairs James's fingers had licked. It burned. He wanted nothing more than to feel the warmth left by his touch. He closed his eyes and said, "I feel sick."

It was as though a sky full of clouds passed over James's face, it was rain and it was fear. Mungo saw the change. It made him look up. They had been sitting close together on the berm but sending clumsy semaphores like it was the Clyde Valley that divided them. James leaned across the distance and placed a kiss on his lips. It was dry and his teeth scraped Mungo's bottom lip. They bumped heads.

Mungo rubbed his forehead. "Did you just headbutt me?"

"We could pretend it was a headbutt if you like?" The smile was fleeing his lips again.

"Don't be daft." Mungo looked both up and down the hill, and then he kissed James quickly on the lips. It was like hot buttered toast when you were starving. It was that good.

They had buried James's mother at Lambhill on a blowy spring day, when the wind stripped all the blossoms from the trees, and the white petals clung to the black mourning cars.

After the funeral, his father had spent his time helping James build the doocot. The whole thing had been his father's idea; pigeons were a good, manly pursuit that would teach James discipline and how to care for something smaller than himself. Besides, if they kept busy building something together, then they didn't have to talk about his mother.

His father missed three work rotations. He stayed away from the rigs as long as he could. His father had promised, "Listen, if ye spend an hour at the doocot every day, I'll be back in no time at all." Then he packed his rig bag and left James to an empty house and all the tears they could never have shed together.

James lay on his bed in a motherless house. The bed sheets were clean but they smelled sour. His father had left them too long on the clothes pulley and it had not occurred to him to turn and air them as they dried. It was these small things that made James feel heaviest. Small things his mammy would just have known to do.

He had done as his father advised. After school he had gone to the doocot and returned before it was dark. He had played with himself and then he had fed himself, and then played with himself some more. Once the fleeting sense of euphoria had ebbed from his body he was left with the stillness of another empty evening. He turned on the wireless in the kitchen and the television in the living room and then he lay on his bed and wondered if he was being punished for something.

He tried to push away the pictures that came into his mind, but they wouldn't leave. They had started in the New Year, when the Catholic boys were put out on the North Field and played shinty with tartan-blue legs. The rain and the wind flayed anyone who would not keep moving in the smirr. They pulled their socks up to try and reach their short hems but Father Strachan shouted at them to stop making such a pitiful show of themselves. "If you are cold," he yelled above the high collar of his long-sleeved fleece, "then run faster."

After battering each other with caman sticks for ninety minutes, the boys were grateful for the lukewarm showers, water that was barely warm enough to return the feeling to their toes and wash the red clay from their legs. James stood under the end jet. He crammed his blue fingers inside his mouth. He tried not to look at Paddy Creek, with his lazy smile and broad, muscular shoulders. He tried to not watch the stream of shampoo as it trickled down his back, and ran between his buttocks. Like the stubborn oose you pick from an acrylic jumper, some unseen static kept pulling his gaze back to the boy. James turned away. He knew if they caught him staring they would have a hundred names for him before he had a name for himself.

James dangled his leg off the edge of his narrow bed. He reached overhead and took the newspaper out from the space between the headboard and the wall. Fetching the cream-coloured telephone through to his bedroom he dialled the number he found in the back of the paper. He could have rung it by heart. He dialled it partially three times before his fingers found the courage and committed to dialling the whole thing. There was a mechanical click and a tinny recording welcoming him to the party line.

A place where boys like you can meet boys like you.

He couldn't tell how many men were on the line, but there were many voices in the dark. Some were like his, the heavy Glaswegian glottal, but others came from faraway parts of Scotland, with sing-song or refined voices, well-educated or shamed into sounding their vowels properly. They were talking and they were laughing. He listened to them talk about music, and the bars they liked and pubs they sometimes went to, where they could meet, places where landlords were more tolerant and would let them enjoy a pint in peace. Some older men came on and were fishing harder than the others. They would ask bluntly for what they wanted, words James didn't know the meaning of but liked the sound of. Sometimes the men would find the thing they were hunting for and the two of them would agree to meet and click through to a private, more expensive line.

Usually James didn't say much. It was comforting just to listen. Tonight, he could tell that some of the men were already touching themselves. The first time he had called, it was enough to shock him, to clamp his hand over the receiver and giggle nervously. But he got used to that rhythmic paddling sound; the way the receiver was cupped between their chin and chest, how they breathed hard and shallow through flared nostrils as they used their hands for other, dirtier things. It would start easily — or it would have already started by the time he rang on — a man (it was always an older-sounding man) would ask someone to describe himself and that someone would. The younger man would tell them all about the map of his body, the colour of his skin, the way his hair created a peach fuzz across his stomach and under the hard muscles of his arse.

"A swimmer's body, not very muscular like, but lean, you know?" the Dundonian was saying.

"I like that," panted the Perthshire farmer. "How many fingers can you fit inside?"

They would be gathered together, a semi-circle of strangers, and as they listened to the young man, they would hope that the beautiful things he said about himself were true.

The farmer spent his mess. Some lines went dead, some new sounds added to the crackle. There was another voice in the background, a melodic, light voice, the voice James had come to listen for in the crowd. *Hah-llo,* it said. "Is there anybody out *theeere?*"

"Fraser, is that you?" asked James.

"Oh, guid." The cheerful sound of a Gaelic speaker, turning himself to English. "I was hoping you were on here, Tonalt."

James had lied when they had asked him his name. *Donald,* he had said, or in reality it sounded like *D-awnaul-Dh,* heavy with a flat Glaswegian *D.* He much preferred the way Fraser sang it. *Tonalt.* "I finally listened to that song, Tonalt," Fraser said. "I stayed up half the night until it came on the radio."

"And did you like it?"

"I did," said the boy with real pleasure. His voice sounded gauzy and light, like he was hidden in a wardrobe with the phone cupped close to his lips. "I even taped it, but the cassette is chewy. I think next time we're in Inbhir Nis I'll need to get it on vinyl. But the ol' lade is sick to the teeth of it already. She said I should be saving for headphones first."

James liked how he dropped Gaelic words into his sentences; they stuck out, like half-hammered nails. The boys had once spent an hour laughing over the Gaelic translation of gay slurs; the party line went silent while Fraser presented and then repeated the words: Càm, *càm.* One by one, the disembodied men parroted the word, like an evening class full of study-abroad students. *Fliuch, boireanta,* or James's favourite, the unimaginative conjunction of boy and bum: *Gille-tòiin.*

"I could send a vinyl to you," said James. "If I knew where you lived."

"That's all right, Tonalt. Maybe some

other time." Fraser buffed the offer away, there were ears on here from all over, it would be indiscreet. "My dad and I sailed to Tober Mhoire at the weekend. There was a lost pigeon in the harbour, a gormless, grey thing, and I thought of you."

"He might be mine," laughed James. "I'm no getting the hang of pouting. I've lost more birds than I catch."

Fraser tutted. "Too bad. Just stick in there . . ."

"I'll stick it in ye, son," said a gruff voice. It made James flinch. For a moment he had forgotten they were not alone.

"I'll stick it right up ye."

All afternoon they lay in the long grass and watched the clouds roll down from the Campsie Fells. Mungo was glad they were lying down, for if he had been standing he would not have known what to do with his limbs. Waves of loveliness ebbed over him followed by waves of shame. They came like Jodie alternating the hot and cold taps and trying to balance a bath with him already in it. This time, though, he couldn't pull his legs to his chest and escape it, he would be burned or he would be chilled as it happened. There was no pulling away.

The boys lay a discreet distance apart.

James's pinkie found his and they knotted them together like they had that first night in James's bedroom. "Do you mind?" It was tentative, all politeness and consideration. Constant searching for the next stair in the dark.

"Naw, I don't mind," said Mungo. "James?"

"Aye."

"Does your da not like me?" It had been weighing on him. "What did I ever do to him?"

"Nothing. 'Asides, it's me he hates. No you."

"How can yer own da no like you?"

James rolled on to his elbow. He kept opening his mouth to talk, but each time he swallowed his words and said nothing.

"You can tell us. I'm good at keeping secrets."

Eventually, James told him about the chatline, about the number from the newspaper he had carried with him, ever since he had been unable to stop thinking about Paddy Creek. ". . . The chatline was nothing dirty. Just voices, boys talking to one another about music, about where they liked to buy clothes and stupit things like that. Sometimes you'd get an older man and he would ask you dirty things but mostly it was just young lads talking and having a good time and telling jokes."

James sat up and pulled his knees to his chest. "There was one boy, wee Fraser, he had the funniest accent you ever heard, he'd tell you something dead-dead-sad and you'd have to be careful not to laugh cos it sounded like a mad chirpy bird. I liked him best. His dad had a sheep farm, he used to complain that there was nobody around him but blackface lambs, that he spent whole days just wandering and being by himself. To him it was pure murder, but to me it seemed like he could be himself, all day, and not pretend. I wanted to know what that felt like."

"But how is this about your da?"

James shook his head. "I'm getting to it. But you have to understand that I hardly ever said a word." He wiped the dirt from his palms on to his denims. "Ah didn't know it would cost a fortune, did ah? Honest to God. My da came off the rig and opened all the bills. He called the phone company when I was at school and they told him what the number was for. 'A sex line for men who like men,' they said." James shook his head. "It wasn't *only* that. Honest."

Mungo sat up. He felt Jodie turning on the hot tap over him, and he was up to his neck in shame.

"Ma da knows. He knows what I am." James took a punishing gulp of the whisky. "He hasn't looked at me right since."

James was bigger than him, a whole head taller, a whole year older. There was a dark road and James was on it. Mungo knew he should not follow, if he didn't step on to the road, he could still turn away. James looked at him, and as though he could read his mind, he laid his finger on Mungo's twitching cheek and said, "Don't be lit me Mungo. It's not too late for you."

But it was already too late. It had always been too late. When they were younger, Mungo and Hamish had been playing in the bathroom. They had filled the scalloped sink and they were slamming Action Men together in an underwater battle. Hamish was resting his weight on the lip of the sink, and Mungo couldn't see, so he jumped up and did the same. There had been the tiniest fracture in the porcelain — Mo-Maw had dropped a glass ashtray into it one time — and now the weight of their play breached it and the water poured everywhere. Just before the sink split, Mungo put his hand over the crack and tried to hold back the water — it worked, and then it failed, and he was soaked and bloody from the chipped porcelain. He tried all afternoon, but there was no way to put the crack back together.

Mungo raised himself on his elbows and kissed James. Even more than the others, it felt like his first proper kiss, clumsy and with too much pressure on his lips. He buried the tip of his nose in James's cheek and gasped when he felt the secret warmth of James's tongue. It thrilled him. The tongue tasted sweet like cream and powdered vanilla, and his mouth was hot like burning peat and golden tobacco.

It was James who put his hand on Mungo's chest and pushed him gently away. It was not safe on the hill so near to the prison.

The Rattray lay on its side and James began spinning the front wheel, seeing how fast he could make it turn. "Did she deserve it?" he asked after a long while. "The wee wummin whose husband nearly kilt her?"

Mungo didn't want to think about Mrs Campbell and her purple eye, not now. "No. You cannae deserve a belting lit that."

James put his foot against the tyre, it stopped instantly. "How no? Ask ma da."

"Is he handy with his fists?"

"Naw. He is fast with the back of his hand though. Ye should know he will kill me if he finds out what we just did." James spun the wheel again and laughed. "He'll kill you first though."

There it was again, the road, the path, the turning, the warning. "Naw man. I'm a Hamilton," he said bravely. "I'll shank the Fenian bastard."

James pushed him over. "Yer a dirty Fenian kisser now, ya daft walloper."

The tap, the hot water, more shame.

"He can never find out, Mungo. He's bad. I mean it." James pumped the wheel. "Like, it was my job to do the dishes when I was wee. Sometimes I'd forget to shut a cabinet or close the drawer all the way. It'd be almost closed, but like, not one hunner per cent. His favourite game was to wait until ye had just fallen asleep, you know that lovely feelin' where ye stretch out your toes and properly sink into the mattress and float away. He'd time it jist perfect. He'd wait and then barge in, the big light blaring, and wake you up and make you get up and close the cabinet door. He'd slap the back of your head all the way to the kitchen and slap you all the way back to bed again."

"Just for an open cabinet door?"

"Aye. He'd pass it all day and just leave it ajar. He could have shut it himself wi' one finger."

"Even Ha-Ha isn't as twisted as all that."

"One time our Geraldine sat on the coffee table and her fat arse broke the glass. She blamed me and he leathered me and then every weekend for a year I was apprenticed to a glazer's in Parkhead just so I learnt the value of glass. I was only twelve."

"How much is it worth, then?"

"How the fuck should ah know? My job was to sit in the empty van when it was double-parked." He stopped the tyre again. "I spent a whole year of weekends in that white van. Afterwards my father had the cheek to ask me how I don't make any friends."

"I'm sorry."

"It's not your fault. But I meant what I said the other night." James picked through the ruins of the cake. He rolled the decorative bear in his palm. It was a cheap plastic thing. It had been poorly printed and the misalignment made it appear as if it was half melted. It was too childish a thing to be wearing a sash that said "Sixteen." James was emancipated now. He could do what he liked. He was a man. "I'll stay for as long as I can. But when I have to go, I will go."

James made to throw the bear away but Mungo stopped him. He took the bear from James's hand. He licked the sugar from it, and when James wasn't looking, he dropped it into his pocket.

James pedalled into the city, heading downhill, back towards the East End. The Rattray flew through the smirr, it sliced and turned, thin and fast as any whippet. Mungo held his body away from James like before, but now, when he held on to his waist, he used his whole hand and gripped the sharp bone at the top of his hips. He allowed his thumbs to slowly creep up under James's Fair Isle jumper and brush against the warm skin. It was a nothing that felt like an everything.

When the traffic thickened the boys took to the pavement, riding against the evening rush, bumping up and down each wet kerb. The rain clung to everything it touched. It dripped from the end of Mungo's nose and coated his eyelashes, which made the glare from the headlights explode like a concussion.

"I thought you had a bird?" asked Mungo, over the growl of a corporation bus.

"A doo?"

"No-o. A robin big breast, a pair of blue tits. A lassie."

"Who? The girls from the fountain?" James stopped pedalling and rested on the razor saddle, sliding himself between Mungo's legs. They coasted slowly downhill together, closer than they had been all day. "No, I don't have a bird," James said. "But I was trying my hardest to get one. After my da found the phone bill he called us every name under the sun. He threw me out and I went to sleep in the doocot, propped up a'cos of all the glass on the floor. It was about half past eleven when he came to the doocot. He tried to kick it down with me inside. He would have wrung the neck of every doo, and mine as well if I had let him. I had to climb out of the top trap and dreepie down the back edge. He dragged me through the streets and called us names I'd never heard afore. He was roaring so loud that there were wummin hanging out of windows from Culloden to Ballindalloch."

Mungo rested his chin on James's shoulder.

"In the morning, he said I could only live under his roof if I got a girlfriend. He said I could 'even get her pregnant' if I wanted. He didnae care either way. But I needed to get a bird, or I would have to leave his house." Headlights streaked across them. "I promised to try. After all, I'd still not done anything I couldn't undo, not really. So, I'd go to the park with a fresh packet of fags and try to find someone to winch. I knew a couple of lassies from my class who didnae have fathers. To them I was just a walking ice cream van. They use me, I use them."

Mungo's face was stinging with the threat of a gift taken back so suddenly. He opened his legs slightly and released James. The damp air filled the space where the other boy had been.

They rolled past the prison and, without a word, James shifted on the narrow seat. He filled the space between them and this time he pushed his spine into Mungo's cavity. Each bony vertebra was a knuckle that pressed into the places that hurt the worst. Mungo exhaled into the sandy hair. His arms disobeyed him as they wrapped around James's waist. He laid his face against the Shetland wool and inhaled the grease of the lanolin and the musk from his armpits. James leaned back into him as hard as Mungo was pressing forward. A diesel lorry chugged by, its air brakes hissing in the rain.

Then James said, "We don't . . . We don't have to do anything like that again. I mean, if ye don't want to?"

SEVENTEEN

There was a bend in the river where a tilting birch tree grew too close to the bank. The soil was worn away and the dissolving riverbank was held in place by a mesh of exposed roots. Mungo floated the body behind him and tucked the old man under the canopy of roots. St Christopher would be safe in this dark hollow, where the eroding earth and the tree formed a hidden pocket.

His rod and fishing bag hadn't floated far, but Mungo searched and could not find the man's tweed bunnet. His teeth were chattering as he pulled himself up on to the riverbank. The rain fell heavy as hailstones.

His whole body was shaking by the time he made it back to the campsite. The belongings Gallowgate had dumped on the ground were scattered and ruined; Ludo pieces had blown across the shingles and his favourite sketchbook was a sodden, bleeding mass. The flaps were open on the tents and the mouth of the larger tent was submerged in a puddle. The sleeping bag, the fishing supplies, everything was wet. Mungo crawled inside and tried to sweep the puddle out but it was futile. He shrank against the back wall and felt all the adrenaline leave his body.

The sky was dimly lit with a dull blue gloam. The clouds hung low and Gallowgate struggled to find his way back. If it hadn't been for the outline of the ruined bothy, he might have missed the campsite entirely. The rain had hammered the tents and several guy lines had come loose. They were half-deflated and looked defeated. No one had lit a fire.

It was too quiet at the campsite. Gallowgate went to the two-man tent expecting to find St Christopher sulking and sober. He had to reach into the darkness until he felt something that wasn't wet polyester or a puddle of rainwater. His fingers brushed skin. There was a leg, it was cold to the touch. He sparked his lighter and the boy sat up.

"Where's auld Chrissy?"

"He's in the other tent," said Mungo,

though it hurt to speak. "He went to bed in a huff."

Gallowgate made a movement to retreat and check on his friend. But Mungo took hold of his wrist and tried not to let his panic show. "Leave him. If he's sleeping then he won't want any drink," he said. "Besides, I'd rather share a tent with you."

Gallowgate smiled, the white of his teeth looking almost ultraviolet in the last of the blue light. The man shed his anorak in the rain, then he lay on his back and inched out of the sodden denims. Gallowgate swept more of the water out of the tent. He pulled the zipper closed and they sat in the darkness together. There was a spark of the lighter and a tiny tea light candle illuminated the space between them. He had bought it at the shop and it was like the ones the Chinese takeaway put in the window at Christmas; a happy, festive thing. Mungo picked at his wounded cheek, wondering if he could use the candle to set the tent on fire.

"How was the fishin'?" Gallowgate asked, trying to warm himself over the little flame. His naked skin was covered in ink from his ankle to his cuff.

"Terrible." Mungo didn't yet know what he was going to tell the man, he hadn't gotten that far in his mind. He only knew that whatever he was going to do, he would do it in the morning when it was dry, when he could run.

Mungo watched him burst open the backpack and take out the tinned ravioli and the Isle of Skye whisky. He handed the boy a tin and Mungo realized he hadn't eaten since the night before. There was a ring pull and the lid separated easily. It was sharp as a razor blade. Mungo licked it, found a comfort in its sharpness, and placed it carefully to the side. Then he held the tin over the tea candle, tried to warm the cold pasta, but it only sent big black puffs of smoke into the air, so he gave up, and ate the ravioli cold. He was ravenous, shovelling big handfuls of the mushy pasta into his mouth and breathing through his nose to swallow it quicker. Gallowgate unscrewed the whisky and offered it to him. Mungo drank it in easy gulps, quickly becoming used to the taste.

"Are ye looking forward to going home the morra?"

Mungo wiped his mouth with the back of his hand, it left a smear across his chin. "Aye. When will we leave?"

"Och, no rush," said Gallowgate. He wasn't interested in the food. "Let's gie auld

Chrissy a chance to get that bastardin' trout, eh?"

Something that had felt like hope dampened inside Mungo. Gallowgate reached out his hand and locked it around the boy's kneecap. "Here!" he said. "How did ye get that?"

There was a gash on Mungo's calf, it wasn't deep but it was long. He must have cut it on a sharp rock when he was pushing the last of the air from St Christopher. Gallowgate poured some of the whisky into his open mouth. He leaned over Mungo's calf and let it dribble out. It hit the gash and burned. Mungo struggled to pull his leg away but Gallowgate gripped him by the back of the knee. He laid the length of his hot whisky-soaked tongue against his cut. Then he licked the blue shin bone like it was a sugary ice pole. "Saliva is meant to help. Does that feel better?"

"I don't want to do that." It was the flattest voice he could manage. Mungo pulled his legs underneath himself and tucked them inside his cagoule.

Gallowgate took another throatful of the whisky, the tea light throwing his shadow against the side of the tent. "If ye don't want to do *that,* how comes ye saved me the sleeping bag next to yours, eh?" Gallowgate removed a burr that had stuck to Mungo's face. He burned it over the candle.

Mungo realized he had made a mistake. He had only worried about hiding the truth about St Christopher, not what might come after. Gallowgate twisted like he was uncomfortable. He stretched out his left leg, where there was an inked banner above his knee that read in bold blue letters: *No Retreat, No Surrender.*

"It's funny," said Gallowgate. "After your mammy telt us the stories about you ah thought ye would've jumped at the chance to get away for a wee weekend. She is disgusted by you, ye know. She practically begged us to take ye away. She's terrified ye'll become a wee soft boy like the Fenian ye were messing around wi'."

Mungo's face was pulling and he could tell his eye wanted to twitch despite the swelling around it. His spine was against the side of the tent and he could feel by the tilt of his body that he was as far away as he could squeeze himself. Gallowgate reached out his hand again, he cupped it around the back of Mungo's neck and dragged him back towards him. He tilted his head and locked his lips over Mungo's. It was an insistent kiss, his tongue pushing Mungo to part his lips. Mungo thought about opening his mouth then, allowing the tongue inside, and biting down on it, ripping it out whole, till it lay fresh and quivering like some of the butcher's meat that Mo-Maw liked so much.

"Stop." He couldn't push Gallowgate away from him, so he collapsed, allowed himself to become heavy and slip from his grip. *"I don't want to do that."*

Gallowgate's lips were wet with his own saliva. There was hurt in his eyes. "Well, we'll see." He wiped his mouth and drank more of the whisky. " 'Asides, what makes ye think ah'm going to let you go home to Glasgow if we're no pals? Ah cannae have ye running around all over the place telling tales on me, can ah?"

"I won't tell." Mungo meant it. His family already thought of him as something less than a person and he couldn't bear the shame. He pictured Chickie Calhoun in his dead mammy's flat, with his comfortable indoor shoes and the way he used his spectacles to keep the feathered hair out of his eyes. He knew how the scheme looked at Chickie. *"Please."*

Gallowgate looked like he was weighing something heavy in his heart. He was shaking his head and looking at Mungo with a great pity. "Ah don't know if ah can trust

405

you, Mungo."

Underneath the waterproof sheet the ground had been pulsing from the pouring rain. Tiny rivers of water tried to find their way past the tent and around the boy to lower ground. Now Mungo's head felt like it was spinning too. Everything was shifting. This was the sixth face Gallowgate had shown him: the victim, the hurt person, the one who was disappointed in Mungo.

He tried to steady himself with thoughts of Glasgow, of Jodie and the warm front room of the tenement flat, the way the air smelled of static on the days when they cooried in together away from the world and watched television.

"You can trust me," he tried to smile.

Gallowgate wrapped his hand around Mungo's wrist. The tent shuddered in the wind. "Ah mean, if we're no pals, mibbe ah should stop being so friendly."

EIGHTEEN

For the past few days he had been lousy with optimism, stupid, stocious with happiness. But now he lost all his bottle. All his new-found confidence ebbed away, and his shoulders took on their familiar slouch. Mungo made himself smaller again, and cringing, he held the gift behind his back and wished he hadn't said anything at all.

James lay sprawled upon the navy-blue carpet, his head resting against his father's settee, his neck at an angle that looked broken. "C'mon. Don't be lit that."

"Just forget it."

James sat up and wrapped himself around Mungo the way monkeys did — maybe this is what Mungo had wanted all along. James was peering around him and snatching for the parcel. Mungo held the box at arm's length, but James's arms were longer. "Awright. Fine. Get off of me."

"You don't want me to get off of you, not

really." James was grinning, but he did as Mungo asked.

Mungo sank back on his haunches and reluctantly handed him the small gift. It was wrapped in a hand-drawn paisley pattern, made up of a hundred swooping pigeons, with wings outstretched and tipped with stripes, swirling across a sky full of puffy clouds. He had drawn it specially for James and he had held his breath as he sliced the page from his sketchbook. Hours upon hours of meticulous linework with a fine-nibbed pen, intricate as Toile de Jouy wall-paper.

James unwrapped the cassette and turned it in his hands. "What's on it? It's no rave music, is it?"

Mungo shrugged. "Naw. It's nothing. Just some stuff I like from the charts."

James set the cassette aside, like it didn't matter much to him. Mungo picked at his cheek. He tried to pin down the hurt that already piqued the muscle to stop it spreading. It was only a cassette, after all, but by the way he felt when James put it to the side it could have been his heart. Then James did something unexpected. He smoothed the paper flat and holding it up to the sunlight he looked at it like it was the most magnificent thing he had ever seen. Mungo watched his fingers trace the spirals tenderly. "Is this for me as well?"

"Only if you want it."

"Aye, I love it."

"You don't have to say that."

James sat forward and kissed him. It was all so familiar now. They had moved beyond the clumsy petting and munching. Mungo would stop frequently to apologize, he felt so inept, and James would cradle his face and guide Mungo's lips back to his. Now their kisses were soft and tender and offered without the fear of refusal. A kiss lasted hours. They lay with their mouths together and Mungo cupped his nose in the divot of James's cheek, and then they led each other in a silent ramble, one would change the direction and the other would follow, over and over until an arm went dead, or the microwave pinged. A hand might slip under a T-shirt but it never dared to do anything else. Mungo knew he wanted to spend his life doing this, just kissing this one boy. There was no need to rush.

Mungo winced. The skin around his lips was chapped with too much tenderness. They looked bee-stung and had swollen slightly and grown rosy in colour.

"Shall we take a wee break?" Usually, James didn't stop, he just kissed over the bud of Mungo's cheek, down past his earlobe and across the pale skin beneath his shirt collar. They had been lucky. A few times they had gotten carried away and Mungo had spent a tense twenty minutes pacing in front of the hallway mirror checking for love bites, James hovering behind him, juggling ice cubes in his hands.

They lay in a nest of their own filth, discarded schoolbags and empty crisp packets. Cereal bowls ringed the carpet in front of the large television, like it was an altar. Half-watched videocassettes were strewn around, stripped of their fake encyclopaedia cases, alongside unfinished homework that had been abandoned in favour of kissing and staring. Mungo thought that if *Lord of the Flies* had been more like this, he might have paid some attention.

He had been surreptitiously borrowing articles of James's clothing, intimate things, that he swapped out for his own perfectly clean, if not especially nice gear. It started with a pair of thick socks, after he complained that he was cold, even though James's flat had central heating that left him dehydrated and with a dull headache. Then he stole a too-big pair of boxer shorts from the clothes pulley, and wore them for three days in a row, under his school trousers, bunched up like Victorian bloomers.

All week they had floated in the mornings from the doocot to separate schools, then back to the doocot, before spending long evenings in James's front room: top floor, facing the moody sky, far from the eyes of anyone else. When they separated to their own bedrooms, across the back middens, they spent hours gurning at the window, feigning being murdered, and flicking each other the finger all while trying not to laugh too loud.

He had been mooning across the divide one afternoon while Jodie was clearing the dirty dishes. "But, soft! what light through yonder window breaks?"

"Whut?" Mungo was resting his cheek on the glass, enjoying the cool condensation.

"What's her name?" asked Jodie.

"None of your business." He felt more gallus now. No longer a solitary soul.

"Keeping secrets. That's not very nice." She tickled his ribs, inspected his sore lips.

"Secrets!" he howled unkindly. "You're like the Finders Keepers of secrets." He poked her in the belly and she flinched. He hadn't known what he said. He was referencing the adverts they had loved on Saturday mornings, where American lassies wrote silly little secrets and locked them safe, in

411

the belly of a stuffed bear. Smiling wee lassies who hadn't had a teacher's wean in their gut, stupid wee lassies with no real secrets worth keeping.

Jodie slapped his hand from her stomach. "Ye get more like Hamish every day."

"God, Jodie, I'm sorry. I didnae think. I didnae mean it."

"Make your own dinner, Romeo." She threw the tea towel at him. "And if your girlfriend scabs your face that sore, make sure and think twice afore you put anything else near her."

The slow hours he spent away from James felt overwhelming. His legs thrummed with a restless energy that irritated Jodie. The hours felt filled with nothing. It was time to sleep and eat and think of things to tell him when he saw him again, stupid little things hardly worth repeating, but he knew James wouldn't mind.

As they lay around James's living room one afternoon, James had seemed restless, swinging his shinty stick while they watched television. He sat up suddenly with a demented look upon his face. He was giggling to himself as he draped a blanket and then a bath towel across his shoulders. He pulled his woollen hat upwards till it sat on the very top of his head and resembled a peaked mitre. "Wait. Wait." James held his caman as though it was a ceremonial mace, and then he turned to face Mungo. He extended his right hand, holding his index and ring fingers aloft as though he was hailing a bus. "Guess who I am?"

Mungo snorted. "Ah dunno. A bam in a bath towel?"

"Naw. I'm you."

There was a mug of tap water they had been sharing; it somehow made the water taste sweeter to be drinking from the same vessel. Mungo motioned for James to pass it to him. "Fuck off, James. How's that me?"

James threw his arms wide in a show of saintly grace. He flicked his fingers in an invitation for the believers to come forward and adore him. "Come to me, my child."

Mungo thought about it. He wanted to obey.

"It's you. It's St Mungo." James turned his profile to the daylight. "It's the statue they have of you above Kelvingrove Museum. Have you no even seen it?"

Mungo had never been to Kelvingrove, and although it was only a few miles away, he had never been to the West End. To admit this would bring out a feeling of inferiority in him and he wanted so badly for them to remain equals, the very, very

413

same. Mungo rolled his eyes and motioned for the communal chalice again.

James handed him the mug of tap water with a papal flourish of his hand. "Bless you, my son."

Mungo took a long slug of water. "Wait. Are you wearing your big sister's trackies?"

James looked down quickly. "Naw!" They were the same trackie bottoms he had been wearing for the past three days. They could do with a wash. "Piss off. Don't come wide with a holy saint, son." Mungo was laughing to himself when James looked up again. "How? Is that a bowl cut you've got?" He stepped forward and tugged on Mungo's forelock. "Wait, you *do* have a bowl cut?"

They had crossed this line a day or two before. They had wandered from timid tenderness to affection wrapped in insults. It was a lovely place for two boys to be: honest, exciting, immature.

"It's not a bowl cut." Mungo slurped the metallic water. He peered at James over the chipped edge. "Besides, nice try, wingnut. Your first miracle as a holy saint should have been to fix those massive ears."

"Don't you like ma ears?" James was towering over him.

"Aye," he grinned. "But can you move a bit to the left? I cannae see the sky."

James made a grab for the mug. He tipped it and poured the water on to Mungo's lap. "Piss yourself often, do ye?"

Mungo hooked his leg around James's and brought him easily to the carpet, water sprayed everywhere. He had found someone he could say the cruellest things to and they would not leave. He didn't care anymore if his lips were sore. They kissed and sucked and bit and lay on top of each other all the way through the evening news and well past the sour trumpets of *Coronation Street*. As much as they had kissed it had not yet gone any further. It was enough to put his hand up James's shirt and feel the broad muscles of his back undulate as he rubbed himself against Mungo. James preferred to keep his own hands in the crook of Mungo's back, softly stroking the downy hair that was growing above his buttocks. It made Mungo feel sleepy, it made him feel safe.

They pushed against each other harder now. He could feel James stiffen through his thick trackies. He moved his hand and used the back of it to rub where it was warmest, then he turned his palm to it and cupped it gently. James let out a low sigh. He pressed his forehead against Mungo's, his breath was sweet with sugar and cereal milk. "Do ye want to?"

"I dunno." Mungo was not sure what he was asking. So far James had been walking down a path ahead of him, while Mungo trailed behind. He led Mungo almost by the hand and several times when he stopped to look at him, it hurt Mungo to feel that the boy with the sticky-out ears might have already been down this road with someone else. He had wanted them to walk it for the first time together.

James raised himself on to his elbows, the front of his trousers tented and damp. As he left the room Mungo felt abandoned, exposed. Pulling his knees to his chest, he wondered what he had done wrong.

"I wanted to show you something." James came back into the front room, a magazine in his hand. He was flicking through it, looking for something in particular, and Mungo knew from the naked contorted bodies and the cheap sound of the paper what the magazine was. "I visited my aunt once in Dundee. They sold these in the bus station. I missed two buses home before I grew the courage to buy it."

"They let *you* buy it?"

James shrugged. "Aye, twelve ninety-nine *is* twelve ninety-nine, after all."

The magazine was full of bloated Americans. Men with swollen muscles and lines of amber tans that showed the ghost of their missing swimming trunks. They didn't have the long, thin limbs of him or James, the soft downy trails of hair, or the white skin that flushed when you touched it, that turned blue or pink depending on temperature, on emotion. Everything about these Americans was artificially plump; they were shaved and plucked, lying on their backs, legs in the air, more like Christmas turkeys than men. There was a painful rictus on their faces, glazed eyes, false winces of pleasure. One man was grinning at the camera while he choked his floppy cock, strangling it like it was an empty tube of toothpaste.

"No way. He's shoved it up his arsehole." Mungo was pointing at two baseball players on a slatted bench.

The magazine was not allowed to show a fully erect penis, but by how the men were arranged together, the idea was clear. He had thought about the curved hillock of James's arse but the centre, the dark hidden part, was not yet something he had thought much about. On the next page, there it was, a man on his back, his legs in the air, his fingers probing himself. It looked painful.

"Aye," James laid his head on Mungo's shoulder. "That's what we do."

"Who's *we*?" scoffed Mungo.

"People lit us."

"Well. Who is the man and who is the woman?" Mungo asked sincerely.

"Well, *you* are the woman."

He shook James from his shoulder. "*You* are."

The pictures aroused him. Sometimes — when Jodie was in bed, and Hamish was sleeping at Sammy-Jo's — he would take his brother's stiff magazine full of buttery soft women. He liked the spreads with men in them the best and so he folded the page, turned the women to the back, and gave them a little rest. The first time he had doctored a page he had been too firm with the paper. Afterwards, no matter how he tried to smooth it, the telltale crease remained; it would surely grass him up. It was torturous to erect the screeching ironing board without waking his sister. Even after he ironed the page to the point of lifting the inks, the faint crease was still visible. The line still separated the woman from her own mouth and the flaccid cock that she tickled with the tip of her tongue.

James turned the page and amongst all the Americans and their army jeeps — even the cars looked bloated — was a realistic vignette of a bus conductor and a cheeky truant. It looked like the top deck of a Glasgow corporation bus, but the conductor had the boy over his knee and was leathering him with the flat of his hand. The schoolboy was grinning at the camera.

"He must have forgotten his monthly Transcard," said James.

"Probably tried to get away with a half-fare."

"Aye, he looks about forty-five."

James tore the magazine from his grip. Mungo watched it sail across the room, but the images were already burned on the back of his retinas. They would be there, later, projected on to the underside of his duvet, like the pictures they played up at the Parade Cinema.

The first time Mungo saw James naked, the closeness of him made it hard to take it all in. Mungo wanted to push him away, pin him on the floor, stand over him, and just simply look. But they twisted together, brow to brow, mouth on mouth, and everything was like peeping through a crack in a door: an eyeful of alabaster and rose, the glacial blue of inner arms with their veins like violet rivers, the chafing at James's elbows that Mungo wanted to kiss so badly, and the fields of fevered carnations blooming high on his pale collarbone. The boy was all growing bones and unblemished skin; a paint chart of the softest whites.

Lying on his back, he had ribs like the hull of an upturned boat, two tiny pink nipples, comically small for such a broad chest. The hollow cavity of his stomach collapsed under the canopy of his ribcage. His pronounced hip bones spoke of a framework he had not filled out yet, but from the muscles of his back, and the globes of his buttocks, it was clear that he would. His body was covered in a fine dusting of white-gold hair, as though pollen had settled upon him. He sparkled faintly in the gloomy daylight.

The feathered mustiness of his armpits and the down that dusted his arse cheeks tickled the tips of Mungo's fingers. His skin was a bigger and more unexpected landscape than anywhere Mungo had ever been and he was glad to explore it. He travelled along the train tracks left behind by the tight boxer short elastic, the touch of it ribbed and musical under his fingertips. They explored each other, their gangly limbs wrapped together, clumsy and inexperienced, hands too hurried, greedy fingers too eager to rush on to other delights. Their bodies parted and James lay with his forehead pressed against Mungo's and his breath, all toffee and milky tea, was hot against his face.

They used their own hands on their own bodies now. Apart but together. They stole pleasure for themselves, shared it through the mixing of their breath, faster, shallower, until James's bottom lip snagged on the tip of Mungo's nose, and his breath grew faster still, his lips sticky over dry teeth. They kept pace with each other. Then just as quickly as it had started, James arched his back, and it was over.

Mungo was dazed, happy, until James left him splayed on the carpet for the second time that afternoon. Mungo reached out for him but James had already rolled on to his knees and was wiping the mess from his own stomach. Kneeling below the bay window, he turned his back to Mungo and there was a pattern of creases from the carpet across his kidneys and flank. He reached for the dregs of a family-sized bottle of ginger and the plastic creased and collapsed as he swallowed it in thick gulps.

The passion had blown across them too quickly. Now James sat there knotted. The rivets of his spine and the struts of his ribs looked like a Govan carcass. When he finally turned, he pushed his back tight against the wall and sat there staring at the floor. They were only a paisley rug apart, but they were not looking at each other, separated as though by a teacher that could no longer tolerate their disruptiveness.

"What did I do?" asked Mungo. *What did I do?* It was what he had been trained to say. Never *what's wrong with you?* or *are you okay?* Only *what did I do?*

James coughed his hacking rattle. He rubbed at the centre of his chest. Sometimes his ears and his gappy teeth gave his face a friendly, cartoonish feel, but not now. Now, in the dying light, when he tilted his head and stared at Mungo under the bone in his brow, the muscles in his jaw tightened and his gaze crossed the room, as cold as a draught. His speckled green eyes were like the slate tiles, more grey than green now, sharp and flinted. "Do you think I'm funny?"

"Funny-ha-ha, or funny-peculiar?"

"Peculiar. Do you . . . Do you think I'm like Poor-Wee-Chickie?" James sucked on his inhaler.

Mungo didn't know what to answer. He tried hard to see what James was saying but he couldn't imagine James hiding in a ground-floor flat, with no fresh air in his hair, and no wide grin on his face. "We don't have to do that ever again."

"You won't tell anyone, will you?" Fear replaced the shame in James's eyes.

"No. How? Will *you*?" He knew he wouldn't, but the bond required that he state it out loud.

"Never." He made the sign of the cross and this seemed to relax him slightly. He wiped the snot from his nose. "Look at this fucking mess. Auld Jamieson is back in three days. He'll skin me if I don't find a lassie."

"He's gonnae skin ye anyhow," said Mungo. "He sounds like my Hamish."

James's eyes were ringed and sore looking. He had travelled so far since he had lain with Mungo; such a distance to cross in seven minutes. "I don't know how you cope."

Mungo was picking the lint out from beneath his toes. "It's got easier since I met you." He tried to coax a smile.

"Ha. Do *you* want to be my girlfriend this weekend when ma da's home?"

"What? Get a wig? Pretend to be wee Mairead from up the Parade?"

"I knew it. I knew you were the woman." James laughed his half-choked laugh.

Mungo would have done anything to have kept him there, with that grin back on his face. "What are you looking at, ya big-eared

423

basturt?"

"Nothing," said James. "I just like looking at you. It's a shame in a way. We've lived across the back middens from each other for our whole lives."

"S'okay. We have three more days before your da gets back."

"Three more days," James agreed. "Then no more Chickie Jamieson."

Mungo lunged at him then and cracked his fist off his chest. He dared him to strike back. Violence always preceded affection; Mungo didn't know any other way. Mo-Maw would crack her Scholl sandal off his back, purpling bruises curdling his cream skin, then she would realize she had gone too far and pull him into the softness of her breast. Jodie would scold and demean his poorly wired brain and then, feeling guilty, make a heaped bowl of warm Weetabix and white sugar. Hamish would wind him with a fist and sit on his chest. When Mungo started calling for help, Hamish would clamp his hand over his face, that hot hand whose fingers covered his eye sockets and whose meat crammed into his open mouth. They would sit there for a long time, Hamish crushing the wind out of him, until Mungo acquiesced, easy as flattened grass, soft as an Easter lamb.

First came the hurt, then came the kiss. Wrapping his long arms around him, James raised Mungo off the floor in a bear hug. He squeezed with all his might until Mungo couldn't breathe. He hoped it would never end. Then James farted, a long, growling thunder. It stunk heavy and rancid, pure dairy and white sugar. Mungo braced himself against James, but he could not get free. And he was glad.

The Jamiesons' bathroom was a creamy mint colour. Of the four shelves above the toilet, only one still held any toiletries. Mungo picked through the canisters of deodorants, fungal foot spray, and a rusted tube of haemorrhoid cream. At the back was an old-fashioned shaving kit, with a badger brush and a straight razor; he had never seen anything like it. Mungo took Mr Jamieson's shaving brush down from the shelf. He sniffed it. The traces of lather smelled like men from another time. It had the bright tang of menthol and pine, and the faint medicinal whiff of aniseed, almost like carbolic soap. He ran the soft badger bristles across his bottom lip, enjoying their tickle.

As he waited for the bath to fill, he traced the brush across his collarbone and then down his neck, across his bare chest and around his left nipple. As he did so he tilted his head back and looked up at the patterned ceiling. Mrs Jamieson must have lowered it herself. She had nailed pins around the perimeter and then strung twine back and forth in a decorative pattern that looked something like macramé. There was a bowl of potpourri on the cistern, but when Mungo sniffed it, it no longer held any scent. Other than this, there was nothing that suggested a woman had ever lived here.

Their bathwater was lukewarm by the time they both climbed in. Mungo got in first and claimed the end without taps. He felt clammy, like he had just passed the worst of a fever, but happy and peaceful in every corner of his skin. James got in and poured his long legs around him. He rested a heaped plate of sausage rolls on the toilet seat and Mungo nodded at the party treats. "Who's the missus now, then?"

James didn't rise to it, instead he ripped into one of the pastries. A dozen buttery flakes stuck to his chest and dissolved on his damp skin. The rest floated on the water like leaves in a puddle. Mungo popped one into his mouth. The gristly meat was scalding hot. He ladled tepid bathwater into his open mouth.

James was wearing his fisherman's cap again, chewing and laughing with an open mouth. Mungo reached out and pulled the cap from his head. "I'm no gonnae sit in a bath with you if you're wearing a bunnet. It's too weird."

James covered his ears with his hands. "I wish someone had pinned them back. You don't know what it's like. You try going to school wi' these. Never even think to sit at the front of a class."

"I don't mind them."

James squirted brown sauce into his mouth. He shoved in another steaming roll and grinned through the sausage meat. "I think you might like me."

"Mibbe." Mungo lowered his chin on to the water. "I only have to look at them for three more days. I think I can hold my boak that long."

"Three days." James had forgotten for a moment. The green eyes turned to grey again.

Mungo shoved his toes under James's balls, until the boy squirmed and a wave of water hit the carpet. Then he sat forward and, grabbing James's cheeks, he pushed upwards till James's fat lips parted in a forced smile. "Listen, if I only get three days

I don't want to spend it with a moody bugger."

Mungo lay back down in the bath, while James glowered and rubbed at his face. "I bet I could kick the shite out of you."

"I bet you couldn't."

"Only because ye've got hauners." He tilted his chin in a challenge. "You only talk to me lit that because of Ha-Ha."

Mungo nodded. "Correct. So watch your Fenian mouth or I'll tell my big brother you showed me your willie."

"But you *liked* it." He sent a tidal wave of bathwater over Mungo.

"Aye, but I won't tell him *that.* Will I?"

They lay back in the dissipating warmth. Mungo took James's foot in his hand. He hadn't looked at it closely before. His sole was surprisingly soft, it smelled of nothing at all. He put James's big toe in his mouth, and they sat like that, with unflinching expressions, until James cackled first and tried to pull it away. Mungo picked a piece of sock oose from the tip of his tongue and under his breath he said, "You're no fit to drink my bathwater."

"Whut?" James was dabbing his finger into the water and eating the pastry flakes that were still bobbing there.

"It's just a funny thing Mo-Maw says all

the time. Some auld woman in the butcher's will run her eyes the length of her and she'll be like, *'Auld cow, she's no fit to drink my bathwater.'* I mean, imagine a line of wummin with thermoses in the hallway and Hamish working a velvet rope. 'Not you Irene, you cannae come in. I don't like the look o' thon orthopaedics. Nae bathwater for you.' "

"I wish I could meet her someday. The bold Maureen."

Mungo shook his head. "No chance. She would give me a showing up."

"She sounds like a laugh."

"Our Jodie doesn't see it that way. But I don't mind her, she's only a danger to herself." Something bright glimmered inside him. He held James's foot to his face and dialled the soft underside as though it were a telephone. "Hallo-hallo. You want an appointment with Mrs Hamilton? Elevenses for three? Usual table, sir?"

It was ticklish. "Aye. Why not . . ." James started coughing again. He reached for his inhaler.

Mungo let go of his foot. "You need to see a doctor. I don't like it when you hack like that."

James rubbed at his bare chest, he tried to catch his breath. "It's nothing."

"It's not nothing. I think it's the doos."

"Probably." He tried to steer the conversation away from the birds. He wanted to wipe the concern from Mungo's brow. "It feels nice to have someone worry about me though."

Mungo slowly lowered his face under the water and tried to hide a broad smile. He bobbed back up. "Does it now? Do you think you're my boyfriend?"

"Only if you're my girlfriend."

Mungo pressed his knee outwards and against the inside of James's thigh. It made the blond boy writhe for submission. "Okay! We'll no tell Mo-Maw *that,* but aye, I'll be your boyfriend, Mungo Hamilton, for the next three days, anyhows."

It had been his turn to forget for a moment. Mungo lay there a while, thinking about the time that was left, rationing his allocation and deciding on how he would spend the sweetness. Of course there could be more of this on the far side of Mr Jamieson's visit, but that hardly seemed to matter. He was feeling childish — why did James's father have to come home at all? James watched Mungo's face darken. He made the boy turn around in the bath, until Mungo was settled and lying against his chest. They sent slops of bathwater on to

430

the carpet. Mungo said, "Okay. You can meet her, but only for a minute."

When James spoke again his lips were against Mungo's ear. He bound Mungo's wrists, held him still. "Good. Who knows? Maybe I can date yer Maw and be yer new da. Two birds with one stone. After all, you're turning out a wee bit funny."

Mungo went early, to see her for himself, and if he had to, to keep her away from the worst of the drink. James knew where to come and when. She kissed him and then she tucked him under the snack bar counter, out of view from the regulars. Mungo was gazing up at her while she charmed customers with snatches of gossip and false smiles. When she looked down at him the smile slid off her face.

Mo-Maw stole sleekit mouthfuls from a polystyrene cup. When she wasn't looking, he checked the cup. It was filled with fortified wine that smelled like cold medicine and rotted fruit. She must have been drinking and refilling the same cup for a long time. The lip of it was ruined with lipstick and she had chewed all along the edge.

The snack bar smelled sweet with fried onions. The late-night radio played soft rock from Mo-Maw's youth: Dr Hook, Eric

Clapton, Kenny Rogers. Mungo sat on the plastic cooler and she handed him a tub of bread rolls. "If yer gonnae bother me at ma work, then ye might as well make yersel useful."

Her new perm had set tighter than she had wanted. Between filling rolls with potato scones and fatty bacon, she tugged at it and tried to steam it straight, holding it out over the sizzling griddle. "That Pauline, the glaikit bitch. She had the nerve to charge me eighteen poun' for this. For this! Ah went to her house and had her weans climbing all over me. By the time I came out I was looking like Orphan-fuckin'-Annie." She tugged until she winced. "Sun'll come out tomorrow. My arse."

"It looks awright." It looked like she had been electrocuted.

"Couldnae even get a decent cup o' tea out of her."

Mungo was ripping the guts out of the bread rolls and eating the soft dough. With a plastic knife he spread bright-yellow margarine on both sides. He thought he was doing a thorough job, he imagined the drivers would want their rolls dripping with grease, but Mo-Maw slapped his hand with the fish lift. "Stop eating they rolls. And stop wasting so much bloody margarine. Big Ella will be on me like a rash." She went back to relaxing her perm. "Why are you here anyway, is it money?"

"How, do you have some?"

"Naw."

"Then I came because I missed you."

She tickled him under the chin. "Ah suppose you do. Ah'm sorry, ma darlin'. Have you been stickin' in at school?"

Mungo wiped some margarine from the front of his jumper. "Not exactly. I was hoping I could leave soon. Get an apprenticeship or a job or something."

Mo-Maw crouched beside him and lit a cigarette. She smoked it under the counter, hunkered out of view. "Ah wish you would stay in school."

"I don't think it's for me. I think I'd be better off working."

"Then do what ye like. Ah can't force ye. Fat load of good school did me." Then she squinted at him. "But Mungo, see if ah get the School Board at ma door, ah tell ye, yer feet will no touch the ground."

"You won't. They'll be glad to see the back of me."

"Aye, well, yer almost a man now. Time ye grew up and paid yer own way." She took a long drink out of the half-chewed cup. As she opened the bottle of wine to refill it, the metal Buckfast cap rolled away across the greasy floor. "Ah, bugger." Mo-Maw shrugged and took a long swig from the bottle as though she had better finish it now. She offered it to Mungo.

He shook his head. "And I wish you wouldn't."

"It's got a wee buzz. It keeps me gaun through the night." Then she added, "And it makes me mair fun. Men prefer women that are mair fun. Ah get better tips."

Of all the alcohol Mo-Maw enjoyed, Mungo feared Buckfast wine the most. He had heard Ha-Ha's boys refer to it as the "Commotion Lotion." Its high alcohol content mixed with its high caffeine content meant it made his mother blindingly drunk and too jittery to subdue. Mungo tore at a bread roll and held the doughy guts out to her. Mo-Maw pushed his hand away. "Have ye seen the shape of me? If I get any heavier this caravan will pop a wheelie."

He crammed the bread into his own mouth. "How's Jocky?"

Mo-Maw suddenly became animated. She spun and splayed her hands out wide, and Mungo could tell he had struck a seam of gold. There was such excitement on her face that, combined with the tight perm, she looked like she was convulsing. "Oh. Ma.

God! Ah cannae believe ah didnae tell ye already. Jocky found some widow's wedding ring that a wee house-robbing basturt tried to fence through his pawnshop. He got a cash reward, but better than that, he's on a promise of a caravan in Burntisland for two weeks. Can you believe?"

There was a hole in the calf of her sheer tan tights. Mungo traced it with his finger. "Can I come?"

Mo-Maw brushed his hair away from his face and made a little moue. "Oh, sorry son. It's still what morning telly calls the honeymoon period. We have to focus on *us* the now. It's very important." She clawed at her waistline. "Oh these tights are killin' me. Ah should know better than to stand at this griddle and smother myself."

He pushed his finger into the hole. "Can I?"

She huffed, and then she nodded. "Aye, go on. If it'll make ye happy."

Mungo felt the stubble of her leg hair against his knuckles. He tore at the hole and the tiny stitches ran away, they poured down her leg like raindrops. He pushed more fingers inside the tear and he tugged them apart. The tights ripped from her ankle bone up beyond the line of her skirt. He burst a hole in the other leg and ripped that one

435

too. Mo-Maw clung to the counter and squealed in delight. They had loved this game as children. When her tights had become laddered beyond decency, she let the children rip them. They never split at the gusset or the toe seam so they made a game of pulling their mother out of her chair by her stocking feet, dragging her giggling across the floor until, finally, the pale softness of her legs thudded to the carpet, like chicken meat escaping from a string bag.

"Oh, I can breathe again." Mo-Maw stepped out of her destroyed tights. She stepped back into her trainers. Mo-Maw put her foot up on the low shelf, picked at some ingrown hairs, and traced a finger along a varicose vein. "That one ah got from nursing you. Such a needy wean. You would never let me put ye down."

Something in the darkness caught her attention. Mungo watched her lean out and peer beyond the glare of the fluorescent light. "Hello there, son. Can ah fill you a roll?"

Mungo sat up and peered over the top of the counter. He was there, shifting nervously, at the very edge of the light. James Jamieson was scrubbed pink from a hot bath, his hair slick and neatly parted.

Mungo grinned at the effort, he would noise him up about it afterwards. "Mo-Maw, this is my pal. This is Jamesy."

"Wait. Ye've made yersel a wee pal?" He watched her calf muscles tense as she leaned into the darkness to shake his hand. "Pleased to meet you, son. Ah'm Maureen, ah'm Mungo's big sister."

Mungo opened the caravan door and jumped down into the dirt. He could tell Mo-Maw was appraising James favourably. However, when James turned his back to say hello to Mungo, Mo-Maw pushed behind her own ears and mouthed silently, *Shame about those.*

"How did youse two start playing the gether?" she asked.

"Jesus. Come on, we don't *play.*"

"Ah don't know the slang, do ah? So when did youse two start going to the bingo the gether? Bridge? Canasta?" She pulled a smart-arse smile. "Is that better?"

Mungo's eye started to pulse. "James has a doocot. He raises pigeons."

Mo-Maw mugged as though she might be sick. "Ah don't know how ye could, beady-eyed wee buggers. Ah swear they just need to see me and then they try an shite on me." She was peering at the tawny boy as she leaned out of the serving hatch. Mungo wished she would button her blouse. James let himself be pored over. Mo-Maw cocked her head in recognition and fell back into the snack bar. "Here now, are you Jimmy Jamieson's boy?" Before James could answer, Mo-Maw slapped the counter. "Ye bloody are. I can tell. Ye're a big handsome wan just like yer da."

James didn't answer, but he looked uncomfortable. Mo-Maw took a polystyrene cup and poured James some of her wine. "Here, ah winched him once. Years ago. Your granny had a conniption when she heard I was a Protestant. But ah've always believed in bringing the religions the gether."

James reached up and cradled the cup with both hands, as though it were a communion chalice. "Thanks for doing your part, Mrs Hamilton."

Mo-Maw had warmed to the young man instantly. She raised her cup in salute. "But here, Mungo, think how different it would be if Mr Jamieson was your da." She snorted, and waved her hand. "No, wait, what am I saying? James, think how much fun it would be if ah was yer mammy. Eh?"

"I'd like that," he lied. The front of his teeth were already staining with wine. "I like your perm."

"See!" Mo-Maw had a weakness for compliments, she never seemed to care if they were sincere or not. She pointed accusatorily at Mungo. "He's only been my son for five seconds and already a nice word. Now that's how ye talk to a wummin."

NINETEEN

The second time they lay together the greediness of the first fever had broken. Now there was no hurry, no selfishness. Afterwards, they lay in the glare of the three-bar fire and turned only when the heat became too much. The electric fire was crowned with a layer of fake plastic coals in imitation of a real fireplace. There was a tinny fan underneath the coals that whirled and sent an artificial firelight dancing across the ceiling. Mungo lay back on the blue rug and watched the flames flicker. James told him how his mother had come to hate this fire. She had loved it when they were children, but as her end came nearer, she said the flames made her think of hell.

Mungo held him tight. James walked his fingers across Mungo's belly. He allowed himself a daydream as he traced his imaginary walker across the pale stomach, into the gullies of his hips and across the rise in his breastbone. Mungo's skin was a snowy plain, a landscape of unblemished emptiness. James teased the line of fine hair that ran down the centre of his stomach. He blew on it and said it reminded him of the grass verges between two fields.

"Imagine living somewhere quiet like this. What it would be like to see as far as you could, nothing but fields and not a soul for miles and miles."

His talk of leaving had begun to irritate Mungo. He wanted James to be here, in the now, not staring into the far distance, worried about his father's return. Mungo ran his hand over his body, he pushed his luck. "Why would you leave? You already own all this."

"Is it mine?"

Mungo nodded.

James used the edge of his hand. He ran it across Mungo's sticky belly like he was slicing him up. "In that case, how much do you think I would get for it if I subdivided it and parcelled it off for a Barratt estate?"

"Nothing. Nobody else wants it."

James tweaked at the faint line of pubic hair that ran from Mungo's cock to his navel. "I dunno. How many head of cattle do you think I could feed on this?" He lowered his muzzle to Mungo's belly and grazed lightly.

Mungo relaxed under the light kisses. "If you left, where would you go anyhows? Edinburgh?"

James collapsed across him. "Nah. I went wi' the school once. Four poun' for a cheese sandwich. Too fuckin' stuck-up. Can ye imagine what they would say about how we talk?"

"London?"

"No way. *Really* expensive. 'Asides, ye get mad riots down there, don't ye? In Brixton and that. It looks rougher than the Calton." He started singing "Guns of Brixton" to himself, a fair distance from the actual melody. *"Yeese kin crush us, yeese kin bruise us, but yeese'll huv tae answer to, ohahwoaoh, the Orange drums of Cahhl-ton."*

The Clash reminded Mungo of Hamish; he had once stomped a boy to unconsciousness while singing "Police and Thieves." Mungo slid his hand over James's mouth to silence him. Then he pushed two fingers between his lips just to see what it felt like. He probed the soft fat of his cheek, the scarred ridges of his back molars. He was quiet a long while, recording all these private textures.

James spat out the fingers. "Ardnamurchan."

"Ard-na-*how*?"

"Murchan. It's Gaelic for *jutting out into the sea* or something. We went there when my mammy was sick. It was the last holiday we took as a family. It's just this quiet, lonely wee bit of Scotland that sticks all the way out into the sea. There were definitely way more sheep than people and the road was so narrow they only let one car go at a time. There was one day, when it was too dreich for my mammy to be outside, that I went walking by maself. I found a quiet bay, you had to scramble down the cliffside to reach it. It was terrifyin', but I could see there was something down at the water's edge. When I got down there, there was a cluster of old stone bothies just abandoned by the people that used to live there. A whole village. Poof, up and gone."

"*Poof?*" Mungo chuckled.

James rolled over and continued his lazy grazing. "It's the most secret place I've ever seen. There's another less hidden beach on the far side of the peninsula that wraps around into a horseshoe and has perfect white sand beaches and crystal-clear water all year round. White sand, pure white, like sugar. They dared me to go for a swim, and I did, all the way out to a big skerrie and back."

"The sea air would be good for your cough."

"Well then, mibbe that's the place. Ma da said it's hard for the farmers to get good help, on account of it being heavy remote. He stopped at one farm and tried to sell Geraldine cos she was moaning of carsickness."

Mungo ran his fingers through the flaxen hair. He wanted to shake him, to scream. Instead he tried his hardest to look unbothered and said, "If you wait till I'm sixteen then we could split the cost. It'd be cheaper."

James stopped his grazing. It would be seven more months before Mungo turned sixteen, before he could finish school and not have the Social come after him. It seemed a lifetime. "What if I can't hide till your birthday?"

"*Fourteen,* only fourteen more shore leaves with your da. It's not that much when you think about it lit that." He held up his fingers. "Look, it *almost* fits on two hands."

"He will kill me, Mungo. I know he will. What if I can't make it to then?"

James lay his head on Mungo's stomach again, he rubbed his face on his belly like his nose was itchy. Mungo liked to look at the untouched pinkness behind his ears, how the wheat-coloured hair curled slightly, and was a thousand different shades as it crept towards the nape of his neck. Of all the intimate parts of James he was discovering this was his most favourite. He liked to think he was the only person to care about it.

There was a blackhead forming on his neck; Mungo dug at it with his nails. "You can make it. You have made it so far already. I'll go anywhere with you. But if I leave afore I'm sixteen there'll be bother. I need to be sure Mo-Maw is awright. And I can't lump her on our Jodie. Cos I need to be certain Jodie makes it to college. She's worked too hard for it."

"Mo-Maw seemed fine to me."

"You've no seen her with a good soak in her. When Jocky ends it, somebody has to be there for her."

James rolled over to face him, he squinted in disbelief. "Chickie Calhoun."

"Whut?"

"Ye'll be Chickie Calhoun. I get it now."

"Stop saying that."

"I can see exactly what you want and it's not guid. If yer no careful, you'll be stuck here with her, with Mo-Maw, for all your days. A wee bachelor living on the third floor with his poor mammy and shuffling about in a cagoule to buy his messages. Suffering Jesus. The best part of your day will be standing outside the butcher's and talking to the other old wummin about the weather. Then you'll carry your fish supper home in a string bag and lock every snib behind yourself. And for whut?"

"For her."

"Then ye're as daft as ye look."

"Yeah, you wouldnae understand." He inhaled sharply as if he could suck the cruel words back out of the air. "I'm sorry, I'm sorry." He felt James go stiff as a board.

"Aye, I'm sorry my mammy is dead an all."

"I didnae mean it."

James scowled up at him. "I suppose I could wait. I suppose I could try harder with the fountain girls. See if you ever grow the fuck up."

"Aye. Do that. If you must." Suddenly he wanted James off of him, but Mungo didn't have to ask because James sat up and wiped the spume from the corner of his mouth. "How can you be like this?"

"Lit what?"

James leaned forward and turned off the electric fire. The flames on the ceiling flickered and died. "Christ's sake, Mungo. You must be steamin'. Have you forgotten what it's like out there? If they knew, they would stab us! Rip us from balls to chin just for something to talk about down the pub."

"I know."

"We're lower than shite to them."

"I know."

"Those lassies. I'd only be doing this for you."

"*Me?* I never asked you for anything."

The boys were staring at each other. James was colouring, digging at the gap in his front teeth. "Can you no see? If I stick around for you then I need to follow his rules. If I'm under his roof I need to try."

It was a trick, it felt like one of Ha-Ha's. This is for your own good. *Blam.* I'm only doing this because you asked for it. *Blam.* You will thank me later. *Blam.*

They had slid further apart; all sharp shins and hollow clavicles, nothing but angular bones wrapped in blue-white skin. They drifted on the sea of navy-blue carpet like calved icebergs that were pulling away from each other. Mungo reached for his discarded clothes.

"Where are you going?"

"Away."

"Naw."

"Don't fuckin' tell me what to do."

447

James grabbed his ankle and started dragging Mungo back across the carpet towards him. The carpet burned. His body filled with electricity. Mungo was unsure how to feel, he knew he wanted to kick him in the face, but what he wanted more, infinitely more, was to be tethered to his side.

James wrapped his arms around Mungo until the twitching stopped and the desire to flee abated. They wrestled for a while. He tried to tilt Mungo's chin to look him in the eyes. But again and again Mungo wriggled free and buried his face in his neck. He didn't want to be reasoned with. He didn't want to be all grown-up.

"Don't be so fuckin' moody."

"You can talk," said Mungo, except his lips were pressed against the muscles of James's shoulder, so the sound that escaped was unintelligible.

"Whut? Whut?" James tickled him. He only wanted one more smile. Mungo dribbled pools of slaver across his skin. James didn't wipe the spittle from his shoulder, he didn't ask Mungo to move, even after their arms had fallen asleep, and their legs began to prickle with pins and needles. They sat wrapped in one another for a long time, long enough for the chill to enter the room. There was the distant jingle of an ice cream van. James kissed him. "Ye have nothing to worry about. Yer ma girl now. Until ye can come away wi' us. I'll do what I can." James pressed his fingers between Mungo's ribs, played a silent tune, and moved them up and down as though Mungo was an accordion.

In the end, three more days of happiness became only two and a quarter. Mungo felt short-changed, stopped short, swindled. All day, he had a sense that something promised had been stolen; like when you chose the biggest bag of crisps, opened it, and it was mostly just empty air.

"Are ye sure ye want to come?" asked James. He had asked the same thing four times now. It was already the gloaming and the park was getting dark. Far from the amber glare of the street lights, the evening was a watery type of grey.

"I do," said Mungo. He knew if he didn't go, he would hide at home, and the horrors he could imagine would feel one million times worse.

The boys stunk of the same cheap after-shave. Their armpits were caked in aerosol deodorant that they had applied so thickly that it slithered like whipped cream beneath their shirts. James rammed his shoulder into

Mungo's and knocked him from the path. "Listen, don't torture yourself, awright? I *have* to go through with it."

"Don't worry about me." Mungo tried to smile and found that he couldn't. "Mibbe they will do a two-for-one special. Poke one lassie, get one poke free."

"I dare ye to suggest a loyalty programme." He laughed, green eyes blazing. "And then run as fast as ye fuckin' can."

The park had only just started to come into spring leaf. There was a break in the cold rain, but everything was still dripping wet. A black path wound through the grass like a slick tongue. The fountain girls were huddled along the back of a rotted bench, bobbing and beady-eyed, like the cold pigeons that waited for the pensioners who came with the end of a loaf. Men's jumpers were pulled down over foreshortened school skirts, and their hair was gelled and scraped away from their faces. Each of them had a fringe, spindly and stiff, that they had rolled and lacquered over a round brush. Now they shot out and curled over their bright faces like awnings on a shopfront.

"What did ye bring us?" asked Nicola, the largest of the three girls.

James emptied the pockets of his anorak and produced a small bottle of MD 20/20, a ten-packet of Embassy Lights, and up his sleeve was a rolled-up copy of *NME* with a haloed Morrissey on the cover. He laid them on the bench and stepped back.

"That magazine is ancient. Who is that on the cover?" asked Nicola, her mouth a cage of metal braces. It was one of James's sister's magazines, almost a decade old by now. Nicola peered at Morrissey with a look of disgust, saying she would have preferred something with Take That, EMF, or The Shamen.

"Bout time you learnt some of the classics."

"You like the same stuff as my Granny Eileen." Nicola sniffed. "Anyway, I thought you had chucked us the rubber ear."

"Aye," agreed the smallest and prettiest girl. Her skin was clear and pale as moonlight, her fine bones made her look even younger than she was. Her face told that she was still discovering how to use makeup, and she looked like a child, painted and rouged from her mammy's dresser. But she took a drag on her cigarette and when she spoke she had a voice deep as a man's. James told Mungo later that Ashley had seven elder brothers at home and that she had a mouth like a publican on Old Firm day. She said, "It's a pure disgrace the way ye can keep three beautiful lassies waiting. I've got half this splintered bench up my hole, all because ah've been sat here waiting for the grand Prince Wingnut to arrive."

Mungo saw James fidget with his wool bunnet. "My doos were sick."

"Naebody cares about yer stupit pigeons. It's embarrassin'." Ashley glanced towards the park gates. Then she yawned. "Ah could have been away wi' Jimmy Fitzsimmons. His big sister's got a new sunbed."

"Don't say that," James said. "You know I think ye're a pure honey."

Mungo must have flinched. He knew what he was here for — he had begged James to let him come along — but it still hurt to hear his lips make sweet words for someone else. Ashley ran her eyes over him. "An' who's this wee bender?"

James introduced him. "He telt me he liked your Angela." He nodded at the girl who hadn't spoken.

"Ma name is *Angelique*." She pronounced it *And-Jahr-Leak-Ee*. "Get it right." She scowled at Mungo. He knew her vaguely from the talk of the streets; she excelled, strangely enough, at German, and could swim further and stay submerged longer than any boy on the scheme. "Are you Ha-Ha's wee brother? Ah telt him no to chase

Sammy-Jo. Everybody knows she only wanted a wean so she could get away from her maw and get a council house of her own."

"She'll have a long wait," said Mungo. "She can't leave till she's sixteen and even then her mammy will have to throw her out to show emotional distress or something."

"Aye, that's what I telt her. Gullible bitch." She laughed bitterly. She had already warmed to Mungo. "Yer much better looking than yer brother."

"Do you kiss better an all?" asked Nicola, who was still holding Morrissey at arm's length. The girls all erupted in squeals of laughter. Suddenly they were fifteen again, only children after all.

"What did ye bring us?" asked Ashley. James already had his hand on her knee, he was moving his lips from her earlobe down to her fine neck.

Mungo dug around in his cagoule pocket for three bars of Terry's mint chocolate.

Nicola immediately tore into it. "Whut? I've no had my dinner. My mammy's at the infirmary with my wee brother. He swallowed an Easter ornament."

James's lips were locked over Ashley's. Their mouths were opening and closing so wide that Mungo could see the muscle strain on James's jaw. It was more of a mauling than a kiss but Ashley was swooning, encouraging him with little groans of pleasure. The ash from her cigarette dangled and fell on to the wet ground.

The other girls ate the chocolate and passed the bottle of Mad Dog between themselves. "Here, if you mix them, it tastes like one of they fancy cocktails."

Mungo stood in the middle of the damp pathway and tried not to watch James. The girls flicked through the magazine, laughing at the dated haircuts on pop groups that had long since disbanded, and ignored Mungo entirely. He was certain he could walk away and no one would call after him. Angelique eventually looked up at him and studied him for a moment. Her face was peppered with pretty ginger freckles. "My mammy says you have roulettes. Is that true?"

"Roulettes?"

Angelique blinked half a dozen times in quick succession. Her tongue hung out of the side of her mouth like a strangled dog's. "Do ye?"

Mungo watched the double-decker buses chug along the Parade. He imagined himself on the top deck, going somewhere, anywhere away from here. He didn't know if he had Tourette's — he didn't want to know. When his blinking and ticcing had first become noticeable, Jodie had taken him to see the doctor. Dr Chaudhry had not seemed too concerned. She asked Mungo if there was stress in his life, if he was experiencing a particularly anxious time. Jodie had started laughing — not her usual affectation, but a nervous giggle that worsened the more she tried to hold it in. It was infectious, and Mungo began to laugh at the sight of his sister struggling to maintain her composure. Dr Chaudhry had become annoyed with them, and accused them of wasting her time. Jodie eventually gathered herself, and apologized, and said yes, she believed Mungo had stress in his life, and that it was nothing especially new.

The doctor said the stuttering facial muscles were not anything to be worried about, not yet. She said that they should increase the vitamins and magnesium in Mungo's diet, but that if it didn't calm down in six to nine months they should return, because it might be a sign of nerve damage or, more likely, Tourette's. Fourteen months had passed and Mungo hadn't returned to the doctor. He would rather not know and live in the faint hope of the ignorant; praying that it might clear up one day, in the same way his eruption of teen-age acne had come and gone.

"I don't know," said Mungo.

At that moment five men appeared on the crest of the path. They passed under a canopy of trees and dipped in and out of the gloomy daylight. Each man had a single golf iron over his shoulder, and they walked, bandy-legged, towards the young lovers. Mungo froze. James stopped mauling Ashley and looked to the advancing men, trying to discern if they were neds or actually golfers. Imperceptibly, the boys rose on to the balls of their feet. As the men came closer, one of them was swinging his club as though the youths were a thicket and he wanted to clear a path through them. Mungo stepped back and on to the grass, and the men passed by without incident. Mungo and James shared a glance. They didn't take their eyes from the men until they faded from view.

"So, which one of us do ye like?" asked Angelique.

"What?" Mungo turned back to the girl. He shrugged. "I think ye're both lovely."

'Well ye cannae kiss us both, we're no perverts."

"Ah should go wi' him," said Nicola, the chocolate clotted on her braces. "Ah winched his brother."

"What, is it a family account?"

"Naw. Ah'm just saying, everybody already knows ah've been wi' a Hamilton. This one wouldn't count a whole different person. It's like a half-point or somethin'. It's no as bad."

"Wie du willst," said Angelique in gruff German. She took up the *NME* again and was flicking through the pages. "But I'm no standing at the bushes keeping edgy for ye."

Nicola stepped off the bench and held out her hand like he had asked her to dance. Her assertiveness terrified him. She led him across the path and into some muddy ground surrounded by thick rhododendron bushes. It was a gloomy kind of dark in the centre. With no hesitation, she pressed up against him and took him in her arms.

Nicola was easily a head taller than James, and Mungo had to arch his back and stand on his toes as her mouth reached downwards and clamped over his. She smelled of fresh apple shampoo and like she lived in a house full of smokers. He could feel the jagged edge of her braces as she opened her mouth wide as a bin lid.

Mungo tried to match what she did and started counting from a thousand back to zero. He made it to 944 before she pushed

him away. Nicola began smacking her chocolatey lips, as though she tasted something
she hadn't enjoyed. She peered at him in
the darkness. The last of the daylight, dying
somewhere far away, glinted in her pupils.

TWENTY

Mungo stood just beyond the bend in the road and watched them through the smirr. He picked at a patch of green paint that was clinging to the rusting fence. As he watched the laughing girls, he pushed the shard between his nail and nail bed, gritting his teeth as the paint flake cut into the soft skin.

The girls were huddled in the dry doorway. They were struggling against each other, two pushing inwards while the smallest one tried to hold them at bay. It looked like a fight but they were shrieking with glee and talking so loudly that women had gathered at their windows. Nicola easily reached over Ashley's head and held her finger against the old close buzzer. The electric intercom shrieked. The sound carried down the narrow street, *tweeeee-eee-eee-eeee, tweeeee-eeee-ee, tweeeeeeee-ee.*

"Ah'm gonnae murder you," Ashley

459

hissed, but she was clearly delighted. She turned to run, but Nicola had hold of her anorak hood, so she threw her ringed fingers over her face, splayed wide enough to keep watching what was happening. "Ah'll die of embarrassment."

"Hallo. Is anybody there?" It was James's voice, as friendly as it must have sounded to the masturbating men on the chatline.

The girls took turns to squeal into the intercom declarations of love for him and confessions of how Ashley was mad in the passion. Ashley tried to clamp her hands over her friends' mouths, but they twisted free, and it was a battle she didn't really want to win.

"If ye come out to the park, Ashley says she'll let you dae *whatever* ye want to her."

Ashley shrieked. "Oh. My. God. I cannae believe you jist telt him that."

Mungo did not hear the rest of their nonsense. He was too busy watching the top floor window. Mr Jamieson had his hands in his trouser pockets. His back was arched in pride, he was rocking on his heels. He stood in his window and watched the foolish schoolgirls declare true love for his son. Mungo watched the smile pull at his top lip.

■ ■ ■ ■

"Have you been chewing the telly remote again?" Jodie pounced on him as he came in the door. It wasn't a question, and she didn't wait for an answer. Most of the time he wasn't aware he was doing it, but he liked to chew the grey remote. It fit perfectly inside his mouth, and he could push it all the way into the back and clench his molars down on to it until he felt calmer. The plastic squeaked satisfactorily, and it was strong enough that he could clamp down his hardest, till he was vibrating with the effort. Crushing the remote between his back teeth focused the current that ran through his body. He hadn't chewed it in a while. But this afternoon, he had found a familiar comfort in it. Jodie pulled a sour face as she wiped it on her skirt.

There were six books laid out on the carpet: three fine art books, a dog-eared novel, a manual of Fair Isle knitting, and a book of traditional Scottish weaving. Each book was opened to a specific page and pinned down by something personal of Jodie's. She had arranged them in a semicircle.

"What are they?" he asked sulkily.

461

Jodie blinked once, very slowly. "*Those* are books."

"What are you going to do with them?"

"I'm going to read them."

"But how?"

Jodie gave him one of those looks that tired women give to stupid boys; it was hard to tell if she felt sorry for him or sorrier for herself for having to suffer him. She looked worn out in her work uniform. Her ice cream costume was prim and old-fashioned with its raspberry piping and scalloped collar, but Mungo could see that it needed ironing and he resolved to wash it for her. Jodie still wore the kirby grips that held her paper hat in place, and as she drew them out, she used them to point at the books. "Actually, I got the books for you."

"But how?"

"Stop saying that. For goodness' sake. It's *why*, not *how*. *Why* did I get them for you. Are you going to talk like a schemie wee bam your whole life?"

Mungo kicked his trainers off. "Didnae realize I was such an embarrassment to you."

"Don't you want to go somewhere in life, Mungo?" Jodie was out of patience. "Sakes. I got them because I need to talk to you." She dropped heavily to the floor. Sitting in

462

the semicircle, she pushed one of the books towards him like it was a Ouija board. It was a white-covered book with drawings of different-coloured boxes stacked one on top of the other: *Ellsworth Kelly, The Museum of Modern Art*. The cover was already yellowing, but when Mungo checked the inside flap, the library ticket showed it was the first time it had been checked out.

"I had to ask the Mitchell Library for their copy. I've been waiting on some of these for a few months."

Mungo flicked through the book; page after page was covered in organized hatch marks or supremely controlled line drawings. Rectangles of fine lines that collided to make patterns and depth of tone from their layered repetition. It was very controlled. He found it calming. "Why are you doing this?"

Jodie sighed. She reached into her school-bag and pulled out an official-looking letter. Handing it to him, she spoke in short, complete sentences, almost as though it would be better parsed out this way. "I've been accepted. Unconditionally. I start in September. I'm going to university."

"Glasgow?"

"Yes. To study Biology."

He lunged at her and crushed her with his

body weight. Underneath him, he could feel her relax as though she had been stiff with tension. They lay against the settee and she returned his embrace. "That's bloody amazing." He chanted into her hair. "I knew it. *I knew.*"

When they sat up again, she was weeping with relief. Her face was slick with tears and her hair was sticking to her damp cheeks. "God. I'm glad you're happy. I was worried. I got this letter last week and I had nobody to tell. *Haaah-ha.*"

He picked at his cheekbone as his memories of James tinted with feelings of guilt. He had been a glutton with his three days. He had been selfish. "Wait just a minute, okay?" Before she could protest, he spun from the room. When he returned, he had a plate with a towering sandwich on it. There were eight layers of bleached white bread and between each layer he had smeared thick raspberry jam. Mungo had carved it into a rough cylindrical shape, then he sliced it into quarters. He crowned the cake with a blue birthday candle that was half-spent.

Jodie clapped her hands and counted the slices of flattened bread. "*Huit-feuille.* My compliments to the chef."

"I dunno what you are banging on about,

but if you close your eyes, I bet it tastes just like Victoria sponge."

They sat cross-legged on the carpet and Mungo cheered as Jodie blew out the candle. She didn't tell him what she had wished for. They tried to eat a slice each, but only Mungo made it further than one bite, scarlet jam gathering in the corners of his smile.

"Are you. Going to be. A doctor?" He couldn't eat, talk, and breathe at the same time.

She picked at the sweet sandwich. "No, I want to learn about the ocean. I'm going to specialize in Marine Biology. S'pose that's one thing to thank Fat Gillespie for. All that time on the Ayr coast and I realized I didn't know anything about the sea."

"Can't ye just watch David Attenborough and learn about it lit that?" Mungo crammed more bread into his mouth. " 'Asides, I wonder. How long. The bus will take?"

"What? To the sea?"

"No. To university. You'll have to change buses in town you know."

Jodie slid her plate away from herself. "I won't get the bus."

"Well you can't *walk* that far." He was

incredulous at her stupidity. Jodie was never stupid.

"No, you're right." She wiped the corners of her mouth. "I'll need to move to the West End. Into the halls of residence with the other students."

An image of James flashed across his mind. "But I can't move."

"I know." She pushed his hair away from his face. "The halls have single beds. I need to go alone. You'll need to stay here. *Haaah-ha.*"

"Oh." Several expressions crossed his face. He slid from happiness to disbelief and finally tried to cover his own rejection and embarrassment with a stoic tightening of his lips and eyelids.

"Mungo, you're bleeding everywhere!" Jodie shot to her feet. There was blood on the carpet and the cover of the Ellsworth Kelly book. Jodie hated anything to happen to a book. She mostly kept hers in the safety of her bedroom, safe from their double lives as tea coasters or dustpans to sweep ciga-rette ash on to. Jodie took his bleeding hand into her own. "You have a piece of metal stuck into your thumb."

"I do?"

"Mungo, how could you not feel that?"
Jodie used her teeth to pull the shard of

paint from the nail bed. Without a second thought, she put his whole thumb into her mouth and sucked the blood from it. Mungo could feel her quick tongue worry the edge of his nail. She drew it out and looked at it closely again. "Stupid bloody boy. How could you not know you had a piece of metal in your nail? You're gonnae need a tetanus jab."

"It doesn't hurt."

She was squeezing the nail, inspecting it for more rust and then cleaning the blood that came forth.

"When do you leave anyhows?"

"What?" She had forgotten all her news in her concern for his thumb. The earlier joy that had flooded his face had now drained away. His cheekbone was already twitching as his eyes reddened with a hurt he was trying to hide from her.

Jodie sat in Mo-Maw's comfy chair. She pulled Mungo towards her and at first he resisted. But Jodie held tight. "C'mon. You're never too big for a cuddle." She drew her brother on to her lap and held him close to her. He was much taller than her now. His gangly legs twisted upon themselves till they were both curled up, like two Siamese cats, cradled in the softness of the burst recliner. "You're getting too heavy for this."

She took his bleeding thumb and inserted it into his mouth. He sucked on it for a while. He could taste her spittle, it tasted like sweet raspberry jam. "My little baby is growing up."

"Cansh I come vishit?" He was lisping around his bleeding thumb.

"Anytime you want. I'll even dandle you like this in front of strangers, if you like."

He toyed with her cabled ponytail. "Well done, Jodie. You're a credit to yourself. I didn't mean to thspoil it."

She pointed with her toe at the books on the floor. "I thought we could talk about some things that might inspire you."

He took his thumb from his mouth to see if it was still bleeding. It wasn't but he went on sucking it. He started to bite down on it, grinding, testing it, then clenching it between his back teeth.

"You like to draw, don't you? Maybe you could do something with that when you leave school."

Mungo gazed at the books. Then he dropped his head again and nuzzled into her shoulder. "Naw. I'm not smart like you."

Jodie could hear his molars squeak against his thumb, it raised the hair on the back of her neck. "You're smarter than you think. And perfectly capable." She squeezed her

468

brother. "Hey? Is this about Mo-Maw?" Mungo didn't answer her. Jodie watched her brother as his eyes slid towards to the soundless television. Something dimmed in his gaze.

She hadn't needed to ask if it was about Mo-Maw. Everything about this boy was about his mother. He lived for her in a way that she had never lived for him. It was as though Mo-Maw was a puppeteer, and she had the tangled, knotted strings of him in her hands. She animated every gesture he made: the timid smile, the thrumming nerves, the anxious biting, the worry, the pleasing, the way he made himself smaller in any room he was in, the watchful way he stood on the edge before committing, and the kindness, the big, big love.

Jodie often marvelled at it, but mostly she hated it: the way he gave Mo-Maw love without thought of reward. Or maybe it was that he heaped and heaped it on in the hopes he would get a fraction of it in return, like his love was some undervalued currency. It made her think of the lassies in her Home Economics class who came back after the summer holidays, with their hair in beaded braids and all their tan on the fronts of them, from the burned tip of their noses to the top of their sore-looking thighs. Two weeks in Benidorm and now they spoke of being millionaires, but their newfound wealth was in pesetas, and Jodie knew they were worth just as much as they always had been.

Mungo's capacity for love frustrated her. His loving wasn't selflessness; he simply couldn't help it. Mo-Maw needed so little and he produced too much, so that it all seemed a horrible waste. It was a harvest no one had seeded, and it blossomed from a vine no one had tended. It should have withered years ago, like hers had, like Hamish's had. Yet Mungo had all this love to give and it lay about him like ripened fruit and nobody bothered to gather it up.

Mrs Campbell had once said Mungo's forgiveness was biblical, but Jodie didn't care much for the Bible, she thought it was stupid of him to be so easily exploited. She thought it was a little bit sad, a little bit weak. Her brother had all this love and forgiveness for an elfin wee woman who thought about herself first and last and in between. She was a terrible mother. Jodie didn't like to say that about another woman, but she was. She was terrible. Hamish knew it. Jodie knew it. She wondered when Mungo would too.

Mungo sighed in a way that shook her

bones. She could see the television reflected in his limpid irises; his pupils had expanded, his gaze was unfocused. "I wish you would talk to me, Mungo."

He answered her without looking at her. "I talk to you every single day."

"No. I jist wish you would tell me what you are feeling."

"Feelin'?" He thought about it for a moment, and then said, "I'm hungry again. But I can't be bothered to get up."

Jodie shoved him away from her.

He was Mo-Maw's youngest son, but he was also her confidant, her lady's maid, and errand boy. He was her one flattering mirror, and her teenage diary, her electric blanket, her doormat. He was her best pal, the dog she hardly walked, and her greatest romance. He was her cheer on a dreich morning, the only laughter in her audience.

Jodie shunted him again but Mungo only grumbled and curled tighter around her.

Her brother was her mother's minor moon, her warmest sun, and at the exact same time, a tiny satellite that she had forgotten about. He would orbit her for an eternity, even as she, and then he, broke into bits.

Jodie flicked the tip of his nose. "Sputnik."

"Whut? Shh. I'm watching this."

Jodie ran her fingers through her brother's hair. Mungo smelled of a strange new deodorant, something animal and loud. It was the type of scent the boys in her year smothered themselves in, it was full of pheromones and held promises of a fight or a fingering. It didn't suit him. She sniffed the top of his head.

"Pack it in!" He shifted like he was uncomfortable. As he slowly resettled beside her, he took care to make sure he wasn't squashing her. Jodie thought about how Mungo had moulded himself so entirely around Mo-Maw, how she had formed him into the exact component piece that she had been missing, and now that she didn't need him anymore, he was stuck in this weird specific shape. She wondered what lay ahead for her baby brother. What woman would love him now? She hoped for someone who would be grateful for his good looks and reticent ways. Someone who would feel blessed by his quiet attention, who would take all his love and keep it safe. There would be girls who would want to mother him forever, who'd be reduced by the helpless dip of his eyes into some primitive need to cook and clean and care for him. There could be others who would exploit him, who would feel so low about themselves that they would see his love for them as weakness, something he should be punished for.

Mungo's eyes came back into focus. He turned his head to meet her gaze. He frowned. "Who the fuck are ye staring at?"

"You. Mungo. I like you. You're good stuff."

Mungo looked a little surprised.

Jodie returned his attention to the books on the floor. "I know she doesn't take an interest in you. But that doesn't mean you shouldn't take an interest in yourself."

"Eugh! What wummin's magazine did ye get that guff from?" Mungo wiped his thumb on his denims. "Anyhows, I think I'll just sell speed for Hamish. There's guid money in it."

Jodie slapped him in the centre of his chest. He blinked in shock. "Listen, I will cuddle you anytime you want, Mungo. Even if we are eighty-five you can sit on my knee till you break my hips, awright? Just *please* don't get tangled up with Hamish."

Mungo nodded slowly. She could tell it pained him to lie to her.

She dropped the subject of education, hoping that if she left the books where they lay he would start to sniff around them for himself. They sat curled up together and watched the end of *EastEnders.* And then Jodie ate the rest of her slice of bread cake just to please him. She went to bed and was unable to sleep, shivery with sugar, and feeling guilty about her brother.

"Where the fuck have you been?" Hamish had a wild-eyed look to him as he let Mungo into the McConnachie flat. It was the middle of the day and he wore a pair of boxer shorts that hung off his wiry frame and flapped about his lean, muscular legs. He slumped on the edge of the settee and resumed watching his television programme; children's nonsense about squeaking puppets on a moon made of cheese.

Adrianna was in her bouncing chair gazing up at her father. The baby was gurgling to herself, her fat fist in her mouth, her chin slick with spit. With his bare foot Hamish pressed on the bouncing chair. He pumped it like he was a machinist who had been told there was no overtime pay. He was distracted by the television and was bouncing it too hard. On the table was a decent amount of speed that he had been dividing into clear baggies. Mungo wondered how long he had been hunched like this, chronic with adrenaline.

Hamish asked him again. "Where have ye been?"

"Nowhere."

"I telt Jodie four days ago I needed yer help."

Mungo mimicked the cooing noises he had heard Mrs Campbell make at her grandchildren. He plucked the baby from the chair before Hamish did it a harm. He stepped quickly to the side, fearful of blocking the television and the squeaking mice. The baby was damp, slick with sweat. He undressed it, better surely to be out in the dry, cold air than damp and warm in its onesie.

The mice blasted off in a rocket. Hamish made a deep inhalation, like he had forgotten to breathe and suddenly discovered the magic of it again. He looked down at the amphetamine piles on the table and then up at his brother and daughter. Mungo did not speak until he was spoken to.

"So, where have ye been?" Hamish had been chewing his bottom lip.

"Just around." Mungo doused the little girl in some talcum powder, the baby blinked in surprise. He rolled her in it, like he was breading chicken.

Hamish threw his arm around the speed. "Watch it wi' that, you." Then he thought again and snatched the talcum from Mungo. He loosened the top and added a handful to the amphetamine and stirred it through. He dabbed at it and licked his finger to see if it was too much. He winced.

"It's perfumed."

"I see that now. What do ye mean, just *around*?"

Mungo wrapped the baby in a towel and sat her on his knee, glad to have the talisman of her between Hamish and himself. "I dunno, I've been here, where else would I be?" He tried to divert the questioning. "Did you need something?"

"Did I need something?" Hamish pulled a sour face. "Naw. I'm out here trying to build a family business and look after a greetin' wean. All the while I've got to creep around cos I smashed a polis just because you were wanting to play doctors and nurses wi' a ginger glue huffer. Naw. Ah'm fine, Mungo. Thanks for asking but I can manage."

On the television two stuffed bears were reading a book to each other while a gormless blond man pretended not to be surprised. Hamish watched it a while and ran his tongue around his mouth. He seemed to be unable to stop biting at his own lips. "So, is it a girl?"

"Is what a girl?"

"Whoever the fuck you have been just *around* with."

"No."

Hamish blinked once behind his thick lenses. Then he laughed, a false, deep, threatening laugh. "I see you are feelin' gallus the day. I admire that. However, I will still slap ye across this room, even if ye are holding my daughter. So, do us both a favour. Cut the shite."

"I've just been around, Hamish. I've made a pal."

"Aw I see. Here I am getting ready to do battle and yer playing like a wean. Did ye enjoy making mud pies? Or are ye more of a fly-my-kite-across-Glasgow-Green kind of rascal?" Hamish was not expecting a laugh. "Who is he?"

"Nobody you know." Mungo tried to sound easy.

"Try me."

Mungo could feel that he was running out of road. "His name is James."

Hamish sucked on his front teeth. "Wee Jimmy Gilchrist? Gimpy Jimmy? Rabbie's twin, Jamesy-Samesy? Don't make me guess. Jimmy *who*?"

"James Jamieson."

When they were smaller, there was a puggy machine at Mo-Maw's favourite bingo. Mo-Maw called it "the babysitter" and for twenty minutes' peace she gave them each a handful of coins. When you dropped a coin in it, you listened to it bounce off a series of pegs and rattle into the machine's belly. The drop took an eternity before the machine lit up and blinded you with its party lights. Sometimes the coin bounced its long route only to miss the trigger and fall out of the machine again. Hamish hated that, the anticipation and then the disappointment, he huffed on his coins and polished them until they gleamed, thinking this would make a difference. Now Mungo tensed up and watched and waited for Hamish's proverbial penny to drop. He hoped it would slide past him, not trigger him, and then Mungo could pretend to drop it and James's name would roll under the settee.

"James Jamieson?" Hamish shook his head. Then his glasses shifted upwards slightly as he wrinkled his nose in recollection and then disgust. "You don't mean that wee papist?" All his lights were ablaze now, and as he sprung to his feet, he drew his arm back.

Mungo recoiled in the chair, he pulled his knees to his chest and held the baby between them. Hamish tried to reach around the laughing girl but Mungo moved her quickly like a human shield. "We're just pals. We just hang around the gether." He was almost screaming. Hamish stepped back, he loosened his fists and the blood returned to his knuckles. He started pacing the front room. Mungo knew not to speak unless he was spoken to. He dared not lower the laughing shield.

When Hamish finally spoke again, he was sitting on the edge of the coffee table, knee to knee with his brother and eye level with his child. There was a mess of clean baby clothes on the arm of the chair. Hamish started folding them carefully and talking sweetly to his daughter as though Mungo was not even in the room.

"You will stop hanging around with him."

"Hamish, c'mon."

"Listen. You *will* stop hanging around with him."

"You can't tell me what to do anymore."

Hamish nodded once, Mungo watched the muscles in his shoulders tighten and then relax. He whispered sweet nothings to the dribbling baby. *You're a lovely wee thing aren't ye?* And then he added in a low voice, "You will stop hanging around with him and on Saturday night ye'll be next to me when the Billies kick the fuck of out the

479

Bhoyston."

"But I don't have any other pals."

Who's a gorgeous wee thing? "It's the one we've been waiting for. They have their two best fighters coming back from a stint working down in Liverpool. They've been bamming us up for months now. Ye'll be there and ye'll chib the Fenian bastards."

"I don't understand, Hamish. Why? Why do we have to fight them?"

Hamish kissed the baby's fat belly. *Ye're getting a wee fat tummy just like yer mammy, aren't ye.* "James Jamieson lives in the tenements over the back green, right? He has a doocot behind the new-build houses?"

Mungo wanted more than anything not to have to answer that question. "Mibbe."

"Mibbe! Ha!" *Ooh yer Uncle Mungus thinks he's a right hardman.* Hamish went on folding the tiny outfits. "Mibbe!" Hamish chuckled to himself again. He was genuinely impressed by his brother's sudden boldness. "Think yer wide as fuck, do ye? Think yer smarter than the rest of us?" Hamish shook his head. "Well, yer Jodie Hamilton's double, right enough. Ah should have nipped that in the bud years ago."

"All I said was I don't know why we have to fight the Catholics."

"See, Jodie's problem is she thinks she's

slummin' it wi' us. She always has. All she's been doing is biding her time till she can get the fuck away. D'ye think when she gets where she's going she'll want to know ye?"

"She's my sister. She'll always be my big sister."

"Ah bet Jodie disnae even think of you as her brother. She thinks of ye as the unwanted wean who was dumped on her who she's had to raise. And she's fuckin' sick of it. Talk about resentment."

"That's not true."

"Jist you wait to the day you meet her on the street and she crosses it to avoid ye. Jodie cannae wait tae get the fuck away from ye. Ah'll bet ye a hunner quid."

Mungo slid back in the chair. He wrapped his arms around the baby and held her close, the top of her head smelled sweet, like talcum and powdered milk. The brothers sat in silence for a while. The gormless man on the television was gluing some toilet tube rolls together to make a child's telescope. Hamish watched it with a slack mouth. Mungo could do nothing but wait.

Hamish didn't turn back to face his brother. He was engrossed by the man who was turning rubbish into treasure. "Are ye listening to me, Mungo?"

"Aye."

481

"Well heed me when ah say, if ye don't show face on Saturday night, ah will go to that doocot. Ah will go to the doocot and ah will lock the papist in. Once ah have locked him in, ah will set fire to it with him inside. James Jamieson will scream for his mammy, but he will roast." Hamish paused, and then he asked, "Do you understand me?"

Mungo nodded, although Hamish did not turn around to see it.

The man on the television glued pieces of blue- and rose-coloured film to the end of the paper telescope and suddenly it became a kaleidoscope. The screen filled with pretty colours. Hamish was grinning madly. He turned back around and gently laid his hand on Mungo's knee. He rolled his tongue around his mouth as he thought about what Mungo had asked. "And your earlier question about fightin' Catholics. It's about honour, mibbe? Territory? Reputation?" The baby reached out and grabbed Hamish's pinkie. Hamish smiled sweetly. "Honestly, ah don't really know. But it's fuckin' good fun."

Twenty-One

Mungo made three separate pilgrimages to Glasgow Cross over the course of two days. It took him forty-five minutes to walk down there and, feeling defeated, an hour and twenty to lumber back home.

The pawnbroker was tucked away on a tatty back street behind the Saltmarket. There were a few half-shuttered shop fronts where the owners were pecking out a living, and a utilitarian-looking pub that wrapped around the corner. Every now and then, a man would shuffle out into the daylight like a cuckoo, blink up at the sky as if trying to judge the time of day, and finding the damp weather unchanged, shuffle back inside. Mungo had been delighted to catch a glimpse inside the boozer and spy a cluster of stout women dancing together, gyrating across the floor like washing machines that had juddered loose from their brackets.

The back street had a feeling of a shortcut

to it, a quick way to travel from the Briggait to the Barras. Mungo bought a poke from the chippy and leaned against the lamp post. He enjoyed watching the different types of people come and go: the hawkers and housewives, the slick yuppies and the slick junkies. A troupe of middle-aged dancers in tap shoes and silver leotards emerged from a side door. The women scuffled down the street, twirling and giggling, sharing some in-joke and passing around a single cigarette. They soft-shoed around Mungo, red lips smiling as they went.

On each of the trips Mungo had watched the pawnbrokers from different vantage points but he had never seen his mother, and he had yet to summon the courage to step inside. The claret exterior was covered in gilded letters, proudly offering the "best cash for ladies jewellery" and a "massive selection of engagement rings." Yet when Mungo peered through the shuttered windows all he could see was stuff that looked like discarded tat. One window held televisions and stacked stereos, a jumble of dated electronics that were wrapped in their own wires as though they had been hastily removed. Another window held a mixture of cumbersome musical instruments and a smattering of labourers' tools: a used angle grinder, old-fashioned wood planes, and a proud shelf of Stanley knifes that made Mungo think of Hamish's boys. There was a display case of photo frames and trinket boxes, heavy bric-a-brac made in a tarnished metal that looked worthless to him, but when he peered at the little price sticker, it made him straighten up in shock. There was a display of fine-looking cameras, of a kind that Mungo had never seen anyone use in real life.

Mungo was pretending to consider a shelf of christening spoons, but really he was glancing up at the stocky man behind the counter. It was hard to see much of Jocky. The interior was dimly lit and he was tight-faced as he counted his money, safe behind the Perspex security screen.

Mungo had almost summoned the courage to step inside when a van bumped up the kerb with a shudder. A young workie in a black donkey jacket rushed into the shop, lugging what must have been a saxophone or a tuba in a battered case. Mungo stepped away and went back to the windows.

"Excuse me. Do you know how pawnbrokers work?" asked a posh-sounding young man.

Mungo was startled by the voice beside him. He turned to the young man. He had

485

been standing before the Japanese cameras and had an intelligent, quiet expression that said he might even know how to use one.

Mungo answered him. "Naw. Sorry. I've never pawned anything myself."

"Okay. Thank you." The young man was tall and angular, his body drowned in an oversized black parka. His ebony hair was overlong but neatly parted. There was worry sitting in the corners of his mouth.

"Look, it cannae be that hard," said Mungo. "What have you got for pawnin'?"

The young man slid his holdall from his shoulder. He opened it carefully and Mungo peered inside. Nestled amongst some soft cloths was a collection of porcelain ornaments; Mungo could make out a coy shepherdess and several frolicking kittens. "I don't even know how much to ask for?"

"Me neither." Mungo shrugged. "How much do you need?"

"As much as I can get. I'm starting at the hairdressing college next week. I wanted to buy some new scissors and that."

Mungo's eyes scanned the window again, he thought he had seen a pair of electric hair clippers somewhere. For a while they both peered into the pawnshop and watched the workie haggle with Jocky. The labourer was moving animatedly, as though he was

486

recounting some yarn about the pedigree of the saxophone, but through it all Jocky's face remained an impassive mask.

"My mother was never a big fan of pawnshops." The man said it in such a way that he seemed to be talking to himself. "She found them quite a low place, dead common. A necessary evil, she said."

"Why don't ye ask her how they work?"

The young man's eyes flickered to meet Mungo's gaze and then they fled again. "Well. I can't."

The workie came banging out of the shop. He had a thin wad of notes in his grasp, "Ye're a parasitic little pirate. Conning guid, hard-working folks out of their fuckin' treasures. Ye should be ashamed of yersel." He slammed the door with such force that the window shutters rattled in their casings. The workie turned to Mungo. "Listen pal, do yersel a favour. Whatever ye've got to pawn, take it elsewhere. Nothin' but a robbin' aul' basturt in there. He'd have the teeth out of your granny's heid."

Mungo was at a loss for words. He felt winded. The labourer had thick, dark lashes and eyes of such a pale shade of blue that Mungo couldn't help but stare. He had been unprepared for the rare beauty of this man. The man's lips were generous against a powerful jawline, and even in his anger he was smirking, his eyes twinkling. "Can ye no talk, mucker?" Something in the knowing way the young man was smiling back at Mungo said that he was used to having this effect on people. "Is it a séance I'll be needin' to reach ye?"

Mungo recovered himself too late. He willed his eye muscles not to betray him. "Aye, I can talk. I heard what you said."

The worried young man with the black hair stepped forward then. "Mister. If I shouldn't pawn my stuff in there, would you know of a place I could take these?" He tilted the bag towards the workie, the man seemed unimpressed as he peered inside.

"Are ye robbin' yer mammy's good china to buy yersel some smack?"

The young hairdresser bristled. "No. Of course not."

The man smiled. Mungo had to look away to stop staring. He would dream about this man later, he would think about how his thick fingers crammed into the pockets of his jeans, how there was chafing on his muscular neck where the coarse wool of his jacket irritated his stubble. The man laughed. "What is it wi' you two? Is it yer first night on earth?" He looked inside the duffel bag again. "Auld Jocky is better for shanking blades and the odd oboe. Ah'd take these out to the West End, look along the Byres Road. They've got fancy houses and antique shops out there. There are *actual* pedlars of other people's old shite, if ye can fuckin' believe it." With that the workie put his money in his breast pocket. He strode across the pavement and got back into his van, the engine came to life with a great rattling shudder.

He leaned out the window and said to the hairdresser, "Haw, you wi' the trinkets. If ye want a lift ah'm heading out yon Finnieston way. If ye don't mind a wee walk I can drop ye close enough to the West End?"

The young man nodded and walked around to the passenger side. The workie was watching Mungo. He leaned out of his window and tapped his hand on the door as though Mungo should come closer. Mungo crossed over to him, and the workie said, "Here, how old are you?"

Mungo hesitated a moment. "Nearly sixteen."

The man smiled and Mungo felt his pulse quicken. The workie pointed at the side of the van. "Can ye read that sign?"

Mungo gazed at where the man was pointing. *Davey MacNeil. Plumbing, Bathroom and Kitchen Fitting. Fair price — fast work. Duke*

Street. Tel: 554 6799. Mungo nodded, he was confused. "Aye, I can read it."

"Can ye remember it?"

Mungo glanced at it again. "Aye. So?"

"Guid. Ah'm Davey. See when you turn twenty-one, can I take you for a drink? Will ye gie us a wee phone?" The workie winked at Mungo, his blue eyes sparkling with mischief. Mungo must have nodded, but he wasn't aware of it. Davey released the handbrake and the van trundled off. Mungo watched it join the evening traffic.

A new voice cut into his thoughts. "Haw. Whit's yer game, pal?"

Mungo turned on his heel. Jocky was standing in the doorway of the pawnshop, he had a claw hammer in his hand. "Ah've seen you every day this week, just watchin' the place. You one of the young Tongs? Think ye can fuckin' rob us?"

Mungo shook his head. "Naw. I'm no from the Calton. Are you Jocky?"

"Whit if ah um?"

"I'm looking for Maureen Buchanan. I'm Mungo. I'm her boy."

Mungo wasn't sure what he had expected, but he had a feeling that the man would have been annoyed at his sudden appearance. Mo-Maw had given him the impression that Jocky didn't like the messy bits of

490

her life, that he and his siblings were like the used plates that she kicked under her bed and hid beneath the bed skirt. Jocky surprised him when he lowered the hammer and said, "Right, Will ye be wanting a cup of tea?"

The inside of the pawnshop was more cluttered than the windows. There was a battalion of upright hoovers along one wall, and behind the security glass were the cases of rings that the signwriting promised. Mungo peered at them, he knew nothing about the fashions of ladies' jewellery but all the women he knew had quick, busy hands and these rings seemed heavy and impractical. Jocky locked the door, he led Mungo behind the counter and into the storeroom at the back. He rinsed two tea mugs and filled the electric kettle. There was a rail of wedding dresses gathering dust.

"Do you sell everything?"

"Aye. Every manner of thing if there's money in it." Jocky shovelled heaped spoonfuls of powdered milk into the mug. "But it's no really about sellin'. It's about haudin'. Sugar?"

Mungo nodded. "I've never been in a pawnshop."

"Och, there's nothing to it. It's just a big storage shed. Money lending, int it?" Jocky offered Mungo a biscuit, and when he took one, Jocky pushed another on him. He pointed at a low stool for Mungo to sit on. "That fella ye were talking tae. He brings his trumpet in here every so often. Every time he pretends like ah came up the Clyde in a banana boat. But ah gie him a couple of poun' for it, and then when wages day comes, he buys it back for a wee bit more than ah gave him."

Mungo chewed the soft biscuit. "So, how much do you want for my mother then?"

Mungo had meant it as a joke, but Jocky handed the boy a cup of tea and carried on as though he hadn't heard him. "There used tae be guid money in it. Decent families needing a wee bit o' cash to tide them over tae Friday. But now it's aw junkies rippin' electronics out of their mammies' flats and puntin' it fur skag." Jocky nodded at a stack of record players. "And who wants tae buy used stuff anymair? It's aw new, new, new wi' people these days. It breaks: they bin it. It doesnae go wi' the wife's latest haircut: they bin it."

Mungo looked around the storeroom with a different perspective. What had first seemed like a bounty of treasures waiting to find new homes now seemed like a dumping ground for unwanted relics.

Jocky slumped on his stool with a groan. He was a short man and stout, but his fat hadn't slackened into corpulence yet, there was still a muscularity to him; he looked like he could handle himself in a fight. He slurped on his tea. "What the polis can never know is ah make a killin' wi' blades and shanks and the odd shooter. Thank fuck the Young Teams are aw fightin'. That's where aw the money is these days, drugs and violence. The rest of it widnae buy ye a lick of an ice cream cone."

Mungo wondered if Hamish had ever been here.

"Did ye know there is a vogue to weapons? Like an actual fashion trend? Some of these fighters carry on like they were lassies buying dresses in Paris. 'Oh naw, ah don't want a bowie knife — every cunt already has a bowie knife. Ah want somethin' mair elegant. Somethin' that screams *me*.' " Jocky chuckled as he lit a cigarette. He offered his packet to Mungo, but Mungo declined. Now that they had discussed the pawn business there seemed nothing left to talk about, other than the woman who was strung between them and tied them together. It seemed like neither of them knew how to broach the subject of Maureen. The silence went on for an uncomfortably long time.

Jocky smoked his fag. Mungo's tea cooled.

"You don't look anything like her. Maureen, that is."

"I know. She's says I look lit my da but . . ." Mungo didn't bother to finish the sentence. "How is she anyhows?"

"Fine. Ah saw her this mornin' as she was comin' in frae her work." Jocky exhaled a long plume of smoke. "Does she always drink that much?"

Mungo thought about it a moment. "If ye can keep her happy, distract her, then she drinks a wee bit less. She's best when she's got something to look forward to. It doesnae have to be big. Tell her you'll take her to the pictures on a Friday. Mibbe tell her you'll take her shopping in the town centre. Jist wee promises to look forward to."

"You know aw the tricks."

"Our Jodie knows better than me. Jodie says it's like minding a sugary wean."

Jocky laughed. "Ah have one of those baby bouncing chairs around here somewhere."

"I bet she'd fit in it."

"She never said ye were funny." Jocky glanced at his wristwatch, it was a heavy silver thing that called attention to its own value. "Ye should go on up the road and see her. She'll be awake now. Ah can gie ye the address of the flat."

"No. It's awright." He lowered his chin into the neck of his cagoule. "Can you do us a favour? Please don't tell her I came here. She asked me not to."

Jocky leaned forward on his stool and his gut sank between his thighs. "Look, son. Ah didnae know she had weans of her own. Honest. As soon as ah found out, ah papped her."

"Naw. Don't do that. We won't get in the way."

"Och, it's no *that*. Ah'd known yer mother for three weeks. She'd telt me how she loved prawn cocktail and Tom Selleck afore she even telt me she had weans. What did ye want me to dae?"

"Honestly. It's awright."

"Ah papped her so she would go up the road and look after youse. What type of wummin doesnae go home to her weans?"

Mungo didn't know how to respond to that. His mother was like a carnival magician, she was forever working some sleight of hand, sucking in her paunch, or turning different faces to these men. Jodie had said it was like how McCallum's the baker kept turning their old wedding cakes in their window when the icing had yellowed in the sunlight. By the time some poor punter sliced into the fruit cake, it'd be too late to complain that it was claggy and unappetizing and soaked in rank old booze.

Jocky swirled his cup, he swallowed the dregs of his tea. "Ah think she worries that youse don't need her anymair and that she'll be left wi' nuthin'. She says ye're all growin' up too fast. That must be hard for a mammy."

It wasn't true; Mungo felt like he would always need her, but he was never allowed to admit that out loud. "My brother said she's cracking on with her life, and so we should crack on with ours."

Whenever he thought unkind thoughts about Mo-Maw, he tried to remember the stories that his mother had told him about her own childhood. About how she was the youngest of four girls, and how, after her mother had died, her father, a grain-hodder on the Clyde, had taken the girls and parcelled them out to anyone who would be able to give them a good home. It had been an ordinary Wednesday when the adults came to the house in their Sunday clothes and carried the sisters away.

It had been agreed not to tell the girls in advance. Instead, each of the couples planned a fine day out: outings to the zoo, or shoe shopping, and then in the evening they took the girls back to their new homes and that was the end of it, no discussion. No one had been able to take all four sisters, so Cathy, the eldest girl, had gone to live in Ballachulish where she could help Granny Buchanan around the croft. Alice and Jean had been sent to England to different cousins of their mother's and had made quiet successes of their lives. Only Maureen, at three and half years old, had remained in the East End of Glasgow. She had been taken in by a childless couple, a scrap merchant and his wife, who lived over the back middens. It was near enough where her father could keep an eye on her, which he did, until he married again and moved through to Falkirk to work on the Union Canal. She hadn't seen him since she was six.

Mo-Maw said the scrap merchant and his wife were good people, phlegmatic but harmless. Mungo believed her, because Mo-Maw could find the skelf in any caress, and so she would have said if they'd been cruel, or miserly, or otherwise. But as easily as Mo-Maw had come into their lives, she had drifted out of it again when she was fifteen. In the evenings the scrap merchant had liked to sit with large leather headphones on, listening to the wireless, old dancehall songs from before the war, or the endless football commentary. His wife had sat on the settee next to him, flipping through her programmes on the television, together but alone. Mo-Maw said that was how she had found them, and that was how she had left them.

Mungo looked down at his feet, his big toe was bursting through the seam of his trainers. "Do you love her?"

Jocky answered too quickly. "Naw. Naw, ah don't."

Mungo looked up at him.

"Listen son, at ma age love is a nuisance of a thing. What ye want is some easy company on a Tuesday night, a bit of help runnin' the hoose, and if yer lucky a bit of nookie as long as ye can both lie on yer side while ye're at it." Mungo didn't laugh at the joke. Jocky dropped his dout into his mug. "What ye want is an easy life. There's nothin' easy about love."

Mungo finished his tea. He put the mug in the sink. "Will you do me a favour?"

"Another one?"

Mungo nodded. "If she asks you if you love her, just tell her 'aye.' She deserves it."

The man didn't answer one way or the other. He got up off his stool with a wince. "It does the spine nae guid to be standing at yon counter all day. If ye want ma advice, when ye go out into the workin' world, try and choose a profession that keeps ye movin' aboot. And be wary of sittin' amongst the refuse of other people's lives."

When they went back through to the shopfront, there was a young woman banging against the locked door. She had a VCR in her arms and a desperate look on her face. When she saw Jocky she bounced on her toes and looked like she might weep. Jocky sighed wearily. "If the skirts get any shorter, they'll start doing without them all the gether."

He drew a couple of pound coins from his trouser pocket and slipped them into Mungo's hand. "Listen, ah like yer mammy, ah do. But she needs to cut back on the cheeky juice. Ah've got weans of ma ain to be worryin' aboot. She cannae be sitting around aw day drinkin'."

Mungo nodded as Jocky unlocked the door. He stepped out into the sunshine just as the silver dancers went twirling up the street.

The doocot door was open to the fair weather. James's head was lowered in concentration. He was humming to himself as he mended the broken hinge on a cage. Patient and self-taught, James knew how to fix or build almost anything; the slates were already on the roof, he didn't need anyone's help.

As James worked, Mungo gazed upon him. He liked to watch him unawares. He didn't know how much longer he would be allowed to do that, and he wanted to dub him on to the videotape in his brain while he still could.

The last time he had seen James, the hair at the nape of his neck had come to a ticklish point, like a little duck tail. Mungo had liked to touch the tip of his nose to it while James napped. Now his hairline was pink and precise where it had been edged by a straight razor. Mungo could picture Mr Jamieson holding his son's head in his hands, asking him about Ashley, as he lathered his neck with the badger brush. Mungo swallowed the little ball of jealousy that rose up inside him. It slunk down his throat and bounced off his ribcage. He could feel it roll around inside him, like a marble dropped into a children's toy.

James put down his pliers and drew a bird from the cage; it panicked as his hands encircled it, but he squeezed lightly and it stopped its nervous bobbing. Mungo watched the fingers cradle the pigeon, half-wild, half-stupid, and he was jealous of the bird, and its ignorant blinking. Mungo stepped into the doocot and kissed the secret pink skin behind James's ear. He had tried, but he could not stay away a full week.

James flinched, his eyes darted beyond Mungo back into the daylight. "Don't do that. Not here. Not now."

The look in James's eyes made it clear there would be no long fingers to hold him tight and make him feel calmer. He had a terrible urge to break something now, to tear the rickety shelves down and set all the birds free. Mungo stood with his arms by his side. He forced himself to remain very still.

"It's almost over. Two more days and then he's gone again. We are *so* close." James was shaking his head. "He's gonnae leave early to go see that wummin in Peterhead. Just two more days and we can be by ourselves."

"Yeah, until next time." He knew he was being callow.

"I cannae help that." James kissed the pouter and put it back in its cage. He busied himself before he grew calm enough to ask, "What have you been up to anyhows?"

"Nothin'." He didn't want to talk now. He had no generosity in him to be good company. He found himself looking up at the small skylight, wondering if James could escape through there when Hamish came for him. "Absolutely fuckin' nothin'."

"You need a hobby."

Here was yet another person telling him what he needed, how he should act, the person he should be. Another person who didn't think he was enough just as he was.

James watched him turn to leave. He was talking to Mungo's back as he dipped at the low doorway. "Ma da took us to Celtic Park. I haven't been to the fitba since I was twelve. The whole match he stood there with his arm around me like he used to, proud, like. After the fitba, he treated Geraldine and me to a curry up in the West End. He took us to the pub and bought me ma first pint. He lied to the barman, telt him his son had just turned eighteen."

"At this rate you'll be sixty before I'm sixteen."

"He's had the best week he's had since my mammy died. I didnae want to spoil it for him." James was twisted-looking, embarrassed at his own happiness. "He hardly mentioned his fancy-wummin."

Mungo tried to breathe through his hurt. All he wanted was the long fingers to wrap around his ribcage and hold him still, stop him floating away, let him know somebody cared. There was a long nail with a shackle padlock hanging from it, he ran his torn thumbnail along it and felt the metal scrape his wound open again.

"Another thing. He said he could get me a job on the rig."

Mungo pushed his skin on to the nail. "Oh?"

"He said he didn't see why not. They're moving him to a new oilfield, on to a newer rig they're building, called the Gannet or something. He said when I turn eighteen, he could get me in for caterin' or janny work, maybe as a roustabout. Given time, I could work up to be a derrickman or driller. He said that's where the money is."

"That's guid."

"If I worked offshore with him, we could spend more time together."

"Won't Ashley mind?"

"Who gies a fuck about her?" James dipped his head to look Mungo in the eyes, peering under the curtain of his fringe. "I wouldn't go, you know that. It's just nice to be asked. Let me enjoy that, for Christ's sake."

"Do you like her?"

"Who?"

"Ashley."

"Naw." James seemed irritated. He busied

himself by scooping bird pellets into a cup. "I sort of hate her. Every single thing she says is either stupit or about herself. She moans if I don't give her attention every five minutes. Her hair always looks wet, but it's dry and hard as a fuckin' rock and when she touches me, you can tell she's counting in her head, like she's adding it to my bill. But . . ."

Something else had snagged on Mungo's mind. "Have ye shagged her yet?"

"Naw." James pushed the meat of his palms into his eye sockets. "But she keeps asking me to. Her maw and stepda are away in Majorca next week. Empty house."

"But." It was a small voice that came next. "We haven't even done that yet."

"I know." James seemed tired now. He was just a wee boy, acting like a man, pretending to be a different type of man.

Mungo pulled his finger off the rusted nail. "I'm glad you are fixed, James. You've worked hard to get better. You deserve it."

"I'm not *fixed,* Mungo. Ah'm just a liar."

"Yeah, well." Mungo tapped the shards of glass from the sole of his trainer. "I'm too many other bad things. I don't want to be a liar as well."

For a moment James looked like he was going to correct him — he was already a liar — but he bit his tongue. He crossed the rat glass towards him. In the half-light, he put his index finger on the nape of Mungo's neck. It was the slightest of touches, a hand that could easily turn to a bully's flick if someone came across the scabby grassland. In a downward motion he gently stroked the line of fine hair that grew there. Mungo tilted his head forward and closed his eyes. He wanted it to last.

"This is what you do when a bird gets distressed."

"Is it not kinder to jist snap their necks?"

James laughed. "It'll be over soon. Then we can pick any direction and ride our bikes there."

"And what about Ashley?"

"You ask too many questions."

"If you do shag her, I would understand." It was a gamble to say it, he could lose, but he needed to say it regardless. "But, like, I will also die."

"Nah. You're harder than ye look." James stopped stroking his neck and drew his knuckle gently across the twitching cheekbone. When Mungo opened his eyes ten digits were splayed before him, he added his own hands and extended four more, then James folded one away. "Look, only thirteen left now. Ma da has only thirteen more shore leaves til you turn sixteen." He seemed like he wanted a smile from Mungo before he left. Just one single smile. Mungo would not surrender one.

Mungo found himself staring at the countdown. It had seemed innocent as an advent calendar a few days ago. But now he pictured Jodie with her bags already packed, Ashley sprawled on her parent's bed, and Hamish, wild on his own supply, with a bottle of siphoned petrol in his hand. Thirteen fingers, thirteen shore leaves, was a distance too far to imagine. They wouldn't both make it. Not safely. Not together. "I can leave now, if you can? Tonight. Who cares if somebody phones the polis? Who cares if the school sends out the Social Work? We can hide. Let's just fuckin' go."

James chewed the inside of his cheek. It was worse than he had thought. He reached beyond Mungo and closed the doocot door. In the darkness his strong fingers encircled Mungo, they pressed against his ribs and moved around to his spine as the long arms snaked around him. Mungo suffocated himself against James's chest, he found the prickle of Shetland wool solid and comforting. James's breath felt hot against his crown. "I listened to your mixtape. I stand in the dark at my window and listen to it every night. I thought you said it was all top forty but it's only one song over and over."

"I felt embarrassed. I lied."

"I love the Smiths." Mungo rubbed his face on the lambswool. "But how come Morrissey didnae think there was panic on the streets of Glasgow? There's plenty of fuckin' panic here."

"Probably because Glasgow rhymes with fuck all. Well, anytime I hear it I will think of you. Ya handsome wee devil." He tilted his head towards Mungo's lips and kissed him deep on the mouth. Then he shoved him back to arm's length and shook him slightly. "Cheer up. I love you, Mungo Hamilton."

"Don't." Something in him could not stand to be loved.

"How no? I can love you if I want."

"It'll just make it harder for me. When everything gets spoiled."

James took his hands away. Mungo felt like the doo again as the anxiety flooded his body. Without opening his eyes, he could hear the rusty hinges of the heavy door, could feel the cold, weak light on the pink of his eyelids.

"Not everything good goes bad."

Mungo wanted to believe that.

James took up the pliers again. "Only two

more days. We can be the gether again. Can you come over on Saturday night? He should be on the last train back to Aberdeen by then."

"Aye, okay." Mungo tried his best to sound nonchalant, when in reality he would look forward to that moment for every minute in between. Then he shook his head, and his hair fell over his eyes again. "Wait, naw. I can't come on Saturday night."

"How no?" James looked crestfallen.

Mungo would never admit it, but he liked to see James's disappointment, the slight swing back of power. It was a twisted payment for the starvation he had suffered the past week. "Nothing. It's jist our Hamish's nonsense."

"Can't you just tell him no?"

Mungo laughed at the absurdity of the idea. "*That's funny.* Let me tell him I don't like his glasses while I'm at it."

"What can be that important it cannae wait?"

"I hate it. But there's a fight planned for Saturday night across the Royston bridge. The Bhoyston have been bamming them up. He said I needed to be there to give them hauners. It's a reputation thing. I'm a Hamilton." He skipped over the threat about burning James alive. "Hamish wouldnae take no for an answer."

"So, you're just gonnae go and chib some Catholics?"

"Honestly, I'm brickin' it. But I was hoping to jist show face, then stand at the back, like." Mungo found a bottle of penicillin on the shelf. He shook it like it was a maraca.

"But I'm a Catholic."

"You're no really. It's no the same, you're different. You don't even go to chapel."

"It's *exactly* the fuckin' same." He turned his shoulder on Mungo and said just loud enough for him to hear. "Ye're a wee coward."

Idiot. Weakling. Poofter. Liar. Coward.

"You do well worse things to hide yourself."

"At least ah don't hurt other people."

Mr Jamieson would be hurt, Ashley would be hurt too, but she would recover swiftly. Mungo did not want to breathe life into these people and bring them back into the doocot between them. "These Catholic fighters, the Bhoyston, they want to hurt me as well. If I don't stand up to them, I'll run into them one day in the Trongate or the Briggait, and they'll slash me from here to here." Mungo ran his fingernail from his earlobe to the corner of his mouth. He pressed so hard it left a bloodless line that

509

flickered and faded. It was pure Ha-Ha talking.

James was hunched over the broken hinge just as Mungo had found him. It was strange to see; it was like he had never even visited, as though he had not altered James's day one bit. His life would go on without him. "If you fight the Catholics, don't come on Saturday. Don't come near me on Sunday or Monday or ever again. If you do that, I don't want to know you."

TWENTY-TWO

Mungo dared not fall asleep. It was his third night at the lochside and his head was bobbing on his shoulders. Gallowgate was in no hurry. He rolled a mean cigarette from scavenged baccy and smoked it inside the collapsing tent. As he told his stories he held the glowing tip too close to the combustible fabric. Mungo didn't care anymore. Let it burn.

By the last light of the tea candle, the inked man advanced upon him slowly, territorially, painted knuckles on the ground. He touched him almost tenderly and caressed the boy with a gentleness that made Mungo feel sick. Mungo put his hand over Gallowgate's mouth — he couldn't bear to hear him say sweet things — but Gallowgate took it the wrong way. He licked the inside of Mungo's palm, nibbled from the meat to the fingertip, his tongue slipping in and out between his fingers.

511

The tenderness quickly evaporated and the inked man began pawing at him, forcing rough hands inside Mungo's clothes. His greed possessed him, his eyes looked bottomless in the candlelight, and he scratched the boy as he grabbed at his flesh. Mungo didn't want what came next. He spat into his own cupped hands and then wrapped them around Gallowgate's swelling. In the flickering light, he worked as quickly as he could to give the man what he wanted, and to send him back into the darkness.

When Gallowgate was spent, he lay back and threw his arms out to the side as though he had been crucified. He reached out to the boy and ruffled his hair, a look of satisfaction upon his face. Mungo listened to the rain beat against the tarpaulin. A question burned inside him, he asked the universe as much as he asked Gallowgate, "Does this mean you're a poofter?"

Gallowgate had slithered across the floor and had begun to snake his naked body around the boy. Now he shoved him away. The distance felt good to Mungo. "Call me that again an' ah'll knock ye out."

Mungo must have dozed because it was already brightening when Gallowgate woke him. The man crawled naked from the tent and went for a piss. Mungo could see the clear morning light through the flaps, it seemed the rain had stopped for a spell. He wrapped the sleeping bag around his shoulders and followed Gallowgate out to the shoreline, feeling safer in the open rather than the sweaty, fetid trap of the tent. The prehistoric boulders were slick again with rain, and new pools of water were already busy with flies. Gallowgate stood at the water's edge. Even his back was a tapestry of tattoos; a life-like pair of women's eyes were painted on his shoulder blades, the eyelashes flicking up like feathery wings. Only his buttocks were untouched, and glowed a ghostly white.

Mungo stared at the one-man tent. It no longer resembled a shelter and lay almost completely flat, a red puddle on the grey shore. It didn't look like it could house a man's body. Mungo pulled the sleeping blanket tight around himself, he walked away from the pissing man and crouched by the water. The face that stared up at him was not his own.

It seemed Gallowgate was impervious to the cold. The last of the drink was burning him from the inside out. "So, what do ye want to do the day?"

Run, run all the way home. But Mungo

pushed his face into the frigid water, let the loch chill his tic. Then he shook himself, steadied himself, and shrugged. "Should we not pack up and think about heading back?"

"You sick of me alreadies?" Gallowgate shook the last dribble of piss from the end of his cock. He frowned at the boy.

Mungo sat back on his haunches. Ha-Ha had trained him well. They were a lot alike, Gallowgate and his brother. They were moody, self-made demigods who demanded constant offerings and could turn vengeful for no reason. Mungo saw the trouble forming. He crossed the short distance and placed a placating kiss on the man's lips. It was the first he had ever offered him.

Gallowgate beamed at him proudly. Now he was convinced of his own allure, happy that he had known what was best for Mungo all along. All the boy had needed was a guiding hand, a father figure to show him the way. Gallowgate flicked his own chin upwards, his sharp teeth tugged on his bottom lip. "See, we are pals." He encircled Mungo's waist with his arm. "Ah think ah'm gonnae show you how to catch some rabbits the day."

"Seems a shame to kill a thing and not even eat it. Can you take it on the bus?"

"Course ye can." He was studying Mungo

closely. " 'Asides, yer maw'll love it. She's gonnae be expecting to hear about yer adventures. And if we catch two she can have a new pair of slippers."

Mungo lowered his gaze. "Don't worry about Mo-Maw. She'll have forgotten I was even gone. She'll be worried about herself, as usual. 'Asides, I learned how to build a fire and peg a tent and . . ." Mungo put his lips to Gallowgate's ear and whispered the last part.

The man flushed. "Ya dirty wee bastard." He bit the boy's neck. "Ah knew what you were like the first time ah saw ye."

Mungo's jumper hung over his knuckles, he blew warm air up his sleeve. "Let's just go. We can catch those rabbits another time."

Gallowgate thought about it for a moment. "Awright then. Do ye promise?"

Mungo nodded.

Gallowgate let go of the boy and turned towards the red tent. "Let's get this auld bastard on his feet and we can get going then."

Mungo caught the man's pinkie with his own. "Do we have to? I mean, can't we just leave him here. He'll find his own way home."

"That's a laugh."

"I can't be his friend and your friend. I can't."

The man pulled Mungo under his armpit and hugged his head hard, twisted it like all the bullies he had ever known. "Don't worry about that. Ye're ma special pal now. But ah cannae leave him here. That tent belongs to a fella at ma work. Ah'll be out sixty poun' if ah don't return it to him. He's gonnae ask me for money anyhows, cos auld stinky baws has been fartin' away all night in it."

All that lying, all that forced tenderness had been for nothing. Mungo's stomach lurched as Gallowgate kicked the guy line. The last of the air blew out and the red tent collapsed with a defeated sigh. There was the faint hummock of a sleeping bag, but it seemed impossible that the tent could hold the body of St Christopher, no matter how rotted and hollowed out the man was. Gallowgate stepped on the sleeping bag. Then he tramped up and down the length of the collapsed shelter. "Where the fuck is he?"

Mungo was bone-tired. He was so plain-spoken and honest that guile exhausted him. It was sapping the last of his energy to pretend he felt anything but hatred for this man. "I don't know. Maybe he's gone fishing?"

Gallowgate stumbled along the waterfront,

his shrivelled cock bouncing comically. He peered up and down the banks of the loch. "At this hour? Where'd ye see him last?"

Mungo didn't know what to say. He spread his sleeping bag. He threw it open like a pair of quilted wings and revealed his thin body. It lay in the centre like some knock-kneed offering.

Gallowgate shook his head. "Naw. C'mon. There's nae time for that. We have to find him."

Mungo wrapped himself up again. He lied as best he could. He told a half-truth about the day before, how St Christopher had been a terrible fisherman and so he had taken him to a spot where the fish seemed lazy and easy to catch. Then he told Gallowgate how he had lost all of his little sprats and grown frustrated even there. The saint had bloodied feet when he came back to the campsite, and scratching for a drink and finding none, he had sealed himself into the tent in a huff. That was the last the boy had heard from him before Gallowgate had returned in the gloaming. "Maybe he's gone home?"

"Naw. He must've had the bad shakes." Gallowgate was pulling on his rain-soaked clothes. It was a sick relief when he covered the eyes on his shoulder blades.

"He was definitely tremblin'. It looked somethin' awful."

"Then we need to find the auld arsehole. Ah cannae leave him here and expect to show ma face up at the probation office." With that, Gallowgate trudged towards the trees.

Mungo wrapped the sleeping bag tight around himself, certain now that the chill was coming from inside him. He wanted to cast it off and run the other direction. He could bound over the rocks and boulders and make for the other treeline. He was sure he could run faster than Gallowgate; Mungo had seen the damage the drink had done to the man. But where would he run to? What way was home? The man stopped; he snapped his fingers and whistled as though the boy was a terrier. Mungo nodded and followed him into the understorey.

Everything was dripping wet underneath the trees. Soon the sleeping bag was sodden. It grew heavy and Mungo was tired, so he laid it over a fallen tree and shivered in his shorts and cagoule. The way Gallowgate was creeping through the undergrowth unnerved him. It was like he didn't want to wake the spirits that slept there. He tried not to picture St Christopher waking from his place below the birch tree, pointing a bony finger in his direction, the right side of his sallow skull caved in.

In the distance, on the far side of the river, a roe buck browsed a low clump of goose-grass. It stopped Mungo in his tracks. He held his breath as the deer raised its head and looked in their direction. Its eyes were as dark and wet as two peeled plums. The deer flicked its ears, scanning the forest for any unfamiliar sounds. On its head was a small set of underdeveloped antlers, and it made Mungo wonder where the deer's mother was. Gallowgate crept nearly to the riverbank before the young buck startled and disappeared with a flick of its tail. As suddenly as it had appeared it was gone again. Gallowgate was beaming with delight. "Now, ye have to tell Maureen about that. Ah get a bonus point for that, don't ah?"

The river was higher than it had been yesterday, and it looked more violent than Mungo had remembered it. Gallowgate was scanning the riverbank for a sign of his crony but Mungo's eyes were fixed on the rushing water. He stood near the point where he had bludgeoned St Christopher, and imagined he saw a glint of silver sovereign lying on the riverbed.

"Over here," said Gallowgate as he bent by the riverbank. He had the tweed bunnet in his hand. It had washed on to a boulder and the wet wool had stuck it there. It was a drab, dull grey and Mungo had missed it in his panic. Gallowgate was turning it in his hands, he held the sweated label out to Mungo. *Christopher Milligan.* The man was no saint. Mungo was sure he would remember that name forever.

"Fuuuuuuuuccck." It leaked out of Gallowgate in a long groan. "We need to keep lookin' for him. If the daft bastard's fallen in, they're gonnae think ah killed him. Ah'll end up back in Barlinnie for sure." For the first time that weekend there was a look of real fear in his eyes.

Gallowgate walked further downriver. Mungo could see the birch tree at the bend but there was no sign of the man's body. He had hidden it well. He tried to reassure himself of what a quiet place this was. Of how the only footprints had been theirs and how the ram's skull had lain undisturbed for years, decades perhaps. They would never find St Christopher. No one ever would. It was as good a grave as the man deserved.

Gallowgate wasn't moving carefully anymore. He was wildly scanning the riverbank and slipping on mossy stones; frightened for what he might find, worried for what he might not be able to find. He stumbled downriver, moving closer to the loch. Mungo drew in his breath as Gallowgate rounded the next bend.

It must have taken only a few seconds, but it felt like several minutes. All Mungo could see was that Gallowgate's back had straightened as he pulled himself up to his full height. Gallowgate's right arm extended and he was pointing at something in the distance, not at the birch tree but at a shallow bay further downstream. The man said nothing. But as Mungo turned the corner, he knew what he would find.

The heavy flood must have dislodged St Christopher from the rooted cave. It had carried him downriver some and beached him on some sharp rocks. The body was lying face up and his eyes were wide open. The man's head was trapped between some large boulders, his neck certainly broken. The lanky body was full of false life, bobbing in the current. Mungo's heart stuttered. From where he stood it looked like the saint was floating peacefully on the surface, quietly contemplating the heavens.

TWENTY-THREE

The falling darkness ate the clouds out of the sky. As the lights came on in the slick streets the Protestant boys began to pour out of the tenement mouths and crow at one another like nocturnal scavengers. Mungo watched from the third-floor window as the older Billies congregated outside the Paki shop on the corner. They gathered in the light of its open doorway, fluttering like colour-blocked moths. From high above, Mungo could tell they were jumpy and unpredictable with adrenaline, looking forward to a fight, dreaming of their own glory, anything that would put a shine on their name. They hung on each other affectionately, wide manly hugs, bodies never touching but full of love and rage, eager to stab and maim the Royston Catholics.

Mungo pressed his face against the cold glass. He rolled his forehead back and forth. The room behind him was too hot and much too close. The electric fire was on high, filling the air with the stale smell of lager and sweat, and giving off a needling static that made his head sore. The condensation on the window felt good after a long day spent inside, hovering and worrying as Mo-Maw cracked can after can, running her tongue along her teeth, moaning about how Jocky had papped her again.

The day had started as innocently as a tea party. At first Mo-Maw had sat them both down and poured them tumblers of heavy ale. She pinned Mungo and Jodie against the settee with lurid stories of how Jocky had done her wrong: how he had promised her a week in Burntisland and then invited his weans to join (the nerve of this prick), how he had kept a house full of drink and moaned if she enjoyed it just a *wee* bit (the parsimonious basturt). Mungo watched his sister become marble-faced as Mo-Maw droned on in self-pity. When the urge became too much, Jodie excused herself and quietly left without telling them where she was going. It was the tinder that lit the fire. Now Jodie would be sulking at the café or the library, and Mo-Maw wanted company — Tattie-bogle demanded an audience — somebody, anybody to listen to her tale of unrequited shoves.

Mungo pretended to draw as Mo-Maw chapped on different doors in the close, not ready to be alone, not ready to be without Jocky. Mrs Campbell turned her away gently. Kindly, timorous Mr Robertson didn't even answer. But then Mr Donnelly opened his door and it was sickening to hear his mother cajole the widower for company. "God sakes, it's Saturday night," she said it over and over, "come on, come on, come on!" Mo-Maw escorted him downstairs and led him into their flat, coaxing, pulling on his sleeve as though he were a stray, or a beast to the blade. The man had hastily packed a plastic bag with all the leftover drink he had in the house and here she slipped it from his grip.

At first, thirsty Donnelly had shown a polite interest in Mungo, nodding and listening as Mo-Maw made him tell of the things he had learned at the doocot. On cue, the lean man had said how bright he was and how proud Mo-Maw must be — both of which were a fiction. Mo-Maw smiled wanly before her eyes glazed over and filled with a faraway look. It was the look that the melancholy singers got at Hogmanay; the old men who gathered in corners and burst into mournful song, ruining good spirits, making old women cry. "Ah've given the best of my years to raising those three. And what did ah get in return?"

Mungo babysat them as they got drunk. From how Donnelly gawped, his mother must have been the loveliest thing the lonely widower had seen in a long time. Donnelly had gotten dressed in shoes, blazer, and hat, simply to step over his own threshold. His manners were from another time and he seemed too ashamed to admit that he wanted to stay. So the man sat in his Harris blazer, baking in the heat but unable to take it off. He would shift, uncomfortable on the soft couch, and stick his fingers in the neck of his threadbare shirt.

Mo-Maw curled her legs under herself and sat on her flash trainers. She asked the man questions as though she were a daytime telly host, knowing full well that men liked it best when they talked about themselves. Mungo smirked. Anybody could see she wasn't listening to the answers, but she kept the man talking and drank more than her fair share.

With the stifling heat of the room Mungo wished she would fall asleep; then he could take the old man by the elbow and lead him to the door, thank him for coming, and hand him the dregs of the carry-out. It was getting late, he would need to go soon, leave his mother and take his place beside his brother. It would not be possible to get out of it. Not this time.

He had spent the afternoon brewing up excuses. Mungo thought about blaming it on Mo-Maw's return, explaining that Mr Donnelly from the top floor was trying to get his brogues under their table. Hamish hated Mr Donnelly, but it would not be enough to get Mungo excused; Hamish would burn James alive as easily as he set fire to the stolen Capri.

Mo-Maw had dipped her eyes a couple of times in the heat, her permed head lolling on her chin, but each time Mr Donnelly would light a cigarette and hand it to her with a nudge. The nicotine would pull her back towards the living and she would start a wearisome story about caravans and snack bars. Mungo drew an interminable spiral. It seemed her happiest memories were all housed on wheels, temporary, and without foundations.

The pair of them smiled at something in the far distance and bobbed drunkenly on the sofa like they were adrift on their own small boat. Mungo thought how it wouldn't be long now until he could put her to bed. Then he could throw the windows wide to the fresh air, clean the ash off the carpet, and head out into the night. Mo-Maw paused in mid-ramble and drew luxuriously on her cigarette; the ash was a long finger that threatened to burn a hole in her tan leggings. She closed her eyes.

Mr Donnelly reached inside his thick blazer and pulled out a thin wallet. He rifled through some notes and stopped at a small blue five; he considered the determination on Mungo's face before pulling out something bigger, browner. The sound of money made Mo-Maw's eyes flutter open, and she seemed surprised to find a cigarette clamped between her lips. Mungo and Mo-Maw stared at the bank note like it had said something. "Why don't ye away and take yersel to the pictures, eh?"

Mo-Maw made a delighted face, like she was watching Mungo unwrap a lovely Christmas gift. "Would you look at that. What do you say, then?" Her manners suddenly remembered. It was a funny thing, to be in such a sorry state but still mindful of the social graces of others.

Mungo looked at the note and thought about all the things he could buy. What he wanted more than anything was a bus ticket with James. A ticket to somewhere far away, where he could be himself and James would be safe. He didn't want to take the money, but he found himself leaning forward. "Thank you, Mister Donnelly."

The man's eyes narrowed again. The note made a crisp, clean sound as it passed between their hands. Mungo sat for a minute until the man turned to him and said, "Well then?" He took a draw on his dout. "Away ye go tae the pictures." The adults stared at Mungo expectantly. Mo-Maw nodded once, deliberately and slowly.

Mungo tidied his sketches away. He folded the banknote again and again and again, and as he did a new feeling settled over him, a self-loathing that he was a boy who had sold his own mother. He stood up and extended his hand towards the widower. "Right, I'll see you out."

"Whut?" The man's little black eyes took an age to focus.

"I'm going to the pictures, so I'll see you out. You can't stay here, alone, with my maw."

Mo-Maw and the widower looked at one another. Mr Donnelly cycled through several expressions; swinging from confusion, to suspecting he was the butt of some sick joke, to settling on a look that said he thought he had been conned. "Maureen?"

"Mungo, ye cannae talk to Mr Donnelly like that. This is my house."

Mungo was too tired to laugh. He reached over the coffee table and took the man by the elbow. Mr Donnelly squirmed like a child resisting bath time. Mo-Maw slapped Mungo's hand. She sat forward and made to stand up, but Mungo pressed her back into her settee. He thumbed over his shoulder. "Mr Donnelly, do you really want me to go get our Hamish?"

The man looked to Mo-Maw for support, but she was loose-jawed. Mungo took the man by the elbow again and hoisted him to his feet. With his other hand he snatched up as much of the man's possessions as he could manage. Mungo escorted him to the front door, and as he left the man blinking in the bright close he slipped a can of lager into one hand, and his hat into the other.

When he went back into the living room, Mo-Maw had her arms folded like a huffy toddler. She was scowling at the darkening sky. Mungo dropped into the armchair and began to lace up his trainers.

"Ah don't know who the fuck you think you are!" she spat.

"Aye? Me neither."

She had been gearing up for a fight but this disarmed her. Mungo pulled his cagoule over his head. They sat in silence for a moment before he said, "You're my maw.

You're my only maw. I just want guid things for you."

Her tongue was clamped between her teeth as she poured the dregs from several glasses into her own. "And there's not a single fuckin' thing on the telly." Mo-Maw moved in slow motion. Her concentration betrayed how drunk she was. "Anyway, yer a liar. Ye're just like they other two. Ye only want me happy so I can make your life easier. Ye only care about what ah can do for you. And ah'm sick of it."

Mungo came out of the close and joined a pack of Proddy boys heading to the waste ground. He fell into formation amongst the baby-faced warriors. He swung his meatless legs in imitation of their gallus way of walking; his shoulders about his ears and a sour scowl on his face. This swagger was a uniform as ubiquitous as any football top. It had a gangly forward motion like a big-balled, bandy-legged weasel, head swung low, eyes always fixed on the prey ahead, ready to lunge with either a fist or a silver blade. Mungo tried his best to wear the uniform but he felt like an imposter. It was a poor imitation.

The smirr wetted them to the skin. The fine mist found its way into the cracks of clothing and pushed through their shoes, making their white socks damp and grimy. It ate them from the feet up, inching inside their denims and soaking them through to their underwear. The spitting rain was only visible when they stepped into the pools made by the orange street lamps. These orange lights gave a feeling of warmth that had been missing in the grey daylight hours. Now and again the boys stopped and huddled underneath them. They passed half-bricks and homemade shanks between themselves as if they were swapping toys.

Mungo was shivering by the time they reached Ha-Ha and the older boys. It was clear that Ha-Ha had bumped some speed; it showed in the way he was grinding his jaw and dancing like a shadow-boxer. He clapped his brother on the back. "Ye made the right decision, fuckwit. Shame really, ah like bonfires. They're pure lovely to look at."

Now, as one disorganized rabble, the boys turned the corner into the darkness. Sprayed across the waste ground were wooden boards and old pallets; debris that the younger boys had turned into ramshackle forts and dens. Sat in the mud and weeds it looked like a medieval settlement. Some of the dens had low doorways and were built atop patterned scraps of linoleum. Some had fancy feminine touches and sticks of once-fine furniture. Ha-Ha kicked the side of the smallest hovel. Five or six small boys spilled out of it and soon the whole settlement swarmed like a tiny village. One of the bigger boys flashed a torn pornographic page at Ha-Ha, a woman on her back with her legs splayed.

"Who's that?" asked Ha-Ha as he passed the woman around. "Yer maw?"

Mungo wanted to stay in the shanty town. It reminded him of the goodness of the doocot. These boys had been getting along, co-operating constructively in the process of building the little village, making something good out of nothing, just like James had.

Ha-Ha snatched the dirty picture and tucked it safely inside his anorak. "Who's comin' up the bridge wi' me? Let's fuckin' do this!" Like an Orange piper, Ha-Ha marched the boys on through the weeds and into the night. They whistled their fight song in fair tonal unison. Mungo hung back. He could see that some of the boys were still as young as nine or ten, a few were in T-shirts or light knit tops and most were occupied in licking the dribbling cold off the ends of their noses. There were a handful amongst them, Ha-Ha's closest lieutenants, who were more than grown men. They carried heavy ceremonial swords, taken from Masonic fathers, and lengths of lead pipe stolen from pulled-down tenements. The ginger-headed boy still had his arm strapped across his chest, but in his other hand flashed the silver teeth of his mammy's serrated bread knife.

There were no street lights over the waste ground but Mungo could see the man-made glow of the bridge ahead. The narrow footbridge spanned the motorway, connecting the Protestant scheme with the Catholic scheme that lay on the far side. This was a bridge that no young Protestant fighter would ever cross alone.

The motorway was pulsing with Saturday day trippers returning from a jaunt to Edinburgh Castle; contented weans who had rubbed the snout of Greyfriars Bobby.

Mungo could see hooded figures loitering at the mouth of the bridge. There must have been another ten or fifteen Protestant boys, all older than himself, all standing tight-faced in the cold rain. They parted to let Ha-Ha through. It was a great turnout. Ha-Ha looked swollen with pride.

Someone crouched in the dirt and picked up a rock in one hand and a ginger bottle in the other. Like potato farmers, the smaller boys began digging for other missiles. Mungo looked down and saw a half-brick, red and heavy, a relic from some other battle. He dug it out, its edges sharp and violent, and straight away he wanted to put it down, to turn and head back to James.

One of the hooded Billies turned his way, taking a long draw on his fag. "Ah see we finally got young Hamilton out here. Bout time, shitebag." The man's mouth was a collection of broken teeth. He had a grin like a graveyard full of wrecked headstones. "Ah thought ye were gonnae let the family name doon. Turn out to be a fuckin' bender."

Mungo did his best to pull himself up to his full height. He knew that it didn't matter what he said next, it only mattered how he said it. "Haw, fuckface. If ye like they wooden pegs ye call teeth ah'd shut yer fuckin' mouth." The hooded boy had come too close to the truth. Mungo rolled the brick in his hand as his fear turned to adrenaline. He sensed Ha-Ha nod approval somewhere over the sea of warriors and one by one, the boys turned away from him.

The mass of fighters now numbered forty or so. As the traffic rushed by beneath them, they huddled under the single pool of street light with hands and ears tucked deep into anoraks and sang Rangers songs. As they sang, their warm breath escaped over the top of their chimney-stack necklines. They told dirty stories and lied boastfully of fucking each other's mothers. It was decided that a blond boy — square-jawed for eleven — had the most fuckable mammy. Several of the older Billies stepped forward and claimed to be this boy's father. "You look lit me," one crowed, "Naw. Sure. Ye look mair lit me." They amused themselves for a time by extending their fists and having the boy crawl back and forth in the mud to kiss their gold-plated rings, which he did, grateful to have been noticed by his elders.

Someone passed around a bottle of Buckfast and the men drank it down in gulps. A couple of the younger ones reached for it, eager to earn respect, and then pulled faces as the sour wine hit the back of their throats. Mungo shifted nervously, feeling his wet socks squish between his toes, and folding and unfolding the ten-pound note in his pocket. He thought about how James had turned away from him in disgust. Then, without wanting to, he thought about Ashley and how her eyes flickered backwards when James kissed her neck in the park. She would soon know James like he never had.

A high ululation sailed over the heads; someone was on the bridge. In an instant, bricks were raised up, and silver blades pulled from pockets. Two of the boys drew long rusting swords from the legs of their trackie bottoms, and Mungo noticed one of the smallest boys had a log splitter that he needed both hands to hold up. As quickly as the weapons were drawn the crowd began to part. Boys pulled back into two rows, creating a narrow gauntlet. Through it came a tight-faced girl. She was pushing a wobbly pram with a sticky-looking child in it. She wore the same baggy tracksuit as the boys, distinguishing herself as female through her large hoop earrings and her light-pink trainers. The girl pushed the plastic pram over the shortcut of waste ground. The squeaky wheels slipped on the weeds and shoogled the baby about. "Aw, grow up. Ye should be bloody ashamed of yersels." The girl carried herself like a warrior queen, her hair scraped back and caught into a bejewelled headband. Several of the plastic gems were missing, their bezel casings looked empty as gouged eyes. When she had safely passed the Billies, she sneered and shouted back, "I hope they Catholics kick the shite oot o' ye."

The boys looked from one to another, searching for a leader, someone who would tell them how they should feel about this

536

insult. A loose bottle flew through the air and smashed at her feet. The boys let out a single unified whoop.

The sticky wean started to cry. Having been raised in the fighting way of all Glasgow women, the girl took the bait. She let go of the pram and shot back across the dirt, wet ponytail whipping behind her, her chewed claws out, ready to tear them to ribbons. She caught the hair of the gobbiest lad and brought her fist down on his neck and head. The boy tried to run, but she had him by the hood and kept hitting him. The other boys stopped their laughing. The bottle thrower shrank into the crowd. The battered boy wriggled out of his hoodie and stood there shirtless and shivering in the rain, dodging out of claw range. It was the most degrading thing that could happen to a fighting man: to be so publicly skinned by a girl.

Mungo slid to the edge of the rabble. He dared himself to run while the crowd was distracted. The men started to circle the shirtless boy, trapping him and pushing him towards the spitting girl like a hen at a dog fight. Her nails tore long pink streaks of skin off of his arms and the scalping of his fair hair was audible even over the excited squeaks of the boys. Each time he freed himself, the Billies moved to block his escape, pushing him back towards the young mother. She kicked into his pure white body, blackened him with her muddy feet.

From out of nowhere another bottle spun through the night air; it shattered across the temple of one of the smallest boys and when it did, it sparkled like the lights at the school disco. As he fell, the small boy's blood sprayed a wide arc across the shirtless boy.

They had all been distracted by the furious girl; they hadn't noticed the group of Fenians standing on the apex of the narrow motorway footbridge. The Catholics stood grinning in the dim light, each dressed in a uniform of green and white hoops.

The Billies started to swarm like a leaderless hive until Ha-Ha's voice mustered them to action. "Haud it the gether." And then: "Kick their fuckin' cunts in."

The gang reorganized and with a hateful roar, the first of their projectiles sailed up through the air and into the bright motorway light. The Bhoyston danced backwards, letting the glass shatter at their feet. They watched the weapons turn to glitter, and then one by one their green tops flashed in the bright light as they launched back down on to the waste ground. The Catholics held the advantage; by shooting downhill their weapons travelled further and found their targets more easily. Half-bricks made a dull thud and crack as they caught boys in the ribs. Other boys jumped and danced like nylon scarecrows as bottles of piss exploded at their feet.

The air was thick with volleys of religious hate, but the boys were enjoying themselves, having the time of their young lives. The Bhoyston soon found their half-bricks and stones returned to them, dirty and wet from the Dennistoun mud. Rocks thrown by the younger boys missed the bridge altogether and clattered dangerously to the busy motorway below. There was a blare of car horns.

Mungo was rooted to the spot. The brick had slipped from his fingers and his legs disobeyed the order to run. As missiles flew all around him, some of the wounded boys started to retreat back to the little wooden village; they had purple welts on their blue arms and bloody hands clamped over ears that were surely ringing with pain. Half-grown men fell to the ground clutching split skulls, the bravest warriors screaming for their mammies.

The night went suddenly quiet, the sound of splintering glass and stone on bone stopped. The Bhoyston on the bridge had thinned, their casualties retreating back to Royston. The Dennistoun Billies started to clap their cold hands together, roaring over the motorway. The shouting gave the scared boys courage and it coalesced in a bawdy, shouty round of "The Sash My Father Wore." The Bhoyston had lost control of the high ground. When only a few remained, some of the older Billies picked up their hammers and swords and charged the bridge. The Billies threw their arms wide as though they were scaring grouse from the heather. But not Ha-Ha. Ha-Ha ran with purpose, determined to catch the Fenians. Mungo watched his brother pursue the last of the Catholics back into Royston, well beyond the point where he was safe. The edge of his tomahawk glinted in the car headlights.

The wounded Protestants let out a cheer. Bobby Barr, the broken-armed ginger, raised his serrated knife into the air. "If ah ever see that wee Tim bastard wi' the bleached hair ah'm gonnae knock the fuck out of him." The other boys made similar pledges: the revenge they would take, who had fought well, whose bottle had found its target. The bragging and showmanship made Mungo's stomach lurch. It seemed cowardly. He slunk into the darkness, glad it was over.

He had done what had been asked of him and, best of all, he hadn't hurt anyone. Mungo burned to tell James this: he would go there now, he would run, he would press his face into the tenement buzzer and declare proud, mad love as Ashley already had. Why should he not? Mungo was drunk with the hope of it. He threw his head back, enjoying the rain on his hot face, and exhaled all the air he had been hoarding inside.

He had half-turned towards the estate when it caught him on the side of the head. The crack was so loud that he thought his skull had exploded, it was a sound like a hockey stick hitting a tight, water-filled drum. His vision exploded like the sky on fireworks night. Then everything went white.

The side of his head was hot with pain and, with his hands still in his pockets, he fell sideways into the mud. When the bright light faded and he could finally open his eyes he saw the Billies scatter like spooked sheep; some tucked their tails in tight and ran in a gallop, others ran backwards, flailing under the blows of their attackers. Mungo lay on the ground and watched the green and white hoops tear through the royal blue. Only one or two of the bravest stood their ground with weapons drawn. They were soon run through, fresh faces sliced open with box cutters, tennis rackets cracked over skulls. He watched Bobby Barr run as a boot flew into his kidneys. His face had twisted in pain, but all the wind was booted from his body and he couldn't even scream.

Mungo was writhing in the dirt, blinking, when soft brown eyes looked down at him and there was a flash of a perfect, dazzling smile. He was a beautiful boy; dazed as he was, Mungo was still winded by his beauty. He had the broad-boned nose of a proud Sheltie and dark eyebrows under thick black hair, parted as neat as any parish priest's. He seemed to be saying something, but Mungo couldn't hear him over the din in his skull. Mungo raised his hand to ask for help. Then the boy's foot rose up high and came down like a hoof on the side of Mungo's head.

The white flooded back. It felt like when he sat by himself in the darkness and Jodie turned on the big light, the bare bulb with no lampshade, and it burned his skull. The foot came down again and again, trying to sever his head from his body. Mungo could hear the rubbery squeak of the trainer against his face. He could taste the blood from his ear and the salt from his eyes in his mouth and in a delayed reflex he pulled his hands up to cover his face.

The stomping took on the rhythm of a happy jig. Mungo couldn't see through the pain. The foot came down again and then travelled the length of his body. Then the beautiful boy walked the length of Mungo. He did it in marching strides, like a cartoon Nazi. He turned above Mungo's head, goose-stepped on his heel and made to walk back down the fallen body. The next foot never fell.

Ha-Ha was there, the tomahawk above his head, and he cleaved it down on the beautiful Catholic and the boy fell like a wasted sapling. The side of his brother's face was scarlet. There was a curtain of his own blood falling from a line that stretched from his ear to his mouth. It was already raised and puckered white at the edges, like the torn fat on a rasher of bacon. Ha-Ha tapped Mungo with his toe and then he turned, axe above his head, and started hacking at the forest of Fenians.

Mungo lay on the wet ground. He could not lift himself from where he had been stamped into the earth. He would have frozen but for the inferno of his pain. And as the fighting raged above him, he closed his eyes.

The Catholics retreated over the motorway bridge. Mungo could hear Ha-Ha roar after them, singing sweet promises of chibbing and buggery. He lay in the mud and the spitting rain was cool against his face. He gently probed the inside of his mouth with soiled fingers; he had torn through the fat of his cheek and at least one of his back teeth was cracked. The mud protested as he tried to stand. Several times his legs slid out from under him and he fell back into the grass. When he eventually freed himself, he saw how he had left a perfect outline, like a snow angel that had been pressed into the filth.

Other boys had not been so lucky. There was a crowd gathered around a twelve-year-old who had liked to skateboard and always helped his granny wash the outside of her windows. Mungo had seen him out on the high ledge as his granny clung to his waist. On the other side, some Billies had caught a flame-haired Catholic boy, and in a circular ceilidh, they were taking turns to dance on him. He would be lucky to live.

Mungo held his hands to his ringing head as he stumbled across the battlefield. He was having trouble breathing. He feared that his ribs might be broken as he inhaled the damp night air in little lopsided sips. His eye had scabbed shut already and there was dirt trapped under the swelling; he could feel it scrape against his eyeball. It caused a blinding pain to put weight on his left foot, but because the pain shot up from his ankle through his hip bone, he couldn't tell which parts of him were calling for attention. He wanted to sob, to cry for the waste of it all.

Ha-Ha would see tonight as a defeat. Those who could still fight would be shamed into returning next week to save face. It should be over, but Mungo knew better. It was more of a beginning than an ending.

Mungo stumbled on and swallowed his hurt just like he had been taught. His tears caught in the back of his throat where they mingled with his own blood. He gulped until he had choked on too much, and then he hauched black spittle into the grass. He was glad that he could not see the redness under the dim lights.

Young men hurried in all directions. All the dauntless warriors were limping home, bragging of their glories, screaming threats of retaliation. But by how they tucked their tailbones Mungo could see that they were shaken. They were gulping, chewing on their hurt until they could be across their front doors. They kept their chests puffed out until they could be safe in their mammies' arms again; where they could coorie into her side as she watched television and she would ask, "What is all this, eh, what's with all these cuddles?" and they would say nothing, desperate to just be boys again, wrapped up safe in her softness.

The first of the polis sirens echoed off the tenements. The young men who could still run started running. Mungo came to the cluster of dens. The little settlement was destroyed; the shanty town pushed flat and broken to bits. The gutted porn magazines lay upon the grass, and the open-mouthed women, their faces twisted in agony or pleasure, lay scattered about like dead villagers.

When he reached his street, he felt an anger for the happy glow coming from the different flats. Families would be tucked in together, eating fish suppers and watching the Saturday night variety shows. When he came to his close, he struggled to climb the stairs. Inside the Hamilton flat it was dark and quiet. Jodie was home from the café and already in her bedroom; Mungo pressed on it gently, almost pleadingly, but her door was snibbed tight.

The living room was empty. It hung with a low cloud of stale smoke, flat ale, and sweat. Under the fug was a memory of Mo-Maw's vanilla perfume — the one they had chipped in for and bought her for Christmas — and he was sad to not find her on the couch, snoring off the drink.

Mungo flicked on the electric fire and struggled out of his wet clothes. It took an age to undress; every ordinary movement caused an extraordinary pain and he had to stop often to catch his breath and summon the courage to continue. It was hardest to take off his cagoule — he found he couldn't lift his arm over his head — and by the time he was in his boxer shorts, there were tears of rage and hurt streaming down his face. He downed a mouthful of leftover lager from Mo-Maw's glass. It stung the tear in his cheek, but the drink tasted sad and flat and the smell of it made him long for her, made him want to lie next to his mother.

Out in the hallway he listened at her bedroom door. He could hear Mo-Maw's rolling snore coming from inside. Mungo knew he was too old for these feelings, he knew that Jodie would disapprove, but as he reached for the handle all he could think about was how much he wanted to climb into bed beside his mother and feel safe in her arms. He cracked the door slowly, the room was dark but for the faint orange glow coming in through the undrawn curtains.

"Maw?" he whispered.

Mungo inched along the wall until he bumped into her bedside table. There was a tinkle of tea mugs and perfume bottles. In the faint street light he could see his mother's pale face above the sheets. Her head was turned to the side, and she was asleep. Mungo watched her for a moment. Her make-up had smeared on the pillow and there was tension in her face, a puckering in her eyelids, as though she was caught in the purgatory between the drink and its sugars. *"Mo-Maw?"* His bottom lip began to tremble with self-pity. Mungo peeled the candlewick away from his mother; he turned to slip in beside her but as his one good eye adjusted to the dark, he realized that her tiny frame made too large of a hummock in the bedspread.

Mungo lifted the sheets slowly.

The street light washed across the strange bodies. The old widower from upstairs was nestled beside his mother. He was burrowed below her armpit, his mouth was clamped to her breast, his long arms wrapped around her waist. He was like an undernourished tick suckling at her side and it took a moment for Mungo to make sense of the tangle of limbs, for his mind to arrange the horror into something that made sense.

It was as though they had been in the middle of some dance when they had both fallen asleep, or had simply given up.

Perhaps it was the sudden cold air. Perhaps it was the faint light. Mr Donnelly opened his little black eyes. As he lifted his mouth from Mo-Maw's skin, there was a long slaver of spittle. He unfurled his body like some rodent in a nest. His thin hair was sweated across his face and as he blinked and looked up at the boy, his eyes were like two puddles in the darkness.

Mr Donnelly had not expected the placid boy to turn on him. When Mungo grabbed the man by the hair and dragged him out into the close all the old chancer could say was "Aye, nae problem chief, ah didnae mean any bother." It rolled off his tongue in a jovial manner as though he was a first-footer who had stayed too long after the Hogmanay bells.

Mungo hurled the man on to the hard stairs. He paced the landing, flagellating himself, slapping his own face, cracking his fists off his temples. It was this that unsettled the old man the most. His fury sent Mr

Donnelly cowering into the corner of the stairwell, where he sank to the floor with his hands covering his head. Mungo was angry at the man, but he was angrier with himself. It was a nightmarish sight to see the man without trousers but with his old blazer and shirt on and his tie still knotted. His bare legs were pallid against the concrete and the tip of his shrivelled cock was hanging below his shirt hem, tacky in the close light. Mr Donnelly had seen his opportunity and taken it, he hadn't bothered to waste time on swooning or sweet teases. It was a low way to live.

Mungo spat on the man, a great shower of directionless spittle.

"Thank you, son. Aye, thank you." The old man seemed grateful to have gotten off so lightly.

Leaving Mr Donnelly hunkered in the close, Mungo went inside and locked every lock. He returned to Mo-Maw and pulled the sweated bed sheets across her. She didn't stir. Her head was tilted backwards, her mouth open and ghastly with her own smeared lipstick. *Tattie-bogle.* He would pretend she had been Tattie-bogle all along. Without glancing at her pinkest flesh, he lifted the empty shell of her most gently and stuffed the sheets underneath her. It brought her splayed legs back together. Then, as though he was preparing her for burial, he wiped the last of the paint from her lips. She lay there, drunk out of her memory, looking like a baby that would not sleep without being swaddled.

The struggle with the old man had roused Jodie. She was growling to herself like she could not wait to be gone from this madhouse. He heard her fill a mug with tap water. Then she sealed herself back inside her bedroom.

Mungo couldn't sleep after that. Inside and out he was in agony. He crawled on to his bed and felt rotten for all the mistakes he had made, all the poor-me's he could conjure: Jodie and the baby, Ha-Ha and the Bhoyston, Mo-Maw and the dirty money, but most of all for James.

He had been so scared of Ha-Ha that he had ruined the best thing he had ever known. Now, in the darkness, he knew that Ha-Ha would not keep his word, not for long — he never did. It was only a matter of time before James would be hurt, and for what? For liking Mungo Hamilton, the ruiner of all good things.

TWENTY-FOUR

As the sun broke over the tenements Mungo
went to the bathroom and cleaned the blood
and mud with a damp cloth. He crunched
two of Jodie's painkillers and smeared Mo-
Maw's tubes of ointment over his ribs till
they were thick with pungent grease. He
wrapped his kidneys in strips torn from of
an old cotton duster and tested the bruises
that were spreading up his flank. His out-
sides looked as dead as his insides felt. It
seemed only right.

There was a congealed split under his
hairline where the hockey stick had cracked
his skull. He cleaned the swollen area and
then covered it with a bunion plaster, the
only thing he could find that was adhesive.
Mungo tried to hold the edges of skin
together while it set, and he combed his
hair, still matted in places with his own
blood, over the flesh-toned rubber. When
he swept it back from his face there was a

bruise around his temple so he took some of Jodie's foundation and spread the too-orange cream from the outside of his eye up to his hairline.

It hurt to pull clean clothes over his body and the bandages and the pain meant he could not bend properly as he packed his schoolbag. He burst his piggy bank and wrapped the pittance inside Mr Donnelly's tainted note. Unpinning an old school photo of Jodie from his wall he placed it safely into the pocket of his cagoule. It didn't take long to pack the things he loved, and when he was finished his bag was still light enough to lift, despite his tender sides.

He forced himself to wait and try to eat the end-slice of the bread. Wincing, he ate it slowly, while the cut inside his cheek screamed. As he chewed he stared across the back greens at James's darkened windows. He hadn't hurt any Catholics, surely that was worth something. They had both done what they needed to hide their true selves. He would show James his bruises and James would understand that. James would put Ashley aside and then they would leave together on a fast bus, going in any direction Mungo pointed.

Mungo closed the door behind him. He stumbled down the sleeping close as weak sun spilled through the stained-glass windows. When he reached the ground floor he was surprised to find Chickie Calhoun stepping back into the close mouth. Natalie was tugging on her leash, her beady eyes bulging out of her skull. Mungo nodded politely and squeezed past them. He had his hand on the heavy door before Poor-Wee-Chickie spoke.

"Is the circus in town?"

"Pardon me?" Even in his low state he remembered his manners.

The little man stood in the shadows at the deep end of the close, the dog leash wrapped around his hand. "Well, you're creepin' about with a face full of make-up and a packed bag. So I figured maybe ye were running away to join the Ringlings."

Mungo smiled although he didn't feel like it. He reached for the heavy door again.

"Listen, if I were you, I'd wait a wee minute afore going out there. The polis have been up and down that street so often the council will need to lay some new carpet." Mungo peered through the frosted glass. It was the start of a fine Sunday morning outside. The sun had pushed wide cracks in the thick clouds and it promised a blue sky when it could manage. Still, sure enough, two unmarked CID cars crept along the street; they were conspicuous on a street where few could afford motors of their own. They rolled slowly to catch unawares any boys still trapped out from the fighting. Poor-Wee-Chickie nodded towards his own front door. "Son, have you eaten anything hot yet?"

"No."

"Well, come in then, let me make you some liver."

"I don't like liver, Mister Calhoun."

"Och, naebody likes liver, son, but you look like you could use the iron."

Over the threshold, Poor-Wee-Chickie locked all the deadbolts behind them. He drew off his anorak and put on his cooking cardigan, buttoning it all the way to the neck. He pushed the purple liver around in an old pan then put it down in front of the boy, still quivering and bloody. The smell of it turned Mungo's stomach, but he brought his knife through it to be polite.

"Can you no eat?"

Mungo shook his head. "I'm sorry. My mouth hurts."

Poor-Wee-Chickie fished around in the pocket of his cardigan and put on his reading glasses. He took Mungo's head in his hands and told him to open wide. "Awright, haud still." He used a pair of eyebrow tweezers and pushed against Mungo's cheek. There was a tug, and he pulled out a sliver of tooth from the cheek fat; it was long as a sliced almond. "Ye'll need to get that tooth looked at." He handed Mungo a water glass cloudy with cooking salt. "Rinse with this and the cut will do much better."

Mungo swilled the salty water with a wince. He did it again and spat the bloody water into the sink.

"Are you awright, son? Yer face is twitching somethin' rotten."

Mungo pinched his tic. "Sorry, Mister Calhoun."

"Och, no need to apologize to me." Poor-Wee-Chickie was indulging him. "But don't grab yer face too hard, ye'll spoil yer lovely foundation." He took Mungo's face in his hands for the second time that morning. He watched the blinking tic for a moment and then with the tip of an old tea towel he wiped the boy's face. With careful fingers he was gently blending the thick foundation better, feathering it away at the edges. "After the fine-upstanding-family-men-of-the-roofers-union drove me out of the business, I went to work at the King's Theatre. I jist minded the back door, but sometimes they used to let us watch the big stars, you know, while they put on their make-up and wigs and that. I was *mad* for Dorothy Paul, so I was."

Mungo Hamilton, never one to cry, started to cry now. He ground his top teeth into his bottom lip but it would not be controlled.

"Here, here, it's awright. You can let it out. I mean, auld Dorothy is no the singer she once was, but ah wouldnae greet about it, son."

Mungo found himself choking between laughter and tears.

"Let it out. It'll do you good."

"I don't know how to do that."

Poor-Wee-Chickie refolded his tea towel. He pointed out into the back green. "Ye know, I knew a brave wee sodjur once. He was parading up and down that back wall out there." The man mimicked a rigid little soldier, marching with pride. "He had a wee wooden gun and one of his mammy's old berets; pure proud as anything, he was. I was just standing at my window watching him have a great time, pretending to shoot the opposing army of weans, all of them screaming into walkie-talkies, chucking fake grenades, the whole pantomime. When all of a sudden, this big general came up ahind him and kicked the sodjur off the wall. Just shoved him without blinking. Oh, it was a pure sin! This general was in the *same*

557

army, can ye believe it? He just shoved his own man off the wall lit that." Chickie shook his head. "Anyway, this brave wee fella fell about four feet, hit the midden roof, rolled once and fell eight feet on to the paving slabs. *Blamm!*" Poor-Wee-Chickie winced as he slapped his hand on the countertop. "That wee sodjur didn't even make a sound. He was winded but he was brave. Any other wee boy would have screamed for his mammy. But not this little sodjur. This wee army man jist stood up and got on with it."

Mungo let out a low gut roar. He had balled his fists and was trying to shove them backwards into his brain through his eye sockets. His face was bright red.

"It's awright son, let it out. Every brave sodjur gets tired and cries at some point."

Poor-Wee-Chickie didn't rub his back or pat his shoulder, he just stood there and gave Mungo the space to scream inwards into himself. He lit a cigarette and when the boy finally took his fists from his eyes he asked, "Does the boy with the slate roof like you as much as you like him?"

Mungo flinched.

"It's awright, I won't tell anyone yer secret." He crossed his heart and saluted the boy. "On ma Girl Guides honour."

Mungo looked at Chickie through swollen eyes. Poor-Wee-Chickie who stood behind net curtains and saw everything had arrived at the very heart of it. He could see clearly what had been going on. "He did, Mister Calhoun. He liked me a lot. But I've ruined everything."

"Och! Weans! Everything seems a hunner per cent more dramatic at your age. It'll pass." He handed him a clean tea towel.

"Do you honestly think so?"

"Aye."

Mungo wiped his face. "He asked me to run away with him and I asked him to wait. Now I don't think we can hide much longer."

Poor-Wee-Chickie was thinking again; he had tilted his head to the side and was running his tongue along the back of his teeth. "I want to show you something. Don't run away now. It's no a big kiddie-catching net, no matter what the other weans might say."

He was gone only a short while, but long enough for Mungo to wipe his face on the tea towel and feel stupid. When he returned there was a burgundy book in his hand, a diary with "1957" stamped in gold deboss. Flicking through the pages, he saw that each cream surface was warped with tiny, obsessive script. Chickie's feelings were crowding the page, and when the page was full, they twisted and continued up along the margin.

Tucked in between the pages were two black-and-white photos. The first photo was square with a white frame. It showed a young man with thick hair, standing out-doors and leaning against the open window of a tenement. He had a broad Sunday paper folded in one hand and a short cigarette in the other. His face was tilted upwards towards a rare sun and he wore a heavy wool jumper and some high-waisted trousers. He was carefree and laughing at whoever was taking the photo.

The man in the photo was handsome and had the confidence of youth. Everything lay ahead of him. It was all unspoiled. "Ye were bonny, Mister Calhoun."

"*Were?* Cheeky bugger. I have a jawline that could etch glass."

In the next photo six teenage boys were in the back green of a tenement, this same tenement, sitting cross-legged on trampled grass and beaming at the photographer. Two of the boys sat slightly to the side on an old Mackintosh coat laid out like a picnic blanket. It was the smallest thing. The six were smoking after a football match, but those two seemed special, ever so slightly separated, an island of their very own.

Poor-Wee-Chickie pointed at the man sitting next to him on the coat. A towheaded boy with a dimpled chin and a crooked smile. "That fella's name was Georgie. A kind boy, really, truly kind and considerate. We trained through in Ayr for the Merchant Navy the gether. On the first day he felt bad for me when he saw I didnae have socks thick enough for the boots so he gave me a pair of his. My mother had given me money for a sandwich and a bottle of ginger at the train station back to the city, I saw he didn't have any so I made sure he got half of mine. That's all it really was, wee things. Over the next three months, it was just wee kindnesses here and there. I loved him, though. He gave me my first kiss. My best kiss."

Mungo was struck dumb.

"He asked me to emigrate to Australia with him."

"Why didn't you?"

"Och, I had a hunner good reasons back then, none of them make much sense now. Usual shite: ma mammy wisnae well, ma daddy never came back from the war, ma sister would be left to cope by herself, I didnae look guid in short trousers. Utter nonsense. All stories I telt myself to cover my fear. Australia! My wee arsehole was twitching like a rabbit's nose." Poor-Wee

561

Chickie sighed as he filled the kettle. "Still, you know, ah suppose ah did what any guid son should do. At least my mammy was happy all her days."

"That was decent of you."

Poor-Wee-Chickie shook his head. "No, you're missing the point. It was cowardly. I wanted that badly to go with Georgie. I've spent the last thirty-odd years imagining it. I just didnae have the guts."

"Was there nobody else?"

"What. Around here?" Poor-Wee-Chickie pulled at a loose thread on his cardigan. "People became scared to death of me. They think what I have is catching. What man would get close to me?"

Mungo looked at the photographs again. The laughing boys, the happy teenager smoking and reading the paper. Poor-Wee-Chickie had been surrounded by love. Where had it all turned for him? "Where's Georgie now?"

"Och! Georgie is married now, so mibbe it was for the best. He writes to me sometimes. He always asks me if I go back to Ayr and I tell him I do, but I never have. I couldnae face it."

"What should I do, Mister Calhoun?"

Poor-Wee-Chickie ducked his head slightly and looked deeply into Mungo's eyes.

"That's easy son. Put yourself first for once."

Mungo drew his school bag over his tender shoulder. He nodded at the liver. "I'm sorry, I can't eat that."

Poor-Wee-Chickie laughed. "Och, that's awright. Natalie loves liver. She'll be in pure heaven." He checked the sliver of sky peeking above his net curtains, and as he sighed, he caught Mungo staring at him. "Och, don't worry about me, son. Ah'll take a wee dauner up the shops, get something nice for ma dinner. Mibbe there's a guid film on later."

It was still early. Mungo waited for a break in the CID patrol before he emerged from the close mouth and lurched along the road. His leg throbbed as he stood on the corner and vacillated between heading to James's tenement and the doocot. If he went to the tenement, James might not let him in, and the neighbours would hear him plead into the intercom. He could not stomach the shame of that.

So he went to the doocot and hunkered out of view on the far side of the shack. The sun came over Glasgow as he waited for James to do his morning feed and exercise. As he waited he rehearsed everything he wanted to say, but it all sounded clumsy, the small things too small, all the big feelings, overwrought and showy as an American film. He didn't have to wait long. He heard James's cough before he saw him.

When Mungo emerged from the far side of the doocot, James wouldn't look at him. He opened the heavy locks and stepped into the darkness as though Mungo was not even there. *"Whrooup, whroooup, whrooup."* The birds sang it back to him.

"I'm ready. I will go anywhere you want to go." For all the rehearsing, Mungo couldn't control himself now. Ashley and Ha-Ha had already wedged too much between them. He needed James to know the depth of everything he felt. It would tumble out of him, even if James shamed him with it later.

James didn't turn around. He was holding a jug of cold water up to each cage, letting the birds drink through the bars like prisoners. It was reinforcing in their small brains that he was a benevolent jailer. That he alone loved them, and he alone would take care of them, if only they promised to return whenever he released them. He wouldn't look at Mungo. "Anywhere? That's brave of ye." It didn't sound as if he meant it. "How is yer self-loathing gaun?"

"We have to go. Now."

"Do we? Funny that. You being ready to leave just when things get a bit better for me." He took a small sepia hen from the cage and stroked her neck. She was not drinking the morning water. "Ah thought you would be happy for me. Ah didnae expect you to be jealous."

"I'm no jealous."

The stiffness in James's shoulders softened slightly. Then he coughed, his damp, raking rattle. "Ah don't think ah want to go anywhere with you. Ye're as bad as your brother."

"I didn't do it." He was circling now, trying to push himself into James's line of sight, but the other boy always found something to tilt away towards. James denied him the comfort of his gaze. "I want you to know I didnae hurt anyone last night. I went. I did as Hamish asked but I didnae fight." He lifted the side of his cagoule to show the navy bruise, but even at the nylon rustling, James did not turn. "I let them hit us and stamp on us and I didnae even fight back."

"That doesn't make you any less of a fuckin' bigot."

Idiot. Weakling. Liar. Poofter. Coward. Pimp. Bigot.

Mungo wanted to say he had done it for

565

James. He had done it so Ha-Ha would not hurt him, so he would leave the one thing Mungo loved in peace. But what was the point now? Either way James seemed lost to him. Mungo tried one last time, but the word escaped him quiet as a sigh. "Please."

James wouldn't look at him.

Mungo picked up his school bag and turned to leave. Where would he go if he was not following James? He knew then that he would go nowhere. He would go straight to Ha-Ha and stand in his line of sight so that he never felt the need to hunt for this Catholic, never felt the need to set fire to him.

"I wish I wasn't like this, James. I wish I was all right but I'm not. You don't have to be like Chickie. Ashley is gorgeous and it's a lovely thing that your da loves you. Those are good things. I lied. I am jealous."

There were mongrels sniffing in the doocot grass. Old men, their eyes obscured by flat caps, stood nearby and whistled gruff commands. Everything would go on as it always had.

"No. Ye're wrong. He doesnae love me." James turned and squinted into the light. "He doesnae even know me."

The heavy cake of Jodie's foundation looked like a crusted scab in the morning sun. The skin around his temple was already purpling with blood. There were heavy bags of worry under Mungo's eyes and the side of his face was swollen both on the inside and out.

"Fuck sake!" James crossed the rat glass and put his hands on the sides of Mungo's head. He tilted him like he was an ashy doo. His eyes searched the wounds, and his fingers pulled on his bottom lip to check his teeth.

"*Ssssttt,*" Mungo winced.

"Where does it hurt?"

He didn't know where to start. "Nowheres. I'm fine."

James was pulling at his cagoule, raising his jacket to his chest. Seeing the outline of heel prints under the ointment, still blooming and darkening across his pale trunk, he laid his fingers gently on it. "Sweet suffering fuck."

"I didn't hurt anyone. I wouldn't do that."

James was turning the pale boy around, his eyes scanning every inch of his torso, his fingers running the outlines of his pain. Mungo tried to laugh the hurt away. "Catholics, man. Everybody thinks they're the good guys."

James jammed his knuckles into his eye sockets. He was repeating *okay,* over and over, like it was a chant. The blood had drained from his face. He stood that way, thinking, chanting, for a long while. "Fuck it. Awright, we'll leave."

Mungo shook his head despite himself. "Naw, I was being selfish. You'll be awright. You can go away to the rigs. You can have weans with Ashley."

James clamped his hands on either side of Mungo's head. "It's too late."

Mungo winced. Then he smiled, a tremulous, fleeting thing. "Are you sure?"

"Aye." His thumbs were caressing Mungo's bottom lip. "Ah think ah have more than enough saved. We can go north and rent a caravan for the whole summer. Ah can find work. We'll be awright."

The men who were walking their dogs in the early sunshine glanced their way. The boys separated. They stood a respectable arm's length apart and laughed and smiled at each other like they were demented. James sank to his knees, his eyes were swivelling back and forth as he thought about all that would need to be planned.

Mungo sat on the grass beside him. His teeth were rattling now. The pain caught up to him and the last of his body heat was leaching through the welts on his side. James drew off his own jumper, the barley and gorse Fair Isle, and then he helped remove Mungo's cagoule and redressed him in the knitwear. Up close there were a thousand different colours all running through the knit, not only the porridgey cream and golds, but also bluebell blues, mossy browns, and an acidic, punkish pink. Mungo wanted time to sit and study it closely, all these little things he had never noticed before. It was alive with the warmth of James, he felt him all around him. Mungo chewed the right cuff, the wool squeaked between his teeth. It calmed him down.

"Better?" James helped pull the cagoule back over Mungo's head and zipped the neck closed all the way to the top, taking care to avoid pinching his chin.

Mungo folded himself over the soft school-bag, suddenly very relieved, and more tired than he could say. He let the weak sun wash over him. "Today?"

James shook his head. "Tomorrow maybe. I need to go see Mac Munroe up in Cran-hill. He'll be desperate to buy the doocot off us. He's been keen to fly my prize pouters for ages. Between the cages and the birds there has to be about four hunner pound all in. That'll be a big help to us."

James went to the doocot and exercised his doos while Mungo slumped on the grass and felt bad about his meagre savings. James retrieved his flask and sandwiches and they ate a shared breakfast together as the pigeons circled overhead. The tea was milky and sweet and it soothed the cut in his mouth. There was no school today, there would be no school tomorrow. The boys made lists of things to pack; useful things like bandages, firelighters, sleeping bags, and then many impractical things: a ghetto blaster, tins of heavy Ambrosia rice, and James's mourning suit, in case farmers expected a formal job interview. Afterwards they lay on their stomachs in the morning sun, nothing more to say, drunk with relief at what lay ahead. James snaked his hand across the grass and lifted the back of Mungo's jumper. He ran his fingers through the downy hairs at the base of his spine. Mungo closed his eyes.

"Do you think people will like us?"

"In Ardnamurchan? Ah dunno, we don't really need people to like us. We just need them to leave us alone. There's hardly any people there, ah think it'll be awright."

No women watching from windows. No gossiping voices at the landing below you. No Ha-Ha wanting him to man up. No Jodie wanting him to grow up. Mungo could not imagine. "Will you tell your da?"

"Aye. Ah've already written the letter. Ah wrote it last year after he battered me for the chatline." James stroked the base of Mungo's spine, ready to pull his hand away should one of the dog walkers come too close. "Will you tell Mo-Maw?"

Mungo thought about it. "Naw. I'll tell Jodie. She'll know how to break it to Hamish and Maureen. 'Asides, they willnae want to know me after they hear what I am."

"Maybe Jodie will." James trusted in the legends of her good-heartedness. It spoke as many lovely things about him as it did about her. "Mibbe one day we can tell her where we went."

"Aye. Mibbe."

"Mungo, you do know we can't ever come back here? Once they know, we'll be as bad as Chickie Calhoun."

Someday Mungo would tell him what he knew but for now all he said was "He's no all bad. He's awright. We're awright."

"Whut? No shuffling to the Paki shop in your cagoule, making soup for Mo-Maw, living for the guid weather when you can watch bin men take their taps aff in the summer sun?"

Mungo was grinning, spit pooling in the side of his open mouth. "You're a cheeky basturt for a Catholic. You still have to apologize for saying all that cruel shite to me."

"Ah was just keeping the Protestants in line. Yeese think ye run this town."

"That was kind of you, wingnut." Mungo snickered as he twisted James's ear.

James batted his hand away. He looked up at the sky full of birling birds. There was some other man's hen in the sky. She was a drab, eggy yellow against the ash-grey clouds, but now and again the sunlight hit her and she shone like gold. One of James's pigeons started to circle her, a plump little bully that he called Henry-the-Weighth. The pair dipped out of view behind the tenements and in that moment, James knew that his bird was lost forever. It would have devastated him only hours ago, but now he huffed, and felt strangely happy for Henry. He chuckled to himself. "Here, ah realized something the other day. Do you remember that chatline ah telt ye about? Well, ah realized ah started phoning it well before my mammy died."

"Aye. So?"

"She must have been getting those bills for months. She must have seen what those numbers were for, and just paid them. She never let on. She never said a word."

It took a moment for Mungo to realize

what it was James was telling him. "Oh. She knew about you. That's guid."

James whistled at his birds. "Aye. That's guid."

Mungo turned his face away from James. The sunlight was making the crown of his head warm, and he wanted to feel it kiss his other cheek. "Just think. This time next week. No more John Donne."

"Who?"

The soft fingers on his spine had lulled him into a stupor. "It doesnae matter."

The sun would hold. The boys closed their eyes.

While the boys had been watching the birds fly over the scheme, Hamish had come upon the doocot from the park side. Like a deer-hound he had the instinct to start at the widest point and sweep inwards, coursing his quarry back towards home. He had come through the park and then slipped between the missing railings in the iron fence.

Earlier that morning he had gone to the flat to look for Mungo and found Mo-Maw slumped at the kitchen table with her head in her hands. Last night had been a blur of adrenaline, flashes of emerald green and white and spit and blood. But through it all

573

he could clearly picture his baby brother lying in the dirt, choking on his blood, while the gleeful Fenian stamped down upon him. When Hamish saw Mungo's bloodied, discarded clothes in the hallway, and found Mo-Maw weeping to herself at the table, he imagined the worst. He shook her. She looked up. She screamed.

For a moment Hamish had forgotten about his own torn-up face. Mo-Maw's screaming brought Jodie through from her bedroom. His sister stood in the kitchen doorway, her hair curled around a tonging iron, the plug dangling from the end where she had ripped it from the wall. It was unlike Jodie to be at a loss for words. She stared at Hamish, and at the blood that was already seeping through the bandage, and as she stared, the tongs singed through her hair and a long, ringleted clump came away in her hand.

Mo-Maw had been nursing a hangover, she hadn't been weeping for Mungo, she thought he was still in his bed. Hamish guffawed at his own stupidity.

Hamish cast no shadows. Mungo didn't know what instinct made him look up from the long grass, what shift in the air made him glance over his shoulder. But when he rolled on to his side, Hamish was standing over them, blood dripping down his neck.

Mungo had thought it would be too early for his brother to be up, too soon for the father of a young baby to be dressed and prowling. Still, here he was — a ginger bottle full of siphoned petrol in his hand.

There was a sour grimace on Hamish's face and his teeth were grinding from the speed. Bleeding and raw, the left side of his face was covered with a large white bandage, but the ointment and coagulating blood seeped through the thin muslin adhesive. The outline of it looked like a half-grin, like one of those carnival drawings you turned upside down to make it either grimace or smile. Hamish had been slashed from his earlobe to the left corner of his mouth, a rusty carpet blade having sliced through most layers of his skin. He must have been in the Royal Infirmary, being stitched together, most of the night. He had taken a bump of speed and had not yet been home to sleep. The stitches were not holding.

"I thought ye were fuckin' dead." His eyes were wild.

"Hamish, it's no what you think." Mungo could only fear how much he had seen, how much he had heard.

There were real tears streaming behind the thick lenses. It was this detail that scared

Mungo the most. Hamish was shaking his head like he didn't want to believe it. The two boys lying side by side in the grass. The Fenian's hand tickling the base of his brother's spine. Hamish let out a single choked sob. "Naw, Mungo. Ye cannae be one of them. Ye cannae. Ye just fuckin' cannae."

James's hand — the same gentle fingers that had caressed Mungo's skin — was lying in the grass, supporting his weight. Hamish stepped forward and brought his boot down upon it. He stamped down twice, all the force concentrated in his heel, and the thick sole of his Doc Martens made a terrible crunching sound. James rolled on to his side, terror blanching his face. He curled into a defensive ball and cradled his broken fingers in his other hand. Mungo went to him.

James's mouth was open wide, but he made no sound. He started crawling backwards, away from Hamish, trying to make it to the doocot. Hamish lifted his glasses and wiped at his wet eyes. He turned his gaze to the Fenian, then he swivelled it back to Mungo. A dark look of relief swept over him. He had the answer he needed, even if it was not the truth.

"Ah. I understand now. Ye're being diddled by this fucker, eh? This dirty Tim bastard that likes to have his way with wee boys. Typical. I blame the fucking priests."

Hamish crossed the grass towards James. It was what he wanted to believe. It was a far easier thing to understand than the other truth, that Mungo had lain with this boy and enjoyed it, that Mungo had dreamt of the cereal sugar on James's breath, that he had taken him in his mouth, or nuzzled his nose into the soft blond down at the crack of his arse, or rubbed himself against James in a cold bath till they made soft bubbles in the flat water. Hamish could not be the brother of a deviant. He would not be the brother of a poofter.

"Ye're a fuckin' child maleshtur."

James Jamieson did something strange then. He stopped trying to get away.

The young man nodded only once, very faintly, as if he had swallowed a pill with no milk to wash it down. He looked at Mungo now and the left corner of his mouth pulled back in acceptance of what would come next. *I understand. It's okay.*

Mungo was too late to see what they were not saying. Hamish had rushed forward before it dawned on him. "No! Hamish. Don't!"

The first kick caught James on the underside of his chin. It split the soft skin and cracked his disobedient teeth to pieces. The second kick came down on to the middle of his face and sent a spray of blood skyward from his broken nose. The boy stopped moving. He lay, wheat and crimson in the sunlight, his head tilted backwards, his arms wide, like a saint waiting for ascension. Mungo was still on his knees. His hands were clasped in prayer. It had taken only two kicks to destroy James Jamieson.

Hamish would not let Mungo go to his side. Mungo darted around his brother, but as he knelt over James, Hamish took a firm grip of his hair and dragged him away.

Hamish unscrewed his ginger bottle and doused James in petrol. It poured out in a galloping stream. Mungo rammed his shoulder into Hamish's gut and tackled him. He used whatever strength he had left to shove his brother away from the body. Mungo struggled but Hamish was stronger, faster. He huckled him to his knees, he put his boot into Mungo's ribs and Mungo became helpless as a newborn calf. With his right hand he twisted deep into his hair, with his left, he gripped the back of Mungo's jumper and dragged him on all fours towards the housing scheme. "Get a haud of yersel. I've saved ye, Mungo. Ye'll thank me one day. I saved ye."

At first Mungo let himself be pulled away, he was glad of every footstep he put between his brother and James's body. But as they reached the pavement, Hamish stopped and roared back at the Catholic. "I'll be back for you. I'm no fuckin' finished."

Mungo twisted wildly. He used his nails to pierce the back of Hamish's hand, but Hamish knew what he was doing. He brought his elbow down into the tender bruise on Mungo's face, again and again, until submission flooded over Mungo. Then he dragged his brother on his knees back towards the tenements, stopping every now and then to shake him, and tell him to quit his fucking greetin'.

TWENTY-FIVE

It turned out to be a beautiful day. The loch was alive with sunlight as Mungo helped Gallowgate drag the dead man back to their campsite. They kept dropping him and St Christopher's bony body rolled away and disappeared beneath the horsetail ferns. Each time they picked him up again, Gallowgate took care to brush the muck from the sallow skin. There was real grief etched on Gallowgate's face as they dragged his friend across the carpet of pearlwort moss. Mungo couldn't look at the body. He wished the dead man would shut his eyes.

They laid St Christopher inside the two-man tent; Gallowgate had insisted on the decency of it. They couldn't get him all the way in because his soaked tweeds stuck to the damp floor and he wouldn't budge any further without bringing the structure down upon himself. So he lay there, his legs sticking out from the kneecap down, as Gallowgate gathered clumps of purple heather and sprinkled them on his chest.

Mungo searched for dry wood to start a fire with, while Gallowgate sank three lager cans, one after the other, without speaking. There was no dry wood and it was a pitiful fire, smoky and slow to catch, but it burned well enough for Mungo to place two tins of ravioli into the flames. He sat across the firepit and watched Gallowgate sink into the drink, finishing the lagers and swilling the spirit bottles for the last dregs.

"He looked after us in the jail." Gallowgate spoke into the fire. "He shared his commissary. Always gave us a few of his smoked douts when he knew ah was short."

It seemed like no great charity to Mungo to receive the blunted leftovers of someone's cigarette. But Gallowgate looked moved by what he was saying.

"Naebody in the jail would talk to me at first — neabody but auld Chrissy. From day one, he was ma pal."

"Was it bad inside? Was it hellish?" Mungo wanted to know. He tried not to look at the dead man's feet.

"Ah dunno, it was jail, win't it? It could be good and bad. It was overcrowded, two men to a single cell and you had to eat yer meals on yer bed. They kept us all in the same wing. All the guys that were inside for sex crimes. The governor had taken a notion to try and rehabilitate us. He let us organize activities, gave us a yellow tea kettle. I think they were studying us."

"They don't keep you apart?" It didn't seem right to Mungo. How could it punish someone to surround them with people who liked the same things they did? Mungo thought about the first-year boys at school. How every autumn they would lose their minds for football stickers. They would huddle in concentration as they bartered for what they wanted, and moved as one large, writhing mass.

"No. They lump you the gether. There were some right monsters in there. Men that chopped up wee lassies in their Easter dresses. Other men that wouldnae leave me alone at night." He emptied the last of the whisky down his throat. Gallowgate buried his chin into the neck of his bomber jacket. He was staring at the man's protruding feet. "Auld Chrissy was different, though. His father used to own a famous butcher's out on the Paisley Road. They saved up for years and bought a second shop further down in Govan. Chrissy was to run it by himself."

"Why didn't he?"

"He did, for a while, and it did really guid.

He'd learnt the skills of the trade from his father, and wi' two shops the quality of meat was better and the prices were just that wee bit lower. It was goin' great guns."

"How come he looked like a pure jakey, then?"

Gallowgate glowered at Mungo. "Watch yer mouth."

No apology would cross Mungo's lips. He went back to picking at his midge bites. "So? What happened with the butcher's?"

Gallowgate shrugged. "He got done for a Saturday boy. He had taken a shine to an eleven-year-old that used to scrub the trays at the end of the week. His father used to work for auld Chrissy and the boy would come in for a few hours and make deliveries and stuff like that. Chrissy thought the boy was fond of him. Chrissy couldnae help himself."

Mungo found he could look at the feet now. The fear he had felt pushed to the back of his mind and suddenly he didn't feel that bad. It was like the shuffling of Ludo cards, remorse sliding to the back, and on top lay something like relief. St Christopher was a very bad man.

"Do you think it hurts to drown?" Mungo had to know.

"How the fuck would ah know? He looked

like he cracked his face in. Ah cannae tell if he did that afore or after he went in the watter."

Mungo felt the knuckles in his spine relax, and he breathed in fully for the first time since they had found the body. He saw now the uneven wear on St Christopher's shoes; the leather soles were worn away on the inside of each arch; the saint was pigeon-toed. "So, like, you don't know how he died?"

Gallowgate shook his head. "Naw. The only person that'd be able to tell for sure is the coroner. They'll cut him open and look."

Mungo nodded, although he barely understood. "After that do you think it'll be okay? He was just an old man who drowned, *right*? We could just leave him here. Why would they bother looking for us?"

"Naw." Gallowgate stared at him for a long time and then he snorted at the boy's naivety. He had forgotten he was talking to a child. "It doesnae work like that. As soon as they find out they've got a dead sex offender out in the middle of nowhere they'll look into it."

"How?" It made no sense to Mungo — surely a dead bogeyman would be a blessing.

"Because when one of us shows up dead

they want to know who we were wi' last. Or more importantly, who was unlucky enough to be wi' *us.*" Gallowgate was becoming jumpy. "Ah don't want to go back to the jail."

Mungo collapsed back against one of the mossy boulders and closed his eyes. He felt empty, yet at the same time, he felt lousy with a knot of feelings he could not untangle. He had to get home. What would they say about him now? He was more of a hardman than Hamish could ever imagine. He wasn't the shy little boy with the spazzy face. He wasn't the poofy Fenian lover who was no good at fighting. They had broken into his body. He had killed a man. He had bludgeoned him and then he had drowned him. It was a funny feeling, to know that he was more of a man than Hamish would ever be, and also less, at the very same time. He had to go home. He could never go home again.

His mother had given him to a pair of child molesters with a bag of dog-eared comic books and a Ludo game, fun for the whole family, ages 6–14. She had thought that they would make a man of him; that they would show him things to put him right, things that a father should have taught him, things that she could have taught him if only she tried, things he would never even need to know if he lived his whole life in Glasgow, which he would, because that's what everybody he knew did.

Mungo's face was wet with tears again. Gallowgate came to him, he put his arms around his shoulders and kissed his hairline. "We can fix this. We can take his body out into the loch and sink it."

The ravioli tins were bubbling and Mungo used this to scuttle away from Gallowgate's embrace. He hunkered like a sulking primate. He sat the scalding tin on the ground and began to pick the pillows out one by one. The sauce burned his fingers but he would not stop.

The midday sun streaked across the Munros on the far side of the loch. The pockets of snow were moving. Mungo watched them walk across the sharp crest of a crag before he realized it was actually a herd of disorganized sheep looking for the sweet green grass that grew between the rocks. He found his disposable camera amongst the assorted junk in his cagoule pocket. He wound on the noisy film and tried to take a photograph of the wandering snow. Then he wound it on another frame and tried to take a photo of Gallowgate. The man hissed. He put his hands over his face. It didn't matter — a small trickle of river water poured from the plastic case.

As they ate, Gallowgate seemed keen to know what Mungo would say, and what he would not say, when he returned to Glasgow. They spent a long time getting their story straight; Gallowgate feeding the boy a line, and Mungo feeling like there was a hook in his mouth. When Gallowgate spoke to him it was in the tone of voice that Mungo hadn't heard since that evening in the tent. It was like they were best pals again, the two of them united against the world. "So, what will you tell yer family about this weekend?"

Mungo stopped chewing. "Just that I had a nice time. I liked the water. I saw some hills."

"Naw, I mean, what will ye say about us? Auld Chrissy and that?"

"What is it you want me to say?"

"Mibbe just tell them we were dead sound. That we taught ye how to build a fire, how to fish. Tell them ah spent my entire two weeks' giro getting us up here. Tell them that." Gallowgate used his tongue to dig some gristle out from behind his bottom lip. "When they ask, where will you say ye slept?"

Mungo nodded to the two-man tent, or

what was left of it.

"Naw. Better tae tell them we put ye in the one-man tent. Make sure and be clear that they understand ye had the whole thing tae yersel. Tell them that ye were scared or some shite, that the deer and the rain were creepy as fuck at night." He hooted like a sad owl. "Tell them that ye braved it any-hows. Aye, tell them that ye had a whole tent tae yersel."

"Okay."

"So what will ye tell them?"

Mungo's eye stuttered. He felt slightly mad. But Gallowgate would not go on until he responded. "I'll say that I slept in this wee tent down by the water's edge all by myself. I'll say that it was cold at night. It was terrifying." His voice was as flat as new tarmacadam.

Gallowgate dug some food out of his back molar and flicked it across the shingle. He didn't like the flatness in Mungo's voice. He was squinting at the boy as though he could not be sure if Mungo was being face-tious or not. "Mind and tell them about the big roe buck you saw. They'll picture that above everything else. And castles — mam-mies *love* castles."

"Okay."

"And how will ye explain them bruises?"

Mungo shrugged. "They won't care."

"Well if they do, tell them you tumbled down a hill. These hills get awfy slippy in the thaw. Ye can stave yer whole face in with one wrong step. Daft wee humpty dumpty."

"Awright."

They were quiet for a long while after that. It was pointless to bother chewing the mushy food, so Mungo just moved it back and forth in his mouth till it was a sludge he could swallow. Gallowgate was watching him the whole time. "Look, it'll do ye no guid to feel sorry for yersel."

"What do you mean?"

"Ah'm no daft. Ye might be tempted to tell tales when ye get up the road. Start spreading lies about me just so everybody feels sorry for ye."

It took effort for Mungo to swallow the next mouthful.

"Pity only feels guid for a minute. It gets stale awfy quick and then it starts to fuckin' stink. But I suppose if ye tell them your lies then ye can have a good greet and ye'll get a couple of lovely hugs. Ye might even get a fish supper out of it."

"Okay."

Gallowgate hauched, his bottom lip gleamed with spit. "But know this — the people ye tell will never look at ye the same

589

again. Yer mammy will feel heavy rotten. She'll take a wee drink and tell somebody, just so as to feel better. That's what wummin do; they cannae be trusted to haud their own watter. Then that person will tell somebody else and then they'll tell somebody else, and afore ye know it, every bastard on the scheme will know how you let two strange men fuck ye in the woods."

"But I didn't."

He looked like he felt sorry for the boy. "Naw. But is that what ye want people to think?"

Mungo shook his head. "No."

"Cos they will." Gallowgate jabbed his thumb in the direction of the dead saint. " 'Asides, if the Hamiltons want tae start somethin' wi' the polis, then we'll aw need tae explain *that.*"

He was hungry but he could eat no more. After a while, Mungo stopped his quiet crying. He turned his face towards the loch and wiped his eyes discreetly. "What if St Christopher's picture is in the evening paper?"

Gallowgate answered with a sad laugh. "Naebody will put his picture in the paper. Naebody will miss him." The man swirled the last of the lager cans, but they were empty. He sat staring at Mungo for a time, a darkening glower, before he asked. "So how long exactly have ye been lying tae yer maw?"

Mungo was confused. "I don't lie."

"Come on." Gallowgate seemed suddenly irritated. He rubbed his temples, his head was surely louping, crying out for one more drink. "Ye've been lying about that Fenian. Ye've been lying about being a wee bender."

"I'm no —"

"See! Ye're lying now."

Mungo's hips had seized in the cold and he stood up with a wince. He moved further away from the man and crouched closer to the weak fire. "A minute ago you wanted me to lie."

Gallowgate snorted. All the syrup in his voice had evaporated. "Aye, yer guid at it. Ah'll gie ye that."

He wasn't a good liar, but he didn't feel like fighting anymore. He gave in, like he always did, and he shrugged.

Gallowgate tossed a mossed stone at his feet. "So, will ye keep yer story straight?"

Mungo hesitated, not because he felt defiant — he knew he wouldn't be able to stomach the look on Mo-Maw's face if he ever told her the truth — he only hesitated because he was tired. Gallowgate's mercurial mind moved too quickly for him. He was tired of his leash being jerked by this man as though he was a dog that couldn't keep up. He was tired of the damp cold that rose off the loch, tired of the pathetic, worn brogues that were sticking out of the tent. Mungo met Gallowgate's eyes for the first time that afternoon and there, in the centre of his brow, was a slight knotting, the first flicker of doubt, fear perhaps. Mungo was glad to see it. He paused and savoured it a half-second longer. "I'll no tell anyone. Promise."

"Oh, Mungo." He sighed. The man's face changed again, and now he looked at the boy with profound sadness. "Ah telt ye, there's no fuckin' way ah'm going back in that jail."

Gallowgate forced the last of the ravioli into his mouth and smeared the red sauce across the back of his hand. Then he spent a time licking his palm and smoothing his short, straight fringe against his forehead. His eyes fell out of focus and he seemed to lose himself in his thoughts. Mungo sat in a daze until Gallowgate leapt to his feet. "Right. Ah need ye to make a pile of stones, heavy ones but small enough so we can fit them into pockets and the lining of his coat." Gallowgate pointed out into the silent water. "About five or six metres out, the edge drops off in a shelf, from there the loch could be a hunner thousand metres or so deep." Mungo must have looked reticent, because the man added, "Dinnae worry, there's nae monster in this loch."

Mungo didn't believe him. He was glad to turn his back to Gallowgate. Scotland was made of splintered rock and he soon gathered a large pile of heavy stones. Gallowgate dragged the dead man from the tent, then he carried him to the water and waded out into the deep as if he was going to baptize him. Mungo followed almost reverentially, head bowed and with an armful of offerings. Gallowgate waded out about six metres into the water before he had to tilt his head backwards to breath. "Hurry up," he spat, "fill his pockets as fast as ye can."

Mungo took the stones and stuffed them into St Christopher's waistband, into his jacket pocket, into his trousers. Gallowgate motioned to him for more and he waded back to the shore for another armful. He slid the last pebble into the saint's open mouth.

Gallowgate showed a great strain on his face, his lips were bloodless and blue. The dead man must have been heavy with all the rocks. Suddenly Gallowgate dropped below the water and Mungo imagined him giving the body one last shove into the nothingness. There were some bubbles and then it was still again. Mungo could picture the glimmering cataracts receding into the dark.

Gallowgate surfaced with empty arms, sputtering and huffing from the cold. His teeth were chittering as they waded back towards the shore. When the water was between his chest and his waist, Mungo felt Gallowgate's hand grab his wrist. "Wait. Do ye know any prayers?"

"Naw."

He pulled the boy back towards him and held him in his arms like he wanted to steal all his warmth. Mungo braced his hands against Gallowgate's chest. He didn't want the man's affection. But Gallowgate held him tight. Then he tried to kiss him.

"Please, just let me go home."

Gallowgate was looking deep into his eyes. His sincerity was unsettling. "Mungo, ah want ye to know, wee Maureen didnae say bad things about ye. What ah said the other day, it wisnae true."

Mungo was too empty to care now.

"She said she named ye after a saint. That after she did, ye never once made her regret that. She said that you were the softest, sweetest boy she had ever known."

Mungo felt his feet leave the ground as Gallowgate embraced him. The man clung to him and began to kiss his neck. He was sobbing and muttering that he was *sorry* as his lips searched Mungo's chin then his cheek for the softness of his lips. Mungo thought he was apologizing for the bad things that had happened, for the pain in his gut, for the dead body. But then the man forced his kiss on Mungo, his hands shifted to his throat and he pushed him under the water.

It was incredibly still beneath the surface of the loch.

Mungo opened his eyes; the water was so clear that he could see the strain on Gallowgate's face, the roped muscles protruding on his inked neck as he tried to drown him. He felt the air inside his cagoule buoy him up to the surface, only to be countered by the force of Gallowgate's fist punching down into his belly, into his heart. He had the sensation of being alone again, the desire to float away into the quietness of the loch, his pockets filled with wildflowers.

Mungo remembered the disposable camera in his pocket — it was a foolish thing to think of but it had been stupid of him to forget to take it out. Now he would never be able to show Jodie the beautiful castle, he could never show James the bleached ram's bones. *James.* He wanted to go home so badly then. He didn't care about Hamish or Mo-Maw or Gallowgate; he wanted to see the oil rigger's son one last time and kiss the pink softness behind his sticky-out ears.

That was a thing that could never happen.

Gallowgate stopped punching into the boy. His hands clamped around his throat again as he choked the last of the air out of him. Mungo was barely aware that his own hands were flailing, grabbing for the sky. He was grabbing for Gallowgate's face, but he couldn't reach, his arms were too short. He saw St Christopher in his last moments and knew now how much drowning burned. Funny that. He saw the Catholic boy and his beatific smile as he marched the length of him.

With Gallowgate's hands on his throat the last air pockets in his clothes tilted his body till it was inverted and his feet were skyward. He felt the disposable camera and Gallowgate's discarded lager can slide out of the kangaroo pouch. It was all shifting inside him, turning upside down, Jodie's school photograph, James's birthday bear. Then something came to his mind, something he had forgotten.

He fumbled the blade Hamish had given him. He gripped it tightly and swung it into Gallowgate's stomach. His hand stuck there, pinned to the man, and he had to tug hard to pull it out before he could swing it again into his ribs. The loch water was freezing cold, but he could swear he felt the warmth of the man's blood pump over his fingers. He swung wildly, again and again, until the hands released his throat and he floated out into the loch.

Mungo was out beyond his depth by the time he regained a normal breath. He was way beyond St Christopher's body and he couldn't feel the bottom. There was a sucking current and several times he was pulled under the surface. He could imagine the sightless saint reaching up from the depths and wrapping his long fingers around his ankles. It took the last of his energy to tread the water. Everything felt like it would be better if he just sank. If he just gave in.

As he was struggling up and down, he caught brief glimpses of Gallowgate. The man stumbled from the loch. He was clutching his side and his good Italian denims were ruined with a black inky liquid. Gallowgate made it to knee-depth before he sat down in the water. He plonked down on his backside like a toddler. He searched his pockets for cigarettes, and finding them ruined, he tossed them into the loch. Then he tipped over.

It could be another trick.

Mungo treaded water as long as he could and then he doggy-paddled to the shallows. He gave Gallowgate a wide berth as he struggled to reach the shore. It took him some time to come near. He was circling and dripping and shivering, inching closer and closer by degrees.

The tide was a pretty pink colour. The man's face was half-in, half-out of the water. Gallowgate's green eyes were open and his right hand gripped a boulder, like he could rise up at any moment. It took a long time, but eventually Mungo summoned enough courage to come close enough to read the ink on his knuckles. *Evan.* He wondered if that was Gallowgate's real name. He prodded the man with his toe. Then he stepped back and waited.

Gallowgate was still bleeding into the water. His blood was unfurling in scarlet swirls. It looked like the man was being consumed by medieval flames. Mungo picked at his cheek and watched him burn for a while.

In his search for cigarettes, Gallowgate's wallet must have fallen out of his pocket.

Mungo fished it out of the shallows. It was almost empty of money — there were no bank cards or credit cards — but in the plastic identification sleeve was a monthly bus pass. Mungo studied the scowling picture. He read the name out loud: *"Angus Bell."*

Tucked into the billfold was a single postcard. It was a photo of Angus Bell in ill-fitting prison gear standing before an artificial Christmas tree. In the bottom right corner it was decorated with holly and bells, and stamped in a Victorian script: *"Thinking of you at Christmas-time."* Mungo turned it over. There was a second-class stamp attached, but no address, no festive message.

Twenty-Six

May evenings were bright enough that they did away with the need for the flickering fluorescent lighting. The natural light gave an unnatural glow of health to the fellowship. The top table called the meeting to order, and as the alcoholics took to their chairs and began with their announcements and affirmations, Mo-Maw sat in the very front and centre, stiff and upright and earnest, a teacher's pet. She was trying hard to show Mungo that anybody could change.

Mungo stood in his usual place by the hot tea urn, only half-listening as the top table ran through the Twelve Steps with unusual gusto. They were cheered by the turn in the weather and encouraged by the half-dozen new faces and the high amount of returning fellowship. Their good mood was not contagious. Mungo filled six polystyrene cups to the brim with scalding black tea. He organized the cups, balanced them precariously along the edge of the folding table.

Skrriit, skriiit, skrriiit, skrit, skrriiiitt, skrit.

He ran his thumbnail along the polystyrene about a centimetre from the bottom of each cup. Slicing his nail into one, he moved to the next and when he had sliced along all six cups, he started again into the groove he had made in the first. The anticipation distracted him, gave him something to look forward to; waiting to see which cup would fail first and burn his legs with hot liquid.

Behind him, the fellowship welcomed all the new members. They listened patiently to those who felt brave enough to share their journeys, until Mo-Maw cut into the end of one man's speech, when she stood to share her story. Mungo had heard it all before.

Skrriit, skriiit, skrriiit, skrit, skrriiiitt, skrit.

"Hallo, ma name's Monday-Thursday Maureen and ah'm an alkahawlick."

"Hallo, Maureen."

"Ah've been struggling with drink, on and off likes, for about twelve years. Ah know, ah know." She let out a well-practised giggle. *Wait for it,* he thought. "Ah don't look nearly old enough but it's true. Anyhows, where was I? Aye, well, ah'm a single mother." Slight pause for sympathy. "My man's been dead nearly sixteen year and it's been hard raising ma weans on ma lonesome. It would be hard enough with one, but ah've been blessed with three and I tell you, they're all so challenging you would barely believe it. Ye never get a minute's peace. Ye turn yer back to help one and the other is up to his neck in some bother. Boys are the hardest, int they?" There was a faint murmur of agreement. Mo-Maw seemed underwhelmed by the lukewarm response. Her voice went up an octave, there was the quiver of poor-me's at its edges. "It's hard to raise a boy without a man around, you try your hardest but sometimes they don't turn out quite right."

Skrriit, skriiit, skrriiit, skrit, skrriiiiitt, skrit.

Mungo pressed his nail a little harder. It was the fourth cup that failed first, a torrent of scalding black tea shot out of the hole. The spray hit him in the thigh and poured down his right leg. Mungo gritted his teeth. He moved his thumbnail to start on the fifth cup.

Someone wrapped a hand around his wrist. Every-Other-Wednesday Nora had popped to the ladies and found him making a nuisance of himself.

"*Weh-ll,* look at the mess ye've made, ya silly article. Away. Out of it." She was already mopping up the mess as she shoved him roughly out of the hallway.

Mo-Maw didn't break her affirmation monologue, but she heard the commotion and threw her son dirty looks over the heads of the crowd. They glided like spears over a battlefield. "That!" She raised the back of her hand to him. "That, ladies and gentlemen, is the reason ah take a guid drink." Forty heads turned as one to see this poor woman's burden for themselves. Mungo waved. He had so little to fear now.

The Hamiltons had gathered like a council of feuding union bosses, each of them gesticulating furiously and trying to talk over the top of the others. Hamish told his mother and sister what had happened as Mungo hung his head, his fingers still stinking of petrol. It was to be Hamish's narration of events: the older Fenian boy molesting his naive little brother. The room fell silent. They looked at Mungo with alternating faces of pity and shame as though he was a china plate that had a bad chip and they were deciding if they would keep it or not; such a lovely thing to be so ruined.

Mungo watched, cold as the Clyde, as the three of them started roaring at each other again: assigning blame, listing their failings, casting up the selfish natures of others. When Mo-Maw and Hamish finally ganged up on Jodie for "not raising him right," Jodie swept her hand along the mantelpiece and broke every picture frame in the house.

Mo-Maw said, "Ah'm tired of you thinking ye are the main attraction around here."

As they were gathering up the glass, Mungo saw his chance. He slipped out the door.

The mud had already dried on his knees as he ran back to the doocot. The back of his head sang where Hamish had dragged him through the streets and now faces loomed down at him from the tenement windows; children crowded around their mammies, everyone had a seat, keen to see what the next embarrassment in the Hamilton pantomime would be.

Mungo was winded by the time he reached the patchy grass. The door to the doocot was slamming in the wind and at first it raised his spirits; James was here, he was hurt, but he would be alive.

There was too much blood on the grass for Mungo to ignore. It was flattened where he had lain, and there were splintered shards of his front teeth, luminous in the mud. Mungo picked them up and put them carefully in the pocket of his cagoule.

But James was in the doocot, it would be all right.

Mungo held the swinging door firm and peered into the darkness. He was looking for the pool of bronze light; the golden hair that refracted the shaft of sunlight into every corner of the dark loft. But James was not there. All the doocot cages were open, some of the doors were hanging loose, the hinges he had carefully maintained were ripped from their bearing screws. There was a solitary doo flapping in the corner, unable to gain any flight. His left wing was extended, it was broken.

Mungo stepped back out into the daylight. There were some pigeons sitting on the new slate roof, but in the grass beyond the doocot were the rest of James's prize pouters, dead and flung about. A few looked like they'd had their necks wrung. There was a cluster of three, the bleached doo, the ashy hen, and a new bird that Mungo had never seen. There were golf tees next to their bodies, and these bodies had no heads. Someone had held them still, for a great laugh, while someone else took a swing with a putter. The sun was not yet fully overhead in the sky, and everything beautiful was all already ruined.

Mungo stepped back inside the doocot. The injured bird was still flapping in panic. He just wanted to hold it like James would, run his fingers along its throat and settle it down. He cooed to it and bobbed gently like he had seen James do. It rested for a moment and he snatched it up and held Little Mungo in his hands. Its heart was thumping against its breast. It was in so much pain.

Whroup, whroooup, whrooup. He chirped into its matted nape till it calmed itself. *Whroup, whroooup, whrooup.* He wept as he wrung its poor neck.

He went to the Jamieson flat, but peering through the letter box, he could tell that no one was home. When he came back home, he was told that Hamish had gone out searching for him again. Jodie had hidden her brother in the warm airing cupboard. She was holding his T-shirt over his head and turning him to look at his bruises. "What Hamish said, is that what really happened? Was that Catholic boy doing dirty things to you?"

"Naw."

Jodie stopped rubbing Germolene into his bruises. She brought her lips close to his ear. "Were you doing bad things to each other?"

"Aye."

She kept rubbing the pink ointment between his ribs but all the colour had left her face. The immersion boiler clicked on and filled the cupboard with a suffocating heat. He used to enjoy that.

"I'm sorry," he said.

"You could get the jail for what you were doing." She was handling him too roughly, scrubbing the lotion into his bruise like it was a stain she could lift with a good brush. "They used to lock men up for that. *Haaah-ha.*"

"I can't help it."

Jodie brought her face so close to his he could count the freckles on her nose. "Do you want to catch AIDS? Is that what you want? Because you *will* catch it. They're aw getting it. That Fenian boy could have it and give it to you, simple as that." She snapped her oily fingers.

"James wouldn't do that."

"Wouldn't he? What on earth would you know about the ways of men, eh?" Jodie scoffed and he could see the little hard bits of Mo-Maw in her now, sure as knots in a fine wood. She was hurting him as she rubbed the lotion into his skin, and he could tell that she meant to. "You're a daft wee boy. A tender-hearted eejit." She spun him and slathered ointment across his kidneys. "We're aw knocking our bloody pans in, try-

607

ing to make something of you, trying to make a man of out you. And what are you doing, eh? Carrying on like a daft lovesick lassie. It's time you toughened up."

He repeated himself. "I can't help it."

Jodie spun him to face her. She shook him hard. "God sake! You have to help it. You can't be like that and expect to be happy about it."

Mungo went to the rear of the meeting room and slid down the tall iron radiator. The hot fins felt good against the bruising. The welts had not started to shrink yet, but they had stopped blooming their terrible purple flowers, and Jodie had said that was a good sign.

The warmth of the radiator spread through him, it made a deep clanging sound and a constant hissing that lulled him into a state of sleepwalking. From the floor he could see under the tideline of the plastic seats. He watched the members' legs fidget anxiously with boredom or fresh shakes. Some of the alcoholics were eager for the meeting to be over, others were worried about what would happen when it was. Faces turned to one another as they said the final benediction. The meeting adjourned, and the fellowship gathered around the urn and passed around plates of gammon sandwiches.

They congregated in groups of four or five and shared their news. Mungo couldn't hear what they were saying, but he appreciated the way they laid hands on each other's arms, and when they spoke, he liked how everyone listened and seemed to feel it deeply in their own bones. It was a funny thing to observe; near strangers who had shared some of their deepest shames, their most vulnerable moments, were now gathering to make small talk about the weather or if Cranhill-Cathy would make it to the regionals in the ladies curling tournament. They had told the most heartbreaking truths, and now in the space of twenty minutes, they were laughing about Hyacinth Bucket.

Mo-Maw was near the front stage. She chatted with Mount Ellen-Ellen, a woman more mean-mouthed than herself, and occasionally they looked over to Mungo and shook their heads. The circles half-rotated as though dancing a lazy ceilidh and two new members joined the pair of women. They were shaking hands and making small talk about nothing in particular: different sides of the city, how meetings in other schemes compared to this one, how the top table here did a great job in making everyone feel like family. *Family,* Mungo thought, *whose real names Mo-Maw would never know.*

He watched Mo-Maw pick the flatness out of her perm, running her eyes appraisingly up and down the new men, ladling them both equal amounts of charm, until she knew which one liked her soup best.

Mungo had never seen the men before, but he had seen the likes of them. The older man seemed to like Mo-Maw. He kept leaning closer to her and smoothing his thin hair across his waxen head. The younger man was more out of place. He seemed only a few years older than Hamish, and by the way he took pride in his appearance Mungo could see the drink had not yet brought him so low. His trainers were a painful white, and his hair was gelled forward and cut in a short Caesar cut.

Every-Other-Wednesday joined the circle. She shook hands with the new members and was swatting at the younger man in a girlish fashion. He was not returning her flirtations. Mungo watched her put her hand on Mo-Maw's arm and say something about the hot tea that made Mo-Maw shake her head. As one, the alcoholics all turned and looked in Mungo's direction.

Just as swiftly they closed their backs to him in a wall. He knew Mo-Maw was pumping them for sympathy, sharing his supposed shame at the hands of the Catholic boy, explaining how he was not turning out right, and as a single parent, a woman, she did not know what to do about it. The men nodded a well-timed *poor you,* and it travelled along the wall like a Mexican wave. The younger man, the one with the Caesar haircut, mimed a long fishing rod that he flicked out over the linoleum tiles. Mo-Maw scratched at her perm again. Then she nodded once. *Okay,* she was agreeing, *if it would be no bother.*

No bother at all. They shrugged and then they were all laughing like old friends.

She beckoned Mungo over, her hand outstretched like a fine lady's.

"Mungo, this is Mister Christopher, and this is . . ." she paused. "Sorry, whit did ye say yer name wis again?"

TWENTY-SEVEN

A scald of panic caused him to flee. For a time, he raced around mindlessly, gathering things, dropping things, stumbling and falling. He bolted into the forest, only to return to the loch, legs twitching, before bolting back in the other direction. It took all the willpower he had, but he eventually stilled his body even as his mind screamed at him to run. Feeling overwhelmed, he stood in the middle of the ruined campsite and closed his eyes and clamped a hand over his mutinous face. Mungo tried to steady his thoughts and think what Hamish would do if he were here. Hamish would do the dishonest thing, the self-serving thing. He would destroy what he could and hide the rest. Then he would lie and pretend like it never, ever, was.

Gallowgate was heavier than he looked, denser, meatier than St Christopher. Mungo could not haul him out to the underwater shelf alone, but he dragged the body as deep as he could and loaded his pockets with small skimming stones. His teeth chattered as he waited for the body to submerge. Mungo stood on the body. He bounced three times and watched Gallowgate's last breath bubble to the surface. He could still see the whites of Gallowgate's eyes as he came to rest on the loch bed.

Mungo tidied up the campsite as best he could. He filled the plastic shopping bags with all their scattered debris and then weighted them with small rocks and hurled them into the loch. Tucking the tents into their rolls, he buried them alongside the fishing rods, deep under the thickest ferns where the ground was peatiest. He tidied his own ruined, childish things into his backpack and slung it over his shoulder. Trembling with the last of his adrenaline, he crouched at the edge of the loch and cleaned the dirt from his face, pumiced the worst of the blood stains from his nylon shorts.

As Mungo leaned over the water he focused on his reflection. He wondered what it was the men had recognized in him. Where was this signal he could not see, the semaphore he had never meant to send? Was it in how his eyes never quite met theirs, how they turned themselves down submissively? Was it in how he stood with his hands limp at his side, his weight on one leg? He wanted to find the signal, and he wanted to end its transmission.

The men had looked at him as though they knew what lay inside his soul, things he still had not even admitted to himself. They knew the inescapable shame of it, how isolated it made him feel, and they had used that to separate him from his home and do as they pleased.

His tears fell and distorted his reflection. He thought about James, and the lovely things they had done on his navy carpet. Three days of happiness, three days marked with Chinese burns and clumsy caresses. Greedy little kisses that were full of bumping teeth and shy apologies. It was wrong to compare their loveliness to the things the drunkards had forced on to him. They were not the same thing, Mungo reminded himself. They were not the same at all. They were not.

He thought only of James then. Did he still wear James's white-sugar kiss on his skin, is that what these men could smell? Could they see it, clear as a stain?

Mungo sat back and wiped his tears with the sleeve of James's jumper. He washed the tip of Hamish's shanking knife then stood up and swung his arm to throw it into the loch. Something occurred to him, a lesson he had learned about the unexpected visits of violence. He was still so far from home. He turned the knife in his hand and dropped it into his kangaroo pocket.

Gathering his things, he walked in the direction he thought they had originally come. He tiptoed through the nettles and wound his way amongst the pine and birch trees. He never saw the ram skull on the way back.

Eventually he came to a pitted access road, and for no better reason than to walk towards the slow summer sun, he turned right and followed the daylight. It was early in the afternoon, and between the trees, the clouds were white and moved quick in the sky. After two miles the road ended in a metal cattle grid and he turned again, trying to use the position of the sun to find true south. The road was empty, but every now and then a car would pass him and he would hold out his hand for either direction, unsure of where he was, or where he was headed.

After a few hours a car finally stopped. It was a green Land Rover Defender that was all mucky metal and set high up off the road. It stopped beyond him, a short way up the road, and he had to jog to reach it. As Mungo drew level the man peered down at him and it seemed like he had stopped only to gawp at the dirty boy in the ripped cagoule.

"Boy, where are ye awa' tae dressed like that?" He had the song of the countryside in his accent.

Mungo tugged his shorts down over the embarrassment of dirt on his legs. He wanted to say to the man, *I don't know. Where should I go?* But instead he hung his head and told the stranger he was trying to get to Glasgow. The man ran his eyes the length of him. He said he was going only as far as the big town — some Gaelic sounding place that Mungo had never heard of — but that if Mungo came with him, he would surely find better connections to the south from there.

Mungo glanced up and down the empty road, unsure if he could trust this man. He considered the stranger, tallied his light-blue eyes and his soft jowly face against the way he tapped his hand impatiently on the steering wheel. His shirt was freshly laundered, a sharp crease ran down the sleeve, and Mungo took that as a sign that some woman cared for him, that he was worth something to someone. Mungo havered on the road. The man asked him if he was getting in, and in the end it was a strange thing that decided it for him: Mungo could see two dogs in the back seat, fat, cuddly, tail-thumping beasts.

The man was watching Mungo closely as he pulled the seatbelt across his chest. Despite the bright sun, the man reached forward and turned on the heat vents full blast. The two Labradors in the back seat — one the colour of toast, and the other the colour of tea — took turns to shove their heads into the front and sniff at the boy. They inhaled deeply, and snuffled his crotch as though they were fascinated by the stories he held there. Mungo must have looked uncomfortable because the man gripped their collars and pushed them into the back. "Sorry about that. This is Crystal and that one is Alexis. Never let your wife name your pets."

The Defender lurched as the man threw it back into gear. They drove along pitted roads in silence and Mungo kept his gaze on the road ahead, grateful for every single fence post, every solitary sheep, they put between him and the loch. The man's waxed jacket was slung over the back of Mungo's seat. It smelled of damp places, foustie from waterproofing wax, and Mungo began to worry what he might smell like to this man. When he thought the man was not watching he scratched at his crotch and then slowly brought the fingers to his nose. If he stunk, the man said nothing. The dogs were already dozing on the back seat.

Saying he knew a shortcut, the man turned off the A-road and on to a narrow B-road. The track curved around a denuded hillside and in the thinnest places it became a single lane. The man had to pull over occasionally to allow cars to pass in the opposite direction. Each time he did, he waved at the other driver as if he knew them. His hands were broad and strong, the backs were mottled with liver spots, but the fingernails were the scrubbed pink of a life of leisure. Mungo wondered if the man was retired.

"So, what are ye doing all the way oot here?"

"Nothing. Camping."

"What? By yourself?"

"Aye."

The man reached forward and angled all the air vents towards the boy. "Hope ye don't mind me saying, but ye don't half look like ye've been through the wars."

Mungo laid his hand over the worst of the scrapes on his leg. "I fell down a hillside."

"Aye? How many times?"

Mungo missed the smirk on the man's lips. He answered him earnestly. "Just the once. I slipped."

The man seemed like he would say no more about it. The toast-coloured dog was licking her forepaws, chewing the pads with frantic little nibbles. Then the man said, "Ye know, I have four sons of my own. Guid boys. I've learned that they never get hurt when they're by themselves. It's when they're together that they get awful clumsy. Together they trip, they fall through the skylight into the lambing shed, they dare one another to ride their bikes into dykes, they chuck themselves into bonfires for laughs. Funny that." The man opened his glove compartment and took out a roll of fruit pastilles. He offered them to Mungo. Mungo politely took one and his mouth flooded with saliva. The man protested and pushed the whole packet on him. The dogs sat forward at the sign of food, before the man elbowed them away. Mungo was glad of how the sugar rinsed the taste of loch water from his mouth. He sucked the first sweetie and tried not to wolf it down. He felt the man's eyes linger on the side of his face as he considered the bruises and the matted hair. "So who was it that shoved you down that hill, then?"

"Nobody."

"Really?" The man was holding the wheel steady as they bumped through the puddles in the road. "Since the minute I picked ye up, ye've been sitting pressed up against that door like some mongrel."

Mungo looked down at himself, and he was indeed perched on the edge of the seat, as far away from the man as he could be. His hand had been worrying the door handle. "Sorry." Mungo eased the seat belt. He relaxed into the centre.

"Look, no need to be sorry. I'm Calum, by the way. I should have said that earlier."

"David," said Mungo.

"Well, nice to meet you, David." The man saluted him with his left hand. His wedding ring glistened in the sunlight. It seemed like it was embedded in to his finger, like a brace slipped around a young sapling that was now stuck, as though the tree had grown up around it. "So, ye heading home?"

It was a simple question but it gave Mungo pause. All weekend he had dreamt of the East End. The image of the tenements lay before him, but "home" didn't feel like the right word anymore. "I suppose so."

"Brave of ye to be oot here on your lonesome. Not sure I'd let any of my boys do that."

"It's awright."

Calum pulled over to allow a camper van full of hippies to ease on by. He drummed his hands on the steering wheel. "Where's yon tent then?"

"My what?"

"Tent." The man nodded at his small backpack. "If you were camping, then where's your tent?"

Mungo swallowed the pastille. "Oh. I must have lost it."

The man slid into first gear and laughed again. "Aye. My boys would like you. They're simple country boys but they think that they're slick. Ye would make them look like masters of espionage." There was no cruelty in his laughter. He had an easy way about himself. Calum seemed like the type of person that enjoyed talking to his neighbours. But also like the type of person who didn't get to talk to his neighbours very often, and so when he did, he could spin talk out of nothing. Clumps of mindless sheep grazed along the verge, they started to thicken and block the road ahead. Calum slowed the Defender again, he pumped the horn to scatter them. "We're a long way from the toon, David. But if you won't tell me your stories then that's all right. I won't pry." He raised his hands in defeat.

After that they drove on in silence for fourteen minutes; Mungo sucked on his pastilles and kept his eyes on the clock. The vents had brought the warmth back to his skin but it couldn't quite penetrate to his bones. He considered telling Calum about the loch side, about his mother and the bargain she had made with the men. He wondered if he told him about it, would he feel lighter, would the pain draw out of his gut like a clog from a drain. As he sat worrying about the dead Glaswegians, he became aware of the man glancing at his face. It jolted him from his thoughts when Calum said, "The roads are a terrible state. Are ye carsick? An awful white face ye've got there, David."

Mungo put his hand over his tic. "Do I? No, I'm fine. I'm sorry."

Calum leaned in and said, "Don't tell anybody, but Alexis there likes to eat the spew whenever any one of my boys gets carsick." He reached back and tickled the brown dog under her chin.

"That's horrible."

Calum agreed with a chuckle as he turned them back on to a two-lane road. The hills stretched in every direction, Mungo could not see a single tree. "Did I tell ye about our youngest boy, our Gregor?"

Mungo had been so numbed by his own thoughts that he wasn't sure if the man had told him about Gregor or not. "Sorry. I don't think so."

"Am I boring you?"

"No, of course not."

"Well, yon Gregor's the one who always gets carsick. He's an awful traveller yet he's my son that's destined to see the world. What a cruel irony, eh?"

Mungo didn't know what irony meant. "How do you know he'll see the world?"

"A father can tell. Gregor's a good lad. A bright, fresh-air mind. Always helps his mother around the house without being asked, but he's a wee bit . . ." The man paused as though he couldn't find the correct word. "Artistic. *T'chut.* Do ye know what I mean by that?"

Mungo gave a small nod. He wasn't sure if what the man meant, and what he understood, were the same thing.

"Forgive me if I've read you wrong, David. But would I be right in thinking ye are a wee bit artistic yourself?" Calum didn't wait for an answer. "See, I know lots of men would be bothered by that. But I have no problem with ye if you are. I'm just saying . . . Och, well, I dunno. I say the wrong thing sometimes." The sunlight was strobing through the clouds and on to the windscreen. Mungo took the opportunity to look at the man. He had a kindly face, it was handsome underneath the weathering, it had been strong before the sagging. His eyes were a clear, bother-free blue and his hair was a neat crown of curls, white and tight as lambs' fleece. "Our Gregor never shuts up, he's like his mother in that respect, but I don't mind. Sometimes I have to sit back and marvel at the nonsense that flies out of his mouth. What an imagination this boy has. I honestly don't know where he gets it from."

Mungo rolled another sweetie around in his mouth. He had thought it was strawberry, but now he wondered if it was blackcurrant.

"If he can get his hands on a length of old curtain and a couple of table lamps, then you are getting a three-act play and an extra matinee for free. He just stands in front of the fireplace and makes it up. Songs, jokes, big heart-breaking dramas — utter nonsense, you understand, but thoroughly entertaining." Calum laughed again but Mungo could tell that he was forcing it. He turned to Mungo to see if he was laughing along with him. He was not.

Mungo didn't know why the man was telling him about his son. Why tell him about this one particular son out of the four sons he said he had? The pastille was sticking to his splintered molar.

"Gregor's almost fourteen. I'd like him to find some work around here, but the wife says he's going to leave us one day. She says he has to go off in search of people that like the same things as him." Calum gestured at the empty hillside. "I suppose there's no life for him here."

Mungo turned his face as though he was considering the empty hillside, but he was looking in the wing mirror, staring at his own reflection and wondering again what it was that people could identify in him.

The man was running along with his own thoughts now. Not really asking for Mungo's conversation but speaking aloud whatever crossed his mind. "Do you think he could be happy? In the city?"

"I don't know."

"Do you have many arty friends?"

Mungo thought of James. He shook his head. "I don't have any."

Calum worked his jaw left and right. "Well. I just want him to know that I'm proud of him. No matter what. Ye know?"

"I think so."

"Your own father must be proud of you," Calum said. "But I hope you don't get in bother for that lost tent."

Mungo turned his face away again. The wing mirror was cracked and affixed to the body with electrical tape.

"Ye're a guid lad, David. I've chewed your ear enough." The man patted Mungo's knee. It was a heavy hand, possessive, and accustomed to being in control. Mungo flinched at the touch but the man's hand didn't linger. It didn't ask for more. Mungo watched it return to the steering wheel. "Ye get a wee sleep if ye want to. I'll wake ye when we get to town."

Mungo could smell the freshness of him now; the aftershave that smelled like every single nice thing the boy had ever inhaled, but crushed together all at once. Mungo laid his head against the headrest, and half-closed his eyes. Through the canopy of his lashes he considered the man's fingernails again, pink and broad and healthy. There was a peek of pale unblemished skin where his shirt met his wrist. These were not hands that worked the land in all weather. They spoke of days sat reading books in the sun. If you could tell things about a person from only a hand, then Mungo would have to admit he was a little jealous. This man was worth more than a hundred-hundred of him. Life looked good and easy. Mungo could imagine that his sons loved him. And that he loved them in return.

TWENTY-EIGHT

It was the end of a long, muggy dusk by the time he reached Glasgow. It took eight hours of faithfully getting into cars and aboard buses he didn't quite know the destination of, but he wasn't afraid any longer.

On two occasions the bus driver wouldn't let him aboard; he had almost no money, plus he was filthy. But there were three occasions when they did, when the driver took pity on him, punched a ticket that didn't exist and waved him on for free.

Mungo was in a daze as he walked slowly home from Buchanan Street station. The city air was hot and close. It stayed light until late this time of year, and carousing louts still had their shirts off, scalded pink from the long weekend, drunk on the last of their holiday wages and not yet willing to go home. He walked past the new Strathclyde University campus, the old Rottenrow hospital, and climbed up and out towards the East End.

All roads to home took him in front of the oppressive Royal Infirmary and the dirt island with the rusted snack bar. Mo-Maw was already at her serving hatch. She was chatting with some ambulance drivers. Even from this distance, he could tell by the artificial width of her smile that she had taken a good drink. He considered passing on by without even saying hello, when he noticed Jodie and Hamish were there, sitting at the skelfy picnic table. They had a poached look about them, as though they had been waiting a long time.

They drew their eyes the length of him as he crossed the dirt. Their reaction was typical of each of them. Mo-Maw fell to melodrama; her cries flew out to him, but her voice was calling, *look at me, look at me.* Hamish set his jaw in a lock; Mungo could see him narrow his eyes behind his thick lenses, determined to let the women show their hands before he played his. He peered past Mungo and seemed disappointed the two alcoholic men were not with his brother.

Only Jodie seemed truly pleased to see him. She wiped her face on her jumper sleeve and folded her arms around his middle. Mungo could feel the heat from her crown where she had sat in the sun the whole bank holiday Monday, just waiting to see her brother again. His arms hung limp at his sides. He found he could not hug her back.

Mungo wanted nothing more than to share his pain with them. To make them feel the slow terrifying hours he had felt. But Gallowgate was right, he could never share the hurt, because it would cloud their eyes and some part of them would wonder what he had done to deserve it. There were tears in his eyes, but he held them there and steadied his lip. He wouldn't give them the satisfaction of pity. He wasn't their baby anymore.

"What happened?" screeched Mo-Maw as she pulled Jodie off of him. "Ah haven't had a minute's peace since ye phoned us."

"Nothing." He shrugged like she had asked him what he'd had for school lunch.

He had worried her on the telephone, or perhaps she sobered up and realized she didn't know where her youngest son was, or who he was with, but now Mo-Maw was concerned in a way she rarely was for others. Mo-Maw's eyes were wild about his face. She turned his hands in hers and ran a finger along the pale boundary where his hair had protected his skin from the sun.

She found the saint's finger marks on his neck and licked her thumb, tried to scrub them away with her spit. They would not lift. "Your face. What the fuck happened to it?"

Mungo nodded at his brother. "He happened to it. It was like this when I left."

"Was it? It looks worse."

"You're imagining it." He picked at his scabby chin. "I fell a couple of times. It was slippy on the hillside. Maybe I banged it again."

Mo-Maw peered along the road. "Well, where are they, then?"

"Who?"

"Ye know, whatshisface and the lanky one."

"Away." Then he added casually, "They said they would see you at the AA meeting on Thursday."

"Are you really all right, Mungo?" Jodie handed him a cup of flat Coke and he drank it in messy gulps.

"Aye, I'm brand new. How are you?"

Mo-Maw was clutching his face too tightly. She seemed annoyed at him now, for intruding on her peaceful weekend. "Why the fuck did ye phone and worry us like that then?"

Mungo shook his face free from her greasy

fingers. "What do you care?"

Mo-Maw rested her weight on one leg and put both her hands on the same hip. The Nike trainers had been through the washing machine, their stitching was separating and the fancy logo had rubbed off; they were fake. "Don't think ye can go on one fishing trip and come over all cheeky bastard on me now." She was raving to herself, turning on the dirt island, talking to any strange driver who would nod sympathy at her plight. "One weekend away doesnae make you a man. Ye're not too big to go over my knee."

Mungo stared right through her. First, he had not been man enough; now he was too much.

He turned to his sister and handed Jodie a pile of skimming stones from the loch-side.

She pressed her forehead against his and whispered. "You'll tell me how it was. Won't you? In the airing cupboard?"

"I saw a roe buck and a dead sheep. It rained. That's about it."

Jodie reached her hand out to push his hair away and he stepped away from her. He could look at Jodie, but he wouldn't let her touch him again. If Jodie, of all people, could not love him, all of him, perhaps he

632

could not be loved.

Mo-Maw was chanting to herself. "All better, all better. See, he's fine. He's back now. *He's fine.*" She was flapping and turning on the dirt. Mungo could see she was relieved. But the relief was for herself.

The infighting had started on Saturday morning when Jodie had asked her mother where Mungo was, and Mo-Maw had answered vaguely, *fishing.* It had dawned on them too late. It had occurred to them that Mo-Maw had never known the men she had sent her son away with. But Mo-Maw had become defensive and she insisted there was safety in the company of men; what safer place was there for a young boy to be? What harm could come of it: a few fish, some fresh air, a hot bonfire. It was only Scotland. The bad things that happened here happened on the very streets she had sent him away from.

Hamish crossed the dirt towards them. He grabbed the lip of Mungo's cagoule pocket and, tugging on it possessively, he peered inside. "Whut? Nothin' for us?" Mungo had thought it would be impossible to look at Hamish but he found that he could. In fact, he found he could look at him without blinking. Mungo bored his eyes into the bridge of his nose until Hamish stepped back. He let go of his little brother. "Haw! Any chance of service here?"

It was that, this single sentence, that let him know it was over. Full stop. The taxi driver, with his gut hanging over his money belt, said he needed his black pudding roll, and that he was pure gasping for a small tea with two teabags. Mo-Maw scuttled back to her serving hatch. The bank holiday weekend was over. He was home. It would be a thing they would never talk about again. Like the never-was baby, or James, the boy who Mungo had loved.

Mungo watched as his siblings gathered up their belongings. He saw them with an unusual clarity. It was already over for them. It would never be over for him. He just had no one to tell.

Mo-Maw was gone from him, he knew that now. She was Jocky's burden, and if not Jocky's, then some other mug's, someone who thought he could handle her. He should have been relieved, but he hated that he felt abandoned.

Jodie would leave forever. It would be gradual at first, but then she would finish university and her absences would stretch. Hamish had been right all along. She would round out her vowels and suppress her glottal stop. She would like her bread to be brown and her films to be foreign. Perhaps she would meet someone at uni who she could quietly love, but she would never bring them home at Christmas. She would have a house full of stray puppies if anyone let her. Mungo could imagine her adopting ex-police dogs, so many dogs that her small flat would smell of incontinent Alsatians.

Hamish winked at him. And Mungo knew then that he would not leave.

He would be dragged behind Hamish into all the idle violence they could manage. He would need to find a girl, he would need to get her pregnant quickly, he would try his best to love her. He would work when he could, and he would steal what he could, and on Thursdays and Saturdays he would sell ten-pound eccies to university students outside the Sub Club and the Arches. He would fight the Bhoyston until he got too old and then he would go to Old Firm games and get into rammies outside the Louden Tavern and sing his supremacist songs every twelfth of July. He would need to become the man that Hamish expected him to be.

"Do you want a bath?" Jodie was heaving her satchel on to her shoulder.

But Mungo wasn't listening.

Across the road, outside the monstrous

infirmary, was a figure. Mungo had not noticed him at first. The buses to the East End were idling in the holiday traffic and the figure kept dropping out of view. The young man was waiting patiently, like he was about to cross the road, but the opportunity came, and he stayed where he was. He would never cross that road.

Around his feet were a pile of mismatched bags, lumpy and bloated, stuffed with soft clothes, full of his life. He wore two heavy coats despite the summer heat. There were black stitches on his pale chin and both his eye sockets were dark blue where his nose had been broken. His ruined fingers were splinted and bound with pink gauze that was already grimy with dirt.

He was watching, and he was waiting, and he was leaving all at the same time.

They stood and regarded each other over the four lanes of traffic. It felt like an eternity. Every time a white van would block his view, Mungo's stomach lurched and he held his breath until it moved again and he was sure the boy was still there, with his packed bags, still watching and waiting. There he was, James-Guid-and-True.

James raised his broken hand in a half-greeting. It was discreet, tentative, like they were only strangers. But it was only for

Mungo. It was for no one else.

Mungo smiled something small and timid. James returned it, and they let their grins widen slowly, slowly, until Mungo knew what he was going to do, where he was going to go. The only place he would ever want to be.

Jodie had gone to see James when Mungo had telephoned Mo-Maw from the lochside. She had pressed his buzzer, but he would not answer, would not let her in. Jodie had hammered all the buzzers on the panel. She had waited until a neighbour admitted her and then stormed the stairs. On her knees at his letter box she told James the story of what had happened — or told it to the empty hallway, since James hid in the shadows.

His face was pummelled, and he would not open the door to any Hamilton. He stood frozen in the hallway and looked at the ripped-out phone jack. "Mungo hasnae phoned," James lisped from the darkness. "He couldnae phone us, even if he wanted to." Jodie let go of the flap. From what she glimpsed through the letter box she could tell she had interrupted his packing.

Mungo put one hand on the traffic barrier and prepared to vault it. He turned to say goodbye to Jodie. As he did so, a navy car emerged from the bank holiday traffic. It bumped up on to the waste ground and kicked up some gravel as it settled. Two polis got out of it. They wore no uniforms, but by the arrogant way they carried themselves, Mungo could tell that they stank of pork. He looked around for his brother to confirm it. Hamish was already sliding towards the shadowed side of the snack bar.

"Don't worry!" Mo-Maw squealed, as though she had planned a grand party. "It's for me. It's for me."

She wiped her hands on her pinny and rushed to greet them. She pushed at her frizzy hair and rebuttoned the top shank on her denims over the soft fat of her belly. Jodie tutted at her vanity. They were not good-looking fellas, but they were ages with her, and they had better-paying jobs than Jocky. "Not to worry officers, ma boy, ma wee darlin' boy is back."

After Mungo had telephoned her, she had taken a good soaking. She had called the polis and reported him missing. Back in their police car, the responding officers had looked at each other in bewilderment. Who gives their wee boy away to strange men? Now they were here for the third time this weekend. The first time they had been curious. The second time they had let their disgust show through. Now they looked sick at the sight of her.

"Everything's fine," she said again. Her arms were flung wide like she was going to hug them, then show them the door and marshal them off her dirt island.

"Aye? Glad to hear it, Mrs Hamilton."

"It's Buchanan," she said. "Ah never marriet their father, ah never got the chance. So it's *Ms*. Ms Buchanan, thank-ye-very-much." Mo-Maw usually went by the name Hamilton, it took less explaining, and it gave everyone a sense of belonging. The only time Mungo heard his mother issue this correction was when she was talking to men.

The officers were unsmiling. They looked down on this small woman and would not be corralled. The stockiest of the two had a ratty mullet, better suited to a radio disc jockey.

The polis were scowling at the three young Hamiltons, a pack of strays who were now spread far across the waste ground. They discounted Jodie almost immediately and focused instead on Hamish and Mungo. They had a stony-faced way of staring, but Mungo knew they were observing him closely and cataloguing every little detail. He could feel their eyes travel across his scuffed knees and up across his sore face. He worried that they could see all the things he didn't want them to.

The polis had a deliberate way of holding their silence for too long, well past the point of it becoming uncomfortable. It made Mungo want to rush in and fill the void. Hamish had taught him how to wait it out; how to start at the letter A and list all the animals he knew in his head, and when he was done with animals, to begin again and this time list all the fruit. Hamish said that to think of vegetables and dogs' names and countries was the best way to keep your expression inscrutable.

Mungo was thinking of koala bears when one of the polis finally spoke. The mulleted officer shook his head grimly. "There's been some bother, see. The body of a man was found today in a loch. Somebody had stabbed him and then tried to sink him. Based on what you telt us, Mrs Hamil—, sorry, Ms Buchanan, we wanted to see what . . ." The polis looked at his pad. *"Mungo?"* He shook his head in pity at a name destined to get belted in any playground. ". . . what young Mungo might know about it?"

"Bodies don't sink, not for long," said the other policeman. He was losing his hair, but he had been brave and cropped it close. He was gruffer than the first.

"Decomposition," said Jodie dryly. "Rotting fat turns to gas. Everybody knows *that*." Mungo didn't. He was irritated by the fact that even in this moment, Jodie couldn't help but show off.

The detective nodded in admiration. He pouted in open surprise that Mo-Maw could have a child this bright. "Aye, right enough. Smart wee lassie ye've got there, Ms Buchanan."

"Aye. She's a real pleasure. A talking bicyclopedia. Do ye want to borrow her?"

The gruff man frowned. "Ye keep givin' yer weans away. Are ye planning on opening a lending library?"

Jodie shifted in embarrassment. The sarcasm of it was lost on Mo-Maw.

The detective explained how Strathclyde Police had phoned Balmaha, Balquhidder, Loch Lomond, and Inveraray to ask if there were any sightings of Mo-Maw's missing boy. The Inveraray police had said no, however, they had just found a drowned body which was not suspicious in itself, but the body had been stabbed and was wearing a designer outfit of Italian denim, which was very unusual. The fishing warden had been patrolling for licence violations and had found the body partially submerged, its pockets filled with dozens of small stones. The body should not have risen so quickly; Gallowgate was not a fat man and the water was cold. He would have stayed submerged for weeks if he had been weighted properly.

When the police had hauled the body to the small village and called the mortician to come collect it, it had caused the stir of the century. The postmistress had instantly recognized Gallowgate and said he had a quiet boy with him. She said they both had thick, uncultured Glaswegian accents, that the boy was surrounded by a sadness, and that they had stolen chocolate bars and owed her a pound fifty.

"Ah'm glad Mungo came home. Yer lucky that everything worked out. But we do need to talk to the boy." The mulleted detective turned his head from one brother to the other. "So, which one of youse is the bold Mungo Hamilton?"

Jodie and Mo-Maw did something strange then. They turned not to Mungo but to Hamish. In pure instinct, they looked to Hamish because he would know what to do. He was the man of the house. Their eyes seemed to implore, *Handle it, Hamish.*

The first detective kicked the ground like he had lost a bet. It was not the brother he had thought it would be. Hamish was certainly the shorter of the two, but this boy was slightly too old to fit the description. But the mouth of the balding detective pulled tight in a knowing grimace. As soon as he had clocked Hamish, he had thought him capable of violence.

Hamish stepped forward almost immediately. He didn't blink, he barely nodded. "I am. I am Mungo."

Gallus eejit. The officers would not play daft for long.

It could be the last time he ever saw James. Mungo knew it now. He turned because he wanted to look on him for as long as he possibly could, to remember the smile that made everything better, the mouth full of happy gappy teeth. He wanted to see if his cheeks had turned their usual bluish-pinkish tartan in fresh air.

James's broken hand was raised in a frozen greeting. In his many coats he again resembled the statue of St Mungo at Kelvingrove, reaching out, welcoming followers.

James was biting his split lip. The rushing traffic blew his tawny hair over his eyes, the wheat and the barley, the sticky pulled sugar of it caught and ate the last of the sinking sun.

The broken hand swivelled then. He

turned his bandaged knuckles towards Mungo and the splinted fingers that had caressed the soft down at the bottom of his spine twitched faintly, discreetly. The swaddling made the gesture crude, inarticulate, but Mungo understood.

He beckoned him only once. Once was enough.

Come, it said. *Come away.*

ACKNOWLEDGEMENTS

I am so grateful to my family, the gallus Glaswegians that I was blessed with, and the wonderful friends that are lumped with me. I wouldn't be here without you.

I am indebted to my editor, Peter Blackstock, and to the Grove Atlantic team: Morgan Entrekin, Judy Hottensen, Deb Seager, John Mark Boling, and Emily Burns. Thank you to my fellow ugly duckling (his words) Ravi Mirchandani, and to Camilla Elworthy, Jeremy Trevathan, Stu Wilson, Gillian McKay, and the talented folk at Picador. Love and thanks to Anna Stein, Claire Nozieres, and Lucy Luck for taking such good care of Mungo, and to Grace Robinson, Julie Flanagan, and Will Watkins for all their support. Thank you to Mungo's friends from o'er yonder, Cathrine Bakke Bolin, Daniel Sandström, Susanne Van Leeuwen, Lina Muzur, and Valentine Gay.

I survive on the encouragement of my

early readers, so many beers are owed to Patricia McNulty, Clive Smith, Valentina Castellani, Margaret Ann MacLeod, Tanya Carey, and Tina Pohlman for the loan of their hearts and minds.

Thank you, above all, to Michael Cary, who has always believed.

ABOUT THE AUTHOR

Douglas Stuart is a Scottish-American author. His *New York Times*-bestselling debut novel *Shuggie Bain* won the 2020 Booker Prize and the Sue Kaufman Prize from the American Academy of Arts and Letters. It was the winner of two British Book Awards, including Book of the Year, and was a finalist for the National Book Award, PEN/Hemingway Award, National Book Critics Circle John Leonard Prize, Kirkus Prize, as well as several other literary awards. Stuart's writing has appeared in the *New Yorker* and *Literary Hub.*

Douglas Stuart is a Scottish-American author. His New York Times-bestselling debut novel Shuggie Bain won the 2020 Booker Prize and the Sue Kaufman Prize from the American Academy of Arts and Letters. It was the winner of two British Book Awards, including Book of the Year, and was a finalist for the National Book Award, PEN/Hemingway Award, National Book Critics Circle John Leonard Prize, Kirkus Prize as well as several other literary awards. Stuart's writing has appeared in the New Yorker and Literary Hub.

The employees of Thorndike Press hope you have enjoyed this Large Print book. All our Thorndike, Wheeler, and Kennebec Large Print titles are designed for easy reading, and all our books are made to last. Other Thorndike Press Large Print books are available at your library, through selected bookstores, or directly from us.

For information about titles, please call:
  (800) 223-1244

or visit our website at:
  gale.com/thorndike

To share your comments, please write:
  Publisher
  Thorndike Press
  10 Water St., Suite 310
  Waterville, ME 04901

THE
WAY HOME

GEORGE PELECANOS

First published in Great Britain in 2009 by Orion Books,
an imprint of The Orion Publishing Group Ltd
Orion House, 5 Upper Saint Martin's Lane
London WC2H 9EA

An Hachette UK Company

1 3 5 7 9 10 8 6 4 2

A CIP catalogue record for this book is
available from the British Library.

ISBN (Hardback) 978 0 7528 7543 9
ISBN (Export Trade Paperback) 978 1 4091 0127 7

Printed in Great Britain by Clays Ltd, St Ives plc

The Orion Publishing Group's policy is to use papers that are natural,
renewable and recyclable products and made from wood grown in sustainable
forests. The logging and manufacturing processes are expected to
conform to the environmental regulations of the country of origin.

www.orionbooks.co.uk

For my father, Pete Pelecanos

Last night I dreamed that I was a child
out where the pines grow wild and tall
I was trying to make it home through the forest
before the darkness falls
— *Bruce Springsteen, "My Father's House"*

PART ONE
BAD CHRIS

ONE

No ONE could say why it was called Pine Ridge. Wasn't any pines around that Chris could see. Just a group of one-story, L-shaped, red brick buildings set on a flat dirt-and-mud clearing, surrounded by a fence topped with razor wire. Beyond the fence, woods. Oak, maple, wild dogwood, and weed trees, but no pines. Somewhere back in those woods, the jail they had for girls.

The facility was situated on eight hundred acres out in Anne Arundel County, Maryland, twenty-five miles from Northwest D.C., where Chris had grown up. At night, lying in his cell, he could hear planes coming in low. So he knew that they were near the Baltimore airport, and close to a highway, too. Some days, if the wind was right, playing basketball on the outdoor court or walking to the school building from his unit, he'd make out the hiss and rumble of vehicles speeding by, straights going off to work or heading back home, moms in their minivans, kids driving to parties or hookups. Teenagers like him, only free.

Of course, he had been told exactly where he was. The director of the district's Department of Youth Rehabilitation

Services, the superintendent, the guards, his fellow inmates, his parents, and the lawyer his father had hired to represent him had explained it to him in detail. He'd even been shown a map. But it was more interesting for him to imagine that he was in some kind of mysterious location. *They are sending me to a top secret place in the woods. A facility for boys they cannot control. A place that can't hold me. I will now plan my daring escape, ha-ha.*

"Chris?" said his mother.

"Huh?"

"Is something funny?"

"No."

"You're grinning."

"Was I?"

"Chris, you seem to be treating all of this very lightly."

"I don't mean to, Ma. I was thinkin on something, was all it was."

"You were thinking *about* something," said his father.

Chris smiled, causing the muscles along his father's jawline to tighten.

Chris Flynn was seated at a scarred wooden table in the Pine Ridge visiting room. Across the table were his parents, Thomas and Amanda Flynn. Nearby, several other boys, all wearing polo shirts and khakis, were being visited by their moms or grandmothers. A guard stood by the door. Outside the room, through a square of Plexiglas, Chris could see two other guards, talking to each other, laughing.

"How's it going, honey?" said Amanda.

"It's all right."

"How's school?"

Chris glanced around the room. "I go."

"Look at your mother when she's talking to you," said Thomas Flynn.

Instead, Chris stared into his father's watery eyes. He saw a husk of anger and hurt, and felt nothing.

"I'm asking you," said Amanda, "are they treating you all right? Are people bullying you?"

"You don't need to worry about that. I know how to jail."

"You," said Flynn, his voice not much louder than a contemptuous whisper.

"Do you have one of those level meetings coming up?" said Amanda.

"Not that I know."

"They're supposed to have them monthly. I'll follow up with our attorney. He's in contact with the superintendent."

"Fine."

"Let's pray," said Amanda.

She laced her fingers together, rested her hands on the table, and bowed her head. Chris and Thomas Flynn dutifully did the same. But they did not speak to God, and their thoughts were not spiritual or pure.

When Amanda was done, the three of them got up out of their seats. Amanda looked at the guard, a big man with kind eyes who surely would understand, and she embraced her son. As she held him, she slipped three folded twenty-dollar bills into the pocket of his trousers.

Amanda broke away from him, tears heavy in her eyes. "We're doing everything we can."

"I know it."

"You're in my prayers. I love you, Chris."

"Love you, too, Mom." He said this quietly, so the other boys would not hear him.

Neither Chris nor his father made a step toward each other. After a long, empty lock of their eyes, Chris gave Thomas Flynn a tough nod with his chin, turned, and left the room.

"Should we try and talk to the superintendent before we leave?" said Amanda.

"What for?" Flynn shook his head. "Let's just go."

ALONG WITH an escort guard, Thomas and Amanda Flynn walked out of the building toward the gatehouse, Thomas in front of Amanda, his heavy steps indenting the mud beneath his feet. Inmates, between classes and lunch, were moving from unit to unit, their arms behind their backs, one hand holding the wrist of the other, accompanied by a guard carrying a two-way radio. All of the boys were black. Flynn had seen one Hispanic kid, waxy eyed and wired on meds, on his last visit, so maybe there were a few Spanish here, too, but that was immaterial to him. What weighed on him was that Chris was the sole white inmate of the facility.

My son, here with all these . . .

Flynn stopped himself before ugly words spelled themselves out in his head.

He rang the bell on the door at the rear of the gatehouse, looking through bars and Plexiglas to get the attention of one of two uniformed women behind the counter. Like most of the female guard staff Flynn had seen here, these women were wide and generously weighted in the legs and hips. He and his wife were buzzed in, and they passed through the same security aisle, similar to those used in airports, they'd entered. Neither of the guards looked at the couple or spoke to them as Flynn and Amanda collected their keys and cells.

They exited the gatehouse and walked along the chain link and razor wire fence to Amanda's SUV, parked in the staff and visitors' lot. They did not talk. Amanda was thinking of going to early mass on Sunday and lighting a candle for Chris. Flynn, as he often did, was thinking of what had gone wrong.

By Flynn's reckoning, he had begun to lose his son somewhere in Chris's freshman year of high school. At the time, Chris was playing football and CYO basketball, getting decent grades, attending Sunday school and mass. He was also smoking marijuana, shoplifting, fighting other boys, and breaking into cars and lockers. This was all happening at the same time, when Chris was about fifteen. To Amanda, Flynn began to refer to his son as if he were two people: Good Chris and Bad Chris. By the time Chris was sixteen, only Bad Chris remained.

As a teenager and into his twenties, Flynn had blown his share of marijuana, so he detected Chris's use right away. Flynn could see the high in Chris's eyes, the way he would laugh inappropriately at violent images on the television screen, or his sudden interest in their Lab mix, Darby, playing tug-of-war or wrestling him to the ground, things he would never do while straight. Of course, there was the smell that always hung in Chris's clothing and, when he had copped, that unmistakable skunky odor of fresh bud in his bedroom.

It didn't bother Flynn horribly that his son smoked marijuana. In fact, he told Chris that he had no moral objection to it but felt that it was, basically, a waste of time. That for an already marginal student like Chris, it could impede his progress. What bothered Flynn, what became alarming, was that Chris began to smoke marijuana to the exclusion of everything else. He stopped playing sports. He stopped going to mass and hanging out with his church friends. He quit his job at the coffee shop in Friendship Heights. His grades edged toward failure. He seemed not to care about the loss or what his degeneration was doing to his parents.

Amanda still thought of Chris as her little boy and couldn't bring herself to discipline him like a young man. Plus, she was certain that the Lord would step in and, when He deemed it appropriate, blow the black clouds away and give Chris the wisdom to get back on the righteous path. Flynn's response was elemental and not carefully considered. He believed in Darwin over fairy tales and aimed to reinforce his position as the alpha dog of the house. He put Chris up against the wall more than once, raised his closed fist, and walked away before punching him. So Chris knew that his father was willing to cross the line and kick his ass, but the knowledge did nothing to alter his behavior. He didn't care.

Chris was charged with possession of marijuana. The arresting officer did not show up for court, and the charge was dropped. Chris got in a fight at school and was suspended. He strong-armed a fellow student for his Walkman on school property and was arrested and expelled for the remainder of the year. He received community service time. Chris and his friend Jason were caught on camera looting the lockers of their high school basketball team while the players were at practice, and were arrested and charged. An adjudicatory hearing was scheduled. Chris was videotaped vandalizing and stealing from cars in the back lot of a Mexican restaurant. His father paid off the owners of the restaurant and the owners of the vehicles, thereby avoiding the involvement of police. And then there were the final charges and the conviction that led to his incarceration: assault, possession with intent to distribute, leaving the scene of an accident, reckless driving, driving on the sidewalk, fleeing and eluding police. With each succeeding "incident," with each visit to the Second District station on Idaho Avenue to pick up his son, Flynn grew more angry and distant.

Kate would be eighteen now. We'd be looking at colleges. We'd be taking photos of her, dressed up for the senior prom. Instead of visiting that little shit with his prison uniform and his pride in knowing "how to jail."

Christopher Flynn was the only surviving offspring of Thomas and Amanda Flynn. Their first child, Kate, died two days after she was born. The death certificate listed the cause as "respiratory distress syndrome," which meant that she had suffocated. She was a preemie, and her lungs had not fully developed.

At the time of Kate's birth, Thomas Flynn was a young uniformed police officer in D.C.'s Fourth District. He had signed up impulsively, successfully passed through the academy, and upon his graduation he almost immediately realized he had made a mistake. He was dispassionate about the job and did not want to lock up kids, making him unsuited to be a soldier in the drug war. Flynn resigned and took a position as an account representative for a carpet-and-flooring wholesaler whose sales manager, not coincidentally, was his former high school basketball coach. Flynn's intention was to learn the business, establish contacts, and eventually go out on his own.

Soon after Kate died, Amanda became pregnant but lost the baby in the first trimester. Despite assurances from her obstetrician that she was healthy, Amanda, who along with Flynn had dabbled in cocaine in her youth, blamed her past drug use for Kate's premature birth and death. She believed that she had permanently damaged her "insides" and could no longer carry a child to term. "My eggs are dirty," she told Flynn, who only nodded, preferring not to argue with her, in the way that one does not try to reason with a loved one who has begun to mentally slip away. Amanda had by then welcomed Jesus into their lives, and Flynn found it increasingly difficult for the three of them to coexist.

Kate's death did not ruin their marriage, but it killed a piece of it. Flynn barely recognized in the humorless, saved Amanda the funny, spirited woman he had married. Despite the emotional gulf between them, they continued to have sex frequently. Amanda still secretly hoped to have a healthy child, and, born again or not, she had a body on her, and Thomas Flynn liked to have it. Chris was born in 1982.

As the problems with Chris progressed, Flynn found himself thinking more and more of Kate. She was with them for only two days and had no discernible personality, but he was haunted by her and obsessed with what she might have become had she lived. Chris was real, a stained reminder of Flynn's failings as a father. The Kate he imagined was a charmer, lovely, well mannered, and successful. Kate would surely have looked upon Flynn with loving eyes. He fantasized about the daughter he would never have, and it made him feel optimistic and right. Knowing all the while, from the evidence of his business and his everyday life, that reality was usually far less intriguing than the dream.

"Tommy?" said Amanda, now seated beside him in the SUV, Thomas Flynn in the driver's bucket and fitting his key to the ignition.

"What."

"We should schedule a meeting with our attorney. I want him to keep in contact with the warden."

"You want to help him, huh?" Flynn glared at his wife. "I saw you slip Chris that money."

"He might need it."

"I told you not to do that, didn't I?"

"Yes, but —"

"*Didn't* I."

"Yes."

"He's going to buy marijuana with it. They get it from the guards."

"I can't just leave him in there with no resources. He's our son."

Flynn held his tongue.

TWO

THE FIRST time Chris took a charge, for loitering and possession of marijuana, he was all nerves, standing in this room they had at the 2D station, waiting for his father to come and take him home. He was expecting his pops to spaz on him, put a finger up in his face, give him the lecture about responsibility and choices, maybe make some threats. But his father entered that room and, first thing, hugged him and kissed him on the cheek. It surprised Chris and, because there was a police officer in the room, embarrassed him. If his father was soft like that, someone might get the idea that Chris was soft, too.

"I told you not to touch him, sir," said the police officer, but Thomas Flynn did not apologize.

Chris should have expected his father to support him. If he had thought about it, he would have realized that his father had always taken his side against teachers and school administrators in the past, including those times when Chris had been in the wrong. Thomas Flynn had even physically challenged a security guy at Chris's middle school back when Chris started getting in trouble. The security guard had said, "Your boy needs to see a psychiatrist, somethin. He's not right." And his

12

father said, "If I want your opinion, young man, I'll kick it out your ass." His father had a temper, and he was also in denial about who Chris was. But Chris knew who he was, even then.

It came to him one morning, lying in bed, after his mother had woken him up to go to school. He was in the seventh grade, thirteen years old. It occurred to him that he didn't have to get up and go to school if he didn't want to. That his parents couldn't force him to go. They couldn't, in fact, force him to do anything. Most kids would do what their parents said because they were the parents and that was how it worked, but Chris did not feel the way those other kids felt, not anymore. It was like something in his brain got switched off at the same time that something else, something more exciting, had been ignited. He still thought of his mom and dad as his parents, but he was no longer interested in pleasing them or doing what they thought was right. He didn't care.

His father's attitude changed after Chris began to get in trouble time and time again. It was partly the repetition of the incidents that wore his father down, but it was also the nature of them.

Chris liked to fight. He wasn't an honors or AP kid, and being good at fighting was a way of showing that he was someone, too. If it was a fair fight, meaning he wasn't picking on a retard or a weakling, then it was on, and someone was about to get hurt.

He rationalized robbery, too. If someone was stupid enough to leave cash in a locker, or have designer shades or a cell phone visible inside a parked car, then he was going to break into that locker or car and help his self.

He had bad luck, though, and he got caught. His old man would come to pick him up from the school office or the police station, and each time, his father's face was more disappointed and less forgiving. Chris wasn't trying to hurt his parents, exactly. But in his mind it was written like this: They have unreasonable expectations for me. They don't realize who I am. I am hard and I like to get high. I don't want to be their good boy and I don't want the things they want for me. If they can't face that, it's their problem, not mine.

"Why, Chris?" said his father, driving him back from the Mexican restaurant, Tuco's, where he'd been caught vandalizing and stealing from cars. "Why?"

"Why what?"

"Why are you doing this?" His father's voice was hoarse, and it looked to Chris that he was close to desperation.

"I don't know. I can't help it, I guess."

"You're throwing it all away. You've quit on everything, and you get high all the time. You've got a police record, and your grades are . . . they're *shit*, Chris. Other kids are studying for the SATs and looking at colleges, and you're breaking into cars. For *what?* What could you possibly need that I haven't given you? I *bought* you a car; why in the world would you want to damage someone else's?" Flynn's fingers were white on the steering wheel. "You live in one of the most upscale neighborhoods in Washington, in a nice house. You're trying to act like someone you're not. Why? What's *wrong* with you?"

"Nothing's wrong with me. I'm me. That SUV you bought me, it's fine and all that, but I didn't ask you for it. Far as my grades go, what's the point? I'm not going to college. Let's be real."

"Oh, so now you're not considering college?"

"I'm not *going*. I don't see any reason to go, because I'm not smart enough. Look, accept me like this or don't. Either way, I'm going to be who I am."

This was before the final incident, which started in the lot behind the drugstore on the west side of Connecticut Avenue, up by the Avalon Theater.

It was a midsummer night, and Chris and his friend Jason Berg, whom everyone but Jason's parents and teachers called Country, were walking out of the drugstore with a vial of Visine they had purchased and a bunch of candy and gum packs they had stuffed in their pockets and stolen. They had been drinking beer and smoking some bud, and were laughing at something that struck them as funny because they were high.

A pound of weed was stashed in the back of Chris's vehicle, under a blanket. They had bought it earlier in the evening from a connection on the D.C. side of Takoma and were planning to sell most of it off to their peers and keep an ounce for themselves. Jason had an electronic scale, and their intention was to bag out the marijuana the next day at his house while his parents were at work.

Jason was a big kid, tall and muscled up. He had a buzz cut and still wore braces. People thought he was stupid. He had the mouth-breathing, shallow-eyed look of an idiot, a lumbering walk, a stoner's chuckle, and he was into NASCAR and professional wrestling. Because of those interests and because he was white, the black kids at school had dubbed him Country.

Jason did nothing to discourage the impression others had formed of him. Truth was, he wasn't stupid in the least. His grades were middling because he didn't try during tests or turn in homework, but he had scored very high on his SATs, despite the fact that he had gotten massively baked the night before the exams. He was the son of a Jewish attorney who was a partner in one of the most prominent firms in the District, but he kept this and his intelligence hidden from the kids at school. The hard yahoo stoner was a preferable costume to him over the smart, privileged Jew.

Chris Flynn was of Irish Catholic extraction, shorter than Jason but not by much, and broad in the chest. He too wore his blond hair close to the scalp. He was fair skinned, green eyed, and had a lazy, charming smile. His one physical flaw was the vertical scar creasing the right side of his upper lip, acquired when he walked into an elbow during a pickup game that had gotten out of hand at the Hamilton Rec in 16th Street Heights. Chris liked the scar, and so did the females. He was handsome, but the scar told anyone who suspected it that he was no pretty boy. It made him look tough.

He *was* tough. He and Jason had proven it on the basketball courts and in situations involving hands. They did not hang with other white kids, the skateboarders and punk rockers and intellectuals who populated their high school, and were proud of the fact that they had earned respect, mostly, from the young black men who were bused in from the other side of town. Whether they were liked or not was beside the point to them. Everyone knew that Chris and Jason were on the edge, and that they could ball and fight.

"I think that Chinese girl behind the counter saw us pocket this stuff," said Chris, as he and Jason headed for Chris's SUV.

"What's Ling Ho gonna do? Get up after us?"

As they neared the Isuzu, Chris saw a group of three boys getting into a late-model Volvo station wagon parked down the row of spaces. One of them gave Chris a look, glancing at the old Trooper with the safari roof rack, and smiled in an arrogant way.

"Is he muggin me?" said Chris.

Jason stopped and hard-eyed the kid, who was now slipping behind the wheel of the Volvo. "I'll drop him if he does, son."

"They must be private school," said Chris. "You know those bitches can't go."

Chris and Jason, public-school kids, imagined themselves to be more blue-collar than the many kids in Ward 3 who attended private high schools. For Jason Berg it was an affectation, as his father was in the top 1 percent of earners. Chris, too, was living in a financially comfortable home environment, but he'd inherited the chip on his shoulder from Thomas Flynn.

Chris and Jason got into the SUV. Chris turned the ignition while Country messed with the radio. Despite his moniker, Country listened exclusively to hip-hop and go-go, and found something he could tolerate on KYS. It was a Destiny's Child thing that was popular and bogus, and they talked about that for a minute, and then Chris pulled down on the transmission arm, still talking to Jason and looking at him, and reversed the SUV. Both of them were jolted by a collision. They heard and felt the impact at the same time, and Chris said, "Shit."

He looked over his shoulder. They had hit the Volvo, passing behind them, and the three boys were getting out of the right-side doors because the Isuzu was up against the driver's side. Chris cut the engine and took a deep breath.

"You hit the right car, at least," said Jason with a grin.

"My father's gonna go off."

"What now?"

"'Bout to see what the damage is," said Chris. "You stay in here."

"Sure?"

"Positive. I don't want no trouble tonight. Remember, we got some weight in the back. I'm serious."

"Holler if you need me."

"Right." Chris left the keys in the ignition and got out of the SUV.

He walked toward the boys, now grouped in front of the Volvo. The largest of them was wide and strong, a football

17

player from the looks of him, bulked up in the weight room, but he had nonthreatening eyes. The driver was Chris's size, prep school definitely from the square-hair, clean-shaved looks of him, and standing with his chest puffed out, which meant he was insecure and probably scared. The third kid, small and unformed, had pulled out a cell phone and was talking into it as he walked away. After sizing them all up quickly, the way boys and men do, Chris decided with some satisfaction that there wasn't one of them he could not take. Knowing this chilled him some and allowed him, for the moment, to stay even and cool.

"My bad," said Chris, facing the driver, the boy who'd given him the look. "Guess I wasn't payin attention."

"You *guess*," said the driver. "Look what you did to my car." Annoyed, not giving Chris any slack, not giving him a "That's all right" or an "It happens."

Chris shrugged and his eyes were dead as he looked at the driver. "Said it was my bad."

Chris checked out the Volvo, saw that the left front quarter panel and the edge of the driver's door carried a dent. He then looked at the bumper of the Isuzu, which was not scratched but showed a bit of gold paint that had come off the Volvo's body.

Chris thought of his old man, and the day he had brought the used SUV home and presented it to Chris. It was a corny-looking vehicle, the old, boxy Trooper, which his father said had style and looked "cool." Nerdy was more like it, but whatever. Chris would have preferred an Impala SS or Buick Grand National, but he took it. One thing his father was right about, the Isuzu was a tank. Shoot, it had put a hurtin on a Volvo.

"Somethin funny?" said the driver.

"Nah. I was just . . . look, let me give you my *in*surance card."

"My *in*surance caahd," said the small one, having rejoined the group and slipped his cell into his pocket. The football player looked down at his feet.

Chris's jaw tightened as he drew his wallet and found the card in his father's name. He held it out for the driver, but the driver did not take it.

"Show it to the police," said the driver. "They're on the way."

"That's who your boy called on his cell?" said Chris.

"Yeah."

"Wasn't no need to do that." Chris replaced the card in his wallet, feeling his heart tick up a beat. "We supposed to exchange information."

"We *'posed* to," said the small one. "Look at him. His eyes are glassy, Alex. He's fucked up."

"How do I know if that card is real?" said the driver, with that same smart look he had given Chris when he'd mugged him and his vehicle.

"Leave it alone, Alex," said the football player to the driver.

"See, why you got to say that?" said Chris, staring at the driver, regretting that he had asked the question, not wanting the boy to speak, not trusting what he would do if the boy kept pushing it.

Adults were now standing in the lot, watching.

You want to see some drama? I'll give you something to look at.

Chris felt himself move his weight to his back foot, as his father had taught him to do long ago.

Punch with your shoulder, not your arm. Pivot your hip into the punch. Punch through your target, Chris.

"I don't have to tell you anything, Ace," said the driver. "Just talk to the police."

"*Alex,*" said the football player.

"Okay," said Chris, his face hot as fire. "I guess there's no need for words."

He threw a deep punch and it connected. The driver's nose felt spongy at the point of contact, and it shot blood as he fell to the ground.

Chris did not look at the football player but turned to the small one who had jumped back a step. Chris almost laughed. He said, "You're too little," and turned and walked back to his vehicle. A couple of the adults were shouting at him but not moving to stop him, and he did not turn his head.

He got behind the wheel. He turned the key in the ignition. Jason was laughing. Colored lights had begun to strobe the parking lot, and Chris looked left and saw the 2D cruiser enter the lot from Morrison Street, and then another one behind it.

There was no right or reason. Chris's head was a riot of energy.

THREE

———

WHERE YOU about to *go*, dawg?" said Jason. His face showed no fear or care, and it amped Chris further. "We blocked in behind us."

"Not on the right," said Chris.

"That's one-way to the right, comin in. You'll be going against traffic."

"I can deal with that." Watching as a uniformed officer in the lead car stepped out of his vehicle. "*Fuck* this."

Chris pulled the console's transmission arm toward him and locked it into drive. He cut the wheel right and gave the Trooper hard gas. The SUV went up the driveway, toward a car coming in, and Chris took the Trooper up onto the sidewalk. People shouted out behind them, and Chris swerved and drove across the sidewalk, behind the bus shelter on McKinley Street. A panicked pedestrian leaped away from their path, and then they were off the curb and straight onto the street.

"Red light," said Jason, indicating the signal at Connecticut.

"I see it," said Chris, and he blew the red. A sedan crossing north on the green braked wildly and three-sixtied, its tail end

21

sweeping and missing them, and Chris punched the gas and blew up McKinley's rise going east.

"Ho, shit!" said Jason.

"They're comin," said Chris.

One of the squad cars had hit its sirens and light bar and was maneuvering through the intersection, which had been blocked by the car that had spun and stalled.

Chris stepped on the pedal and kept it pinned to the floor. The gas flooded into the carb, and the Isuzu wound up and took the hill fast, sailing over the crest. It was a narrow street, and a boxy sedan was headed straight for them. Jason said, "Chris," and the sedan swerved to the right and swiped a parked vehicle, sparks illuminating Chris's side vision as they passed. He ran a four-way stop and in the rearview saw the squad car gaining on them, and the one behind it doing the same. The sirens grew louder.

"They about to be on us," said Jason.

"Hold on," said Chris.

He made a right on Broad Branch Road, barely braking. The first squad car squealed a right and fell in behind them. As they neared the Morrison Street intersection, Chris saw a car coming in from the east and Jason gasped as they jetted through the four-way and the oncoming car braked into a ninety-degree skid. They heard a metallic explosion as the skidding car pancaked the squad car behind them, and Chris made a crazy sharp right onto Legation Street. The top-heavy Isuzu went up on two wheels, and Jason's face turned white as milk as he raised his arm to grip the handle mounted on the headliner. Chris kept the wheel steady and put the Trooper back on four, then quickly turned into an alley that he knew elbowed off to the left. He followed the angle of the elbow and when he felt they were out of the sight line of Legation, he put the Trooper beside a wooden fence and cut the lights and engine.

Chris and Jason laughed. They stopped and got their breath, looked at each other, and laughed some more.

"You *dusted* 'em," said Jason.

"They don't live here, man. They don't know these streets like we do."

"The po-po gonna be angry like hornets," said Jason.

"Word."

"When you ran that red on Connecticut . . . shit, I thought that car was gonna do us."

"That car had brakes, too."

"We gonna be legends, son."

"Yeah," said Chris.

Colored lights faintly lit the alley as one of the squad cars slowly passed by on Legation. The boys sat there, hearing sirens that were different than police sirens, closer to those on fire trucks or ambulances, and voices coming from speakers, and they speculated on that. After a long while it was quiet and Chris decided to risk it and make their way from the alley, which had been a good hiding place but was also a trap. He did not hit the headlights until they were back on Legation.

Carefully, Chris crossed Connecticut Avenue and then took 39th Street south. Down near Fessenden, Jason claimed he saw a stripped-down Crown Vic, which could have been a police vehicle, creeping a nearby street, and because of this, and because they still felt invincible, Chris put the Isuzu into four-wheel drive and jumped off-road and onto a hill. They caught air going over the hilltop, and with exuberance Jason said, "Rat Patrol!" and then they were down the hill and rolling across the wide expanse of Fort Reno Park, where Chris and Jason had seen Fugazi and others perform in the summer, and where Chris's father, Thomas Flynn, had come as a teenager in the seventies to see hard rock bands do Deep Purple and Spanish bands try to do Santana. Satisfied that they had not been followed, they dropped back down onto asphalt at Chesapeake and took it east, back across Connecticut and into the beautiful upscale neighborhood of Forest Hills.

It was a section of Northwest whose residents were wealthy in a living-off-the-interest way. Large homes of brick and stone, deep and wide, lushly landscaped lots, Frank Lloyd Wright knockoffs, many embassies, and, down Brandywine toward Rock Creek Park, towering contemporaries housing gyms and indoor movie theaters. In the past, Forest Hills had been the exclusive base for Washington's most wealthy Jewish residents, so for many years D.C.'s less enlightened had called it Hanukkah Hills. Chris and Country knew it as a good place to get high.

Chris pulled into their usual spot at the dead end of Albemarle, where it ran into a striped barrier at the woods of Rock Creek, and cut the engine. Their place was past the light of the last streetlamp on the road. It was dark here and very quiet. Unless they turned around, there was no exit, but they weren't worried; they had never been hassled here before, not even by embassy police.

Chris pulled a couple of beers from the brown paper bag resting on the floorboards behind his seat and opened them both. Jason rolled a tight joint, sealed and dried it with fire, then lit it. They passed it back and forth, drank warm beer, and listened to the radio turned low.

"You used to come here with your mom and pops, didn't you?" said Jason, when they had smoked the joint down. Both of their heads were up, but without the new-high joy of the first smoke of the night.

"Once a year, in the spring," said Chris. "Darby, too, back when he was a puppy. We'd hike that trail they got. You get onto it back up Albemarle, near Connecticut."

He meant the Soapstone Valley Trail, a one-mile hike up and down hills, through an arm of Rock Creek Park. It was one of those city secrets, a wonderful green place, old-growth trees and sun glinting off running water. Chris had thought of it as his family's place when he was a kid, because they rarely saw anyone else on the trail, and because they had claimed ownership on a tree. There was a big oak down there, rooted in the valley floor, on whose trunk his father had carved their names with his buck knife. Thomas and Amanda in a heart when they'd been married, and then, in another heart, Chris when he was born. His father had put Darby's name in a smaller heart as well. When they were down there, Chris and his father would throw rocks and try to skip them in the creek, and sometimes his father would pick up a stick that was shaped like a gun and Chris would find one, too, and they would play war, his father coming from behind a tree and pretending the stick was a machine pistol or some such thing, his mouth making the sound of it spitting bullets. In his mind he could see his father doing this, younger, without that disappointment on his face. But it was just a memory. It didn't make Chris feel anything at all.

"Chris?"

"Huh?"

"What are we gonna do?"

"Go home, I guess."

Jason stubbed out the roach in the ashtray and put it inside a matchbook, which he stowed in his jeans. "What if Johnny Law's waitin on us?"

"Why would they be waitin on *you?* No one even saw you, Country. You stayed in the car the whole time."

"True."

Chris stared out the windshield. "You think someone wrote down my plate numbers?"

"Not the way you shot out that parking lot," said Jason with an unconvincing smile. "I don't see how they could."

Chris sat there, stoned, hoping and wishing that this were true.

"I can't take the weed home," said Jason. "This funk is potent. It stinks."

"I'll stash it under the deck of my house," said Chris. "We can bag it up at your place tomorrow, after your parents go to work."

Chris took a circuitous route back to their neighborhood and stopped the Trooper a couple of blocks away from Jason's house, a Dutch colonial on the corner of 38th and Kanawha. Jason and Chris shook hands and said good-bye.

Jason walked down the street. When he turned the corner, Chris drove off, but not in the direction of his own house. He had too much energy, and he needed to work it off. He headed south, where his girl, Taylor, stayed with her mother, on Woodley Avenue, a street of modest row houses in Woodley Park, between Connecticut Avenue and the zoo. Taylor's mother would be sleeping now, but Taylor would be up and ready. She'd let him in.

TAYLOR DUGAN had put Chris's two remaining beers in the freezer to rechill them quickly, then brought them back down to the basement, where Chris was sprawled out shoeless on the couch. Taylor's mother, a divorcée who worked as a lawyer for a trade association downtown, was in her bed and snoring, two floors above. Though it was tempting, Chris and Taylor never raided the mother's liquor cabinet while Chris was visiting late at night. Taylor's mother, like many alcoholics, counted her drinks and memorized the levels of the bottles, no matter how trashed she got, and Taylor did not care to get busted by her mom.

Taylor was a slim young woman with short dyed-black hair, a nose ring, freckles, and blue eyes. She had changed into boxer shorts and a V-neck white T-shirt after going upstairs to get the beer.

Taylor handed Chris his beer and put hers next to a 35 mm camera that was on an old table set before the couch. She went to a bookshelf, removed a paperback, and found a stash pipe with a hole in each end, one to light, one to draw from. In the middle, a small amount of marijuana was fitted in a screened chamber.

"You want some?" she said.

"Sure," said Chris.

He got up on a chair and cranked open a casement window, and then she joined him. The chair wobbled beneath them and they giggled as they each took a couple of deep hits and blew the exhale out into the night.

"Whew," she said, as she stepped down onto the carpet.

"You need some more?" said Chris.

"No, I'm good."

"Because I copped tonight. I got a pound out in my truck."

"That's not all you did tonight."

"Oh, man. You should have seen me."

"Were you scared?" said Taylor, flopping down onto the couch. Chris had already told the general story, but she was buzzed now and wanted to hear the details.

"Nah, not really," said Chris, walking to the table to get his beer, careful not to step on the sketchbooks scattered about the carpet. "I mean, I didn't think on it all that much. It's like that shrink said to me, the one my parents made me go to? 'It's all about choices, Chris.' Well, I made one."

Taylor picked the camera up off the table, framed Chris through the lens, and snapped a photograph. "Why'd you take off?"

"I dunno. That boy practically begged me to hit him. I mean, what, I was supposed to take the weight for *that?* I hate the police. I don't like explaining myself to them. I don't even like to speak to them if I don't have to." Chris took off his T-shirt and dropped it on the floor. "Hot in here."

"Uh-huh," said Taylor.

Chris tipped his head back, took a long swig of beer, and let her have a look at his flat stomach. Taylor took several more photographs of him like that and placed the camera back on the table.

"How far did they chase you?"

"A good long while," said Chris. "It was like *Cops*, only they didn't get me. Shit *was* sick, Taylor. I blew a red light on Connecticut Avenue at McKinley, and cars were spinning out in the intersection."

"Bad Chris," said Taylor.

"That's me."

Taylor was at that public arts school, Duke Ellington, and liked to paint and stuff. Chris had met her at a Blessed Sacrament dance when they were both in middle school. She had come over to *him*. Told him later that she'd noticed him straight off, that he looked different from the other boys, that he wasn't trying too hard and that she liked his aloof manner, whatever that meant. They had been together, friends and lovers, for a couple of years. He wasn't worried about the other boys at her school, who she said were "fey." He guessed that meant they were faggies or something, 'cause it rhymed with *gay*.

"I'm just a bad boy," said Chris, smiling slowly.

"Did you bring any protection?"

"Didn't know I'd be seein you, girl."

"We'll improvise," said Taylor.

Chris said he was good with that, and Taylor laughed and opened her arms.

Chris put his beer down and went to the couch. His jeans were tight before their mouths met. She stroked his belly, and her breath was hot and smoky as they kissed. She moaned as they made out, and Chris thought, *God, this girl can do it.* Taylor pushed him away, crossed her arms, and drew her T-shirt over her head. She came back to him naked above the waist, and Chris ran his strong hands over her slim hips and up her ribcage, and he found her small breasts, circling her hardening nipples with his thumbs, and she took one of his hands and put it inside her boxer shorts. He did what she liked until Taylor couldn't stand it any longer and she climaxed under his touch. She finished him deftly the same way.

It would be a long time before he would get with a female again. Later, when he was masturbating at night in his cell, bitter because she had stopped taking his calls, but still, wanting Taylor again so badly he thought he would shout out her name, he would regret settling for a hand job in her basement the last time he saw her. He should have put it in her. So what if he didn't have a condom? Okay, she could have got pregnant. What difference would that have made to him then?

"Are they going to get you, Chris?" Taylor was in his arms on the couch, on top of him, her breasts crushed against his chest.

"Nah, I'm straight. I can get the Volvo's paint off my bumper, and there's plenty of Troopers out there the same color as mine. Long as they didn't read my plates, I'll be fine."

"Maybe you got lucky."

"I could have."

"Why'd you hit that boy?"

"I was really tryin not to. Used to be I'd get angry and just fight, but this time was different. I tried to hold back, Taylor. If he hadn't pushed me so hard, run his mouth like he did, all this shit tonight, it wouldn't have happened."

"It's over now."

"No doubt."

"I don't want you to get hurt."

"They can't hurt steel," said Chris with a weak smile.

Taylor hugged him tightly. "I applied to a college I want, Chris. I'm trying to get into the Rhode Island School of Design."

"That's the art school, right?"

"My counselor says it's one of the best."

"I hope you get in."

"What are *you* going to do?"

"Don't know. First thing, I need to get out my house. I can't take livin with my father. When I turn eighteen I figure I'll get a job. Me and Country will find an apartment somewhere. Maybe sell weed on the side, but do it real quiet."

"That's your plan?"

"For now," said Chris. "Yeah."

Taylor said nothing else and soon fell asleep in his arms. Chris untangled himself without waking her and covered her with a blanket. He dressed and left the house quietly, went to his Trooper, and drove toward his house through backstreets. There were few cars out. It was very late.

He drove west on Livingston, the street where he lived, and a car turned off 41st and fell in behind him. The car was a big square sedan, and it was then that he knew. Several squad cars were parked on his block, and their light bars were activated as he neared his house. The air had gone out of him, and he simply put the Isuzu in park in the middle of the street and let them come to him. They leaned him over the hood of his Trooper and cuffed him, and one of the uniformed men said, almost in admiration, "That was some real fancy driving, son." Chris said, "I guess someone got my plate numbers," and the uniform said, "*Oh*, yeah," and Chris remembered that he had a pound of marijuana in the back of his vehicle and he idly wondered what that would do to compound the charges. "You don't even know the trouble you're in," said the uniform. "The woman who hit our cruiser at Morrison, where you blew that stop sign? Mother of three. She's in Sibley's emergency room with severe injuries. They collared her and taped her to a gurney. And that kid in the parking lot is gonna be breathing through his mouth for a while. You broke his nose."

Chris raised his head and squinted through the red and blue shafts of light coloring his yard. His father was standing outside their clapboard colonial, framed beneath the portico he'd built himself, his hands buried in his pockets, his eyes black and broken.

"You made your folks real proud tonight," said the police officer.

Chris didn't care.

FOUR

THOMAS FLYNN obtained a bond and made Chris's bail, twenty-seven hours after he'd been booked. At the arraignment, in a courtroom down in the Indiana Avenue corridor of Judiciary Square, Chris was released to the custody of his parents until the date of his trial. He was represented by Bob Moskowitz, a boyhood friend of Thomas Flynn's who was a private-practice attorney. The *Washington Post* court beat reporter, interested and aggressive because Chris was a white kid and his "night of crime" had made the TV news, tried to ask Chris questions, but Chris made no comment by order of Moskowitz and was hustled out of the building by his father, who held him roughly by the elbow.

Moskowitz followed them to their house, where he met with Thomas, Amanda, and Chris to discuss the status of the case and their general plan. They sat in the living room, where Thomas had built shelves to hold his collection of history and other nonfiction books. Amanda served coffee that neither Moskowitz nor Thomas Flynn touched.

"I've been contacted by Jason Berg's father." Moskowitz wore a caterpillar mustache and was forty pounds too heavy

32

for his height. "After questioning Jason, the police and prose-cutors are satisfied that Jason was not significantly involved in the night's events to the degree that he should be charged."

"You mean," said Flynn, "his father's wired down at the courthouse, and he got his son off."

"There's no doubt that Mr. Berg has some suction. But more likely the prosecutors feel they can't make any charges on Jason stick. Jason never got out of the SUV, so there was no contact or conversation between him and the boys in that parking lot. And of course he wasn't the driver. They're going to focus on Chris."

"What about the pound of marijuana?" said Flynn. "Jason had nothing to do with that, either?"

"He says it wasn't his."

"It was mine," said Chris.

"Shut up," said Flynn.

"Tommy," said Amanda.

"So, what, they're gonna let that idiot off in exchange for his testimony against Chris?"

"Country's my boy," said Chris. "He wouldn't do that."

"I told you to shut the fuck up," said Flynn.

"*Tommy.*"

"I don't think they're going to compel Jason to testify," said Moskowitz with deliberate calm. "His father told me that he had no such indication from his contacts down there. They feel as if they have enough evidence and witnesses to make their case without Jason's testimony."

"What's going to happen to my son?" said Amanda.

"I'm going to give him the best representation possible," said Moskowitz. "Chris?"

"Yes."

"We'll speak in more detail, obviously. But what I want to

ask you now concerns your alleged assault on Alexander Fleming, the boy in the parking lot. It's important, because this is the act that triggered everything that followed. If you had reason to hit him, if you felt threatened or were defending yourself —"

"He didn't threaten me or nothin like that," said Chris. "I can't even say that I was defending myself."

"Why did you hit him, then?" said Moskowitz.

"I was angry," said Chris. "It wasn't what he said so much as how he said it. Actin like he was smarter than me."

"And what did he say to you?"

Chris shook his head. "I don't remember."

"God," said his father.

"Unfortunately," said Moskowitz, making a show of glancing at his watch, "I've got to get to an appointment. Will you walk me out, Tom?"

"Let's go."

"Amanda," said Moskowitz, taking her hand and squeezing it as he rose off the couch. "Chris. You're to stay here in the house unless otherwise directed. You understand that, don't you?"

"Yes."

"Okay. Don't worry. We'll get through this."

Bob Moskowitz and Thomas Flynn walked to a Mercedes sedan parked on Livingston. Moskowitz stowed his briefcase in the trunk, shut the lid, and leaned against his car.

"Talk to me, Bobby," said Flynn.

"Honestly?" said Moskowitz. "This is going to be a challenge, to say the least. Individually, a few of the charges are minor, but compounded they are significant. That, together with the fact that Chris has a history, will give the impression that the incident follows a pattern of violent, reckless behavior.

There's the robbery of the locker room, the fights at the school. He has that assault-and-strong-arm arrest and the possession charge on his record as well."

"That was a while back."

"It's there. You have to remember, people were seriously injured because of his alleged aggression and negligence on the night in question. That woman's back injuries alone appear to be the kind that will plague her for the rest of her life. The boy whose nose Chris broke? His father was a major donor to our own D.C. Council member. Unfortunately, the events made the news and now Chris will be tried, in effect, in the public eye."

"What are you getting at?"

"We'll aim to get some of the charges reduced or thrown out. But I'm almost certain that something's going to stick. What I'm going to recommend to you . . . Well, hear me out. You're going to need to keep an open mind."

"Go ahead."

"The US attorney is making a hard push on this one because of all the publicity. Chris is *not* going to walk. The best thing we can do for him is plead guilty on some of the charges. I mean, we can roll the dice and go to trial, but a conviction in court can result in a stay in an adult prison. Juvenile jail is not the worst that can happen to him."

"My boy's going to jail?"

"Possibly. If so, I'd say that it would be for a relatively short period of time."

"You're talking about that place for juvenile offenders the District's got."

"Pine Ridge," said Moskowitz. "I'm telling you it's *possible*. Of course, I'm going to try to prevent it."

"That's all black kids out there, isn't it?"

"I'm guessing it's about ninety-eight percent, yes. The rest are Hispanics."

"They wouldn't send a white kid from this neighborhood to that place, would they?"

"It's rare. But it has happened. There's only one facility that houses D.C. juveniles who habitually commit these kinds of crimes. He's not exempt from serving time there because he's comfortable and white."

"I can't . . ." said Thomas Flynn, his voice trailing off.

"There's something else you need to prepare for," said Moskowitz. "We've only discussed the criminal aspect of this. There will probably be some litigation in civil court as well."

"Meaning?"

"You're going to be sued, Tommy. Your insurance company, sure, but probably you as well. All those people who got hurt or whose cars were wrecked because of Chris's actions? They're going to claim negligence on your part for letting a boy with Chris's history get behind the wheel of an SUV that you bought for him. It's convoluted, but there it is."

"Can they do that?"

"My brethren are probably lining up to feed at the trough as we speak. They'll certainly try."

Flynn opened his mouth to speak but said nothing. Instead he shook his head.

"I know this is rough," said Moskowitz, putting a hand on his friend's arm. "It all seems insurmountable right now. But look, I see this kind of trouble in families all the time. They get through it eventually. You will, too."

"Let me ask you something, Bob. Your oldest son, how's he doin?"

"He's fine," said Moskowitz.

"I'm asking you, where is he in life right now?"

Moskowitz looked away. "He graduated high school a couple of months ago. He's headed to Haverford in the fall."

"Don't tell me to look on the bright side."

"Tommy —"

"Everything's fucked," said Flynn.

AMANDA FLYNN made Chris a sandwich while her husband and Bob Moskowitz stood talking outside the house. She did it quickly, so as not to annoy Tommy. Tommy would say that Chris, who could take a vehicle his father had bought him and use it to lead police on a high-speed chase, who could punch out a kid in a parking lot for no reason, who could cause a woman to go to the hospital taped to a stretcher, who could carry around a pound of marijuana in his car, who could manage to get kicked out of public high school in the District, who could quit church and sports and everything else, could certainly manage to make a sandwich for himself.

Amanda did not see it that way. She looked at Chris, knowing all that he had done, and saw a young man who had been locked up for a day and night, who was confused and ashamed, who had to be hungry, who needed to be fed. Thomas looked at Chris and saw failure and an insurmountable problem. She saw her little boy. Amanda thinking, *With everything he's done, he's still my son.*

"Here, honey," she said, putting a turkey and Swiss on white down in front of him, mayonnaise, lettuce, no tomatoes, his sandwich, how he liked it. A glass of apple juice, Chris's preferred drink, set beside the plate.

"Thanks, Mom."

As Chris ate, Amanda looked through the living-room window and watched Bob Moskowitz drive away. Thomas Flynn stood on the lawn momentarily, checking the beeper hung on his belt line, replacing it, rubbing at his face. Then wheeling around and walking heavily back toward the house, sullen, his eyes to the ground. Amanda saying a wordless prayer that he would not enter their home and immediately explode.

Flynn came through the door. He looked at Chris, eating a sandwich off a TV tray, and shook his head in disgust. He looked at Amanda and sharply pointed his chin toward the center hall stairway. She followed him up the stairs.

It came to Amanda, when she was trying to "understand" Tom in moments of tension and conflict such as these, that it must be odd for her husband to have to act like an adult and deal with adult problems in the home in which he had grown up. Walking behind him up the stairs, she imagined him as a little boy, taking the steps two at a time, going up to his room to play or to wrestle with his big brother, Sean, now a Boeing executive in Chicago with whom he had little communication. She wondered if Tom, alone at night with his private demons, talked to his parents, whose spirits surely were in this house, and in his desperation sought their help.

It wasn't difficult to imagine him as a child. She had known him since their days at Blessed Sacrament, the Catholic school at Chevy Chase Circle that went from K through eighth. They were boyfriend and girlfriend through high school, and had married against her parents' wishes when Thomas was twenty and she was nineteen. Her father was dismayed that she was making this decision at so young an age and openly discouraged her from marrying a young man who had no intention of going to college.

"He wants to *work*, Dad," said Amanda. "He's ready to make money now."

"And what about you, Amanda? You're going to throw away a chance to go to college, to have that experience?"

"I'm with Tommy," she said.

Amanda had known he was the one as soon as she'd seen him, a black-haired, green-eyed Irish boy, walking cocky through the halls of BS. He was a tough kid, quick to fight, a basketball player who haunted the courts at Friendship, Lafayette, the Chevy Chase Library, and Candy Cane City, and later was point guard and the sole white player on his Interhigh team. He was not a good student, and, with the exception of American history, a subject that fascinated him, he had no interest in books. He liked to have fun, fucked off in class, drank Budweiser from cans, and smoked any kind of weed that was offered to him. His father, an Irish immigrant complete with brogue, worked for the Government Printing Office. His mother was of Irish stock, American born, and proud to be called a housewife. They bought the clapboard house on Livingston on the cheap, when nonprofessionals still lived in Friendship Heights and Chevy Chase, D.C., and upper Northwest neighborhoods were heavy with Irish Catholics. Thomas Flynn delivered the *Washington Post* all through high school, even during basketball season. On his route lived Red Auerbach, whose Celtic-green Mercury Cougar was usually parked in the driveway of his home, two blocks off Nebraska Avenue. Tommy Flynn always put Mr. Auerbach's newspaper at the top of his stoop, just outside the door.

Amanda had grown up on 31st Place in Barnaby Woods, on the east side of Connecticut Avenue, in a brick colonial that looked like several others on her street. Her father worked for an unidentified government agency, traveled frequently, and never talked about his job. Friends and neighbors assumed correctly that he was CIA.

Flynn had his buddies but spent most of his time with Amanda, a full-figured girl with strawberry blonde hair and fair skin, physically mature and sexually precocious at the age of fifteen. The two of them enjoyed their marijuana, alcohol, mushrooms, and downs, and, when they were in the company of kids with money, finger-thick lines of cocaine. They were faithful to each other and made it everywhere, in the front and backseats of Flynn's 442 Cutlass, on a blanket in the high-grass field at Glover and Military, and on the green of Rock Creek Golf Course on summer nights. Tommy couldn't get enough of her lush figure, and Amanda liked the wheel.

After high school, they married and rented a row home in pregentrified Shaw, still dirt cheap at the time. Flynn took retail jobs, then entered the MPD Academy and briefly worked as a police officer. Kate was born and died. Flynn's father dropped dead of a heart attack, and soon after that his mother, Tara, was diagnosed with pancreatic cancer and was gone in six weeks. His parents had willed the house on Livingston to Thomas, leaving their pitifully meager savings to their elder son, Sean, causing a rift between the brothers that would never heal. Flynn quit the MPD and moved with his wife into the Friendship Heights house in which he'd been raised. Amanda found Jesus, had a failed pregnancy, then carried Chris successfully to term. All of this occurred in the space of two and one half years.

Thomas Flynn walked into their bedroom, waited for Amanda to join him, and closed the door behind her. He used his right hand to pop the knuckles of his left. When he started the mangling of his joints, Amanda knew he was attempting to control himself and also that he would fail.

A shock of black hair had fallen over his forehead. He didn't look all that different than he had as a teenager. A little thicker and some lines around his eyes, but that was all right. She still found him handsome and often wanted him and his touch. Because of fatigue, and because their differences on the handling of Chris had put something impenetrable between them, they made love infrequently. Sometimes it was good, and occasionally it was eye-popping, but when it was over, Tommy's black mood would always return.

"What is it?" said Amanda. "You're not going to lecture me, are you?"

"I see you made Chris a sandwich."

"And?"

"Did you serve it to him on his Star Wars plate?"

"I fixed him some lunch. You think I should let him starve?"

"Let the kid make his own lunch. He's old enough to stick a knife in our hearts. He can build a sandwich by himself."

"Okay, Tom. Okay."

"You're not helping him, Amanda. He doesn't need an enabler or a personal chef. It's pretty obvious that the gentle way doesn't get results with him."

"I'm keeping the lines of communication open."

"I tried that and it doesn't work."

"You tell him to shut up. Then you tell him to shut the *fuck* up. That's not communication."

"It's what he deserves."

"He deserves our support. And I don't want to lose him."

"We've already lost him."

"I don't believe that. Look, I know you're angry. But he needs to know that we still love him."

"Fine." Flynn's beeper sounded. He checked the number on the display and took a deep breath. "My mailbox is so full it's not taking any more messages. I can't keep ignoring the business."

"Go to work," said Amanda. "You need to."

"I will. But listen, don't let Chris leave the house. He's going to tell you he's only going up to the store, or he's *only* going out to see his girlfriend. It's a violation of his terms of release. Don't let him play you, do you understand?"

"I *get* it, Tommy."

Flynn looked her in the eyes. He dropped his hands to his sides and softened his tone. "Amanda."

"What?" Now he was going to apologize.

"I'm sorry. This stuff with Chris has knocked me down, obviously. I'm all messed up."

"I know. Go to work. It's all right."

She *wanted* him to go. It was better here when he was not around.

Flynn left without touching her. He left the house without speaking to his son.

THOMAS AND Chris Flynn had little communication over the next few months. Chris continued to see the same psychiatrist that Thomas and Amanda saw as a couple, but Chris refused to meet as a family. At home, Amanda and Chris spoke regularly and cordially, and she cooked for him and did his laundry. Thomas and Chris spoke to each other only if necessary. Often they were in a room together and did not speak at all.

Thomas Flynn kept busy with his carpet-and-floor business and met Bob Moskowitz occasionally to discuss Chris's upcoming hearing. Fall arrived, and as other students returned to their high schools, Chris remained home, sleeping late, watching television, and killing time. He spoke often with Taylor on the phone but had infrequent conversations with his friend Jason Berg, and finally had none at all.

When Chris's case came up on the court's docket, everything seemed to accelerate. Chris pled guilty, and Moskowitz made a well-reasoned and passionate plea for lenience. But the judge was well aware of the criticism he would receive if he were to show mercy to the white kid from upper Northwest who had made the print and broadcast news, especially in light of the boy's history of theft, reckless acts, and violence. In accordance with D.C. juvenile justice procedure, he committed Chris Flynn to the custody of the District of Columbia. It was decided that society and the District would be best served if Chris were to be incarcerated with other young men until it was determined that he had achieved an acceptable degree of reform. And that was it. Chris kissed his mother, said nothing to his father, and was led away, shackled in handcuffs and leg irons, to a van that would transport him to the juvenile detention facility at Pine Ridge, in Anne Arundel County, Maryland.

That night, Flynn and Amanda ate a meal at home and turned in early. Amanda slipped under the covers and turned her back to her husband. He listened to her sob quietly and when her breathing evened out he knew she had fallen asleep. But he couldn't sleep or even close his eyes. He got off the bed and, in his boxers, went downstairs to the dining room, poured bourbon into a tumbler, and drank it down neat. He poured two more fingers from the bottle and took it out to the living room and stood by the mantel over the fireplace, where Amanda had set up framed photographs, the usual array of family and friends.

Thomas Flynn looked at an old photo, taken at the annual St. Patrick's Day parade down on Constitution Avenue, when Chris was two years old. Thomas had put Chris up on his shoulders so he could see above the crowd, and Chris's tiny hands were wrapped around his father's thick index fingers. And then there were those days that Flynn would ride his old

Nishiki ten-speed on the bike path of Rock Creek Park, Chris strapped into a seat mounted over the rear tire, a smile on his chubby face as the wind hit it and blew back his hair, Flynn reaching behind him and squeezing Chris's hand. Flynn could feel the warmth of those hands, the way they clung to him, even now. He remembered how proud he had been the day of the parade, how proud he was to have people see him and his son together on that bike, how certain he was then of his role as provider, protector, and father.

It was no longer about Chris's disturbing behavior, or his indifference to fitting into society, or his trouble with the law, or his marijuana use, or the embarrassment Flynn felt around the friends and acquaintances whose sons and daughters had stayed on track and were heading for college.

Chris was in prison. It felt final and irreversible, and Flynn did not know what to do.

He placed his empty tumbler on the mantel and listened to the tick of the clock mounted on the wall. It was very quiet in the house.

Chris Flynn had spent nearly every night of his life here on Livingston Street. Now it was as if he had never lived here at all. There would be no muffled sounds of the television behind his closed bedroom door, no floor-rumbling bass of his stereo, no low chuckle as he talked on the phone with his girl, no heavy, clumsy footsteps on the stairs. Chris was gone, and the silence he had left behind was a scream in his father's ears.

It was 1999. Chris was seventeen the day he entered juvenile prison. Thomas Flynn was thirty-nine years old.

PART TWO
UNIT 5

FIVE

THE GUARDS called it a room, but it was a cell. To name it anything else was a lie.

It was a six-by-nine-foot space containing a floor-bolted cot and thin mattress, a particleboard desk and chair, and a steel shitter and piss hole. There was a barred window giving to a view of a dirt-and-mud field, leading to a twelve-foot-high fence topped with razor wire. Beyond the fence was a forest of oak, maple, wild dogwood, and weed trees, but no pines. The door to the cell held Plexiglas in its cutout. Comically large Joliet keys, so named because they were originally manufactured for use in Illinois's Joliet prison, unlocked the steel doors.

Wake-up was at 6:30 a.m., then group showers, check-in, and breakfast. Then school, 8:30 to 2:00, Monday through Friday. Regularly scheduled recreation, canceled as often as it occurred, dinner, visiting hours, and psychiatric counseling with staff who barely spoke English. The intended illusion was of routine, just like for boys on the outside.

There were a dozen units housing offenders of various degrees of criminality. The most violent boys, those convicted of second-degree murder and manslaughter, and sexual offenders, who were few, were housed together in Unit 12. That they were designated with the highest number, putting them by implication at the top of the pecking order, was a distinction not lost on the other inmates.

Chris Flynn lived in Unit 5, an L-shaped, low-slung brick building, with fourteen other young men. The residents of each unit wore the same color polo shirts, short sleeves in the summer, long in the winter, and system-issue khakis. They were allowed to wear lace-up shoes and sneaks. Their shirts had distinct colors so that an inmate could quickly be identified by his unit. The boys from Unit 5 wore maroon.

Classes were held in a building the size of a small-town elementary school. It was set apart from the housing units, close to another building that held a cafeteria that sometimes doubled as an auditorium, complete with stage. The warden and other administrators, including the central guard detail, kept offices in a separate structure.

The classrooms looked like the classrooms at Chris's former high school, each with a blackboard, a cluster of old chairs, an opaque projector that only one kid admitted knowing how to operate, and the usual silhouette cutouts of Frederick Douglass and George Washington Carver that the boys spit on and occasionally ripped off the wall. Teachers came to work every day, same as any other teachers, but faced more resistance and saw less progress or success. Chris could not imagine why anyone would want that job and guessed that these folks were do-good types, people his father called "crunchy granolas." What he didn't know was that Pine Ridge was a dumping ground for teachers who could barely cut it in the D.C. public school system.

"Does anyone know who the president of the United States was at the time of Martin Luther King's assassination?" said the teacher, Mr. Brown, a young black dude the boys called Mr. Beige, on account of he talked white. Mr. Brown's clothes were threadbare, further lowering his status in the boys' eyes.

"Roosevelt," said Luther, a boy who talked incessantly to hear his own voice and always gave the wrong answers.

"That's incorrect, Luther."

"Coolidge, then."

"Gump," said a boy wearing blue in the back of the room. "Boy, you just naming high schools."

They were in history class, the maroon shirts of Unit 5 mixed in with the navy blue shirts from Unit 9.

"No, it's not Calvin Coolidge, either. But nice try, Luther. Anyone else?"

Chris thought he knew the answer. He was *certain* Ali knew. Sure enough, when Chris turned his head and looked at him, Ali Carter, seated at the desk-chair beside him, was staring down at the floor, mouthing the word *Johnson*.

Ali was smooth skinned, handsome, with a swollen upper body built by doing push-ups in his cell and dips wherever he could. He wore eyeglasses, which somewhat lessened the effect of his bulldog chest, and at five-foot-six was one of the shorter boys at the facility. Ali was in on an armed-robbery conviction.

"Nobody?" said Mr. Brown. "Okay. It was President Johnson, also known as LBJ. Who knows what those initials stand for?"

"Lonnie's Big Johnson," said Lonnie Wilson, a horn dog who tended to turn any conversation toward pussy or his dick.

"It ain't near as big as mine," said a boy.

A seated guard, one of two stationed in the room, chuckled, his fat moving gelatinously on the action. The other guard, a tall older man named Lattimer, who the boys called Shawshank because he looked like the graybeard in that movie, told Lonnie to watch his mouth and show respect.

"President Johnson and Martin Luther King had a cordial but sometimes rocky relationship during the civil rights era," said Mr. Brown.

"A sex relationship?" said one of the boys, and several of the others laughed.

"That's enough," said Lattimer.

"Perhaps 'rocky' is too strong a term. It's probably more accurate to say that their relationship was one of guarded respect," said Mr. Brown, gamely plowing ahead. "Understandably, Dr. King became increasingly frustrated with the slow progress in achieving his goal of racial equality in America, and was also frustrated with the escalation of the Vietnam War. . . ."

Many of the boys sat slumped in their chairs, some with their arms crossed, some looking away from the teacher, a couple with their eyes closed, stealing sleep. Understandable, as the most blatantly inattentive of them could neither read nor write. Ali, by far the smartest boy in the class, understood what Mr. Beige was saying, but the majority of the other boys did not. Just as many did not have any interest in the subject matter and felt that it had no relevance to the reality of their lives. All of this stuff with Dr. King and Lonnie's Big Johnson had happened before they were born, and wasn't no Dr. Anyone coming to save them and pull them up out of this jail.

". . . Ironically, it was Lyndon Johnson, a product of the South and its racist environment, who signed the Civil Rights Act of 1964, which gave all citizens in this country, regardless of their color, the right to vote."

"He was a leader," said Chris, not intending to speak but recalling something his father had said about Johnson at the dinner table one night. His old man was a history buff. The living room of their home was full of books on presidents and war.

"Black folk couldn't vote before then?" said Ben Braswell, a big dark-skinned boy with soulful eyes who lived in Chris's unit. Ben had stolen many cars and had been caught one too many times.

"Until then," said Mr. Brown, "some white people in power found loopholes and obstacles to prevent African Americans from participating in the process. The Civil Rights Act made any kind of racial discrimination illegal."

"What you think about that, White Boy?" said a husky voice behind Chris.

Chris did not turn his head, knowing that it was Lawrence Newhouse, who some called Bughouse, doing the talking. He did not feel threatened by Lawrence, nor slighted by the tag, which had been given to him his first day in. Everyone had another name in here, the same way soldiers did on the battlefield, and White Boy, though a supremely uncreative moniker, was as good as any other. Lawrence was stupid running to illiterate, unnecessarily abrasive at times, but not considered dangerous unless he was off his meds, though everyone knew he had shot a boy on Wade Road, which had been his ticket in. He was thin and had almond-shaped eyes and skin that in certain lights looked yellow.

"Asked you a question," said Lawrence.

Chris shrugged, the rise and fall of his shoulders his response.

"What, you can't speak?"

"You mind?" said Ali, turning his head to glare at Lawrence. "I'm tryin to hear this shit."

Ali had no intention of defending Chris, but Lawrence annoyed him. Plus, there was that old thing between them. Ali had grown up in Barry Farms, a Section 8 complex in Southeast, and Lawrence had come up in the Parkchester Apartments, a neighboring housing unit. Neither of them were crew members, but there was a rivalry between the young men of the dwellings, a long-standing beef that no one, if pressed, could dissect or explain. Nonetheless, Ali Carter and Lawrence Newhouse had been assigned to the same unit. Boys with a history of animosity, gang related or otherwise, were mixed in with one another and were expected to work out their differences.

"I say somethin to you, Holly?" said Lawrence.

"My name is *Ali*."

"There a problem?" said the old man, Lattimer.

"I'm about to see you outside, little man," said Lawrence under his breath.

But instead, when the class was done and the boys filed out, Lawrence Newhouse took a wild swing at a guard for no apparent reason and was subdued by several other guards and hustled down the hall into an empty room, from which the boys could hear shouts and sounds of struggle. The next time the boys from Unit 5 saw Lawrence, just before lockdown that night, his cheek and upper lip were swollen. He and Ali passed each other in the recreation room but said nothing and made no hard eye contact. A couple of the young men, who did not particularly care for Lawrence, dapped him up. Fights between inmates were inevitable and sometimes necessary, but they bought you nothing. When you swung on a guard, you were going to take a beatdown for sure, but you earned a little piece of respect. Even from your enemies.

CHRIS HAD been inside for several weeks and had been in no fights yet. He had been the recipient of many shoulder bumps and hard brushes, and given out a few, but they had come to nothing. As for his color, he absorbed the usual comments and chose not to respond. Truth was, it didn't bother him to be described as a cracker. Had he called someone a nigger, there would have been immediate go, but there was no corresponding word for whites that would automatically start a fight. Because of Chris's indifference, the other young men grew tired of using his race as a launching pad for aggression and dropped it.

Not that he was feared. He was on the big and strong side, but this did not deter anyone. In fact, it made the smaller boys more eager to drop him. But the deliberate bumps were perfunctory and did not escalate to anything approaching real violence.

The nature of Chris's crimes gave him a certain mystique that was useful on the inside. He was the crazy white boy who had cold-cocked a kid for no reason, led the police on a high-speed chase, and outrun them. When asked, Chris told the story true, but in its telling it did sound as if he had no regard for consequences or respect for the law, when in fact, on the night in question he had just acted impulsively. Chris believed it was wise to take this rep as a gift and did nothing to dispel the notion that he was a little bit off.

The other thing that served him well was his ability to play and sometimes excel at basketball. The Pine Ridge half court, out in the field, was an asphalt surface land-mined with fissures and weeds, equipped with a slightly bent rim with chain netting. The rim was unforgiving, but once Chris learned its idiosyncrasies, he was good with it, and word quickly got around that he could ball. At first he wasn't chosen for pickup because of his color, but the guards forced the issue, and soon he was out there, getting hacked and bumped like everyone else. Playing those games on Saturday afternoons, and holding the court and bragging rights with what would become his team, which included the tall and athletically gifted Ben Braswell, was the high point of his week.

There were no other peaks. The boys were indoors most of the time, and the atmosphere in the unit buildings fostered depression. With clouded Plexiglas substituting for glass, little light entered the structures, so even on sunny days, their world seemed gray, colorless, and grim.

By design, the boys did not have a say in the rules or conditions at Pine Ridge. There was no suggestion box. The boys took orders or they didn't. They were ordered to go from one place to another, to keep in line, to get out of bed, to get in and out of the showers, to get to the cafeteria and to leave the cafeteria, to hurry into class and to leave class, to move into their cells. The guards didn't ask. They shouted and they commanded, often with obscenity-laced language.

Chris found himself bored with the sameness of his life inside. He was smart enough to know that he was being punished, that the boredom, the attitude of the guards, the tasteless food, the scratchy old blanket on his cot, all of it was intended to make him want to act right so he could be released and not return. But still, the treatment and surroundings didn't have to be so harsh all the time. The boys *got* it, they knew they weren't on some field trip, but it seemed counterproductive to get shit on day after day. After a while, the way they got treated felt less like punishment and more like cruelty.

So with bitterness they acted out and broke rules. They talked out of turn in class and swung on guards and one another. Many smoked marijuana when they could get it. It was brought in by a guard who walked it through the gatehouse by taping it under his balls, and it got paid for by money the boys' relatives gave them on visiting days. The weed, stashed in ceiling tiles, was occasionally potent but frequently was not, and most times it produced headaches over highs, but it was something to do.

Because the scent of marijuana was often in the air at Pine Ridge, and because the high was evident in the boys' eyes, this indiscretion was not a secret and the boys were piss-tested and strip-searched at random. They knew they would most likely be caught and that a drug offense would potentially increase their time inside, but most of them didn't care. The warden ordered urine tests on the guards, too, and some of them came up positive. The guard who was selling, a man who arrogantly drove his BMW 5-series to work and thereby generated suspicion, was eventually served a warrant at his residence, where a search turned up several pounds. He was fired and prosecuted, but another guard saw an opportunity and stepped into his shoes. Wisely, this guard continued to drive his old Hyundai.

It was said by some that the juvenile prison system tainted everyone, employees and inmates alike.

Not all succumbed to the atmosphere. There were guards who did their jobs straight and felt they were achieving some kind of good.

Pine Ridge's superintendent, Rick Colvin, was one authority figure most of the boys liked. He managed to remember their names and ask after their well-being and their families. He was decent, and the boys felt better when he was on campus. But Colvin was not always around. His was a nine-to-five job, and his absence was felt at night. The regular guards went home in the evening, leaving duties to the crew of the midnight shift, who the boys considered to be the scrub members of the security team. Ali said, "The low end of the gene pool get the shit hours," and it seemed to be so. These were also the men and women who woke them up in their cells at 6:30 in the morning. They rarely did so with empathy or kindness.

THE NIGHT after Chris assured his dad he knew how to jail, he was in the common room of Unit 5, hanging out on an old couch, reading a paperback novel, not paying attention to what he was reading because as usual the boys in what was called the media room next door were arguing about what they were watching and what they would be watching next on the scarred television mounted high on the wall. Also in the common room was an old Ping-Pong table, looked like a dog had been chewing on its corners, where two boys played. One of the boys liked to slam the ball and then ridicule his opponent about his inability to return the slam. It was hard for Chris to concentrate.

Ali Carter was seated in a fake-leather chair with riveted arms, ripped in spots. It was comfortable and he had commandeered it. Most of the other furniture here had been purchased out of a correctional facility catalogue, items made of hard plastic, indestructible and impossible to sit in for long periods of time. Ali, like Chris, was reading a book, but he did not seem bothered by the noise.

Chris had been given his book by the reading teacher, a young woman named Miss Jacqueline who wore white shirts with black brassieres underneath and tight pinstripe pants to their school. Miss Jacqueline came to school twice a week and worked with the boys individually, and after she visited she was the subject of much talk in the units and fantasies that led to masturbation when the boys got into their cells. Chris had heard Shawshank, the old guard, talking to Superintendent Colvin one day, complaining about Miss Jacqueline's style of dress, and how she "oughtn't be looking like that in here," and how she was driving all the boys crazy, walking around with her behind "all tight and full in them pinstripes." Chris agreed, but he liked looking at her just the same, and he liked the way she smelled of lavender when she leaned toward him. It was nice of her to give him the book, too.

"All right," said Ben Braswell, entering the room, tapping Chris's fist, and sitting down beside him. "Those pieces took my head up, man."

Chris had bought some marijuana with the money his mother had slipped into his pocket and had passed a couple of buds on to Ben.

"What I owe you?" said Ben.

"Nothin."

"I'll get you later, hear?"

"We're straight," said Chris. Ben never had money and had no way to get it. No one visited him, ever.

"We gonna ball this weekend, son?"

"No doubt," said Chris. "Better play while we can. It's startin to get cold out."

"Cool weather means gobble time," said Ben. "They'll be servin a special dinner on that day, too. Turkey and stuffing, cranberry sauce, everything. They did last year, anyway. It was tight."

Thanksgiving was just another day to Chris. But he said, "Sounds good."

He didn't want to taint Ben Braswell's vision of the upcoming holiday. More than any other boy Chris had met at Pine Ridge, Ben saw the brightness in things. His attitude was positive, he was never cruel to be cruel, and he didn't bully anyone out of boredom. Ben kept stealing cars, though, and the court kept putting him back inside.

"Hey, Ali, what you reading, man?" said Ben. "That book looks thick."

An open hardback book rested in Ali's lap. He took his eyes off the page and looked over the top of his specs at Ben. "Called *Pillar of Fire*. Miss Jacqueline gave it to me, said it came out just last year."

"That's a big-ass book."

"You can read it when I'm done, you want to."

"I ain't gonna read shit, Ali. You know that."

Because you can't read, thought Chris.

"It's about that time Mr. Beige was speakin on," said Ali. "The Civil Rights Act, Dr. King, LBJ, all that stuff. You know, that president Chris called a leader."

"He was," said Chris.

"Yeah?" said Ali.

Chris concentrated, tried to arrange his thoughts in a logical manner so he'd sound as if he knew what he was speaking on. For some reason, he wanted to please Ali.

"He did good, even though he wasn't all pure inside. My father told me that Johnson was . . . he was a product of his environment."

"Your pops meant that Johnson was racist," said Ali.

"More like, he couldn't really help what he was."

"Way I heard it, the man told nigger jokes at the dinner table," said Ali.

"Maybe he did," said Chris. "But he signed that act because it was the right thing to do, even though he might not have been feelin it in here." Chris tapped his chest. "That's what I meant when I said he was a leader."

"Okay," said Ali. "You're right. Not only that, he lost the South for his party when he did that, and they ain't never got it back."

"What the fuck are y'all talking about?" said Ben.

"You ain't all that stupid," said Ali, looking directly at Chris for the first time. "You just tryin to act like you are."

Chris blushed. "My father told me that, is all."

"Your father read books?" said Ben.

"History books and shit. He's got a library, like, in our living room."

"Your father," said Ali with a small smile. "Your living room. Books. A library."

"*What?*" said Chris.

"How you end up in this piece?" Ali shook his head and lowered his eyes back to his book. "You don't belong here, man."

IN HIS cell that night, Chris lay on his side on his cot and looked at a charcoal sketch that Taylor Dugan had done of him, taped to the wall. It was made from a photograph she had taken of him in her mother's basement, the night he was arrested. The sketch showed him shirtless, drinking a beer, with a cocky, invincible smile on his face. It had come to him through the prison mail, along with a note that simply said, "Thinking of you and miss you." On the bottom of the sketch, Taylor had put her signature. Underneath his figure she had printed the words "Bad Chris."

That's me.

It was *me. And now I'm here.*

The smile in the sketch seemed to mock him, and Chris turned his back to it. He stared at cinder blocks and felt nothing at all.

SIX

THOMAS FLYNN'S business was called Flynn's Floors. Despite the name, which he'd chosen because of its alliterative effect, the majority of his work was actually in carpet. He avoided wood flooring jobs, which were prone to costly error, and for the same reason he turned down work that involved ceramics. "I prefer not to deal with that," he'd tell customers. "It's outside my comfort level in terms of expertise." To builders and sub-contractors, he'd simply say, "I don't fuck with tiles. You can fix a carpet mistake. With ceramics, you screw up, you've got to eat it."

He catered primarily to the residential trade, with a smatter-ing of commercial work in the mix. Much of his business came from referrals, so he spent a good portion of his day calling on potential clients in their homes, checking work that his instal-lation crew had already done, and putting out any attendant fires. Amanda handled the paperwork end of the business—inventory, bills, receivables, payroll, insurance, and taxes—from the office they had set up in the basement of their house. Flynn was a good closer and could mother his crew and talk dissatis-fied clients down, but he had no interest in the clerical aspect of the business, while Amanda was efficient in paperwork and the collection of moneys. Their talents were complementary and they knew their roles well. Take one of them out of the equation and Flynn's Floors would not have been a success.

Flynn drove a white Ford Econoline van with a removable magnetic sign on its side, advertising the company name and phone number. His crew, headed by a hardworking El Salvadoran named Isaac, rode around in an identical van that Isaac drove home at night and parked on the grass of his Wheaton home off Veirs Mill Road. Chris, when he was still speaking to his father, called the vans the Flynn's Floors fleet.

Like many salesmen, Flynn did not believe in showing up at a client's house looking like he made more money than he needed. He felt that it was prudent to look humble and hungry. His work clothing was plain and square, Dockers from Hecht's, polo shirts bearing the company patch when it was warm enough, long-sleeved cotton-poly blends in the winter and fall, Rocksports on his feet. For a while he had gone through the Vandyke phase, in the rebel yell manner of a white Major League baseball player, but he saw too many guys with double chins doing the same thing, and it screamed middle-age desperation when in fact he wasn't there yet. Amanda said it made him look pleased with himself rather than honest or smart. He shaved it off.

Flynn looked in the mirror and saw what others saw, a guy who went to work every day, who took care of his family, who made what would always be a modest living, and who would pass on, eventually, without having made a significant mark.

He had been fine with this in the past. His aim was to instill values, work ethic, and character in his son, and to see him through to adulthood, when he would become a productive member of society and in turn pass this along to his own children. That was what he felt he was here for. That was how all of this "worked." But when Chris jumped the tracks, Flynn's belief in the system failed. There just didn't seem to be a point to anything anymore. He knew that this attitude, this inability to find purpose in his daily routine, was a sign of depression, but knowing it did not restore any sense of meaning to his life.

It was true what some folks said: When your kid is a failure, your life has been a failure, too.

Still, he continued to go to work. He had bills and real estate taxes, and the responsibility of maintaining employment for Isaac and his crew, who had families they were supporting here and family members they took care of in Central America as well. "It" hadn't worked out for Flynn, but that didn't mean these men and their loved ones had to suffer, too.

And then there was Amanda. Flynn loved her deeply, though he often spoke to her dismissively and they were no longer the friends they had once been. They communicated, and occasionally they came together in bed, but for Flynn the dying of their friendship was the most awful result of the troubles with Chris.

"I got a call from the superintendent," said Bob Moskowitz.

"Yeah?" said Flynn. "What'd he have to say?"

Flynn and Moskowitz were at the bar of the Chevy Chase Lounge on Connecticut Avenue, Flynn's neighborhood local. Flynn was drinking a Budweiser. Moskowitz was kidding himself with a Bud Light.

"He said that Amanda has been calling him fairly frequently."

"And what, he doesn't like it?"

"Colvin's a good guy. But he's got, like, two hundred and seventy-five boys he's responsible for in that facility."

"He's busy."

"Yes. The thing is, Amanda's not calling him with any significant problems or queries. After visitation, she calls Colvin and says stuff like 'I saw Chris and he looked a little thin,' or 'Chris sounded congested.' I mean, they're feeding them out there, Tom. If those boys get sick, they care for them. Guarantee it."

"You're saying Amanda has to stop with the bullshit calls."

"They're not going to release Chris just to get his mom off their back. And it's not helping his case."

"Colvin and them aren't used to parents who give a shit."

"They aren't used to parents who nitpick everything," said Moskowitz. "I understand she's scared for Chris. Outraged, too. But I think she needs to, you know, deal with this in a more internal way."

"Okay. I'll talk to her." Flynn had a pull off his beer and placed the bottle back on the stick. "Did Colvin say how Chris is doing? Or did he just phone you to crap on my wife?"

"Colvin's all right. And Chris is doing okay, too. Maybe too resigned to his incarceration, if you know what I mean."

"I do."

"He doesn't seem to care one way or another about his situation, and that's problematic, because he's got a level meeting coming up. I'm going to advise him to, like, sit up straight in his chair. Tell the review board that he recognizes and regrets his mistakes and that he wants to better himself. That he *will* better himself and is looking forward to the day he'll be released."

"That's good, Bob."

"You could do the same when you see him next."

"He doesn't really speak to me much. Mostly he communicates with his mom."

"I'm saying, you could speak to *him*."

"Right," said Flynn.

Speak to him. That's what the shrink, Dr. Peterman, said in their weekly meeting. And Flynn would nod and say, "You're right. I should try."

Dr. Peterman's office was in Tenleytown, on the corner of Brandywine and Wisconsin, over a beauty parlor, where Mitchell's, the sporting-goods store where as a teenager Flynn had bought his Adidas Superstars, used to be. Flynn wondered if the high rent was added into his tab. Like many men, Flynn did not care to talk about himself or, God forbid, his feelings. He continued to go to their sessions because it made Amanda happy, but as a concession he made sure that he complained about the impending visit on the drive to the man's office. Predictably, he called the shrink "Dr. Peterhead" when speaking of him around Amanda, and brought up more than once the fact that the doctor had a copy of *I'm Okay, You're Okay* displayed on the bookshelf behind his desk. "What," said Flynn, "is that the fountain of knowledge from which Dr. Peterhead drinks?" And Amanda would say, "Please don't be sarcastic when we get there, Tommy."

Flynn was polite in the man's presence, and not unduly sarcastic. Dr. Peterman was a pleasant young guy with a prematurely receding hairline, seemed pretty normal for a head doctor, and not overly analytical or mommy obsessed. Flynn looked around the office, at the usual pedestrian watercolors hung on the wall, at the beanbag chairs for those who liked to get comfy on the floor, at the self-help books on the bookshelf, at *that* book, and he was silently amused.

One day Dr. Peterman set up an easel and on it was a poster showing an imaging photograph of a brain shot from several angles. The man liked his props. The doctor pointed at a section of the brain, seen from a bird's-eye view, that was colored green.

"What are we looking at?" said Dr. Peterman.

"From that overhead angle?" said Flynn. "It looks like a set of nuts."

"Thomas."

Dr. Peterman smiled charitably. "You're looking at a brain, of course. Specifically, the brain of a sixteen-year-old boy. This area in green is the limbic system, which regulates emotion. You can see that it is dominant in terms of geography. Now this blue area, representing the prefrontal cortex, is for reasoning. You can see that it's much smaller. That's because it develops more slowly than the limbic system." Dr. Peterman removed the poster to reveal another poster beneath it with similar imaging photographs. "Now, here is the brain of the same boy, but the photos were taken several years later. The boy is now a man in his twenties. And you can see here that the blue and green areas are represented equitably, more or less. Reasoning has, in effect, caught up with emotion."

"The kid matured," said Flynn.

"In layman's terms, yes. Teenage boys act with emotion more frequently than they do with reason. There's a physiological reason for that."

"But this thing with the brain must be true for all boys," said Flynn.

"I know what you're getting at. Why does someone like Chris find so much trouble and another boy find none at all?"

"Environment," said Amanda.

"Right," said Flynn. "But why Chris? You could understand some kid born into poverty, who comes from a broken home, who's around thugs and drug dealers; I mean, that kid's got problems coming out of the gate. You might not *excuse* it, but you can understand why a young man like that finds trouble. But a boy like Chris . . . why?"

"That's one of the things we're here to talk about. But I bring it up to show you that this is not a permanent state of mind for your son. It's going to improve."

Amanda reached over and squeezed Flynn's hand. The doctor had made her feel better, and Flynn supposed that in this regard, the session had been worthwhile.

THE HOLIDAYS came and were difficult. Then New Year's Eve, the turn of the century, which was supposed to be the biggest party of their lifetimes but which they did not celebrate, and then a return to routine. Low interest rates had encouraged folks to buy homes or take out second mortgages and remodel, which was good for Flynn's business. He and Amanda were kept busy, and Flynn's crew had steady work. The greater profit they experienced, however, was offset by the extreme increases in Flynn's insurance rates. As Moskowitz had predicted, Flynn had been the target of civil suits. The settlements, in total, had been costly.

Amanda visited Chris weekly, sometimes with Flynn, sometimes alone. She thought Chris had grown more receptive to their visits, but Flynn found him sullen and unchanged. On joint visits, it was Amanda who generated conversation and kept things moving along. Chris and Flynn continued to keep each other at arm's length.

Chris had advanced several levels since he had arrived at Pine Ridge. The monthly level meetings consisted of a kind of informal review where the opinions and testimony of administrators and guards came into play. An inmate was required to achieve Level 6 before he would be considered for release. Chris was now at Level 4. His progress was encouraging to Amanda, and the news of it seemed to brighten her outlook. To Flynn, she looked younger than she had in a long while.

Thomas and Amanda continued to see Dr. Peterman. One cool day in late March they made the familiar drive to his office, complete with Flynn's running commentary on Dr. Peterhead, the watercolors, the books in his office, and his fees. Amanda did not mind. She was just happy that Flynn was cooperative and coming along.

As he did with every visit, the doctor returned to the issue of the gulf between father and son. For his part, Flynn contended that Amanda was too soft on Chris. Flynn said that while he disagreed with her, he understood Amanda's approach and that someone, he supposed, had to continue to nurture their son, but he could not bring himself to do it. Eventually he admitted that he was too wounded by Chris's attitude and actions to speak to him in a loving way. And then, perhaps because he was embarrassed by this admission, Flynn claimed that his hardline stance was part of a larger strategy.

"Somebody's got to show him the iron fist," said Flynn. "Let him know that what he's done has been unacceptable. Amanda can be the one to pour juice into his sippy cup and give him hugs."

"Oh, please," said Amanda.

"I'm saying, you've got your role, Amanda, and I've got mine."

"Why don't you switch roles?" said Dr. Peterman. "Amanda can adapt a bit of a tougher stance and you can do the nurturing."

"What," said Flynn, "you want me to wear a skirt?"

Dr. Peterman smirked nervously and blushed a little. "Well, I wouldn't put it quite that way."

Flynn looked at his watch. A quiet settled in the office and they all knew the session was done.

Flynn and Amanda walked over to the Dancing Crab and had lunch and a few beers. Amanda called Flynn a Neanderthal but laughed about his comments in Dr. Peterman's office, and in her eyes he saw light and youth. That afternoon, they made love in the quiet of their bedroom. She fell asleep as the sun streamed in through the parted curtains. Flynn stepped over their Lab, Darby, who was sprawled out and napping on his cushion, and got dressed and left the house.

He drove down Bingham Drive into Rock Creek Park and stopped at a turnoff lot, where he cut the engine, his van facing the water. He and Amanda had come here one day as teenagers after they had eaten mushrooms from a plastic bag. Their spot was a beach of fine pebbles and sand, and they had lain down upon it. Tommy Flynn had taken Amanda's shoes off and massaged the balls of her feet and her toes, and as the psilocybin kicked in, they laughed without reason and uncontrollably for what seemed like a long time. Flynn could barely imagine having so little responsibility again, so little weight on his shoulders. To look up and see no clouds blocking the sun.

I'm just disappointed, thought Flynn. *That's all it is. I've been a failure as a father, and there's nothing ahead of me that looks promising or new.*

In one of their sessions, Dr. Peterman had looked straight at him and said, "Why do *you* think Chris has gone down this road, Thomas?" And: "Is it possible that Chris was trying to please you or emulate you in some way? By your admission, you were a pretty tough kid. Did Chris feel he had to be that way, too, in order to garner your respect and your love?"

Flynn had taken no offense. Peterman was smart and he was onto something. The doctor *knew*.

Flynn tried to think on his early years with his son. How he had continually emphasized the physical over the intellectual with Chris. John Wayned him up with instructions to never show weakness and "step aside for no man." He had taught his son how to fight but never shown him the value in walking away from one.

Pivot your hip, Chris. Aim for two feet behind your target and punch through till you get there. If you're going to throw it, make sure it counts.

While other fathers were reading books to their sons and pointing out countries on the globe, Flynn was showing Chris how to shoot a gun in the woods and teaching him the police ten codes. It became a kind of shorthand between them. Chris would fall down and scrape his knee, and he would reassure his father that he was 10-4. Or Chris would call his father on the car phone, wondering where he was, and ask, "What's your ten-twenty?" The code 10-7 meant out of service, but Chris learned from Flynn that to cops it also meant dead. So when Flynn buried Chris's deceased hamster in the backyard, Chris said, "Mr. Louie is ten-seven."

Flynn had taught his son that an off-the-ten code for an officer in serious trouble was a Signal 13. In elementary school, when Chris was just beginning to act up, he would come home and tell his father that he had been sent to the office, but that the offense was minor and nothing to worry about.

"It was no Signal Thirteen, Dad."

"That's good, Chris," said Flynn with a smile.

The boy had spirit and fire, character traits that annoyed teachers but would serve Chris well as an adult. That's what Flynn had always believed. But in this, and in everything else pertaining to the raising of his son, he now felt that he'd been wrong. Chris had been headed for serious trouble for a long time, and Flynn had missed the signals. It was as if he had been watching his kid drive a car, in slow motion, straight into a brick wall. Watching it, letting it happen, without so much as a shouted warning.

It's not Amanda's fault that Chris is what he is. It's mine.

Speak to him.

I should try.

SEVEN

"How's it going?" said Thomas Flynn.

"It's goin all right," said Chris.

Chris had just seated himself at the table across from Flynn. Chris's eyes were cool and he sat low in his chair.

"Where's Mom at?"

"She wanted to come."

"Why didn't she?"

"I talked her into staying home today. Thought it might be good for you and me to see each other alone."

Chris sat back and crossed his arms. "What are we supposed to do now?"

"Talk, I guess."

Chris looked around the room. A couple of other boys, one in a black polo, one in a forest green, were being visited as well. The boy in black had a male visitor. Chris took mental note of this because it was rare. He returned his attention to his father.

"I'm not trying to be hurtful," said Chris. "But, really, I don't have all that much to say."

"You say things to Mom."

"Honestly? Mom doesn't tell me to shut the fuck up. Mom never called me a piece of shit."

"I shouldn't have said those things," said Flynn. "I was wrong."

"How did you expect me to respond to that, Dad?"

"I didn't think it through."

"It sure didn't make me want to change the way I was."

"I know it."

"It didn't make me want to put my arm around you or get on my knees and beg you to forgive me. It just made me feel nothing. It was like you weren't trying to be my father anymore and you didn't want me as your son. I felt like, *so be it*. You know?"

"Yes, I do," said Flynn. He looked down at his hands, tented on the table. "I took everything that happened . . . I took it too personally, I guess. I let my emotions get the better of me."

"So what you tryin to tell me now?"

What are *you trying to tell me?* thought Flynn. He bit down on his lower lip. "I'm trying to tell you that I'm sorry about the way I reacted."

Chris did not comment. A silence settled between them.

"Your mother said you called her last week."

"Yeah?"

"I'm saying, she was pleasantly surprised. Normally you don't call us at home."

"They only give me ten minutes a week on the phone. Before, I was using that time to call my friends."

"Why'd you change up?"

"My friends stopped taking my calls."

"Jason, too?"

"I haven't spoke to Country in a long time."

"What about your girlfriend?"

Chris shrugged and shook his head. But Flynn could see that he was wounded.

"You'll make new friends," said Flynn.

"I got friends in here."

"That's good, Chris. But I'm saying, when you get out, it'll be a new start. New friends, everything."

Chris looked away.

Flynn breathed out slowly and said, "Mom told me you're doing well in school."

"I'm gonna graduate. A real high school degree, not some GED."

"Excellent. With a degree in hand you could test into a community college."

"That's not gonna happen."

"What, then? What will you do?"

"Work, I guess. I don't know."

Flynn used one hand to crack the knuckles of the other.

"Don't get frustrated, Dad."

"I just don't want you to make that kind of crucial decision without thinking about it."

"I don't want to go to college. You didn't go, and you turned out all right."

"*Don't* . . . don't compare yourself to me. Back in my day, with only a high school degree, you could still make something of yourself. But now there are two distinct societies, Chris, plainly separated. The educated and the uneducated. You don't just go to college to learn. You go to mingle and forge a permanent network with people who all move up the chain together. Don't go to college and there's going to be a ceiling on your earnings. The pool will be limited on who you date and marry. Not only will you probably live in a lower-income neighborhood, but so will your children, and their peers will be lower income, too. Don't you see how it works? There are people who strive to make it to the upper level of society and then there are the other people who stay down below."

"It was you who was always cracking on the lawyers and doctors in our neighborhood. Saying how they came from privilege and money, and how they had a leg up. Being all sarcastic about how they never got their hands dirty or broke a sweat. Like how you sweated every day."

"Chris—"

"You don't want me to be like you?"

"You're not listening to me."

"I guess I'm just one of those other people. The ones who stay down below."

"God*damn* it, Chris."

"Anyway. All this talk about the future? It doesn't mean nothin to me. I mean, I'm in *here*. This is what I got to deal with now." Chris swept his arm around the room as if he were showing his father something grand. He pushed his chair back and stood away from the table. "Thanks for coming by. Tell Mom I was askin about her, hear?"

Flynn put his hand on his son's forearm and held him a bit too hard. He knew that he should tell Chris he loved him and that now was the time. He tried to say the words but he could not.

"Sir?" said the guard on duty. "There's no physical contact allowed."

Chris pulled his arm free. He stared at his father for a moment, then made a chin motion to the guard, who let him out the door of the visitation room. Flynn watched his son walk back into jail.

* * *

THE BOYS were sitting around in the common room on a cold night in early spring, cracking on one another, talking random shit, and killing time until lights-out. None of them were anxious to go to their cells, where a few would study, fewer would read books for pleasure, many others would masturbate, and most would simply go to sleep as their bodies wound down and the shield they felt they had to carry fell away. Though cell time was the one truly quiet, introspective time of their day, it was also the loneliest, and the most difficult to face.

Ali Carter and Chris Flynn were seated on the couch, and Ben Braswell was in the fake-leather chair with the rivets in the arms. Luther Moore and Lonnie Wilson were playing Ping-Pong. Lattimer, the old graybeard guard they called Shawshank, was in a hard-back chair too small for him. The boys liked him well enough for what he was, but they would not defer to him and give up a seat more suited to his age, size, and authority.

They could hear Lawrence Newhouse in the media room, arguing with a boy, trying to get time on the computer, an old, slow machine with a blinking cursor that sat next to a dot matrix printer. Lawrence's tone was becoming more threatening by the sentence, but Lattimer was not moving from his chair.

"You better get in there, Shawshank," said Luther. "Lawrence sound like he ready to blow."

"Scott's in there," said Lattimer. Scott Stewart, a fellow guard, was built like a Minotaur. "He can handle it."

"Scott's swole," said Ben.

"They need to get Bughouse out this unit," said Ali. "Put him in Unit Twelve."

"He ain't that kind of bad," said Lattimer. "Lawrence just be talkin, mostly."

"Either get him out or put me somewhere else," said Ali. " 'Cause I cannot stand to be around that fool anymore."

"Won't be long till you're gone anyway, young man," said Lattimer, trying to make eye contact with Ali. "Stay focused on those books and walk that straight line. You keep doing what you been doing, you'll be all right."

"They can put *me* somewhere else," said Lonnie Wilson, laying down his paddle, signaling to Luther that their game of table tennis was done. Both of them came to join the group but remained standing, as no one was about to move over and make room for them to sit.

"Where you want to go?" said Ben.

"Unit Six," said Lonnie, running a hand across the crotch of his khakis. "What you think?"

Lattimer rolled his eyes. Unit 6 was the girls' building, out in the woods somewhere, out of sight from the boys' camp. It was on Pine Ridge acreage, surrounded by its own razor wire–topped fence. The conversation was about to go where it usually went this time of night.

"Boy," said Lonnie, "I would punish the *shit* out them girls in Unit Six. I would be like a bull in one of them Chinese shops."

"Don't be runnin your fingers through their hair, though," said Luther.

"I know it," said Lonnie.

"They put razor blades in their braids!" said Luther.

"You don't know nothin, Luther," said Ali.

"I know enough not to touch their braids."

"It's a lot of gray girls they got out there, too," said Lonnie.

"White Boy would like it out in Unit Six," said Luther, and Chris felt warmth in his face.

"Them pale skins are runaways and hos, mostly," said Lonnie. "But I got love for all the girls. I don't care what they did to get locked up or what color their skin is. Shoot, I'll even get with a Mexican. They pink to me, too."

"What about, like, Asia girls?" said Luther.

"*'Specially* them. I'm all about equal opportunity."

"If they got to squat to pee, you gonna take the opportunity," said Luther, and he and Lonnie Wilson smiled and dapped each other up.

"Do they let those girls have dogs out there, Shawshank?" said Ben.

"Hell, no," said Lattimer.

"Warden Colvin said we might get puppies," said Ben.

"For real?" said Chris. He missed Darby.

"I saw Colvin today and he said we might. Every unit could have their own."

"We could have us a pit," said Luther. "Or a rot with a head big as a horse. Five would have a fierce-ass dog."

"Nah," said Ben. "It wouldn't be a dog we'd use to fight. It would be like a pet."

"Ya'll ain't getting *no* kind of dog," said Lattimer. "Some of these boys in here, they'd torture those poor animals. And a lot of you are allergic to dogs and don't even know it. You'd be surprised how many."

"'Nother words, your people gonna try to stop it," said Ali, looking hard at Lattimer.

"They'd be *right* to stop it. It's not in my contract to pick up dog shit."

"It's not about dog shit," said Ali. "It's about keeping us low. Any time the superintendent try to do somethin nice for us, the guard union blocks him."

"That's not true."

"Sure it is. You know it, too."

"You're a smart young man," said Lattimer. "So I'm gonna tell you something, because I believe you can understand it. This ain't no country club out here. Y'all are here for a reason. You've done wrong and now you here to learn and be reformed. You know what re-formed means? It means you were one thing, and then you get formed into something new. What the superintendent don't seem to understand is, you boys need to learn consequences, not get rewarded for what you done. And that means you don't get served ice cream sundaes after dinner or get to talk to fine young women during your reading class. And you sure don't get the right to have no pets. You see your way out of here? You can eat all the ice cream and have all the women and dogs you want. That's what law-abiding citizens get to do. But you ain't that. Not yet. You got to *earn* that."

A crashing sound came from the media room, and all turned their heads. Lawrence Newhouse was cursing, and struggling from the sound of it, and though they did not say it, the boys assumed his conflict was with the big guard, Scott. And then Lawrence came airborne out of the media room, with Scott moving strong toward him, and Lawrence was falling, and before he hit the ground Scott had grabbed his shirt and lifted him back up to give him more of what he'd already had. Scott threw him against a wall of shellacked cinder block. His face hit it pretty hard. Scott put Lawrence's right arm behind his back and twisted it up, getting control of the young man.

"Boy, you just had to get on my last nerve," said Scott, and he began to push Lawrence out toward the cells.

Most of the boys had lowered their eyes. None of them liked Lawrence, but when the guards won, it was like they had been robbed of a piece of their manhood, too.

As Lawrence passed he looked at Ali, who had not looked away, and said, "What the fuck you staring at, Holly?"

Ali said nothing. Lawrence spit a mouthful of blood in the direction of Ali and Chris. Scott hustled him down the hall.

"Bughouse always be tweakin," said Luther Moore.

"That boy just angry," said Lattimer.

Ben Braswell looked at Chris. "You think we might get a puppy, man?"

"We might," said Chris, though he knew Ali was correct. The guards' arm of the FOP union, which tended to fight any reforms the superintendent proposed, would find a way to stop the boys from having pets.

"You got a dog at home, right?" said Ben.

"Yeah," said Chris.

"You're *lucky*," said Ben. Chris could feel Ali's knowing stare but did not look his way.

"Time for y'all to get to your bedrooms," said Lattimer.

The boys got up from their seats without objection and headed to their cells.

As they walked, they could hear the old man still speaking to them, giving them his parting words of inspiration. "Another good day for you fellas. Another day closer to your goal. You get right with God, you gonna get right with yourselves."

The boys went down the narrow hall, where Lattimer would wait until they entered their six-by-nine spaces, then use his Joliet key to lock the steel doors behind them. From his own cell, Lawrence Newhouse was alternately screaming and laughing. His anguished wail echoed in the hall.

"Ain't no God in here," said Ali.

Chris walked into his cell.

THE NEXT day, while Chris and Ali were walking in the hall between classes, Ali took a fist in the back of the head, for no apparent reason, from a boy named Maximus Dukes. Ali tripped and fell to the floor, severing the bridge of his glasses. Without even thinking of himself, Chris was on Maximus, throwing him up against the wall and delivering several body blows and one solid uppercut to the jaw before Maximus could return fire. He was a big boy and Chris's rain had not hurt him, and he came back strong. Chris took a glancing temple shot and one deep right to the solar plexus that blew half the wind out of him, but he kept his feet, and several more punches were thrown before the guards charged in and stopped the fight. It had been meaningless, and there was no rancor between any of them again. Because neither Chris nor Maximus had gone down, their reps had been elevated. The fight cost Chris his Level 5, but he would achieve it at a later date.

Of the many things Chris learned at Pine Ridge, one would be embedded in his mind for years after his release: When you or one of your own is attacked, retaliation is mandatory, no matter the consequences or repercussions. It has to be on.

The guards had seen Maximus blind-punch Ali. Wasn't any need for Chris to step in. But it wouldn't have been as satisfying to see the guards strong-arm Maximus and lead him down the hall. When Chris swung on the boy, his blood got up in a righteous way, and he felt like a man. He wished his father had been there to see that he'd stood tall.

EIGHT

FOR SECURITY reasons, doors had been removed in the bath-room stalls, so the boys voided their bowels in full view of the other inmates. It was something Chris had to get used to quickly. Let it bother you, you'd have to hold your shits till you got back in your cell. That wasn't natural, and no one liked to stink up their rooms.

On the same level of indignity was the morning ritual of group showers. There were no privacy curtains or barriers of any kind, and if someone was modest or ashamed, he had to get over it, that is if he wanted to be clean. The open area was meant to discourage violence, and perhaps it had been a wise idea, as there were rarely serious altercations in the showers. The best Chris could say about the experience was that it was fast. If you lingered in the shower more than a little bit, the tepid water would go cold.

Chris and the other boys did not worry about nonconsen-sual homosexuality in the showers or anywhere else inside the walls. It was the most dreaded aspect of prison for a boy on the outside looking in, but the truth was, oral and anal rape were extremely rare at Pine Ridge. The boys in juvenile had not yet gone to that level of degradation that occurred in adult male prisons. There were scattered consensual homosexual relations here, but, somewhat surprisingly, it was not an issue of derision among the boys who were straight. They knew who among them had gone that way, but didn't berate them to their faces or, for the most part, behind their backs. Those boys were just as tough as the other boys, and no one was going out of their way to find a fight.

What took away their dignity was the presence of the guards, who watched the boys shower though a Plexiglas window. The fact that they, fully clothed and outfitted with security gear, could stare at the inmates, naked and completely vulnerable, seemed wrong. Thing of it was, you didn't know what they were thinking while they were looking at you. Chris was reminded of that one summer when his mother had persuaded his father to vacation with a wealthy neighborhood family, the Rubinos, who had invited them to their house on Martha's Vineyard. The house was steps away from a nude beach, and from the start, even though the Flynns had been assured that they did not have to "participate," his father had been annoyed. Many families went naked, including their prepubescent sons and daughters, and there were also grown men on the same beach, naked and alone, and Thomas Flynn said, "Why would a father let his little boy or girl go nude in front of those men? You don't know what's going on behind their sunglasses." Amanda had said, "Don't be rude, honey; we're guests here," and his dad muttered something about "bored rich people" and left it at that. That was their first and last vacation with the Rubinos. Years later, when Steve Rubino cashed out of his law firm and left his wife and kids for a twenty-two-year-old GW student, Thomas Flynn said, "You know what Rubino was doing up on that beach? He was *shopping*. I told you that guy wasn't right."

Chris smiled, thinking of his old man. They had a word for the way he was. Crum-something. Always complaining but doing it in a funny way.

"What you grinnin on, White Boy?" said Lawrence Newhouse, standing beside Chris in the shower.

Chris shrugged, giving Lawrence nothing.

"Thinkin about your home?" said Lawrence. "Bet you got a nice one. A real nice family, too."

Chris recognized the mention of his family as some kind of threat, but it had no weight or meaning. For a moment, but only for a moment, he thought, *Bughouse is right*. But to let himself dwell on what he'd had, and on his mistakes, was not productive. He was here now, and it didn't matter where he'd come from; he was the same as everyone else inside Pine Ridge. Locked up and low.

"Why you never speak to me, man?" said Lawrence. "You too good?"

Chris did not answer. He stepped out of the spray and reached for a towel smelling of body odor that hung on a plastic knob.

"We gonna talk, *Christina*," said Lawrence.

Chris dried himself off and walked away.

A MAN who had done time at Lorton, and who had written poetry there and eventually a series of popular street-lit message novels aimed at juveniles, came to speak to the inmates of Pine Ridge late in April. The residents of Unit 5, wearing maroon, and Unit 8, wearing gray, were ushered into the auditorium, having walked from the school building through a cold rain.

Many of them were soaked and shivering as they sat in their too-small chairs and half-listened to the speaker, who started his talk with the usual I-came-from-the-same-streets-as-you, I-made-it-and-you-can-too platitudes that went through them faster than the greasy Chinese food they used to eat in the neighborhoods they'd come up in.

Ali Carter and Chris Flynn sat in the row of chairs farthest back in the room. Ali was wearing his glasses, a piece of surgical tape holding them together at the bridge, and a kufi skull cap, finely knitted. The cap was allowed for religious reasons, despite the facility's no-hat policy. Ali had confessed to Chris that he had been named by his mother after the boxer and held no Muslim beliefs. He wore the skull cap just to mess with the guards, who didn't like the boys asserting their individuality, and to take a minor victory where he could.

"When I wrote *Payback Time*," said the writer, whose nom de plume was J. Paul Sampson, "I was thinking of young men just like you. Because I was once where you are now, and I understand that revenge is a natural impulse. I understand that you *think* it's going to make you feel good."

"Not as good as gettin a nut," said Lonnie Wilson from somewhere in the crowd, and a few of the boys laughed.

J. Paul Sampson, immaculate in a custom-tailored suit, plowed on. "But revenge, my young brothers, is a dead-end street."

Ben Braswell was a row ahead, seated among gray shirts. He was listening to the book writer and nodding his head. In the front row sat Lawrence Newhouse, defiantly slumped in his chair, arms crossed. A half-dozen guards, including Lattimer, and a few teachers, including the school's earnest, bearded young English teacher, Mr. McNamara, were standing around the perimeter.

"Where I was," said J. Paul Sampson, "in lockup? It was full of men who felt they'd been disrespected, and because of that, they acted on impulse and got violent. With the passage of time, as the years went by in prison, they couldn't even tell you why they'd killed. Because what they did was unreasonable. You know what that means, don't you, gentlemen? There was no *reason*."

In one of the rows ahead, a young man in a gray polo shirt had turned his chair slightly so that he could look to the back of the room. His gaze was focused steadily on Ali.

"Why's that dude eye-fuckin you?" said Chris, keeping his voice low.

"Calvin Cooke," said Ali, leaning in close to Chris. "Boy's from Langdon Park, over there off Rhode Island Avenue. It's a Northeast-Southeast thing. I guess he feel the need to stare."

"So?"

"He just bein unreasonable," said Ali with a small smile.

Ali often got singled out for intimidation because of his short stature and, due to his eyeglasses, his studious appearance. Some called him Urkel as he passed. The ones who said nothing had taken note of his big chest.

"I'm here to tell you that the life I have now is better than the one I had," said J. Paul Sampson. "I made a choice when I got out of prison, and I'm a successful and productive member of society today. You can make the same kind of choice."

Luther raised his hand. "Do you get paid?"

J. Paul Sampson chuckled nervously. "Yes, of course."

"Do you get pussy?" said another boy, and the auditorium erupted with laughter. A guard pulled that boy roughly out of his chair and led him from the room.

"Show respect to Mr. Sampson," said the English teacher, McNamara. "He took valuable time out of his day to come here and talk to you. Listen to what he has to say."

There were murmurs in the room, and the boys' posture slackened further.

"I got a question," said Lattimer, stepping forward from the back of the room. "I knew you were coming to speak, so I read one of your books. You know that one, *Brothers in Blood*?"

"Yes?"

"The boy in that book is bad, almost all the way through. He's in a crew, he gives other kids beat downs, he drops out of school. To him, all the authority figures, including the police, is hypocrites and fools. Then in the last chapter, the boy comes to his senses and turns his self around."

"That's right. The message is, you can make many mistakes, but it's never too late to change."

"See," said Lattimer, "I kinda figured out what you're doing. What they call the formula. You're getting kids all jacked up on one hundred and eighty pages of violence and disrespect, and then you add ten pages of redemption in the end that they not even gonna read. What I'd like to see is a whole book about a kid who doesn't do any wrong at all. Who stays on the straight even though he may be living in a bad environment, because that's the right thing to do. Because he knows the *consequences* of being wrong."

Scattered mumblings came from the crowd: "You stupid, Shawshank," and "Why you got to talk?" and "Sit down, Mr. Huxtable."

"I try to tell the truth, sir," said the author amiably. "My books reflect the reality of the street."

"A little more respect for authority is all I'm looking for," said Lattimer. "That's what these boys need to read about and learn."

"I appreciate your comments."

"Got to give Shawshank credit," said Ali, staring at the boy from Langdon Park, who was still staring at him. "Man believe what he believe, and you can't move him off it."

"Shawshank's a rock," said Chris.

Luther raised his hand. "Can I be a book writer, too?"

"You can be whatever you want to be," said J. Paul Sampson. "If there's one thing I want you gentlemen to take away from this today, it's that."

"I want to be one now," said Luther.

"It's a goal to strive for," said J. Paul Sampson, exasperation replacing the fading brightness in his eyes. "But it takes time. Like anything worth having, you need to work for it. Being an author is like having any other job."

"I don't want no job," said Luther. "*Fuck* that."

LAWRENCE NEWHOUSE had been put on heavier meds, rumored to be in the lithium family, and when his behavior improved it became contagious. Unit 5 was more peaceful when Lawrence was subdued, and at times the atmosphere was nearly congenial. There were arguments, but the fire in them died quickly, and people laughed at Luther's dumb jokes and listened patiently to Lonnie Wilson's boasts and three-way fantasies though they had heard them many times before.

Ali and Chris were in the common room one night, Chris sprawled out on the couch. A guard was nearby, but he was sleeping. Many of the boys from the unit were in media, watching television, Joneing on one another, cackling at whatever was onscreen, debating whether the male actors were real or soft, talking about the girl actors and what they'd do to them if they had the chance. Someone was riffing on an actress, twisting her name, predictably, into something obscene, and Ben Braswell was laughing. Also laughing, in baritone, was Scott, the big guard.

"You high?" said Ali, putting the book he was reading down on the floor beside the ripped fake-leather chair where he sat.

"Nah," said Chris. "Just chillin."

"You look like you're high."

"I'm not."

" 'Cause you need to stop doin that shit."

"I *been* stopped," said Chris.

"You know they gonna make you drop a urine. And you got that level meeting comin up. Ben does, too."

"I haven't given Ben any weed," said Chris. "Not for a while."

"That's good. Ben needs to drop a positive so he can get out this piece. Just like you do."

"Ben gets out," said Chris, "he's just gonna steal a car again and come right back in. That's who he is."

"Ben wants y'all to think that. He tells everyone how he was born to hot-wire, how he loves to get behind the wheel of a vehicle, how he can't stop himself, all that. Truth is, it's a crime he can do where he doesn't have to hurt no one. All he wants is to get his self put back inside these walls."

"Why would he want that?"

"Because this is the only place where he feels right. I'm not talkin about that three-hots-and-a-cot bullshit you hear all the time. You notice nobody ever comes to visit him? I mean, we all got *some*one, right? Ben got nobody. His crackhead mother died young and then he got moved to foster homes, and every-where he lived was shit. In here, at least he got friends. In the classroom, he listens, even though he doesn't understand half the stuff the teachers be sayin, and you know he can't read. The fact that anyone notices that boy or calls him by his name is good to him. Bad as it is, this here is his home."

"He can't stay, though."

"No," said Ali. "Neither can you. Won't be long before I'm out, too."

"You're always saying how I don't belong here—"

"You don't."

"What about you? How'd someone smart like you fuck up so bad?"

"Which time?" said Ali.

"I hear you," said Chris, thinking on his many mistakes, how he'd piled them on top of one another without consideration or even a glancing thought.

"The last time, though," said Ali, shaking his head, "with my uncle? That's what got me put away."

"Talkin about the armed-robbery thing."

"Yeah. My mom's half brother, he ain't but five years older than me. He's ignorant and weak, I see it now, but me bein a dumb-ass kid, I looked up to him at the time. He was more like a father to me than an uncle. I'm sayin, when he put his eyes on me, I wanted him to see a man. So when he asked me to come along with him, and told me I had to hold the gun and do the thing, on account of I didn't know how to drive the car, I did it. You think I'm smart and maybe I am. But I wasn't smart that day."

"So now you got yourself a Pine Ridge education. You learned."

"Not the way they wanted, though. They tryin to break us down to nothing, so we can get reborn. But all their commands and speeches don't mean shit to me. I learned on my own. I'm not what they think I am and I'm not gonna be what they expect me to be. Once I'm out, I'm not coming back, but not because of anything they did to me in here. I'm gonna be right because I *want* to be." Ali jabbed a finger at his own chest. "For me."

"Nuff 'a that high-and-mighty talk," said the guard, who had awakened. "You boys need to get to bed."

Later, in his cell, Chris lay atop his scratchy wool blanket with his forearm covering his eyes. The unit grew dead quiet as one by one the boys fell asleep. Chris was not tired. His head was full of contemplation and, for once, regret. He sat up on the edge of his cot.

Chris stood and went to the wall where he'd taped Taylor Dugan's drawing. He looked at his image, shirtless, eyebrow arched, mouth in a bold smile, his hand holding a beer, and it did not make him feel proud or amused.

Bad Chris. He was not sure who he was, but he was certain that he was no longer the boy in the drawing. Nor did he wish to be.

Chris peeled the paper off the wall, ripped it apart, and dropped the pieces in the trash. He went back to bed and fell asleep.

NINE

ON A cool, cloudy Saturday in May, a three-on-three basket-ball game was in progress on the asphalt court out in the middle of Pine Ridge's muddy field. Chris Flynn, Ali Carter, and Ben Braswell were in maroon, up against Calvin Cooke, Milton "the Monster" Dickerson, and Lamar Brooks, all wearing gray. Lawrence Newhouse stood out of bounds, as did a boy named Clarence Wheeler, wearing navy blue. They had called next and would choose one from the losers of this game to round out their team. A rotund guard, Mr. Green, stood on a weedy patch of dirt, observing, a two-way radio in hand.

Chris had the ball up top. He was being covered by Lamar Brooks, a quiet boy who had no offense but whose darting hands were quick. Lamar was trying to slap the ball away, but Chris had turned his hip and was protecting the pill. Down below, Ben had boxed out Milton, a kid in on multiple drug charges, who was Ben's size. Ben had his hand up and was calling for the ball.

Out beyond the imaginary three stood Ali, loosely matched with Calvin Cooke, the Langdon Park boy who had lately been mugging and shoulder-brushing him in the auditorium and cafeteria. Cooke wore his hair in small twists and had flat eyes

91

and a smile of pain. He was in on a firearm conviction, having beaten a murder charge in court. The prosecution's witness, too frightened to testify, had muted up on the stand.

Chris faked a chest pass to Ali, then bounced one around Lamar and in to Ben, who caught it, turned, and hooked it up. On a normal hoop it would have dropped, but this iron granted no favors, and the ball bounced off the back of the rim. Ben threw his ass out on Milton, got his own rebound, and passed it to Ali. Ali was the shortest man on the court but had the greatest vertical leap. He went up, way over the outstretched hand of Calvin, and put one through the chains.

"All right," said Chris.

"You gonna play defense on that retard?" said Calvin to Milton. "Or you gonna let him pick apart your candy ass?"

"Wasn't my man made that bucket," said Milton.

"Mini Me lucky," said Calvin.

Chris walked the ball to the top of the key and looked at Lamar.

"Checked," said Lamar.

Chris bounced the ball over to Ali. Chris clapped, and Ali tossed it back. Lamar was three feet away, playing him loose, so Chris went up and gunned it. From out here, he knew it had to be all net or a kiss off the backboard. It felt right as it left his fingers, and the chains danced.

"Splash," said Ben.

"Luck," said Calvin. "None 'a these bitches can play."

"Six-nothin," said Ali, and Ben grinned.

Mr. Green's radio crackled. He listened to its message and his face told the boys that it was urgent. He said, "Copy that," and turned to the inmates. "Ya'll play on. I got an emergency situation I got to attend to. I'm gonna be right back, hear?"

The boys watched the overweight guard jog laboriously

across the field toward one of the unit buildings. They could see heightened activity there. Guards streaming in, a guard posted at the door. It meant that there had been some kind of violence.

"Now that Tubby the Tuba gone," said Calvin, "we can play for real."

"Look to me like they *been* playin," said Lawrence Newhouse.

"I ask you somethin?" said Calvin. "Take a pill and dream you a man, Bughouse."

Lawrence, his eyes glassy from his meds, smiled at Calvin Cooke. A wind came up and whipped at the boys' shirts and cooled their sweat.

"Ball up top," said Chris.

"Checked," said Lamar.

"Cover that Gump," said Calvin to Milton.

"I got him. Get your mans, too."

"He too scared to come inside," said Calvin.

Chris dribbled and faked a move to the left. In his side vision he saw Ali slashing into the lane and he put English on the rock and bounced it in. Ali took it and put the ball down on the asphalt and made his move, driving toward the basket with Calvin in front of him. Ali did a jump-step thing and elevated, and as he went up, Calvin threw a forearm into Ali's shoulder. Ali released a shot as he fell back. He landed hard, and the ball clanged off the back of the iron.

"Don't even walk past the front of my house," said Calvin.

Milton pounded his fist. "Eastside."

"Ball," said Chris.

"That wasn't no foul, White Boy," said Calvin. "Your boy flopped like Reggie Miller."

Ben reached down, grasped Ali's hand, and pulled him up off the asphalt.

"You all right?" said Ben.

"I'm straight," said Ali. "Play it."

"See?" said Calvin. "Your own man say that shit was clean."

"Don't matter what Holly say," said Lawrence. "You fouled his ass."

Lamar Brooks quietly stepped off the court. Clarence Wheeler, the boy in the navy blue polo shirt, took a few steps back and separated himself from the group.

"What you say?" said Calvin, stepping up to Lawrence.

"I said you got him. You throwin forearms 'cause you can't fuck with Unit Five."

Calvin smiled. "And you a stone faggot."

"Then *do* somethin," said Lawrence.

Calvin Cooke's right fist whipped out and connected. Lawrence's head snapped back and he lost his legs and dropped to the ground.

Calvin grunted with effort as he kicked Lawrence in the ribs. He pulled back his foot to kick him again.

"Don't," said Ben, moving quickly and wrapping his arms around Calvin from behind. Calvin struggled wildly in his grasp. Ben lifted him off his feet. "Don't!" he said in an imploring way.

Milton Dickerson charged Ben, and Chris stepped in front of him. Dickerson hit Chris like a nose tackle, and it knocked the wind from both of them as they went down.

Chris broke free and rolled away. He caught his breath and got to his feet.

Ben had Calvin in a hug and was swinging him, attempting to gain some kind of control but stumbling back.

Ali shouted, "Let him go, Ben!"

Ben whipped Calvin around, and Calvin's head caught the steel pole of the backboard. When it hit, it sounded like a bell.

Ben released him.

Calvin fell to the ground, landed on his back, and for a moment was motionless. Blood began to flow from one of his ears and bubbly saliva poured out the side of his mouth. His eyes were open and crossed, and his body began to spasm.

"Help," said Ben, horrified, his voice soft and low.

Several guards ran across the field toward them. Chris looked at Ali, and Ali lowered his eyes and shook his head.

Chris lay down on his stomach and waited. He felt his arm twist up violently behind him. He felt a knee grind into his back.

IT SEEMED as if it took a long time for the emergency medical technicians to arrive. When they came, the ambulance driver drove the vehicle very slowly across the muddy field, as if he were wary of getting stuck. The boys were being led toward the guards' building then, and they watched the ambo pass.

They were taken to separate rooms and interrogated by Pine Ridge authorities and police. Warden Colvin and a visibly agitated Glenn Hill, the director of the Department of Youth Rehabilitation Services, were in attendance. When the interviews were done, Chris and the others were taken to their cells, where their dinners were brought to them. Chris did not touch his food.

They found out later that Calvin Cooke had suffered what one of the guards called "a cerebral hemorrhage caused by trauma." It was said that the slow response time by the emergency people had allowed Calvin's brain to swell up and that was why his condition would not improve.

In a J. Paul Sampson novel, the boys from Calvin's unit would have been out for revenge on the boys of Unit 5. There would have been eye-mugging, shoulder brushes, talk of getback, and maybe another minor tragedy of some kind, but in the last chapter the boys of the two units would have met in another contest on the same court where Calvin got his dome crushed, and the game of basketball would have united them. They would have agreed that revenge was a dead-end street and decided to honor the spirit of Calvin and shake hands and walk away as comrades rather than enemies.

The reality was, no one thought to avenge Calvin. The boys in his unit understood that what happened to him was an accident he'd brought upon himself, the cost of boasting and stepping to someone, and anyway, they never did like him much. Calvin did not return to Pine Ridge, and no one spoke of him. When he died two years later, of infection brought on by bedsores, he had been forgotten.

In his cell, Chris lay on his stomach, his arms dangling over the sides of his cot. On the floor in front of him was an open notebook, a pen resting on a blank white sheet of paper. Chris could hear Ben Braswell, speaking to himself and crying, from his cell down the hall. He could hear the guards out there in the hall, walking back and forth, talking and chuckling, making one another laugh to try and cut the boredom of their suicide watch.

In his mind, Chris saw a spring day down on the Soapstone Valley Trail in Rock Creek Park. Darby galloping clumsily though a carpet of leaves, Chris's mom in a new down vest, a shade of green that was her favorite color. His father swinging out from behind the trunk of a tree, a stick in his hand, making machine gun noises, a lock of black hair fallen across his forehead. Chris jumping from rock to rock across the creek, the sun dancing off the water.

Chris picked up his pen. Across the paper he wrote: "Signal 13."

In his bedroom on Livingston Street, Thomas Flynn woke suddenly, startled from a dream.

PART THREE
SIGNAL 13

TEN

THE JOB was north of Logan Circle and south of U Street, in a section of the city that people in the past had broadly called Shaw, but now got called Logan by many real estate agents and some residents. In midtown the homes were row houses, mostly, some topped with D.C.-signature turrets, all backed by alleys. There were houses here and there whose disrepair went back generations, but the majority had been restored and remodeled, and the general impression was one of transformation.

A white Ford cargo van rolled down U Street, its two occupants in matching blue polo shirts, taking note of the sidewalk parade, people strolling past restaurants, bars, and boutiques. Different skin colors, a mash-up of straight and gay, non-flash money and hipsters, heads, hustlers, and intellectuals, young couples, bike messengers, old folks who remembered the fires of '68, everyone trying this new thing together. It wasn't perfect because nothing is, but down here it seemed as good as Washington had ever been, and for some, it was a dream realized.

To Chris Flynn, it just looked like a nice place to live. But he figured that he would never be able to afford to buy a place in this zip code. Weren't any carpet installers who owned property here. The ones who carried mortgages here, he reckoned, had gone to college.

"Dag, boy, it sure is different than it was," said Ben Braswell, his big frame sprawled on the bench, his arm on the lip of the open passenger window.

"It was the Metro system did it," said Chris, thinking on something his father had once said, explaining the positive changes in the city. "Every place where they opened subway stations, the neighborhoods improved around them. Public transportation got all this shit going again."

"Took, like, twenty-five years to happen."

"Point is, it happened."

"Yo, man, pull over," said Ben, rubbernecking the diner that bore his name. "I need a half-smoke *now*."

"After this job, maybe," said Chris.

"Chili, mustard, onions," said Ben, his gentle eyes gone dreamy. "Sweet tea. Maze on the juke . . ."

"We don't do this installation, we don't get paid."

"How we supposed to work if we don't eat?"

"How you supposed to pay for your half-smoke if you don't work?" said Chris.

"True," said Ben.

Chris was going to have to disappoint him. There wasn't time to stop anywhere because they were already behind. After this install they'd have to drive back out to Beltsville in Maryland to pick up the roll for the next job, then head over to a home in Bethesda to complete it. Ben would understand.

Chris turned left off U into the residential section of the neighborhood. "If we get done quick, we'll have time for lunch."

They found a spot on the street close to the job site. A real estate agent was standing outside the row house, talking on her cell, a look of annoyance on her face as she spotted the van, recognizing the magnetic sign on its side that read "Flynn's Floors."

"Wait here," said Chris. "Let me get up with this woman before we unload."

Chris got out of the van and approached her. She continued to talk on her cell and did not acknowledge him. She was in her midfifties, with a short, spiky, gelled hairdo. She was blond, heavily made up, and had crinkle-bunny lines from age and too much sun. Her petite figure seemed shapeless under her loose, sleeveless purple dress.

The "For Sale" sign mounted on a post behind her had her photograph on it, arms crossed, smiling, with two young people, also smiling, standing behind her. In big letters, the sign said, "Mindy Kramer," and below it, in smaller script, "The Kramer Dream Team."

"I've got to go," said Mindy Kramer into her phone. "They finally got here." She shut the cell's lid with an audible snap and looked at Chris. "You are?"

"Chris." He did not use his last name unless asked.

"I expected you earlier."

"We got hung up on another job—"

"And now I have to leave and meet a client on Capitol Hill. I'll let you in and then I'll come back and lock up when the job is done." She looked past him to Ben, seated in the van, slouched, his blue Nationals W cap worn sideways on his head. "Mr. Flynn said his crews were bonded and insured. I assume that includes you and your partner."

"Yes, ma'am."

"Let's take a look at the room."

She marched up the granite steps that led to the front door. Chris turned to the van and did the darting-tongue thing, and Ben smiled. Chris followed Mindy Kramer into the house.

Chris admired the structure and its craftsmanship as soon as he walked inside. Chair rail molding in the dining room, wide-plank hardwood floors in the center hall, plaster walls. No furniture, though. Whoever once lived here was gone.

"This way." Mindy Kramer cut a right through open French doors.

Chris stepped in, rapping his knuckles on the door frame out of habit and curiosity. As he expected, it was solid wood, not the Masonite he saw in so much new construction. The space was about fourteen by twelve, he guessed, and would be called a library on the listing, as it held a wall of built-in book-shelves. He looked down at the worn carpet that covered the floor.

"It should be a pretty straightforward job," said Mindy Kramer. "I went with the cable. Mr. Flynn said the loop pile would be fine for a medium-traffic space."

"It'll work," said Chris, pulling his Stanley tape measure off the belt line of his Dickies where he kept it clipped. He laid down the tape and measured the length and width of the room, which was close to his estimation, and mentally noted that his father had ordered a larger roll than was needed to do the job. This meant that he hadn't liked Mindy Kramer or that he foresaw complaints from her or multiple post-job visits. When the customer showed arrogance or attitude up front, they tended to pay extra. Chris's father called this the "personality defect tax."

"Is what you brought sufficient?"

"Oh, yeah," said Chris. "It's gonna be fine."

"There's a walnut floor under this carpet, but it needs sanding and refinishing. Nice hardwood is preferable to carpet when you're selling a home, of course, especially to younger clients, but I don't have the time or inclination to go that route. I just want to get some carpet down and bring in a few pieces of furniture here and there so I can flip the property. I bought it at auction for a song. The previous owner was a gay gentleman who had no surviving heirs. . . ."

Chris nodded, trying to keep eye contact with her. All she was doing was bragging on how savvy she had been and how much money she was going to make. Telling a stranger this because she was insecure. He was not impressed.

"We'll get started," said Chris. "It shouldn't take us long."

"Here's my card," said Mindy Kramer, handing him one. "Call me on my cell when you're almost done and I'll shoot back over and give it a look. Tell me your number, Chris."

Chris gave her his cell number. She punched it into the contacts file of her phone and typed in a name.

"I'm going to call you Chris Carpet," she said, proud of her cleverness, "so I can remember who you are when I scan through my contacts."

Whatever, thought Chris. But he said, "That's fine."

Mindy Kramer hit "save" and glanced at her watch. "Any questions?"

"That'll do 'er," said Chris, giving her the redneck inflection that she no doubt expected.

Ben had already slipped his kneepads over his jeans and was tying a leather multipocket tool belt around his waist when Chris emerged from the house. Ben and Chris wore the same type of belts and in their pouches they kept their pro-shop razor knives. As Ben finished tying his belt off, Mindy Kramer got into her C-series and, cell phone to her ear, sped away.

Chris put his pads on, and he and Ben went around to the

back of the van. They untied a red towel from the end of the out-hanging carpet and removed the roll and its sister roll of padding. They carried the carpet inside, came back and got the padding, took it up the steps, and placed it beside the roll they had stowed in the hall. It was hotter in the house than it was outside, and both of them began to perspire. They had done one job already, so it was the second time they were sweating into their polo shirts that day.

"In here," said Chris, and Ben followed him into the library.

Ben sized up the job, liking that there was no furniture to move and that the space was virtually square. "Looks easy."

"Can you take up the old carpet?"

"What, you too busy to help?"

"I gotta check in with my father. I'll only be like a minute. I'm sayin, get started, is all."

Ben commenced taking up the old carpet in the library. He started in a corner as Chris walked from the room and reached into a pocket of his Dickies for his phone. He wandered down the hall to what had been a living room and punched in his father's number.

"Hey," said Thomas Flynn. "Where are you?"

"Down at that job off U Street."

"The Dream Team there, too?"

"Just Mindy. She had to bolt, but she's coming back. We were late gettin down here. That job in Laurel set us back about an hour."

"I'm in the warehouse. My guy says you were late getting *started* this morning."

"A little." Chris was a bit annoyed that his father was still checking up on him so closely. At the same time, he told himself that it was business, only business.

"Ben sleep in again?"

"Wasn't Ben, Dad. We were just a *little* late. We did the job in Laurel quick, but the guy had a problem with the bubbles. I had to talk to him for a while. Explain why it looked that way."

"They all belch about the bubbles, son. Did you tell him they'll flatten out after he walks on it?"

"Yeah, I told him."

"The bubbles go away. They do flatten."

"I know. So that's done, and now me and Ben are gonna knock this out."

"And then that job in Bethesda, right?"

"Yes. We'll get that done, too."

"It's money for all of us," said Flynn.

"Right," said Chris.

He walked down the hall, slipping the phone back into the pocket of his work pants. He could hear Ben chuckling, saying, "Chris, come *in* here, man," and then, almost in wonder, "Oh, *shit*." For a moment, it reminded Chris of Ben's voice coming from his cell down the hall at Pine Ridge, how Ben had talked to himself at night, how his talking had bothered others, how it had been a comforting sound for Chris.

Chris stepped into the library. Ben was sitting on the faded, scuffed walnut-plank floor, the worn carpet and corroded padding peeled back. A piece of the floor, a cutout, had been removed and was propped up against the wall.

There was an old Adidas gym bag, the kind with the stiff handles that was popular before Chris and Ben's time, on the floor beside Ben. It had been zipped open.

Chris could see cash. Green money in stacks, held together by bands.

"Oh, *shit*," said Ben, grinning up at Chris.

Chris felt a rush of excitement. Found money did that to a man, even a rich one.

But Chris did not smile.

THOMAS FLYNN warehoused his inventory at a space on Sunnyside Avenue, a long loop of road holding cinder-block and concrete structures in an industrial park in Beltsville, Maryland, north of College Park. Flynn didn't own the space, called Top Carpet and Floor Install, but paid in-and-out charges to keep his goods there. TCFI's main business was installation, subbed out from one of two big-box retailers serving the PG County do-it-yourself trade.

Flynn stood before a large wooden stage at the head of the warehouse. The stage had holes in it and air was blown up through the holes, a hovercraft effect that allowed one worker to handle a large piece of carpet and spin it around while he laminated or cut it.

Beside Flynn was one of Isaac's crew, a young curly-haired man named Hector who wore a blue polo shirt displaying a breast patch company logo, the L's in "Flynn's Floors" depicted as vertical, slightly bent carpet rolls. Amanda had come up with the design, along with the idea that the employees wear the shirts. She said that with the shirts the installers looked as if they worked for a "real" company. Flynn agreed to it, with the childish condition that his polo shirt be red, to separate him from the others. Also, with his black hair, he felt that red looked good.

"You gonna take that Berber roll with you, right?" said Flynn.

"That job is not today," said Hector.

"I need to get it out of here. Otherwise I've got to pay, like, rent for it. You've got Isaac's van, haven't you?"

"Yes."

"C'mon, I'll help you put it in."

They found the roll in Flynn's section. He checked its tag, on which was written the customer's name, and he motioned for Hector to grab an end.

"The Berber popular," said Hector, grunting as he lifted.

"I can move as much as they give me," said Flynn.

He was, and always had been, a good salesman. He sold like a factory rep, not an untrained retail salesman with an eye on the clock or a better job. He was a professional carpet-and-floor man. He knew the product thoroughly, explained its advantages, and, because he was a good listener rather than a fast talker, made many deals.

The problem was not with sales. Through referrals and his own acumen at closing, Flynn had as much business as he could handle. The problem was with installations and installers.

Flynn still had Isaac and his crew, and they were golden. Isaac had been with him for many years and would be with him as long as Flynn had work. Isaac had built on to his house in Wheaton, one of the many unconventional "Spanish mansions" seen in the area around Veirs Mill and Randolph roads, had a daughter in college and a son who was learning the installation trade. He would never live in El Salvador again. Isaac's crew came and went, usually leaving the country due to unpaid taxes or immigration complications, but even though the faces changed, to a man they did quality, responsible work. No wonder Flynn's mantra was Thank God for Hispanic workers.

Flynn and Hector loaded the roll into the van.

Hector looked at Flynn sorrowfully and said, "No more job today."

"We didn't make much money today," said Flynn, always

careful to use the inclusive pronoun. "But we will tomorrow. I've got something for you every day this week."

"Okay, boss."

Hector drove the van out of the lot, Flynn thinking, *Yeah, these Spanish guys like to work. Not like Chris and his crews of parolees.*

There were plenty of installers with tough pasts. Ex-offenders, bulls, and badasses of various colors and ethnicities, all on the young side. None had gone to college. This wasn't the place for students looking for summer jobs. Flynn had tried one or two out, and they hadn't been able to cut it. It was hard, demanding work. The goods were heavy and bulky, and much of the job time was spent on one's knees.

Many of the installers drank heavily at night and used marijuana and other drugs. Flynn could smell the alcohol in their sweat, could see the misery in their eyes nearly every morning. Unhealthy skin pallor was another giveaway. When Flynn interviewed a potential worker, he took note of his teeth. A guy had fucked-up teeth, it meant he came from little means or was raised by people who didn't care enough about their own kid to see to his dental hygiene. Whites from East Baltimore had the worst choppers.

Because it was hard work, and because the success of his business depended on their diligence and conscientious manner, Flynn compensated his installers relatively well. A sharp, hard-charging bull could make fifty, sixty grand a year installing carpets, but guys like that were rare. Chris's guys were lucky to make twenty-five to thirty thousand. Flynn put a little extra on Chris's check, due to the fact that he was a crew chief, so Chris made about thirty-five.

Thirty-five tops, thought Flynn, as he walked into the TCFI offices to drop off a check.

"Hey, Tommy," said a young woman behind one of two computers in the office.

Flynn couldn't remember her name. She was usually outside smoking in the morning when he came by, a gregarious Laurel girl, chubby, with a Route 1 hairstyle, one of those burn perm things.

"How's it going, sweetheart?" said Flynn.

"It's Susie."

"I knew that. Sweetheart suits you better, though." Susie smiled, and Flynn dropped an envelope on her desk. "Give that to the boss, will you? I don't want him to send the cavalry out after me."

"Your son was in this morning," said Susie.

Susie made eye contact with the girl seated behind the other computer, a pretty, fair-skinned strawberry blonde, voluptuous for her thin bone structure, couldn't have been more than two or three years out of high school. Flynn had noticed her before but had never heard her speak.

"Say hello to Katherine," said Susie. The girl looked down at her desk in a self-conscious gesture and smiled.

"Nice to meet you, darling," said Flynn.

"And you," said Katherine.

"Chris never says more than a couple of words to me," said Susie, once again glancing at her office mate. "Course, I'm spoken for. But he doesn't mind talking to Kate."

"It's Katherine," said the woman, gently correcting her co-worker.

Kate would be twenty-seven now.

"Chris is just shy around girls named Susie," said Flynn, forcing a grin. "Not like me."

"He doesn't even look like you," said Susie. "All that blond hair."

Again the girl named Katherine looked down at her desk.

"He got that from his mom," said Flynn, then comically puffed out his chest and made a bodybuilder's pose. "But he got the beef from me."

"Get out of here, Tommy!" said Susie, her boisterous, wheezy, Marlboro Light–inflected laughter trailing Flynn as he left the office.

Out in the hot sun, he put on his shades and walked to his van.

Kate would be twenty-seven. Amanda and me would be getting her ready for a wedding, or visiting her where she works, some professional job in New York City, maybe, or Chicago.

Flynn passed a guy he knew in the parking lot but did not say hello.

Chris is twenty-six. No college, time in prison, his days spent on his knees, laying carpet.

Flynn opened the van's driver's-side door.

Thirty-five grand a year, tops.

He got into the van and fitted his key to the ignition.

What's going to happen to my son?

ELEVEN

SHOULD WE count it?" said Ben Braswell.

"No," said Chris, staring at the money, shaking his head slowly. "I don't even want to touch it."

"You don't want to know how much it is?"

"Zip up the bag and put it back in that hole," said Chris. "Then seal it up again with that cutout piece. We'll get this new carpet down and move on to the next job."

"You're serious."

"I am."

Ben stood up, went to the window that gave to a view of the street, and opened it. He meant to cool the room, but the air outside was still, and there was no discernible relief from the heat.

"Why?" said Ben, walking back to join Chris. "Why you don't even want to talk about this?"

"It's stealing."

"You just told me yourself, the dude who lived here died, and he had no kin. You can *see* how old this bag is. Prob'ly the man who lived here last wasn't even the one who buried it. And you *know* that real estate lady didn't bury no money. Whoever

111

put it under this floor got to be buried now, too. So how is this stealing? From *who?*"

"It's not ours," said Chris.

"It ain't nobody's, far as I can tell."

Chris ran his hand through his longish blond hair.

"Forget this," said Ben, and he got down on his haunches and reached into the bag. "I gotta know."

Without removing the band, he slowly counted one of the stacks of money, bill by bill. His lips moved as he mentally tabulated the sum.

I've seen this movie, thought Chris. Innocent, basically good people found some money and decided to keep it, rationalizing their act because the cash belonged to no one. The money corrupted them, and they betrayed one another and were ultimately brought down by their own greed, a basic component of their human nature that they thought they would overcome. It always ended up bad.

Ben finished counting the one stack, then counted the number of stacks in the bag and multiplied.

"It's damn near fifty thousand in here," said Ben.

"Now you know," said Chris. "Zip up the bag and put it back."

Ben pointed a finger at the money. "That's two times what I make in one year, Chris. Working on my knees. I could buy something nice for my girl, take her out to dinner to one of those restaurants got white tablecloths. I could have some real clothes, and not the off-brand shit I got now. A pair of designer shades—"

"Put it back."

Ben stood up and faced Chris. He was going for confrontational, but he couldn't get there. There wasn't anything like that inside him. Instead, he looked hurt.

"How you gonna *do* this to me, man?"

"I'm doing you a favor."

"Nobody would know, so what's the harm? You can't tell me I'm wrong."

"My father gave us a chance here," said Chris. "Wasn't anybody else looking to hand us a decent job, was there? Someone does find out, it's his reputation we'd be messin with. That's *his* name on the truck."

"And yours," said Ben.

"What's that supposed to mean?"

"Means that I got nothin. Someday, whatever your father's got, whatever he built up, it's gonna come to you."

Chris moved his eyes from Ben's. "I've never taken anything from him but a paycheck."

"Comes a time, you will." Ben's features softened. "You *know* I appreciate what your pops did for me. But this thing we're talkin about here, it could change my life."

"It's already changed," said Chris. "You don't see it yet, is all. I'm sayin, there's no shortcut to where we're trying to get to. Just work, every day. Same as how it is for everyone else."

"Don't you want more?"

Chris stared at Ben. "Put the bag back in the hole. Let's finish the job."

"Damn, you just *stubborn*."

While they were laying down the new carpet, Mindy Kramer called and said she was on her way to the row house. She arrived shortly thereafter, just as they were finishing the installation. Mindy eyeballed the work, walked on it, questioned the bubbles, and carefully inspected the line where the carpet met the bead at the edge of the wall.

"I guess it's fine," said Mindy Kramer, constitutionally incapable of telling them that their work was satisfactory. "I need a little time to let it marinate. If I have any problems, I'll call Mr. Flynn."

"Any concerns you got," said Chris, "he'll take care of it."

They cleaned up the work site and packed the old carpet and padding in the back of the van. On the way out the door, Ben looked for an indication of an alarm system and saw none. He and Chris climbed into the van and took off.

Driving down U Street, Chris said, "Hungry?"

"You *know* I am."

"I'll buy."

"That's gonna make us late to our next job."

"I'll handle my dad," said Chris. "You earned lunch."

Ben adjusted his W cap on his head and slouched in the bucket. "I coulda bought a whole restaurant with what I left back there. I had what was in that bag, I could eat a hundred half-smokes every day for the rest of my life."

"You'd get sick of half-smokes," said Chris. "You'd shit like a horse."

"In my gold bathroom."

"Okay."

"And I'd have a butler to wipe my ass."

"Every man should have a dream," said Chris. He pulled the van to the side of the road and locked it down.

They walked toward the diner on U.

"I don't like wearing these things," said Ben with petulance, fingering the short sleeve of his Flynn's Floors polo shirt.

"Neither do I," said Chris.

"You *know* what it reminds me of," said Ben.

"I'll talk to my dad."

Ben Braswell pushed on the door of the eat house. He was hot and tired, and still thinking about the money. Chris was, too.

ALI CARTER sat in a rickety chair behind an old metal desk, manufactured and used by federal government workers before he was born. On the other side of the desk, in a chair just as suspect as Ali's, sat a young man named William Richards. He wore a Bulls cap, Guess jeans, a We R One T-shirt, and Nike boots. Richards was seventeen, full nosed, slightly bug-eyed, and annoyed.

"Mr. Masters said you been fighting him on the uniform shirt," said Ali.

"That shirt stupid," said William.

"It says you work for the company. It identifies you so when you do those events, the clients and the kids know who you are."

"That shirt got a picture of a clown on it. *And* balloons. I can't be walkin down the street wearin that mess."

"The clown's part of the logo," said Ali with patience. "You work for a company that sets up parties for kids. That logo is what makes people remember the business."

"The younguns where I stay at be laughin at me, Mr. Ali."

"So put the Party Land shirt in a bag and wear another shirt to the job. When you get to the site, change up. That'll work, right?"

William Richards nodded without conviction and looked away.

They were seated in a storefront office situated on a commercial stretch of Alabama Avenue, in the Garfield Heights section of Southeast. Ali was a junior staff member of Men Movin on Up, a nonprofit funded by the District, local charities, and private donors. Though there were many such organizations, set up in churches, rec centers, and storefronts, to help young men find their way and stay on track, Men Movin on Up was specifically designed to work with offenders, boys on parole or probation and boys awaiting trial. Its director, Coleman Wallace, was a career social worker and activist

Christian who had grown up poor and fatherless in Ward 8. A lifelong Washingtonian, he stayed in contact with many locals from his generation, and he put his hand out to those who had made it and asked them without shame to donate their money and volunteer their time to help young men who, like them, had come up disadvantaged. This group occasionally brought the boys to their places of work, counseled them, coached them in rec basketball, and took them on day trips to ball games and amusement parks.

Occasionally they made a difference in the boys' lives. There were many disappointments, failures, and setbacks, but Wallace and his friends had long ago stopped laboring under the illusion that they were going to save the collective youth of the city. If they could reach one kid, plant a seed that by example might grow into something right, they felt they had achieved success.

Ali was the sole staff member on the payroll. Coleman Wallace had hired him right out of Howard, where Ali had earned a bachelor's degree at the age of twenty-five. Coleman was attracted to Ali's intelligence and commitment, and also to the fact that Ali had done time at Pine Ridge and made the complete turnaround from incarcerated youth to productive member of society. He was smart and accomplished but also had the cachet of the real. His history bought him respect from the clients.

Also, Ali's relative youth was an attraction. Coleman Wallace was well aware that many of the boys he counseled could not relate to him, a middle-aged man. Most of them didn't even know that the organization's name, Men Movin on Up, referred to the Curtis Mayfield lyric. Or that the hand-lettered lyrics framed and hung on the office wall were from Coleman's favorite Curtis composition. Nine out of ten in this current crop didn't even know who Mayfield was. To these young men,

Ali Carter was go-go and hip-hop, and Coleman Wallace was slo-jam, tight basketball shorts, and way past old-school. Coleman needed an Ali Carter to help him connect.

Ali's focus was on getting the young men jobs and making sure they held them. To do this he communicated with parole officers, defense attorneys and prosecutors, and the staff of Ken Young, the recently hired reform-minded director of the District's Department of Youth Rehabilitation Services. He dealt with the members of the District's Absconding Unit, who tracked down kids who had skipped supervision, and he reached out to potential employers throughout the area, in particular those who had seen some trouble in their own youth and were willing to give his kids a try.

Without realizing it or having it in mind, Ali Carter was becoming connected and making a name for himself in the city. He liked his work and tried to forget that he was earning little more than minimum wage, which left him close to the poverty line.

"Any other problems?" said Ali.

"That man just aggravate the shit out of me, man," said William Richards.

"Mr. Masters?"

"Mr. *Slave*master. He *al*ways tryin to tell me what to do."

"He's paying you ten dollars an hour. It's his right to tell you what to do."

"I don't need that job."

"He's trying to introduce you to the culture of work."

"Huh?"

"Mr. Masters knows how hard it is to come back from jail time. He doesn't want you to have to go through that. He's trying to teach you how to work so that work becomes routine for you."

"I don't need him to teach me that. I know how to work and I damn sure can make some money. That's one thing I can do."

"Listen to me. It's important that you have a legitimate job right now and keep it, so that when you go to your hearing, you can stand before the judge and say that you're gainfully employed. Do you understand, William?"

"Yeah." But his slack posture and lack of eye contact said that he did not.

"Did you get your paycheck?"

"Here in my pocket."

"What are you going to do with it?"

"Take it that check-cash place round my way."

"They charge you big for that, don't they?"

"So?"

"I been tellin you, you should open a checking account at the bank. They charge much less than that store does. And they'll give you an ATM card. You can manage your money better and get to it any time."

"My mother got to take me to that bank, right?"

"To open the account? Yes."

"She too busy."

"You asked her?"

"No, but I'm about to. Next week." William stood abruptly out of his chair. He drew his cell from his jeans, opened it, and checked it for text messages.

"We straight?" said Ali.

"Huh?"

"Look at me, William." Ali stared into his eyes. "You're good with this job, right?"

"Yeah," said William. "But I'm not wearin no clown shirt. That ain't me."

Ali watched William slip out of his office. He didn't reflect on William or strategize on what to do with him next. At seventeen, William was at a point in his life where he had to choose a path for himself. Ali would be there for him if need be, but he wouldn't spend an inordinate amount of time on him if he continued to display his current level of resistance. Ali had many boys, and though they rarely expressed it verbally, some of them recognized the value in the hand that was being offered to them. It was unproductive for Ali to focus on one who was not willing to meet him halfway.

For the next hour, Ali made some phone calls. One was to a midlevel manager at the new baseball stadium, where Ali had been trying to get a couple of his boys put on. He knew that there were plenty of workers needed at the concession stands as well as less-desirable positions of the janitorial variety. Thus far the stadium officials had been unresponsive. The manager had said something about the need to present a more polished face to the public. Ali actually understood this from a business standpoint, but he vowed to be persistent. He'd call Ken Young. Young had direct dealings with stadium officials and the ear of the mayor, who had hired him from out of town.

There was a cursory knock on the glass storefront door, and a man pushed through it. Almond-shaped eyes, skin that in some lights looked yellow. He now wore his hair in braids. He was twenty-six but looked ten years older. Ali could see that he was high.

" 'Sup, *Holly?*" he said.

"Lawrence."

"Can't your boy visit a minute?"

Ali nodded warily as Lawrence Newhouse crossed the room.

TWELVE

Damn, boy," said Lawrence Newhouse, looking around the office. "You oughta fix this joint up some."

"We got no money to speak of," said Ali. "None extra, anyway."

"Still," said Lawrence.

The space consisted of two desks, one for Ali, one for Coleman Wallace; a computer with slow dial-up service that they shared; and file cabinets. Also in the room were a foosball table with a cracked leg, a television set with no remote, a roll-in blackboard, several chairs, and a ripped-fabric couch. Ali did his best to make it a place where the boys would feel comfortable hanging out. Everything had been donated. It wasn't nice, but it was good enough.

"What can I do for you, Lawrence?"

"Wonderin why I stopped in, huh."

"Been a while."

"Bet you think I'm lookin for work, somethin."

"No, I didn't think that."

"I *got* work, man. Got this thing where I detail cars."

"That's good."

"What you doin here, it's for young men at risk. You know I'm not at risk."

"And you're not that young," said Ali.

Lawrence chuckled and pointed a finger at Ali. "That's right."

"So what can I do for you?"

"It's about my nephew. Marquis Gilman?"

Ali knew him, a nonviolent boy of average intelligence, funny, with lively eyes. Marquis was sixteen, up on drug charges, a recent dropout of Anacostia High School. He had been picked up several times for loitering and possession. His heart wasn't in his work. He was a low-level runner who didn't care to run.

"Marquis is one of my clients," said Ali. "I'm tryin to help him out."

"He told me. Want you to know, I appreciate it. He stays over there at Parkchester, with my sister and me. She's havin a little trouble containing him. You know how that is. Boys that age just don't think right. They wired up stupid in their heads."

Ali nodded. He wouldn't have put it that way, but Lawrence had the general idea. No one knew more about teenage brain scramble and bad decisions than Lawrence Newhouse.

"I'm lookin out for him, though," said Lawrence. "I got no kids myself, so he as close to one as there is."

For a moment, Ali thought of his own uncle and shook his head.

"What's wrong?" said Lawrence.

"Nothin," said Ali.

"So let me tell you why I'm here. Marquis said you tryin to hook him up with a job."

"I'm trying. So far we haven't had much luck."

"What, you tryin to put him in a Wendy's, sumshit like that?"

"At this point, we need to find him a job anywhere. Then, if he doesn't want to return to school, I'll get him started on earning his GED. Get him used to work and study. Change his habits. Marquis has all the necessary tools."

"That's what I'm sayin. He's better than some fast-food job. I mean, he could do better right now. I been talkin to Ben Braswell. You know I still stay in contact with my man."

"And?"

"Ben workin with White Boy, laying carpet. Both of them make good money at it. That's the kind of thing I'd like to see Marquis get into. Learn a trade, and I'm not talkin about operatin no deep fryer."

"I don't think Marquis is ready for that right now. It's a man's job, for one. Heavy lifting and hard work. And it's a trade that requires experience. You have to know what you're doing."

"White Boy's father got the business, right?"

"Chris's father owns it," said Ali. "That's right."

"Then he could put Marquis on. I mean, shit, he put Ben on, and you know Ben ain't no genius."

"Chris's father already hired some guys from our old unit. Remember Lonnie and Luther? Plus Milton Dickerson and that boy we used to ball with, Lamar Brooks. Lamar's the only one who worked out, and he left to start his own thing. It was me who asked Mr. Flynn to give them a try, so I can't go back to that well right now."

"Marquis ain't never been incarcerated. He was in that pretrial jail at Mount Olivet, but no hard lockup."

"Marquis isn't ready," said Ali, holding Lawrence's gaze.

Lawrence smiled. "All right. Maybe I'll just talk to Ben. See what he got to say."

Ali rose from his chair, telling Lawrence it was time to go. Lawrence stood, and the two of them walked toward the door.

"Damn, you all swole," said Lawrence, looking Ali over. "I remember when you was one step off a midget. You always did have a chest on you, though."

"I got one of those late growth spurts," said Ali. He was now a man of average height with a fireplug build.

Above the door, where boys who were exiting the office could read them, were framed, hand-lettered lyrics:

> *We people who are darker than blue*
> *Don't let us hang around this town*
> *And let what others say come true.*

"What's that mean?" said Lawrence, pointing at the lyrics.

"Means, don't become what society expects you to become. Be better than that."

"Damn, boy, you like Crusader Rabbit and shit."

"Not really."

"What you gonna do after you save all these young niggas down here? Run for president?"

"I think I'll just stay here and work."

Ali held the door open for Lawrence, who walked down the sidewalk toward his vehicle, an old Chevy, parked on Alabama Avenue. Two young men stood outside the storefront, talking loudly, laughing.

"Y'all want to come inside?" said Ali.

"What for?" said one young man.

"You can watch television."

"Ya'll ain't even got cable. Or a remote."

"Play foosball if you want," said Ali.

"That shit broke," said the other young man, and he and his friend laughed.

Ali went back into the office, thinking, *He's right, it is broke.* He made a mental note to get some duct tape and fix it, when he found the time.

THOMAS FLYNN'S last stop of the day was at a Ford dealership in the Route 29 corridor of Silver Spring. It was where he bought his E-250 cargo vans and had them serviced. He dealt with the manager, Paul Nicolopoulos, a good-looking silver-maned guy in his fifties taken to double-breasted blazers and crisp white oxfords. Nicolopoulos always introduced himself as Paul Nichols to his clients, just to make his life easier. Increasingly, many of his customers were Hispanics and other types of immigrants, and they had trouble with his name, which his proud Greek immigrant grandfather had refused to change.

"Just give me the cheap stuff," said Nicolopoulos, watching Flynn measure the space with his Craftsman tape. They were in the used-car office, set up in a trailer. Nothing about it was plush.

"I'm gonna sell you the olefin," said Flynn. "Twenty-six-ounce commercial, level loop."

"The service guys walk through here all day with their boots on, and they're not delicate. It's like they got hooves."

"The olefin's made for high traffic. It's not pretty, but it's plenty tough."

Flynn drew the tape back into the dispenser and clipped it onto his belt. He produced a pocket calculator and began to punch in numbers. He typically took the cost, added his profit, then tacked on the personality defect tax or, if he liked the client or owed him something, gave him a discount. In this way he arrived at a final figure.

"Don't hurt me," said Nicolopoulos, watching Flynn calculate.

"I'll only put the head in," said Flynn.

"Pretend that I'm a virgin," said Nicolopoulos.

"I'll be tender and kind," said Flynn.

"Afterward, will you brush the tears off my face?"

"I'll take you to McDonald's and buy you a Happy Meal."

"Thank you, Tom."

Flynn closed the calculator and replaced it in his breast pocket. "Twenty dollars a square yard, including installation and takeaway."

"Is that good?"

"I dunno. Did you give me a good price on my vans?"

"I did the best I could."

"Me, too," said Flynn.

"When can you put it in?"

"Early next week."

"Perfect," said Nicolopoulos.

Out in his van, Flynn called in the order to the mill. He phoned Chris, who was still in Bethesda with Ben, and checked on the status of the job. The two of them were slow, but Chris was conscientious and did decent work. Flynn tried not to lose patience with Chris, though sometimes, depending on his mood, he did become agitated. The trick was to avoid comparing Chris and Ben's work to that of Isaac and his crew. No one was as fast or efficient as Isaac, but in general Chris and Ben were fine.

Which wasn't the case with some of the other ex-offenders Flynn had tried to help. At the urging of Chris's friend Ali, he had hired, at various times, several men who had once been incarcerated at Pine Ridge. A couple of them, genial guys named Lonnie and Luther who had been in Chris and Ali's unit, had issues with drugs and alcohol, rarely reported to work at an acceptable time, and dressed inappropriately. Another, a large man named Milton, could not grasp the mechanics of installation. Flynn ran a business that grew and was perpetuated by referrals, and who he sent into his clients' homes made or broke his reputation. He had to let them go.

There was one guy, a quiet, polite Pine Ridge alumnus named Lamar Brooks, who Flynn had hired and who had acquitted himself well. Lamar was ambitious, had his eyes wide open, and quickly learned the trade. After six months he bought a van and tools, went out on his own, and started an installation service, subcontracting for small carpet retailers in the Northeast and Southeast quadrants of the city. Flynn saw the failure of Lonnie, Luther, and Milton as insignificant in the face of Lamar's success. And though Chris did not verbalize it, Flynn sensed that Chris appreciated his efforts on behalf of his friends, and that alone had been worth the aggravation a few of these young men had caused.

"So you guys are almost done?" said Flynn into his cell.

"Should be out of here in a half hour," said Chris.

"What are you doing tonight? You want to come to dinner?"

"Can't."

"You have plans?"

"Yeah."

"I met a young lady named Katherine today," said Flynn. "Works over at TCFI?"

"Uh-huh."

"Are you seeing her?"

"A little."

"Don't be so effusive," said Flynn.

"I'm busy here."

"What's her story?"

"I gotta get back to work, Dad."

"All right. Come by for dinner sometime; your mom misses you. I've got a book to give you, too. Guy named Paul Fussell."

"I've read Fussell."

"Have fun tonight," said Flynn.

"I need to finish this job. . . ."

"Go."

Flynn headed home. It had been a decent day. No serious fires, no major mistakes. Not too busy, but he had closed a couple of deals, and there would be steady work for all his people in the coming week.

Inside his house, he greeted Django, an adult Lab-pit mix they had adopted fully grown from the Humane Society at Georgia and Geranium after Darby's death. Django had gotten off his circular cushioned bed that sat beside the couch in the den, and met Flynn at the door after hearing Flynn's van pulling into the driveway, the distinctive sound of its Triton V-8 jacking up the beast's ears. Django's tail was spinning like a prop, and Flynn rubbed behind his ears and stroked his neck and chin. Django weighed eighty pounds and was heavily muscled. The pit in him was most visible in his blockish head.

Amanda's car was out on the street, so Flynn knew she was home, despite the utter quiet in the house. In the early evening she liked to pray the rosary in their bedroom. She would be up there now, making the sign of the cross, reciting the Apostles'

Creed, touching the crucifix and then the beads as she proceeded into the Our Father, the three Hail Marys, and the Glory Be.

He had come to accept Amanda's devotion to Catholicism and Christ. He no longer thought it was square or weird, or a Stepford wife phase she was going through, as he had when she became deeply religious in the early days of their marriage. He was thankful for the comfort that religion gave her, even as he was unable to buy into it himself. He had learned to share her with the one he had once called "Uncle Jesus," whom he thought of as an unwanted relative who had camped out in his home, and in turn Amanda had stopped trying to convert him.

Flynn grabbed the plastic wrapper from that morning's *Washington Post*, which Amanda saved daily, off the kitchen counter. Django began to bark, knowing that the plastic container was no longer a protective cover for the newspaper but was now a shit bag for his nightly walk.

"Let's go, boy," said Flynn, and ecstatically the dog followed him down the hall to where Flynn grabbed his harness and leash off a peg.

They walked their usual route through Friendship Heights, Django stopping at the houses where he knew other dogs lived, barking excitedly at the canine faces that were barking at him through doors and windowpanes. When Amanda walked Django, she stopped to talk to neighbors and occasionally strangers, but Flynn was not gregarious that way and politely nodded or said hello but kept up his pace. He was a workingman in a neighborhood of what he thought of, rather archaically, as professionals and yuppies, and as an adult he felt he did not fit in here, despite the fact that this had been his home almost his entire life. Sure, he ran a successful business and cleared six figures every year, but to his knowledge he was the only homeowner in Friendship Heights who drove a cargo van to work, and he believed that people looked at him and saw a guy who was not as educated as they were, not as accomplished, and, on some level, not in their class.

This was largely in Flynn's mind. In reality, most of the neighbors liked Thomas and Amanda Flynn and had never been anything but friendly and inclusive. Flynn knew this, yet he could not keep those feelings at bay.

He stopped, as always, at the rec center and playground near their house. There in the grass Django sniffed about, found a spot he liked, and commenced to take a crap. Flynn looked at the playground, where young parents stood talking to one another while their children played. "I'm going to enroll Emily in the French-immersion program," and "Skyler loves science; we're taking him to the Smithsonian tomorrow," and "Dylan is strong at soccer; we're looking at a sleepaway camp for him this summer. Maybe he'll get an athletic scholarship someday!"

Enjoy it now, thought Flynn. *There's nothing but heartache ahead. Okay, some of you will be luckier than I was. But not all of you. So enjoy your dreams.*

Flynn made a glove of the plastic bag and scooped up Django's shit.

Amanda was standing over the granite kitchen counter, chopping a red onion for a salad, when they returned. Beside the cutting board sat a ziplock bag containing chicken breasts in a marinade of salad dressing. Flynn guessed he would be grilling the chicken shortly. His plan was to pour himself a bourbon over ice and take it out on the deck while he worked.

"Good day today?" said Amanda. Django pressed his nose into her thigh by way of hello.

"Not bad," said Flynn, going to the sink. He pushed down on the plunger of a liquid-soap dispenser, turned on the faucet, and began to wash his hands. "You?"

"I had to pay the insurance for our guys. But a couple of receivables came in, too."

Flynn ripped a paper towel from a roll and dried off. "Our son's got a girlfriend, I think."

"Yeah?"

"She works in the office at the warehouse. Nice-looking girl. I doubt she's educated. . . ."

"Don't be such a snob."

"I'm not."

"I didn't go to college. You saying you have regrets?"

"Hell, no."

Amanda stopped chopping momentarily as Flynn walked behind her and placed his hands on her waist. She was twenty pounds heavier than she had been as a teenager but carried it naturally. She had kept her curves, and the thought of her naked still excited him. He pulled her shoulder-length hair away from her neck and kissed her there and took in a clean smell of soap and lotion.

"How do you know she's his girlfriend and not just a girl?"

"Just a feeling I had," said Flynn. "She has your hair color and build. You know what they say about boys trying to date their moms."

"Stop."

Flynn saw the lines at the corners of her eyes deepen and knew that she was pleased. "I don't blame him." Flynn cupped her breasts and kissed the side of her mouth.

She turned in to him. They kissed and in no time it went from love to passion. Finally her skin became flushed, and she chuckled low and gently pushed him away.

"That was nice," she said.

"We're done?"

"Why does every kiss have to lead to sex?"

"Because I'm a man?"

"A caveman, you mean."

"They don't bother with kisses."

"Go pour yourself a drink."

"Trying to get rid of me?"

"Not entirely," said Amanda.

"So, later on tonight . . ."

"Perhaps."

Flynn walked toward the dining room, where he kept a small bar.

"What's her name?" said Amanda to his back.

Flynn said, "Kate."

He made a drink. He drank it rather quickly, and reached for the bottle on the cart.

THIRTEEN

BEN LIVED in a one-bedroom unit in a group of boxy red brick apartment houses set near the Rock Creek Cemetery in upper Northwest, steps away from Northeast. The neighborhood was not dangerous, nor did it carry an air of tension like the foster homes in which he'd been raised. After the rush hour traffic died down on close-by North Capitol Street, a commuter route in and out of the city, the atmosphere was fairly quiet. His apartment got little sun, was furnished with Goodwill and Salvation Army stuff, and roaches scattered when he turned on the kitchen light.

Ben's place was nothing to brag about, but it was the first living quarters he'd ever had to his self outside lockup. It was his and it was fine. Only bad thing was, the management didn't allow pets. He wanted a dog.

Ben didn't own a car or possess a driver's license. He hadn't been behind the wheel of a vehicle since his days of joyriding and grand theft. For a while he'd been barred from getting a license, but he was clear to obtain one now. Chris had been urging him to take the test. It would be easier on Chris, and make Ben more valuable to Mr. Flynn, if he could drive the vans. He supposed he would do so eventually, but he was not in a hurry. He preferred to take small steps.

Other than for work, Ben had no need for a car. He was on a bus line, and he was not far from the Fort Totten Metro station. You stayed in the District, it was easy to get around.

He liked to take walks in the cemetery, eighty-some acres of hills, trees, monuments, and headstones, some of the nicest green space in D.C. He entered at the main gate, at Rock Creek Church Road and Webster Street, and walked up past the church to the high ground, where the finest, most ornate monuments were located, and down a road so narrow it did not look like a proper road, to the Adams Memorial, his favorite spot. A marble bench faced the statue, the monument shielded by a wall of evergreens. On his weekends off, he'd sit on the bench and try to write poetry. Or open a paperback novel he had slipped into the pocket of his jeans.

Ben could read.

He had been at Pine Ridge until the age of twenty-one. The incident with Calvin Cooke had kept him behind the fence and razor wire, even as his friends had been set free. At eighteen, Ali and Chris had rotated out when they'd achieved Level 6. Lawrence Newhouse had been released, violated the conditions of his parole, was reincarcerated at the Ridge, and went on to do adult time for gun charges, first at Lorton before it closed, and then at a penitentiary in Ohio. By the time Ben had walked free, he was the old man of the facility. The guards had clapped him out, the way faculty did for kids graduating elementary school.

Under supervision, he lived in several halfway houses with other men. He stayed to himself, kept his appointments with his parole officer, walked by unlocked cars without stopping, was piss-tested regularly, and always dropped negatives. Chris, by then employed by his father, put him on as an assistant and taught him the carpet-and-floor-installation trade. Ali, then a student at Howard but already working the system, found out about a special night program at UDC, funded by the District and local charities, set up to educate ex-offenders. Ali got Ben enrolled.

There he met his teacher, a kind and patient young woman named Cecelia Lewis. In the schools of his youth, and his high school classes at Pine Ridge, he had worked with instructors who tried to get him to read, and corrected him, always corrected him, when he could not make out words, and he became ashamed and got to where he hated to look at books. Miss Lewis read *to* him, which no one had ever done. She read from newspapers, comic books, books written for teenagers, and then from adult novels, not fancy ones, but clearly written books with good characters that anyone could appreciate and understand. She would read from a book, and he would hold a copy of that same book and follow along, and after months of this, twice a week at night, the words and sentences connected and became pictures in his head. He was reading, and a door opened, and when he went through it he felt as if things were possible now that had not been possible before. It was like putting on a pair of prescription eyeglasses for the first time. The world looked new.

Of course, he fell in love with Cecelia Lewis. He picked flowers from people's gardens and window boxes on his walk to the Red Line train, handing them to her when he arrived at her classroom, and he wrote poems, sensing they were awful but giving them to her anyway to let her know that she had reached him deep.

They never did make it to bed. They never even kissed. When he finally expressed his feelings to her, she told him that it would be inappropriate for a teacher to have that kind of relationship with her student, that it was certainly not him, that she did care about him as a person, whatever that meant, and that they should remain friends. Her eyes told him something different, they said she was into him, but he understood her reticence and didn't press it further. When the semester was over, he never saw her again. No matter. Cecelia Lewis had changed his life, and there would always be a place for her in his heart.

Ben had a girl now, nice woman named Renee, built low to the ground, lived over in Hyattsville and worked at a nail salon. She was easy to get along with. They stayed in mostly, had pizza delivered, sat together, and laughed. She didn't complain about Ben watching his basketball on the TV, didn't ask why he seldom took her to restaurants or clubs. Maybe she knew that he was uncomfortable in such places and, in general, out in the world. Renee was just cool with it. She was all right.

Ben's cell sounded. Its ring tone was that old Rare Essence "Overnight Scenario" joint that Ben loved. He checked the ID and answered.

"Wha'sup, Chris?"

"Checkin up on you."

"I'm fine."

"You're not cryin over that bag of money, are you?"

"I wished I had it. But I'm not blown by it."

"So what're you doin?"

"'Bout to take a walk. You seein your redhead tonight?"

"Uh-huh."

"Should I call you in the morning and wake your ass up?"

"No need. I'll swing by and get you, same time as usual."

Ben ended the call. He slipped *Of Mice and Men*, a worn Penguin edition he had bought used, into the rear pocket of his jeans and headed out the door in the direction of the cemetery. There was still an hour or so of summer light, enough for him to sit and read in peace.

CHRIS LIVED in a house that had been converted into three apartments on a street of single-family homes in downtown Silver Spring, just over the District line in Maryland. He had chosen it when he'd seen the built-in bookshelves in its living-room area, a place to house the many biography and US history titles that he read and collected. Ali had gotten him hooked with the Taylor Branch books on Dr. King and the civil rights movement, which were two volumes when Chris was incarcerated and had grown to a trilogy after his release. He liked anything by Halberstam, the unconventional takes on the world wars by Paul Fussell, David McCullough's entire body of work, and war memoirs like E. B. Sledge's *With the Old Breed*, which he felt was the finest book of its kind ever written. He was inspired by these extraordinary writers and their subjects, even as he was aware of and resigned to his own very ordinary life.

His place was small but entirely adequate for his needs. He did not have many possessions other than his books, and he kept a neat and uncluttered apartment. He lined his shoes up in pairs under his bed, heels out, as he had done beneath his cot at Pine Ridge. He had a small television set and bought the most basic cable package so that he could watch sports. Every morning, before he went to work, he made his bed.

The other tenants of the house were the Gibsons, a young punkish couple, the husband a rock musician, the wife a private music teacher, and Andy Ladas, a middle-aged man who kept to himself and smoked cigarettes on the porch at night as he slowly drank bottled beer. The four of them took turns mowing the lawn with regularity, and the couple went beyond the call and landscaped the yard, keeping the property in better shape than many of the homeowners on the block did. Despite this, there were rumblings on the neighborhood Listserve about keeping future renters off the street. If they wanted him gone, fine, he'd go. He'd had the sense that he'd be moving around frequently, anyway. That his would be that kind of nomadic life.

But he was feeling different lately, since he'd been going out with Katherine. Yeah, she meant more to him than the other young women he'd been with since coming out. If pressed, because he was not one to talk about such things, he'd even admit that he was in love with her. But also, he felt that this change in outlook had to do with his age. Just as it felt normal to rebel as a teenager, settling into something more permanent felt natural as he moved into the tail end of his twenties.

After a long shower, Chris dressed in Levi's and an Ecko Unlimited button-down shirt, which he had purchased from the Macy's up in Wheaton. Most of his peers from the neighborhood he'd grown up in shopped at Bloomingdale's and Saks in Friendship Heights, or the Rodeo Drive–like stores that lined a block of Wisconsin Avenue across the Maryland line. Chris did not have the money to shop in those places, nor was he particularly cognizant of trendy fashion. The Macy's where he shopped seemed to market to their black and Hispanic base in the Wheaton location, and he was cool with that. More accurately, he made do with what they offered. He could afford to shop there.

Chris drove the van over to PG County. It still held the old roll and padding, fitted between the buckets so that the rear doors would close, from the Bethesda job. He was headed to pick up Katherine at her parents' home in University Park, a township of colonials and restored bungalows south of College Park.

Katherine's father, James Murphy, was a tenured professor in arts and humanities at the University of Maryland. Her mother, Colleen, worked at a downtown think tank specializing in energy policy. Both were brilliant and perhaps overeducated to the point of social retardation. Their son had earned a bachelor's degree but had no desire to go to graduate school and was working in New York as a boom operator on feature films. He was respected in his field, but his parents felt he had underachieved.

Their daughter, Katherine, had disappointed them completely. After graduating in low standing from Elizabeth Seaton, the Catholic girls' high school in their area, she had floundered in PG Community College, dropped out, and had been working in the office of a warehouse for the past year. And now she was dating a man who installed carpet for a living and apparently had been incarcerated in his youth.

Chris understood their negativity. They were basically good people and in other circumstances they might have welcomed him into their home, but they wanted the best for their daughter. Admittedly he was not an exemplary prospect, but he cared for Katherine, respected her, and would protect her. He worked with his hands, but he worked hard and honestly. None of this was reassuring to her parents, but he was who he was, and for now it was the best he could do.

He stood on the stoop of their house and rang the doorbell.

Colleen Murphy answered. She was a tall brunette whose perpetually serious nature had taken a toll on her looks and spirit. Katherine had gotten her fair complexion and reddish hair from her father.

"Hey, Mrs. Murphy. How you doin?"

"I'm fine, Chris."

"Is my friend ready?"

"Yes, just about. Would you like to come in?"

"Nah, this is fine."

Chris had called Katherine from his cell when he was a few minutes away from the house, hoping she'd be waiting when he arrived, hoping to avoid this.

Colleen Murphy stared at him, looking down on him slightly because she was up a step in the door frame. He moved his eyes away from hers and looked around at the old-growth trees on the property, the azaleas framing the stoop, and a large triple-trunk crepe myrtle with scarlet blossoms. A Sunfish sailboat, covered by a tarp, was set on a trailer beside the house.

"Nice yard," said Chris lamely.

"Yes," said Colleen Murphy.

"Does Mr. Murphy sail?"

"Occasionally."

Thankfully, Katherine came down the center hall stairs. She wore a green-and-rust shift with green T-strap sandals, and she had one of those black band things in her strawberry blonde hair. She brushed past her mother and met Chris outside the door.

"See you, Mom," said Katherine.

"Take care, Mrs. Murphy," said Chris, saluting stupidly, immediately wishing he hadn't. Katherine kissed him on the cheek and took his hand, and they walked across the yard to his van. Chris thinking, *Her mom hates me*.

Colleen Murphy watched as her daughter and Chris Flynn got into the van. At that moment, she had no animosity in her at all. She was thinking of a time when her boyfriend, Jimmy Murphy, had picked her up from her own parents' house in

Burke, Virginia, back in the midseventies. How they had laughed and held hands on the way to his car, a gold Ford Pinto station wagon with synthetic wood-paneled sides. How tall he was, how strong his hand felt in hers, how she couldn't wait to have those hands on her breasts and ribcage.

She turned and went back inside her house. James Murphy would be in his office, working. They would have a quiet dinner with little conversation. She would turn in early, and he would come to bed after she had gone to sleep.

In the van, around the corner from her house, Katherine told Chris to pull over to the side of the road.

"Where?" said Chris.

"Here. That house has been unoccupied for the last six months."

"So?"

"Just do it."

"Okay."

When he put it in park, she leaned across the carpet and padding and kissed him deeply.

"What's that for?" said Chris.

"My apologies. For keeping you waiting."

She rubbed the crotch of his jeans. He placed his hand on her muscled thighs, and she opened her legs as she unzipped him and pulled him free.

Chris laughed. "Right here?"

"There a problem?" she said, working him until he could take it no longer. He moved her hand away.

"*Damn*, girl."

"What?"

"I'm about to bust."

"You afraid you're gonna mess up the seats?"

"More like your hair."

"Quit boasting."

"I'm sayin, I'm a young man. I got velocity."

"C'mon, let's get in the back."

"For real?"

She kissed him. "Come on, Chris."

Afterward, they went to dinner at a pho house in Wheaton, because they liked the soup and it was cheap. The restaurant was in a commercial strip of Laundromats and Kosher and Chinese grocers. The diners sat communally at tables similar to those found in school cafeterias. Except for Chris and Katherine, all of the customers were Vietnamese. No one talked to them, or seemed to notice the sweat rings on Chris's shirt or Katherine's unkempt hair. At the end of the meal, Chris bought an inexpensive bottle of Chilean red at the deli next door, and they drove back to his place in Silver Spring.

They made love properly, but no less energetically, in his bed. Chris had lit votive candles around the room, with his small stereo set on WHUR, playing the old EWF tune "Can't Hide Love." The candles and the music were on the corny side, but Chris was a D.C. boy all the way, and Quiet Storm was in his blood. His parents had listened to Melvin Lindsay, the originator, spin Norman Connors and Major Harris when Thomas and Amanda Flynn were young and making love on hot summer nights just like this one.

Katherine, lying naked atop the sheets beside Chris, reached over and traced her finger down the vertical scar above his lip.

"Your dad finally talked to me today," said Katherine. "Susie sort of made him. In her own sloppy way, she let him know that you and I were together."

"Did he call you honey or sweetheart?"

"I think it was 'darling.' "

"That's my pops. He has trouble remembering names. Odd for a salesman, but there it is. He'll remember yours now, though."

"Why's that?"

"My parents had a baby named Kate who died before I was born. Dad still talks about her. Like she's going to come back and be everything that I'm not."

"Your father cares about you, Chris."

"Like you care for a lame dog. You know Champ is never gonna win a show or a race. But you look after him anyway, out of the kindness of your heart."

"It's not attractive when you feel sorry for yourself."

"I'm not. I *never* do. I'm sayin, this is how I think it is from his eyes. I don't have a problem with who I am. Far as I'm concerned, I'm doing fine. But my pops looks at me like I'm some kind of cripple. My past still eats at him, Katherine. There's got to be a reason for the troubles I had, and he needs to know why. Look, my parents didn't cause me to jump the tracks, and I never meant to hurt them. I was selfish and full of fire, and I wasn't thinkin right. That's the best way I know how to explain it. Truth is, my fuckups were mine and mine alone."

"When I dropped out of college," said Katherine, "I could hear my parents whispering, and then arguing, behind their bedroom door. It was all about the bad decisions they thought they had made along the way. How they should have moved out of PG County, or put me in a better high school, got me away from my friends and other bad influences. How they should have pushed me harder to get better grades. But I just plain didn't *like* school, Chris. I didn't like it when I was a little kid. Not everybody goes to college. Not everybody can get more education than their parents, or make more money than them, or live in a nicer house than the one they grew up in."

"I hear you. But they want it for you anyway."

"It's natural for them to feel like that."

"Way your mom looks at me, seems like she's made her mind up that I'm not the right one for you."

"My mom'll come around," said Katherine. She moved beside him and pressed her flat belly against him. "You know, if you weren't an installer, if I hadn't dropped out of school and taken that dumb job in the office . . ."

"We wouldn't have met."

"So everything's been to the good, far as I'm concerned."

They kissed.

"This is right," said Chris, holding her close.

"You can feel it, can't you. We're supposed to be together, Chris."

"Yes."

He told her about the bag of money that Ben had found earlier in the day. He told her that he'd convinced Ben to put it back in the space under the floor.

"You made a good decision," said Katherine. "I guess."

Chris chuckled. "You're not so sure, either."

"Who wouldn't think twice about keeping it? But it seems like it would come to bad if you took it. I mean, it's not yours. Technically . . ."

"It's stealing. What I'm worried about is, did I do right by Ben. At the time, I *thought* I did. I felt like I was tryin to protect him by leaving that money there."

"But you're not positive now."

"Back in Pine Ridge, Ali told me that I was always going to be taken care of in some way, 'cause of my father and mother. And he was right. But Ben, he's got nothin. No family and no kinda breaks. To him, fifty grand in a gym bag is a gift from heaven."

"He's not angry with you, right?"

"No, we're straight."

"So why are you stressed about it?"

Chris stroked Katherine's arm. "I'm just worried about my friend."

FOURTEEN

BEN BRASWELL heard a knock on his apartment door. He got up from his chair, walked barefoot and softly to the peep, and bent his tall frame to look through the glass in the hole. He sighed audibly, stood to his full height, and considered his next move.

There was little chance that Lawrence could know that Ben was home. If Ben stood here quietly, eventually Lawrence would give it up and go. Ben knew that a drop-in by Lawrence meant that Lawrence's hand was going to be outstretched in some way. But Ben could not just stand behind the door like a coward, and it wasn't in him to be deceitful. Lawrence, low as he was and could be, was a man. He deserved respect until it was no longer warranted. Ben unlocked the deadbolt and opened the door.

"My boy," said Lawrence Newhouse.

Ben raised his hand warily and they touched fists. Lawrence's eyes were pink and the smell of weed was on him.

"What you doin here, man?"

"Can't a friend visit?"

"It's late."

"Night owl like you? Shit. You was always the last one asleep at the Ridge. Talkin to yourself in your cell at all hours. Remember?"

"Come on."

Lawrence walked in. Ben closed the door behind him, leaned his back against it, and crossed his arms. Lawrence went to a chair that had been new in the 1970s and had a seat. Ben dropped his arms to his sides and spread himself out on a worn sofa near the chair.

"I got work tomorrow," said Ben.

"That's good," said Lawrence. "Wished I did, too."

"Thought you had a detailing thing."

"I do, but it's slow. Gas prices go up, people don't be drivin their cars. They don't take 'em out the garage, they don't feel the need to clean 'em. You know how that is."

"You got a place of business?"

"Nah, my shit is portable, man. I bring my supplies in a grocery cart and wash and detail the whips right at the places where people stay at. Most everybody got a hose. If they don't, I carry one with me. All my, you know, transactions are in cash, so I don't have to fuck with no taxes. Don't pay rent, either. I got a good thing. But like I say, right now it's slow."

Some business, thought Ben. *But at least Lawrence is doing something halfway straight. Least he's not shootin at anyone. Or getting his ass beat regular.*

"Why you come to see me?" said Ben.

"Damn, boy, you just short and to the point, ain't you?"

"Told you, it's late."

Lawrence rubbed sweat theatrically from his yellowish forehead. He head-tossed his braids back off his face. "Hot in this piece."

"Air's on. Maybe it's you."

"Hot and small. Feel like I'm in a coffin in here and shit. You know I don't like these small spaces. Reminds me of when I was inside."

"You free to roll out."

"Let's both go out. Have a drink. Little bit of vodka on a nice summer night like this?"

"I got no extra for that."

"I got you. Bottle's sittin out in my car. All's we need to do is stop and get some ice-cold juice."

Ben looked down at his bare feet. It was warm in the room, and a cool vodka drink sounded good. Might be a way to get Lawrence out of this apartment and out of his world. Drive around and sip some, find out what he wanted, then say good-bye.

"What say you, Big Man?" said Lawrence.

"Let me get my shoes," said Ben.

As Ben went into his bedroom, Lawrence inspected the leather tool belt hanging on a hook by the front door. In one of its pouches he found a razor knife with a hooked end. He replaced it as he heard Ben's heavy footsteps heading back into the room.

"Let's get that drink," said Lawrence.

They bought a large bottle of cold grapefruit juice at the 7-Eleven on Kansas Avenue and emptied half of it out in the parking lot. Lawrence drove back down Blair and then North Capitol while Ben filled the bottle from a fifth of Popov vodka. He closed the lid of the juice bottle tightly and shook it, mixing the vodka and grapefruit.

They passed the bottle back and forth. Lawrence turned left on H Street and drove east. Ben relaxed and sat low in the seat. He kept his arm on the lip of the window and held his hand palm-out to catch the air. The car was an old Chevy Cavalier and it barely contained him. But he felt good. The vodka was working pleasantly on his head.

"I got this nephew," said Lawrence Newhouse.

"Uh-huh."

"Name of Marquis. My sister's boy."

"Okay."

"Sixteen years old. Had a few problems here and there. Loitering, possession, like that. He's up on charges right now, but they gonna slap his wrist, most likely. He's not cut out for that business no how. I tried to tell him, you gonna be in the game, at least show some heart. But the boy didn't listen. Police came up on him and he said, 'Here.'" In illustration, Lawrence touched his wrists together so that they were cuff-ready. "He's thick like that."

Maybe he took a look at you and saw what the life would get him, thought Ben.

"Kids be hardheaded sometimes," said Ben.

"Exactly." Lawrence looked over at Ben. "Gimme that bottle, man. You hoggin that shit."

Ben handed him the bottle. Lawrence drank sloppily, and some of the vodka and juice rolled down his chin. He fitted the bottle between his legs and made a sweeping gesture with his hand toward the street.

"City don't look like it did," said Lawrence. "Got bars and clubs for white people now in Northeast. On *H* Street. You believe it? Graybeards down by my way talk about H Street burning down during those riots they had, what, forty years ago. Took a while, but now the white folk got their hands in this, too. They were waitin on it to hit bottom all along so they could buy it up cheap. Just like they did on U."

As usual, Lawrence had oversimplified the situation and taken the conversation into the realm of conspiracy. There were all kinds of people, owners and customers, in these new bars and restaurants, not just whites. They were young and they dressed better than Lawrence and Ben, and probably had more school. They had a little money and they wanted nice places to sit and hang with their dates and friends. One or two of these nightspots had opened up, and then they started to multiply. It was progress, and people got displaced because of it, and that was a shame, but Ben didn't feel it was all to the bad. On this street here, there were lights on in windows that had once been dark, and jobs for people who needed work, and folks spending money to keep it going. Anyway, once the ball started to roll, wasn't anyone could stop it.

"No Metro on H Street," said Ben, recalling what Chris had told him earlier in the day. "That's why it took so long to turn."

At 8th, near the bus shelter that was always crowded with locals, a group of young men were running across the street, stopping traffic, yelling at the occupants of cars.

"It ain't turned all the way yet," said Lawrence.

"What about your nephew?"

"Right. Ali Carter's trying to help him out. Ali's at that place down on Alabama Avenue, Men Move Upstairs, or whatever they call it. He's workin with at-risk kids, finding them jobs and stuff. I *respect* that, you know?"

"So?"

"He means well, but I feel like he selling my nephew short. Tryin to put Marquis into a *Mac*-Donald's or a Wendy's."

"It's somethin."

"But he's better than that. Boy needs a real job. Like the kind of work you and White Boy do."

"What about it?"

"I was thinking, you know, White Boy's father could maybe

put Marquis on. Teach him so he learns a trade. So Marquis doesn't have to take some dumb-ass job where he got to wear a paper hat and get laughed at."

"Lawrence, I don't know. I mean, we got our crews set. I don't see Mr. Flynn hiring anybody new right now."

"You can ask, can't you? This for my nephew, man."

"Yeah, I can ask."

"You my boy, B. You know this."

They drove down to the new baseball stadium on South Capitol Street. Ben had not yet seen it except in photographs. There was no game that night, but the stadium was lit up and they parked and admired it, and finished what was in the bottle. A security vehicle drove by, and its occupant shone a light in their car, accelerated, and turned a corner up ahead.

"He gonna come around again," said Lawrence, cranking the ignition of the Cavalier. "They always got to be funny."

Lawrence drove east on M Street and they went past a corporate headquarters of some kind. The road wound and dipped down along the old marinas, where modest powerboats were docked, some sitting beneath colorful Christmas lights strung overhead, tucked in along the banks of the Anacostia River. Lawrence kept on cruising and pulled over near a land leg of the Sousa Bridge, in a spot where old men and kids sat on overturned plastic buckets and fished during the day; it was deserted now.

Lawrence reached under his seat and found a joint of weed he had freaked in a Black & Mild wrapper, and he slipped it into the breast pocket of his oversize shirt.

"Let's walk," he said.

They got out of the car and crossed the road. Lawrence used a lighter to fire up the blunt, and by the time they had made it to the railroad tracks it was live. The road down here dead-ended eventually, so if the police were to roll through, which they did often, it would be trouble. But Lawrence only carried enough weed to eat and be done with if need be. The police could make out that you were high, they could smell it on you, they could even see the smoke coming out your mouth, but they couldn't do shit if you had none on you. Lawrence knew the law, or so he told anyone who would listen. He felt that he was slick like that.

He offered the blunt to Ben, who took it and drew on it deep. Ben loved to get after it, but he only smoked occasionally with Chris outside work, and sometimes with his girl, Renee. He was careful to get his head right in places where he was comfortable and around people he trusted and felt safe with. Tonight, though, he made an exception. Lawrence was all right. He *could* be, sometimes. It would be bad manners to turn him down. Also, Ben was near gone on the alcohol. When he got like that, he craved a little marijuana to take him up further and, at the same time, even out his high.

They walked the tracks and smoked the joint down. Laughing and wasted, they returned to the car. Lawrence got the bottle of Popov from the Cavalier, and the two of them sat on the hood, facing Anacostia Park across the river, watching the lights from the bridge lamps play on the water, passing the alcohol back and forth, drinking warm vodka and feeling its burn.

"Pretty from here," said Ben.

"East of the river?" said Lawrence. "Nicest part of town, you ask me. That's the high point of D.C. High and green. You ever been on the grounds of Saint Elizabeth's?"

"Can't say I have."

"They got a bench on the top of a hill where you can sit and look down at the whole damn city. I mean, it's nice."

"Why were you there?"

"I got sent there. Understand, I wasn't crazy or nothin like that." Lawrence looked at Ben, then looked away. "I just didn't want to be in regular lockup no more. I'm talkin about when I was incarcerated in the *a*dult facility. People always muggin you and, you know, *challenging* you. I got tired of it. So I acted all messed up."

"What'd you do?"

"It ain't all that important what I did. Point is, I got moved. They transferred me over to Saint E's for a little bit. Had some good-ass meds in there, too."

Ben reached for the bottle. The lights on the water had blurred, and the bridge split apart and kind of flew off and came back together.

"Sounds tough," said Ben.

"Well, it was better than the joint. But I could only fool them white coats for so long."

"Anyway, it's all behind us."

"Yeah, it's past," said Lawrence. "I ain't goin back to none 'a that."

"Neither am I."

"I just wish shit was easier." Lawrence took the bottle from Ben's hand and swigged from it. He wiped vodka from his chin. "I guess I'll be workin the rest of my damn life. Ain't gonna be no money tree growin in my yard."

"There is such a thing, though. For real."

"*Shit.*"

"I saw one. Wasn't no tree, though. It was a bag."

"Fuck you talkin about, man?"

"I found a bag of cash today," said Ben. "Me and Chris did, on the job."

"How you gonna lie like that?"

"I'm not. I counted it myself. And I put it back where it was my own self, too."

"What, you just left it there?"

"Uh-huh."

"For what reason?"

"There were fifty thousand reasons to take it. Right now, I can't say why I didn't. But that ship sailed out the harbor. Can't do anything about it now."

Lawrence handed Ben the bottle. "Where was that at, B?"

Ben told him the story, and the row house address, and, because Lawrence deftly and gently prodded him, every other detail that he could remember. And when he was done talking, realizing that he was too drunk and high, and that he had to be up for work early in the morning, he asked Lawrence to drive him home.

Lawrence grinned and said he would.

FIFTEEN

"COME DOWN here," said Thomas Flynn. "Dream with me."

Thomas Flynn was in the home of Eric and Linda Wasserman. He was on his knees in their living room, pitching carpet. A large book of samples was open beside him.

Linda Wasserman, a blonde in her midthirties, stood over Flynn, her arms crossed. Her husband was at work and their child was at sleepaway camp. She had a toned body, a perfect dye job, immaculately pedicured feet at rest in designer sandals, and lovely skin. Flynn reckoned she spent a great deal of time working out and getting worked on. He was in the presence of new Potomac money.

"Come on down here," said Flynn again.

"Should I?"

"Absolutely!"

Linda Wasserman got down on all fours. She was looking to replace her living-room carpet with something nicer. The Wassermans had recently bought the house and inherited its shag carpeting and scuffed-up floors.

Flynn was there to guide her and make a sale. He was trying not to concentrate on her tight, perfect ass, which was small enough to fit into one of his hands. It would be like palming a basketball. *You could actually carry her around the house*, thought Flynn. *She's light enough. Put her in one hand and rest her on your hip, hold a beer in the other, and walk her to the bedroom.*

What's wrong with me? thought Flynn. And in his head he heard a reply: *Nothing that isn't wrong with any other man.*

"Now what?" said Linda Wasserman.

Flynn had his fingers deep in one of the samples, and he was kneading it while looking into her eyes.

"Put your hand on this," said Flynn. Meaning the sample.

She reached out and stroked the carpet sample. As she leaned forward, her breasts became pendulous beneath her pullover blouse, one of those jobs with an oval cutout and a little string tied at the scoop of the neck.

"Plush pile," said Flynn. "It's sheared several times to give it a velvety sheen. Imagine walking on this. You're not going to want to wear shoes in this room, I can tell you that. Neither are your guests."

"We don't actually use the living room much."

"Perfect. This is low-traffic carpet."

"It is nice," she said. "Is it expensive?"

"Yes," said Flynn. With her, the high cost would be a positive. But not too high. They weren't stupid rich. "It's not overextravagant, mind you. It's the Benz of carpet, rather than the Ferrari."

"Hmm." She caught him glancing at her breasts and quickly got to her feet. "I'm going to have to discuss this with my husband, Mr. Flynn."

"Of course," said Flynn, standing more slowly than she because of his aging knees. "My wife and I always talk about these kinds of purchases before we come to a decision. Let me just size this out and give you an estimate."

While he was measuring the room, his cell rang. He read the caller ID, prepared himself mentally, and answered. With one finger he made an "excuse me" sign to Linda Wasserman, then he walked out of the room.

"Thomas Flynn speaking."

"Mr. Flynn, this is Mindy Kramer."

"Hello, Mindy—"

"I need to see you down at the job site right away."

Clearly she was agitated. But with these aggressive, hard-charging types, it could be nothing more than a few drops of soda spilled on a hardwood floor by a worker, or a piece of the old carpet left behind on the site. A negotiating ploy to get the price of the job down.

"Is there a problem?" said Flynn.

"A *very* serious problem."

"With the product or the installation?"

"The installation. Maybe the product. *I* don't know."

"So I should send my guys down."

"I'd like you here, too. Frankly, I have no faith in them at this point."

"Can you just elaborate a little bit so I know what we're talking about here?"

"I don't have *time*. The police are here, Mr. Flynn, and I have to go. On top of the subpar work that was done by your men, this house was broken into last night."

"I'm sorry to hear that. Okay. I've got to finish up here, but it won't be long."

"I'll see you shortly."

Flynn phoned Chris and asked him if he knew the nature of Mindy Kramer's malfunction. Chris, on a Northwest job with Ben, told him that the install at her row house had been clean and error free. Flynn caught a bit of hesitation in Chris's voice that did not comfort him.

"Finish up what you're doing," said Flynn, "and meet me down at the house."

Flynn gave Linda Wasserman her estimate, deliberately not allowing his eyes to drop below her chin as he explained the pricing and terms. He shook her hand and headed back down into the city.

FLYNN SPOTTED a Third District cruiser on the street as he pulled up near Mindy Kramer's row house. He went through the unlocked front door and followed the sound of Mindy Kramer's distinctive voice to the kitchen at the rear.

The kitchen door opened to a small deck whose steps led down to the alley. Mindy Kramer and two young uniformed officers, a woman and a man, were standing on the deck. Mindy was smoking a long, thin white cigarette, gesturing with it as she spoke to the two rather uninterested-looking police.

"I don't have an alarm system," Mindy Kramer was saying, as Flynn joined the group. "I'm flipping this place, so I'm not going to invest in one. And you don't want to try and sell a home with bars on its windows. I mean, the house is unfurnished, so what's there to steal?"

"Whoever broke in didn't know that till he got inside," said the female officer.

"That's right," said Flynn, just to inject himself into the conversation.

The female police officer looked at Flynn. "And you are?"

"He's here for something else," said Mindy Kramer, by way of both introduction and dismissal, waving at him with her cigarette, waving him away.

The male officer drifted and eyed the severely splintered doorjamb. It looked to Flynn as if a jimmy or crowbar had been taken to it. It had been an unprofessional and successful effort.

"It could have been kids," said Mindy Kramer. "Or a junkie. I don't care who it was. But you'd think the neighbors would have heard something. A couple of people on this block have dogs, for God's sake."

"We'll knock on some doors," said the female officer. "See what we can find out."

"Aren't you going to dust for prints?" said Mindy Kramer.

The female officer looked at Flynn for a moment and light danced in her eyes. They could "dust" the whole house, but, short of walking into the 3D station himself and confessing to the crime, this particular perpetrator, who apparently had stolen nothing, would not be brought to justice.

"First thing, I'm gonna need to fill out a report," she said.

"Ach," said Mindy Kramer, rolling her eyes. It was as if the officer had told her that she was about to be strip-searched.

"Excuse me," said Flynn. "About that problem."

"Go have a look at it," said Mindy Kramer. "You'll see what I'm talking about right away. I have to stay here and help her *fill out* a report."

Flynn exchanged another commiserating look with the officer before moving away.

He was not in love with the police, but he was empathetic about the job they did and the people they had to deal with every day. He had never once regretted his decision to leave the MPD, but he was glad he had experienced that life, if only for less than a year. The brevity of his tenure aside, the man in blue had never left his blood entirely.

He owned a .38 Special, which had been the MPD sidearm

in his day, before the force switched over to the Glock 17.
Though it probably wasn't true that all police felt naked without a gun after their retirement, it happened to be true for
Flynn. Despite the District handgun ban, recently lifted, he
had bought the revolver hot from one of his installers and kept
it loaded in the nightstand beside his bed. He liked knowing
that there was a firearm within reach. Given the relative safety
of his neighborhood, his decision to own an illegal gun was
emotional rather than rational. He realized he'd pay a heavy
price if he was caught with it, but he was willing to take the
risk.

"Pardon me," said Flynn to the male officer, as he stepped
around him and went through the open kitchen door.

Flynn went toward the front of the house, into the center
hallway, and cut left into the library. He inspected the work
that Chris and Ben had done. It had simply been a sloppy performance. One side of the carpet was misaligned with the wall
and slanted away from the bead. On that side, nearest the built-
in bookshelves, the corner of the carpet had not been laid
properly and appeared to have been pulled up and hastily put
back down.

"Chris," said Flynn, shaking his head. Flynn knew that he
had measured correctly and he had double-checked the size of
the roll when it had come into the warehouse. This was on
Chris and his friend Ben. They just hadn't done the job with
conscience or care.

He went to the spot that looked worse and got down on his
knees. He lifted the corner to check on the padding and saw
that a cutout had been made in the hardwood floor. With one
knee holding down the bent-back carpet, he got his fingers
under a notch in the cutout and lifted it away from the floor.

A kind of basket, fashioned with wood slats, had been built

in beneath the floor. It was meant to hold something, but it held nothing now. Flynn actually scratched his head. The concealed cutout and basket were nothing to him, and asking Mindy Kramer about them would only be a further complication. He replaced the panel, put the carpet back down, and phoned his son. Chris and Ben were headed south on 16th Street, just five minutes away.

When they arrived, they came straight to the job site where Flynn was waiting.

"Hey," said Chris.

"Chris," said Flynn, "what's this?"

Chris breathed through his mouth, his eyes darting nervously as he revisited the work they'd done. What Flynn used to call his "what the fuck did I do" look. Ben stood beside him, silent, not able or willing to look at Flynn. Flynn smelled the alcohol sweat coming off Ben and could see a hard night and shame in his eyes. He wondered how long he could carry this man. When poor performance began to affect Flynn's business, he had to reconsider the hire. Even if it was his own son.

"That's not how we left it," said Chris.

"C'mon, Chris. Don't play me like that."

"Listen to me, Dad. We did this job right."

"Yeah, okay."

Chris thumb-stroked the scar above his lip, something he did unconsciously when he was struggling with a problem. "What are the police doing here? We saw 'em in the back of the house when we came down the hall."

"Somebody broke in last night," said Flynn. "It's got nothing to do with this."

Flynn noticed Chris glance at Ben, and he saw Ben stare

down at his shoes, his posture slackening. Something wasn't right.

"Maybe whoever broke in came in here and messed up our work," said Chris.

"Please," said Flynn.

"I'm *tell*ing you. We did the job correctly."

"I don't have time for this right now," said Flynn. "You two get to work and correct it. I've got to go back out there and make some sort of price adjustment for the customer. It's gonna cost me, but hey, what's a few hundred dollars."

"Take it out my check," said Chris.

"You know I don't do that," said Flynn. "Go on, get to work."

Flynn left the room. Chris stared at Ben, who would not meet his eyes.

"You heard him," said Chris. "Let's fix this shit."

CHRIS AND Ben refinished the job properly while Thomas Flynn dealt with Mindy Kramer and adjusted her bill. When they were almost done, two young police officers came into the room where they were working and had a look around. The female officer asked Chris what he was doing, and he told her that they were correcting a new-carpet install that had been done the day before. Chris and Ben said nothing further. If they had been asked other questions, their responses would have been similarly to-the-point and minimal. They did not hate police, but neither did they trust them or have any desire to cooperate or fraternize with them.

The day had cooled little by early evening, when Chris pulled into the small parking lot behind Ben's apartment house, finding a spot shaded, somewhat, by a thin-armed maple. Chris pushed the transmission arm up into park and let the motor run. Ben had his elbow resting on the lip of the window and was staring out toward the cemetery. They had spoken very little on the ride uptown.

"You gonna talk to me now?" said Chris.

Ben turned his head and looked into his friend's eyes. "I didn't take the money, Chris."

"You told me that already."

"You believe me, right?"

"I do. But you know who took it."

Ben nodded slowly. "Had to be Lawrence Newhouse."

"*Shit*. You told Lawrence?"

"Uh-huh."

"Why him?"

Ben briefly shut his eyes, as if that could erase what he had done. "Lawrence came past my spot last night."

"He just dropped in for no reason."

"Nah, he wanted something. *You* know that. Ali's been tryin to help his nephew out. Young man's up on charges, I expect. So Ali's lookin to, you know, help him get a job at a McDonald's, someplace like that. Lawrence don't think that's good enough for his nephew. He wanted to see if your father could put him on."

"I'm not doing that," said Chris. "I'm not getting involved with Lawrence or anyone in his family. I wouldn't do that to my old man."

"I told Lawrence the same. In a different way, but I told him. And then I went for a drive with him, just to get him out my apartment."

"I would've shown him the door."

"That's what I should've done, but I didn't. We ended up down by the river, and Lawrence got me all fucked up on weed and alcohol. You know I can't hold my drink. I started to talk behind the vodka. I'm not making an excuse. I'm just sayin, I was trippin and that's what I did. I can't even tell you what I said to him. I mean, I was that far gone. But I woke up this morning and I knew I had told him enough and that I had messed up bad."

"Shit, Ben."

"I know, man. I'm sorry."

"Sorry don't fix this."

"I could talk to Lawrence. He still stays down there at Parkchester. Ali could get up with him through his nephew."

"What for?" said Chris.

They sat there for a while without speaking. They thought about what to do, and it came to Chris that there was nothing to do. There was no one to return the money to. There was simply a basket, now empty, underneath a floor in an unoccupied row house. No one would miss the money or know that it had been there or that it was gone.

Naturally, their thoughts drifted toward regret and then resentment. Why hadn't they gone ahead and taken the money themselves when they had come upon it the day before? If taking it had no consequences, and it appeared that there would be none, then what had been the wrong in it? Now Lawrence Newhouse had the money, and he didn't deserve to have it. Lawrence would blow it on bad clothing, strippers, potent weed, and stepped-on cocaine. And Chris and Ben would be ass-broke and back at work at seven in the morning, sweating through polo shirts they hated to wear.

"Bughouse," said Chris under his breath. He managed a small incredulous smile.

"Stupid," said Ben, shaking his head. *"Stupid."*

"Anyway," said Chris.

Chris and Ben shook hands.

"Same time tomorrow?" said Ben.

"I'll pick you up."

Ben left his tool belt in the back of the van and shut the doors. Chris watched his friend go into the stairwell of his building, then pulled from the lot and headed out of the city. By the time North Capitol became Blair Road, his bitterness had dissipated. He was thinking of a cool shower, a cold beer, and Katherine.

In his apartment, Ben Braswell washed up and changed his clothing. He phoned Renee to see if she wanted to hook up that night, and she said she did. She'd come by with a pizza and a Blockbuster movie when she got off work, around ten o'clock.

"See you then, girl," said Ben.

"That's a bet," said Renee.

He took a catnap on his sofa. When he woke, the room had darkened. He got up, went to the window, and parted the blinds. There was still light left in the day.

Ben slipped a paperback into the back pocket of his jeans, left his place, went along the black iron fence to the open gate at Rock Creek Church and Webster, and entered the cemetery grounds. He was headed toward the Adams Memorial, where he would sit on the marble bench shielded by evergreens and read until dark.

He stepped down a road so narrow it was no kind of road, then went off it, taking a shortcut across a stand of graves. The dying sun settled on the headstones and threw shadows at his feet.

SIXTEEN

MINDY KRAMER ate in the same place most every weekday. It was a Thai restaurant up in Wheaton, off University Boulevard, in an area heavy with Hispanics and Orthodox Jews, where nothing was upscale and fast-food wrappers and cigarette butts littered the streets.

The restaurant itself had little ambience, holding eight four-tops and a half-dozen deuces, with the standard royal family portraits hung on plain blue walls. But the food was clean, the service mostly efficient, and the specials went for four dollars and ninety-five cents, including a choice of spring rolls or watered-down lemongrass soup.

Thai Feast was out of the way from Mindy's core business, which was down in Dupont, Capitol Hill, and that broad area of Shaw that included the neighborhood she and her fellow real estate professionals called Logan. Mindy made the half-hour trek out to Wheaton because Thai Feast had become her base camp. The girl who always served her, Toi, gave her the same deuce by the window, leaving it unoccupied until her arrival, and had her ice water and iced coffee on the table shortly after Mindy had taken her seat. As Mindy made her calls and answered e-mails from her BlackBerry, Toi was busy fetching the spring rolls that came with the special and making sure the main dish that Mindy had chosen would come out right behind it. The bill was always seven forty-nine, and Mindy always left one forty-nine in the tip column of the check, exactly 20 percent.

Mindy Kramer was all about routine and organization. She had married at twenty-two, had one daughter, Lisa, and divorced her layabout husband at twenty-five. She had raised and supported Lisa by herself as she got her license and grew her business. Now she had an office in Northwest, where "a girl" handled the phones and paperwork. Mindy had trained and polished two young sales protégés who, along with her, made up the Dream Team. Unfortunately, Lisa had made the same mistake as her mother and married a young man who had no energy or ambition outside the bedroom. She was now single with two little girls, ages six and four, of her own. Because she felt that Lisa was not emotionally equipped to be a proper mother to them, Mindy often took the children, Michelle and Lauren, with her to the office or dropped them off at summer day camp.

She handled all of this because she was efficient. *And* she looked good. At fifty-five, she was toned, well-dressed, and properly made up and manicured. There wasn't one gelled, spiked, highlighted hair out of place on her head.

"How is your family, Toi?" said Mindy Kramer, as she added the tip and signed the credit card voucher before her.

"They are well," said Toi with a smile.

"I'll see you tomorrow," said Mindy.

"Thank you so much," said Toi, her smile frozen in place.

Mindy Kramer got up and, smoothing her sleeveless lavender shift down her thighs, her purse in hand, left the restaurant, donning her oversize sunglasses as she walked toward her C-class, parked in the lot.

Watching Mindy through the plate glass window of Thai Feast, Toi let her smile fade. She couldn't stand this weathered shrew with the stupid haircut, who would never round up the tip one penny to an even one fifty, who asked about her family but never really listened to the reply or looked into her eyes. But this was what you put up with every day. It was work.

Mindy got into her Mercedes and turned the ignition. She glanced at the Anne Klein watch on her tan, lightly freckled wrist. She was exactly on schedule to make her meeting down at the row house in Logan. She had gotten a call from a gentleman that morning, telling her he was interested in taking a look at the house. It had been a week since the break-in, and several months since she had bought the home at auction. The market was extremely soft, her interest rate had not been optimum, and the clock was ticking. But, like all good sales professionals, she was an optimist. Perhaps this would be the client she had been waiting for. It could very well be Mindy's day.

THERE WERE two men standing at the top of her row house steps as Mindy Kramer pulled into a nearby space on the street. Her immediate impression, looking at them through the windshield of her sedan, was that these men could not be her potential buyers. They looked more like workmen than clients.

She got out of her car, smile in place, and walked across the sidewalk and up the steps to greet them. She kept her smile rigid as she got a good look at them, thinking, *God, why are they wasting my time?* She would qualify them quickly and let them know with diplomacy that this was too much house for them and that perhaps she could find them someplace else, in a neighborhood, say, where trailer trash was more welcome.

"Mindy Kramer," she said, extending her hand to the larger of the two men.

"Ralph Cotter," he said, vise-gripping her hand, showing her a row of grayish, cheaply capped teeth. "This is my friend Nat Harbin."

"Pleasure," said Nat Harbin. Tattoos of some kind showed on his veined biceps beneath the rolled-up edges of his T-shirt, and tattoos sleeved his forearms. He wore black ring-strap boots.

Cotter had not released her hand. She looked at his and saw a tattoo, like a four-leaf clover, on the crook of it. Cotter let go of her, stepped back, and smiled.

Both were in their late thirties and both wore jeans. Harbin in a black T-shirt and Cotter in a windbreaker with a white oxford underneath. Harbin had some sort of chain going from his wallet pocket to his belt loop. He was short and wiry, with a bushy mustache that appeared to originate in his nose. His eyes were flat and brown. His long brown hair was parted in the middle and it was unclean.

Cotter was tall, broad, and strong, with a big chest and an unchecked gut. His black hair was also on the long side and swept back behind his ears. He wore a dark walrus mustache on a face with high, pronounced cheekbones. His eyes were black, mostly pupil, and did not appear to be threatening or unkind.

Mindy prided herself on reading people. She was in a business that required such a talent, after all. These two were strange, stuck in a time warp, perhaps new to the city, and uninterested in current fashions. But they weren't here to do her any harm. In any event, there had never been a situation that she couldn't handle.

Mustaches, wallet chains, boots . . . costume macho. *Gay*

bikers, thought Mindy Kramer. *Okay, I'm projecting. Gay would fit fine here, though. But do they have the dosh to buy this house?*

"You gentlemen are both interested in the property?" she said. "You're considering it . . . together?"

"Yeah," said Ralph Cotter. "Can we have a look inside?"

"Of course!"

Mindy opened her small purse, where she kept her Black-Berry and keys, and negotiated the lockbox hung on the door-knob.

"No alarm system?" said Cotter.

"No need," she said, looking over her shoulder and up be-cause he was so tall.

"Street looks peaceful enough."

"You notice no bars on the windows, either. We really don't have those kinds of problems in this neighborhood. It was dicey at one time, but" . . . she opened the door . . . "no lon-ger."

They stepped into a foyer, where a staircase led up to the third-floor bedrooms and a hall went straight back to the body of the house. The little one, Nat Harbin, shut the door behind them. The closing of it darkened the foyer, and Mindy switched on a light.

"Where did you find out about this home?" said Mindy. "I always like to know if my advertising dollars are well spent."

"Drove by it and saw the sign," said Cotter. "Then we got on the Internet and learned the particulars."

"So you've read the entire listing."

"We know the price," said Cotter patiently. "We can han-dle it."

"You gentlemen are in what business?"

"Don't worry, we qualify," said Cotter. Not annoyed, just matter-of-fact. "Let's see the house."

"Okay," said Mindy. "We'll start with the kitchen."

They went down the hall. The one named Nat eyed the layout and various rooms as they went along, but Cotter kept his focus on Mindy. He looked down at her head, noticing her scalp showing through all the clumps of hair glued together and sticking up straight. There didn't seem to be much to her under that dress. She had an ass but not enough of one. She had small cans and she was old. He didn't mind the old part, but he liked a woman with big tits.

"Here's the kitchen," she said, casually sliding a dimmer switch mounted on the wall and bathing the room in a yellowish glow. "Granite countertops and stainless steel appliances, as you can see."

Granite countertops were now as remarkable as toilet paper holders in bathrooms, and stainless steel surfaces had no bearing on the quality of the appliances themselves, but the public was gullible. Who was Mindy Kramer to educate them when she was merely trying to move a house?

"Nice," said Cotter, nodding his head.

"And all new," said Mindy. She placed her purse on the granite counter. "Do you two like to cook?" Neither of them answered, and Mindy said, "This is a very diverse neighborhood, you know."

Cotter and Harbin looked at each other and laughed.

Mindy scratched at her neck. It was something she did when she became a bit self-conscious and insecure, and she hated herself for succumbing to the reflex now. These two were vulgarians. They were not going to buy this house, nor could they afford to. They were wasting her time.

"Internet said this place had a library slash den," said Nat Harbin. "Can you take us to it?"

"Yes, but . . . please understand, I have a very busy schedule today."

"We'd like to see it," said Cotter, still smiling, his capped teeth perfect and ugly in the yellow light. "If you don't mind."

She led them back down the hall. She stumbled, catching the toe of one Stuart Weitzman sandal on the walnut floor, and Cotter grabbed her elbow with his big hand and steadied her.

"Easy now," he said, and as he held her elbow with one hand, he lightly stroked her bare arm with the other. Bumps rose on her flesh.

She went into the library and they followed her. She crossed her arms and looked out the window that gave to a view of the street, and then back at the men. The one who called himself Ralph Cotter stood blocking the door. The little one, Nat Harbin, was looking at Cotter expectantly, waiting for a signal or direction.

"Get to it," said Cotter.

Harbin bent forward, hiked up the left leg of his jeans, and pulled a knife from a tie-down sheath inside his boot. The knife was hardwood handled, with a heavy-duty pommel and a spine-cut surgical-steel blade.

Mindy Kramer hugged herself and looked down at her feet.

"That's right, honey," said Cotter. "You just stand there and mind your own."

Harbin went to a corner of the room, lifted a bit of the carpet, and cut cleanly beneath it in a filleting motion. He pulled back a triangle of the Berber and with his knee kept it pinned down. He found the notch in the cutout of wood floor and lifted the piece away, and when he saw there was nothing in the basket that had been fashioned beneath it, he said, "Shit."

"Nothin, huh," said Cotter.

"It's empty," said Harbin.

Cotter shook his head. "That's a problem."

"Where is it, lady?" said Harbin.

"Where is what?" said Mindy Kramer in a small voice, keeping her eyes to the floor.

"I had somethin in that hole," said Cotter. "It belonged to me."

"I don't know anything about it," said Mindy.

"Look at me," said Cotter.

Mindy willed herself to raise her eyes and face him. "I swear to you. I don't know what you're talking about. I bought this house to flip it. I've never lived here. I've never even looked under that carpet, not once."

"Rug looks brand-new to me."

"I replaced it, just a week ago. Not me, of course . . ."

"Who?"

"I used a local company."

"Who *exactly?*"

"I've got the information. I keep a file on all the work I've done here. Warranties and such."

"Where?"

"It's in the kitchen."

"Let's go."

Cotter stepped out of the room to let her pass, Harbin close behind her, knife in hand. They all went back down the hall, and in the kitchen Mindy maxed out the dimmer switch and pulled open a drawer near a stainless steel gas cooktop. On top of a stack of use-and-care manuals was a manila file folder, and she withdrew it. She opened the file on the granite countertop, her hand visibly shaking as she rooted through papers and found the one she was looking for.

"Here it is," she said, handing it to Cotter.

He examined the piece of paper. The name of the company and the billing address were at the top of the page. The cost of goods and the labor were line-itemed in the body of the bill. At the bottom, in the total slot, the number had been changed and initialed.

"Flynn's Floors," said Cotter. "And you dealt with . . ."

"The owner. Thomas Flynn."

"Looks like he gave you some kind of break on the price."

"It was an adjustment. His installers did a poor job. They had to come back and redo the work."

Cotter and Harbin exchanged a look.

"You wouldn't recall the names of the *in*-stallers, would you?" said Cotter.

"I . . ."

"C'mon, honey. You're doing good so far."

Mindy Kramer chewed on her lower lip. "I'm going to reach into my purse. I need to get my BlackBerry."

"Do it," said Cotter.

She took her purse off the counter, opened it, and retrieved her phone. She scrolled through her contacts and found the one she was looking for. She had entered it using a memory device so that she could recall it easily.

"Here's one of them," said Mindy, handing him the phone.

"Chris Carpet," said Cotter, squinting to read it.

"I didn't get his last name."

"Describe him for me."

"Young. Big, with blond hair."

"You said there was two of them."

"The other installer was black. Young and strong, like his partner. Tall. That's all I can remember about him. I'm sorry—"

"That'll be fine. Write down Chris Carpet's phone number on the back of the bill for me, will you?"

Mindy found a pen in her purse and did as she was told. Cotter took the bill of sale, folded it, and slipped it into the pocket of his windbreaker. Then he stepped forward and pressed himself against her. His cock grew hard. Because of his height and her lack of it, he pushed it against her belly. She turned her head to the side. A tear sprung loose from one eye and rolled down her cheek. He felt her body shiver against his.

"Don't cry, honey," said Cotter.

"I can't . . . help it."

"You wanna know what I had in that hole?"

"No."

"I had money."

"No . . ."

"How about our real names? Wanna know what they are? Bet you're curious."

A string of mucus dropped from Mindy's nose and came to rest on her lip. "I'm not."

"Course you're not. You think if I tell you my name I'm gonna go ahead and kill you. Ain't that right?"

Mindy's tears flowed freely and she closed her eyes and shook her head. Cotter stepped back. A triangle of urine had darkened the crotch of her dress.

"Look at that," said Harbin. "She tinkled."

"I'm not gonna kill you, Mindy," said Cotter. "Not you. I don't need to." Cotter put his hand into the pocket of his jeans and pulled free a cell phone. He flipped it open and punched buttons clumsily with his thick thumb. "I got a phone, too. Not as fancy as yours, but hey. Here we go."

Cotter handed her the phone. She looked at the screen and made a small choking sound from deep in her throat.

"You recognize those little girls, right? Kinda hard to see 'em, I know, 'cause I was far away. But that's them. That would be your granddaughters, right?"

Mindy did not answer.

"Say it's them," said Harbin.

"It's my granddaughters," said Mindy Kramer.

"Okay," said Cotter. He pointed to the ink on the crook of his hand. "Now, do you know what this is?"

"A clover?"

"It's a shamrock, honey. Means I'm part of something, kind of like a club. We got members in prisons all across the country. We *run* the prisons, matter of fact. Got a lotta members who are out and in the world now, too. All of us, in this club, forever. When you ride with the rock, you're protected. And if anything bad does happen to you, you're avenged. Families, children . . . we'll kill 'em all and not even think on it twice. It's part of the blood oath we take to get in. Do you understand?"

"I think so."

"I hope you do. You know what we were doing this morning? We were parked outside your office, watching you bring in your granddaughters, watching you bring them back out. After, we followed you to where you dropped them off, at that rec center outside the elementary school. What was that, Thirty-third Street? Yeah, that's where it was. Where I snapped these pictures from my phone."

Cotter reached out and took his cell from Mindy Kramer's hand.

"You never met us today," said Cotter.

Mindy Kramer nodded.

"You ain't gonna talk about this to your priest or rabbi, or your shrink, or nobody else. You're not gonna warn Chris Carpet that we're looking to speak to him, either."

"I won't."

"Because if you do, my little friend here will visit your grand-daughters."

"Please, don't—"

"He'll cut their heads off and skull-fuck 'em both, *Mindy*. Do you get it?"

Mindy Kramer nodded.

"Say you do," said Harbin.

"I get it," said Mindy.

"I think she does," said Cotter. "C'mon."

Harbin sheathed his knife. He and Cotter walked down the hall, straight out of the house, closing the door behind them and taking the steps to the sidewalk, not caring if they were seen.

When Mindy Kramer heard the shut of the door, she dropped to the kitchen floor and sat with her back to the cabinets, weeping, her head between her knees, chest heaving, mascara running down her face. She made no move to phone the police or anyone else. She sat there and waited for the fear to leave her. She sat there for a long while. What they had taken from her would not come back soon. Maybe it would never come back at all.

THE MEN walked to their car, a 1988 Mercury Marquis they had picked up from a cancer-ridden old man in West Virginia. From the long-term lot at Dulles Airport they had switched out plates, and the car now bore D.C. tags. The sedan was boxy and black, with a landau roof and red velour interior, a fake-fur-covered steering wheel, and a V-8 under the hood.

Ralph Cotter and Nat Harbin were not their names. The big man with the walrus mustache was Sonny Wade. He had chosen the fake names from two of the many novels he had read while incarcerated at the federal prison in Lewisburg, Pennsylvania. In those books, Cotter had been a stone killer and Harbin had been a career burglar. It was at Lewisburg that Sonny Wade had met the little man, Wayne Minors, who had been his cell mate. Wayne did not read books.

Sonny got himself positioned in the driver's seat and turned the key in the ignition. Wayne looked tiny beside him, as if he were Sonny's child, if Sonny could have had a son his own age. Wayne's features were compressed toward the middle of his face, folding into one another, so he looked like a piece of fruit that had begun to rot. Wayne drank and used speed, but his longtime cigarette smoking had done the bulk of the damage to his looks.

Wayne lit a Marlboro off a butane flame as Sonny pulled out of the spot on S Street. They were headed toward New York Avenue, where they had a room in a flophouse motel populated by unwitting tourists, assorted losers, prostitutes, alcoholics, drug addicts, and people on the government tit.

"She wasn't so full of herself when we got finished with her," said Wayne.

"She won't speak on this to anyone," said Sonny.

"She pissed her panties."

"That she did."

"Kramer's a Jewish name."

"Uh-huh."

"You hear what she said about us being together? And askin, do we like to cook?" Wayne's eyes crossed slightly as he considered this. "It was like she thought we was faggots."

"She thought *you* was," said Sonny.

"Your daddy was," said Wayne.

They were silent as Sonny wheeled the radio dial, trying to find something he liked, settling on a station playing a Rascal

Flatts song. Wayne smoked and studied the city as they passed through it, looking at the whites and the blacks together in these neighborhoods, wondering how a father could let his daughter live among these low coloreds in a shithole such as this.

"Those installers took my money," said Sonny after a while. "Had to be them."

"We'll get it back." Wayne pitched his cigarette out the open window. "Sonny?"

"Huh."

"Why'd you tell that woman I'd fuck those little girls and cut their heads off? You know I wouldn't do no such thing. I wouldn't kill a kid. I'm a gentleman. I ain't like that."

"And I'm no AB. I was just puttin the fear into her, is all."

"I'd kill a nigger," offered Wayne.

"You might could get your chance," said Sonny. "But we're gonna talk to Chris Carpet first."

SEVENTEEN

CHRIS, ALI, and several younger men were in a Saturday afternoon game on the basketball courts at the Hamilton Rec Center between 13th and 14th in Northwest, in an area known as 16th Street Heights. When he was available, Ali liked to have Chris hang out with his boys, so that they could see by example an ex–juvenile offender who had managed to reenter society in a positive way. Chris wasn't about giving speeches or deep advice, but if it meant simply showing up to ball, he was there.

Chris had asked Ali to bring the boys to Hamilton, as the fenced-in courts were in good shape, and the red, white, and blue nets were kept intact. He'd been playing there since his teens and found the quality of players fairly high. It was here where an errant elbow had split his lip and given him his scar, which Katherine later told him was the second thing she'd noticed about him and liked, after his eyes. Ham Rec now held value to him for that alone.

Ali had driven out from Southeast in his mother's beat-up Saturn with William Richards and Marquis Gilman, Lawrence's nephew, in tow. They had invited in two young men who lived on Farragut Street and gone three-on-three for a few games. Chris had bulk and a jumper, and Ali still had his vertical leap, but the teenagers had them on speed. The games had been hard fought but without major conflict, the players evenly matched, and all had been sweated out and satisfied when it was agreed that they were done.

Chris stayed on the court and worked with Marquis, showing him his box-out move and telling him to watch the extra step on his drive to the bucket. Marquis, still gangly in his youth, looked Chris in the eye when spoken to but disagreed that his pretty move was a violation.

"That's a jump step, Mr. Chris," said Marquis.

"It's an *extra* step," said Chris. "Just 'cause they don't call it in the NBA doesn't mean you can do it out here."

"I'll do it when I go pro, then."

"You're not goin pro, Marquis. But you *could* be a good pickup man. If you didn't travel with the ball every time you drove."

"Okay," said Marquis. "I hear you."

Ali returned with some bottles of water he had gotten out of the Saturn's trunk. William Richards, who had been sitting by himself near the playground, got up and joined them. Ali offered him a bottle, but he waved it away.

"I don't want it," said William, his Bulls cap cocked sideways on his head. "That water's hot."

"Wet, too," said Ali.

"I'm gonna walk down to Kennedy and Georgia, get somethin to drink at the Wings n Things."

"They closed that place," said Chris.

"Whateva they call it now, they still got cold sodas," said William. "You comin, Marquis?"

"Is it all right, Mr. Ali?" said Marquis.

"Yeah, go ahead. Keep to yourselves, hear? I'll come by and pick you two up on my way out."

The two young men walked east on Hamilton, then cut north on 13th. Ali and Chris went to the black Saturn, parked behind Chris's van. Ali sat on the hood and took a swig of warm water.

"Marquis is all right," said Chris.

"Ain't nothin wrong with him," said Ali. "He got some issues at home and with his peers at those apartments, is all. Marquis only did dirt 'cause his friends did. He's just tryin to belong to something, man."

"You get him legit work?"

"I'm about to hook him up at a Wendy's, if the manager ever calls me back."

"Ben said Lawrence came to see you."

"He wanted me to put Marquis up with your pops. I wouldn't even ask. Wendy's is a better start for him at this point. That boy's gonna be one of my success stories."

"No doubt," said Chris.

"You seen Lawrence lately?"

"No. Ben and him were together one night recently. But I wasn't with 'em."

Chris hadn't told Ali about Lawrence and the bag of cash. Lawrence had been putting that money up his nose, most likely, or watching it bounce on his dick since he'd broke into the Kramer house to take it. Chris was trying to forget about the money, and for the most part he had.

"Man looks old," said Ali. "But he's the same Lawrence."

"Bughouse is Bughouse," said Chris, repeating something that had been said often in their unit, many years back.

Ali took a long drink. Chris bunched up his shirt and wiped sweat from his face.

181

"Appreciate you coming out today," said Ali.

"I just came to play basketball."

"It's more than that. The boys like seeing you. You got a nice way with them, man."

"I don't mind hangin with them, when I have the time."

"You ever think of changing up? Doing something different?"

"What, you asking me to come work with you?"

"I make less than you do," said Ali. "So I wouldn't suggest that. I'm talking about switching careers. You love reading those books of yours so much, why don't you use it? Good as you are with kids, you could be a history teacher, somethin like that."

"You mean like Mr. Beige? He didn't look all that prosperous to me."

"Teachers make decent money now, Chris, and it's getting better all the time. In some cities schoolteachers make six figures, they hang with it long enough."

"But I can't be one," said Chris.

"Sure you can."

"Armed with a high school degree?"

"So get yourself enrolled in a community college, then transfer to a university or state school when you make grades."

"How would I support myself?"

"You'd work, just like you do now. Work during the day and go to your classes at night."

"That would take forever."

"Those years would go by quick. You could earn your teaching certificate and get out there and do some good. They got this Teach For America program, where people come fresh out of college and go to work in disadvantaged school districts—"

"Nah, man."

"Why not?"

"That's not who I am," said Chris. "I'm a carpet installer, Ali."

"You could be more."

"Okay, Shawshank."

Ali chuckled. "Shit. That old man just didn't know when to quit, did he."

"Like you," said Chris, eyeing his friend and tapping his water bottle to Ali's.

"Well, let me go pick up those knuckleheads," said Ali, getting off the hood of his mother's car.

"My father's having his employee barbecue tonight at his house," said Chris, retrieving the van keys from the pocket of his shorts. "You gonna come past?"

"Your pops walks backward when he sees me," said Ali.

"He asked me to tell you to come by. Even though you made him put Lonnie and Luther on the payroll."

"Don't forget Milton."

"Yeah, Milton couldn't operate the tape measure. But my old man does like you. Not that I can figure out why. Prob'ly cause, out of me and my friends, you're the only one who's had any success."

"You're doin all right, too, man."

"Right." Chris walked toward the white van. "Come by, hear?"

Ali said, "I will."

LAWRENCE NEWHOUSE walked up the road in his long T-shirt, along the Barry Farms dwellings, this particular block a two-story strip of tan motel-style structures with chocolate doorways and arches. Time was, in his youth, he and his boys at

Parkchester would have been beefing with those at the Farms, and he supposed the young ones still did the same, but that was past for him. People looked at him as he went along, eyeing him but not hard, like he wasn't worth the time it took to fix a stare. At twenty-six, Lawrence was old. He had not taken care of himself, what with his poor diet, drinking, all manner of smoke, and powder when he could get it. He looked close to forty.

He had a plastic bottle of fruit punch in his hand. He had bought it at the local Korean place, having woken up, still in his club clothes atop the sheets of his bed, with a vicious thirst. He'd spent a bunch of money the night before in that strip club he liked on New York Avenue. He'd spent it on hard liquor and dancers, the usual shove-the-bills-in-the-string thing, and on a gram of coke he'd copped in the bathroom from a young man he'd met at the bar. The freeze had made him shit soon as he'd taken his first bite of it off the end of a key. That's what he got for buying coke from someone he didn't know. Wasn't much more than laxative, but it kept him awake. And it got one of the dancers interested enough to come outside with him and swallow his manhood in the backseat of her man's car. Which had cost him another hundred. He didn't remember driving his Cavalier back to Southeast, but it was parked in his spot, so he supposed that this is what he had done.

Money went quick.

Lawrence walked across a small dusty playground with monkey bars and the rusted, spidery frame of a swing set. At the edge of the playground a steel pole with no backboard was set in concrete. Around the pole was a tribute to a boy named Beanie, a loose arrangement of teddy bears, ribbons and banners, empty Hennessey bottles, and photographs, a commemoration of Beanie's short, fast life and death by gun.

Then Lawrence was on Wade and heading toward the Parkchester Apartments, stepping around boys he recognized but did not speak to who were grouped at one of the entrance-ways, and going into a stairwell holding the usual stagnant smells of things that were fried, eaten, or smoked.

He went into his place.

It wasn't his place, exactly. It was Dorita's, his half-sister. Dorita was on government assistance, had three children by two different men, and let him stay here. When she was short on food or needed Nikes for the kids, he gave her cash, if he had it. He had it now, but Dorita didn't know.

Her two younger kids, Terrence and Loquatia, were on the carpet, watching a show on a widescreen plasma television Dorita had bought on time. Loquatia, eleven and already running to fat like her mother, had her hand in a bowl of Skittles, running her fingers through the colored bits. Long as Loquatia was touching food, she was cool. Her little brother was staring at the cartoon lobster on the screen but daydreaming, thinking on something called a galaxy, which he had learned about in school. He had an active imagination, and his teacher suspected he was highly intelligent. The teacher had phoned Dorita to tell her about an accelerated program available at his elementary, but Dorita had yet to call her back.

Dorita sat on the living-room sofa, her feet up on it, cell phone in hand. There was no man currently in her life. She was thirty-two, and her stretch-marked belly spilled out from beneath her tight shirt. At two fifty, she had eighty pounds on Lawrence. They had the same mother but looked nothing alike.

"Where you been at?" said Dorita.

"I went down to the Chang's," said Lawrence.

"And you ain't get me nothin?"

"Wasn't like I went to the grocery store." Lawrence head-shook his braids away from his face. "Where's Marquis at?"

"Mr. Carter came past and picked him up. Before you woke up. Marquis said they were going to play basketball."

"Okay," said Lawrence, annoyed but not fully understanding why. He appreciated that Ali was trying to help the boy, and he also resented it.

"You snored last night," said Terrence, and Dorita laughed.

"So?" said Lawrence. "You farted."

Terrence and Loquatia laughed.

"If you goin to the Chang's, you need to tell me," said Dorita. "We could use some soda in this house."

"I ain't no shopping service."

"You could contribute," said Dorita. 'Stead of just taking all the time."

"Least my mother didn't name me after a corn chip," said Lawrence, saying the same tired thing he had been saying to his sister since they were kids.

Dorita did not respond, and Lawrence went to his room.

It wasn't his room, exactly. He shared it with the two younger kids. He had strung up a sheet between their beds and his single bed to give him some privacy. Didn't leave much space, but this was what he had. Free rent, you couldn't complain. Anyway, he was about to be out of here.

About to be.

He pulled aside the sheet, flopped down on his bed, and draped his forearm over his eyes. Underneath the bed, the bag of money. He felt he had to keep it close. But what was he going to do with it? That was the thing that was fucking with his head.

He knew he should be looking for a nice place of his own. Maybe go to one of the Eastern Motors and trade up off that hooptie he had. But then he'd be in an apartment by himself, no one to talk to, no one to Jone on, and driving a car that was newer, that's all. He'd already spent a couple of thousand on women and fun. Beyond that, wasn't anything that he could see to buy that would make him happy.

What he wanted, what he'd always craved, was to have friends and pride. He'd thought that money would help him get those things. But to get it, he'd tricked the one dude who'd *been* his friend, the only boy who'd stepped in and stood tall for him back when he was getting his ass beat regular at Pine Ridge. And now he, Lawrence, had gone and done him dirt.

Sometimes, no lie, he hated the sight of his own self in the mirror.

Lawrence rolled over onto his side. In the heat of the room, sweat dampening his long T-shirt, he went to sleep.

ALI CARTER lived with his mother, Juanita Carter, in a vinyl-sided duplex town home on Alabama Avenue in Garfield Heights, across the road from the offices of Men Movin on Up. The development was on the new side, the yards were still clean, and the several hundred homes that had been constructed here had replaced some problem-ridden projects that had been good for no one. Houses here were still being sold for about three hundred thousand dollars, with low-interest loans and no-money-down offers in effect. A chain grocery store, the Seventh District Police Station, and Fort Stanton Park were within walking distance. Communities such as this one, housing longtime residents and newcomers alike, had been appearing in several spots in Southeast. Only those who were unreasonably resistant to change could say that this was not a positive development. For Ali, it was a huge step up, and a world away from where he'd been raised.

Juanita Carter had not been a bad mother to Ali and his sisters in any way; she had merely been born poor. Her start at the back of the line had crippled her, and by the time she had made a family, her lack of higher education and unfortunate choices in men had put her at a severe disadvantage. She and her kids lived in the Barry Farms dwellings, and she had no choice but to raise them in that rough-and-tumble and occasionally toxic atmosphere. After earning her GED, she started taking health care classes while working on the cleaning crew at the old D.C. General Hospital. But while she was bettering herself in order to move her family out of the Farms, Ali was entering his teens, a dangerous time for a boy to have little supervision at home. Juanita blamed herself to this day for the trouble Ali and one of his sisters, who eventually was lost to the streets, had found. But Ali knew it wasn't her. It was him, and the fact that some young men just had to touch their hand to the flame to see for themselves that fire was hot.

"Where you off to?" said Juanita, as her son entered the kitchen in his pressed jeans and a sky blue Lacoste shirt, picking a pair of sunglasses out of a bowl on the counter that held his things.

"Chris Flynn's father is having a cookout," said Ali. "For his employees."

"You don't work for him."

"No, but he's been good to some fellas I know. At least, he tried to be."

"So you gonna, what, show your appreciation to this man by eating his burgers and potato salad?"

"I'll prob'ly ask him for some more favors, too." Ali put his hand in Juanita's bowl of things, set beside his, and looked at her sheepishly. "Can I get your car?"

"If you say you're not gonna drink."

"You know I don't even like it."

Ali took the keys and kissed his mother on the cheek. She was a small woman of forty-two with big brown eyes and a pretty smile. It was from her that he had acquired his modest height and handsome features.

In the past, they had experienced conflicts, but as adults, they made a good team. They had cosigned for the loan on the house and together they had made it work. She was an attendant at a dialysis center on 8th Street on Capitol Hill, and had learned to budget herself, watch her purchases, and still walk down the street in relative style. He stayed with her to pay her back, in some way, for the trouble he'd caused her as a youth. Both knew he'd be gone when he found someone special and started having kids of his own. She seemed to want it more than he did.

"Any girls gonna be at this barbecue?"

"Nah, Mama. We're all members of the He-Men Women Hater's Club."

"I wonder sometimes."

"Huh," said Ali. He had his eye on this one girl he'd met at church, but his mother didn't need to know that yet.

"Don't drink tonight," said Juanita, as her son headed out the door, her car keys in hand.

"I won't," said Ali.

She watched him go, thinking, *I'm not trying to get on you or nag. I don't want anything to happen to you. That's all it is.*

You've come so far.

EIGHTEEN

CHRIS CAME down into Rock Creek Park on the winding Sherrill Drive, took Beach for a piece, and came up out of the park on Bingham, the east-west cut-through his father had showed him as a child. He drove the van up the long hill of Nebraska Avenue and headed west on McKinley. Katherine was beside him in the shotgun bucket, and Ben was on the collapsible second-row bench. As he tended to do when he reentered his old neighborhood, Chris grew quiet.

They stopped at the red light at McKinley and Connecticut Avenue. To their right were the fenced-in courts of the Chevy Chase Rec Center, where Chris had played under the lights and stars in various summer leagues. Across the avenue, to the north, was the Avalon, the theater where he had smoked weed in the men's room with his friends before movies, now an independent operation showing art films.

"See those blocks of concrete?" said Ben, pointing a long finger between Chris and Katherine at the planters on the sidewalk past the bus shelter, lined along the sloping driveway entrance to the drugstore at the southwest corner of Connecticut.

"Yes?" said Katherine, suspecting what was coming, having heard the story of Chris's night of crime.

"Those are, like, monuments to Chris," said Ben. "They put 'em up there after he drove his truck 'cross the sidewalk."

"That wasn't me. That was some other dude."

Chris accelerated through the intersection on the green and glanced at the concrete barriers as he drove past.

"My legacy," said Chris, and Katherine reached over and squeezed his hand.

Driving west on McKinley, Chris pulled to the right as far as he could to allow a late-model Audi to pass. The coupe came alongside him, and Chris looked to the driver for the courtesy nod. Their eyes met. The driver, a good-looking man around Chris's age with a salon haircut and a clean open-necked white shirt, smiled nervously in recognition.

"Hey," said the driver, with a finger wave.

"How's it goin, man?" said Chris, returning the smile.

Neither of them stopped. Chris's heavy foot gave the van a bit too much gas.

"Who was that?" said Katherine.

"A kid I ran with from the neighborhood," said Chris.

"Looks like he prosperin, whoever he is," said Ben.

"He got out of law school last year," said Chris. "My father says he's with a downtown firm now."

"You never mentioned him to me," said Katherine.

"Yes, I did," said Chris.

"I guess I don't remember."

"No big deal," said Chris. "He's just a guy I used to know."

THE COOKOUT was in the backyard of the Flynns' clapboard colonial on Livingston. Depending on the level of business, Thomas Flynn employed six to eight men, but they came to this annual

191

event with children, wives, girlfriends, and one or two unin-vited friends. The yard was not large to begin with, and it was full.

Amanda Flynn had laid out a food spread on a table set on their screened-in porch, which led to an uncovered deck, where Flynn was busy barbecuing burgers, chorizo sausages, half-smokes, and chicken breasts on his commercial-grade gas grill. Amanda and Isaac's wife, Maria, were moving back and forth from the kitchen to the porch, putting out sides, paper plates, napkins, and utensils, catching up with conversation as they worked. Flynn had a spatula in one hand and a bottle of Bud in the other. Within reach, on the rail of the deck, was a party ball of Jim Beam and shot glasses for anyone who cared to join him. Nearby were two iced-down coolers, one stocked with beer and white wine, the other holding sodas and water.

Music was coming from outdoor speakers mounted on the ceiling of the screened-in porch. It was a mix of Spanish-language pop with dramatic vocals, which everyone enjoyed to some degree but would become a bone of contention and dis-cussion as the night wore on. Ben had brought his Rare Es-sence and Backyard Band tapes, Maze's greatest hits, and the new Wale to drop in later, when folks got loose. One of Aman-da's jobs was to keep her husband away from the stereo, espe-cially after he'd had a few drinks. This was not the crowd for Thin Lizzy or Lynyrd Skynyrd, and no one here, with the ex-ception of Thomas Flynn, was into Bruce.

Renee, Ben's girlfriend, had joined them late, after she came off work at the nail salon. In her evening clothes and heels, she was overdressed for a cookout, but she looked good. Kather-ine, in a sundress, her hair down, was in conversation with Renee, as Ben was spending much of his time playing with Django, the Flynns' dog.

Also in attendance was Lonnie Wilson. Though he had not worked for Flynn's Floors for several years, and his employment had been short-lived, Lonnie liked a party and could not pass up free food and drink. He had brought along his wife, Yolanda, and their two children. Pussy-crazy Lonnie, who had talked incessantly about all the women he was going to slay when he left Pine Ridge, had married Yolanda, the first girl he got with when he came out. Despite the fact that Lonnie had been unable to hold a job and their money problems were deep, Lonnie and his family were a tight unit.

Darkness had settled on the yard. Chris, Ali, Ben, and Lonnie stood around an outdoor fire pit, drinking beer from bottles, talking, and looking into the fire that Chris had lit using wood stacked beside the alley garage. Thomas Flynn had built the pit years ago. Flynn had leveled the dirt, constructed the base and walls with cinder block and mortar, covered it with decorative stone veneer, grouted it, and capped it with concrete he cut and mitered himself.

Chris could not have constructed such a fine piece of work. He was not a natural handyman like his father. He was not even a particularly good carpet man, though he had learned enough to do satisfactory installations. Truth was, he wasn't suited to his current job, but it had been made available to him and was what he had.

"Look at this dog, man," said a gleeful Ben, holding a rubber toy by its U-shaped handle, the other end death-clenched in Django's powerful jaws, the dog pulling furiously, his rear legs dug in, his eyes rolled back in his square head. "You see pit when he's got somethin in his mouth."

"The ID card at the shelter said 'Labrador mix,' " said Chris. "They put that tag on all the dogs, even the beagles. People want to adopt Labs."

Ben let go of the toy. Django dropped it at Ben's feet, sat, looked up at him, and smiled.

"He wants to play more," said Ali.

"If I had a dog like this, I'd play with him all the time," said Ben. "But it wouldn't be right for me to keep him in my apartment all day while I was at work."

"Dog's all ass," said Lonnie.

"That's the pit in him," said Ben.

"All that power in his ass, I bet he can fuck like a machine, too," said Lonnie.

"Not anymore," said Chris. "My parents had him fixed."

"See, man, why they have to do that?" said Lonnie.

"Someone should do it to you," said Ali.

"I'm not done, though," said Lonnie. "I'm gonna have a big family. I'm into kids, see, and I got the means to make 'em. Also, Yolanda is fertile as mess. I'm like one of them sperm banks you read about, and Yolanda's the vault. Couple times a day, I got to make a deposit."

"That doesn't even make sense," said Ali.

Chris looked up to the deck, where Isaac was talking intently with his father. Chris felt a slight pang of jealousy. Isaac was a better worker than Chris, more skilled, more diligent, and more conscientious. Isaac deserved to get a shot at running Flynn's Floors someday, more so than Chris. What hurt Chris was the realization that his father had to know this, too, and would be torn by his loyalty to his son and this exemplary employee.

"Hey," said Hector. "I was wondering where all the women was."

Hector, the young, curly-haired worker from Isaac's crew, stepped into the circle, playfully elbowing Ben to move him aside. Hector tapped Chris's beer bottle with his own.

"If it ain't Hector the Dick Inspector," said Ben.

"You inspect the *vergas*," said Hector pleasantly. "I will work. And faster than you, my friend." In the light of the fire, with his glassy eyes and wide grin, he looked a bit drunk.

"Ali, Lonnie," said Chris, "this is Hector."

Hector nodded, then gave them a small bow. "Nice to meet you."

"You, too," said Ali.

"Hector works on one of our crews," said Chris.

"The *best* crew," said Hector. He was a competitive type and could back up his boasts.

"I thought your name was Mary," said Ben.

"My name is not Mary," said Hector.

"Sure it is," said Ben. "Mary Cone."

Hector's face contorted as he figured it out. Then he smiled with delight and pointed his finger at Ben. "*You* are *maricone!*"

They laughed and drank more beer. Katherine and Renee joined them, and the circle enlarged. Everyone took a step back from the fire. They were all sweating, and the alcohol was not cooling them down. Kids ran through the yard, and one of Isaac's crew was dancing with a young woman in the light of a torch to a Tejano ballad playing on the stereo.

"Where's your shadow tonight?" said Chris to Lonnie. "He usually comes to this thing."

"Luther?" said Lonnie. He shook his head. "I don't get up with Luther too much anymore. Luther *lost*, man."

"He druggin?" said Ali

"Luther's doin everything wrong," said Lonnie. "Just runnin with the wrong people, basically. One of 'em he met at the Ridge originally. Remember DeMarco Hines?"

"From Twelve," said Ali, naming the unit housing the most violent boys.

"Last time I seen Luther, I told him, it's time to get away from those kinds of people and stop all that nonsense. You too old to be in that game. But he wouldn't listen. Thing is, Luther isn't bad, not like DeMarco."

"Luther had no business being in Pine Ridge to begin with," said Ali. "You put someone in with boys who got sickness for real, he's gonna catch a virus."

"Luther got arrested as a runner one too many times," said Lonnie. "Police would jump out their cars and grab him, and then he kept violating his parole. That's all it was."

"Imagine the law, on foot, catchin a young kid like that," said Ben.

"We used to look back and laugh at the police while we was runnin from 'em," said Lonnie. "But that boy was just too slow."

"Bad luck," said Hector, trying to contribute to the conversation.

"There's the other kind of luck, too," said Chris. "I saw an old friend of mine, earlier tonight. Eight, nine years ago, he was your basic fuckup, just like me. Now Jason's a lawyer, looks like fresh money. And I'm . . ."

"Chris," said Katherine.

"All because he stayed in the SUV," said Chris, "and I got out."

"Who you talkin about, man?" said Lonnie.

"My boy Country." Chris raised his bottle in weak salute. "The one who didn't get out of the Trooper."

No one commented. Chris tipped his head back and killed his beer. Katherine looped her arm though his and touched her thigh to his.

"I'm gonna get something to eat," said Ali, pouring the rest of his beer out onto the grass. "I already broke a promise to my mother. I gotta put some food in my stomach before I drive home."

He walked across the lawn and up the steps to the deck. Thomas Flynn stood before the grill, flipping the last of the burgers. Ali went to him and put a hand on his shoulder, and Flynn took a couple of steps back in mock retreat.

"Don't worry, Mr. Flynn. I don't want anything."

"Not tonight."

"I'm not working tonight. But you know I'm gonna have to come back *to* you."

"That's what you do."

"I can't accomplish anything without folks like you," said Ali. "Anyway, want you to know, I appreciate your patience."

They looked at each other with respect, and Ali reached out and shook Flynn's hand.

"Do a shot with me," said Flynn.

"Nah, I don't mess with that stuff. But thanks."

Flynn pointed his chin out into the yard. "I see Lonnie and his brood made it."

"Lonnie went forth and multiplied."

"What was his friend's name? The one who could never show up for work on time."

"Luther. He's not doing so good."

"They can't all be success stories."

"I know it."

"Last time I saw Luther, I spotted him ten dollars until payday."

"You never want to see Luther again, just give him ten dollars."

Flynn waved his spatula toward the screened-in porch. "Go on, get something to eat."

"Thank you."

Ali headed for the food table, and Flynn poured a shot of Beam. He sipped it, watching his son, his friend Ben, and their girlfriends standing by the fire pit out in the yard. Chris and Ben looked older than their years. He had seen them wearing the shirts they had on tonight many times before. Chris had missed the experience of high school sports, the senior prom, cap-and-gown day, and so much more, and now he was a man too weathered to enjoy his own time. Flynn lowered his head in regret.

"What are you brooding about, Tommy?"

Amanda had appeared at his side.

"Nothin, Amanda."

"I had a nice talk with Katherine earlier."

"Pretty girl."

"Smart, too," said Amanda. "It's obvious she and Chris are in love."

"I'm happy for him."

"You don't look too happy to me."

Flynn drained his shot and placed the glass on the railing. "I was having a quiet moment, is all. Until you interrupted."

"Stop focusing on what Chris isn't and be thankful for the good in him. He's doing fine, Tommy."

"Okay. I'm okay, you're okay."

"And ease up on that bourbon. You still have to make your little speech, remember?"

Flynn picked up the oversize bottle of Beam, still capped, and pretended to swig from it. Then he stumbled broadly across the deck.

"Quit screwin around, Tommy."

"I love you guys," said Flynn, his eyes comically unfocused. "I really fuckin . . . *love* you guys, man."

"Stop it."

"You mean *that* speech?"

"Just stop." Amanda stepped forward and shouted out to the adults and children in the yard. "C'mon, everybody! Come eat before it gets cold!"

Flynn reached out and touched her ass. She swatted his hand away deftly, turned, and quick-stepped toward the screened-in porch.

"WHEN YOU start a company," said Flynn, "you're thinking about yourself. Your wife and kids, maybe, if you're lucky enough to have them. But my point is, you open a business to make money. That's your goal."

Flynn was on the deck, a shot of bourbon in hand. He was no longer acting, but in fact was now half drunk. Amanda stood beside him, concerned, loving, patient, and somewhat proud. He had built the business and earned the floor. For his troubles, he could be sentimental and smashed for one night.

Below them on the grass stood the employees and their companions, looking up at Flynn. Whatever they were feeling, and it ranged from loyalty to indifference, they were paying attention and respect. Some were finishing up their plates of food, some were still drinking, and others were completely sober. Isaac had Maria and his kids close by. The other children were running and playing in the yard.

"What you don't expect, when you get yourself into this, is the feeling of responsibility and affection you get for the people you employ and have the privilege of working with every day. Now, I've had many employees over the years. For most of them, they and their wives and children have been better off and had better lives after coming to work for me. That's quite an accomplishment. It's the one I'm most proud of, you want the truth.

"I'm also very fortunate to be able to work with my family. You know my lovely and extremely capable wife, Amanda." Flynn reached to his side and squeezed Amanda's arm. "And my son, Chris, is an integral part of our installation team. But they're not the only ones I've come to think of as family. I'm thinking of Isaac, of course, who has been with me for a long time. Isaac, you know this company doesn't work without you."

"Thank you, boss," said Isaac, his posture erect.

"But it's all of you, really," said Flynn. "Friends and family are what we're about. Together, we are gonna prosper. When we do a job and do it right . . ."

"It's money for all of us," said Chris under his breath, a rush of affection for his old man washing over his chest.

"It's money for all of us," said Flynn. "I know we've had a little downturn in business this summer. Hell, everybody's taking gas in this economy. That's nothing but a blip on the radar screen. So we didn't make much money this month. But I promise you . . ." Flynn paused dramatically ". . . we will to-morrow."

"Yes!" said Hector, too emphatically.

"Easy, Mary," said Ben.

"*You* Mary," said Hector, with a lopsided smile.

"That's it," said Flynn. "See you at work on Monday."

There was some mild applause as Amanda turned to him, put her hand around his waist, and kissed him on the mouth.

"Damn, I'm good," said Flynn, a lock of black hair falling across his forehead. "Henry at Agincourt had nothin on me."

"Save some of that bravado for the bedroom."

"For real?"

"Yes."

Chris said, "We're taking off." He was standing at the foot of the stairs, watching his parents, waiting for them to finish.

"You're not driving, are you?" said Amanda.

"Katherine is," said Chris. "Don't worry, she barely drank."

"That's one lovely young woman," said Flynn.

Chris nodded. They watched him join his group, saying good-bye to Ali, who was still talking to Lonnie.

"He's the effusive type," said Flynn.

"Come on," said Amanda. "Help me clean up."

Chris, Ben, and their girlfriends walked out of the backyard.

TWO MEN, one large and one small, sat in a black Marquis, parked down Livingston, a good distance from the Flynn home. The old Mercury, though well maintained, was out of place among the late-model imports of Friendship Heights. Sonny Wade and Wayne Minors had not been here long and did not intend to stick around. They had come to check out the business address for Flynn's Floors and were surprised to discover that it was a residential location.

"Party's endin," said Sonny.

"For them it is," said Wayne.

A young white couple and a young black couple moved across the front yard of the colonial and came to a stop near a white work van. It looked like they were about to split up.

"By God, look at the titties on that redhead," said Sonny.

"I'd make a tunnel outta them bad boys," said Wayne.

"And what would you drive through the tunnel?"

"You know what they say about little dudes."

"They got little pricks?"

"Ho," said Wayne.

Sonny picked up a cheap 8 x 21 monocular he had purchased at a surplus store and put it to one eye. "Our gal Mindy said it was a black and a blond, large and young. They're both big. Could be them."

"What you gonna do, walk up and ask 'em?"

"Keep your eyes on the white boy." Sonny handed the monocular to Wayne, picked up his cell from the red velour seat, found the number he was looking for in his contacts, and punched it into the keyboard.

They waited.

"He's answering," said Wayne with a short giggle.

"Hello," said Sonny. "Is Chris Carpet there?"

"Who is this?" Chris's annoyed voice came through the speaker.

Sonny hit "end" and took the monocular back. Looking through it, he said, "Boy's staring at his phone like it's gonna tell him somethin."

"But now he's got your number on the caller ID."

"Why would I give a fuck? He's the thief. He stole from *me*. What's he gonna do, go to the law?"

"Should we follow him to where he's goin?"

"I'm thinking," said Sonny, stroking his walrus mustache.

Katherine took Chris's keys and the two of them got into the white van. Ben and Renee walked toward her black Hyundai, parked up by 41st Street.

"That coon's really got some size on him," said Wayne.

"The white boy looks like a tougher nut, though," said Sonny, squinting. "The way the other one walks, all loose . . . somethin about him says soft to me."

"You know what they say: Cut a tall boofer, he falls like a big tree."

"I got Mr. Carpet's number," said Sonny. "We can get hold of him anytime. Let's follow the black one and see where he goes."

NINETEEN

BEN AND Renee woke up late on Sunday and spent most of the day indoors, lounging, ordering in, and making love. They watched a Martin Lawrence movie that Renee had brought with her and several innings of a Nationals game on cable. Ben walked her to the parking lot in the early evening and kissed her good-bye through the open window of her Hyundai. They had laughed all day and were right for each other in the bedroom. He was thinking that she might be the one.

Ben went back to his apartment. On his nightstand he found a paperback novel, *Blood on the Forge*, that he had been struggling with at first but getting into of late. He rubbed his fingers over the handsome cover. To him, it was like touching gold.

He was challenging himself these days to take on reading material that was a bit more difficult. Ben knew who he was and where he wanted to go. He was never going to be accomplished by society's standards, or rich by anyone's, but he was comfortable with his limitations. For many, life was about the pursuit of status, but it was not so for him. Ben's was all about the quest for knowledge, and his vehicle was books.

He thought of work as a means to acquire food and shelter. Friends and Renee kept him socialized and sane. He tried not to stress on his broken childhood or troubled teens, and mostly managed to steer his mind clear of dark places. He was past that, and looked forward to learning something new every day.

Ben sniffed the short-sleeved Timberland button-down he'd worn the night before, decided that it did not stink, and put it on. He went to the front door and took his keys off a peg bar mounted on the wall. He had his cell, his wallet, and his book, which he had slipped into the back pocket of his jeans.

He left the apartment, crossed the street, and walked along a black iron fence. In the apartment house parking lot, from inside an aging sedan, two men watched.

Ben entered the cemetery gate at Rock Creek Church and Webster, walked down the wide road around the church, and took the very narrow road to the Adams Memorial. As it was a weekend, the memorial had visitors, an elderly couple whose car was parked nearby. Ben moved on, finding a spot atop a stone retaining wall near a large pond. He began to read.

Shadows lengthened as the sun dropped. A Hispanic groundsman finished his edging and, his day done, drove a motorized utility cart up the slope toward the physical plant. A little while later, a security car rolled by, and its driver, a middle-aged gentleman who knew Ben on sight, tapped the face of his wristwatch, telling Ben by signal that it would soon be time to go.

Ben waved at him and held up five fingers. The driver nodded and drove on.

Ben stayed longer than he intended. Though the light was dying, he was at a point in the novel that he could not walk away from. In the book, three black brothers, country boys from the South, had come north to work in the steel mills, and now their fates were being laid bare. Ben was transfixed.

An old black car drove slowly down the road. It came to a

stop near Ben and sat idling like a crow at rest. Ben looked down at the pages of his book. He looked back at the car. The engine had cut off. A big man with a walrus mustache got out of the driver's side, and a small man with wiry tattooed arms and a bushy mustache stepped from the passenger side. The big man, wearing a windbreaker and jeans, looked around, saw no one, and walked toward Ben. Ben put the book down and eased off the stone wall. He stood with discomfort, unsure of what to do or where to put his hands.

As the big man neared him, Ben said, "Somethin I can help you with?"

"I sure hope so." The man drew a semiautomatic pistol from where it was holstered beneath his windbreaker. He pointed the gun at Ben, then waved its barrel toward the old sedan. "In the car."

"I didn't do nothin," said Ben.

"Yes, you did." He waved the barrel in the same direction once again. "Do what I say. Quick."

Ben looked around. It was near dark and no one, visitor or employee, was in sight.

The big man locked back the pistol's hammer. "Run, you got a mind to."

Ben willed himself to walk toward the vehicle. The man with the gun was behind him as the little man opened the passenger door to let Ben in.

"Up front," said the big man.

Ben got in and the door shut after him. In his side vision he saw the big man hand the little man the gun. He heard the little man get into the backseat as the other one settled into the driver's seat.

"Remember this," said the big man. "My friend will shoot you dead."

Ben couldn't speak. He felt the car lurch forward. His fingers dented the red velour seat. They drove slowly through the cemetery, up the hill and around the church. The security vehicle came just as slowly in their direction as the big man deftly went through the gate and pulled out onto Webster Street.

"We just made it," said the little man.

"Yeah, they're about to close that gate." The big man with the high cheekbones looked over at Ben. "What's your name, fella?"

"Ben."

"You can call me Sonny." His smile showed perfect gray teeth.

THEY DROVE around without apparent destination until it was full dark. Ben listened to the random, pointless banter between the two men, much of it concerning female singers, the discussion starting with the merits of their talent and quickly veering off toward cup size. The little one smoked and commented frequently on what he saw out the window. The city and its residents did not please him.

Ben tried to think of the reason for his abduction, and he could not. He had no enemies that he knew of. He'd been straight for a long time, and in his recollection had done no one wrong.

The car stank. His abductors had awful body odor, and Ben suspected that he did, too. He had sweated into his shirt.

At several stoplights he considered jumping out of the Mercury but decided against it, fearing that the little one with the stove-in face would shoot him. He would have to sit here and hope that these two would not harm him. There was nothing else he could see to do.

Sonny caught Ben noticing the shamrock tattoo on the

crook of his hand, wrapped around the fake-fur-covered steering wheel.

"You dig my ink?" said Sonny.

Ben did not answer.

"C'mon, fella. Ain't no need to be silent. We gonna converse, eventually."

They drove south on a downward slope of North Capitol and traveled under the New York Avenue overpass.

"You know what my tattoo is?" said Sonny.

"It's a four-leaf clover," said Ben.

"Why don't no one ever get that?" said the little man.

"It's a shamrock," said Sonny. "Means I'm part of a club."

"He's talkin about the Aryan Brotherhood," said the little man.

"Shut up, stupid," said Sonny. "Let me tell it how I want to."

"My name is not Stupid."

"Shut up, *Wayne*."

Sonny stopped at the red light on K. A panhandling drunk came across the street from the east corner of North Capitol, out of the shadows of a shuttered church. As he neared the driver's side of the Marquis, Sonny turned his head to him and said, "Get your dirty ass gone." The man retreated without a word.

On the green, Sonny turned left onto K Street. They entered an old tunnel with water-stained walls, lit by globe-topped streetlamps. From above, Ben could hear the clomping sound of a train moving on tracks.

"I hope you're not frightened," said Sonny.

"I'm not," said Ben quickly.

"I'm glad you're not," said Sonny. "I want you thinkin clear. We gonna go someplace now and have a quiet conversation. Okay?"

Sonny drove several blocks, hooked a left onto 6th Street, and parked along the curb. They were beside an old, boxy, three-story building surrounded by a chain-link fence, standing out in a residential neighborhood of row homes. Metal security screens and plywood were fitted in its large windows, and a sign announcing the coming of the Ward Six Senior Wellness Center was posted on the south face. Ben had seen buildings such as this, shuttered or laced with creeping ivy, around the city. He guessed that this one, like the others, had once been a school.

"Wait," said Sonny. Two young men were walking down the sidewalk in their direction, talking loudly, and when they had passed, Sonny tossed the keys over the seat to Wayne and said, "Get the things."

Wayne handed Sonny his gun and got out of the car. Sonny kept the gun low and pointed at Ben. The trunk opened, and Ben could hear Wayne ratfucking through it.

Wayne returned and opened the passenger door. He was wearing latex gloves and tossed a pair to Sonny.

"Don't worry," said Sonny, noticing a twitch in Ben's lip and the sweat bulleting his forehead.

"Put your hands behind your back," said Wayne.

Ben looked at Sonny.

"It's all just a pre-caution," said Sonny, fitting the gloves on his hands.

Ben allowed the little man to cuff him. When Sonny was satisfied that the street was clear, Wayne pulled on Ben's arm and brought him out of the car. Wayne locked the Mercury, and the three of them went north on the sidewalk, along the school, whose main entrance faced 6th. Ben made out a naked flagpole mounted over the wide front doors, and big letters that spelled out "Hayes School."

"Round the side," said Sonny. Wayne pushed on a gate that had been padlocked but was open because its chain had been severed by a pair of cutters, now in the Mercury's trunk. Ben moved off the sidewalk and walked onto the asphalt and weeds of the property.

"Hey," said Ben. He was encouraged by the sound of his own voice, and he screamed, "Hey!"

Wayne jumped up and punched him behind the ear. Ben stumbled, and Sonny grabbed his left arm and righted him.

"That wasn't smart," said Sonny. "Now, you just relax."

From a nearby porch, out front of one of the houses on 6th, Ben heard someone laugh.

They went to the north face of the school, out of the glow of streetlamps. There were two windows on the ground floor covered by heavy wire screen, and one in the center holding a square of plywood painted white. Wayne removed the plywood, which he had kicked in earlier that day. Ben saw only complete darkness there and in fear he turned away from it, but Sonny spun him and pushed him from behind. As Ben fell into the room, it was illuminated, slightly, by the beam of a mini Maglite held in Wayne's hand. Wayne moved the flashlight beam and it hit on eyes that glowed. Ben heard the fluttering of clawed feet and saw animals, big as cats, scatter back into the shadows. His stomach dropped.

"Rats gotta live someplace, too," said Sonny.

Wayne used his butane lighter to put fire to candles pushed into the necks of beer bottles placed in a circular shape on the concrete floor. A child's chair with a plastic seat and steel legs was set in the center of the circle. As the old classroom revealed itself, Sonny gestured to the chair and said, "That's for you."

Wayne refitted the plywood to the frame as Sonny helped

Ben down into the chair. Its seat was small, and Ben had to rest on the edge of it to accommodate his arms, cuffed behind his back. His rolled his shoulders to alleviate the ache in his neck. He saw a bottle of water standing on the floor and he licked his parched lips.

"I know it's uncomfortable," said Sonny, standing before him. Sonny picked up the bottle, drank from it, then placed the bottle back on the floor. "So let's get this over with and we'll all go home."

Wayne moved through the light and crouched down on one knee, half of him in darkness. Then he stood and moved beside the chair. Ben did not look at him. He focused on the big man. He seemed to be reasonable and he was the one in charge.

"You know that thing I told you 'bout my tat?" said Sonny. "You ride with the rock, you take a blood oath to the Aryan Brotherhood. Well, I didn't take no oath. I put this ink on after I got out the federal joint. If any genuine AB saw me carryin it, he'd cut my throat. I just put it on my hand to make an impression with folks that need to get a certain message. Like Mindy Kramer. You know her, don't you, Ben?"

Ben's eyes betrayed him, and Sonny chuckled low.

"Course you do." Sonny shifted his weight from one foot to the other. "I wasn't bad enough to be Aryan Brotherhood. I'm not ashamed to say it. I don't even *sub*-scribe to their notions of race. I don't hate African American people. Want you to know that. This here ain't got nothin to do with the color of your skin. Truth is, the modern Aryan Brotherhood ain't even about hatin blacks, Mexicans, or Jews. It's about power, money, and control. Now, Wayne here, he does have a bit of a problem with, what's that they call it, *people of color*. Wayne wanted to get in, but they don't let itty-bitty boys like him into the club. I'm a big man, as you can see, but I look like queer bait next to them ABs. They are some big specimens. They're honest-to-god animals, Ben."

"Can I get a drink of water?" said Ben.

"Not just yet," said Sonny. "To finish my point: Me and Wayne were just cogs in the machine at Lewisburg. We did favors for the bad boys. Runnin errands and such. They called our kind peckerwoods."

"They called *you* it," said Wayne.

"Not that I wasn't capable of doing bad things," said Sonny. "Wayne, too. Got to give it to my little friend, because he can be fierce. But I wasn't interested in that power thing. I only wanted to have what I worked for. I like a roll of folding money in my pocket, and when I get it I expect to keep it. Do you understand?"

"Yes."

"I *had* some money," said Sonny. "Fifty thousand dollars, give or take. Me and an associate, fella named Leslie Hawkins, took off four jewelry stores in the Baltimore area over the course of, I don't know, five or six months. Wasn't any kind of trick to it. You put a gun up in someone's face, they gonna give you what you askin for. I was a young man at the time, about your age, and I had a kind of energy comin off me that was very convincing. The Jews and the slopes who we were robbin, they knew we meant business. Me and Hawk, we made over a hundred grand on those jobs after we fenced it out. I gave him half, even though the only thing he did was drive a car. And it was all clean. I wore a mask when I was workin, a hood with cutout eyes, like a hangman's bag. So the cameras didn't pick up on shit. The problem wasn't that the law knew who I was. The problem was Leslie Hawkins. I should have known better than to partner up with a man had a girl's name."

"Please," said Ben, sweat stinging his eyes. "Can I get some water?"

"When I'm done," said Sonny. "Hawkins got pulled over one night by a state trooper for a busted taillight. Leslie panicked and booked, thinking they had made his vehicle from the robberies. Led the police on one of those high-speed chases you see on the tee-vee, and of course he got caught. Dumbass had his share of the money in the trunk of the car. He spilled soon as they got him into a room. Hawkins put me in for the robberies. That wasn't no surprise. Through the underworld telegraph, I'd heard he got picked up, and I figured it was just a matter of time before the law got around to me. So I went to visit my uncle, who lived here in D.C."

"Hot in here, ain't it?" said Wayne.

"It is stuffy," said Sonny, and he removed his windbreaker and tossed it aside. The semiautomatic was holstered in a leather rig looped over his shoulder and chest.

"I need a drink," said Ben, desperation entering his voice.

"My uncle came from the same place I do," said Sonny, ignoring the request. "What passes for mountain country, way up in Maryland. Ever been there, Ben?"

"No."

"Well, my uncle had one of those alternative lifestyles, and they don't exactly tolerate that kind of thing up there. So he moved down here to the city, got a job managing a fancy furniture store, had a partner for a while, bought a house. Carved out a nice life for himself. I never had no problem with him or who he was. Matter of fact, I loved him. Now that he's gone, makes me feel a little bad that I buried my money without his knowledge in that library-slash-den of his before I got arrested. He died while I was in the joint, and then his home went to auction. But I won't go on about it. You know the rest. *Don't you, fella.*"

"I didn't take that money," said Ben.

Sonny drew the gun from its holster. It was an S&W .45 with a black grip and a stainless steel slide and body. Sonny worked the slide and dropped a round into the chamber. He squinted as he inspected the gun.

"Shaved numbers," said Sonny. "I reckon I'm in big trouble if they pick me up."

Wayne laughed.

"Plus, I'm a parole violator," said Sonny. "I haven't reported to my supervisor but one time since I got out. Never did pee in no cup. I just left and picked up Wayne, my old cell mate, and came straight down to War-shington via West Virginia to get my money. Imagine my surprise when I found out that my money is gone."

"I didn't take it."

"Yeah, I'm in a world of trouble if I cross paths with the law." Sonny stepped close to Ben. The flames from the candles reflected in his black, empty eyes. "But I don't care. I want you to know it. I plain don't give a fuck."

"I saw it," said Ben. "It was in an old gym bag. But I didn't take it."

"'Scuse me if I can't believe that."

"We left it there."

"You mean, you and your partner, Chris. The both of you."

"That's right," said Ben, holding Sonny's stare. "We saw it, but we left it where it was at. Someone broke into that house after and took it. I know because we had to go back and fix the carpet."

"It wasn't you. It was someone else."

"Yes."

"So you told someone 'bout the money."

"No," said Ben.

Sonny cocked back the hammer of the gun and locked it in place. He touched the barrel to the corner of Ben's eye. Ben turned his head, and Sonny pressed the tip of the barrel tighter to his flesh.

"Liar," said Sonny. "I'm only gonna ask you one more time. Who took my money?"

"I . . . don't know."

Sonny held the gun in place. Ben heard clawed feet gaining purchase on concrete, and a scampering sound. He closed his eyes.

"I was wrong about you," said Sonny, standing straight, dropping the gun to his side. He took several steps back. "I thought you was a soft one. I guess now I'll have to talk to your friend Chris. 'Cause you damn sure ain't gonna talk. Makes me think you got the code of the jailhouse in you. You ever done time, Ben?"

"Juvenile," said Ben softly.

"Me, too," said Sonny. "They had me up in that boy's reformatory in Sabillasville. I wasn't so bad when I went in. But they cured me of any goodness I had by the time I came out. That's what that place did for me. It made me well."

"I'm thirsty."

"I know it, fella." Sonny holstered his gun. "Wayne?"

Wayne's tattooed arm arced into the light. Ben gasped as he saw the blade swing toward him, and his eyes crossed as the knife pierced his chest and entered his heart.

The force of the blow knocked Ben off the chair. Wayne stood over him and with his face contorted, he grunted and came down with the knife, rabbit-punching, stabbing Ben's torso, his abdomen, his neck. Ben writhed and cried out, and Wayne did not stop. Ben went into shock, and chopping sounds filled the room as Wayne worked on.

"Wayne," said Sonny.

Wayne stood, spent with exhaustion. His latex gloves and forearms were dark with blood. The front of his T-shirt was soaked with it. Bloodied hair had fallen about his face.

"He ain't nothin now," said Wayne, his eyes bright. "Is he, Sonny? *Is* he."

"You did end him," said Sonny. "Get his wallet and cell if he has one. Seal this shithole up and I'll meet you out at the car."

Ten minutes later, Wayne Minors crept out of the shadows of the school property, opened the gate, and looped its padlock and chain through the links of the fence so that it appeared to have been undisturbed.

On the street, Sonny Wade sat patiently behind the wheel of his Mercury, waiting for his little friend.

TWENTY

CHRIS FLYNN stopped by Ben's apartment house on Monday morning, as he usually did, to pick him up for work. Normally, as Chris neared Ben's place, he gave him a heads-up via cell or, if they couldn't connect in that manner, through a text message. But Ben had replied to neither, so Chris got out of the van, walked into the building, and knocked on Ben's door. He tried it the soft way and even gave it the cop knock, but there was no response.

Heading back to the parking lot, he phoned Renee.

"Ben over there?" he said.

"Uh-uh," said Renee. Her voice was raspy, and Chris assumed that he had woken her up. "He stayed at his place last night. We were together all afternoon."

"You haven't spoke to him since?"

"I called him late to say good night, but he didn't pick up."

"Well, he's not in his apartment," said Chris. "Either that or he's in bed and not answering the door. Not answering his cell, either."

"Ben wouldn't do you like that." After a pause Renee said, "Now you got me worried."

"He'll turn up," said Chris.

"Call me when you hook up with him. I'll text him soon as we cut off, and if he gets back to me I'll hit you up."

"Okay, Renee. Thanks."

Chris called his father. He briefly considered telling him that Ben had phoned in sick, but he decided to be truthful, take the hit, and say that Ben was MIA.

"This is bad," said Thomas Flynn. "You've got two jobs today."

"I know."

"Why would he do this to us? To *you*."

"We don't know that he's done anything. You should wait to speak to him before you pass judgment."

"Thanks for the lecture. But see, I'm trying to run a business. If he went out and overdid it, and now he's got the Irish flu, that's not something I can excuse."

"You don't know that. He could have taken a walk and got hit by a car. Could be he's lying in a hospital bed right now, somethin like that."

"If you think so, then maybe you ought to call the police."

"No," said Chris, too quickly. "I don't think we need to go there just yet."

"Fine. You better get on out to the warehouse, then. I'll pull Hector off Isaac's crew, and the two of you can work today's jobs."

"Okay, Dad. Okay."

Chris stood by the white cargo van but didn't get in right away. Ben had no relatives that Chris knew of, and a small circle of friends. It was possible that Lawrence Newhouse had got up with him and they had been clubbing, drinking, or drugging, spending some of the money Lawrence had stolen. Chris would be disappointed in Ben if that were the case, but it was understandable. Ben was a young man, and maybe he was still bitter about having left the cash in the row house and wanted to try some of it out. Chris didn't know how to get up with Lawrence and he really didn't care to. But Ali would find a way to reach Lawrence. And it could be that Ali had heard from Ben.

Chris phoned Ali and had a brief conversation. Later in the day, while Chris was doing an install, Ali reached him on his cell and told him that he had spoken to Lawrence, who claimed he hadn't seen or heard from Ben.

Chris and Hector finished the job. Hector was animated as always, moving quickly while he talked, humming and making jokes. Chris worked quietly, with a gathering sense of dread.

THAT EVENING, Amanda stood in the kitchen and listened as Flynn spoke to their son from their house phone. Amanda could hear the impatience in her husband's voice, and noted the way he cradled the receiver a little too roughly at the end of the conversation.

"He went by Ben's apartment with Renee," said Flynn. "She's got a key. Ben's stuff is intact. Doesn't look like he packed up anything or took a trip."

"Chris is worried," said Amanda.

"Yeah, he's worried. But he doesn't want to call the police. It's partly because he doesn't know what Ben is into. Could be, you involve the law, you're gonna get the young man in trouble. But there's that other thing, too. These guys, with their histories, they've got that code. They don't like to give up information, and the last person they want to talk to is a police officer."

"Do you think Ben's done something wrong?"

"I don't think of him as a guy who holes up in a motel room

218

with an eight-ball and a couple of whores, if that's what you mean."

"I don't think of him that way, either."

"So I should probably call the police myself. Report him as a missing person."

"That means they're going to come here and take a statement. His past might come up in the course of the conversation. Chris's, too."

"It might. If they've done nothing wrong, then it's not a problem, right?"

"Right," said Amanda, without conviction.

"Look, Ben is my responsibility. More than anyone else who works for me, this company is his only family. Do you get that?"

"Yes."

"Do me a favor and go down to the office and pull his file, okay? I'm gonna need the information at hand."

Flynn punched a number into the phone as she left the room.

MONDAY HAD brought tension, but Tuesday was worse. Renee called in sick to the nail salon, and Chris's installations were completed in a satisfactory but perfunctory manner. Even Hector, for a change, was subdued.

Flynn had reported Ben as a missing person to the MPD, but he knew from his brief experience that they would be busy with crimes of the here-and-now and would not actively investigate his disappearance, which, after all, could be nothing more than a young man gone out of town. Ben would be just another name added to a database, the daily sheets, and eventually the missing persons Web site.

From Chris, Flynn learned that Ben often haunted the

Adams Memorial in Rock Creek Cemetery. Because he had been in Brookland doing an estimate on his last call of the day, Flynn decided to stop by the cemetery grounds on his way home on the chance that he might speak to someone who was on duty Sunday or find something of importance.

In the main office, near the front gate, he was directed to the office of security, where he found a middle-aged man who had been on patrol Sunday evening past. This man, a Mr. Mallory, said that he knew Ben as described by sight but not to name, and that he had seen him sitting on the retaining wall near the pond, reading, and that he had indicated by signal that the cemetery would be closing and that Ben should prepare to leave. Mr. Mallory had not seen him go and could recall no suspicious visitors or unlawful activity for the remainder of the night.

Flynn thanked him and drove down to the pond. There he found a copy of a book called *Blood on the Forge*, still wet from a late-afternoon thunderstorm typical to Washington summers, face-up on the stone wall. Inside the cover, Ben had printed his full name.

Flynn called the police, used the case number as reference, and reported his discovery to a nameless listener with an uninterested voice. He then phoned Chris and told him what he had found. Chris agreed that Ben would not have left his book behind, even if he were done with it. Chris did not tell his father that he was certain now that something bad had come to Ben.

That night, Chris drove the streets, looking for his friend.

ON WEDNESDAY morning, three brothers, Yohance, Ade, and Baba Brown, residents of the neighborhood of Trinidad and all under twelve years old, were walking south from their row house with a bat, one mitt, and a tennis ball, looking for someplace to play, when they came upon the old Hayes School at 6th and K, Northeast, now fenced in and shuttered. They saw the possibilities in the broad north face of the building and its weeded blacktop, and went to the gate to see if they could find a way to dismantle its Master padlock. To their delight they found that the chain had been severed and by unthreading it through the links of the fence, they could simply walk onto the school grounds.

They played stickball against a wall where a rusted sign reading "No Ball Playing" was anchored into brick. They commented on the putrid smell of the area around the school, accusing one another of incomplete wipes and dirty asses, but played on because they had found a spot where they could throw hard, swing freely, and enjoy a summer day.

Around eleven o'clock, the youngest of the brothers, Yohance Brown, noticed that the white-painted square of plywood covering the middle window of the first floor was fitted poorly and askew. He used the bat to push the plywood and watched it fall into the dark of the room beyond. Immediately the awful smell that they had been commenting on hit them full force. Because they were boys, the three of them had to know, and they stepped into the space, now faintly illuminated by sunlight, and, holding the bat as a club, the oldest brother, Baba, led them to where hundreds of flies buzzed deeply and furry rodents scrambled back into the shadows, leaving a thing that had once been a man lying in the center of the concrete floor. What they saw would trouble them into adulthood and haunt the youngest for the rest of his life.

Five minutes later, a 1D patrolman named Jack Harris drove his cruiser east on K and saw a boy run into the street, his arms waving, horror and excitement in his eyes.

*　　*　　*

SERGEANT SONDRA Bryant, a homicide detective in her midforties with almost twenty in, was on the bubble when the body was found, and caught the case. She did not jump up from the seat behind her desk, located in the offices of the Violent Crime Branch behind a shopping center in Southeast. She was a slow, deliberate mover anyway, what with the extra weight she was carrying these days in her hips, belly, and behind. Sondra Bryant was known as a good detective, intuitive and conscientious, as she liked to put down cases for the white shirts and her own pride. But she was in no hurry to get to the crime scene. The victim had been dead for a couple of days. Her thought was to let the techs do their scene work, and meet them on the tail end of their task.

After speaking to two of her children on the phone and attending to a personal item, she got up out of her chair and headed out to find a car in the back lot that she could use. She went by a medium-size detective with a black mustache and a good chest, who was standing in his cubicle, a dead telephone receiver in his hand, staring down at his desk.

"Your kids again?" said Bryant.

"My son," said the detective. "My wife found some marijuana in his bedroom. A package of Black and Milds, too."

"No stroke mags?"

"Those are under my bed."

"Could be worse. She could have found a gun or a kilo of somethin white."

"I know that. I'm just disappointed, I guess."

"It'll pass."

The detective looked at Bryant, carrying her oversize purse, her badge on a chain around her neck. "You caught one?"

"I'm the primary. Kids came up on a body in the old Hayes School. Wanna ride along?"

"No, thanks. I'll send DeSchlong down when he comes back."

"You busy with something?"

"I'm gonna go to the boys' room and practice looking hard in the mirror, so I'm ready to talk to my son when I get home."

"Good luck, Gus."

"You, too."

Detective Bryant drove a maroon Impala to the school in Northeast. She ducked the crime tape, then spoke briefly to Jack Harris, the first officer on the scene, and to the three young brothers, who had been detained for her arrival. She entered the opening in the north wall of the school and held a handkerchief to her face as she had a look at the body, which was being attended to by a Mobile Crime Lab tech named Karen Krissoff, wearing a surgical mask and a smudge of Vaseline under her nose. Portable lights had been set up in the room, and flies buzzed and moved through the blasts of white.

"Karen."

"Sondra."

"How long's he been here?"

"Won't know till we get him back to the ME. The heat and the rats didn't do us any favors. Neither did the flies."

"Cause of death?"

"Multiple stab wounds, so far. Marks on the wrists indicate he was bound or cuffed."

"Any identification?"

"No wallet, no cell, no business cards."

"I need prints on the deceased."

"I already got 'em and sent them out."

"Thanks, Karen."

"Go get some fresh air."

Sondra Bryant went back outside and met up with Detective Joseph DeLong, who had come to assist her. DeLong, known as "DeSchlong" in the unit just because, was an affable fellow who worked many overtime hours after a divorce had left him lonely and rather helpless. Bryant and DeLong split the east and west sides of the street between K and L and canvassed the residents of the houses. This took a couple of hours. Bryant then drove over to the 3500 block of V Street, NE, to the Crime Scene Examination complex. Because of Ben Braswell's priors, there had been a hit on his prints.

Bryant sat at a computer station and typed Ben's name into the WACIES program, which brought up his profile. His father was unknown and his mother had been dead since he was two years old. He had no known relatives or known accomplices. She read his charges, convictions, and history of juvenile incarceration. She then switched programs and searched the missing-persons database, and her hunch came up aces. The man who had reported him missing, a Thomas Flynn, was identified as his employer.

Sondra Bryant picked up the phone.

THOMAS FLYNN took the call. He listened intently, asked a few questions, and told the detective that his son, Chris, was the person closest to Ben. He mentioned Ali Carter and told her the name of the place where Ali worked and the nature of his business. He told her that Ben had a girlfriend named Renee. He agreed to meet with Sondra Bryant later that night and have Chris in attendance. Flynn would supply Renee's full name and contact information, which he could get from Chris, when Bryant arrived. He was trying to be as cooperative as possible.

Amanda stood beside him, tears streaming down her face, when Flynn phoned Chris at his apartment. After he gave his son the news and told him the few details he knew, there was a long pause on the other end of the line. When he spoke, Chris's voice was even.

"I'll call Ali," said Chris. "Me and Katherine will go over to Renee's place. I think we should tell her in person. Then I'll swing by your house and talk to the detective."

"You okay?"

"Yeah."

"Chris, I need to ask you . . . I promise I'm only going to ask you this one time."

"I don't know anything, Dad. I don't know why Ben was killed."

"I'll see you in a little while. Take care."

When Flynn hung up, Amanda said, "How is he?"

"Same as ever," said Flynn unhappily. "Tough."

Flynn phoned his friend, the attorney Bob Moskowitz.

AFTER CHRIS spoke with Ali and Katherine, they agreed to go together to Renee's apartment on Queens Chapel Road, not far from the District line. Chris and Katherine met Ali in the parking lot, and they steeled themselves before going inside. Predictably, Renee became hysterical upon hearing the news of Ben's violent death. Thankfully, her mother was there, so Chris, Ali, and Katherine were not entirely helpless in the face of the young woman's loud outbursts of emotion. Her mother, a devoted churchgoer with a quiet manner, had sedatives in her purse for whatever reason, and gave one to Renee. Chris hugged her on the living-room couch for a long while, Renee sobbing and shaking in his arms. After a while her breathing evened out and she lay down there, her mother sitting by her side. Chris, Katherine, and Ali quietly left the apartment house.

"I gotta go speak to the homicide detective," said Chris to Ali, standing by their cars in the lot. "Lady named Bryant. I expect she's gonna get up with you, too."

"She already called me," said Ali. "I'm hooking up with her first thing in the morning."

"You might want to put her up with Lawrence."

"You think—"

"I don't think anything. Lawrence was with Ben recently. That's all."

"Listen," said Ali, "I've got to go to a funeral tomorrow in Northeast. Boy I was working with who didn't make it. I figure you're not going in. . . ."

"I'm not."

"Come with me, Chris. I don't feel like being alone to-morrow."

"All right. Swing past when you're done with the detec-tive."

They gave each other backward glances as they walked to their vehicles. Chris joined Katherine, waiting for him in the van.

THOMAS AND Chris Flynn sat in the living room of the Flynns' home with Detective Sondra Bryant and Bob Moskowitz. Bry-ant had a small notebook in hand and was making notes in it with a Parker pen. Amanda and Katherine were in the kitchen, quietly talking. Django was asleep at Chris's feet.

Bryant had remarked that it was unusual for an interviewee

who was not a suspect to ask for the presence of a lawyer at this point in the process. Thomas Flynn was forthright and told her that his son and Ben had been incarcerated together as juveniles at Pine Ridge, that both had led straight and productive lives since, but that the scars of the experience made Chris extremely cautious about speaking with police.

"I get it," said Bryant. "All right, Mr. Moskowitz. Is it okay for me to speak with your client?"

"Chris will answer any questions you have," said Moskowitz, who had found diet religion and was now a slim bald man nearing fifty whose suit was too large for his frame.

Bryant asked Chris a series of questions. He answered a bit robotically and with little eye contact but did so to her satisfaction. He had a hard exterior, but she could see from his red-rimmed eyes that he had cried at some point in the evening and was grieving. He obviously came from a good family, or at least one that was intact. She believed that he had no direct involvement in his friend's murder and felt, with a lesser degree of certainty, that he had no knowledge of the causes or circumstances surrounding Ben Braswell's death. But she was unconvinced by Chris's repeated claim that Ben had no enemies and had done nothing wrong.

"I had a look at Ben's record," said Sondra Bryant. "There was an incidence of violence at Pine Ridge that kept him incarcerated for a longer period time than was indicated by his original conviction."

"That was an accident," said Chris. "Ben was just defending someone. He wasn't trying to hurt anybody. That kind of thing wasn't in him."

"Maybe the boy he hurt had relatives or friends who didn't see it that way."

"No," said Chris. "This wasn't a revenge thing. Everybody liked Ben."

"Somebody didn't." Bryant had a sip of water and placed her glass back on the table. She looked at Thomas Flynn. "I know this is difficult. May I speak freely?"

"Go ahead," said Flynn.

"We have a saying in our offices. A gun murder is often business. Killing by knife is almost always personal. This victim was stabbed, many, many times. He had been cuffed or had his hands tied. It's possible he was tortured."

"Ben didn't do anything to anybody," said Chris very quietly.

"I believe he's answered the question, Detective Bryant," said Moskowitz.

"Right." Bryant closed her notebook and dropped it into her purse. "We'll speak again. In the meantime, I'll leave you good people and let you have some peace. Have a blessed evening."

"You do the same," said Thomas Flynn.

He and Moskowitz walked her outside. Moskowitz was seeking a few words with her away from Chris, and Flynn intended to ask about the procedure involved in the release of Ben's body. He wanted to know how he could get authorization to gain possession of it.

Chris stayed in the living room, rubbing behind Django's ear. Soon Katherine joined him, kissed his mouth, and sat close to him on the couch.

When Flynn reentered the house, he went to his bar cart in the dining room and poured himself several fingers of Jim Beam. He killed the drink quickly and poured another. He saw Amanda looking at him from the kitchen.

"What?"

"Easy with that," said Amanda.

Flynn tipped his head back and drank.

Out on the street, far down Livingston from the Flynn home, two men sat in an old black Mercury. They were waiting for the man called Chris to emerge from the house that doubled as the business office for Flynn's Floors. They intended to follow him. They wanted to see where he lived.

TWENTY-ONE

THE FUNERAL service for Royalle Foreman, nineteen, was held at a large Baptist church on Nannie Helen Burroughs Avenue in Burrville, in the 50s in far Northeast. Ali and Chris arrived early, pulled into the parking lot, and sat in Juanita Carter's black Saturn, letting the air conditioner run. They talked about Ali's conversation with Detective Bryant earlier that morning, and they spoke fondly and bitterly about Ben. They were in no hurry to get out and stand in the summer heat by the front door of the church, where a line had already formed.

"Looks like it's gonna be full," said Chris.

"Royalle touched a lot of people," said Ali. "He played football for Ballou before he dropped out, and he shined. That right there gets you some positive notoriety. He had a charming smile on him, and he was funny. People *liked* Royalle."

"What happened?"

"The usual. Peers pulling him down. No one at home strong enough to keep his head in the books or tell him to stay indoors at night. He was a repeat offender. Possession first, then sales. Nonviolent stuff, but after multiples they're gonna lock you up. He did a little time with the hard boys out at Pine

230

Ridge. Did a second jolt on a parole violation, and that set him up with new contacts and problems. I was tryin to work with him, and I did find him some employment. I had him with this auto body dude I know, as an apprentice. But Royalle couldn't stay out his own way. He had some kind of long-standing beef with someone, over a girl. Last Saturday night a car, three deep, rolled up on him in while he was walkin to his aunt's house, where he stayed. He took one in the neck and bled out right on the sidewalk. Another bullet had eyes for a row house window. Kids in there had the presence of mind to get down on the floor when they heard the first pops."

"City kids learn young," said Chris. "The police know who did it?"

"No witnesses. I'm guessing that some of the young men at this funeral know who was in that car, and who the shooter was. But they won't talk to the police."

"They're gonna settle it themselves."

"No doubt," said Ali. "You know, I went to court and pled for lenience on behalf of Royalle before they sent him back to the Ridge a second time. I was tryin to get him into this charter high school they have now, where the kids eat and sleep on the premises."

"Like a boarding school?"

"Exactly. Gets the boys out of their environment but doesn't put them into a prison environment. Judge wouldn't listen. I guess he was reading those editorials in the newspaper about how the juvenile justice system is letting too many bad kids back out on the street. You know, 'I grew up black and poor, and now I'm a professional journalist. You have to be extra tough on these boys and keep them locked up. I made it; why can't they?' All that bullshit. No question, some boys, the gunmen and killers, they do need to be jailed and off the street.

But Royalle wasn't one of those boys. Juvenile prison just kept him low."

"They're letting them in," said Chris, watching the line move.

"Yeah, let's go."

They walked across the parking lot, now nearly full. Chris and Ali wore sport jackets over open-necked shirts and jeans, in the medium range of dress for those who had come to the funeral. The majority of the attendees were young, some in suits, others in T-shirts bearing Royalle Foreman's likeness with mentions of love, the Lord, heaven, and RIP.

In the lobby, Chris took a program and looked up at the memorial wall adorned with more than a hundred photographs of deceased teenagers and young adults from across the city, victims of shootings and other violent acts. Ali tugged on Chris's jacket, and the two of them walked into the sanctuary, where female ushers were handing out Kleenex and paper fans to sweating mourners. A large video screen was set up behind the pulpit and altar, and on it was the image of Royalle Foreman lying in an open casket. Gospel music played through a PA system. A receiving line had formed, and a woman in it was crying loudly.

A minister stood in the pulpit and leaned into a lectern's microphone. "Please turn off your cell phones. And please, let me remind you, there is no drinking in the parking lot."

Chris stood in a pew beside Ali. He closed his eyes and said a silent prayer. He was not religious, but he felt, in an uncomplicated way, that there had to be something higher, some reason that he and the people he loved were here and alive, and others had been taken. In his mind he saw Ben, a dog beside him, both of them walking in a field, the dog's tail switching back and forth, Ben smiling. It should have made Chris happy to envision his friend this way. But instead his thoughts went to violence, and he found that he was no longer speaking to God but fantasizing about murdering the men who had murdered Ben.

"No," said Chris very softly.

Not in church.

ALI HAD an appointment to meet with Ken Young, the most recent director of the District's Department of Youth Rehabilitation Services, and Reginald Roberts, the superintendent of Pine Ridge. Because it was Young's day to visit Pine Ridge, Ali had planned to meet them both out there. Chris, after a bit of prodding from Ali, agreed to come along. He knew that Ali wanted company. Also, he did not want to go back to his apartment and be alone with his thoughts.

They drove out to Anne Arundel County in Maryland. The facility was less than thirty miles from the city, but it was country, with stretches of highway running past woods, the occasional new housing community, warehouses, government agencies, and company headquarters. It felt a world away.

Ali turned off the two-lane and went down a long road that wound back into more country and dense stands of trees. Chris felt a sense of dread creep up on him. He wondered if Ali, who made the trek out here regularly, still felt it, too.

"No pines," said Chris.

"None that I ever seen," said Ali.

They passed the site of the new facility, which was close to completion. A Democratic senator from Maryland had fought the building of it, as had representatives of neighboring residential communities, arguing that the D.C. jail for youths should be located in the District of Columbia, but they had failed, and construction had gone on as planned.

"Ken Young put some of the boys to work on the crews here," said Ali. "A lot of it was straight labor, but a few of them apprenticed with tradesmen and carpenters. When they get out, they'll have skills. The new facility is gonna have a wood-working shop in it."

"What about private showers?"

"That, too. The housing units are gonna be more like dorms than bunkers."

"Where'd this guy Young come from?"

"Some big city with problems like ours. The mayor found him. He had years of experience implementing what they call the 'Missouri model' for juvenile rehabilitation. Basically, it stresses nurturing over hard punishment. Preparing these boys to succeed, playing to their strengths and interests rather than keeping them low. Bunch of states have picked up on it. It's not cheap, but it pays off later on, when you've got fewer boys graduating to adult prisons."

"Young must have enemies."

"They talk about the negative impact on the community when you let jailed boys out and put them under supervision. But when you lock up kids without looking at other alternatives, you *destroy* communities. There's gonna be some failures, naturally. But there's gonna be some success stories, too."

Ali parked in the lot among cars belonging to guards and administration. They walked along the link-and-razor-wire fence to the gatehouse. As if on cue, clouds had moved in, and inside the fence the palette was gray. *This is how I remember it,* thought Chris. *This is how it always seemed to me.*

They passed through the security office of the gatehouse. Ali had called ahead and had Chris's name added to the visitors list. Then they were inside the fence and moving toward the ad-ministrative offices, weeds and dirt beneath their feet. A group of boys were walking from one building to another, accompanied by a couple of guards. One of the boys chopped another in the back of the neck while the guards weren't looking.

"Knuckleheads," said Chris.

"That ain't never gonna change," said Ali.

"They don't make them walk with one hand grabbing their wrist behind their back anymore."

"Young stopped that, too. I mean, shoot, they're caged up in here. Where they supposed to go?"

They met Reginald Roberts, Pine Ridge's latest superintendent, in his office. Roberts had modest height, a bodybuilder's physique, and wore his hair in braids. He was a reform warden, handpicked by Ken Young. Young was tall, thin, middle-aged, and shaggy haired, unable to stay seated, with the kind of nervous energy that kept him standing next to the wall. Roberts took a seat behind his desk, and Chris and Ali settled into chairs before him.

"Chris here is a Pine Ridge alumnus," said Ali. "I've spoken of him before."

"Good to finally meet you, Chris," said Young. "Ali also told me that your father has employed some of our graduates."

"He's tried," said Chris.

"We appreciate it," said Roberts.

"I'm sorry for the loss of your friend," said Young. "Ali mentioned this morning that the two of you were tight. I read about his death in the paper."

"The whole paragraph?" said Chris.

"Ali says that all three of y'all were together out here," said Roberts.

"Unit Five," said Ali.

"I closed that one," said Young.

"Anyway," said Roberts. He pushed a manila folder across

the desk toward Ali, who picked it up. "Let's talk about these boys right here."

For the next half hour they discussed inmates who were about to come out, either released to their families or to residential treatment centers. Ali reported on the progress of several young men and talked about others who were struggling and might be headed back into the facility.

"You might want to make a bed up for William Richards," said Ali.

"When he was in he talked about culinary school," said Roberts.

"Half the boys say that," said Young. "When you ask them what they're gonna do, it's the most popular response. 'I'm about to go to culinary school.'"

"We're gonna graduate a lot of chefs," said Roberts.

"There's always McDonald's," said Ali. "That's one way to start."

"Coupla years ago the big thing was barber college," said Young. "I had this one kid, Morris Weeks, said in his last level meeting that he wanted to go to 'haircut academy.' He had just got off punishment for cold-cocking a guard. I said to him, 'Morris, who's gonna put a scissors in your hand when you're always acting so violent?'"

"Boy learned, though," said Roberts.

"He did," said Young. "Morris got a chair in a shop on Georgia and Piney Branch Road."

When they were done, Ali and Chris shook hands with Reginald Roberts.

"Walk with me, guys," said Ken Young.

They left the building and headed toward another. Chris could see the basketball court, its pole and backboard standing out in the field.

"That rusted old hoop," said Chris.

"We're gonna have a nice court in the new place," said Young.

They entered the school building and walked through its halls. Guards were standing outside the doors of the classrooms, all with handsets. Many nodded perfunctorily at Young and a few gave him more genuine greetings as they passed. Down the hall, an inmate, his arm pinned up behind him, was being pushed out the exit door by two guards.

"Who's that?" said Young to a burly guard wearing a Cowboys ball cap. "Is it Jerome?"

"Yeah, that boy swung on Bobby."

"Take him out and let him cool down."

"That's what we're doin, Mr. Young." Chris saw the guard roll his eyes slightly at the guard beside him.

They walked on. The colors of the walls were brighter than Chris remembered. Paintings done by inmates were pinned up on bulletin boards.

"We've got a new foundation running the school," said Young, seeing surprise on Chris's face. "New teachers. The classes are smaller because I have fewer numbers in lockup. Almost sixty percent of the boys here are Tier One, the high-security youth. Only about ten percent are low security. The majority of the kids committed to the DYRS are in their homes or in residential treatment. They don't belong in cells."

"I see you got them doin art," said Ali.

"Yeah, and there's a literary magazine. We even put on a Shakespeare play for officials at city hall. And I had some boys hook up with AmeriCorps, went down to Mississippi to rebuild some homes after Katrina. I'm trying everything."

"Some of those guards didn't look too happy to see you."

"We call them youth development specialists now," said

Young. "They don't like that, either. Matter of fact, a lot of them wouldn't piss on me if I was running down the street on fire. The union reps gave me and Reginald a vote of no confidence, tried to have us fired. And they've fought to retain abusive or incompetent guards that I've let go."

"I read all that stuff on the op-ed page," said Ali. "Their solution is to, what, keep kids locked up?"

"Seems to be."

"What'd you do, forget to kiss that columnist's ring? You damn sure aren't gonna win a popularity contest with the press."

"I'm not looking to," said Young.

Outside the school, Young led them to Unit Five. He got a key from a chain hung on his belt loop and unlocked the building's door.

"I don't know," said Chris.

"Come on," said Young. "They're going to tear it down soon. You should see it one more time."

"I see it every day," said Chris, as he stepped inside.

The smell got him. He had forgotten that. It was unidentifiable, but it suggested stillness and decay. They went into the common room. The Ping-Pong table was gone, as was the fake-leather chair with the arms studded in nail heads. The old couch was all that was left. Its back was now nearly completely shredded, and a spring showed from beneath its worn seat. Beyond the common room sat the media room, now in complete darkness.

Young led them down the hall. Chris looked up at the tiled ceilings where he'd stashed marijuana many years before. Then they were along the rows of doors leading to the cells. Chris feared that if he closed his eyes he would hear Ben's voice, talking to himself the way he used to do at night.

Ali and Chris looked through clouded Plexiglas into one of the small cells. The gray blanket covering the bolted-down cot. The steel shitter and pisshole. The particleboard desk.

"I've got the Joliet," said Ken Young, touching the extra-large key hanging off the ring on his belt line. "If you want to go in."

"No," said Chris.

"I brought you in here so you wouldn't forget," said Young. "The more allies I have, the better it is for me. If people could see this, they wouldn't be so eager to put kids in cages."

"They *should* tear this building down," said Chris. "I'd drive the bulldozer if you'd let me."

Young nodded. "You'd have to get in line."

TWENTY-TWO

CHRIS WAS quiet on the ride back to the city. It was more than circumspection. There was something on his mind beyond Ben and the awful memories rekindled at Pine Ridge.

"What's going on with you, man?" said Ali.

"I'm thinking on something," said Chris. He thumb-stroked the vertical scar above his lip. "When you spoke to that detective this morning, did you tell her about Lawrence New-house?"

"No. I had a conversation with him last night. He said he didn't know anything about Ben's murder. He said he didn't want to talk to police. I expected that, and I had to respect his wishes."

"How was he when you gave him the news about Ben?"

"Bad," said Ali. "He cried, and he didn't care if I heard it. He was blown."

"I gotta tell you something, Ali. I didn't say it to you before because I didn't think it meant anything. But now I'm not so sure."

Chris told Ali about the money in the gym bag. He said that

they had left it in the row house, but that Lawrence had gotten Ben wasted and Ben had told him where it was. Chris and Ben believed that Lawrence had gone to the house and stolen the money. They had done nothing about it because they felt that there was nothing to do.

When Chris was done, Ali said, "And now you think there's something with that money that connects Lawrence to Ben's murder."

"I'm not sayin that."

"Lawrence loved Ben. When Lawrence was getting his ass beat by everyone and their brother at Pine Ridge, Ben stood up for him. He was the only one who did. If there was one dude who Lawrence considered a friend, it was Ben."

"I know that."

"*What*, then?"

"Maybe they went out together and were spending the money. Maybe they ran their mouths off at a club or during a card game. Lawrence could have been braggin on what he had. Or someone thought the cash was Ben's and tried to take him off."

"That's thin."

"Shit, Ali, I don't know *what* I'm talkin about. I'm sayin there might be some kind of connection."

"You're speculating."

"Yeah."

"Then you need to talk to Lawrence. I know you don't like to, but there it is. And if Lawrence does know something, he needs to tell it to the law."

"Right."

Ali looked at his friend. "What else you got on your mind?"

"I don't know," said Chris. "It's like a finger is tapping the side of my head, trying to remind me that . . . I *know* something, Ali. Damn if I can remember it."

"You will."

They came off the Beltway and headed down Colesville Road toward the District line, traffic gathering thickly around them. Oddly, the congestion made them both more comfortable.

"Any plans for Ben's funeral?" said Ali.

"My father is taking care of it," said Chris. "When the police release the body, my dad is gonna have Ben cremated over at Rapp. He's getting him a spot at Rock Creek Cemetery."

"That's where Ben got took, right?"

"Yeah. My father spoke to that homicide detective, and she said that the Rock Creek security guard recalled an old black sedan leaving out the place at the end of the night. He didn't happen to see if Ben was inside it. He didn't say that he found it suspicious at the time. He just remembered it 'cause it was the last car out."

"Safe to say that it started there, though."

"But it wouldn't have changed Ben's opinion of the cemetery. That was his spot. It's where he would have wanted to be buried."

"I thought you had to be rich or connected to get put in that place," said Ali.

"So did I. But my father looked into it and found something that was available. Like anything else, all it takes is money. It's not gonna be a fancy monument or in the prime section of the grounds. It'll prob'ly be a small marker, something like that. Important thing is, Ben will be there."

"That can't be cheap."

"It's thousands."

"Your father's a good man," said Ali.

"He's like most people," said Chris. "He's trying to be good, and most times he is."

"Like you."

"But he wanted me to be better than him. Turns out I was human, just like him."

"That's behind y'all."

"It is for me."

"YOU GONNA lie there all day?" said Marquis Gilman.

"I might," said Lawrence Newhouse. He was on his single bed, on his back, in the room he shared with Terrence and Loquatia. Marquis had entered the room, held aside the privacy sheet, and stood at the foot of Lawrence's bed.

"Let's go shoot around some."

"Nah, I'm too tired."

Marquis could see that Lawrence's eyes were pink. He hated to think that his uncle had been crying.

"Mama told me 'bout your friend."

"Uh."

"You know who did the thing?"

"No."

"Whoever did it needs to be got."

Lawrence turned his head sharply toward Marquis. "That ain't for you to speak on, boy."

Marquis looked down at his Nikes. "I didn't mean nothin."

Lawrence's eyes softened. "This is on me."

"You not workin today?"

"I'm done with it."

"'Cause I could help you."

"I don't want you washin cars. You better than that. I'm still tryin to get you hooked up with my mans. You could learn the carpet trade, 'stead of doin mule stuff."

"I'm sayin, I can work."

"Go on, Marquis. Go play ball."

Marquis left the room.

Lawrence Newhouse hadn't washed and detailed one car since he'd taken the money. The young man he worked with, Deon Miller, was upset with him, because together they'd built up a nice little business. But he couldn't tell Deon why he'd lost his ambition. He'd known Deon since he was a kid, growing up at Parkchester, and smoking weed one day on Stevens Road, they'd made grandiose plans about this thing they were going to do, starting small and ending, in their minds, with a string of locations in Southeast and PG. They'd be known as the entrepreneurs who owned the spots to get the nicest cars in D.C. cleaned and shined. They'd be to cars what Murray was to steaks.

It hadn't turned out so big, but they'd done all right.

Lawrence and Deon took their business to the car owners. They used grocery carts they'd stolen from the Giant, and stocked them with everything needed to impress. Lawrence would go to the big auto parts store, buy their cheap house brands of liquid detergent, wax, wheel cleaner, and tire shine, and pour them into empty bottles of recognizable brand names, like Armor All and Black Magic, that he'd found in the trash. They called their business Elite Shine. If they had a sign, it would have read, "Only the finest materials used to detail the very finest cars." Lawrence had thought of that when he was high.

They were getting a rep around Southeast. Seeing the same customers getting their cars done. What they called "repeat clientele." So it was natural that, just as they were beginning to lift off, Deon would be disturbed and disappointed when Lawrence told him that he didn't want to work no more.

"What, you just gonna give up on everything we built up?" said Deon.

Lawrence said, "I'm retired," and left it at that.

That was before Ben got done. Now that he was gone, nothing mattered. Not even the money.

Lawrence draped his forearm over his eyes. He was sweating and he could smell his own stink.

Why would someone do his boy like that?

Why? was the first question. Then came, Who?

Lawrence burned to know.

CHRIS FLYNN returned to his apartment, put his shoes neatly under his bed, changed his clothes, and went to sleep. When he woke, the bedroom had darkened. He went to the window and opened the blinds and saw that it was night. He had slept heavily for several hours and could not recall if he had dreamed.

Chris phoned Katherine. She asked if he wanted company, and he said that he preferred to be alone. It was not that he did not want to see her. He knew that he would not be good with anyone tonight.

"I'm worried about you," said Katherine.

"I'll call you tomorrow," said Chris.

He showered, microwaved a Celeste pizza, and ate it standing up. He thought of smoking some marijuana he kept in his nightstand but decided against it. His head would be up for a while, but then he'd get to that overthinking phase, and he didn't want that. He grabbed a few bottles of Budweiser out of the refrigerator and put them in a six-pack-sized cooler, along with some ice. He dropped his cell into the pocket of his shorts and left his apartment.

Out on the front porch of the bungalow, Andy Ladas, the black-haired, middle-aged tenant of the three-family home, was sitting in a high-backed chair, drinking an Anchor Steam and smoking a Winston. Beside him was a steel stand-up ashtray of the type once common in barbershops. This was Ladas's position and activity for a couple of hours every night.

"Hey, Andy."

"Chris."

"We alone?"

"The kids got a gig," said Ladas. He was referring to the musician couple, Tina and Doug Gibson, who had the top floor. They were older than Chris but did not look it.

"Case you fall asleep with that cigarette in your hand and catch fire, I'll be out back."

The house was on a corner of the street, at an intersection featuring a four-way stop that was frequently ignored. There was a police station nearby, and it seemed the main offenders were cops. They were the most aggressive speeders, too. Neighborhood activists had petitioned for road humps to slow the cruisers down, which had improved things slightly.

Chris walked through the side yard to the back, where he put down the cooler and took a seat in a green metal rocking chair beside a brick grill. The yard went deep and it had been landscaped by the Gibsons and maintained by all the tenants. It was a nice spot, and he frequently sat here on summer nights. With a view unencumbered by the branches of trees overhead, he could look up at the stars. The sky was clear, and the moon cast a pearl glow on the property.

Chris drank a beer. He thought of Ben and the day at Pine Ridge, and as the alcohol kissed him he felt his shoulders relax. He tossed the first bottle into the grass and reached into the cooler for another. He twisted off its top and emptied its neck.

Chris heard a vehicle come to a stop and looked to his right.

An old black sedan had parked on the street and its engine died.

Chris reached into his pocket, retrieved his cell, and flipped it open, its buttons and screen illuminated. Because he was of a generation that was dexterous with keyboards, he quickly found the contact he was searching for.

Two men, one large and one small, got out of the car, crossed the street, and walked toward him in the yard. Chris studied them and continued to text with his fingers.

He was not thinking of police. He was a boy, and he was calling his father.

He typed the words *I'm at home*.

And: *Signal 13*.

TWENTY-THREE

THE LARGE man wore a windbreaker over a T-shirt and jeans. The small man wore black. They stood before Chris Flynn, still seated in his chair. Chris had slipped his cell back into his pocket. He held a beer bottle loosely in his right hand.

"Get up," said Sonny. "Let's take a ride."

Chris slowly shook his head. "I don't think so."

"We need to have a talk."

"We're talking now."

"Not here," said Sonny.

Chris's eyes disconnected from Sonny's. He drank slowly from his bottle of beer.

"Get up," said Wayne.

Chris looked at him blankly. Wayne's brush mustache seemed to spring from inside his nostrils and lay beneath a flat nose in a deeply lined, imploding face. He appeared to be rotting. His wiry arms were dominated by ink.

"What do you want?" said Chris, returning his gaze to the big man with the walrus whiskers and high cheekbones.

"Somethin that's mine," said Sonny.

"What would that be?"

"Try to tell me you don't know."

"I'm not playing this game," said Chris.

"You will."

"You're trespassing."

"Fuck you, sweetheart. Let's go."

Chris looked at him with lazy green eyes.

The big man held one hand out to Chris and turned it into the shine of moonlight. Chris saw a tattoo on the crook of it.

"You know what this is?" said Sonny.

"Prison ink," said Chris.

"What, *specific?*"

"It's a four-leaf clover."

Sonny breathed out heavily in exasperation. Chris thought he saw the little one smile.

"It's a shamrock," said Sonny Wade. "You ride with the rock, means you're part of a special club. You know what that club is?"

"The dick suck club," said Chris.

Wayne grinned and giggled. Sonny's smile showed perfect ugly teeth, gray in the light.

A car drove by and they all went silent.

"Let's just get this done," said Sonny, and he reached into his windbreaker.

"I wouldn't," said Chris. "Whatever you got inside that jacket, you pull it out, it's a mistake."

Sonny kept his hand where it was but made no move to pull his gun. "I said, let's walk."

"I'm not goin anywhere with you."

"How 'bout I just murder your ass right here?"

"You'll lose what you're after."

"Chris Carpet," said Wayne. "Boy thinks he's a real tough nut."

Chris felt the blood leave his face.

"Shut up, stupid," said Sonny.

A Montgomery County police cruiser drove by on the road beside the house. No one spoke, and the car passed from sight. Sonny's black eyes flickered and he moved his hand. Chris saw the grip of a pistol inch out from the jacket.

"There a problem here?"

Andy Ladas emerged from the shadows of the side yard and stood well back from the two men. In his hand was a flipped-open cell.

"Chris," said Andy. "Is there a *problem?*"

"Is there?" said Chris, staring into Sonny's eyes.

Sonny's hand came empty out of his jacket and he dropped it to his side. He looked at Wayne and nodded shortly.

Sonny looked down at Chris. "See you around, fella."

Sonny walked out of the yard, his little partner creeping along beside him. Chris heard car doors open and slam, and the turn of an engine. He heard the creak of worn shocks and watched the old black sedan roll down the street.

"How long were you back there, Andy?"

"I came off the porch soon as I seen those two walk back into the yard. Those guys didn't look right."

"What did you hear?"

"Most of it. I was about to call nine-one-one."

"Wasn't any need for that. But thanks." Chris stood from his chair and killed the beer left in the bottle. He tossed it on the ground and noticed that his hand was shaking. He picked up the cooler and gripped its handle tight.

"You all right?" said Ladas.

"Yeah," said Chris. "When my dad comes, don't speak on any particulars. Just tell him I'm inside."

He walked toward the bungalow, using his damp T-shirt to wipe away the sweat that had broken on his face.

*   *   *

THOMAS FLYNN arrived shortly thereafter and parked Amanda's SUV sloppily on the road, one set of tires up on the curb. He jogged across the yard to the front porch of the bungalow, where Andy Ladas sat, working on another beer and a smoke. Flynn was winded and his color was up. His shirttails were out, covering the .38 he had holstered at the small of his back.

"Is Chris all right?"

"Yes," said Ladas.

"What's happening here?"

"Couple of guys were talkin to Chris outside." Ladas cut his eyes away from Flynn's. "That's all I know. They're gone and he's fine."

Flynn went into the house. He stepped to the door of Chris's apartment and turned the knob without knocking. It was a small place consisting of a bedroom, living room, kitchenette, and head. From behind the closed bathroom door he could hear the run of a shower. Flynn had a seat in a cushiony chair. He looked up at the crowded bookshelves. On the small table beside him lay a bookmarked copy of *Wartime* by Paul Fussell.

The shower shut off. Soon Chris stepped out of the bathroom, a towel around his waist.

"Dad."

"Everything all right?"

"I'm good."

"You're so *good*, why'd you send me that code?"

"Can I dry my hair off and put some pants on?"

"Go ahead."

"There's beer in the refrigerator, you want one."

Flynn found a bottle of Budweiser and uncapped it while Chris changed. He drank off a good piece of it standing up and finished it sitting in the same chair.

He's taking his time, thought Flynn. *He's figuring out his story and his lies.*

Flynn went back to the refrigerator and got another beer. He was drinking it when Chris stepped barefoot into the room, wearing jeans and a wife beater. His hair had been towel dried and left uncombed. The look on his face was clever and annoyed, as it had been when he was a teen. As if he was expecting a tongue-lashing from his father, was prepared to take it, and would give up nothing in return.

"Well?" said Flynn.

Chris pushed hair back behind his ears. "Couple of dudes came by to speak with me about somethin. I thought there was gonna be trouble, but I was wrong. I apologize for bothering you."

"What did they want?"

"I owe them money," said Chris. "I get into these card games sometimes. Texas hold 'em, like you see on ESPN. Only these are played in basements around town. I was into those two for a coupla thousand dollars."

"Bullshit."

"It was a card debt."

"No, it wasn't. You're lying. Don't forget who you're talking to, son. I had years and years of experience watching you lie to me. You don't look any different to me right now than you did when you were sixteen."

"I'm telling you how it was. I don't know what else to say."

"Say the truth. You sent me that signal. If it was nothing, you could have handled it yourself. If you needed just a little help you could have called the police. Shit, the station house is right up the street."

"I wouldn't call the police," said Chris.

"I forgot," said Flynn. "You don't talk to the *po*-leece."

"That's not necessary," said Chris, and he left the room to get himself a beer.

When he returned, his father was staring down at his shoes.

"I'm sorry," said Flynn. "I was out of line."

Chris dragged a chair beside his father and had a seat. Flynn popped the knuckles of his left hand with his right.

"Calm down, Dad."

"Okay."

"You know I'm tryin."

"I do."

"I go to work every day. I pretty much play by the rules. But you know, some things, some of the bad habits I picked up along the way, and especially the experience of being locked up—"

"I know. It's hard to shake."

"Me and Ali went out to Pine Ridge today. Ali had some work stuff to take care of out there, and I joined him. Bein back in my unit, looking into my cell, it hit me kinda hard. It's tough to get that monster off your back. Wasn't easy for Ben, either."

"You telling me that you and Ben slipped back into some criminal thing?"

"No. I already told you; Ben didn't do anything wrong."

"So those two men were here because of a card debt."

"Yes."

"Bullshit," said Flynn.

The two of them sat there and drank. Flynn finished his and went to the fridge and got another. He caught a look from Chris as he retook his seat.

"You should slow down," said Chris. "You gotta drive home."

"Fuck that," said Flynn. "I'm a grown man, and you sound like your mother."

Flynn took a long pull from his bottle.

"I'm not comin in for a few days," said Chris. "I need some time off."

"How you gonna pay your gambling debt if you don't work? What about the vig? Isn't that what you guys call it?"

"There is no vig."

"On account of there's no debt. 'Cause this card game thing is bullshit."

Chris chuckled. "You can't let it go, can you?"

"That's all right," said Flynn, his eyes a bit unfocused. He drank off more of his beer. "You'll tell me the truth when you're ready, I guess. I don't wanna pressure you or nothin like that."

"Can I say something else?"

"Go 'head."

"When I come back to work, I'm not wearing that polo shirt anymore. I'll wear anything you want, but not that. Me and Ben, we never liked those things. They reminded us of our uniforms at the Ridge. Is that all right?"

Flynn could not look at Chris. He said, "Yes, Chris. It's fine."

Chris cleared his throat. "I'm . . ."

"What?"

"I'm thinking of taking a class or two, spring semester, over at Montgomery College. American history."

"That's nice," said Flynn. And because he was his father, he added, "What would you do with that?"

"Just check it out and see what happens, I guess," said Chris. "Maybe work toward a teaching degree. I dunno. Things are gettin kind of serious between Katherine and me. If I'm gonna be, you know, responsible for someone else . . . I'm sayin, I don't want to be installing carpet all my life."

"I don't want that for you, either."

"Anyway."

"Yeah."

Flynn got up and went to the kitchenette and stood over its sink. He drank deeply of his beer, took a breath, and finished what was left. He placed the bottle along a row of empties on the counter and walked toward the front door.

"I'm outta here, Chris."

"Dad?"

Flynn stopped walking. "Yeah."

"Thanks for coming. When I called, I mean."

Flynn stared at Chris, his eyes sad and knowing. Now would be the time to say the words that needed to be said, but he could not. He waved and walked out the door.

Chris stared at the bottle in his hand. He drank from it, his chest heavy with emotion.

FLYNN STOOD at his bar cart and poured three fingers of Beam into a rocks glass. He sipped at the bourbon and felt it bite as Amanda came into the dining room. Her eyes traveled over him and flickered away.

"I'm just having one before bed," said Flynn.

"I didn't say a word."

"What would Jesus have done, Amanda? If he'd had a son like ours, I mean. Do you think Jesus might have a drink once in a while, just to take the edge off?"

Amanda hugged her arms. "What happened?"

"Nothing. I got there and whatever was going on was over. Chris says he's in a little trouble over a gambling debt."

"Chris doesn't gamble. Does he?"

"No idea. But he's lying about what went down tonight. Still lying to me, after everything we've been through."

"Maybe there's a reason."

"He was mixed up with Ben on something. Ben was killed because of it, and Chris won't tell me or anyone else what it's about. That's the reason, Manda. Chris fucked up again. He's into something wrong."

"You don't know that."

"And you're blind. You always have been."

"At least I didn't give up on him."

"Yes, you did. Call it nurturing if you want to put a sweet name to it, but to me, you just gave up. Because you stopped expecting anything from him. I never did."

"He's our child."

"He's a man. And I can't accept what he is. I won't."

"Give him a chance."

"I always have," said Flynn. "And I'm not the only one. You remember that time he broke into those cars in the parking lot of that Tex-Mex place on Wisconsin?"

"Tuco's," said Amanda. The owner of the restaurant had called them at home. His people had watched Chris do the crime on live camera. He'd been caught by a couple of employees and brought back into the kitchen. Her husband had told the owner he'd make restitution when he picked Chris up.

"When I got there," said Flynn, "I went up the stairs with these Mexicans, or whatever they were, to this little security room they had with video monitors in it, on the second floor. In the dining room of that restaurant the waitstaff was dressed in bright outfits, the music was festive, and everyone was smiling. Y'know, one of those happy ethnic eating experiences for white people in Ward Three. But up in that room these guys looked like some rough Spanish dudes who'd just had a well-to-do kid come to their business establishment and ruin that experience for their customers. I mean, these guys were hot. I had to beg them not to call the police. And I had to stand there with them and watch a tape of my son in that lot, looking around and hesitating before he made the decision to break into those cars. I was saying, 'Don't do it, Chris. *Please*, don't do it.' But he had al*ready* done it. I was watching a tape of something that had happened an hour earlier. Those Mexicans must have thought I was nuts."

"What difference does it make now?"

"The point is, I gave him plenty of chances. The guy who owned the restaurant, he gave the kid a chance that day, too. Chris just kept on screwing up."

"That was ten years ago."

"Right." Flynn swirled bourbon and looked into the glass. "You'll be happy to know that he's making plans, at least. Says he's going to take a couple of classes at Montgomery College in the spring. And apparently he's serious about Kate."

"That's wonderful," said Amanda.

"His blue area's finally catching up to his green area."

"What?"

"Reasoning and emotion. The limbic system and the pre-frontal cortex. Remember Dr. Peterhead's presentation on that easel? Chris's brain is evening out. Now if he can only stop himself from stumbling. Refrain from those criminal impulses he's got. I guess that's a different area of the, the *cortex*."

"You're drunk."

"So?"

"I'm going to bed."

Amanda left the dining room. Flynn listened to her footsteps ascend the stairs.

"I'll be up in a minute," he shouted.

There was no reply. He closed his eyes and drank.

IN HIS apartment, Chris sat in the dark and drank another beer. He had been thinking on something the little man with the thick mustache had said. As the pieces began to connect in his head, murder came to his heart.

TWENTY-FOUR

CHRIS FLYNN sat at a window deuce with Mindy Kramer in Thai Feast. Their view was of several painters' vans and pickups jumbled in a parking lot dominated by a green Dumpster. But neither of them was looking out the window. Before Mindy was her noodle special, a glass of water, iced coffee, and a full cup of chicken–lemon grass soup that had gone cold. Mindy was staring down at the table, her oversize sunglasses and BlackBerry neatly aligned beside the plates. Her hands were in her lap and her fingers were tightly entwined.

Chris had ordered nothing and was drinking water. Mindy had agreed to meet him after hearing the malice in his voice during an early-morning phone call. She knew what this was going to be about. She wanted the conversation to take place in public.

"How did you know?" said Mindy. Her hair was heavily gelled and her makeup was as thick as a cardboard mask.

"One of them called me Chris Carpet. It's the same stupid name you bragged about giving me when you entered it into your phone."

"I meant you no disrespect. It was just a mnemonic device I used."

259

"*And* I got an anonymous call on my cell last Saturday night. The caller addressed me as Chris Carpet. So it all goes back to you."

Toi, the house waitress, came to the table and refilled Chris's water glass. She looked at the untouched food and drink in front of Mindy.

"You are not hungry today, Miss Kramer? Something wrong with the noodles? You don't like?"

"Everything's fine," said Mindy, making a short, impatient chopping motion with one hand.

Toi smiled wanly and drifted to another table.

"Why'd you give up my name?"

"I was frightened," said Mindy. "I thought they'd murder me if I didn't give them a name. Can you understand that? I assumed that you and your partner—"

"His name was Ben."

"I assumed that the two of you found the money and took it. I certainly knew nothing about its existence until the day those animals came into my life."

"You were wrong," said Chris. "We didn't take anything."

Mindy used her thumb to rub at the corner of one eye and smudged mascara onto the side of her face. "I didn't know what else to do."

"Tell me what they looked like."

Mindy ran a hand up and down the goose bumps on her bare arm. "A large man with one of those mustaches that curve down around the mouth. It looked like he had false teeth to me. He had a small tattoo on his hand. A four-leaf clover."

"And the other," said Chris, his eyes losing their light.

"Much smaller. Bushy mustache. An awful, ugly face."

"Their names?"

"The big one called himself Ralph Cotter. He made the appointment and I wrote the name into my daybook. I don't remember what the little one went by. Cotter wasn't his real name. He told me as much."

"Any weapons?" said Chris, and Mindy looked at him quizzically. "You said you thought they were going to kill you. What would they have used?"

"The little man had a knife."

"What kind of a knife?" said Chris.

"He kept it in a sheath tied to his calf. It had a wood handle and teeth on the blade."

Chris mumbled something that she could not hear.

"What?"

"They killed my friend."

"I'm sorry," said Mindy.

"He didn't take their money. He never hurt anyone. He couldn't."

"I'm so sorry."

Chris said nothing and drank water from his glass.

"I have a daughter," said Mindy Kramer. "Lisa's about your age. She's been . . . I don't mind telling you, she's been a disappointment to me. It's not uncommon for a parent of my generation to feel that way, you know. We were so ambitious and hard-charging, and our children seem so, I don't know, unconcerned with what they are going to achieve in life." Mindy sipped her iced coffee and placed the glass gently on the table. "Lisa had two little girls. She's no longer married to the father, and I don't feel as if she's equipped to handle the responsibility of motherhood. So I'm practically raising Michelle and Lauren myself."

"I've gotta get going," said Chris.

Mindy reached across the table, put her hand on top of Chris's, and squeezed it. "They threatened my granddaughters. The big man said the little one would . . . he said the little man would cut their heads off. Do you understand what I went through that day?"

Chris gently pulled his hand free from hers. "Don't speak of this conversation to anyone. Ever. Not even if you get a sudden case of conscience. Especially not if you read something about these men in the paper or see it on the TV news. Don't ever speak on this again."

"I won't, Chris."

"And it's Chris Flynn."

He got up out of his seat and walked from the restaurant. She watched him cross the parking lot to the white work van with the magnetic sign that read "Flynn's Floors." Realizing now that he was the owner's son. She wondered if he was going to kill the men who had visited her and murdered his friend. She was not a violent person, but she found herself hoping that he would do just that.

"You finished?" said Toi, reaching for the main dish of uneaten food. "You want me to box it up for you?"

"No," said Mindy, wiping a tear that had threatened to break from her eye. "Just get me the check."

Toi went back to the waitress station, smiling to herself, thinking of the tall blond man who had humbled the bitch and made her cry.

SONNY WADE and Wayne Minors had moved out of the hotel in the badlands of the eastward strip of New York Avenue. In addition to the foreign tourists, who seemed shell-shocked to find themselves in such a place, the hotel was heavy with low-level criminals of various stripes, people drinking themselves to death, and one-night-stand women, both professional and amateur. Hence, a police car was often in the parking lot, either surveilling the premises or responding to a call. Sonny was aware that their old vehicle stood out, especially in Washington, where everyone, even those without the means, seemed to be driving late-model cars. Plus, their plates were certainly on the hot sheet now. It was not a good idea to stick around.

Sonny and Wayne were uncomfortable in cities, and in this one they felt particularly out of place. It wasn't just that they were among many blacks and Spanish. The white people made them feel different, too. Sonny and Wayne had been institutionalized for most of their lives, and they did not know how to dress, converse, or wear facial hair like straights. In an urban environment, they were socially inept.

After checking out of the hotel, Sonny and Wayne drove down to the bus depot near Union Station. Sonny had suggested it, as he had always had luck making friends in those kinds of places. They were looking for girls of a certain type, and they had what was needed to make their acquaintance: cash and drugs.

They had taken off a meth dealer at gun- and knifepoint in Wheeling, West Virginia, on the way to Washington, after they'd purchased the Mercury. Wayne enjoyed snorting the powder, and though Sonny did not partake, being a Jack-and-Coke man himself, he wanted his little friend to be happy. So they had gone to a bar to find a way to make a purchase. There they met a young dealer who had the distinct body odor and the pale, poorly complected look they were searching for, and when they followed him to his garden apartment to party and cop, they decided to relieve him of his money and premeasured, snow-sealed goods. Sonny ransacked the apartment while Wayne held his knife to the boy's throat. The threat of murder made it easy. Sonny didn't have to show the boy his tattoo.

At the bus station, they found what they were looking for, a girl named Ashley and her friend Cheyenne. Sonny had spotted them first and pegged them as runaways, hookers, or both. Neither had baggage or a backpack, and he guessed they were doing the traditional bus depot hustle. He approached both girls and engaged Ashley in conversation, choosing her because of her generous bosoms, a feature that had always closed the deal for him. Her face was plain, but she was young, and she had a belly on her like many young women did these days, but he didn't mind. While Sonny spoke to Ashley, Wayne stood back against a wall, tapping his foot nervously and head-shaking his long center-parted hair away from his face. Sonny waved him over. As Wayne neared the girls, the one named Cheyenne could not hide her look of revulsion, but she was no prize herself, bone skinny, dotted with acne, lank hair. Her features softened when Sonny mentioned the meth. Wayne added that it was "high-octane hillbilly coke" and didn't burn "too awful goin up the nose."

Sonny and Ashley quickly negotiated a fee.

"Let's do it," said Sonny. "Trouble is, Wayne and me don't have a place to throw no shindig."

"We know a spot," said Ashley. "You studs got a car?"

"A beauty," said Sonny.

Wayne, who figured himself a proper gentleman around the ladies, uncurled his fist and made a sweeping motion with his hand, as if he were pointing to a red carpet.

"Ladies," said Wayne. "After you."

On the way to their destination, they stopped at a liquor store for a big ball of Jack Daniel's, a liter of Coke, multiple cases of Coors Light, and, because Wayne thought they'd like it, a package of wine coolers for the girls.

*   *   *

CHRIS PHONED Ali down at his office and asked for Lawrence Newhouse's cell number.

"I'm ready to talk to Lawrence," said Chris. "I just wanna find out if he or Ben discussed the money with anyone. For my own peace of mind."

"Okay," said Ali.

Chris waited. "Well?"

"I'm gettin it."

"There a problem?"

"You sound different," said Ali. "Your voice got that hard thing to it. The way it used to when you had the need to show the world how tough you were."

"I'm still broke up about Ben. That's all."

"It's more than that. You sound like you got purpose."

"Give me the number, Ali."

"Here it is."

Chris wrote it down. "Thanks."

"You gonna get up with Lawrence, maybe I oughta come with you."

"I'd rather see him alone."

"Y'all could meet right here in my office."

"I'll hit you later," said Chris. "Tell you how it went."

Chris ended the call. Sitting on the edge of his bed, he stared at his cell awhile as if he were deciding, but it was theatrical hesitation. He had already made the decision, and he punched Lawrence's number into the grid.

"Who is this?" said Lawrence Newhouse, his voice raspy and low.

"Chris Flynn."

"What you want?"

"I know who killed Ben."

After a long silence, Lawrence said, "Who was it?"

"Two men. I met them last night."

"So?"

"The money you stole was theirs. They killed Ben over it. It's safe to say that Ben didn't give you up. If he had, you'd be dead now, too."

"Did *you* give me up, White Boy?"

"No."

"Why? All a sudden, you my friend?"

"I'm gonna need your help."

"I guess we should meet, then."

Chris said, "Where?"

TWENTY-FIVE

THE NATIONAL Arboretum was situated on four hundred acres of trees, fields, and landscaped plants bordered by New York Avenue to the north and the Anacostia River to the southeast. Thousands of cars drove along its black fence every day, and the park was open to the public, yet it seemed underutilized by Washingtonians, perhaps because of its ugly gateway and the overinflated reputation for violence of the neighborhoods around it.

Chris Flynn drove his van past the information center and gift shop, located near the New York Avenue entrance, noticing the many Jeep security vehicles parked in the lot. It was in his makeup to take note of such things, and to rank private cops in a low position on his police scale. Private security meant they must not have any serious trouble back here, beyond kids smoking weed.

Couples were hiking along the shoulder and on trails, and cyclists were taking their bikes off the racks of their cars. Chris went down Ellipse Road and saw the Corinthian columns, twenty-two sandstone structures that had once been located on the east portico of the Capitol, now standing in an open meadow. He remembered his parents taking him here as a child, water running under the shadows of the columns down a graduated channel to a reflecting pool, his father grabbing his collar as Chris had attempted to jump in.

He took another road, squeezing by a groundsman hauling hay in a motorized cart. He saw employees but fewer visitors as the van climbed up into more thickly forested areas, the Conifer and then the Dogwood collections. He followed the clearly marked signs and drove up the winding Hickory Hill Road, then parked beside a Chevy Cavalier in a shaded lot near a brick structure that he reckoned housed men's and women's bathrooms. He locked the van and headed toward a trail, passing a woman who was carrying a bucket and wearing an Arboretum shirt. He had arrived at the Asian Collection, a section boasting a variety of plants imported from China, Korea, and Japan, now thriving in the hilly woods.

Chris walked down a steeply graded wood-chip-and-dirt path lined by beveled railroad ties. At the bottom of the grade was a wooden bench in a clearing, where Lawrence Newhouse stood waiting. Lawrence wore an LRG T-shirt with a matching hat, and Nikes edged in red to pick up the red off the shirt. His cap sat high and cocked atop his braids.

They nodded at each other but didn't shake hands. Lawrence sat down on the bench and Chris joined him. Several feet before them was a ledge, and there the land dropped off precipitously. They could see the tops of trees and below, on the ridge floor, the brown ribbon of the Anacostia River, sun glinting off its water.

"This here's my spot," said Lawrence.

"I don't know this place," said Chris.

"That's what makes this shit so special. I used to ride my bike here all the way from Wade Road in Southeast. It's far, but I was young, and I had mad energy. I came all that way to look at this. To sit here and have that kind of peace, it was worth it to me. You ever see where me and Ali come up?"

"Ali drove me up Stanton once."

"Then you know. I was round the corner in Parkchester. Ali was down at the bottom of the Farms, near Firth Sterling Ave. What they called the dwellings. Not houses or apartments or homes . . . *dwellings*. Anyway, Ali and his mom got out. I'm proud of that boy."

"I am, too."

"He tryin to help all them young niggas who think they got to be one way. I thought he could help my nephew Marquis."

"I know Marquis. He's a decent kid."

"He's smart. Talented, too. He just needs to get out of that fucked-up environment he's in. Before it does to him what it did to me."

"Ali was gonna hook him up with a fast-food job, wasn't he?"

"But I wanted Ali to put him someplace better. A place where he could learn a trade. That's why I reached out to him and asked him to get up with you and your pops. But he wasn't willin to do it. Maybe 'cause it was me askin. So I contacted Ben. I thought Ben might speak to you about it. I didn't know nothin about no money until Ben's tongue got loose behind that Popov and weed. I wasn't tryin to do my boy dirt."

"But you did it anyway."

Lawrence narrowed his eyes. "That's right. I stole that money. What, you thought I was gonna let it sit there like you? I'm not that kind of sucker. But I didn't know Ben was gonna get done behind it. Ben was my boy."

They sat there and listened to the birds, and the wind moving the leaves on the trees.

"Who did this?" said Lawrence.

"Trash," said Chris. "Two white guys, older than us. Seemed

to me that they've been in the system a long time. No one who's lived on the outside looks like that. There was a little guy with a big mustache and heavy ink. Looks like he kissed a train. His partner's a beast. Clover tat on one hand. Big gut, big chest. The little guy's the blade man. I'm guessing he murdered Ben. The big one carries a gun."

"Then we gonna need to tool up, too. I can do that."

Chris nodded slowly.

"You know what you're fixin to do?" said Lawrence. "I'm sayin, are you up for it?"

"Are *you?*"

"I ain't never killed no one," said Lawrence. "But when they do one of your own, you got to come back hard."

"That's right," said Chris, with no enthusiasm.

"Unit Five," said Lawrence, and he held out his fist. Chris did not raise his hand. "You too good to dap me up?"

"I'm not about that anymore, Lawrence."

"You done put it all behind you, huh. But you here, though. Right?"

Chris looked away.

"Okay," said Lawrence. "How we gonna contact them?"

"I've got a cell number on my caller ID. I'll set up a meet. I'll tell them I'm ready to give up the money."

"Let *me* have the number. I'll make the call."

"Why?"

" 'Cause *I* took the money, White Boy. Like you said, it's on me. I'm runnin this shit or I'm out."

"I'll do it alone, then."

"No, you won't. You ain't hard enough, *Christina.* You just think you are. But you don't get to the kinda hard that me and them other boys at the Ridge were at, comin from where you did. With your home and your library and your pet dog."

"I did the same time you did."

"But you never did the real time. I'm talkin about the time I did as a child. All the beatings I took, from the men in my mother's apartment to the boys out on the street. The beatings I took in my heart from the teachers who told me I wasn't shit and never was gonna *be* shit. Then in Pine Ridge, feeding me meds just to make me normal." Lawrence shook his braids away from his face and stared down at the water. "I was in Lorton before they closed it. So crowded you were living on top of men who would punch you in the face for nothin. Know what I did to get out of there? I screamed like a baby. I smeared my own shit on myself and I ate it, too. They took me outta there. Put me in Saint E's for a while. They had me in one of them jackets with straps. I musta took everything they had in their medicine cabinet, boy. I couldn't tell the difference between who I was and who I was pretendin to be. When I got released? Wasn't nobody with their arms out and a smile on their face. But when you came out the Ridge, I bet there was someone there for you." Chris did not answer, and Lawrence said, "Bet your mother made you a real nice dinner, too."

She did, thought Chris. His father had put three New York strips out on the grill, and his mother had made onion rings and a big salad to go with the steaks. She had set the table in the dining room with candles, and for dessert had baked him his favorite cake, a rich German chocolate. The dog had flopped down under the table while they ate, resting against Chris's feet. They did not speak much during dinner, but it was not uncomfortable, and afterward Chris went up to his room and slept on clean sheets that smelled of spring.

"We about to do a murder, son," said Lawrence. "Who you want in charge of this shit? You or me?"

Chris reached into his pocket, retrieved his cell, and flipped it open. He scrolled through his contacts and found the number he had taken from caller ID and saved. He handed the phone to Lawrence, who transferred it into his own cell.

"Where they gonna put Ben?" said Lawrence.

"As soon as the police release his body, we're having his ashes buried at Rock Creek."

"That was Ben's thing," said Lawrence. "Me, I want to be right here."

"They don't bury people here, Lawrence. It's a park."

"I ain't say nothing about being buried. Why you always got to act so superior?"

"I wasn't—"

"Let's just go."

They walked up the path together. They crossed the road to the parking area, near the rest room structure. Chris's van was beside Lawrence's Cavalier.

Lawrence nodded to its rear doors. "Ben's tool belt in there?"

"Yeah."

"Let me see it."

Chris unlocked the van, opened its rear, and handed Lawrence the belt. From one of its pouches Lawrence took Ben's double-sided Crain razor knife and felt its weight and balance in his hand. The knife had a contoured wood handle and a heavy gauge three-inch blade that hooked at the end.

"Can I have it?" said Lawrence.

"Why?"

"Poet's justice," said Lawrence.

Chris nodded. "Hit me up."

"I plan to arrange this quick," said Lawrence. "We don't need to think on it too much."

"Right."

"Be ready, White Boy."

Lawrence back-pocketed the carpet knife and walked to his car. Chris's blood pounded in his ears as he watched him drive away.

SONNY AND Wayne had been partying all day in a white asbestos-shingled rambler on a generous piece of land bordering a community center in a place called Riverdale Park. Though the town was only a couple of miles off the District line in Maryland, there were trees and large lots as well as baseball and football fields visible from the backyard, and it felt familiar to both of them. They were comfortable here and relaxed. There were many Spanish in the neighborhood, and some blacks, but that didn't ruin it for them. It was as good a place as they'd been in since they had come to D.C.

The girls, Ashley and Cheyenne, had directed them out here via Kenilworth Boulevard, more miles of shit-laid road to their eyes, so it had been a nice surprise when they pulled into this neighborhood of quiet and green. Ashley said that she and Cheyenne were friendly with the boy, Chuck, who was renting the house. It was a group home for three undergraduates who attended the University of Maryland, and Chuck was the only one who'd stayed for the summer while his roommates had gone back to their hometowns. Chuck came from upstate New York money, had illegal habits, worked in a comic-book store, and was weak but sweet. He'd given them permission to crash there any time and told them where the key would be, under a flowerpot on the front stoop. They three-wayed him when he wanted it, and unlike most drug users, he shared, so it was a good arrangement. Chuck would be cool with them bringing their two new friends over for some fun. He wouldn't mind.

Sonny was outside the house, drinking a Jack and Coke from a plastic cup. Shadows had gathered and faded as night darkened the yard. Crickets rubbed their legs together, and the sound soothed him.

Sonny was high, maybe drunk, but in control. He had taken Ashley into one of the bedrooms as soon as they got there, asked her to strip for him, and told her to walk around. Predictably, she had a rose tattoo at the small of her back and one that matched just above her pubic line. She had cat eyes, freckles on her nose, and melon tits. It took a while, but he became aroused and he called her over to the bed, where he pushed the twins together, made them Siamese, and gave her a friction hump. It never took him long, and when he was done he was done for the day. He sat with her for a while as she snorted meth and he drank his cocktails, and he became bored, listening to her talk about bullshit, faster and faster, and listening to Wayne give it to Cheyenne in the adjoining room, the skinny girl making a whole mess of noise, Wayne showing off to his old cell mate, sending plaster chips off the wall, bottom-knocking that gal fierce, like he was hitting a pound of raw hamburger.

After, they all joined up back in the living room and commenced to partying group-style. The girls got down to panties and brassieres, which they no doubt thought was sexy, but to Sonny's mind just exposed Ashley's fat and Cheyenne's birdlike build and acned back. Wayne had his shirt off, showing off his wiry frame, not an ounce of body fat on that boy at all. They were all doing the crystal except for Sonny, with Wayne pounding Silver Bullets behind the speckled white. Wayne had no bottom for beer when he did meth. Ashley and Cheyenne found a colored station on the radio they liked, and both of them were rapping together to what passed for a song these days, and they got up and did some kind of jungle-jump to it as Wayne clapped out of time and shouted them on. Eventually Wayne and Cheyenne went back into the bedroom, and Ashley drifted off, lit some candles, and drew herself a bath. Sonny took a nap.

When he woke up, the house was quiet. He fixed a drink and went outside and saw that the Mercury was gone. He had a seat on the stoop and as night came he thought of his situation and what would come next.

He tried to envision his future, but nothing came to mind.

It occurred to him that he was where he wanted to be. A lifetime of incarceration, starting at the boys' detention center in Sabillasville, continuing on through several adult facilities, leading to the last, the federal joint in Lewisburg. All that schooling, and what he learned was: Live in the now. Take what you want, have no dreams, ride free. Like it said in the song by that wild country boy he loved: *There are those that break and bend / I'm the other kind.*

His cell phone rang. Sonny flipped it open and answered the call. When he was done talking, he put the cell back in his pocket and nodded tightly.

The Mercury pulled up in front of the house. Wayne got out, carrying a bunch of supermarket daisies, and crept across the yard. He stood in front of Sonny and head-shook his center-parted hair.

"You got that look," said Wayne. "Somethin's happenin."

"Outta the blue, I just got a call from some coon. Said he had my money and was lookin to give it back."

"I don't follow."

"Only Chris Carpet has my number. From the caller ID. So he's got a partner."

"You think it's a trap? Maybe he called the law."

"He didn't even call out for the patrol car when it passed by his yard last night, and that was life and death. He ain't that type."

Wayne grinned and his face folded in upon itself. "So it's on."

"I reckon. Whoever I spoke to is gonna phone me tomorrow and tell me when and where."

"Huh," said Wayne.

"What are the flowers for?"

"They're for my girl."

"Your girl? We paid that little heifer to fuck you, son."

"She's a nice young lady."

"She stinks."

"Watch what you say."

"She stinks like a menstruatin polecat."

"Your mother does," said Wayne.

Sonny snorted as Wayne slipped into the house.

Not much later, an old Honda coupe stopped on the street and a white boy got out of it. He walked gingerly toward Sonny. He was overweight and had long hair and a black T-shirt stretched tight over an hourglass figure. He stopped in front of the stoop where Sonny still sat.

"Who are you?" said the boy.

"Friend of Ashley's. You?"

"Chuck. I *live* here."

"So?"

The boy named Chuck tried to hold Sonny's gaze, but he could not. His shoulders slumped and he stepped carefully around the big man, opened the door to his place, and walked inside.

Sonny smiled.

TWENTY-SIX

CHRIS FLYNN sat shirtless on the edge of his bed and used one hand to pop the joints of the other. He had turned off his cell and had no landline, but now there was an incessant knocking on his apartment door. His van was on the street, so he couldn't pretend that he was not at home. He walked to the door and opened it. Katherine stood in the hall. She was lovely and agitated. Angry even, for her.

"You don't want to see me?"

"I do," said Chris. "Come in."

He stepped aside to let her pass. She came into the apartment and he followed her to the living room.

"You want a beer, somethin?"

"No, I don't want anything."

Chris pointed to a chair. "Sit down."

She sat, and Chris took a seat beside her.

"What's going on with you?" said Katherine.

"I need to be alone, is all."

"Your eyes are dead."

"It's because of Ben. I'm all fucked up behind it."

"Something's happening with you and it goes beyond Ben's

death. I need to know what it is. You've never shut me out like this before."

Chris stared down at the hardwood floor. Katherine had him. They were going to be together forever, and she was the one he could talk to. She was a piece of him and she wouldn't do him wrong. He looked her in the eyes.

"It *is* about Ben," said Chris. "I know who killed him."

"*How* do you know?" said Katherine carefully.

"It was two men. They came to visit me, right here in my backyard. They killed Ben over the money that we left in that house. It was theirs. They must have tried to get Ben to talk about who took it."

"Do you know who took it?"

"A guy named Lawrence. We were locked up with him at Pine Ridge. Ben got drunk and told Lawrence about the money, and Lawrence went back and stole it. The two men strong-armed the lady who owns the house. That led them to Ben, and me."

"And this Lawrence. He still has the money."

"Yes."

"If you know who these men are, why haven't you called the police?"

Chris looked away.

"*Chris.*"

"I'm not gonna do that," said Chris, his voice hoarse. "Me and Lawrence, we're gonna take care of this ourselves."

Katherine got up abruptly and went to the kitchen. She stood over the sink and cupped her hand and ran water into it, drank while the other hand held her strawberry blonde hair back behind her head. Chris watched her splash her face with water. She reentered the room, walking with purpose. Her cheeks were flushed and brightly freckled, and her green eyes were wildly flared. She sat beside him and grasped his hand.

"Say what you're going to do, Chris. Not that jailhouse bullshit talk, either. When you say you're going to take care of it, what are you talking about? Murder?"

"It's the only way."

"What about an arrest and conviction? The right way. The way that doesn't make you a killer and a candidate for prison."

"I can't. Ben didn't give me or Lawrence up. Ben stood tall—"

"*Stop* it." Katherine squeezed his hand tightly. "Listen to what you're saying. This isn't you, Chris."

"There's two of me," said Chris. "There's the person you think you know, and the one who's still inside me. The boy who did dirt and got schooled in that jail. The one you never met."

"I'm in love with the one I met. I could never love someone who deliberately took a life, not when there was a more reasonable option. I couldn't be with him or have his child. Do you understand that?"

"Yes. But I got to do this." He held her hand tightly. "Stay with me tonight."

Katherine pulled her hand back and stood out of the chair. She looked down at him and her lip quivered, but she held on and turned and stepped away. She headed for the door.

"Don't tell my father," said Chris.

Katherine left the apartment, shutting the door behind her without another word.

SHE DROVE straight to the Flynn home on Livingston Street. She cried on the way there but put herself back together before she arrived. After Flynn opened the door, Django bumped against her excitedly and followed her steps closely as she came into the house. Flynn was talking to her, but she was not responding, and he could only go with her, out the back door, onto the deck overlooking the yard. Flynn shut the door, leaving Django on the other side of the glass.

"What is it, honey?" said Flynn, joining Katherine at the rail. "Did you and Chris have a fight?"

She told him of their conversation in the apartment. By now Amanda had come downstairs, but as she moved toward the back door, Flynn raised his palm and she saw the look on his face and stayed inside.

"I knew he was mixed up in something," said Flynn, when Katherine was done.

"But he wasn't," said Katherine. "Someone else stole that money. A guy named Lawrence. Not Chris, and not Ben. The trouble came to them after. They were trying to do right and walk away from it. It came to *them*. Chris hasn't done anything wrong. Not yet."

Flynn pushed a shock of black hair off his forehead. He recalled the day at Mindy Kramer's house, when he'd accused Chris and Ben of botching the job. Whoever had taken the money, that Lawrence fellow, had messed up the good work they'd done. It wasn't them being lazy or sloppy. Chris had been telling the truth that day. As he tended to do, Flynn had assumed the worst about his son.

"Well, it's simple," said Flynn. "I've got to stop him. What he's saying he's gonna do, that's not him. It never was him. He was a stupid, selfish teenager, and he made mistakes. But he couldn't kill anyone. He won't."

"You should call the police, Mr. Flynn."

"I can't do that. Not until I speak to him. I don't know how

far he's gone down the road. If anyone's going to call the police, it has to be him. I'll speak to him and talk him down. I can
do that."

"If you think that's the way."

"I know it is. Yes."

Flynn hugged Katherine. He was perspiring, and she could
smell the alcohol on his breath and in his sweat.

"He won't answer your phone call," said Katherine.

"I'm going to go over there," said Flynn, stepping back.
"Stay here with Amanda for now."

"Okay."

"Thanks for coming here, Kate."

"It's Katherine," she said gently.

"Katherine. Right."

They walked into the house where Amanda was waiting.

"Chris is all right," said Flynn. "I just need to speak with
him. Katherine will explain."

Amanda started to say something, but Flynn embraced her
clumsily and kissed her on the mouth.

"Don't worry."

"Call me," said Amanda.

He nodded, grabbed his keys from a bowl on the kitchen
counter, and headed out the door.

ROMARIO KNIGHT lived in a middle-class home in Hillcrest Heights,
across Southern Avenue, which ran between the District and
Prince George's County, Maryland. Knight's street was quiet
and he kept to himself. He was a bachelor who occasionally
brought women home and had friends over on Redskins Sun-
days. He looked like any man in his thirties who went to work
and made a modest living. By day, Knight wore a uniform as a

meter man for the gas company. He was also a gun dealer who serviced the Southeast trade. Knight's clients came to his place of residence after being screened by third parties.

Lawrence Newhouse stood with Knight in the downstairs rec room of the Hillcrest home. A huge television set, couches and chairs, and a wet bar filled the room, and Redskins memorabilia covered the walls. Knight wore a Sean Taylor jersey and he filled it out. He was a huge man who, even when in shape, had always been fat. In the years he played high school ball in PG, he was known, alternately and randomly, as Papa Doc and Baby Doc. He had the curious distinction of carrying the nicknames of both the father and the son.

Lawrence had put the word out with a boy at Parkchester he reckoned would have such connections, and soon Lawrence got a call on his cell and then was met by another young man, who checked him out, issued some barely veiled threats, and gave him instructions. In the course of a few hours, Lawrence was here, purchasing guns.

A large and a small revolver, a couple of semiautomatics, and boxes of ammunition were laid out on a card table. The weapons still had serial numbers and if confiscated would be traced back to legitimate gun stores in Virginia, where they had been originally purchased by straw buyers.

Lawrence stood beside Knight, looking down at the weapons, experiencing that curious sensation of excitement and dread some men feel in the presence of guns.

Lawrence had shot a boy many years ago. Had he killed the young man, Lawrence's punishment would have been more severe, but the wound was not fatal. Lawrence could barely remember why he had done the thing. Some slight, real or imagined, had sent him after the boy with a Taurus .38, a true

Saturday night special, because Lawrence knew he couldn't settle it with his hands.

"What's that?" said Lawrence, pointing to a small auto pistol with a chrome finish and a laminated wood stock.

"Davis thirty-two," said Knight.

"Does it work?"

"It ain't gonna blow up in your face, *I don't think*. I mean, shit, you said you wanted the cheapest thing I had."

"It's for my partner. I'm askin, will it stop a man?"

"I'm not even about to answer that. The Davis is a gun and it shoots bullets. That's all I can say."

"Okay. I'll take that."

"You said you wanted a revolver for yourself."

"Autos jam."

"They been known to."

"What you got?"

"I brought out a couple pieces you might like. S and W's, both. There goes a thirty-eight, right there." Knight pointed to a short-barreled Chief. "Smith and Wesson make a nice product. You can't go wrong with that."

Knight's voice was unenthusiastic. Lawrence knew he was about to be stepped up to the larger, more masculine-looking weapon set beside it. He knew, but he couldn't help asking the next question.

"What about that big boy right there?" said Lawrence.

"Go ahead and pick it up," said Knight.

Lawrence lifted the gun off the table. He hefted it and turned it in the light. It had a stainless finish, a six-inch barrel, and rubber, finger-molded grips. It felt right in his hand.

"Three fifty-seven combat magnum," said Knight. "That's a pup right there. You squeeze the trigger on that boy, it's like shootin a full can of beer at a thousand miles an hour. Make a nice hole goin in and a mess goin out. It's gonna kick, too. I don't know, you might want somethin more manageable for your body type. . . ."

"I'll take it," said Lawrence.

"You gonna need some bullets, right?"

"Not a whole box."

"I only sell bricks."

"What about a shoulder rig for this one? I can't be putting this monster down in my dip."

"I can sell you that, too."

"How about throwin it in?"

Knight laughed through his teeth and shook his head. They negotiated a price, and Lawrence paid him from a roll he had in his pocket, then stashed everything into a daypack he had brought with him.

Walking to the basement steps, Lawrence said, "Where you get all this Redskins shit, man?"

"Shows. The Internet."

"You go to the games?"

"Not anymore," said Knight. "I hate that stadium."

"We gonna do it this year?"

"Not this year. But we will." Knight put his hand on Lawrence's shoulder at the front door. "You don't know me, man. We ain't never met."

"I heard that," said Lawrence.

He walked to his Cavalier, parked on the street.

AFTER REPEATED knocks on Chris's door with no response, Flynn was let into the apartment by Andy Ladas, who had an extra key. There was nothing there, no note, no notepads to rub that would reveal the secret message, no telltale signs left behind to let Flynn know where Chris had gone. It occurred to Flynn that he knew little about Chris's life as an adult. He was not familiar with his hangouts, his haunts, or the locations of the homes or apartments of his closest friends.

He did have Ali's number logged into the address book of his cell. He phoned Ali, got him, and filled him in on the latest events. Ali said that he would try to contact Lawrence; he had his number and knew where he lived. While Flynn waited in the quiet of Chris's apartment, he helped himself to a beer, drank it quickly, and had another. By the time he was headed for a third, Ali phoned him back.

"Lawrence wasn't answering his cell," said Ali. "I went over to where he stays and talked to his sister. He's been out the apartment all night. She hasn't seen or heard from him."

"Can you get away for a while?" said Flynn. "I want to look for him. Two sets of eyes and all that."

"I can meet you," said Ali. He told Flynn where, a halfway point on Riggs Road, near South Dakota Avenue.

"Twenty minutes," said Flynn.

They drove the streets for hours, but they didn't find Chris.

HE HAD checked into a motel high on Georgia Avenue, in south Silver Spring, just over the line into Maryland. Though it was near the niceties of the new downtown, it had a Plexiglas reception area and the requisite male hooker, dressed and made up as a female, lounging in the lobby. It was not a plastic-sheet flophouse, but it was close.

What it did have was a covered garage. Chris had tucked the van far back inside, well out of view from the street, before he checked in.

He had a duffel bag with some clothes in it, and his shaving kit. He had not bought any alcohol or weed to smoke. He wanted his mind sharp and clear. His thoughts were grim and clouded, and he needed to see through them to some kind of light.

He had turned on his cell, and its ring tone sounded frequently. The calls were from his father, Ali, his mother, and Katherine. He let them go to message. Eventually the calls stopped.

He lay on the double bed of the stark room, watching television but not watching it, thinking. He had used the remote to get ESPN, and now there were highlights of a bicycle race, many men wearing tight shorts and colorful jerseys, navigating a twisting downhill road, and some sort of accident where several bicycles went down. He did not follow the sport, could not identify this particular race, and was uninterested. He had never been a fan of biking. As he reached his teens, he had thought it was nerdy and lame.

His father used to strap him into a seat on the back of his bike and ride him all the way down to the Potomac on the paved trails of Rock Creek Park. He had been very young and his memory was sketchy, and he had not thought of it at all in a long while. What he remembered, mostly, were flashes and sensations. Sun streaming down through the trees. The wind on his face and in his hair. The feel of his own smile. On those rides, when he got up a good amount of speed, his father would sometimes reach behind him and squeeze Chris's hand, reassure him, tell him that everything was going to be all right.

I am not someone who could kill a man. There is nothing in my past and nothing inside me that would allow me to do that. Ben couldn't, and neither can I.

Ben had tried to help Lawrence. Ben had seen something in him that others couldn't see. If Ben were alive, he'd stop Lawrence from what he had planned. Chris knew this. It was on him now to act for Ben.

He relaxed and fell asleep.

His ring tone woke him up. He looked at the caller ID on his cell and saw that it was Lawrence.

"Yeah," said Chris.

"It's me," said Lawrence, his voice gravelly. "We about to do this, son."

"All right."

"I set it up. Got us some iron, too." Lawrence listened to silence and said, "You still with me?"

"Where we supposed to meet 'em?"

"I'll tell you face-to-face. You and me need to hook up and lay it out."

Lawrence gave him the time and the spot. Chris said he'd meet him there and ended the call.

TWENTY-SEVEN

LAWRENCE NEWHOUSE stood in the heat of the bedroom he shared with Dorita's younger kids and slipped a lightweight burnt-orange North Face jacket over his white T. The gym bag, filled with money, and his daypack, containing the guns and Ben's carpet knife, sat on the bed.

He had been up, unable to sleep, for most of the night. He had stayed on his back, on the bed, his forearm draped over his eyes, thinking of what he was about to do. Pondering his strategy, and Chris.

Lawrence lifted the daypack and slipped one strap over his shoulder.

His smart little nephew, Terrence, came into the room. He grabbed his sneaks off the floor and looked up at his old uncle, overdressed for this summer day.

"Where you goin, Uncle L?"

"I got business."

"You a businessman?"

"You know I am."

"I'm gonna be a scientist," said Terrence, his face hopeful

288

and bright. "Look at the solar system through one of them telescopes and stuff."

"You can do it, Terrence. Just keep your head in those books."

Lawrence reached out and touched Terrence's warm scalp. The boy *could* do it. He had the brains. But he needed to get out of this place and away from his mother, who was too busy putting on weight and talking on her cell to get the boy in a position where he could succeed. Lawrence had heard of those charter schools the kids slept at, away from their homes. That was the type of hookup Terrence needed. But Lawrence didn't know how to make that kind of thing happen. It got him confused and angry to think on it, so he reached for the gym bag and gripped its stiff handles in his hand.

"I'll check you later, little man."

Lawrence walked from the room. He passed through the big area off the kitchen, where Dorita was sprawled out on the couch. Her little girl, Loquatia, was seated on the carpet in front of the TV, her hand in a bag of Cheetos.

"Where you headed?" said Dorita.

"Out," said Lawrence.

"Bring me back a soda."

"That's one thing you don't need."

"I ain't ask for your opinion."

"Okay, corn chip."

Lawrence kept moving out the door. He cared about his sister, he supposed, but damn, Dorita wasn't much more than two hundred fifty pounds of waste. He had considered giving her some of the money, but only for a minute. She'd blow it on stupid shit that would come to no good for the kids. Instead, Lawrence was gonna do something with it. One thing right.

Out on the street, he went to his Cavalier. Marquis Gilman,

his teenage nephew, called out to him. Marquis was standing around talking to some boys he shouldn't have been talking to. Lawrence walked to his car, popped the rear lid, and dropped the gym bag and the daypack into the trunk. Marquis was now beside him, looking at the trunk's contents. Lawrence closed the lid.

"You leavin out?" said Marquis, his gangly arms hanging loosely at his side.

"Nah, man. Goin for a ride."

"Looks like you takin off for real."

"I'm straight hood, son. Where would I go?" Lawrence put his hand on his nephew's shoulder. "Look, Marquis . . ."

"What?"

"I'm gonna go talk to Mr. Carter one more time. See if he can't hook you up with some worthwhile employment. But whatever happens, I want you to listen to that man and do what he says. He's lookin out for you. Ali is cool people." Lawrence made a sweeping motion with his hand. "You don't belong on this street. Time for you to make your move or you ain't never gonna get out."

"*You* stayed."

"Does it look like it was good to me?"

Marquis did not answer. Lawrence clasped one of Marquis's hands and put his free arm around Marquis and patted his back.

"See you up the road," said Lawrence. "Hear?"

Lawrence got into his car without looking back and sped away. A couple of blocks from the apartment, he stopped and threw his cell phone down a storm drain. He was done with it and didn't want to be called or traced. He was shedding his skin. He then drove over the Frederick Douglass Memorial Bridge and tossed something over its rail. On the other side of the Anacostia, he turned around, recrossed the river, and rolled back into his neighborhood.

He drove around for a while, till he spotted what he was looking for. Down around Firth Sterling Ave and Sumner Road he saw a boy, no older than ten or eleven, on a men's road bike that looked to be in perfect shape and was way too big for him. Lawrence pulled over and leaned out the open window.

"Young!" shouted Lawrence. "Yeah, you. Don't worry, you not in trouble. I just want to talk to you."

"What you want?" said the boy, who was pedaling the bike slowly in a tight circle.

"You about to make some money."

"What kinda money?"

"Kind you spend," said Lawrence. He killed the engine and stepped out of the car.

FLYNN AND Hector carried a roll of Berber out of the warehouse of Top Carpet and Floor Install in Beltsville and loaded it into Hector's van. Hector was not his usual upbeat self. He had been upset by the killing of Ben and his general air of optimism had been tested. But he was determined to work his way through it. He and the others in Isaac's crew, in the absence of Ben and Chris, had doubled their load and come through for the company.

Flynn's chest ached as he pushed the roll into the back of the van. He stood straight and waited for the pain to pass.

"You okay, boss?" said Hector.

"Fine," said Flynn. "This is going to that Tenleytown job."

"Tito gonna meet me there," said Hector, speaking of a new guy from the Dominican.

"Okay. Then you need to come back and pick up that roll for the lady in Tysons."

"We gonna take care of it. We make it nice."

"Thank you," said Flynn, looking Hector straight in the eye. "I appreciate it. I do."

As Hector drove off, Flynn entered the warehouse, passing the stage where a man spun a large piece of carpet levitated by air, and walked into the office area. Susie, the chubby girl with the fried-perm hairdo, and Katherine were seated behind their desks. Katherine had dark semicircles beneath her eyes. It was obvious she hadn't slept.

Flynn looked at Katherine and made a head motion toward the door.

"I'll just be a minute, Suze," said Katherine, and she got up out of her chair and followed Flynn outside.

They went by a parking area, crossed a narrow road, and stood in the shade of a lone oak.

"You hear from Chris?" said Flynn.

"No."

"We haven't, either. I'm in touch with Ali, and of course Amanda is sitting by the phone at home." Flynn touched Katherine's arm. "I don't want you to worry."

"It's like it was when Ben was missing," said Katherine. "It feels the same way."

"It's not gonna be like that," said Flynn. "Nothing's going to happen to my son and he's not going to kill anyone. Chris is tough and he's got character. This is going to be over with today and it's going to end right. Between all of us, we're going to find him. Okay?"

"I want to believe you," said Katherine.

"I promise you," said Flynn. Hoping that the sick feeling inside him, the helplessness, was not showing on his face.

*   *   *

CHRIS SAW the Cavalier, parked in the lot where Lawrence had said it would be. Chris put the van in a space alongside the Chevy. Chris had followed Lawrence's directions to a community park in Colman Manor, but he was in an unfamiliar place and felt lucky to have found the vehicle. Atop the Cavalier were a couple of loose ropes that went inside the barely open windows. Lawrence had lashed something to the roof of the car.

Chris only knew that he was in Prince George's County, somewhere near the District, having come through a tucked-in community that looked like a country town.

He locked the van, and, per Lawrence's instructions, found a nearby bike path sided by trees. He walked it for what seemed like a long while. Partway in, he realized he had left his cell back in the Ford, but he had come too far to turn back. Eventually he emerged from the woods and found himself on a wide road along a body of water. There were houses and streets on his left. He idly wondered why Lawrence had not told him to park on those residential blocks, which were much closer to the meeting spot. Across the water he could see a large dock and recreation area, and the famous tan-and-brown Peace Cross, a place his father had spoken of, once home to country, rock, and biker nightlife. Now Chris had a better idea of his location. He was somewhere near Bladensburg Road and the old Route 1.

The bike path continued, veering off the road and down a dip, going under a bridge. There he saw Lawrence in the shadows. A bicycle leaned up against a three-pole rail that separated the path and a drop-off to the water. An old white man, not much larger than a boy, was standing there, too. On the ground nearby were several blankets and a cooler.

Chris walked under the bridge and nodded at Lawrence. The little white man, unshaven, drunk, wearing a sleeveless T-shirt, raised his fists over his head and flexed his muscles.

"I'm fifty-five," said the little man, smiling, showing brown nubs that had once been teeth. "And I'll do fifty-five push-ups."

"Leave outta here, old-timer," said Lawrence, not unkindly.

"This is my house," said the little man.

Lawrence produced a roll of cash from his pocket and peeled off a twenty. "Go on, man. Get yourself some medicine. When you come back, we'll be gone."

The little man happily took the money and walked down the path in the direction of Bladensburg Road.

"Where are we?" said Chris.

"That's the Anacostia right there," said Lawrence, nodding at the river. "You know it flowed this far into Maryland?"

"I didn't."

"I'm tellin you, you can't know this city till you get on a bicycle."

"Where'd you get that one?"

"Bought it off some kid. It was stole, I reckon, so he made out all right."

Chris shifted his feet. "Why are we meeting here, Lawrence?"

"It's out the way."

"Tell me about it. I could have parked right in that neighborhood over there, instead of in that park."

"And now you gonna have to hike out a distance to get back to your car. Gives me time to put some space between us, what with me and my two wheels."

"Why would you want to do that?"

" 'Cause you ain't comin with me, man."

Chris squinted. "I thought you bought me a gun."

"I threw that cheap piece off the Douglass. It would have blown up in your face, anyhow. That is, if you had the steel to use it. I just don't think you do."

"You're right," said Chris. "I wouldn't have used it. I'm not about to kill anyone."

"So why are you here?"

"To try and stop you."

"Try, then."

Chris reached out to put a brotherly hand on Lawrence's shoulder. Lawrence slapped Chris's hand away and smiled.

"Don't be touchin on me," said Lawrence.

"There's got to be another way to solve this."

"Not for me."

"Tell me where you're meeting them. We'll have them arrested."

"You know I ain't gonna do that."

"We can talk about it, at least."

"You wanna talk now?" said Lawrence. "What about all that time in the Ridge when you refused to talk to me? When you showed me your back. Callin me Bughouse and shit, when I had a real last name. You think I don't know what y'all thought of me? All 'a y'all, except Ben. That boy had good in him, man. And I killed him." Lawrence poked a finger roughly into his own chest. "*I* did. This here got nothing to do with you. So go home, White Boy. Leave me to my thing."

"Listen," said Chris, taking a step forward.

Lawrence threw a right. It caught Chris square on the jaw, and he lost his balance. He went down on his side to the paved path. He rolled over and got up onto his knees. He had bitten his tongue and he spit out saliva and blood. He stood slowly and unsteadily. The landscape was tilted, and he tried to shake his head and make it straight but could not.

"That's right," said Lawrence. "Surprised you, didn't I?"

"Wait," said Chris.

"I'm about to clean you proper now."

Lawrence planted his back foot. Chris tucked his elbows in and tried to cover up, but he was too slow. Lawrence jabbed through the protection with his left and his fist found Chris's nose. The ring on his finger cut Chris, stung him, and blurred his vision. Chris dropped one arm and Lawrence grunted behind a right that had everything in it and Chris took the punch in the temple and was spun and knocked off his feet. He seemed to fall for a long time. His head hit the iron rail, and for a moment there was faint sensation and a downward float. He did not feel it when he hit the ground.

Lawrence stood over him. Blood flowed freely from Chris's nose. He wasn't moving. Lawrence crouched down and felt for a pulse. He did not find it and he began to panic and touched the artery standing out on Chris's neck. Chris was unconscious, but he was alive. Lawrence folded one of the little man's blankets into a small square and placed it behind Chris's head. He had seen this done on television shows. He hoped that this was right, but he couldn't stay.

Elated and horrified, he swung onto the saddle of the bike and pedaled furiously down the path in the direction of his car.

TWENTY-EIGHT

ALI CARTER stood inside the storefront window of his office on Alabama Avenue, watching William Richards mixing with the young men and women on the street. He had just met with William, and it had not gone well. He'd tried to convince him to return to his job with Party Land, which William had recently walked away from once again, refusing to wear the shirt with the balloon-and-clown logo. Ali was pretty certain that William was back to dirt and running with his boys. He had heard that William was beefing with someone and that this problem was about to boil over. William was too proud and stupid to walk away from it. His future, most likely, was grim. Anyway, Ali had tried.

Ali could not help everyone who came through his doors. Being completely honest with himself, he would admit that he could not help most of them or lead the majority of them to productive futures. If he were to think in terms of grandiose objectives, he would have to give up. It was impossible to pull large groups of young men through tiny keyholes. Ali had modest goals because that was how he got through his day.

Lawrence Newhouse's hooptie, the old Cavalier, pulled up in front of the office, a bike tied to its roof.

Ali watched as Lawrence, in a white T-shirt under a light-weight, rust-colored jacket, got out of the car. Lawrence opened the trunk and withdrew a gym bag. He walked toward the storefront, ignoring the snickers from the young ones on the sidewalk around him.

"Come on," said Ali, though no one else was in the room. "Come inside."

Lawrence entered the office. A chime sounded from a bell mounted over the door.

"Ding," said Lawrence, with a smile. He shook his braids away from his face. "Heard you been lookin for me."

"Come sit," said Ali.

They crossed the spartan room. Ali sat behind his desk, and Lawrence took a chair before it.

"I'm here," said Lawrence.

"Where's Chris at?"

"I had to drop him. That's right. Me."

"What do you mean, *drop him?*"

"I didn't shoot him or nothin like that. I put him down with my hands. He was tryin to stop me from doing this thing I got to do. Gettin all high-horse on my ass."

"Is he all right?"

"He's breathin. He fell down and hit his head. He ain't as rough and tough as he thinks he is. But he's gonna be okay."

"Where is he?" said Ali.

"On a bike trail, under a bridge. Near the Peace Cross, out by Colman Manor."

"Where exactly?"

Lawrence described the short way in and Ali wrote it down. Ali picked his cell up off the desk, and Lawrence listened as Ali spoke to Chris's father with urgency and gave the father directions to his son. As Ali talked, Lawrence took a black Sharpie from a leather cup filled with writing utensils and slipped one into the pocket of his North Face. Ali ended the call and placed the cell phone back atop the desk.

Ali's eyes went to the floor, where the gym bag sat. "What's in that sack?"

"My valuables. You don't think I'd leave them in my car, do you? In this neighborhood?"

"It's not so bad. Me and my mother live across the street."

"I know it. Gotta hand it to you, 'cause you got out."

"You could, too."

"It's too late for me."

"It's not," said Ali. "You don't have to do this."

"But I'm about to."

"I could call the police."

"And have me arrested for what? Thinkin on a murder?"

"I bet if they searched your car, they'd find a gun. That's an automatic fall for you."

"You wouldn't do that."

"Killing those men is not what Ben would've wanted."

"Don't start with me," said Lawrence. "You don't even want to put your hand near the flames I got inside me today. Chris did, and he stretched out."

The chair creaked beneath Ali's shifting weight. "Why'd you come here, Lawrence?"

"To appeal to your sense of right, I guess. To ask you one more time to get my nephew someplace good."

"I'm tryin to. But it takes baby steps to get where Marquis needs to be. Wasn't no leap from where I was to that house across the street, or this job I got right here. You can't just snap your fingers and make it happen."

"Take care of him the best you can. That's all I'm askin."

Ali nodded slowly. "I will."

Lawrence picked up the gym bag and stood from his chair. "Where the bathroom in this piece?"

"In the back."

Lawrence walked past the desk. Ali listened as the toilet flushed and the sink water ran. A couple of minutes later, Lawrence emerged from the bathroom without the bag and stood across from where Ali was seated.

"Place is dirty. You could use some new furniture, shit like that. Maybe a TV set that ain't broke, so the boys could chill in here."

"You forgot your bag."

"No, I didn't."

"What's going on, Lawrence?"

"Take care of your little niggas, hear?"

"I'm doin my best."

Lawrence held out his fist and reached across the desk. "Unit Five."

"Unit Five," said Ali softly. He dapped Lawrence up.

Lawrence grinned. "See you later . . . *Holly*."

Ali smiled a little against a sinking feeling as he watched him step to the door. The small bell chimed as the door pushed out and Lawrence hit the sidewalk.

Ali got out of his chair and walked into the bathroom. There on the closed toilet lid sat the open gym bag, filled with cash. And on the mirror, written in black:

Your boy, Lawrence

Ali jogged out of the bathroom, went to the front window of the storefront, and looked out onto the street.

Lawrence Newhouse was gone.

*　　*　　*

SONNY WADE walked into a bedroom of the white rambler in Riverdale. Wayne Minors sat on the edge of the bed, shirtless and taut. He had been napping, and Sonny's heavy fist on the closed door, ten minutes earlier, had woken him up. Beside Wayne, the girl named Cheyenne slept nude atop the sheets. Raspberries of acne dotted her bony back.

"You been dozing?" said Sonny.

"I get tired after," said Wayne.

"I told you not to take no postcoital naps."

"Huh?"

"We got work and I want your head straight. Here." Sonny reached into his windbreaker and drew a Taurus .9 from where he had slipped it against his belly. "You're gonna need that."

"I got my knife."

"That's only good for close work. 'Less you plan to throw it."

"I could."

"This ain't no carnival. Take the gun."

Wayne took it and placed it beside him on the bed. He reached over to the nightstand and picked up the hardwood-handled knife with the spine-cut steel blade. He fitted it in its sheath, hiked up one leg of his Wrangler jeans, and strapped the sheath to his calf. He put on his black ring-strap Dingo boots, stood, and drew a black T-shirt over his head. He folded up the sleeves of the T-shirt one time to show off his arms and touched his wallet, chained to a belt loop, to make sure that it was secure.

"Say good-bye to your little slut," said Sonny.

"Don't call her that."

"Do it and let's get gone."

Wayne leaned over the bed and kissed Cheyenne's shoulder. His bushy mustache flattened out against her bone. He stood straight and holstered the Taurus in his waistband, under his T.

They walked into the living room. Ashley and Chuck were seated on the couch. There was a bong on the table before them, a ziplock bag of marijuana that was mostly seeds and stems, empty wine cooler bottles, crushed cans of beer. The television was on. They were watching *MTV Cribs*.

"You leavin?" said Ashley.

"It's time," said Sonny, his idea of a warm good-bye. He looked at Chuck, rolls of fat spilling about his waist, staring at the TV, too frightened to meet Sonny's eyes. "You never met us. Is that clear, fella?"

"Yes," said Chuck.

Sonny stood over Chuck and leaned forward. "You speak on either of us, my little buddy will come back here and carve you up."

Chuck's lip trembled.

" 'Preciate the hospitality," said Sonny.

Sonny and Wayne walked from the house. They got into the Mercury and drove over to the community center and park, where brown people were playing baseball on one of the diamonds. Sonny and Wayne got out of the black sedan and broke their cell phones on the hard road and threw the pieces into the woods. Sonny wanted no record of the incoming or outgoing calls they had made while they were in town, nor did he wish to worry on the tracking possibilities of GPS. They'd buy a couple of disposable cells at a convenience store when they left town.

They drove over to Kenilworth Avenue and headed into the city. Sonny had loaded the Mercury with all of their belongings. They had no firm plans or destination but were ticking with anticipation of the violence that was about to come.

Twenty minutes later, they were on New York Avenue. Sonny gripped the wheel of the fake-fur-covered steering wheel and spun it as Wayne lit a cigarette off a butane flame. He blew a smoke ring that shattered in the wind. Looking at it, his eyes crossed.

"What's postcoital mean?" said Wayne.

"Means after you stick her, stupid."

"My name is not Stupid."

"Hmph," said Sonny Wade.

They rolled through the open black gates of the National Arboretum and drove to the information center to get a map.

THE LITTLE man's name was Larry. He had returned to his home under the bridge, a brown bag holding a pint of store-brand vodka and a six of beer clutched under his arm. He had found Chris lying on the path with a blanket under his head. Chris was awake but motionless, looking up at the steel beams beneath the bridge floor. There was blood on his face. Larry wiped at it with a dirty rag, which only smudged the blood further. He covered Chris with another blanket.

"You're gonna be all right," said Larry. "But you need to lie there some."

"I gotta get back to my van," said Chris.

"You been hit on the noggin. You should take it slow."

Chris felt weak and a bit shocked. He peeled off the blanket and tried to get up on his feet. He was too dizzy. He sat back down, waited for the nausea to pass, and tried again. He stood carefully and gripped the rail.

"Who's that?" said Larry. He was nodding at the bike trail that broadened to a road.

Chris looked in that direction. A man with wild black hair was running down the road toward them. His feet were pounding the asphalt and dirt, and their heavy contact raised dust.

"Crazy sonofabitch," said Larry.

Chris issued a blood-caked smile.

THOMAS FLYNN walked Chris to Amanda's SUV and got him into the passenger bucket. He found a packet of wipes in the glove box and cleaned Chris's face, and once it was free of dirt and blood he inspected it.

"I should take you to an emergency room," said Flynn.

"I'm all right. I hit my head when I was falling, is all."

"All the more reason to get you to a doctor." Flynn shook his head, looking at the purple bruising that had come to Chris's face. "Why he'd do this to you?"

"Lawrence? I was tryin to stop him. But it was more than that. In his own way, Lawrence was looking to protect me. He wanted to keep me out of it."

"Do you know where he was going to meet them?"

"I had some time to think about it, lying under that bridge." Chris nodded. "I'm pretty sure I know where he went. It's a spot Lawrence took me to, over at the Arboretum."

"Then you need to call the police."

"Go ahead."

"*You* need to, Chris."

Chris looked at his watch. "It's close to four. He's already there."

Flynn scrolled through the contacts on his cell and found the one he was looking for.

"This is the number for Sergeant Bryant. Call her and tell her what's happening. She'll get some cars over there." Chris did not reach for the cell. "Do it, son. You've got to do what's right."

"I'm tryin, Dad."

"I know it. You've been trying all along. I'm sorry I doubted you."

"Forget all that," said Chris. "It's past."

They looked at each other across the seats.

Flynn held out his phone. Chris took it and made the call.

TWENTY-NINE

HE HAD parked the Cavalier in a small lot near the Capitol columns and untied the bicycle from the roof. It was now late in the afternoon and a drizzle had come that would soon turn to rain. Lawrence swung the daypack over his shoulders and got onto the bike.

He took the Crabtree loop and then Hickory Hill. He rode for miles. The rain cooled him and his pace was steady as he geared up and took the rise. The wind was pleasant on his face and it blew back his braids.

His prize possession as a boy had been his bicycle. When he would go out on long rides, to the Peace Cross, the Aquatic Gardens, and the Arboretum, he was far away from his roach-infested apartment, his smoked-up mother, her various men. He imagined that if he kept pedaling he would come to a place that was safe, find people to hold him instead of slap him, and be with adults who would talk to him with kindness and patience instead of sarcasm and cruelty. He never did find that place. But on his bike, for a short time at least, he could see it in his mind.

He pedaled up the road as the woods grew thick. He was

soaked with sweat beneath his jacket as he climbed the last hill. He passed a motorized maintenance cart, its driver giving him a small wave, as he arrived at the Asia Collection and its parking lot. There were no cars. It was the most out-of-the-way area in the park and also it was raining. There would be few visitors or grounds crew here today.

Lawrence got off the bike. He walked it off the road, past the brick house that held rest rooms, and carefully stepped down a lightly forested hill, holding and guiding the bike. Halfway down the hill he laid the bicycle on its side, partially concealed behind an oak, and covered it as best he could with brush and leaves. It was not hidden, but there was no place to keep it totally out of sight without putting it very far away. He would need access to it in the unlikely event that things went right.

Lawrence lifted the pack off his shoulders. From it he retrieved the Smith and Wesson combat magnum. He broke open its cylinder and thumbed six rounds into its chambers.

"Six is enough," he said, speaking out loud because he was nervous.

He snapped the cylinder shut and slipped the .357 into the shoulder holster he wore under his jacket. He drew the weapon cleanly and put it back in its holster. Then he took the Crain knife from the pack and slid it into the side pocket of his North Face.

He pinned the daypack under the bike and walked up the hill.

SONNY AND Wayne went into the Arboretum visitors' center. There were some old-folk visitors in the lobby and a couple of large female employees. One was complaining to the other about her man. The two white men with the outdated facial hair looked like they did not belong here or anywhere else but went virtually unnoticed because they did not linger. Wayne grabbed a folded information pamphlet that contained a map, and the two of them went back outside.

Crossing the lot, Wayne remarked on the numerous compact Jeep security vehicles and their drivers, rented cops.

Sonny said, "What are they gonna do? Only real police and criminals have guns in this town. Anyway, my Merc's got eight cylinders and they got four."

"What time is it?"

Sonny checked his watch. "Three thirty-five. Our friend said he'd be there at four."

"This *bro*-chure says the grounds close at five."

"We'll be done by then."

Sonny ignitioned the Marquis and took off. Wayne served as copilot as Sonny navigated the roads. Wayne was confused by the icons on the map, which he found overly clever and unhelpful, but signs on the shoulder had English words and clear arrows, and Sonny followed their directions up into the hills.

"How many exits you see on that map?" said Sonny.

"Looks like three. A service road makes four."

"Jesus, they're makin this easy."

Wayne lit a Marlboro, rolling the window down as Sonny arrived at the area, high atop a winding rise, marked "Asia Collection." There was a Cushman utility truck parked on the edge of the road, bales of hay stacked on its flat bed. Sonny put the Mercury into a lined space, head in, facing a small brick structure set down a stone path. He cut the engine.

It was raining harder. Wayne kept his window open, his arm leaning on the door ledge as he smoked, not noticing that he was getting wet.

"That can't be theirs," said Wayne, turning his head to indicate the truck.

"That's a vehicle for workers," said Sonny.

"So there's a third party here in these woods."

"Shame on them if they see us."

"Where's our friends?"

"They'll be here."

"You reckon there's two?"

"Well, there was that Afro American I spoke to. And Chris Carpet. Them and the smoke you butchered. They were all in this together. Criminals, like us. But not as hard as us."

Wayne took the Taurus from his waistband and pushed it under the seat. Its barrel had been cutting into his middle. He pitched his cigarette out the window and found a snow seal in the pocket of his Wranglers and carefully unfolded it. In it was a small amount of white crystal speckled with blue. He put his nose to it and snorted it up. He licked the paper hungrily, crumpled it, and dropped it on the floor.

"That did it," said Wayne, instantly lit. His eyes had begun to spiral.

"Now your nose is gonna bleed."

"Means it's good." Wayne nodded toward the small brick house. "Them's bathrooms?"

"No, it's a mo-tel."

"'Cause I feel like I could shit."

"Clench your sphincter," said Sonny.

Wayne folded his arms petulantly and unfolded them. "I need to walk. Look around. Could be they're lyin in wait."

"Dumbass. You think they parachuted in?"

"I'm sayin I can't sit still."

"Go ahead, then, but roll up that window before you do. That rain's gonna damage my velour."

Wayne closed the window. "You comin?"

"Nope. I think I'll stay dry."

"What if somethin happens?"

Sonny smiled. "I'll hear you scream."

"Or them," said Wayne, and he stepped out of the car.

Sonny watched him go down the stone path toward the rest room structure. It was hard to see him through the windshield, what with the rain. Wayne turned the corner and went around the back of the building and was gone.

LAWRENCE STOOD behind the brick house for a long while, but his nerves got to him when he heard the work truck come to a stop on the road. He looked around the corner and saw a young, heavyset female in an Arboretum shirt get out of the truck, a big cell or two-way holstered to her side. She was a white girl and she wore a rain slicker over the shirt and carried a bucket and hand shovel. If she saw him she'd see a hood rat from the side of town she never drove through, and she would get suspicious and maybe call security. Lawrence guessed she was one of those college girls who had majored in trees and plants. They had a name for that. Whore culture. Lawrence was too nervous to remember the word. But she was not the type to be cleaning out a bathroom. Wasn't no way she'd walk into the men's. Lawrence slipped around the corner and quietly pushed on the door to the men's room and stepped inside.

It was smaller than he thought it would be. Around a green metal divider, along one wall, were two urinals and a green metal stall holding a toilet. On the wall to his right was a white sink, a soap dispenser above it, and to the left one of those hot-air hand dryers that no one liked to use. Beside the sink, an office-sized trash can lined with a plastic bag. The floor was made up of small tiles in various shades of brown.

Rain tapped at the shingled roof. Lawrence heard the engine of a car, sounded like a big one, as it neared and then came to a stop.

He realized then that he had no plan.

In his mind, he had seen himself facing them, his gun hand hanging loosely at his side, his eyes steely, perhaps a small smile on his face, drawing quickly, beating their draw because they were white boys and slow, spinning the gun and holstering it before they even hit the ground. Ron O'Neal. The Master Gunfighter.

But here he was, low Lawrence Newhouse, cowering in a dirty bathroom. Trapped.

If one of them walked in, Lawrence would have to use Ben's blade. The sound of a gunshot would bring the other one, prepared, and that would mean that he, Lawrence, would be doomed.

Lawrence stood in front of the toilet stall. In his quivering hand was the carpet knife. The wood handle was damp with his sweat.

He shook his braids away from his face and tried to raise spit.

WAYNE MINORS had gone around the back of the building with the shingled roof and had found nothing but bright green ivy and a meter on its red brick wall. He had to go, but he preferred to urinate outside. Because he was still a child, he pissed his initials against the bricks. When he zipped up, he moved back from the wall and looked down a gently sloping hill.

He squinted through the mist and the rain. Down there behind a tree he thought he saw . . . yes, it was. A bicycle. Wayne stared at it, his mouth open, breathing through his nose. He got down to one knee and as his pants leg rode up, he drew his Rambo III knife from its sheath.

He gripped the hardwood handle and pressed the heavy-duty pommel and the steel blade against his leg. He went around the corner of the building and looked to the Mercury, parked in the space at the end of the stone path. He made a chucking motion with his chin but could not clearly see Sonny's reaction, or if he had one at all. The windshield was heavy with water.

One bicycle, one man. Ain't gonna be no problem. I'll walk out with a trophy and see the admiration in Sonny's eyes. Because I am his equal. I am not stupid.

Wayne turned and stepped quickly into the men's room.

LAWRENCE GOT a look at the man who had come to kill him as he emerged from behind the green metal divider. He was a little white man, tightly wound and strong, with a thick mustache and slightly crossed eyes. He held a hunting knife.

Lawrence opened his mouth to speak but could not. The little man giggled and came across the room. He was on Lawrence fast as fire, his knife hand raised.

This is the man who murdered Ben, thought Lawrence Newhouse, stepping back against the sink wall, frozen, unable to raise the Crain carpet knife, as he watched Wayne's weapon come down toward his chest.

The blade glanced off the holster and butt of Lawrence's gun. It surprised Wayne and woke Lawrence up.

This is the man who murdered Ben.

Wayne raised the knife again.

Lawrence grabbed Wayne's knife hand at the wrist and pushed him back. He danced Wayne across the tiles and into the green metal divider, rocking it. He had Wayne's T-shirt bunched in his right hand, still gripping the wood of the carpet knife. He spun him and held tight, pushing and lifting him, Wayne's feet grazing the tiles as they headed back to the sink wall, and Lawrence, with great force, slammed him up against the hand dryer. He let go of Wayne's shirt and moved the knife to the little man's neck and broke the flesh with the end, hooking it in beside the artery. Wayne's eyes pinballed in their sockets and he bared his teeth. He made an animal sound and freed his hand from Lawrence's grasp and stabbed at Lawrence furiously with the spine-cut knife. Lawrence gasped as the blade entered his chest again and again. Still, he held fast to Wayne.

Lawrence buried the hook deep and found purchase in the little man's flesh. He grunted with effort and ripped the Crain knife violently and almost completely through Wayne's neck, severing his artery and windpipe. Lawrence was showered in blood.

Wayne's head unhinged in a backward direction as he crumpled and fell. His boots kicked at the tiles. His head, loosely attached to his torso, floated in a widening pool of fluid. He had voided his bowels, and the stench was heavy in the room.

"God," whispered Lawrence.

He stumbled to the divider and leaned against it. He looked down at his T-shirt, drenched in crimson. He winced at the pain and dropped the Crain knife to the tile floor. He listened to the wheeze in his own breath.

Let me keep my feet.

Lawrence drew the heavy revolver from inside his shredded jacket and walked out of the men's room and into the rain.

The heavyset woman was now standing beside her truck. She saw Lawrence and her eyes grew wide. She turned and bucked. Lawrence saw her lift her radio off her hip as she ran into the woods.

He heard the opening of a car door. An old black sedan was parked at the end of the stone path. Its driver's-side door was opening and a big white man with a walrus mustache was getting out. He stood behind the open door and glass. Lawrence raised his gun and pointed it at the man's torso.

Lawrence saw the big man reach inside his windbreaker. His eyes lost their will, and his hand came out empty.

The man smiled. "Where's my friend?"

Lawrence did not reply.

Sonny Wade's hand slipped back inside his jacket.

"You ain't get to do that twice," said Lawrence, his weak voice lost in the rain.

"I can't hear you, fella," said Sonny, and he drew his .45.

Lawrence squeezed the trigger of the magnum. The .357 round shattered the window and blew a quarter-sized hole in Sonny's chest. The slug flattened, tumbled, and ruined everything in its path. When the lead exited, its hole was as big as a fist. Sonny grabbed the top of the open door, and Lawrence walked forward and shot him again. Sonny went down on his back.

It felt to Lawrence that he was floating as he moved crookedly to the car. He stood over the big man, whose shirt was moving in and out where he had taken the first bullet. The second round had entered Sonny's abdomen. His chest and belly were slick with red. Sonny was blinking his eyes slowly, struggling to breathe, the rain hitting his pale and frightened face as he pondered eternity. Lawrence pointed the gun at the big man's face and locked back the hammer. But he did not pull the trigger.

I'm not gonna give him that gift, thought Lawrence. *Let death laugh at him and walk toward him slow.*

Lawrence stumbled to the edge of the parking lot. He saw the path of wood chips and mud lined by beveled railroad ties. He made it there. He looked at his hand and saw that it no longer held the gun. He tripped and fell and slid down the hill. He managed to get back up. He saw the bench at the end of the trail, set before the ledge. He was there and he dropped onto it. He sat and looked across the treetops, down to the Anacostia. It was a wide ribbon of brown, and rain dotted its surface. He heard sirens and his vision began to fade.

This is where I want to be.

Lawrence stared at the river.

When they found him, he was staring at it still.

PART FOUR
THE WAY HOME

THIRTY

On a Sunday late in April, the family attended early mass. They then visited Ben's grave at the cemetery and went to breakfast at the Open City Diner in Woodley Park. Afterward, Thomas and Amanda returned to their house on Livingston, changed their clothes, and put Django in the back of the SUV. They met Chris and Katherine on Albemarle Street in Forest Hills, where they all walked onto the entrance of the Soapstone Valley Trail in a tributary of Rock Creek Park.

They went along a flat stretch, followed the yellow trail markers painted on the trees, and navigated a steep slope into the valley. They stopped to look at a tall oak. On its trunk had been carved a heart enveloping Thomas's and Amanda's names, and the year 1980. A smaller heart was below it, bearing the name of Darby, Chris's childhood dog. A third heart contained the name of Chris and 1982, the year of his birth. Using her cell phone, Amanda took a photo of the tree. Chris and Flynn exchanged a look and they walked on.

Seeing no other hikers or pets, Flynn let Django off his leash. The Lab mix immediately galloped off trail and crashed into the woods in search of the creek, where he could splash in the water. They followed him there, Katherine and Amanda walking ahead of Chris and Flynn. Chris noticed the gray in his mother's hair as the sun, streaming down through the trees, highlighted it and brightened the water where Django played. There was a lightness in Amanda's step.

Flynn tripped on an exposed root, and Chris grabbed his arm before he fell. Steadying him, Chris smelled alcohol on his father and wondered when he had found the time to steal a drink. Chris made no mention of it. He felt that he was perhaps responsible for his father's deteriorated condition. Or maybe his father would have gotten to that place on his own, without the troubles they'd had. In any case, Chris wouldn't lecture him or question him in any way. For a long time it had seemed unlikely that they would all be back here, together and settled, as they were now.

"Thanks," said Flynn.

"That's what I'm here for."

"To prop up your old man."

"You're not so old."

"Feels like I am. I'll never lay carpet again, that's for sure. I can't get up off my knees."

"You've got Isaac and his guys for that."

"And you," said Flynn. "And your boy, what's his name . . ."

"Marquis."

"Yeah, him. How's he doing?"

Marquis was a work in progress. Chris said, "He'll be fine."

With some convincing from Chris and Ali, Flynn had put Marquis Gilman on. It was one of Ali's last acts as an assistant at Men Movin on Up. His boss, Coleman Wallace, had accepted a job in the D.C. government, and Ali had taken over the top spot. Ali was frequently on TV now as a spokesperson and advocate for at-risk boys, and sometimes as a voice of community conscience when boys got murdered. Chris smiled when he'd catch him on television, at press conferences and such. It was funny, realizing that all those cameras and eyes were upon him, knowing where Ali had come from. It was true that Chris was a little envious, seeing that Ali had done something meaningful with his life. But he was also very proud.

Flynn and Chris found a seat on some boulders in a patch of sunlight out on the creek. Amanda and Katherine were playing with Django on the bank, throwing a stick into the water, the dog's tail spinning like a prop as he watched the prize float on the current.

"You did good," said Flynn. "She's a solid woman."

"She is," said Chris. "You finally got your Kate."

"It's Katherine," said Flynn.

The stick went down the creek and neared a bend. Django waited until the last moment and jumped in to retrieve it.

"How's school?" said Flynn.

"It's all right. It's just one class. Most of the stuff, I'm familiar with. I mean, I already read all those history books you turned me on to."

"Stay with it."

"I'll see where it goes."

"And stay with our company. Isaac wants to expand, and we're gonna need your help. It's going to get better for you. Less grunt work and more management."

"There's money for all of us," said Chris, and Flynn blushed a little and smiled.

"Seriously," said Flynn, nodding his chin in the direction of Katherine, her strawberry blonde hair lifted by the breeze. "You're gonna be working for three soon. You'll need that paycheck."

"I know it," said Chris. "I'm gonna keep the day job. But I've also got my eye on something else."

"If you want to be a teacher, pursue it. I'll be there for you if you get jammed up. Me and your mom."

They sat there for a while, enjoying each other's company, saying little but not uncomfortable in the silence. Then Chris got up and joined his mother and Katherine, talking about the wedding and the baby that was on the way. Chris dutifully listened and acted as if he cared about caterers and floral arrangements, but they knew he did not and told him that it was okay to leave them to their conversation and fun. Chris smiled at his mother, kissed Katherine, and turned back to the rocks. Thomas Flynn was gone.

Chris walked through the woods. He got back on the trail and followed its markers south. A cloud passed overhead and the landscape darkened. And Chris thought, *Isn't it so.*

He was not unaware of his good fortune. He had been born in a well-to-do neighborhood, raised in a loving home. When he'd gotten out of Pine Ridge, his father had put him to work and his mother had continued to feed him and buy him clothes even as he passed from boy to adult. At twenty-six he'd come close to killing two men but was stopped by someone who sacrificed himself instead. Chris hadn't been charged or implicated in any way. His call to the police had helped, along with Bob Moskowitz, who was tight with the prosecutors downtown.

Chris knew that for everyone like him, who had good fortune, there was a Lawrence Newhouse, who had none. But it wasn't as if Chris would go untouched. His life would not always be a spring afternoon, sunlight streaming on his mom, a breeze caressing the hair of his beautiful lover, a strong dog joyfully playing in a creek. If he could have looked into his future, he'd have seen much happiness in the family he would raise, and fulfillment in his career, as well as wrenching disappointment, regret, and old age. He'd have seen his mother, alone and suddenly aged, praying the rosary in her room. He'd have seen his father lying on a morgue slab at the age of fifty-five, his face deeply cut from windshield glass, his blood alcohol level impossibly high.

If the storytellers told it true, all stories would end in death. *But that will come in time*, thought Chris. *Not today.*

The clouds broke as he went down a long slope and found his father, standing before the thick oak rooted in the valley floor. Flynn had his open buck knife in hand. He was carving Katherine's name beside Chris's, inside the heart on the family's tree.

"Dad," said Chris.

Thomas Flynn turned and stepped toward his son.

ACKNOWLEDGMENTS

Many thanks to Vincent Schiraldi, director of the Department of Youth Rehabilitation Services (DYRS) of the District of Columbia, for his good work and assistance. Also, thanks go out to the youth, staff, and guards at the Oak Hill juvenile detention facility for their candid opinions and conversations. My lifelong friend Steve Rados provided the carpet-and-floor-business expertise.

For more information on the promotion of a more effective criminal-justice system through reform of sentencing laws and practices, and alternatives to incarceration, go to www.sentencingproject.org.